# T. Csernis & Julia Bland

---

# LIGHT
## NUMEN CHRONICLES VOLUME THREE

## ORIGINAL EDITION

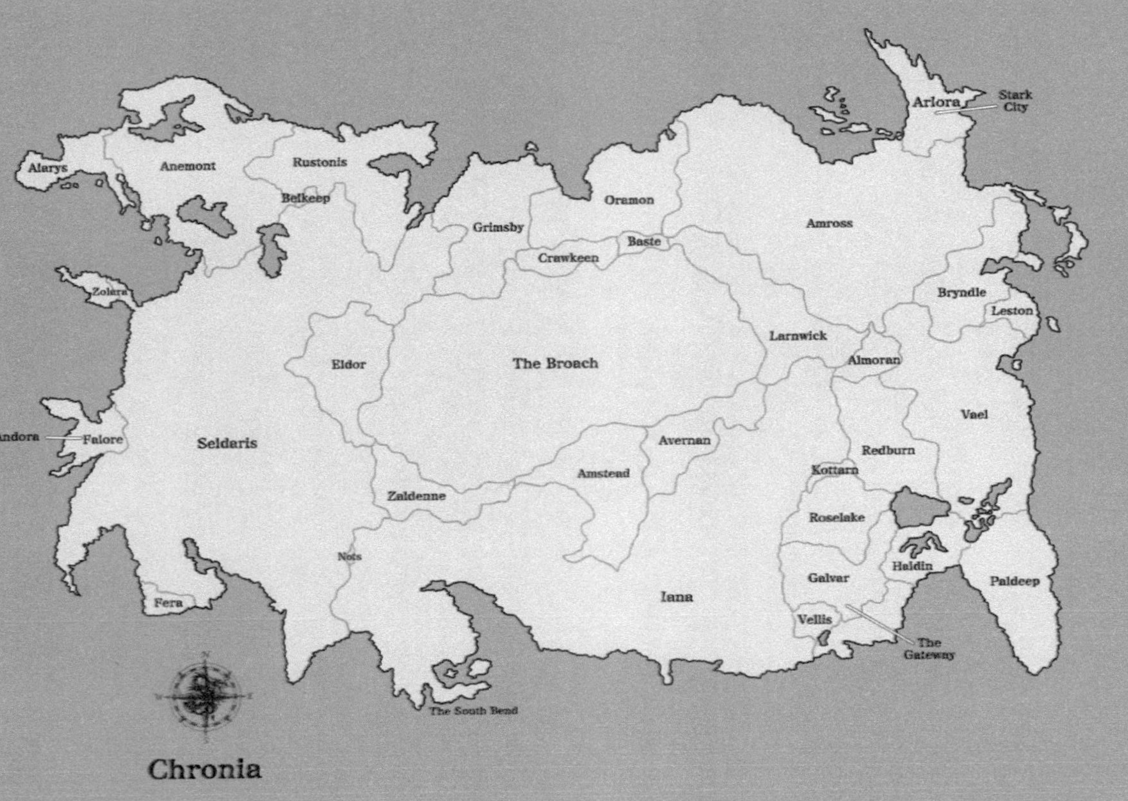

Chronia
Stark City
Arlora
Alarys
Anemont
Rustonis
Belkeep
Oramon
Amross
Grimsby
Baste
Crawkeen
Bryndle
Zolara
Leston
Larnwick
Eldor
The Broach
Almoran
Vael
Andora
Falore
Seldaris
Avernan
Redburn
Kottarn
Amstend
Zaldenne
Roselake
Fera
Nots
Galvar
Haldin
Paldeep
Iana
Vellis
The Gateway
The South Bend
Chronia

# GLOSSARY

--------------------------------------------------------------

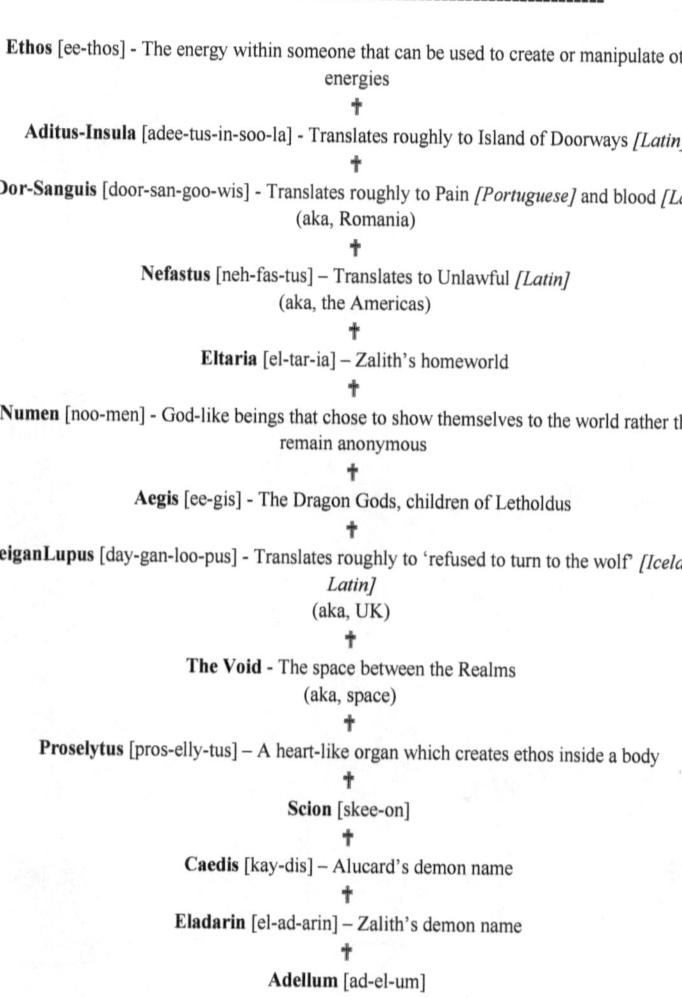

**Ethos** [ee-thos] - The energy within someone that can be used to create or manipulate other energies

✝

**Aditus-Insula** [adee-tus-in-soo-la] - Translates roughly to Island of Doorways *[Latin]*

✝

**Dor-Sanguis** [door-san-goo-wis] - Translates roughly to Pain *[Portuguese]* and blood *[Latin]*
(aka, Romania)

✝

**Nefastus** [neh-fas-tus] – Translates to Unlawful *[Latin]*
(aka, the Americas)

✝

**Eltaria** [el-tar-ia] – Zalith's homeworld

✝

**Numen** [noo-men] - God-like beings that chose to show themselves to the world rather than remain anonymous

✝

**Aegis** [ee-gis] - The Dragon Gods, children of Letholdus

✝

**DeiganLupus** [day-gan-loo-pus] - Translates roughly to 'refused to turn to the wolf' *[Icelantic, Latin]*
(aka, UK)

✝

**The Void** - The space between the Realms
(aka, space)

✝

**Proselytus** [pros-elly-tus] – A heart-like organ which creates ethos inside a body

✝

**Scion** [skee-on]

✝

**Caedis** [kay-dis] – Alucard's demon name

✝

**Eladarin** [el-ad-arin] – Zalith's demon name

✝

**Adellum** [ad-el-um]

# The Months and Currency

-----------------------------------------------------------------

## Months

January – Primis
February – Cordus
March – Tertium
April – Aprilis
May – Quintus
June – Iunius
July – Quintilis
August – Tria
September – Novem
October – Decem
November – Undecim
December – Clausula

## Currency

Copper – Equivalent of $0.01
Bronze – Equivalent of $0.20
Silver – Equivalent of $2
Gold – Equivalent of $10
Coronam – Equivalent of $100
Cidaris – Equivalent of $1 million

# CONTENTS

--------------------------------------------------------------------

## ARC ONE || LATE NIGHTS AND BLINDING LIGHTS



## ARC TWO || THE SLOW DESCENT INTO DEREALIZATION

# ARC THREE || LUPA

ARC ONE
— † —
LATE NIGHTS
AND
BLINDING LIGHTS

# Understanding Alucard's Accent

---

Alucard's dialogue in this edition of the story has an accent. He doesn't pronounce Hs, THs and some Rs. Below are some examples to help you understand his dialogue:

You'll see words like 'ead (head), 'ere (here), and 'owever (however), missing the H.

THs are often ZHs, such as zhat (that), zhis (this), zhe (the), and zhere (there). In other cases, you'll see ozzer (other).

Ws become Vs, such as vhat (what), vhere (where), and vhy (why).

Some Ds become Zs, such as Zamien (Damien), zon't (don't), and Zetlaff (Detlaff).

Fs also become Vs, such as vollow (follow), vriend (friend), and vor (for).

And some Rs become Vs, such as vest (rest), Veiner (Reiner), and Remont (Vemont).

# Chapter One

— ⸲ † ⸲ —

# An Ending's Beginning

| **Zalith** |

A flash of crimson light.

Zalith jolted awake, his senses on high alert, as an ominous rumble of thunder reverberated through the pitch-black sky. The once-peaceful lake water quivered with an unsettling energy, sending loud ripples across its surface. The air, once serene and calm, thickened with an unspoken sense of approaching dismay, suffocating the atmosphere within the seemingly protective cabin where the two demons lay.

"Alucard," he whispered, lightly shaking the sleeping vampire's shoulder.

Alucard, who had his head rested on Zalith's chest murmured, slowly waking from his slumber.

"Wake up," the demon insisted, haste in his voice. He knew what that sound meant, that *light*, and he had to get Alucard out of there.

The vampire frowned as he woke, sluggishly sitting up.

Zalith snatched his trousers from the floor as he did his very best not to look so worried. He glanced back at Alucard's tired, confused face as he pulled his trousers on. "Damien's here," he said, and the moment he mentioned that creature's name, a look of dread struck the vampire's face. "You need to hide," he insisted, getting out of bed. "I'll deal with him."

Alucard stared at him for a moment, almost as if he was trying to process what was happening. But there was no time to waste. Damien had arrived—he was outside, getting closer and closer as each second passed, and Zalith had but moments to try and work out what approach he was going to take.

There was no way Damien could know that Alucard was here—he'd made sure of that. But what he *hadn't* done was make sure that Damien wouldn't be able to find *him*. It was only a matter of time; he'd been so focused on Alucard that he'd forgotten to hide himself, and now he had to face the consequences of his mistake.

He deadpanned and left the bedroom as Alucard got out of bed, preparing to hide in case Damien searched for him.

Swiftly, the demon made his way through the dark cabin and out onto the porch. He set his sights on the horned, winged man making his way across the grass with an evil glare in his eyes, which he fixed on Zalith.

A displeased grimace stretched across Damien's face once he stopped in his prowl and waited for Zalith to approach him. "Eladarin," he called, slowly crossing his arms. "How strange it is to see you…here." He scowled skeptically, looking around.

Zalith didn't utter a word in response. He knew why Damien was there; the Daegelus had obviously come in search of Alucard, but Zalith wasn't going to give him what he wanted. He did, however, step down off the porch and make his way towards him as he watched his every step with both disgust and anger.

When Zalith reached him, Damien eyed him suspiciously. "Where is Aleksei?"

"I have no id—"

Damien abruptly smashed his fist into Zalith's face—it was sudden, but Zalith was expecting to get hurt. He didn't stumble or stutter, but the force of Damien's hit did make him turn his head to the side and take half a step back. The Daegelus could have hit him a whole lot harder, but he was sure that Damien was only just getting started.

As Zalith slowly turned his head to look back at him, Damien scowled impatiently and gritted his teeth. "Where is he?" he asked again, now with much more hostility in his voice.

"I don't know," he insisted, but calmly and vacantly.

Damien appeared to be more desperate than insistent; worry lingered in his eyes, probably because he knew that without Alucard, he was weak and defenceless. He lifted his foot and slammed it into the demon's stomach, sending Zalith flying back and crashing down to the ground. Before he could get up, Damien landed over him and gripped a fistful of his hair in one of his hands, the ground beneath them shattering as he touched the ground.

The Daegelus then forced the side of Zalith's face against the grass, dug one of his knees into his back, and leaned into his ear with a look of malice on his face. "Either you tell me where he is yourself, or I beat it out of you. I know you know where he is; you're covered in his repulsive stench, so don't even try to lie your way out of this," he hissed.

Zalith remained as calm as he could, keeping his anger at bay. "He imprinted on me," he answered.

The Daegelus scoffed amusedly, tightening his grip on Zalith's hair. "Of course he did. What a poor, miserable little creature—what a pathetic ability…and you…such a pitiful little man. I imagine you've already found someone else to fuck around with, haven't you?"

"I don't commit to people," Zalith answered tonelessly, feeding Damien's idea that he was still just as promiscuous as he'd been years ago. "You know that."

Glaring down at him, Damien scoffed once more. "And when did you decide you were done with Aleksei?"

Zalith had to think fast and smart. He knew that at one point, Damien and Lilith were working together, so he had to consider that they might work together again. He didn't want to lie only for Lilith to tell Damien that he and Alucard had still been together not too long ago. "After we escaped Lilith," he answered. "Shortly after you left, she came and took us both. We escaped, and once we were back in Alvenguard, I left him. I have no idea where he is or where he might be, and I don't particularly care, either."

Damien snarled irritably, let go of Zalith, and stood up straight. "Your reputation never fails to proceed you," he sneered, watching Zalith as he climbed to his feet. "Until now—" he snatched his throat, pulled him closer, and glared into his eyes, "—I don't believe a single word coming out of your mouth; in what world would a man-whore such as yourself attack me for someone so meaningless?" he growled, baring his fangs as he searched Zalith's eyes for a hint of panic.

But Zalith wasn't shaken. Damien might try so very fiercely to scare him, but it didn't work. The only kind of fear he had was for Alucard and if Damien somehow found him right now. That wasn't going to happen, though. He'd protect Alucard with his life.

He kept his vacant stare. "I almost died, something that I would not like to experience again, especially after Lilith found us. I can't say leaving him didn't hurt, but I did what had to be done. I don't need that kind of threat or danger in my life," he explained as regret filled his heart; even though what he was doing was to protect Alucard, it felt wrong to lie about his vampire. But he had to.

Damien, however, didn't seem convinced. He tightened his grip on Zalith's throat so that he could barely breathe. "And what are you still doing in Aegisguard if not to see Aleksei?"

"I…" he choked.

The Daegelus glowered and loosened his grip enough so that he could speak.

"I grew tired of living in a land plagued with war. I live here now."

Amused, Damien laughed and looked over at the cabin. "You? Here?" he asked, looking back at Zalith. "Miles upon miles away from civilization…? That's not you, is it, Eladarin?" he asked, tilting his head slightly, a condescending, amused tone in his voice. "Where out here will you find so many innocent little men to prey upon? Unless, of course, your latest boyfriend is inside—I'd love to meet him," the Daegelus challenged, lifting his free hand to point in the cabin's direction.

Zalith kept his eyes on Damien. He knew full well that Damien had been searching the area for signs of anyone else since he arrived, *and* that he knew that Zalith was alone. There was no way he could detect Alucard, and he was sure that Damien was simply testing him…or trying to piss him off as some sort of revenge for Zalith having ripped one of his hearts out a month ago.

The Daegelus then grinned, jerking his hand ever so slightly, instantly sending the cabin up in flames. He waited for Zalith's reaction, but the demon kept his eyes on him, not a flicker of change in his vacant stare.

Of course, inside, he was trying his best to remain as calm as he was. His irritancy was making it hard for him to hold back, as was his worry for Alucard, who was still inside—as far as he knew, anyway. But he couldn't do anything; he had to stand there and continue to act as though he didn't care.

Damien waited, taking his eyes off Zalith to glare at the burning cabin. He seemed to anger as each minute passed and not a sign of anyone else made itself known. Zalith knew how much Damien hated defeat, and he was sure that the Daegelus was going to do something to make himself feel better about being wrong.

The Daegelus snarled, taking his eyes off the cabin as it started to collapse. "Don't think I'm going to let you get away with defying me," he growled. "I should kill you for attacking me…but unfortunately, I need you alive. Perhaps I ought to make you *wish* you were dead." He grinned, pressing the tips of his claws against the left side of Zalith's face. "You think you're smart, you think you're above the rules, don't you?"

Zalith didn't answer, nor did he show any sign of anger. He simply waited.

"I had so much fun over the past four hundred years breaking Aleksei…I think I'll have even *more* fun breaking you."

An amused smile flickered through Zalith's vacant stare. He couldn't help but feel humoured. Did Damien really think he was capable of breaking him down? "How long do you think it will take?"

The Daegelus' smile grew thicker as he started to slowly drag his claws down the side of Zalith's face, cutting his skin as it bled. "You're not the first smart ass I've dealt with, and you won't be the last. I know your kind too well; you hide your fear and uncertainty behind a smile that says you can't possibly be knocked off your little throne of perpetual superiority. But in reality, you are nothing but a small little man— a *lonely* little man who thinks he finds comfort in acting as though he is untouchable. You are *not* untouchable, Eladarin, and you are not in any way superior. You are mortal, you are perishable, and you will learn what it is to truly suffer."

Looking at him, the demon then sighed. "I hate to see us like this, Damien," he said with fake but believable regret.

Damien scowled as he pulled his claws from Zalith's bleeding face, clearly not interested at all in his sarcastic approach. The Daegelus then extended his index finger and pointed at him, his blood dripping off his black claw. "I'm glad you think this is funny," he said, the embers of the fire starting to float their way. "I wonder how funny it will be when you're rotting in the darkness of a place quite like Hell. You've been living on borrowed time since your brave attack, Eladarin, and you'll be sure to understand that."

## | Alucard |

Alucard watched from the cover of the fire, suspended between the space of the real world and the Astral Plane, a place some demons could enter for a brief moment to move from one place to another. It took a lot of ethos to remain in this state, but ever since Damien had removed the runes from his body, he noticed a significant increase in his ethos and understood that Damien had muted a lot of his power.

But as he observed, fighting the urge to race over to them and stop the Daegelus from hurting Zalith, he began to feel strangely…embarrassed. The fact that Zalith wasn't afraid of Damien once made him seem attractive and appealing, but right now, it was beginning to make Alucard feel rather pathetic. Damien was threatening and hurting Zalith in the same ways he'd hurt him all his life…yet Zalith seemed to be making a game of it. Was Damien really not all that terrifying? Was Alucard just weak and stupid? He was beginning to feel that way.

He watched from the shadows of the mountain behind him, unseen, unheard, utterly undetectable. Damien told Zalith he'd be back for him very soon; Alucard was confident that Zalith had already come up with a plan to hide himself from Damien, so that wasn't going to happen.

As Damien disappeared with a horrifying crash and flash of crimson light, Alucard didn't immediately reveal himself. He waited a fair amount of time, watching as the cabin in which he had only got to spend one night burned to the ground.

Zalith seemed furious. He wiped the blood from his scratched face and used his ethos to put out the raging fire so that it didn't consume the forest around them. The demon clearly understood that Alucard wanted to wait a short while before revealing himself just in case Damien was lingering above; he sat on a tree stump, waiting.

Once he was sure that the Daegelus was gone, Alucard emerged from his limbo-like state and made his way out of the fire. He hurried to Zalith, who immediately embraced him, and then rested his forehead against Alucard's to stare into his eyes.

"Are you okay?" Alucard asked before Zalith could.

The demon smiled despite the gashes on the side of his face. "I am. Are you?"

Alucard nodded, silencing his conflicting thoughts; Zalith was all that mattered right now. "'Ow did 'e know you vere 'ere?"

Zalith sighed, pulling the vampire into another tight embrace as he glared at the burning cabin. "He must have been watching the phase-space; I suspect he'd been waiting for me to phase and then followed the trail that rift ethos leaves," he said. But then he took hold of Alucard's hand. "We should go."

Alucard had no need to stall. "Okay."

"We should avoid using the phase space together. I don't want to risk him seeing you."

"I can vly us 'ome," he offered, taking Zalith's hand.

The demon nodded. "Okay. Let's go."

Without hindrance, Alucard dematerialized them into vermillion smoke and began the journey back to Nefastus. All that mattered now was making sure that Zalith was safe. He knew how determined Damien was once he made a promise, and Alucard would do everything in his power to ensure that the man he loved didn't suffer the same pain that he did. Zalith didn't deserve that.

# Chapter Two

# Home

| **Alucard** |

Alucard woke suddenly, gripping the sheets below him as he opened his eyes with a quiet, sharp gasp of breath. He stared at the grey walls across from where he lay, the light of day seeping in through the closed curtains. Despite the fact that it had been eight months since it happened, he couldn't banish the memory of the night Damien had almost found him.

The fear in his heart swelled like a relentless tide, an unyielding spectre that only Zalith's presence could dispel. With a heavy sigh, he turned, reaching out with trembling hands to grasp for the familiar warmth of his demon lover, but he found only cold sheets, leaving him with a familiar hollow ache, a gnawing emptiness that clawed at his soul. It wasn't a surprise anymore, yet each absence carved deeper into the recesses of his being, leaving behind a poignant trail of desolation in the depths of his fiery gaze.

With a despondent frown, the vampire slowly turned back onto his side and guided his arms under his pillow. Every day for the past three months had been the same; he didn't know why Zalith had become distant, but he was afraid to ask. Maybe he was just busy with work; he'd been having a lot of meetings in his office, after all. But that didn't explain why he had to leave so often and so early.

Today would be no different than the last. He'd get out of bed, talk to Luther about the same things, and wait around while Zalith did whatever it was he did with his time. Sometimes, Alucard felt like he might just sleep until noon; dinner was the only time he got to spend time with Zalith, so what was the point in sitting around all day alone?

But he shouldn't sleep all day. Despite the suffocating, crushing sadness and uncertainty, he had work to do.

With a despondent frown clinging to his tired face, he climbed out of bed and dragged himself into the bathroom. He brushed his teeth, tidied his hair, and then dressed into his trousers and white shirt, pulling its sleeves to mask the ugly scars on his arms—how he hated them.

The vampire left the bathroom and headed across the hall to his study. He pushed the door open, closed it behind him, and made his way down the small staircase that had been installed, connecting to his office. As soon as he got down there, his overgrown heap of a dog stood up and panted excitedly. Sabazios—once a shin-height puppy, now a waist-height dog—stared at Alucard, the frantic wagging of his tail slowing as the vampire walked to his desk and slumped down in the chair behind it.

Alucard gazed at his faithful companion, observing the way the dog settled into his resting place, yet remained vigilant as if anticipating words that would never come. Weariness weighed upon Alucard like a suffocating shroud, draining him of the strength to even muster a whisper. He sat there, enveloped by the chilling embrace of despair, a bleak abyss that seemed to stretch endlessly before him. In the dimness of his solitude, even the comforting presence of his loyal friend offered little solace against the relentless onslaught of his own melancholy.

The distant murmur of voices drifted towards him. Beyond the confines of his office, the lounge resonated with Varana's lively chatter, accompanied by the laughter of her companions. Their jovial banter filtered through the walls, a bittersweet reminder of the world outside his desolate realm. Yet Alucard remained detached, indifferent to the frivolity that danced on the edges of his awareness, accentuating the cavernous void within him, and amplifying the stark emptiness of his existence.

To the right of his workspace was *Zalith's* office. Alucard could hear the mutters of both him and his three Alphas, Orin, Tyrus, and Idina—the vampire didn't want to listen to their conversation, but…he missed Zalith so much; he ached for his touch so much that it hurt to think that he probably didn't spare him a thought throughout his day. Why would he? He was busy with his life, and Alucard knew that he should do his best to accept that.

He listened to the voice of the man he loved. He listened to him telling his Alphas to search someplace for Damien's activities, and another for Lilith's; the two Numen were still out to find and kill him and Zalith and had been ever since they'd escaped the Numens' grasp. He didn't want to sit there and think about that, though. Zalith had said that he was going to deal with it, so Alucard sighed away his thoughts and stared sullenly at his desk. Zalith would have told him if the Numen were making a move.

This loneliness…it was like the despair that he'd felt years ago, the despair that Damien forced on him. Who else did he really have, after all? He didn't have anyone to sit around and laugh with; the person he enjoyed doing that with was busy talking to other people. He wasn't mad, though. Why would he be mad? He wasn't the only person in Zalith's life; he felt like he shouldn't expect to be the only one Zalith spent his time with.

The least the demon could do was make him feel like he wanted him, though.

No…he was being selfish. Zalith was busy.

He swivelled around in his seat and stared out into the estate gardens. Perhaps this was what life was like once people had spent a certain amount of time with someone they loved. Perhaps it was normal for things to settle down, for them to both reach a point where they lived together and went about their own business. Was that normal? How was Alucard to know? Who could he even ask?

What was *he* supposed to do? Zalith was spending his time with his friends…or subordinates, whatever they were to him. But Alucard? The only friend he had was a dog, and he couldn't exactly have a conversation with Sabazios, could he? He looked down at the dog and frowned. Sabazios instantly raised his ears and started wagging his tail, waiting to be spoken to, but Alucard had nothing to say.

The vampire slouched back, his despondent stare thickening as he gazed aimlessly into the forest in the distance. But like Zalith, he had responsibilities.

With a tired sigh, he turned to face his desk and set his eyes on a pile of letters. They all consisted of the same thing: Lilith was searching for him, Damien was looking for Zalith. Some of the letters even informed him that the Diabolus had expanded and were now searching the entirety of Aegisguard for him.

One letter from Attila told him that both Lilith and Damien's cults were actively causing problems all over the world, turning settlements and villages into ash for simply knowing of Alucard's existence yet not being able to tell them where he was hiding. Alucard was sure that Zalith was receiving the same news from his people, and he wanted to discuss these problems with him—after all, it wouldn't be long until these search parties reached Nefastus. They wouldn't find his and Zalith's home, though. It had been surrounded by masking and protection ethos *months* ago. But Alucard still felt anxious knowing that the cults were endlessly searching for him *and* Zalith.

A quiet knock came at his door.

He sighed as he lowered the letter in his hands.

His door opened, and to his annoyance, Luther walked in and shut it behind him. "Hey," he said enthusiastically, holding up one of his hands as he walked over to the desk, dressed—as usual—in an all-white suit.

Silence lingered over them as Luther sat down and stared at Alucard, who didn't say anything in response.

"You all right?" the man asked, resting his arms on the table.

Alucard set his eyes on him; they slowly faded to blue as the sunlight hit his face, causing his head to ache. "Talk," he muttered.

"Detlaff's quiet, wolves are quiet, and Ben's doing fine, too. Last time I checked, he was hanging out with a bunch of guys he works with. He seems to be doing pretty well…you know, with his becoming human again and all."

Alucard turned his head, looking out of the window behind him.

"Drac's doing good," Luther added. "The whole sanctuary is doing good, actually."

That snapped Alucard out of his disinterested trance. Not too long after his birthday, he bought the animal sanctuary that housed a female kori serpent, and he sent Drac to live with her. He was glad to hear that the place was no longer in danger of being shut down, but that was all thanks to the unnecessary amount of money he'd come to acquire through his years of work—work that didn't even require much of his attention anymore. Attila and Luther did everything he needed them to.

He didn't want to leave the house, anyway. Sitting in the same building as Zalith was as close as he came to spending time with him; hearing his voice through the walls gave him some sort of comfort, but it also saddened him. He'd rather see him and talk to him than have to hear him talking to other people. But he was convinced that Zalith was content with how things were—if he wasn't, he'd be coming to Alucard, right?

"Are we walking today?" Luther asked.

Alucard took his eyes off the outside and looked over at his subordinate. "Vhat?"

"Walking," Luther repeated. "Today?"

He sighed and looked out the window again. The only thing he'd been doing lately was walking and training with Luther—despite his sadness, he'd not let himself go. His scars already made him feel ugly enough. "*Da,*" he muttered. "Vhat about Attila?"

Luther crossed his arms and leaned back in his chair. "Haven't heard from him in a few days. He's dealing with that little disagreement they've got going on over in DeiganLupus—the humans arguing over land or something dumb."

Alucard rolled his eyes as he rested the side of his face in his hand. "Is zhere ever anyving intervesting vor you to tell me?" he grumbled.

"Well…maybe not interesting, but there *is* something I've been meaning to bring to your attention."

"Vhat?"

"Two vampires were found last night," he said cautiously. "Dead."

Alucard frowned at him.

"Both dumped in an alley, stakes through their chests."

Concern immediately shoved Alucard's dismay aside. "'Unters?"

"We're not sure, but we're looking into it. Dargamoore gets tourists all the time, so we think it might have been an isolated incident, someone who doesn't know about the treaty felt threatened or something, I don't know. We'll find out who did it, though."

"You're vorking vith zhe 'uman law envorcement, *da*?"

Luther nodded. "Trying to, anyway. I need to say, Alucard…they're very rude and hard to work with. I'd much rather investigate this on my own."

"Is zhe law," Alucard denied. "Both peoples vork togezzer. Zhis treaty vas almost shattered vonce bevore; I von't let zhat 'appen again."

"Yeah, don't worry. I got this," Luther assured him.

"Good," Alucard muttered. Luther might irritate him sometimes, but he *was* good at his job. He just hoped that this *was* an isolated incident. The treaty was the only thing ensuring that his vampires had somewhere safe to live; he couldn't afford to lose it.

"Other than that, same old, same old." Luther paused and shuffled around in his seat. "If we're done with that, perhaps we can move on to more personal matters."

"Like?" he muttered, thinking about the fact that he was going to have to speak to all his vampires; they were likely afraid of what Luther just revealed to him, and he wanted to make sure that they knew he'd do whatever he had to to ensure their safety.

Luther answered, "You could tell me why you're so bummed out all the time."

Alucard rolled his eyes, sighed deeply in annoyance, and leaned back in his seat. He had no interest in telling Luther anything about his personal life. He did, however, abruptly feel enough motivation to get up and head for the door. "Ve vill valk," he said.

"Oh, I checked out that new theatre they set up in Dargamoore," Luther said as he walked at Alucard's side, following him out of his office, through his house, and towards the front door. "It's not bad. If you ever want to get out of here for a while, you could come and watch a show with me and Attila," he offered.

"No," Alucard replied, slipping on his shoes before pulling the front door open.

"Don't like shows?" he asked, following him through the estate's grounds. "Well, there's also a new show at the opera, too. It's become really popular lately; some new guy turned up."

"Since vhen vere *you* intervested in opera?"

"There's a lot of things I'm interested in, Alucard. If you asked me, you'd know."

"Vhy vould I ask you?" he uttered, leaving the estate and leading the way along the gravel path.

"Oh, I don't know," Luther said with a shrug. "Perhaps because I'm your friend?"

Alucard stared tiredly as he turned left into the forest.

"Being your friend also means I sit around wondering why it is you've become so sad and quiet recently. You won't tell me, so it leads me to have to make assumptions."

He still had nothing to say.

"Are you and him all right?" Luther asked. "Something's up with you, and I haven't seen you and your demon hanging around with each other *at all* lately. You get into a fight or something?"

"No," Alucard mumbled.

"Then why the hell are you so depressed?"

Alucard stopped walking but didn't turn to look at Luther. This wasn't the first time he'd asked these questions, and he was sure that it wouldn't be the last. But he felt no need to explain himself or his feelings to Luther; he wasn't sure why he wanted to know so much, but it was none of his business.

"I'm sorry if I'm annoying the shit out of you—I probably am," Luther said, leaning against the nearest tree. "But I often have to ask you the same thing a million times before you actually tell me—you've always been like this."

Alucard took his eyes off the distance and glared at him. He hated his voice, he hated how much he just talked and talked and talked. Resisting the urge to order him to never speak again was getting harder. *Much* harder.

Luther shrugged and smirked. "How close to the million mark am I?"

"Var," Alucard snarled.

"All right, well, I'll keep asking," he said with a sigh, stepping away from the tree. He then started to lead the way. "You never really were a talker," he continued as Alucard glared at the back of his stupid head. "Attila and I always placed bets on which of us would get you to talk first. I often won; I like to think I know you better than he does, especially now since he's scared to talk to you alone. You really shook him up, you know," he said, looking back over his shoulder at him.

"Good," he growled.

"Well, you certainly have me a little stumped on this one, though. First time you've dated someone, so, first time I'm dealing with this kind of situation. You know, though," he said, looking over his shoulder at him again, "*a lot* of people find it real helpful to talk to their friends when things go sideways relationship-wise. For example: remember that time Attila dated Bethany? He sat down with me, and we talked a good few hours. Next day? Those two were fine."

"Do you ever stop talking?" Alucard snarled, scowling.

Luther looked ahead again. "Nope."

Alucard rolled his eyes. He didn't want to talk to anyone about anything. So much as thinking about it made him feel like he was suffocating, and the only person he was comfortable talking about his feelings with was Zalith.

He took his eyes off Luther and stared at the ground as he continued following him. All he could think about was how much he wanted to go back to the house, but he'd only feel worse there. His home felt so different now; before, it was more like home than any other place he'd lived, but now that Zalith had become distant and distracted, it didn't feel the same.

*Nothing* felt the same.

He sunk into the dismay; he tried his best not to let it get to him, but who was he kidding? It was *tormenting* him. He had no idea what was going on. What had happened? Why was Zalith so different…so distant, so…absent? He didn't understand. Had he done something wrong? Was Zalith mad…or was he losing interest?

Alucard desperately tried to push the thought aside, to bury it beneath layers of denial, but it clawed its way back to the forefront of his mind with relentless persistence. How could he ignore the stark contrast between then and now? Zalith, once a constant presence, had become elusive, his touches fleeting and rare. They used to have sex at least once a day, and now, it had been two months since they'd been intimate.

The absence of their intimate moments gnawed at Alucard's soul, a haunting reminder of the distance that had grown between them. It had been too long—far too long—since their last embrace, leaving Alucard to drown in a sea of worry and self-doubt. Each passing day without Zalith's affection only deepened the chasm of uncertainty, casting a shadow of despair over their once passionate bond.

Doubt consumed Alucard like a relentless flame, each flicker igniting new insecurities within his tormented mind. The fear that Zalith might not be attracted to him anymore loomed over him like a shadow, casting uncertainty upon his very worthiness of love. What had drawn Zalith to him in the first place? Alucard found himself grasping at elusive answers, his thoughts twisting into a labyrinth of self-deprecation and confusion. The relentless pursuit of physical perfection, the ceaseless efforts to maintain his allure—were they all in vain? A bitter realization gnawed at him, whispering that perhaps it was futile to fight against the tide of Zalith's fading interest. With each passing day, Alucard felt himself teetering on the edge of resignation, the weight of his own inadequacies threatening to drag him into the abyss of despair.

With the ache in his heart growing, he tried his best to focus on what little hope he had that perhaps Zalith was just too busy with work, but everything convinced him that wasn't the case.

What Varana said a while ago lingered like a bad smell, and it began to make sense. *Of course* Zalith was getting bored of him. It wasn't like he was amazing in any way; why would he be any different from the other people Zalith had dated? If anything, he was probably one of the least interesting. What did he have to offer, after all? He had no family, no friends, no exciting job, or interests—he was just Alucard, the boring, worthless little man who failed everyone around him. Why would Zalith be any different in that regard? He knew that something like this would happen, he knew that the demon would get bored of him, but he'd allowed himself to become convinced that he wouldn't.

Why had he ignored his fears?

But then he scowled. He didn't want to jump to conclusions. If Zalith didn't want him anymore, why would he still sleep in the same bed with him every night? Why would he still be living with him? It all confused him so much, and it hurt so sorely to think about it because he didn't understand, nor did he know what to think. He just... didn't know what happened or why these things were happening, and it weighed so heavily on his mind that he felt like he might drown any moment.

"Alucard," Luther called, snapping him out of his thoughts.

He halted in his tracks and lifted his gaze to the horizon. Before him lay the familiar cliff edge, the solemn boundary that marked the end of their journey.

"You okay?" Luther asked.

"I'm vine," he grumbled, continuing forward until he was standing at the very edge of the cliff. He stared down at the river that flowed below, its banks lined with white chalk and limestone.

"Did you hear what I said?" his subordinate asked as they started making their way down the narrow path carved into the side of the cliff.

He hadn't been paying an ounce of attention to him. "No."

Luther laughed slightly. "I asked you if we're doing physical or ethos today."

"I zon't care," he muttered, for he really didn't care which form of combat they trained in together. Nothing else mattered anymore. The sadness and worry he felt for his and Zalith's relationship made him feel so hopeless and defeated. It confused and irritated him, but he couldn't do anything about it. He felt…trapped in some sort of emotional limbo, and there was no one there to help him out of it.

Luther looked back over his shoulder at him. "Physical, then?"

"Sure," he mumbled.

Whatever was going on with Zalith, he was sure that it was only going to get worse, and when the demon eventually decided that he wanted Alucard to leave…well, he wasn't sure if he'd try to fight it or not. He loved Zalith more than anything; all he wanted was for him to be happy. And if the demon would be happier without him, then…maybe there was no reason to fight.

# Chapter Three

— ⟨ † ⟩ —

# A Desolate Situation

**| Alucard |**

Alucard frowned irritably when Luther looked back over his shoulder at him *again*. Why couldn't he just lead the way in silence?

"Hey," Luther called, smiling. "I saw something you might like on my way here."

The vampire waited.

"There's a small island not too far from the Citadel docks, and I'm *pretty* sure I saw some of those Drac lizard dragons out there—kinda lost, don't you think? Maybe we can help them on their way back to Avalmoor."

"Zhey're not like Drac; zhose are bergan serpents. And is migration season," Alucard mumbled. "Zhey go back to Avalmoor in a couple of months vonce gets varmer 'ere."

Luther frowned. "Oh," he replied and looked ahead as they reached the bottom of the cliff. He led the way onto the beach, which was covered in limestone chunks and very small chalk pebbles.

Alucard continued forward, following Luther along the bank of the slowly flowing river until they stopped close to a rather large piece of driftwood. He couldn't hear whatever his subordinate was ranting on about now—he didn't care to listen. He stared vacantly, the world around him becoming mute; all he could think about was Zalith. The demon always occupied his thoughts, but never in such a discomforting way. He couldn't stop asking himself what he had done wrong or what even *was* wrong. Was he supposed to do something to make things return to how they used to be? If he did, he didn't know what.

He felt useless, stupid. There was obviously a reason why Zalith had become so distant and distracted, but he couldn't work out what it was. He wanted to ask—he wanted to talk to Zalith about why they weren't spending time together anymore—but he was afraid of what the answers might be. He didn't want to hear that Zalith had become tired of him. He didn't want to be told that he wasn't wanted anymore. Feeling it was enough.

With a quiet, despondent sigh, he sunk deeper and deeper into the confusing sadness, and the fact that he just wanted to go home and see Zalith made it worse. He couldn't see him. The demon was busy and probably didn't even want to see him—

"Alucard," Luther called.

"Vhat?!" he snapped angrily.

Luther laughed with both concern and startlement as he stepped back. "Calm down, sheesh," he muttered, holding up his hands. "I asked if you were ready."

Ready? It took him a moment to remember that they were meant to be brawling. He didn't feel like it, though. However, he didn't want to stand there and sulk, either. He was sure that he'd only feel worse if he allowed himself to spiral further into the depravity that had gripped him.

He stopped aimlessly staring and set his attention upon Luther. "Yes," he answered.

Luther, who took off his white blazer and rolled the sleeves of his grey shirt up, smirked and took a few steps back. Then, without hesitation, he struck his right first forward—

Alucard dodged easily, leaning ever so slightly to the right to avoid Luther's strike. His subordinate tried again, and again, and again, but each successful dodge only made Alucard's bored scowl increase. He didn't even need to pay much attention; Luther wasn't exactly the best vampire at combat; However, not only did Alucard have everyone else working on keeping the treaty protected but he also didn't want to share his private life with any of his subordinates. Luther was the only exception became, once upon a time, they were friends.

He kept dodging every attack as the thought of Zalith intensified. His almost desperate need for the demon's attention weighed on both his body and mind, and it was tormenting him. He'd become so attached to that man that it felt physically painful not to be with him, and although their relationship wasn't over, Alucard couldn't escape the fact that it had started to feel like the end was nigh.

The vampire raised his arm and smacked away Luther's fist as his attacks became fiercer.

Alucard's concentration remained on the thoughts racing around inside his head. What could have happened? Zalith only started acting differently after Damien showed up again…. What if that had something to do with this? What if the things Damien said and did caused Zalith to rethink how he felt about Alucard? What if Zalith changed his mind about wanting to keep him safe from Damien and the other Numen? What if the stress of that snapped him back to reality? Alucard really wasn't worth the danger and stress that came with hiding from the Numen, was he? Had Zalith realized that? Was that why he was losing interest in him?

Just then, Luther crashed his fist into Alucard's face—the shock snapped him out of his despondent thoughts and left him with nothing but anger. He scowled and snarled, and before Luther had a chance to say a word—before Luther had even pulled his fist back—Alucard slammed his fist into his subordinate's stomach, sending him flying across the beach.

But his anger withered as he watched Luther crash down onto the chalk pebbles. It wasn't Luther's fault; Alucard should have been paying attention to their training. He didn't feel sorry for Luther, but he felt as though he should probably go to him and tell him that he didn't mean to hit him so hard.

With another quiet sigh, he made his way over, reaching Luther as he stumbled back to his feet.

"What the fuck, man?" Luther groaned, spitting blood into the river before tidying his hair. "What the hell did you do that for?"

Alucard scowled and crossed his arms as he watched Luther recover. "Ve're vighting, no? Zhe point is to avoid my 'its, too."

Luther rolled his eyes and straightened his clothes. "*I'm* fighting. You're standing there in a world of your own."

The vampire took his eyes off his subordinate and looked at the river. He wasn't able to focus on anything recently, but today was a whole lot worse than usual. He didn't feel like continuing, nor did he feel like explaining himself. So, he shifted his sights to Luther and frowned vacantly. "You can go 'ome now."

"Wait, what?" Luther laughed, moving closer to him. "We've been out here barely even ten minutes and you're sending me away already?"

"Zhat's vhat I just said."

Luther stared at him with a look of confliction on his face, but as Alucard's frown slowly became a scowl, Luther shook his head. "All right, enough."

"Vhat?" he snarled.

"You, this…" he said, looking around. "The longer you sit and stand around in silence, the worse it's gonna feel. Talk to me, Alucard."

"Go—"

Luther snatched Alucard's shoulder before he could turn his back on him—

Alucard snarled furiously at the feel of his unwelcome touch, spun around, and shoved him away.

Luther took a few steps back and looked as if he was waiting to see if Alucard would attack. After a few silent moments of aggravated glaring, though, he calmed down. With a deep breath, he cautiously held out one of his hands in what looked like a feeble attempt to defend himself if Alucard changed his mind. "I know I've been away for like…over a hundred years," he started.

Alucard deadpanned. He really didn't want to stand there and hear whatever it was that Luther had to say. "Zon't start," he warned him.

He kept talking, though. "Maybe a little longer than that," he said with a frown, lowering his hand. "But back then, you actually used to talk, you know? It took you a long ass time, but you told me and Attila things because the three of us were close. That hasn't changed for me; maybe it changed for you; I don't know what the hell you've been through in the last century—heck, I don't even know what you've been up to in the last *decade*. But I *do* know something's wrong, and you need to know that you can talk to me about it, okay? I'm not just your work subordinate, I'm your friend, too, and seeing you like this isn't really making me feel good. I want to help you with whatever it is."

"Are you done?"

Luther frowned irritably. "Really?"

Alucard snarled and turned his back on him.

But Luther followed. "Okay," he said with a derisive laugh, catching up to Alucard as he walked quickly towards the path that led up to the cliff. "I'm just gonna say it— I'm gonna say it. Something's going on with you and your boyfriend, and you have no idea what to do about it, so you're sitting around hoping things will just get better if you wait, right?"

Alucard stopped walking and scowled back at him. His aching heart was beginning to feel as if it was ensnared in sharp, poisonous thorns.

Luther halted, crossed his arms, and frowned smugly. "I'm right, aren't I? Might even go so far as to say I'm spot-on."

With a roll of his eyes, Alucard turned around and continued walking.

"What happened?" Luther asked, following him up the cliff. "Did you fight? Argue?" he called, keeping up with Alucard's very fast pace.

Alucard wasn't going to answer. He had no idea how Luther was able to guess, but he wasn't going to talk to him about it. He didn't want to talk to *anyone* about it.

Luther, however, evidently wasn't going to give up. With a scowl on his face, he reached out and snatched hold of Alucard's shoulder once more—

With an angered snarl, Alucard swung around, snatched hold of his throat, and pinned his back against the cliff. But before he could yell in Luther's face, his subordinate held up his hands in surrender.

"I'm only trying to help," he insisted.

"I zon't vant your fucking 'elp," the vampire growled.

"No, but I'm going to give it to you anyway."

He glowered at him, gritting his teeth.

"What's going on? Why aren't you as happy as you were when you came to Avalmoor? I'd never seen you so content. Now, you're more depressed than a widow."

With an irritated growl, Alucard harshly let go of him and continued up towards the forest.

Luther caught up to him and looked. "Just talk to me. Let me at least *try* to help you."

Alucard felt conflicted, overwrought. He didn't know what to do or what to say anymore. Zalith's absence and sudden change made him feel so lost and confused that he wasn't even able to keep himself composed. He was just sad. Sad, confused, and alone.

But was he?

He glanced at Luther. The man was reminding him so much of Elvin right now that he wasn't sure whether he wanted to leave or let him help. Before, he felt guilty for turning Elvin away the way he did, and now he was gone. All that bard had ever wanted to do was be there for him—Tobias, too. Everyone. They all tried to be there for him, and now, they were gone.

Alucard looked down at the grass when they reached the top of the cliff. Once before, talking to Tobias helped clear some of his confusion about his feelings for Zalith; maybe Luther could help in that same way. Luther, after all, had known him for most of his life…and Alucard also knew that Luther—unlike Attila—wasn't going to degrade and belittle him for loving another man. He seemed happy for him at times, and maybe that was why he was insisting right now…. Alucard was so confused and hurt and upset that he'd take any kind of help to relieve his worry.

So, he sighed and shrugged a little. "I zon't know," he answered honestly.

"Don't know what?" Luther asked.

"Vhat's going on anymore."

"With you and Zalith?"

He nodded. "Vings just started changing."

"Changing?"

He shrugged again. "Noving 'appened—not veally. Vone morning, 'e just vasn't zhere when I voke up, and zhen every morning avter zhat. I zon't know vhy. As var as I am avare, noving 'appened. I zidn't do or say anyving, so I zon't know if 'e's mad or if 'e's just getting bored of me."

"Why would he get bored of you?" Luther asked with a slight laugh.

Alucard didn't want to answer that. He didn't want to think about all the names Varana had given him from the list of men whom Zalith dated and grew bored of. He didn't want to imagine his name being added to that list.

He shook his head, continuing through the forest. "Ve stopped spending time togezzer. Zhe last time ve veally did anyving vas vor 'is birvday avter Yule. 'E's gone all day and zhe only time I get to see 'im is vhen ve 'ave dinner—and even zhen 'e isn't zhe same. 'E's alvays tired. Ve 'aven't even…been…intimate in months. Virst, 'e stopped initiating vings, and zhen vhen I stopped, 'e zidn't say anyving or ask vhy. 'E 'asn't told me zhat someving 'as 'appened, and 'e vould alvays tell me vings…vell, important vings. I zon't know if I'm doing someving vrong or if…I zon't know," he said with a sigh, giving up.

Luther stared at him, thinking. But then he exhaled deeply and looked ahead as the path that led to the estate came into view. "I don't know what to tell you; I don't know Zalith, and I don't really know what he's got going on. But Alucard," he said with severity in his voice, "if there is some sort of problem that's caused him to become distant, I don't think it's because of you. What could you have done wrong, right? You're there for him, you're loyal—even now, you're there waiting for him when he's done doing whatever it is he does, right?"

He nodded slowly.

"You guys didn't argue or fight…I think *he's* the one with the problem."

"Vhat?"

"Well…he's the one who just started doing these things without warning. *He* stopped waiting for you to wake up in the morning. *He* stopped making himself available so you can spend time together. Did you talk to him about it?"

"No," he mumbled, walking over to the path. "I zon't vant to make vorse. I zon't know if 'e's just busy or…if 'e zoesn't vant me anymore."

Luther stopped walking and crossed his arms when Alucard turned to face him. "Well…I say ask him. If you ask and he says he doesn't want you, so what?"

The thorns around Alucard's heart became sharper.

"It's his loss. From what I know and what I see, *you* haven't done anything wrong, okay? You deserve to be happy, and you aren't right now, are you? I don't know him, so I can't really say much, but…I know *you*. Think about it."

He frowned a little. Everything Luther just said didn't feel helpful at all. It didn't clear up his worry, it didn't help him decide what to do. If anything, it made him more afraid to confront Zalith. *Was* he getting bored of him? *Did* he have a problem that he didn't want to mention for the sake of Alucard's feelings? He had no idea, and Luther had done nothing but make him panic more.

Luther lifted his hand. "I have to go and get back to work, but…I can stay if you want to keep talking—"

"No," Alucard grumbled.

He lowered his hand. "All right, well, if you need me, just…are you sure you don't want me to stay?"

"Go," the vampire muttered. "Do your job. Vind out who killed zhose vampires."

Luther frowned again, but when the vampire turned his back on him, the man disappeared into the air, leaving Alucard alone.

The vampire set his eyes on his home in the distance. Luther's useless rant had done nothing but anger and confuse him. He felt no less despondent and more convinced that Zalith didn't want him anymore.

Luther—what a fucking moron. Why did he think talking to that idiot would help? Everything he said was a waste of time. It made no sense. It was no help.

Alucard scowled frustratedly and made his way along the path. His emotions were all over the place, and he didn't understand why it was so hard to get them under control, why it was such a strain to ignore the paranoia. But emotions were still new to him; before Zalith, all he knew was dismay, despair, and loneliness. And anger. The *rage*. Before he met and fell in love with Zalith, he'd simply shut his emotions off like closing a boring book. But now, as much as he tried, he couldn't ignore the ache in his heart, the hole in his soul. Zalith meant so much to him. He was a part of him, and it felt so very wrong *not* to be spending at least half his day with him.

But he didn't know what to do.

With a sullen sigh, he slipped his hands into his pockets and headed into the manor gardens. He wasn't sure what he'd do once he got into the house, but he was certain that he wouldn't be seeing Zalith until tonight.

# Chapter Four

― ⸲ † ⸳ ―

# Mary-Beth

**| Alucard |**

Alucard walked languidly through the gardens as he pulled his flask from his inside pocket and took a sip of the blood inside. Zalith continued to ensnare his thoughts, and the dismay was overwhelming. He was starting to feel frustrated; he didn't understand what was going on, and not understanding made him feel aggravated.

Part of him felt as though he should keep waiting for things to return to how they used to be, but another part of him told him that nothing would change unless he faced the situation. If he faced it, though, what would Zalith's response be? He was terrified that the demon had lost interest and was simply waiting for him to notice and say something, starting the awkward conversation.

He frowned despondently, approaching the gravel-covered courtyard. But that was when he *finally* snapped out of his despair-ridden mind. Sitting on the bench not too far from the fountain was a blonde woman dressed in a baby-blue off-shoulder dress. The sclera of her brown eyes was red from her tears, which were streaming down her face as she cried quietly into a white handkerchief.

The vampire stopped by the wall and stared at her, waiting to see if anyone would come and claim her—she was most likely one of Varana's friends; why else would there be a strange woman crying outside? She didn't like Zalith's kind of company.

He waited a few more seconds and took another sip from his flask, grimacing as the bland taste struck him, but the woman kept weeping into her cloth. The vampire frowned, sighed quietly, and continued on his way towards his house.

As he got closer to her, though, her cries grew more distressing. No one else was around…and he'd faced so much despair lately that it felt wrong of him to just leave her there. So he stopped a few feet away from where she sat and asked, "Vhy do you cry?"

The blonde woman gasped quietly, wiped away her tears, and glanced up at him. She stared at him with her teary eyes; she opened her mouth to speak but then frowned sadly and looked down at her lap. She shook her head, sniffling again. "I just…got into a disagreement with the girls."

Alucard frowned, looking around again to see if the mentioned girls were coming to collect their friend.

"Oh…I'm sorry. Should I go somewhere else?" she asked sadly as she picked up and placed a white box that had been concealed beside her onto her lap. "I'm probably in the way," she said, her voice strangely croaky. How long had she been crying?

"No…" he answered. "Vhy are you out 'ere by yourselv?"

She took her eyes off her lap and looked around. "Oh, I'm just…waiting for my carriage to take me home. I thought it was better…better to wait out here than in there with…them," she said quietly, wiping her wet face with her rather ghastly-looking handkerchief.

Alucard nodded slowly. Her friends were evidently inside, and they'd most likely come out to get her soon—or not. What did it matter? He wasn't going to stand around with some woman; he needed to figure out what he was going to do with his own sadness—a sadness that was slowly creeping back up on him.

With a slight nod, he turned around and started to head for the front door—

"You're Luca, right?" the woman then asked.

Luca? He stopped in his tracks and looked back over his shoulder at her. "Vhat?"

She wiped her face again and shuffled a little on the bench so that she was facing the direction he was walking. "Luca…Varana's brother."

The sound of that woman's name *always* sent a shiver of irritancy down his spine. Luca? It wasn't that awful—that sour-attituded woman could have called him a lot worse, but she'd chosen to abbreviate his real name; at least she hadn't exposed his real name to strangers.

He nodded a slow, unsure nod—it felt strange to have just been called Varana's brother, but it was a fact…technically. That woman was his sister through their father's ethos, not blood.

"Yes…" he grumbled in response.

Looking up at him, a flicker of confusion danced through her brown eyes as she shrugged her shoulders in discomfort. But a small smile appeared through her tears. "I'm Mary-Beth Thompson," she introduced.

Alucard nodded again. He really didn't feel like talking to her right now. If Varana had gone so far as to give him a nickname, it was obvious that she spoke to this woman and God only knew however many other people about him. He wasn't going to hang around and become the latest gossip for Varana and her friends—the friends he often heard giggling pretty much every day while trying to work in his office.

He looked over at the door to his house, frowned, and then looked back at the woman. "I 'ave to—"

"Do many people know?" she interjected, speaking at the exact same time as him; as she realized that she cut him off, she frowned in startlement. "Sorry."

"Know vhat?"

"That… that you're gay," she said quietly, leaning closer.

"Vhat?" he asked confusedly. At first, he felt confounded as to why it mattered how many people knew he was gay, but then he remembered that he was now living in Nefastus, a land where people often spoke as though they didn't care who someone loved or slept with, but in reality, they did. He wasn't sure what to say in response—whether to confirm or deny the fact.

But Mary-Beth then waved her hand and giggled a little. "Oh, how very rude of me," she said, shuffling over to make space on the bench. "Here, have a seat. Do you want some cake?" she asked almost as if she was in a rush. "They're chocolate raspberry," she offered, opening the white box and revealing three chocolate muffins, each with a few pink raspberries on top. She patted the seat beside her; the sadness seemed to fade from her face.

Alucard felt hesitant. Did he want to sit down with someone who was friends with Varana? Not exactly. He was sure that it was a lure to ask him a whole lot of questions that he didn't want to answer. However, Mary-Beth had been crying and mentioned she'd had a disagreement with the girls, which had to mean Varana and whoever else she was always giggling with. Perhaps Mary-Beth just wanted to talk to someone who wasn't Varana; he was sure, after all, that she was the one who made Mary-Beth sob.

And then there was the cake. He wasn't exactly hungry; he felt very put off by the mere thought of food lately… but maybe he'd want it in a minute. So, he slowly turned around, eyed her for a moment, and sat down.

She handed him one of the cupcakes, closed the box, and rested her arms on it.

He wasn't sure what to say or do, so he just looked down at the cake in his hand.

"I'm sorry if I'm being intrusive," she said, staring at him. "It's just that when we heard that Varana and Z weren't actually ever married and that he was seeing you, we were all really shocked."

He stared at the cake as the mere mention of Zalith dragged him right back into his sadness. He didn't even want to think about how Varana made it seem as though she and Zalith were married; that woman was an entirely different problem, one Alucard had tried not to overthink.

Mary-Beth didn't pick up on his sorrow, though, and kept talking. "Both Cadence and Varana painted quite a picture of you," she continued after a moment of silence. "But I didn't expect your hair to be so red," she laughed excitedly. "It's so gorgeous—and

Cadence was right, you are quite handsome. The devastatingly good looks run in the family, I see," she said with a smile.

Alucard didn't know how to reply; all he could do was stare at the cake and try to fight the drowning dismay.

"Your parents must be stunning," Mary-Beth said. She waited for him to say something, but after a few moments, she smiled again. "What was it like growing up with V? She must have been such a handful, huh?"

He frowned a little as he glanced at her. "I zidn't grow up vith 'er."

"O-oh!" she gasped excitedly. "But I guess that makes sense, considering that you both have different accents," she laughed. His lack of response brought a frown to her face; her eyes then wandered down to the cake in his hand. "You really don't have to eat it if you don't want to," she said, sadness returning to her voice. "It's okay. The girls didn't seem too fond of them…well, Varana, mostly."

The vampire took his eyes off the cake and glanced at her again. "Vhy zidn't zhey like zhem?"

"Well…they did at first, but…." She sighed sadly and looked down at the box. "But then Varana tried it, and she doesn't like chocolate with raspberries, so she spat it out and said it was disgusting, and the other girls did the same thing because they always feel the need to impress her," she explained. "It's an old family recipe, and I was excited to get them to try it—it was a big part of my childhood," she added as tears returned to her face.

Alucard took his eyes off Mary-Beth and stared at the cake. He *really* didn't feel like eating anything; he'd thought that maybe being handed the cake would encourage him, but the thought of any sort of food made him feel sick. Perhaps it was because he'd pretty much been forced back to drinking the blood of humans to keep himself from starving. The downgrade in both the flavour and the effects it had on him made him feel more uncomfortable and strangely tired than usual, and it made any other kind of sustenance seem revolting, just like the cake in front of him.

However, he didn't want Mary-Beth to start sobbing again, nor did he want to be rude and awful like Varana. So, with a despondent exhale, he took a small bite. It tasted exactly how he expected it to taste, as bland as everything else. As his sadness gradually worsened with each day, his sense of taste withered just a bit more. Nothing he ate made him feel anything—no enjoyment, no satisfaction. It was just food.

He looked at Mary-Beth. "Is good," he lied, unsure of what else to say

Mary-Beth's face lightened up in response.

He looked back down at the cake. "Zon't listen to vhat zhat voman says. 'Er sense of taste is dreadvul; zhat is ovten made clear vhrough zhe outvits she chooses to vear," he grumbled.

Mary-Beth giggled and held her hand to her mouth. "It's not that awful. She's just...particular sometimes."

"Particular," he scoffed, looking at the house.

"I'm sorry I didn't introduce myself sooner," she then said. "I've been coming over to your house for months, and I never said hello. I feel horrible."

Alucard shrugged as he looked back down at the cake. "Is vine," he mumbled, tearing a piece of the cake with his fingers. "I 'aven't veally noticed anyvone coming or going." He ate the small tear of cake.

"Oh...really? Well, that's good. I always worry that we're too loud, especially with your offices being so close to where we usually spend our time."

The vampire stared down at the cake; he felt burnt out...like all his energy had faded away, and he was running on his reserves. He wanted to go and lay by himself and try to figure out why Zalith had become so distant—it was still all he could think about. He couldn't remember the last time *they'd* had a conversation...a long, meaningful, or even *relaxing* conversation together. It hurt to think about how much time they weren't spending together, and it hurt more to think that Zalith's time was going elsewhere...maybe to someone else.

"You should come and spend time with us one of these days," Mary-Beth invited, still smiling. "I'm sure you're more than welcome."

Alucard scoffed again. "I know I'm not," he said. He knew that Varana didn't like him, and he didn't like her. The last thing either of them would do was spend time together, especially now.

"Why not? I know that Cadence and Selena would love to meet you."

"No. Varana and I are...not vriends," he grumbled. Saying her name left a disgusting taste in his mouth, a taste worse than the cupcake he was trying to finish to be polite.

Mary-Beth frowned sadly. "Oh...well, I'm sure she'll come around. I imagine she's upset that you and Z are together, but I think she's just going to have to get used to it."

His sadness grew. Could that even be said anymore? Zalith and him...together? It didn't feel like it, and he was terrified that soon, it might be a fact that he and Zalith *weren't* together. He felt like everything was pointing to that conclusion; the lack of communication, the drastic decrease in time spent together, the absence of intimacy— when was the last time they embraced one another or kissed? A hug or a kiss that wasn't short, snappy, and short-lived. He was too sad to try and remember.

"It doesn't bother *me*," she continued. "I haven't seen you and Z together in person, but when I visualize it, you both look very cute together."

Alucard scowled in distress. He missed Zalith so much. Despite the fact that he was in the house just a small distance away, it didn't feel like he was there at all. Alucard didn't feel what he felt before; when he walked into that house, he felt happy and safe...he felt content in a way that he never had before. But now it just felt like walking into his old home—empty…emptiness that projected a horrible feeling of loss, confusion, and loneliness. It didn't warm him knowing that Zalith was within the same walls, it just made him sadder because as often as he thought about Zalith, he was sure Zalith wasn't thinking about him.

A dark-brown carriage led by a white mare then pulled up to the courtyard.

"Oh, that's me!" Mary-Beth said, standing up. "Don't worry, your secret's safe with me," she said quietly. "It's safe with all of us. None of the girls are going to tell anyone about you and Z. He's done a lot of good here, and we'd hate to ruin things for him. Here." She opened the box again. "Why don't you take one of these for Z, too?" she suggested, handing Alucard another muffin.

Alucard stood up as he took it from her.

"Have a nice day, Luca—and it was nice to meet you," she called as she waved and hurried towards the carriage.

The vampire nodded and watched her leave. Then, with a quiet sigh, he glanced down at the cake. The sadness in his heart grew heavier, and he felt conflicted about delivering the cake to Zalith. Did he want to see him? Of course he did, but all the uncertainty and confusion was so overbearing that he began feeling anxious.

One thing he *was* sure about, however, was that he wasn't going to stand outside anymore. He wanted to lie down. So he turned around and headed towards the house. He'd decide what to do with the cake later.

# Chapter Five

⌐ ⋜ ✝ ⋝ ⌐

# Cupcake

**| Alucard |**

When Alucard got into the entrance hall, he slipped his shoes off. His anxiety worsened by the second; his thoughts became louder, and that feeling of loss and emptiness grew heavier.

Maybe Luther was right. Perhaps he *should* speak to Zalith about how he felt. He was so confused, and being confused made him feel frustrated and angry. If he wanted answers, he'd have to ask for them, wouldn't he? But what if the answers he got weren't the ones he wanted? Or what if Zalith was waiting for him to go and ask him why all of this was happening so he could tell him he didn't want him anymore?

Alucard felt stupid for thinking that. If Zalith felt that way, he wouldn't still be around, would he? But then why… why was Zalith so different? Why had things between them changed so much? What was he missing? Was Luther wrong? Was *he* the problem? Could *Zalith* think that *he* was the one losing interest? Was that possible? What if all of this change was happening because *he* had stopped seeking Zalith's attention?

He glanced down at the cake in his hand again and then looked across the hall at the door to Zalith's office. It was open, and his guests had obviously left. It was the first time in a while that Zalith appeared to be free. Maybe…he should go to him. But what if Zalith didn't want to see him?

Alucard scowled irritably. His thoughts were so annoying. Half of them told him to go and see Zalith so he could stop feeling so sad and alone because he missed him, and the other half told him not to because it might make things worse. What should he do? He had no idea. But the fact remained that the cake in his hand was meant for Zalith, and he should probably deliver it to him before it started to dry out and become nasty.

With a conflicted frown, he silenced his thoughts as best he could and walked towards the demon's office. He wasn't sure what might come of his choice, but he just wanted to see Zalith. Maybe he'd find the answer to his worries if he showed him *he* hadn't lost interest; for all he knew, Zalith could be feeling the same way he was and might be just as afraid to approach the situation they found themselves in.

However, when he reached the demon's office and stepped inside, his mind went blank. Zalith was sitting behind his desk, dressed in black suit trousers, a dark grey shirt, and a black waistcoat; he looked as neat and tidy as ever, and the moment Alucard set his eyes on him, the pain, worry, and confusion returned. All he could do was stand there, stare, and try to work out what to say.

Zalith stopped writing, looked at him, and smiled. "Hey," he said, not an ounce of worry or confusion in his voice. He seemed as calm as he always was.

Alucard's sadness grew. He took his eyes off the demon, setting his gaze on the floor instead. He didn't understand why seeing him made him feel so sad—he was right there, yet…he missed him with such distress that he couldn't even begin to try and explain.

"What's wrong?" the demon asked, a frown appearing on his face as he rested his arms on his desk.

He didn't want to start—he didn't know how. The hurt kept him trapped in a still silence. His thoughts were stifled; it was as though he'd opened a book expecting to find words but instead found nothing but blank pages.

"Vhere did your Alphas go?" he asked, that being the only thing that he dared to ask.

"They left," he answered. "What's wrong?"

The invitation was right there. Alucard could tell him what was wrong; he could tell him how sad and alone and confused he felt. But his fear outweighed everything else. So he just gave up before he even started. He felt so useless and hopeless that there probably wasn't even any point in trying to explain. "I'm vine," he lied. "Luther vas just…annoying."

Zalith frowned and leaned back in his seat. "Come here."

He didn't want to move, but as Zalith then stood up and made his way over, Alucard frowned in confusion. When Zalith reached him, he took the cake from his hands, placed it on the nearby table, and pulled him into a tight embrace.

Alucard's confusion became overwhelming as he stood there, unsure of what to say or do. For months, Zalith had barely even touched him, and now the demon was hugging him as though that hadn't been the case. Why?

He moved his arms around Zalith, his longing for the demon's affection urging him to take whatever he could get. He rested the side of his head on Zalith's shoulder as he closed his eyes, trying to fight his torment and the hold it had over him. He tightened his grip around Zalith, a scowl of distress forming on his face as he did his best to hide just how much he missed him.

"It's okay," Zalith said quietly.

Was it? Alucard ignored his racing thoughts. All he knew right now was that this was exactly what he needed. Despite the months of uncertainty, confusion, and sadness, the embrace he now found himself in muted all his worry.

Maybe he was just overthinking. Maybe they were fine. Maybe Zalith was just busy. Maybe he needed to make more of an effort to show Zalith that he wanted his attention. Maybe they were okay. Maybe…maybe everything would be okay now.

*Maybe.*

Zalith then leaned back, kissed Alucard's cheek, and glanced at the cake. "Did you bring me a snack?" he asked with a smile.

Alucard's sadness slowly faded as the thought of things actually being okay started to take hold of him. He nodded and said, "Zhere vas a…Mary…Bev outside. She gave me vone to give to you."

The demon picked up the cake. "That's nice of her," he said, tearing it in half. He then tried some, smirked, and held a piece of it towards the vampire. "I only want half of it," he said, obviously waiting for Alucard to eat the cake he had between his thumb and index finger.

Alucard frowned again, but he didn't hesitate. He ate the cake, but his confusion started to return. Right now, things seemed fine…things seemed normal. Zalith was smiling, smirking, and making him eat things—it was as if the past months of nothing didn't even exist in Zalith's eyes. *Could* everything be fine? Was he simply overthinking everything?

But Zalith then donned a look of regret and sighed quietly. "I have to head out."

There it was. The sharp, painful end to a moment Alucard hoped would linger. His aching heart felt as though a stake had been driven through it, and silence gripped him once again.

"I don't think I'll make it home in time for dinner, but we can talk when I get back, okay?"

The despair constricted him. It was always the same thing. He had to leave, he wouldn't be home in time for dinner, and he wouldn't be there when Alucard woke up the next morning, either. "Vhere are you going?" he asked.

"To Eltaria. There are a few things I have to take care of."

Alucard suspected *that* was where Zalith had been going whenever he couldn't be found around the house. He remembered Zalith telling him that he might have to shift his focus to his homeworld, but why? "Vhat vings?" he asked with a frown.

"It's been brought to my attention that someone may be conspiring among my allies. I have to find, interrogate, and kill him."

The fact that Zalith was heading to Eltaria to deal with something work-related banished a little of Alucard's sadness…but it didn't answer everything. He didn't want to let all his worry and confusion take away the small glimmer of hope he had found, though. They seemed fine right now; Zalith was acting normal—he hugged him…kissed him…and he didn't seem to be hiding anything.

He nodded, looking down at the floor for a moment. He missed Zalith so much that he didn't want this moment to end; he had his attention, he was beginning to feel okay…and he didn't want to spend any more of today without Zalith. "Do you vant me to come vith you?" he offered.

Hesitation smothered Zalith's face. "No," he denied. "I don't want you to get hurt."

Alucard didn't have the energy to argue. What was the point?

"I want you to stay here where it's safe."

Zalith didn't want him to go with him, and he didn't seem to want to stick around, either. But he had work to do, obviously, and Alucard wouldn't keep him from it. "Okay," he said.

The demon smiled slightly as he pulled Alucard closer. He moved a few strands of Alucard's hair out of his face so that he could stare into his eyes. "I love you," he said quietly.

*Did* he? Alucard didn't feel it the way he used to feel it, but Zalith had just said it, so…he had to mean it, right? He tried his best to keep a vacant stare rather than the despondent one that was trying to fight its way onto his face. "I love you," he replied.

Zalith leaned closer and pressed his lips against Alucard's. But their kiss didn't last very long—Zalith did, however, stop to look at Alucard for a moment and kiss him one more time. "I have to go now," he said regretfully.

Alucard lifted his head and looked at him. He didn't want Zalith to go, but he wouldn't keep him from his work—but he wanted…no, he *needed* more. It had been so long since he'd felt something contentful, something satisfying. Their hug was short, and Zalith's kisses were shorter—it wasn't like before. But he felt selfish, he felt awful for feeling as though it wasn't enough. It was different, but…it was *something*. He wouldn't push. He'd take this short moment after months of nothing.

He nodded, trying to keep himself from sinking into sadness.

"I'll see you later," Zalith said with a soft smile.

And then…Zalith walked away, heading for his office door.

Alucard watched him leave. He felt the desire to reach out and snatch his arm to stop him so that he could spend a few more moments with him, but he didn't want to seem clingy or get in the way of Zalith's work.

He stood there, not yet sure what to do with himself. Despite how much he missed Zalith and wished he would stay, he felt a little better. Zalith didn't seem like he wasn't interested, he just…still seemed a little distant, but maybe that was because he was heading off to weed out a traitor among his subordinates.

The vampire sighed quietly and left Zalith's office, retreating into his own. He'd wait until he got home; Zalith said they'd talk once he returned, and maybe then Alucard would be able to talk to him about how he was feeling. Perhaps Luther was right, maybe talking to him was what he should do. But what was he supposed to do until Zalith came home?

As he closed his office door behind him, he looked around slowly. The first thing that came to mind was his dreams; after all this time, he was still having such awful, upsetting nightmares. Eight months ago, he said he'd look into it, but he'd become distracted and unmotivated to do pretty much anything. However, he now felt he had the motivation he needed. Although their interaction had been brief, it made him feel hopeful.

He headed to the book-lined walls on his right, took the books he'd need to investigate dream ethos, and sat on one of the couches. He wasn't sure how long Zalith would be, but the demon said he'd miss dinner. That was okay. Alucard didn't feel like eating anyway. He just wanted to sit, read, and wait for Zalith to get home.

# Chapter Six

# Await

| **Alucard** |

Alucard wasn't sure how long he'd been waiting. He watched the late afternoon become night; he read through most of the dream ethos books, and he was close to being done with his research altogether.

Not only was he tired, but he was also worried; Zalith had been gone for hours, and he didn't know much about what he was doing at all, only that he'd gone to find, interrogate, and kill someone. But who? *With* who? He scowled, resting his book in his lap as he gazed at the black sky outside. He was sure that it was close to midnight, and as much as he wanted to wait for Zalith so that they could talk, his tiredness was beginning to overwhelm him.

The vampire glanced back down at his book, his eyes heavy, his head starting to ache. He looked around his office and attempted to find something to focus on, but nothing helped. He tried reading more pages, but he couldn't comprehend any of the information. He was too tired to concentrate.

Alucard had no idea where Zalith was, so he couldn't even go looking for him. He *could* see how Zalith was feeling through their imprint connection, but…it made him feel anxious. He might not like what he discovered, so he shoved aside the thought and glared at his book. How much longer would Zalith be?

With a tired sigh and despondent frown, he lowered his book and stared at the window again. Maybe he should just stop worrying; it was Zalith, after all, and he knew there was nothing that man couldn't handle.

He shuffled around and laid back on the couch. He tried reading again…and just moments later—to his relief—he heard the front door open and shut. Zalith's voice echoed through the hall with Edwin's—he was telling the butler to make sure that his blazer was cleaned thoroughly. Then, his footsteps came towards Alucard's office.

When his door opened, Zalith came in, smiled at him, and said, "Hey."

For a moment, Alucard just stared at him. He looked exhausted; his hair was messy, his waistcoat was torn at the bottom, and he had blood on his shirt—but it wasn't his own. Alucard knew the captivating scent of Zalith's blood, and that was not it.

The vampire sat up and placed his book in his lap as he watched Zalith walk over to him.

Zalith pulled off his waistcoat, slumped down on the couch beside him, and took off his shirt. He dropped both on the floor—he obviously didn't want to get blood or dirt anywhere. Then, he leaned closer, resting his head on Alucard's shoulder as he sighed deeply and tiredly.

Alucard didn't know what to say. He laid back and made himself comfortable, inviting Zalith to do the same. And then, for a moment, they just lay there. He wanted to ask Zalith whose blood was on his shirt; he wanted to know why he looked so exhausted, but he wasn't sure whether or not Zalith even wanted to talk about what he'd come back from. He wanted to know if Zalith was okay, though, so he looked down at what he could see of the demon.

"Are you…okay?" he asked him, looking him up and down for signs of healing injuries or marks, but there was nothing of the sort.

Zalith moved his hand over Alucard's chest and rested it on his shoulder. "I'm okay," he answered with a huff. "It's just been a long day; I'm tired. What are you reading?"

Glancing down at the book he'd placed in his lap, Alucard shrugged lightly. "I vas looking into dream ethos—maybe I can vind someving to 'elp me stop zhe nightmares I 'ave," he said, picking the book back up.

Still with his head rested against Alucard's shoulder, Zalith nodded. "Have you found anything yet?"

"Not veally," Alucard answered, looking at the pages in front of him. "I've just been looking vor…vings zhat might 'elp. Noving 'as veally stood out to me yet, zhough."

Zalith was quiet for a moment…but then exhaled quietly. "I hope you find what you're looking for."

Alucard frowned; he could tell that Zalith probably just wanted to go to bed. Of course, he still wanted to talk and spend as much time with him as he could, but…it was late, Zalith was tired, and for all Alucard knew, he could be hurting, too. He didn't know what he might have been through, and seeing that his clothes were torn and dirty convinced him that the demon had been through more than simply interrogating and killing someone. Had he been fighting?

It saddened him, but he cared more about how Zalith felt than he cared about himself. They could always talk tomorrow, right? He frowned despondently, hesitation starting to grip him. But…Zalith seemed okay—*they* seemed okay. Why would tomorrow be any different? He could wake up and talk to Zalith over breakfast or lunch…or he could just go to him in his office again. He felt more confident about talking to him now; after all, why would Zalith have come straight to him, and why would he be lying with him right now if he didn't want him anymore?

They could talk tomorrow.

He looked down at Zalith again. "Ve can...go to bed," he said, closing his book. "And...talk tomorrow, no?"

"No, it's okay," he mumbled quietly. "I want to be here with you."

"But...is almost midnight."

Zalith sighed heavily. "Are *you* tired?" he asked, his voice quieter and sleepier than when he'd first sat down.

Was he? Now that Zalith was home, he felt everything but tired. He wanted to talk to him—he wanted to just sit there and have a conversation about anything; it didn't even have to be about his feelings or his worries. He simply wanted to spend time with him. But he was sure that Zalith would fall asleep any moment; he didn't want that to happen, but he didn't really know what to do or if he should do anything at all. He didn't want Zalith to lose the sleep he needed.

He exhaled quietly and placed his book on the table behind him. "Yes," he mumbled. "Ve can go to bed."

The demon murmured quietly. "Okay," was one of the few words Alucard could make out. "Let's go."

But Zalith didn't get up.

Alucard waited, sitting there for a moment. He couldn't get up with Zalith leaning on him, but it appeared that Zalith was so tired that Alucard might have to help him up.

He tried to get up, but Zalith made a disapproving sound, tightened his grip on him, and wrapped his arms around him as if to try and keep him from moving.

Alucard wasn't entirely sure what to do, but Zalith was confusing him. He seemed fine, acting the way he would as if they hadn't just gone months without anything like this. Had the fact that Alucard had gone to him earlier really solved everything? It seemed to be that way.

The vampire hesitated, remaining on the edge of the couch as Zalith rested his head in his lap. He wasn't sure whether he should convince Zalith to follow him up to their bedroom or if it was better to just sleep there. But...it wouldn't be comfortable for them to *both* try and sleep on this couch, would it?

"Ve 'ave to go to bed," he said with a little more sincerity in his voice.

Zalith murmured in disapproval once again, but Alucard wasn't going to let him sleep on the couch. He lightly took hold of Zalith's arms and pulled him up with him as he stood. The demon hesitated but followed Alucard as he started to lead the way out of his office and through the hall.

The demon gripped Alucard's hand, staring tiredly as he followed closely behind Alucard. And together, they made their way up the stairs and towards their bedroom.

Once they got into their room, Zalith slumped down on the edge of the bed, pulled off the rest of his clothes, and crawled under the blankets.

Alucard got undressed, too, and when he lay down, the demon shuffled closer and rested his head on his shoulder once more.

The vampire looked down at what he could see of Zalith; he was sure that he'd already fallen asleep. But that was okay. Zalith was exhausted, and Alucard just wanted him to rest.

He turned his head to the right, resting it on the side of Zalith's. Tomorrow, he was sure that things would be a whole lot better. He'd talk to Zalith and spend time with him… and the past months of confusion and sadness wouldn't weigh on his mind anymore.

At least he hoped so.

# Chapter Seven

## Scars

| Alucard |

Something hit the marble floor.

Alucard's frown deepened as he stirred from his sleep. He gradually opened his eyes, surveying his surroundings through a haze of grogginess. He didn't know what time it was, but he found his bedroom cloaked in shadows, the feeble light of dawn barely penetrating through the curtains. Yet, the stark brightness seeping from the slightly ajar bathroom door stung his eyes, intensifying his discomfort.

He lay there on his back, and it didn't take him long to notice that Zalith wasn't beside him anymore. The vampire looked to his right, hoping that the demon had just rolled over in the night, but he wasn't in bed at all. Alucard shifted his sights back to the bathroom, and when the light turned off and the door opened, he watched Zalith walk out.

Zalith made his way out of the bathroom without a towel or clothes in what looked like a rush. Alucard observed from where he lay as the demon headed into the dressing rooms. Where could he be going, and why was he in a hurry?

Alucard waited, and after a few minutes, Zalith came back out of the dressing rooms in a pair of black trousers and walked towards the bedroom door as he pulled on the white shirt he'd been holding.

But Alucard sat up as a confused scowl found its way to his tired face. "Vhere are you going?" he asked sleepily.

The demon stopped in his tracks and turned to face him. He frowned a little through his tired expression and enthusiastically said, "Eltaria." He didn't seem at all pleased to be going there. He walked to the bed and sat beside Alucard.

For a few moments, Alucard stared at him, trying to work out what he wanted to say. He felt so tired that he couldn't concentrate on anything but what he could see of Zalith's body as he tied his shirt buttons. The first thing that came to mind was how much he missed him, how much he missed his touch, his embrace, and the softness of his lips, but the longer he sat there trying to wake up, the more his mind started racing. The thought of how much he really didn't want to spend another day by himself constricted him, clashing with the growing desire for Zalith's affection. If he wasn't so shy, he'd ask if he wanted to have sex, but he wasn't sure of what Zalith's answer might be.

He frowned sadly. "Vhy?" He questioned and glanced at the clock. "Is…vive in zhe morning."

"I have to check in on the situation; the ramifications for killing the man I killed yesterday may be bad, and I need to be there; I've already been away longer than I should have," he explained, tying the last button.

As Zalith grabbed his blazer from the edge of the bed, Alucard's frown thickened with despondency. If he had known that Zalith was leaving so early today, he wouldn't have given up his chance to talk to him last night—but then again…Zalith had been so tired and making him stay up longer would have been selfish. He felt selfish *right now* for wishing to keep Zalith with him rather than let him go again.

Confliction gripped his heart. He had no idea what time Zalith might be back and if he'd get the chance to talk to him today. Maybe…he could go with him, then he'd get to not only talk to him about his concerns but he'd also get to spend more time with him, something he so sorely ached for.

"I vant to come vith you," he said and went to lift the blanket so that he could get out of bed and get ready.

Zalith placed his hand over Alucard's wrist and stopped him. "No, it's okay, baby; stay here and get some more sleep," he insisted quietly.

"No, I vant to come vith you," he said, a little sterner this time.

The demon stared at him with an overwrought look of hesitation on his face. He then sighed deeply and looked down at the floor, closing his eyes for a moment as he shook his head. "Alucard, I can't…" he muttered, slowly looking back at him. But then he sighed again, gazing into the vampire's eyes. "I want you to stay here," he said sadly.

Alucard wasn't sure what Zalith might have wanted to say, but he didn't need to be told again that the demon didn't want him to go with him. As that fact stabbed and burrowed into his heart, he quickly lost any motivation to fight him. If Zalith didn't want him with him, he'd not force or insert himself.

Both anger and sadness enthralled him as he frowned, a pout making its way onto his face. "Vine," he mumbled, laying back down on his side so that Zalith couldn't see most of his irritated face. He was far too tired and far too upset to get into an argument; that was the last thing he wanted. So, he lay there, glaring at the wall, trying to ignore the ache in his heart.

Zalith sighed quietly and caressed the vampire's hair. "I'm sorry."

Silence grasped them.

After a few moments, though, Zalith pulled his blazer on. "I have to go," he said quietly. He leaned over, kissed the vampire's forehead, and stood up. "Go back to sleep," he said, pulling the blanket up to cover Alucard's shoulders. "I'll see you when I get home."

Alucard didn't reply; his anger and sadness built as each moment passed. He felt like an idiot for believing that he might actually get to spend some time with Zalith today and watching him leave once again made him feel empty. Perhaps he should just get used to it, for it seemed to be the new norm, especially over the past few months. Was this what their lives were going to be like now? Brief moments of conversation, rare minutes of something not even close to the intimacy that they used to share, and lonely, empty mornings?

He closed his eyes, his conflicted feelings at war with one another as he listened to the bedroom door close and Zalith leaving him once again. This *was* how things were going to be now, wasn't it? And he'd have to get used to it.

But could he?

Daylight came. Alucard opened his eyes, the irritating weight of pain in his head greeting him when he woke. As if it were instinct, he rolled over and searched the bed with his hand for Zalith, but he wasn't there. The demon had gone so early this morning, leaving Alucard to his despondent thoughts—but it wasn't just sadness he felt. He felt something angry, frustrated. Why didn't Zalith want him to go with him to Eltaria? Why didn't Zalith seem to want to take a chance to spend more time with him?

There could only be *one* answer: Zalith just didn't want to spend as much time with Alucard as he used to, did he? As much as it hurt, Alucard would have to accept that; but he wanted to understand why—why didn't Zalith want to spend time with him? The things Damien called him for four hundred years came in the way of answers. Boring. Useless. Ordinary. Pathetic. Annoying. He wasn't special, was he? Was Zalith beginning to see that?

Alucard sighed shakily as the sadness tightened his throat. He stared up at the ceiling as he moved his hand from Zalith's side of the bed and rested it on his chest; he didn't know what to think. Yesterday, Zalith seemed normal—they hugged, talked, and kissed; Zalith came to see him once he got home and was acting like his usual, strangely clingy self. But now...now he was back to the confusing, distant demon whom Alucard had come to know in the past months. Now, Alucard was almost certain that this was how things would be from this point on. And all he could do was either accept and live with it...or leave.

He sat up, dragging his hand over the back of his head as his headache started to wane. This was the first time the thought crossed his mind…to leave rather than remain in a place where he felt so sad, confused, and lost. He didn't want to leave; he loved Zalith so much. He wanted to spend his lifetime with him. But he couldn't deny that it was beginning to feel as though Zalith might not feel the same. After all, why would he want to spend his life with someone he didn't even want to spend a few hours with?

With another deep sigh, Alucard did his best to try and silence his conflicted thoughts, half of which were telling him that Zalith was just busy, and the other half told him that Zalith didn't want him the way he used to and was only holding off on telling him because he promised he'd not leave him. But if that were the case, Alucard wouldn't want Zalith to stay with him just because he felt like he had to.

He climbed out of bed and pulled his trousers on as he headed into the bathroom. But when he stood in front of the mirror, he froze. He glared at himself, his anger tearing through his sadness. He didn't want to let Damien's words sink their teeth into him, but…what if it was true? Zalith was acting differently. Why couldn't he go to Eltaria with him? Because Zalith didn't want him to get hurt? Zalith knew how capable Alucard was—that couldn't be the reason. So, what *was* the reason? Was there something going on in Eltaria that Zalith didn't want Alucard to see? Perhaps…some*one*?

No. He didn't want to think like that. Zalith promised him that he no longer did the things that he did when he was younger, the things Varana talked about. He didn't even want to think about what she said or that woman altogether. He just wanted…he just wanted to feel okay.

His eyes shifted to the scars on his neck left by Zalith's fangs; he placed his hand over them and slowly dragged his palm down his chest. Scars…he was covered in so many ugly scars. Before Zalith said that he didn't need to, he'd always done his best to hide them, and now, for the first time since revealing them to the demon, he found himself thinking that maybe he ought to hide them again. He knew how disgusting they were, especially to another demon. Zalith might have said that he didn't care, but what if he did? What if that played a part in why he seemed to have lost interest? The fact that Alucard had been Disavowed, cast out, exiled from every place and everything demon. What if Zalith couldn't ignore that anymore?

Alucard scowled in distress, closing his eyes as he turned his head away from the mirror. He didn't want to see himself; it would only make him overthink more. So he left the bathroom, hiding away from his reflection.

He made his way into the dressing rooms, snatched a black, long-sleeved t-shirt, and pulled it on over his head as he headed for the bedroom door.

Despite his sadness, he still had to get on with his work. And maybe…he'd get to talk to Zalith tonight.

# Chapter Eight

— ᛉ † ᛣ —

# Alucard's Sister

**| Alucard |**

Sabazios greeted Alucard with a happy bark when he stepped out into the hall. The vampire stopped to look down at him, and the dog sat, holding up his paw and panting excitedly as he waited for Alucard to respond to him.

The vampire frowned despondently but crouched and took the dog's paw in his hand. "Vhat's vrong?"

Looking at him, the dog whined quietly. He clearly knew that Alucard was upset and seemed to want to try and help.

Alucard sighed as he stood back up. "I'm vine," he muttered and headed towards his study. He wasn't sure when Luther would arrive; he was awake a little earlier than he would usually get up, but he didn't want to try and get back to sleep. He knew that he'd only be trapped in another awful nightmare and that he'd wake up to find that the comfort he needed was no longer there. So what better to do with his free time than continue looking for a way to stop the dreams altogether?

He made his way into his study and down the stairs to his office. The books he'd been reading last night were still on the same table he'd left them on, and as he slumped down on the couch, he grabbed one of them and opened it to the bookmarked page.

Last night, he'd been reading about crystal ethos, and it was the only thing that made him feel like he might be close to getting answers. He knew about the existence of crystal mages, and he also knew a little about their practice. Last night, he learned that certain crystals could absorb ethos, energy, memories, emotions, *and* dreams—the latter was what he was looking for, and in his hand was a book focused entirely on crystal ethos. If he'd find his answers anywhere, it would be inside this book.

With a quiet sigh, he started reading, and he tried his best to focus solely on the pages.

A while later, a knock came at his door.

For a moment, Alucard hoped that it was Zalith, but he knew it wasn't.

"Come," he called.

The door opened, and Luther walked in.

Alucard wasn't sure what time it was or how long he was reading, but Luther looked concerned, and that snatched his attention away from his books.

Luther closed the door behind him and sighed deeply as he set his brown eyes on Alucard. "I'm surprised to see you up so early."

"Vhy are you 'ere so soon?" Alucard asked with a frown.

"I get here the same time every day; your butler has me wait outside."

"Vhy?" Alucard asked, closing his book and placing it in his lap. "You know I zon't get up until noon; vhy zon't you come zhen?"

Shrugging, Luther took a few steps forward and looked around. "I like to arrive early, just in case," he said with a smile, setting his eyes back on Alucard.

"Vight...." He climbed to his feet and made his way over to his desk. He sat in his chair and leaned back in it as he watched Luther take a seat in front of him.

"So?" his subordinate asked.

Unsure of what he might be asking, Alucard glared at him. "Vhat?"

"How did it go? Did you talk to him?"

Obviously, he was referring to the conversation they had yesterday regarding Zalith. The answer was no, he hadn't been able to express his feelings or concerns to the demon, and he didn't feel like talking about it to Luther. He scowled, keeping his eyes on his subordinate. "'As anyving 'appened? You came in 'ere looking like you 'ad someving to tell me."

"Uh...yeah," he answered. "To start, Freja's sister is getting married—she thought you should know since she'll be uniting her pack with that of the alpha her sister is marrying."

"Vhat pack?" he asked.

"Some little, unimportant group that moved in not too long after you left to live here. It consists of two Alphas, including himself, and seven Betas. Freja insists she needs your permission, so...here I am...asking...for your permission."

Alucard waved his hand in dismissal as he swivelled around in his chair to stare out the window. "Vhatever. Vhat about zhe vampire situation? 'Ave you made progress?"

Luther sounded hesitant as he answered, "Five more vampires were found staked in the city this morning. They were all in different locations."

Alucard scowled irritably and tapped his claws on the arm of his chair.

"A lot of the vampires are worried that they're being purposely hunted, and I mean...that's what it looks like."

Who would do this? Would the humans really risk the treaty like this? Alucard wasn't sure, but a part of him worried that Marcus' gang might be resurfacing; perhaps they were brewing in the shadows since he killed their leader.

"Jasper also says that the watchers have been seeing a couple of strange people checking out the castle—"

"Vatchers?" Alucard asked, glaring at the forest in the distance.

"That's what Jasper calls the day guards…easier to say, I guess. Anyway, as I said, they've been seeing people checking out the castle."

"Vhat people?"

"I don't know. He says they always come at the same times every day."

"And zhose times are?"

"Twelve, three, and six. Always in black robes, hoods, can't see their faces."

"Interrogate vone of zhem," Alucard ordered. He was beginning to feel like he should get involved. His vampires were becoming afraid, and that was the last thing he wanted any of them to feel. Dealing with this before it got too big was probably a good idea, too. Luther *was* good at his job, but Alucard knew that he'd get things done faster if he did it himself. He wasn't going to let any more of his people die. "I vant all zhe invormation on zhe murdered vampires levt on my desk at zhe castle. I vant to know vhere and 'ow zhey vere vound."

"Got it," Luther said with a nod. "One other thing. I found a place *way* outside of Dargamoore—it's linked to the stuff you had me looking for regarding that Charlotte woman. She was a Meridian witch with demon blood, and she was part of a cult—there were two sub-cults inside the Diabolus back then. She was part of one of them; her particular sub-cult focused on creating children. I don't know if that means anything to you, but…knowing that you're Lucifer's son, I assume that you might be looking for any children that these cults made?"

Listening, Alucard remained silent.

"Uh…well, there aren't any…if that's what you were looking to know—"

"Does zhis sub-cult still exist?"

"Well…it looks like it. I did a lot of digging into the Diabolus, and there are still several sub-cults within the larger one itself. Most of them are made up of witches and seers, though."

"Vind out vhat you can about zhe vone Charlotte vas in."

"All right. Might I…know why you want to know about—"

"No," Alucard grumbled, uninterested in telling him about his mother.

Nodding, Luther sighed quietly. "Well, that's pretty much everything I have."

"Go," he mumbled, glancing back at him. "Get vhat I asked vor."

Luther frowned in response to Alucard's dismissal. He didn't get up, and the hesitant look on his face thickened. With a nervous expression, he leaned his arms onto the table. "I imagine…things *haven't* improved since yesterday, huh?"

"I said go."

Again, Luther sighed. "Why do you stay here? If he's making you feel like this, why don't you just…leave? You don't deserve—"

"I zon't need you to tell me vhat I do and do not deserve," Alucard growled, looking back over his shoulder at him. "I told you to leave, so leave—bevore I make you."

He sighed heavily. "I hate leaving you here knowing that you're alone."

Alucard snarled quietly, slowly swivelling around in his seat to face Luther.

"Just because he's off elsewhere doing God fucking knows what doesn't mean you have to sit around here and do nothing. He doesn't own you; you don't have to sit here and wait for him to get back, you know."

Alucard glowered at him. "Vhen did I ever say 'e owns me?"

"You don't have to say it for me to see, Alucard. Where is he?"

"Get out," Alucard warned.

Luther leaned back in his seat and crossed his arms. "You know," he said, watching Alucard's angered scowl thicken. "This all makes a lot of sense when you think about it. The lack of time for you, the change in his attitude, him being gone all day, and I assume he's gone some nights, too. And then there's also the fact that he's a demon. How do you know he's not out there fucking someone else? I wouldn't put it past him; he seems the type."

Alucard clenched his jaw, but before he could snap at Luther, his heart ached horribly in his chest. He didn't want to consider what he'd just heard, but…could that be it? He frowned sullenly and looked down at his lap. Was that why Zalith seemed to be losing interest? Was he getting what he needed from someone else?

"I'm…I'm sorry," Luther suddenly said. "I didn't mean to put it so crudely, I just…the signs are there, and I won't sit here and watch you suffer whilst he does whatever the hell he wants thinking you're still going to be here when he gets back from whoever's bed he's spent the day in."

Alucard remained silent. The more Luther said, and the more he considered the possibility, the worse his heart hurt. He was right. The signs *were* there. But would Zalith really do that to him?

Luther cleared his throat, leaning back in his seat. "It might not even be the case," he said anxiously, almost as if he was afraid that Alucard was about to scold him. "He could just be…busy, or…." He sighed heavily and shook his head. "Alucard, I don't know the full story. But…from what I do know, and from what I've seen, you really don't need to stay here and wait around for someone who doesn't value you. Just…I'm always here for you if you want to talk or get away from here for a while. I just want you to be happy, you know?"

Still, Alucard remained silent. He didn't want to talk about this with him. He just wanted to be alone.

Luther evidently—and *finally*—worked that out. He exhaled deeply and stood up. "I'll see you tomorrow, then, I guess." He looked back at the door and then at Alucard one last time, waiting to see if he had anything to say.

But his silence wasn't broken.

With a quiet sigh, Luther got up and left the office, pulling the door shut behind him.

Alucard scowled in dismay, tears building up in his eyes. He didn't want to think about it, but he couldn't keep himself from wondering…what if it was true? He trusted Zalith—of course he did; he just wasn't entirely sure what to think anymore.

With a sullen frown, he slouched back in his seat and stared out of the window. He just wanted to go back to bed. But he couldn't. His people were being killed, and he needed to find out who was responsible. Until Luther contacted him and told him that he'd gathered the information he asked for, though, there wasn't much he could do but wait.

| **Luther** |

Luther headed through the hall as he wiped his hand over his face. He'd tried his best to help Alucard, but it was like everything that he was saying was going in one ear and out the other. He knew he'd probably stepped over the line several times, but it was hard as hell to get Alucard to talk sometimes.

He highly suspected that Zalith was being unfaithful to Alucard, and his boss— his *friend*—deserved so much better than that. Zalith was likely out there sneaking around with people who didn't even come close to how amazing Alucard was. Obviously, Zalith didn't see that—he didn't respect Alucard. But that was Zalith's loss. Luther didn't care how long it took, he *would* make sure Alucard understood that he deserved better.

With another sigh, he dragged his hand over his face—

"Watch where you're going!" came the astounded exclamation of the woman Luther had just collided with.

Luther stumbled and stepped back, taking his eyes off the ground to stare at the black-haired, crimson-eyed woman dressed in an elegant, emerald-green dress. He stuttered and stood up straight, realizing that he hadn't been watching where he was going, too focused on his thoughts. "Sorry," he said.

But the woman smiled sweetly and laughed as she waved her hand ever so slightly. "Oh, don't worry about it."

He also smiled. It was a while ago, but he remembered seeing her outside with Zalith back when Alucard had only just moved into this place, and he'd also seen glimpses of her here and there around the house throughout his visits. Surely, she was someone close to either Alucard or Zalith—maybe both of them.

"You're Alucard's friend, right?" she asked.

"Luther," he greeted, holding out his hand.

Her smile widened. "Varana," she said, placing her hand in his. "Alucard's baby sister."

His eyes widened in surprise as he pulled the woman's hand towards his face. He kissed the back of her palm and then smirked as she giggled. "I wasn't aware he had a sister—and one so elegant."

Varana slowly pulled her hand out of his as she smiled flirtatiously. She gripped his tie and straightened it, leaning closer. "I've only ever seen you from behind," she mumbled, stroking her hand down over his tie. "How cute I found you from that angle doesn't compare to how I find you from this one."

Luther smirked, keeping his eyes on her as she slowly took her hands off him and stepped back. He'd not deny how beautiful she was, and if he wasn't so distracted by Alucard, he might actually fancy her. But Alucard was his current objective, and he'd not become phased by his sister.

"Sorry," he repeated again, keeping his smile. "I was just on my way out."

"I won't keep you, then," Varana said with a pleasant smile. "It was nice to finally meet you, Luther," she said as he headed for the door.

He looked back over his shoulder at her.

"Have a nice day," she called, smiling as she waved him off.

Luther smiled back at her but then faced ahead once he was out of the house. He ignored the group of three brightly-dressed women waiting by the fountain as he made his way towards the gardens; his thoughts immediately returned to Alucard and what he could do to try and help him out of his depression. But Alucard was a finicky, volatile man, and Luther knew that it was going to take a lot to get through to him.

He wouldn't give up, though. He knew what he wanted—and that was for Alucard to be happy. If Zalith couldn't make him happy, then *he* would. He'd not deny that he was attracted to Alucard and always had been, and now that he knew Alucard was gay—something he'd suspected for a while over the three hundred years he'd known him—he felt more comfortable pursuing him. He didn't care what it would take; he *would* get

Alucard to see that he deserved better than some demon who made him feel unwanted and depressed.

## | Varana |

Varana smiled as she watched Luther leave. She'd seen him quite a few times now and had come to learn that he was important to Alucard. She had already decided that she was going to date him to enrage Alucard, whom she was still furious at for not only still being with Zalith but for being the reason why her best friend was so distant lately. She didn't even want to think about how angry and horrified that made her feel. Alucard was *stealing* Zalith away.

Luther was going to be fairly easy to seduce, she was sure. With looks as beautiful as hers—not to mention her hair which many women would kill for. And her body? One in ten billion. No one came close to how desired she was, and Luther would be no exception. She caressed her own hair and sighed with a smug smile on her face. No man could resist her.

She wouldn't deny that Luther was actually kind of cute, but… she was going to use him to get to Alucard and Zalith. She felt so abandoned lately, and she was confident that this was going to get her the attention she deserved.

With a snide smile, she headed for the door, preparing to join her three friends, whom she'd purposely kept waiting for quite some time now. She had to keep them in line.

# Chapter Nine

— ⟨ ✝ ⟩ —

## Treats for Sabazios

| Alucard |

Alucard stared aimlessly out of his window, sinking into his conflicting thoughts. He was still confused and didn't know what to think about Zalith; why had the demon seemed fine yesterday but was back to being distant and unlike himself this morning? He tried to think of logical reasons, but all that came to him was that either Zalith was busy, or he didn't feel the same way about Alucard that he'd felt a few months ago.

He frowned, looking down at Sabazios, who he hadn't even realized had entered his office. If Zalith was busy—and that *was* his reason for acting strangely—then why wouldn't he have told him? Zalith always told him if he was going to be busy or not, but he hadn't given any explanation for why he was spending less and less time with him, ignoring chances to be with him, and why he seemed to have become less affectionate.

Could Luther be right? Could Zalith's affections be going elsewhere? He didn't want to think that. He trusted Zalith, and he didn't believe he'd cheat behind his back.

Taking his eyes off his dog, he turned to face the door and rested his arms on his desk. He couldn't disregard the fact that he might just be overthinking. Despite what happened this morning, he still wanted to try and talk to Zalith about his worries. Maybe he just needed to do whatever he could to show Zalith that he loved him because, for all he knew, Zalith might be the one who thought things weren't okay between them.

Zalith said he'd be home later, and later nowadays had come to mean around dinner time. So, he'd talk to Zalith at dinner—but he wanted to do more than just talk to him. Zalith was in Eltaria, most likely dealing with something stressful; he'd said he would be dealing with the ramifications that came with killing the man he'd killed yesterday, and something told Alucard that such ramifications weren't simple ones. So, he'd do something nice for Zalith to come home to. Surely *that* would assure the demon that their relationship was fine.

But he also needed to head to Dor-Sanguis and find out who or what was killing his people. Luther hadn't yet told him that he'd got the information he needed, so while he waited, he'd try and figure out what to do for Zalith.

A quiet knock then came at his door. "Vhat?" he called, unsure of who it might be.

The door opened, and with a smile on her face and a box in her hand, Mary-Beth—the crying woman Alucard had met yesterday—came in. She was wearing a beige dress with pink and crimson floral patterns and had her blonde hair styled into a bob. "Good morning, Luca," she said, waving at him with her free hand as she approached his desk. "I'm sorry if you're busy, but I felt bad about how we met yesterday, so I brought some treats for your dog to make up for it," she said, tapping the box she was holding as she stopped a few feet in front of his desk.

Sabazios instantly got up and hurried over to her.

Clearly surprised, Mary-Beth gasped quietly and stepped back. "My, he's so big now," she said, looking down at him as he sat in front of her, panting happily.

Alucard didn't really know what to say to her, so he just sat there and watched her open the box, pull out a small biscuit, and hand it to Sabazios. She giggled when the dog crunched the treat with a content look on his face.

"He's so sweet," she said, smiling as she patted Sabazios' head. "He's so unusual looking.... What's his name?"

"Sabazios," Alucard answered.

Mary-Beth frowned. "Sa...ba...Sabazios?" she said, struggling a little with the pronunciation.

"*Da*," Alucard mumbled. "'E is 'ell'ound."

"Oh..." Mary-Beth said, slowly looking back at Alucard. "Where did you get him?" she asked, handing Sabazios another treat.

Alucard leaned back in his seat, resting his arms in his lap. "A year ago...at a market," he lied. He wasn't sure how she might react to hearing that he'd picked up his pet in Hell.

Mary-Beth nodded, looking down at Sabazios as he chewed on the treat. "He's very polite."

He nodded.

"I like your office," she then said, glancing around. "It looks very nice and cosy."

"*Multemesc*," Alucard mumbled, glancing at Sabazios as he started to whine at Mary-Beth's feet for another treat. "You've 'ad enough," he grumbled, and as the dog gawped at him, he scowled.

Sabazios rolled his eyes and stropped back into his bed.

"Wasn't there a library here before?" Mary-Beth asked. "Where did all the books go?"

Alucard shrugged. "Zhey vere moved into zhe ozzer library."

"Oh. Who decorated for you?"

Unsure of where the conversation was going, Alucard sighed quietly and leaned forward, resting his arms on the table. "People. Zaliv 'ad…interior design person," he muttered.

She smiled as she glanced at him again. But then she made her way over and placed the box of dog treats on Alucard's desk. "I'll leave these here for you."

He looked down at the box and then back up at her. "Did you make zhem?" he asked—she made the cakes she'd given him yesterday, and he suspected that she might have also made the treats for Sabazios.

"I did." She glanced at the chair beside her. "May I?" she asked, and as Alucard nodded, she sat down. "I love to bake things; it's a great pass-time," she explained with a content smile. "I also like to make things for Marcellus—that's my husband—he's always working so hard every day. I like to make sure he has something tasty waiting for him when he gets home. His favourite is cherry tart—it's also my favourite to make," she said, leaning closer to the table with a giggle.

Alucard knew someone called Marcellus—the man he knew and Mary-Beth's husband could possibly be the same man. It wouldn't surprise him if that were the case, and that Varana had befriended Marcellus' wife. Alucard knew that Zalith was planning to construct a government here and that he was interested in the inventors and curators who lived in and around the Citadel. Marcellus was one of them, and Alucard suspected that Varana's befriending of his wife was part of Zalith's plan to become close to the men in question. It was a good plan, one he had used many a time before.

His thoughts then focused on everything else she had said, and it made him think about his choice to do something nice for Zalith once he got home. "'E 'as stressful job, no?"

Mary-Beth sighed. "*So* stressful. He has to deal with hundreds of people each day—the workers, the customers. He's always so worn out when he gets home."

"Vhat do you do?"

"Well," she started, shuffling around as she made herself comfortable, "he gets home, we have dinner, and then I give him whatever I spent the day making. And then we just sit and talk about how our days went. I hardly ever have anything interesting to tell him, but that doesn't matter; it's good to just talk, even if you have nothing to talk about."

"Vhy?"

"Well…I don't know," she said, frowning. "I love Marcellus, and he loves me. I know that I just love to hear his voice and listen to him talk about whatever he has to say, and I know he feels the same about me. It's nice…to just listen to his voice. Marcellus always tells me how my voice is what he wants to hear at the end of each stressful workday; he tells me he misses me all the time. So, that's why I talk to him about anything and everything when he gets home, to make him feel less stressed or worried about work."

He frowned slightly. "But…vhat if you 'ave noving intervesting to talk about?"

She laughed quietly. "It doesn't have to be interesting. I could talk for hours about something boring like baking or gardening, and Marcellus would sit there and listen to me. Don't you and Zalith sit around and talk about anything and everything?"

Alucard looked down at his lap, trying not to sink into his sadness. "Sometimes," he said, remembering the times Zalith had asked him to talk about something just so that he could listen to him, something Zalith hadn't done in a long time.

Mary-Beth smiled. "It's nice, isn't it?"

Alucard nodded. He couldn't think of anything to say in response.

"How *are* you and Zalith?"

He frowned as her question woke his sadness from its brief slumber. Although he had convinced himself that the problem might just be a lack of communication, he couldn't help but think that might not be the case. *How* were he and Zalith? At the moment, things were upsetting and confusing. He didn't understand why Zalith was so different, and as much as he wanted to ask, he felt afraid that Zalith might tell him something that would break his heart—something like…'it's over'.

With a sullen frown, he shrugged. "Ve're…vine."

Mary-Beth frowned sadly. "Just fine?"

Alucard didn't want to talk about it. Discussing it with Luther had gotten him nowhere, and he wasn't in the mood to talk to anyone else about it. He'd already decided that he was going to do something for Zalith and talk to him at dinner; he was sure that talking would fix the distance that had burrowed and been growing between them, and he didn't want to make himself feel any sadder by talking about it.

He stood up. "I 'ave to be somevhere."

"Oh," she said as she got up. "I'm so sorry for taking up your time. I hope you have a good day. Don't give Sabazios too many of these at once, by the way," she said, tapping the box of treats. "They might be a little sickly after three or four," she warned, watching Alucard as he stepped out from behind his desk.

"Vight. Vank you," he said.

"That's okay." Mary-Beth smiled, making her way over to the door. "It was nice talking to you some more, Luca," she said, waving at him as she left his office. "Bye!"

He didn't have a chance to say goodbye, but as she left his office, an awkward smile clung to his face, fighting through the despair. He'd only seen her twice, but he'd not deny that her company felt a whole lot better than that of Luther or Attila. She didn't pry, nor did she expect him to answer questions he didn't want to—*and* she didn't question him when he asked to be left alone. Not only that, but she'd gone out of her way to bring something for Sabazios; he hadn't asked her to do that, and she didn't have to, but she did. It almost seemed as though this Mary-Beth might be looking to become his friend. He liked her enough to consider it.

But right now, he had other things to focus on.

Leaving his office, he made his way up the stairs and into his study. He was going to head to Dor-Sanguis whether Luther had the information he asked for or not. He needed to find out what was going on with his vampires, and he also knew that he could get the crystals he'd been reading about in Dargamoore.

He made his way into his and Zalith's bedroom, took one of his black blazers from the dressing rooms, and then pulled it on as he headed downstairs again.

When he reached the front door, he pulled his fur-collared cape from one of the coatracks. Then, as he put it on over his shoulders, he stepped out onto the porch. Without hindrance, he disappeared into vermillion smoke and began his journey to Dor-Sanguis.

# Chapter Ten

## The Spy



**| Luther, *Dor-Sanguis* |**

It was just coming up to 5 p.m. when Luther got back to Dor-Sanguis. The fact that Nefastus was nearly seven hours behind made him feel a little disorientated after every visit; after months of travelling back and forth, he was still trying to get used to the sudden change from morning to evening.

Once he got to his office, he sorted through all the files and papers he'd earlier gathered on his desk. While he worked, he tried concentrating, but he couldn't stop thinking about Alucard.

He reminisced the times they'd spent together—the good and the bad—and the things they had achieved…well, the things *Alucard* had achieved, but Luther was there to witness it. However, his thoughts consisted mostly of what had been happening *lately*. Before, Luther had become convinced that Alucard was the type that never dated, but not too long ago, he'd learned that to be false and also discovered that Alucard wasn't straight, either. Both revelations somewhat surprised him, and now that he knew, he was debating whether or not he should tell Alucard how *he* felt.

For nearly three hundred years, he, Attila, and Alucard had been friends—closer than friends, even. But Attila was a strongly religious man, and Luther suspected that might be what caused Alucard to take so long to explore his sexuality. Of course, he wished that he could have been the one whom Alucard confided in and not some demon who was obviously taking advantage of Alucard's love and kindness.

The thought of that demon made him furious; knowing that right now, Alucard was probably sitting in his office waiting for Zalith to get home while he did whatever he was doing, and Luther strongly suspected that to be cheating. *That* made him a whole different kind of angry. Alucard didn't deserve to be treated like that; he deserved so much more than some unappreciative, lying, manipulative, unfaithful demon.

Why was he even dating a demon in the first place? In all the years Luther had spent with Alucard, never would he have expected him to be *friends* with a demon, let alone date one. The Alucard he knew hated demons…but evidently, something happened to change his mind in the years Luther had been away.

He sighed, turning his head to the left to gaze out of the window. He knew how volatile Alucard was, and he also knew the extent of his anger—he had seen first-hand just how devastating it was to be on the receiving end of Alucard's fury, and he didn't want to do or say something that might ruin their friendship.

Of course, now that he knew it was possible, he wanted more than friendship with Alucard, but how could he tell him that? Right now probably wasn't a good time; he was clearly having problems with his current relationship, and he didn't want to make him feel any worse than he already did. But what he *did* want to do was make sure that Alucard understood he deserved better than what he was currently getting, and that *Luther* could be the one to give him that.

"It's getting close to three," Jasper called, snapping him out of his thoughts.

Taking his eyes off the sky, Luther turned his head to set his eyes on him. "Any sign of those stalkers?"

"Nothing yet," he replied, standing in the doorway. "Did Lord Aleksei have anything to say about them or the murdered vampires? We've had ten more vampires abandon their homes in Dargamoore out of fear and move back here just in the last hour."

"Hmm," Luther mumbled, looking down at the papers on his desk. He knew he should be trying to come up with a suggestion for the situation, especially since Alucard was relying on him, but he couldn't stop reminiscing. This time, the memory that came to mind was the first time he met Alucard…almost three hundred years ago.

"Uh…hello?" Jasper questioned cautiously.

"How old are you?" Luther asked, setting his eyes on the blonde vampire.

"Uh…two hundred and four. Why?"

"Does it feel…strange to have been alive for so long?"

Jasper frowned and leaned his shoulder on the doorframe. "Not really."

Luther rested his arms on his desk and sighed quietly. "Perhaps…he sees life from a different perspective."

"Who?"

"Alucard," Luther replied with a shrug. "I've watched a lot of humans live and expire; they seem to get through their lives so quickly, and they tend to rush a lot of things: growing up, finding love, marriage, kids. Perhaps, for us, it's different. We know that we don't exactly have a time limit to get a job, meet someone, get married, or have a family. Or maybe we just lose the wish for such things once our mortality is lifted."

Jasper stood there, waiting with an unsure expression on his face.

Luther didn't stop, though. "Do you still possess these feelings? Do you yearn for a family?"

"Well…I mean, maybe one day, but…I'm a vampire," he laughed with a frown. "We can't have kids, so…what would be the point in meeting someone?"

"To spend your life with them, right?"

"I mean…sure. It would be nice to spend forever with someone, maybe…but it's not really something that's been big on my mind. It's not like we have the whole demon soulmates or werewolf mate thing going on; we're not destined to find our other half. For vampires, it's just…luck."

Luther nodded, taking his eyes off Jasper to stare at the empty fireplace. "Maybe…once we reach a certain age, we decide it's time to find someone. I stuck with him for all my years as a vampire, and nothing came of it. Then, when I'm away for a few measly years, he decides it's time to love someone."

"Uh…are you…still talking about Lord Aleksei?"

"Would you feel angry if someone you cared about ignored you for a few hundred years and then shacked up with someone they've known for less than *five* years?"

Jasper, who looked a little reluctant to answer, shrugged lightly. "I mean…yes, but if they weren't interested in me in that way, then it would be my fault for sticking around expecting something to happen. I'd be upset that they didn't feel the same, but I wouldn't be *that* mad, because…well, you can't force someone to feel something they don't, can you?"

He leaned back in his seat and sighed. "Right. Anyway, Aleksei told us to capture and interrogate one of the people that you've seen watching the castle. Inform the watchers."

"What about the scared vampires? We're fine right now, but at this rate, the castle is going to fill up very fast, and we won't have any spare rooms left."

"I'll tell Aleksei about it when I next see him."

With an unsure nod, Jasper left the room, leaving Luther on his own.

Luther exhaled deeply, slouching further into his seat. Alucard had never expressed much to him; he didn't know whether Alucard would be interested in him romantically. Maybe he should just tell Alucard how he felt, no hesitation. But what if that made the vampire angry or uncomfortable? He wasn't sure how to approach the situation because Alucard was hard to read and understand, and his volatility unnerved Luther.

He then scowled. How had Zalith done it? How had that demon managed to break through all of Alucard's towering walls? He wanted to know because then *he* could use the same method. But who would know? He wouldn't ask Alucard; that would be weird of him. But who else could possibly know how that demon had worked his way into Alucard's life? He sighed again, staring out of the window, trying to work out what he could do.

What about Alucard's sister? Varana. He met her this morning; maybe she would have the answers to his questions. He felt a little awful about considering using her to get information about Alucard and Zalith, but he couldn't think of any better alternatives. She might not even want to talk to him, but he'd try for the sake of both his feelings and Alucard; he hated seeing him suffering, and the sooner he knew how to tell him how he felt, the better.

Luther reached into the closest desk drawer and pulled out a quill and a piece of parchment. He didn't think much about his message. A simple: '*Varana, I have been thinking about you since our fateful meeting and hoped you would like to join me for coffee tomorrow morning. Luther,*' would work, he was sure. He folded up the note and handed it to the owl that just swooped in through his open window. Now, all he had to do was wait for her reply.

His attention, however, was instantly snatched by the arrival of who could only be Alucard. In the corner of his eye, he watched the crimson shadow of The Vampire Lord race by; he stood up, headed over to his window so he could look down at the castle's courtyard below, and watched as Alucard landed. As soon as Luther saw him, anxiety gripped hold of him. Alucard had been on his mind so much lately that every time he saw him, he felt angst pool in his stomach—but that was probably because of how much he wanted to tell Alucard about his feelings.

His feelings could wait, though. Alucard wouldn't be here if it wasn't for something important, and he wanted to make sure that he was there if he needed him. So he left his office and headed for the main hall.

## | **Alucard** |

Alucard headed into his castle. He glanced and nodded at the vampires guarding the doors as they greeted him, and when he saw Luther hurrying towards him, he sighed quietly and stopped. He'd like to hope that the man wasn't about to go off on another tangent, but he wouldn't hold his breath.

"Alucard," Luther called with a smile.

The vampire stared vacantly at him as he made his way over, and once he stopped in front of him, he waited.

"Has something happened?" Luther asked.

"You vill show me vhere zhese people 'ave been vatching zhe castle vrom, and zhen I vill interrogate zhem myselv."

"Of course," Luther said with a concerned frown. "But…you really didn't have to come all the way out here. I've got it under control. I've almost got all that information together, too."

Alucard raised his left eyebrow, but he didn't have the energy to scold him. So, he turned around and headed for the door. "Show me."

Luther followed behind him.

"Vhere do zhey come?" the vampire questioned.

"They usually hang out around the tree line of the forest," Luther answered. Then, he caught up with Alucard and walked beside him. "When was the last time you were here, huh? Probably feels like ages. Nice to be home, though, yeah?"

"No," Alucard grumbled. "Every time I come back to zhis godvorsaken place, I am veminded of 'ow much I veally 'ate 'ere."

"Oh…. It's not that bad, is it?"

Alucard stopped walking and glared at him. "Everyvone I ever cared about died 'ere. If vasn't my birvplace, I vould burn to zhe ground." He then continued through the courtyard.

Luther followed. "Not *everyone*," he said slowly. "I'm still here, and Attila's still around. Yeah, he's an asshole, but he's still your friend. And…you've still got Zalith, right?"

Alucard didn't say anything as he led the way down towards the forest. The mere mention of Zalith's name made his aching heart hurt even more.

"I don't know why you care about him," he continued. "I mean…does he care about *you*? Clearly not, seeing as he's left you worrying and questioning his feelings."

Alucard stopped walking again. He didn't understand why Luther persisted and kept bringing up Zalith, and he was aggravating him more and more as each second passed. He didn't want to talk about it—he didn't even want to *think* about it. If Zalith didn't care about him…his thoughts fumbled. For a moment, he frowned, taking his eyes off Luther to glare over at the forest. If Zalith *did* care about him, then why would he be distancing himself like this? Why would he be reducing the amount of time they spent together…and why had he allowed their moments of affection and conversation to become so short? If Zalith *did* care…why had he turned away the opportunity to spend the day with him today?

He didn't want to overthink. With a scowl on his face, he looked back at Luther. "Vhere are zhese people?"

Luther sighed and adorned a look of irritancy. "When will you stop dismissing my attempts to help you?"

"'Elp me?" Alucard scoffed. "You can 'elp me by telling me vhere zhese—"

"What are you afraid of?" he interjected. "That he doesn't want you anymore? That he'd rather fuck someone else? So what? If that's how he feels, then that's how he feels.

It's not your fault; you know as well as I do what demons are like. They're greedy and selfish, and they don't give a shit about the people around them."

Alucard gritted his teeth and clenched his fists.

"Do you really think he's any different because you love him? He's not, Alucard. I know that you care about him, and I know that you love him, but if he doesn't feel the same anymore, keeping yourself in that situation is only going to make you feel worse, and when he finally decides that it's time to stop sneaking around, it's going to hurt more to hear him tell you what you already know. The best thing you can do is leave before he gets the chance to hurt you any more than he already has."

Alucard glared at him, his motivation to yell at him withering as each word left Luther's mouth. He didn't want to hear it, but Luther's voice was like a knife, and it was cutting deeper and deeper. What if all of this really was happening because Zalith was seeing someone else? He didn't want to consider it because he trusted Zalith with his life, and that was more than he'd ever trusted anyone else. He wouldn't ever suspect that Zalith would do something like that to him.

Zalith promised him time and time again that he would be with him forever—he'd even imprinted on him. From what Alucard knew about imprints, it would be literally impossible for Zalith to want someone else…right? He didn't know anymore. An imprint didn't mean they were meant to be together like Alucard wanted, did it? It just meant that they loved one another and always would in a way like no other. But if that were true…would Zalith really hurt him like this?

He took his eyes off Luther, looking down at the grass. Maybe that was why Zalith had stopped touching him as much as he used to. Perhaps that was why they didn't kiss or hug or have sex anymore. Maybe Zalith was getting all of that elsewhere. And thinking about it broke his heart, it made it hard to breathe, and an expression that reflected his pain surely made its way onto his face.

"I-I didn't mean to…" Luther stuttered. "I'm sorry, I'm just…."

Alucard turned his back on him, hiding his tortured scowl. He'd done his best to distract himself from his thoughts, but coming home had only made it worse—*Luther* had only made it worse. But what if he was right?

Why would Zalith do that? Why would he come into his life, why would he love him, help him, and ask him to live with him if he was only going to get tired of him? It didn't make sense.

None of it made sense.

All Alucard could think about now was how much he loved Zalith and how much he didn't want it to be true. He didn't want to lose him, but…if Zalith didn't want him anymore, what use was there in holding on?

"Alucard?" Luther asked, placing his hand on Alucard's shoulder.

With an irritated snarl, Alucard shrugged his hand off and turned to face him. "Zon't touch me," he warned aggressively.

Luther sighed as he stepped back. "I'm sorry if I've upset you. I just hate to see you sad. I've known you nearly three hundred years, and I've never seen you so depressed. I don't know the extent of your situation, but…I want to help you."

"I zon't need your 'elp or anyvone else's," Alucard snarled.

"You've always been so stubborn, you know," Luther said with a frown, crossing his arms. "For once, perhaps you should try not being so standoffish and talk about it. It helps."

Alucard's scowl thickened. "Vhat vould 'elp is if you vould stop prying into my private life and get on vith your job."

"Uh-huh. Well, when you finally decide to stop punishing yourself, I'll be here. I mean, what else can I do? You sit around waiting for someone who doesn't give a shit and ignore the people that actually do."

"I zidn't ask you to."

"You don't have to ask people to care for you, they just do. And the people who care for you don't leave you to feel like…this," he said, gesturing his hands at him. "Surely, he can see how upset you are, but has he done anything about it?"

Alucard frowned, taking his eyes off him.

"Exactly. Whatever, Alucard. Keep pushing me away, but I'm sure you'll work out soon enough who *actually* cares for you." He nodded a little to Alucard's left. "That's your guy over there."

Alucard's attention shifted away from Luther; as he looked over his shoulder, his gaze pierced through the shadows of the tree line and fixated on a solitary figure lurking in the depths of the forest. Their identity was veiled, but it didn't matter to Alucard; any distraction from the weight of his thoughts about Zalith was a welcomed respite, and he seized it without hesitation.

He burst towards the trees, his departure so swift that Luther stumbled in his wake. Alucard paid him no mind; if anything, the abrupt start was a fitting response to the man's persistent annoyance.

Suppressing any semblance of thought, Alucard traversed the distance with preternatural speed, materializing before the shrouded figure in the blink of an eye. His hand shot out, clasping around their throat before they could react, pressing them firmly against the rough bark of a nearby tree. As their startled gasp escaped, the figure revealed that they were a woman.

Pinning her against the gnarled trunk, Alucard deftly removed her hood, discovering a countenance framed by raven-black locks and eyes the hue of polished amber. Her features betrayed a youthful vigour, and the terror etched across her face exposed her inexperience with creatures such as himself.

"Who are you?" Alucard snarled.

She gulped and gripped his wrist with both her hands—

"What do you want?" Luther asked, appearing beside Alucard.

The woman took her eyes off Alucard and glanced at him, her look of terror increasing. But as she breathed frantically in panic, she set her eyes back on Alucard, who waited for her to answer.

"Are you Diabolus?" Luther asked.

Alucard rolled his eyes and glowered at him. "Can you do me a vavour and fuck off?"

Luther scoffed. "No. You told me to deal with this, so…here I am…dealing with it…kind of."

The vampire snarled and set his eyes back on the woman in his grip. He wasn't going to argue with him; he didn't have the energy for it. "Vhat are you doing 'ere?" he asked her.

Staring at him, the woman remained silent.

His patience was dwindling. He tightened his grip around her throat and leaned closer, growling to bare his fangs in an attempt to horrify her further.

Clearly, she thought that he was about to sink his fangs into her neck; she screeched in horror, trying to break free of his grip, but once she worked out that she wasn't going anywhere, she stared back and forth at them both before gulping. "I…I'm…I'm not here to hurt anyone," she said, her voice shaking. "I just…you…you," she said, looking at Luther. "You've been…you were looking into the Diabolus…and…we were supposed to find out who you were working for," she explained.

Alucard glanced at Luther, waiting for him to respond to her.

Luther scowled and crossed his arms. "Huh…guess I wasn't as careful as I thought I was," he mumbled. Then, he asked Alucard, "Do you wanna kill her, or do you want me—"

"N-no, wait!" she insisted. "I'm not with the Diabolus."

"Zhen who are you vith?" Alucard asked.

She gulped and shook her head, but as Alucard tightened his grip, she choked and nodded. He loosened his grip, glowering at her as she caught her breath.

"Y-you were looking into a sub-cult of the Diabolus," she said, glancing at Luther. "We've been looking into the same cult—well…my boss has a particular interest in it, and when we learned that you were searching for information on them—more specifically, on the people who were involved four hundred years ago—we had to find out why."

Luther nodded slowly, and when Alucard permitted him to respond with a slight nod, he asked, "Why do you want to know why I'm looking into it?"

She hesitated, but as she caught sight of Alucard's hostile glare again, she shuddered in fear. "W-well…we're…looking for someone, and my boss thinks maybe you're that someone—or you work for them."

"Who is this someone?" Luther asked.

"A, uh…Caedis."

Upon the mention of his demon name, angst gripped Alucard. Only the Numen and Zalith knew that name, which meant this woman had to be a subject of one of the Numen. But which one?

"Who? I don't…know a Caedis," Luther muttered, looking at Alucard.

"Vhich Numen do you vork vor?" Alucard asked her.

She set her eyes on him as her face seemed to light up in hope. "I…are you him?" she asked, her fear waning.

"Answer him," Luther said, scowling.

She stuttered. "I…he has many names."

Alucard was well aware that two of the three male Numen wanted him dead…or worse. "Vone vill do."

"He…everyone knows him as Death, but those close to him know him as Erich."

Erich? He was the only one of the Numen whom Alucard had never seen; he'd been convinced that Erich might not want anything to do with him, but now he'd learnt that might not be the case. What could Erich want with him, though? All the other Numen had similar reasons for wanting him; they wanted to use him to take each other out, but Erich…. He seemed to have removed himself from any conflict with his siblings. Why now, of all times, had he decided to involve himself?

Alucard scowled. "What does 'e vant vith Caedis?"

"Do you know where he is?" she asked.

"Answer," he snarled, tightening his grip.

"I-I don't know," she choked. "He doesn't tell us anything! He just told us to find out who he was looking for the information for," she said, nodding at Luther. "I don't know what he wants with him!"

Alucard sighed quietly, taking his eyes off her for a moment. He didn't know what Erich wanted with him, but he could assume that he wanted him for the same reason all the other Numen did.

He'd not let this woman run back to him and tell him what had happened here.

Without hesitation, he tightened his grip, depriving her of her breath. She struggled, tears streaming down her reddened face as she tried to fight for her life. But it was swiftly taken from her, and as she fell still, Alucard let her body drop to the ground.

"Get vid of 'er," he grumbled, stepping back.

"You know this Caedis, I assume," Luther said, staring at him.

"No, I just velt like killing somevone," he sneered. "Get vid of 'er body and get back to vork. If you see any more of zhem lurking avound, kill zhem."

Luther sighed and looked down at the body. "Yeah, sure."

Alucard then left the forest and headed for his castle. The people watching the castle weren't involved in the vampire murders, and that didn't relieve him as much as he'd like. He now had *two* problems to deal with. He wasn't entirely sure what Erich wanted, but he wouldn't let him find him. Killing his spies was about as much as Alucard could do right now, not only because he needed to focus on finding out who was killing his people but also because he had no idea where to find Erich or his followers. He was the only Numen was almost a complete mystery to him.

But the ring on his finger kept him hidden from all the Numen. Erich would never know where to find him.

# Chapter Eleven

## ⎯ ⋜ ✝ ⋟ ⎯

# Investigation

**| Alucard |**

When Alucard got back to the castle, he headed through the hall towards the door on the far left. He heard the door to the vampires' part of the castle open; he glanced over there and watched as Jasper came out with a concerned look on his face—and the moment he saw Alucard, he raced over to him.

"My Lord," he said, sounding a little hurried. "Sorry, I...I did bring this matter to Luther, and I'm not sure if he's told you, but the vampires are scared, sir. A lot of them have abandoned their homes and lives in Dargamoore and come back here because they feel like their lives are in threat."

Alucard sighed a little. He didn't want his people to feel like they had to run. Dor-Sanguis was supposed to be the one place where vampires could live without worrying that they might turn a corner and get a stake through their chest.

"'Ow many 'ave moved back?" he asked.

"Since the latest attack, twenty-seven, My Lord. Ten of them arrived just this morning before sunrise," Jasper told him.

"Gazzer everyvone in zhe ballvoom. I'll be zhere to talk to zhem shortly."

Jasper nodded. "Yes, My Lord." And then he hurried off back to the other side of the castle.

Alucard dragged his hand over his face as he navigated the corridors towards his office. He wasn't sure why this was happening or who was responsible, but the possibility that it might be Marcus' little cult had him concerned. The last thing anyone needed right now was a vampire-hating cult sneaking around the city.

He walked into his office, but the information he'd asked Luther for wasn't on his desk. With an irritated sigh, he turned around, left his office, and headed upstairs. He made his way to Luther's office, and of course, there were the papers sitting on *his* desk. The vampire snatched them with a snarl and walked back through the halls.

Along the way, he glanced at each page. The first two murdered vampires were Georgina Hale and Daniel Hemming, and the latest five were Loyde and Sophina Klarke, Noelle Reed, Frank Jameson, and Vicktoria Wess. He felt guilty about the fact that he didn't know them personally, but two of them were vampires from Eltaria. Would Zalith be angry with him for letting this happen? He was supposed to protect these people…and someone was out there killing them while he was sitting at home feeling miserable about something that might not even be true.

He scowled at himself and read through the information; there were locations, addresses, and even sketches of where the murders had taken place. If he was going to get answers, he should start there.

When he got to his office, he stood by his desk and read through everything again, ensuring that he memorised it. The brain fog that had ensnared him while his mind was a victim of Numen tampering may have been cleared, but he still wanted to make sure that he had everything he needed. Then, he put the papers down and headed back towards the entrance hall.

Once he reached the hall, he went into the vampires' side of the castle and to the hall where he'd told Jasper to gather everyone. The darkness was full of staring red eyes, all following him with desperate gazes as he made his way up to the stage. For a moment, he stood there and looked over them; *everyone* was there, even some of the guards, and they all looked afraid.

"Listen to me carevully," he called across the hall. "I'm going to vind whoever is doing zhis; I von't let anymore of you get 'urt. Zhis country and zhe city are your 'ome, and is my job to ensure zhat your 'ome is safe and protected. Vor your savety, vhile I vork, I ask zhat you stay inside zhe castle. If any of you see anyving suspicious or 'ave any invormation about zhe attacks, tell Jasper, and 'e vill tell me. Understood?"

The entire hall called back, "Yes, My Lord."

Alucard then headed back towards the door but waved over at Jasper as he walked. When the blonde vampire joined him, he said, "Make sure zhe day and night guards are on 'igh alert. If you 'ave any new trainees, get zhem on posts, too. I zon't vant anyvone coming vithin ten miles of zhis place."

Jasper nodded. "Understood, My Lord," and then he disappeared into the tense, chatting crowd.

Alucard made his way to the entrance hall, and on his way outside, he saw Luther carrying the dead spy's body.

"Oh," Luther called. "I can get that information in a few—"

"I alveady vound. I'm 'eading to zhe city to investigate zhese murders myselv. I need you to keep an eye on zhis place and make sure zhat everyvone is safe."

Luther looked a little hesitant but nodded. "All right. Do you need help?"

"No." He dematerialized into vermillion smoke and left the courtyard.

He raced towards Dargamoore, and when he landed at the city gates, he stepped inside and immediately turned right. At the end of the narrow, uneven passage was a decrepit tavern, one displaying a sign that said it didn't server vampires. Beside it stood the arched entrance to the alley where Georgina Hale and Daniel Hemming were found with stakes through their hearts. Why would they be near a tavern that wouldn't serve them?

Alucard stood in the alley, which reeked of rotting wood, damp soil, and old beer. There was still blood on the cobblestone. Scratches on the wall. There'd been a struggle there, and Alucard was quite sure that the vampires had tried fighting for their lives. But were humans really strong enough to overpower a vampire in a fight? Only if they had the correct tools…which Marcus' old gang appeared to have. *Could* it be them? Were they back?

The question still remained, though: why were Georgina and Daniel here? His vampires knew very well not to try and step foot in places that said they wouldn't serve their kind, places that had been dedicated to human-only presences. He trusted his vampires not to disobey the rules, and so he could only suspect that their bodies had either been moved there…or they'd been lured into the alley. He couldn't tell for sure, but he was completely confident that Georgina and Daniel weren't intentionally in the alley.

With a quiet sigh, he followed the narrow passage back to the main road. He moved through the bustling crowds; all the humans seemed fine despite the murders. But why would they care about dead vampires? He clenched his jaw but remained as calm as he could. Anger wouldn't help right now.

He turned onto a street lined with food stalls, taverns, and restaurants. At the end of the street where the road forked, he went right, and he found his way to the Harrod Inn, where Loyde and Sophina Klarke were found half-buried in the mud and trash in a small courtyard behind the building.

The place reeked worse than the alley; rotten food, dead rats, and blood. It was enough to force Alucard to hold his hand over his mouth and nose to try and block out the stench. He glanced around, and he saw the gaping holes in the mud where the bodies had been dug out. There was no sign of struggle, and the only blood that he could see was mixed in with the mud…and it led somewhere. There was a clear trail, and by the look of the tracks in the dirt, it looked like someone had dragged the bodies into the courtyard.

But from where?

Alucard followed the blood; when he left the courtyard, the smell of bleach struck him. Whoever had moved the bodies had tried cleaning the blood from the cobblestone sidewalk, but Alucard could still smell it. So he kept following it, and it took him fifty feet away from the courtyard and to the door of a restaurant. Unlike the decrepit tavern he'd passed not long ago, this establishment served vampires. Why did the trail lead inside, then?

The vampire pushed the door open, and the second he stepped in, every patron went quiet and stared at him. He slowly approached the service desk, eyeing each and every person sitting at the tables. They were all dressed expensively, and each of them donned the same snooty expression…apart from a few people at a table by the windows. They looked guilty…*worried*. Panicked.

"Can I help you?" came a voice, snatching his attention.

Alucard turned his head and looked at the woman in front of him.

"Do you have a reservation?" she asked.

"No. I'm looking into zhe vampire murders zhat 'ave been 'appening. Did Loyde and Sophina Klarke 'ave a reservation 'ere?"

The woman looked hesitant. "Oh…um…I can't…really give out that information, sir," she said, holding the clipboard in her hands against her chest.

"Yes, you can," he replied. "Or vould you prever I take zhat board vrom you?"

She looked down at it, frowned worriedly, and then reluctantly handed it to him.

He snatched it from her and flipped through the pages. Loyde and Sophina Klarke had a reservation last night at 8 p.m., and they left at 10 p.m., or so whoever wrote it down would have him believe. The signatures didn't match. Someone had tried to make it look like Loyde and Sophina had left, and Alucard wondered if that someone might be the woman in front of him…or someone she knew.

"Eizer you can tell me who signed Loyde and Sophina out or I can get zhe authorities involved. A vine establishment like zhis vouldn't look very good if zhere vere law envorcement looking avound, no?"

She went a little pale. "I-I don't know, sir. I wasn't on shift last night."

"Who vas? Give me zhe shivt vota."

"I…" she drawled but sighed. "One moment."

The vampire watched her leave and head to the office behind the desk. Then, he glanced around the room again. The people he'd seen looking guilty were trying to hide their faces, taking discreet glances at him. He wanted to question them, but he didn't want to push his luck. The last thing he needed was for one of them to report him and for the council to hound him with questions about why he was working alone on this.

He always worked better alone.

A few moments later, the woman returned with a piece of paper. "This is from yesterday, sir."

Alucard didn't recognize any of the staff names, but if this was Marcus' cult, it was obviously made up of new people, wasn't it? The original cult was dead. Or at least it was supposed to be.

"I need zhe addresses of zhese employees."

The woman shook her head, looking a little flustered. "I-I can't give that information out without a warrant, sir. I'm sorry, but this is the best I can do."

Alucard huffed irritably. He had the names, but that wasn't enough. If he was going to find out who was involved, he needed to talk to them, but how could he do that if he didn't know where they lived? Asking around might get him answers, but that could take *forever*, and he didn't have time on his side. Whoever was doing this could attack again tonight.

"I-if that's all, sir, please leave. We'd appreciate if you didn't upset our patrons," the woman said cautiously.

With a roll of his eyes and an irritated snarl, Alucard left the restaurant. If he wanted to know where the people on the rota lived, he was going to have to ask the city law enforcement for help—which he was already supposed to be doing. They'd have to investigate them, especially since the blood trail led into that building. He just hoped they weren't in on it.

He started heading up the street—

"Excuse me," a man called.

Alucard stopped and turned to face him.

A young, brown-haired human man dressed just like the restaurant patrons hurried over to him. "Sorry, I uh…would've caught you inside, but I didn't want anyone to see."

He frowned. "Vhat?"

The man moved closer and adorned a wary expression. "I know what happened."

Alucard's frown thickened.

"With those two posh vampires. I saw the whole thing."

"You saw who killed zhem?"

"Shh!" he insisted and looked around cautiously. "The whole street is in on it."

Alucard scowled skeptically and glanced up and down the street. Several gazes met his, but they all looked away quickly.

The man pulled out a piece of paper and hastily wrote something down. "Here," he said, shoving the paper into Alucard's hand. "Meet me here tomorrow morning after my shift at 6 a.m. I can help you."

His suspicion then shifted to the man. "Vhy vould you 'elp me? Zhese are vampire murders, not 'uman."

He scoffed slightly. "Believe it or not, there *are* some of us who like your kind. Loyde and Sophina came to this place all the time, and they were always real nice to me even though I was just the dishwasher. They didn't deserve it."

Alucard focused on the man's heartbeat and micro expressions. As far as he could tell, this human was telling the truth.

"I'm Bernie," he told him and then looked around anxiously. "Tomorrow, okay?" he insisted, and then he moved past Alucard and scurried off down the street.

The vampire watched him leave, and then he looked down at the paper. It was the address of an inn. Maybe it was where the guy was staying. If he could tell him who was killing vampires, he wouldn't pass up the opportunity to find out. And if what he told him wasn't enough, he'd give the rota in his other hand to the city law enforcement.

But what was he supposed to do until then?

The vampire started walking up the street, and everywhere he looked, he only saw humans. Those of his vampires who hadn't yet made it back to the castle were likely hiding in their homes, and the fact that things had changed so quickly made Alucard feel worse than he already did. But he'd fix it. He'd make sure his people were safe in Dargamoore again.

He didn't want to head home and wait around, nor did he want to sit in the castle because he knew that he'd just start overthinking again. So while he waited, he thought he might as well find the crystal and alchemy store that he'd been planning to visit after doing his research on dream ethos.

As he made his way through the city, though, Zalith still possessed every thought in his head. Despite recently finding out that Erich was searching for him, and that he might have a lead on the vampire murders, he couldn't seem to think about anything else. Maybe it was because Zalith was such a significant part of his life, and to lose him would feel like losing a part of himself. Or perhaps it was because he loved Zalith with every inch of his soul and heart, and he didn't want to live a life without him. Overthinking wouldn't do him any good, though.

He sighed deeply as he walked through the busy streets and set his eyes on a small store up ahead. Its panelled outside walls were painted black, and the glass windows were old and stained. He hoped that it still sold the things he needed. Maybe he could focus on *that* for now rather than sinking deeper into his confounding sadness.

The vampire headed into the store.

As the owner instantly set his dull, green eyes on him, he called "Good afternoon," in Dor-Sanguian.

It had been quite a while since Alucard heard anyone speak his native tongue, and even longer since he had a conversation in it.

"Can I help you?" the owner asked, making his way over to him.

Alucard closed the door behind him and took a few moments to look around. The walls were lined with shelves upon shelves of curiosities, crystals, alchemy appliances and ingredients, jewellery, herbs, and dried plants.

Alucard looked at the owner as he stopped in front of him. "A small box," he said, holding out his hands to show him the size he was looking for.

The owner nodded and disappeared behind the counter, leaving Alucard on his own.

He remembered quite clearly what it was that he needed and moved over to the shelf where he'd seen a collection of small and large black crystals. He wasn't sure how many he needed of each, so he picked up a fair few pieces of shungite crystal and black onyx. Then, he searched the place with his eyes for obsidian. Most of the crystals he read about were used for banishing negative energies, and since his dreams felt very much like negative energies that were not originally his own, he thought such things would help. After all, most of the time, his dreams were strange visions of things that hadn't ever happened before, and he wasn't sure if it was something else causing him to have them, or if his own mind was betraying him—as usual.

When he located the shelf with a small collection of obsidian on it, he took a few pieces—and that was when the store owner returned with the box he'd asked for. He placed everything he picked up so far into it and then took the box from him.

"Is there anything I can help you find?" the man asked.

"No," Alucard mumbled. He'd much rather be left alone right now.

As the owner retreated behind the counter, Alucard made his way over to one last shelf with a collection of brightly coloured crystals, geodes, and stones. He found what he was looking for—fire agate—took a few pieces, and then walked over to the counter. He placed the box on it and waited for the owner to look through it all.

While Alucard waited, he glanced around the store. Usually, when he came to a place like this, he'd enjoy looking at everything, but right now, he just wanted to get what he'd come for and figure out what to do with the rest of his time.

But he then snapped out of his despondency when his eyes located on a shimmer of gold behind where the owner was standing. At first glance, it looked to be a single, rounded piece of gold sitting in a black box of silk, but once he actually stared at it, he discovered that it was a pocket watch, and it looked like it had carvings, but he couldn't really make out what they were from where he was.

He took his eyes off it and looked down at the counter, waiting as patiently as he could, but for some reason, that random pocket watch seemed to catch his attention more than he might have thought. He stared at it again; surely, if it was in a place like this, there must be something special about it, right? But what? The mystery intrigued Alucard, and he wanted to know.

"Vhat is zhat?" he asked, nodding in the direction of the watch.

The man stopped tallying up the price of the crystals and looked over his shoulder. He then smiled slightly and shrugged. "Oh, just some old thing that's been in here since before I was around."

"You own zhis place…and you zon't even know about your vares?"

The man frowned slightly. "Well…it's more of a…you come here, you see it, you want it type of deal. It's a store of curiosities; you're supposed to feel drawn to things in here. That's what my mother used to say. She was a witch; she owned this store before me."

"Vight," he mumbled. "Vell, I vant zhat, too," he said, looking at the pocket watch again.

The store owner glanced back at it and then wandered over to the shelf. He carefully picked it up, making sure that it stayed inside the box, and placed it on the counter in front of the vampire. "It's probably older than both of us."

"Doubtful," Alucard mumbled, taking it off the counter. Now that it was right in front of him, he could see that the carvings on it were unmistakably carnations, the same flowers Zalith sent him after he returned from Damien's castle almost two years ago.

Sadness quickly swelled inside him the longer he stared at it, the longer he thought about the time Zalith sent him carnations. He still had them…those flowers. He got them stored in resin so that they would stay the way they were forever; he wanted to remember the time Zalith made him feel so wanted…something he didn't feel right now.

With a distressed scowl, he placed the pocket watch back on the counter. "'Ow much is all zhis?" he asked, eager to leave.

"Uh…." The man frowned, looking over the list he had been writing. "Well…I haven't finished—"

With an irritated sigh, Alucard reached into his pocket and pulled out several coronam notes; it was probably more than ten times as much as he would have needed, but he didn't care. He just wanted to leave. So he placed the money in front of the confused man, put everything he needed back into the box, and turned around, heading for the exit.

Once he was outside, Alucard felt a little less overwrought. He hated being in such small, confined spaces.

Alucard trudged along the street, a heavy burden of melancholy weighing upon him like a suffocating shroud. Despite his concerted efforts to evade the overwhelming grip of sadness that had ensnared him ever since the shift in Zalith's demeanour, thoughts of the demon persisted, haunting his every step.

The relentless barrage of memories and unanswered questions gnawed at his consciousness, leaving him feeling adrift in a sea of desolation. Why was he unable to banish these dolorous thoughts, even as they inflicted fresh wounds upon his already bruised spirit? The ache of loneliness seemed to deepen with each passing moment, a constant reminder of his inability to escape the emotional turmoil that consumed him.

He spotted a store to his right with a window full of all kinds of sweet things. As soon as he saw the cherry-topped cupcake, he remembered what Mary-Beth said about her husband, about how she would always make sure he had something nice to come home to.

Alucard still wanted to do something for Zalith. Perhaps he should try what Mary-Beth did. She was married, after all, and she seemed to know exactly what to do for her husband, and that encouraged Alucard to try something similar for Zalith.

He went into the store but hesitated and stopped in his tracks, realizing that he didn't know much about food. What did Zalith even like? He wasn't sure, but that didn't stop him from wanting to get something for him.

The vampire made his way over to the counter, eyeing each and every treat and snack. He was quite sure *he'd* like everything on display, but he was looking for something for Zalith.

He set his sights on a small box containing four different muffins, each decorated with differently coloured frosting and all with two strawberry halves placed on top of them. If he got those, there were four for Zalith to choose from. If he didn't like one of them, then maybe he would like one of the others.

"I vould like zhis," he said, looking at the woman behind the counter as he pointed to the muffins.

She smiled, took out the box, and handed it to him. He paid her, placed the box on top of the other that he was carrying, and then left the store.

He felt a little better now; thinking about Zalith appreciating the cakes kept him from sinking further into dismay, and he'd admittedly gotten the pocket watch for him, too. He hardly ever got Zalith gifts, so maybe that would convince the demon that *he* hadn't lost interest in their relationship…and hopefully Zalith's reaction would help Alucard assume the same about him.

There was still such a long time to wait until it was time to meet Bernie, though, so he thought he might head home, put the cakes someplace safe, and wait a little. Surely, Zalith would come home before he had to leave, right?

# Chapter Twelve

— ⸓ ✝ ⸓ —

# Waiting... Again

**| Alucard |**

It was almost 7 p.m. when Alucard got back home to Nefastus. He hated how long it took him to fly sometimes.

He could see the glow of light coming from Zalith's office, which had to mean that the demon was already home.

Alucard made his way inside and into his office, where he placed his two boxes. He wasn't going to work tonight; he just wanted to go and relax and have dinner with Zalith, so he'd leave the crystals in his office and start working with them tomorrow.

He took off his cape and blazer, and then he took the pocket watch and cakes with him as he went into the hall. However, he stopped when he heard Zalith's voice from inside his office. At first, he thought he might go and tell the demon that he was going to go and wait for him, but he didn't want to interrupt whatever he was doing. They always had dinner around the same time each night, so he was sure that Zalith would join him soon.

The vampire made his way through the hall and into the dining room; two glasses and a bottle of wine had been left on the table for them, and once he sat down, he filled both of them. He placed the two boxes he'd brought with him aside and waited for Zalith to join him. He wasn't sure how much longer he might be, but of course, whatever Zalith was doing was probably important, and Alucard didn't mind waiting.

But the time ticked on, and after a while passed, Alucard began to feel concerned. He glanced at the clock on the mantlepiece, seeing that he'd been waiting nearly forty minutes—maybe Zalith would be finishing up soon.

He shuffled forward, resting his arms on the table as he refilled his glass of wine.

A quiet knock then came at the dining room door.

Alucard looked over there to see Edwin, who stepped into the room. "Excuse me, sir, but sir Zalith has asked me to tell you that he will be another thirty minutes; something unexpected has come up."

The vampire nodded and watched as the butler left.

Then, he looked down at his glass. Another thirty minutes was fine. He still had enough time to have dinner and head to Dor-Sanguis to meet Bernie; his home country was seven hours ahead of Nefastus, though, so he needed to keep double-checking what hour it was. He didn't want to miss the meeting.


Though it was much longer than he anticipated. Over the past *hour*, he sunk into a slouch, staring aimlessly at his empty glass. He thought about pouring another, but he didn't want to get through the entire bottle on his own.

What could be keeping Zalith? Something had obviously happened; not only had Edwin said so, but he'd heard Zalith talking in his office earlier, and he sounded rather tense. Maybe something happened in Eltaria after he left.

But then the door opened again. Alucard hoped it might be Zalith, but disappointment struck and enthralled him when he saw that it was Edwin once more.

"Vhat?" he grumbled, sitting up.

"Sir Zalith will be twenty more minutes," he said, and then he left.

Alucard pouted, resting his arms on the table as he looked down at his glass. Another twenty minutes? He started to feel annoyed, but he also felt awful for feeling vexed that Zalith was taking longer than usual; for all Alucard knew, something serious could have happened, and Zalith could be struggling to deal with it.

The vampire sighed, glancing at the things he bought for Zalith. Perhaps he could use this time to work out what he wanted to say to the demon about his worries and feelings, and what he would say when giving him the gift he'd got him. He felt so nervous about it already and he was sure that he'd feel much shyer when the time to give the watch to Zalith came. He also had no idea how to start the conversation about his feelings….

What did he want to tell him? That he was worried because they weren't spending as much time together anymore? That was *one* thing. He also wanted to know why Zalith had changed, why their moments together had become so rare and so short. Why did Zalith seem so distant? Why was he always gone? Where was he going?

Why was he taking so long?

Alucard frowned as distress started enthralling him, growing as each moment passed. Every minute he spent waiting was another minute his thoughts pulled him further and further into dismay. He didn't want to become angry because Zalith was taking a while; he didn't want to be so selfish as to think that having dinner with him was more important than whatever Zalith was working on. But...*what* was he working on? Why was he taking so long? He'd never missed dinner before, so why was he missing it now?

He sunk deeper and deeper into his conflicting thoughts, his sadness taking hold of him just as it had been these past few days. Zalith stopped doing a lot of the things that he used to do before, and now, perhaps dinner was another thing that would stop happening. Alucard was already convinced that Zalith didn't want to spend as much time with him as he used to, and now it looked as though he didn't even want to spend this minuscule amount of time with him, either.

He didn't want to think like that. He sat up straight and looked down at the two boxes. Maybe he was just busy with work...but it hurt to know that Zalith was allowing the only time they got to spend together to slip away.

Dinner was the only time Alucard got to spend with Zalith anymore; the demon missed it yesterday, and Alucard hoped that he'd not miss it tonight, but...it was beginning to look like he would, and that led Alucard to believe that maybe this would be the case from now on.


But...he waited. The next twenty minutes passed by, and Alucard was starting to think that his assumption that maybe *Zalith* was worried about the distance that had come between them wasn't true. If it was, wouldn't Zalith jump at the chance to sit down with him right now? Alucard knew *he* would.

The door to the dining room suddenly opened, and this time, it wasn't Edwin. Alucard looked over at the door, and as soon as he saw that it was Zalith walking in, he stood up, and relief filled him. His hopelessness faded as Zalith walked towards him, but the hesitant look on the demon's face told him that he was about to hear something he really didn't want to.

"I'm so sorry, darling," Zalith said as he reached Alucard, pulling him into a hug. "One of my very important subordinates has died, and things are beginning to get out of hand. I'm going to have to head to Eltaria to try and get things under control," he explained in a rush.

Alucard scowled despondently. He *knew* something like this was going to happen, but he'd not argue or do anything that might stop Zalith. He had his work, and clearly, right now, it was more important than him.

"I'm sorry again," Zalith said, placing his hands on Alucard's shoulders as he stepped back out of their hug. "Please have dinner without me; I'm going to be gone for at least a few hours. But once things are back in order, I'll be home, and we can spend some time together."

Alucard didn't know what to say or think. All he knew was that it hurt knowing that once again, he'd not get to spend any time with Zalith. But he had told himself this morning that he'd probably have to get used to it, and now, he could see that he really should.

He wasn't sure why he hoped that things might get better since yesterday and why he thought his efforts would do anything. Right now, he didn't even see the point in telling Zalith he'd got some things for him; he wasn't going to stick around long enough, was he?

Alucard wouldn't keep him from his work, though…if that was even what he was doing.

He scowled, looking down at the floor. Why had Luther's words embedded themselves in his mind? Now, because of him, he started suspecting more and more that Zalith's disappearances weren't work-related. He didn't believe Zalith would lie to him like that; the demon was clearly worried and in a hurry. Something *had* to be happening to make him look so concerned. Or maybe…maybe Zalith was just making it seem that way.

With a quiet sigh, he sunk back into his seat. "Okay," he answered.

Zalith frowned and crouched beside him, looking up at him as he stared back. "I'm sorry," he said again, placing his hand over Alucard's. He then dragged his hand up Alucard's arm and to the back of his head, pulling him closer so that he could rest his forehead against his. "I'll be back soon."

Alucard stared sullenly into his eyes. He didn't want to hold him to that. Would he wait for him? Yes, but he wouldn't expect Zalith to be back any time soon. He was always gone so long.

The demon leaned closer and kissed the vampire's lips. He stood up and took a few steps back as he sighed quietly, hesitating for a few moments. "I'll be back later, baby," he said with a smile.

And then he was gone.

Alucard let the dismay devour him. He just wanted to spend some time with Zalith, time that wasn't interrupted by work or one of them being tired. Something always came up, something always happened to stop them from spending so much as an hour together, and it had been happening so often that Alucard felt as if it was time to stop hoping that things might improve.

He didn't know why Zalith was acting so differently, but he was tired of trying to work it out or convince himself that things would return to how they used to be. Things had only been becoming worse; he'd see less and less of Zalith each day, Zalith ignored opportunities for them to spend time together, and Alucard was convinced that Zalith just didn't want to prioritise him anymore.

But he wouldn't get angry. He didn't expect Zalith to choose him over whatever it was that had him so preoccupied. Why would he be more important? He felt stupid for letting himself believe that he might be. Stupid for thinking that his meaningless attempts to show Zalith he wanted to spend time with him would matter.

He leaned his arms onto the table, staring down at it as he let the negative feelings enthral him. Maybe Luther was right. Maybe Zalith was doing this because he didn't know how to tell him he couldn't keep his promises. And why would Alucard be mad at him? Zalith had learned a whole lot more about him since they met, and he'd always suspected that, at some point, Zalith would learn something that he didn't want to know. There were so many ugly things about Alucard—his past, his present…his family— nothing about him was wonderful, and maybe Zalith was beginning to see that.

Maybe Luther *was* right. Perhaps Zalith had been spending his time elsewhere and with someone else; he'd been going to Eltaria pretty much every day for a long time now, and he was always gone in the morning, always coming home at night. How was Alucard to know whether or not he'd met someone else? Someone more interesting, someone who hadn't been cast out from the world that Zalith was a part of. Someone who wasn't meek and pathetic and stupid like him. Someone who hadn't been scarred and broken. And that was okay. Because Alucard knew of his imperfections, he knew of the ugliness that festered inside and out, and the only thing that hurt was the fact that it had taken Zalith this long to see it, that he'd allowed Alucard to believe that he didn't care about his imperfections.

It all made sense. As much as Alucard didn't want it to, it did. The total disappearance of intimacy apart from a kiss here or a hug there; the lack of time they spent together, the lack of touching. Sometimes, he felt like Zalith didn't even look at him how he used to. They rarely spoke, and whenever they did, it felt forced and strange. Zalith was always in a rush to go somewhere and leave.

He just didn't want Alucard anymore, did he? It was as though Zalith was trying to love him but just couldn't. That was what it felt like.

The vampire stood up and left the dining room. He stopped in the middle of the hall, confliction starting to break through his sadness. For a moment, his eyes wandered to the door. Should he even stay here anymore? It probably made things harder for Zalith knowing that he was still in the same house as him; Zalith had been leaving a lot, and maybe that was because he couldn't stand to be in the same house as Alucard.

But where could he go? He could go back to his castle, but he hated it there. This was the only place he ever really felt at home. But was it even home anymore? Without Zalith, everything felt so wrong and strange, and Alucard just felt so desperate for things to go back to the way they used to be.

He didn't want to leave. He loved Zalith more than he'd ever loved anything, and the way things currently were was causing him so much pain and so much confusion that he had no idea what to do or who to turn to. Did Zalith even want him anymore? If he did, why was he acting like this? Why was he always gone, and why had he become so distant? Did he really even love Alucard anymore? Or did he just feel like he had to say he did?

Alucard didn't know. Maybe he'd never know. And he didn't want to think about it again. He just wanted everything to stop for a while; the hurt, the loneliness, the confusion. How could he escape it?

He sighed deeply, turning his head to stare over at the stairs. He wanted to sleep, but he had to go and meet Bernie. His dedication to his people didn't change whether he was depressed or dying. He had to protect them, and he had to find out who was murdering vampires.

With a despondent scowl, he put his shoes and cape back on and left the house. It was time to head back to Dor-Sanguis.

# Chapter Thirteen

⸺ ⸹ ✝ ⸺

# The Dargamoore Saviours

**| Alucard |**

When Alucard got back to Dor-Sanguis, the early morning was dark and damp; rain hadn't long fallen, and the clouds looming above suggested that a storm was approaching.

The vampire rematerialized in an alley not far from the inn where Bernie had told him to meet him. He sighed deeply and stepped out onto the wet street, and then he made his way towards the mahogany and white building sitting between a closed bar and an empty café. The aroma of coffee and cooking bread merged with the smell of petrichor, and the place was silent. It wouldn't be for very long, though.

He hoped that whatever Bernie knew was enough for him to put an end to the murders before whoever was behind them managed to kill anyone else, and he also hoped that it was something he could deal with alone. He knew that he and his people were supposed to work with the city law enforcement when dealing with crimes between vampires and humans, but Luther was right when he said that the humans were rude and very hard to work with.

The vampire approached the inn, but just as he was about to head inside, a quiet voice called from his right.

"Hey, over here." It sounded like Bernie.

Alucard turned to face the direction it came from, and his eyes quickly located the brown-haired human he'd come to meet.

"Come on," he called, waving at Alucard, leaning out from behind the cover of a crooked fence.

The vampire frowned skeptically. While he hadn't detected any deceit on the man's face or in his voice when he spoke to him earlier, a part of him felt as though he should be cautious and ready, so he reached into his blazer and made sure that his colts were secure in case he needed them. Then, he slowly made his way towards the fence, focusing his senses. He couldn't sense anyone else nearby other than the people inside the inn and the bar, but he wouldn't let his guard down.

He stepped around the fence and looked into the narrow alley. Bernie was waiting at the end by an open door that led into the house behind the bar and inn.

"This way," Bernie called. "You can come in."

Alucard moved towards the door, and when he stepped past the threshold, he followed Bernie inside the dark house. "So vhat do you know?" he asked impatiently.

"Well…a lot," Bernie said as he led him into the living room and switched the lights on. "Where do you want me to start?"

"Vherever," Alucard muttered, watching him sit down on the dusty couch. He wanted to know everything he could; any and all details could help.

Bernie invited him to sit in the armchair across from him.

Alucard shook his head. "I'm vine standing."

"Oh, okay," he said with a nod. "Well…like I said earlier, Loyde and Sophina came into the Ruby Lounge at least once a week. They never did anything to upset any of the regulars, but I guess just being vampires was enough to push someone over the edge, right?"

"Vight."

"Do you want a drink?"

Alucard's skepticism grew. It looked like Bernie was stalling, and he was beginning to feel like he should leave, but he wanted to find out whatever he could about what happened to Loyde and Sophina; they were the two Eltarian vampires, and he was sure that Zalith would want answers just as much as he did…no matter the state of their relationship.

He wouldn't let the dismay start consuming him again, though.

"No," the vampire replied. "Do you know who did zhis?"

Bernie didn't immediately answer. He looked like he was thinking while he tapped his fingers on the couch arm. "It's a group," he finally said.

"Of 'unters?"

"Uh…sort of, I guess," he said with a shrug.

"Vhat does 'sort of' mean?"

"They're like…they see themselves as saviours—they actually call themselves the Dargamoore Saviours or something."

Alucard frowned again.

"They say that their mission is the save the people of Dor-Sanguis from the vile undead—vampires. I think they're religious."

"Do zhey 'ave anyving to do vith Marcus' group."

Bernie frowned. "Who?"

Alucard wasn't sure whether his answer meant that this group had nothing to do with Marcus or that Bernie just had no idea who he was and didn't have all the information. "A man who tried to start a movement avound two years ago."

"Oh…*that*," he said, shaking his head. "I don't think so. I've never heard the mention of anyone called Marcus."

"Vhen did zhis group vorm?"

"I'm not sure. All I know is that they first killed the other day. There've been whispers flying around the city that it was them, and…a lot of people seem…glad? I thought that everyone was fine with the treaty, but that's because I only hang around people who welcome it and partake in blood exchanges. But I mean there's always people who are never gonna change or evolve, right?"

Alucard crossed his arms and asked, "And vone or more of zhese people go to zhe place you vork, no?"

Bernie nodded.

"Who?"

"Well…" he drawled, looking nervous. "I-I don't wanna piss the wrong people off. All the rich people in this city are super close with the council, and I don't wanna be stuck washing dishes for the rest of my life, you see, so—"

"No vone vill know zhis invormation came vrom you," he grumbled.

The man shuffled around in his seat. "You see…I'd like to believe you…you know, with you being the vampire leader and all that…but I really am risking my career and entire life in this city. What if someone finds out that it was me?"

He was clearly fishing for something, and Alucard didn't want to stand there and be led around any more circles. So he asked, "Vhat do you vant vrom me?"

"Uh…well, now that you mention it…you *do* have a pretty high standing with the city council, don't you?"

Alucard sighed deeply. "I do."

"Then…you could get me a better job or into Elescaster University, right?"

"I zon't 'ave anyving to do vith Elescaster City."

"But you could like…get me some good recommendations or references, right? If they came from influential people, even not in that city, that would look good for me, wouldn't it?"

The vampire rolled his eyes. "Vine. Vhatever. Now tell me everyvone who is involved in Loyde and Sophina's murders."

Excitement and relief flickered across Bernie's face. "Right, okay. Do you have a pen and paper?"

"I'll vemember."

"Okay…so, Allison and Gregory McFlarren are regulars, and I've seen them hanging around with this man who everyone calls Rorke. Now *he* has always been into shady business; he's been arrested a dozen or so times for countless different crimes, but they could never find any evidence. I saw *him* leave the Ruby Lounge just a minute or so after Loyde and Sophina. And then the next morning, a woman who works in the pop-up market found their bodies while dumping trash in the courtyard. Her name was uh…Ellie. It was in the paper."

"Vhat do Allison and Gregory McVlarren 'ave to do vith zhis?" he asked with a frown.

"Oh, so they left just after Rorke did. Allison works for the city paper, and *she* wrote the article about Loyde and Sophina, but she left out quite a few details…which I'm sure she did on purpose. I saw the murder site myself…before the police got there. I was on my way to work when I saw all the people crowding the courtyard entrance. The report said that the bodies were found with slashes and claw marks and that it was likely a werewolf, but there were no marks on their bodies that could have been made by werewolves. They each had a stake in their heart."

Alucard hadn't read the report, but he already knew that they were staked because Luther told him. Clearly, Luther had been doing his job well and managed to find out some information that whoever was behind this was trying to hide. What Bernie said made that very clear.

"Vhat about Gregory?" he asked.

"Gregory has a brother who works as a chef in the Ruby Lounge; he comes in all the time with his wife because they get a family discount."

Although he didn't have enough information to start hypothesizing much, Alucard wondered if these Saviours operated out of the Rube Lounge. It seemed a little odd that Rorke, a repeat-offending criminal, would be allowed in such a place, and even stranger that the woman who worked for the paper was a regular there. It had to be connected.

"'Ave you seen anyvone else leaving vith or avound zhe same time as Rorke?"

Bernie shook his head. "No, sorry. I don't see very much because I'm normally always out the back washing dishes. I-I know where Rorke lives, though…if that's helpful."

Investigating Rorke looked to be the next step, so he nodded. "Vhere?"

"You know that little hut not far from the farm fields? The one that a little bard used to live in."

Alucard's heart sunk into his stomach. He knew that place. He never wanted to know where Elvin lived back then because he didn't want anyone to use that information against him; he didn't want his enemies harming that kid to get to him. But after Elvin died, he had his vampires find out where he'd been living, and he gave his kitten to one of the farmers.

"He moved out there after getting off a manslaughter charge," Bernie continued. "What kind of guy gets off with no jail time for causing his girlfriend's death?"

Someone who had friends in high places. If Rorke was involved, which Alucard was beginning to highly suspect that he was, he had to find out who his friends were.

"Is zhere anyving else you vink I should know?" he asked, standing up straight. "Anyving about zhe ozzer murders?"

Bernie pondered. "No, sorry. I only knew Loyde and Sophina."

Alucard nodded. "Vight. Vank you vor zhe invormation. If I vere you, I'd lie low vor a vew days until I get to zhe bottom of zhis."

He looked nervous but nodded again. "Just don't use my name…please. Unless I get into Elescaster University," he said with a slight chuckle. "They won't be able to hurt me if I don't live here anymore, right?"

"Mm," he mumbled. "I vill 'ave somevone contact you about zhat in a vew days, too."

Bernie adorned an appreciative smile and stood up. "Thank you."

Alucard nodded and turned around. He headed for the door, and when he stepped outside, Bernie waved from the threshold.

For a moment there, Alucard thought that man might be leading him into a trap, but he was just nervous. And he had every right to be. If the rich, influential people of this city were involved in the murders and covering them up, they could ruin the lives of anyone who spoke out or tried to stop them. But not Alucard. This country was his birthright; nothing and no one could take that away.

When he passed the bar, he glanced in through the window at the clock. It was getting close to midnight. Once he was done talking to Rorke, he ought to head home. He was almost certain that Zalith wouldn't be there, but he wanted to make sure that he was there when the demon eventually did get back. He didn't want Zalith to come home to an empty bed and think that *he* was out with someone else.

But…would Zalith even care?

He didn't want to let the thoughts start overwhelming him again. He had a job to do.

With a quiet sigh, he dematerialized into vermillion smoke and began his journey towards Elvin's old hut; hopefully, Rorke would give him the rest of the story, and by tomorrow, his vampires would be safe again.

# Chapter Fourteen

# Rorke

**| Alucard |**

A frigid wave of remorse cascaded down Alucard's spine as he rematerialized in front of Elvin's old hut. The memory of the night when Damien came seeking retribution weighed heavily upon him, casting a pall of guilt and dismay over his thoughts. He could never absolve himself for his treatment of the bard; despite Elvin's quirks and idiosyncrasies, he had shown genuine concern for Alucard. Yet, in a moment of callousness, Alucard had discarded that bond as though it were inconsequential, and the regret gnawed at him like a festering wound.

Despite the weight of regret, Alucard remained resolute as he stood before the place the bard once lived, grappling with the haunting question of whether his actions had been justified. In the depths of his soul, he knew the answer—regardless of Zalith's altered sentiments, his love for the demon remained steadfast and unwavering. If faced with the same choice again, he would not hesitate to make the ultimate sacrifice, for in Zalith's enigmatic embrace, Alucard had found a love worth any price.

Even if Zalith no longer felt the same.

He didn't have time to stand there and sink into his despair, though, so he sighed away as much of the guilt as he could and approached the door. Rorke was a criminal, and if he *was* involved in the vampire murders, then he was going to be prepared for anything.

Alucard had to be careful; he was still susceptible to the same things as his vampires. As he neared the door, he focused his senses, finding only one aura inside, and it was human. He scanned the entire area around him as far as his senses would reach; there were werewolves in the forest, but their auras matched those of Freja's pack—they were no threat. He detected humans in the nearby farmhouse, but that was to be expected. As far as he could tell, Rorke was alone.

He halted when the question hit him: did Rorke *own* this house?

The vampire frowned unsurely. Would a criminal sign the deed to a home? He wouldn't think so. Either way, he was about to find out.

He knocked on the door and waited.

Someone shuffled around inside.

Alucard kept his senses focused, and when the door slowly creaked open, he prepared to grab his weapons if need be.

The beady eyes of a tall, bald man met Alucard's skeptical gaze. Rorke stood dressed in old, torn clothes and a dark grey overcoat which concealed most of his body. The outline of a sidearm was just noticeable beneath the coat on his right, and the shimmer of silver blades flickered from beneath it as Rorke crossed his arms and looked Alucard up and down.

"What do ye want?" he questioned.

"I vant to ask you a vew questions about Loyde and Sophina Klarke, two vampires who vould vrequent zhe Vuby Lounge," Alucard answered.

Rorke scoffed. "I knew *someone* would come sniffing around, but I never thought it would be you." He quickly pulled a silver blade from under his coat and called, "Get 'im, boys!"

Similarly dressed men burst up from grass camouflage blankets and from around the back of the hut, wielding silver blades as they charged at Alucard.

He should've known that it was a trap. But that didn't change the fact that he was going to get answers.

With an irritated snarl, Alucard lifted his leg and slammed his foot against Rorke's chest before the man took a single step; as Rorke flew back into the hut and hit the wall, Alucard swung to his right and grabbed the wrist of the first man brave enough to attack. The vampire crushed his wrist, and then he savagely tore his bottom jaw off when he screamed hysterically.

He turned around fast enough to grab the arm of another man and pulled him off his feet, launching him at the guy farthest away aiming a hunting rifle. The man fired his shot too late, and the bullet burrowed into the grass as the man that Alucard threw collided with the rifleman.

Rorke growled furiously as he lunged out of the hut towards Alucard. "Fucking get him!"

Alucard grabbed Rorke's arm when the man swung his blade at him, but he didn't see the vial in his hand in time. Rorke splashed the liquid inside onto Alucard's face; it burned agonizingly upon contact, a sting that Alucard knew too well. He yelled out painfully as he shoved Rorke away and stumbled back, trying to wipe the holy water from his skin, but it burned deeper, throwing his senses off and blurring his vision.

Two of Rorke's men grabbed each of Alucard's arms, and then Rorke smashed his fist into the vampire's face with a fierce, excited shout.

The force made Alucard turn his head to the side; his ears started ringing, and the holy water stole his vision, leaving him with a painful, swirling darkness.

"Fuck!" Rorke yelled enthusiastically, laughing—Alucard could feel the breeze shifting around in front of him; Rorke was likely pacing. "The boss is gonna fucking *love* this shit," he called as his men snickered around him.

Alucard gritted his teeth, waiting for his body to fight off the holy water and heal the wounds it left on him. His eyes stung, and the high-pitched ring in his ears started circling him. He tried to concentrate, though. Rorke evidently worked for someone, and he needed to know *who*.

"What about that fucking kid?" one of the men asked.

Rorke scoffed. "'Lil fucking Bernie boy? Fuck him! Kill the little rat. I *told* you all that he was a snitch."

"I wanna do it," another man announced.

"Yeah, yeah, whatever," Rorke muttered. "Bag and tag this undead freak. I'll take 'im to the boss meself."

Alucard scowled angrily. He couldn't see, and his hearing was still swirling, but he didn't need all his senses to kill these assholes. The moment they tried dragging him somewhere, the vampire pulled both his arms free and grabbed one of the men. He wanted to drink from him—he needed it, and it would heal him faster—but they likely had holy water or vampire poisons in their systems; he wasn't going to risk ingesting that. So instead, he tore out the man's throat with his claws and then backed off as he held his hands out in front of him. He still couldn't see, but luciferium crystals would seek them out for him. The vampire twisted his hand, and when he felt the ground rumble beneath his feet, horrified cries broke through the determined grunts and laughter.

The smell of blood filled his nose. He held out his hand, transforming every drop into crystalized shards, something he'd only remembered he could do after Zalith untangled his mind. Once every drop of blood was weaponized, Alucard commanded them to seek out the humans around him. The cries and yells grew louder and more painful as the sound of sharp crystals slicing flesh raced around where the vampire stood.

He exhaled deeply, focusing his ethos and forcing his body to heal his vision before anything else. The world slowly reformed around him; it was colourless at first, but life quickly returned to the forest and farmland.

A struggling, gurgling grunt snatched his attention.

Alucard looked in the direction it came from and set his eyes on Rorke. The man lay in a puddle of blood, both his own and his friends', with a luciferium crystal impaled through his right side.

The vampire moved towards him, clenching his bloody fists as he did. He wanted to kill him, but he needed answers, and Rorke was the best person to get them from.

He stopped and crouched beside him. "Did you veally vink zhis vould vork?"

Rorke spat blood on the grass and then glared up at Alucard. "Fuck you, you undead piece of—"

Alucard snatched the man's face and pulled him to his feet, dragging him free from the crystal. Rorke yelled out in agony as the vampire harshly pinned him against the hut wall, and when he glared into his eyes, Rorke gritted his teeth and growled furiously, trying to fight.

"Tell me who you vork vor," Alucard snarled.

"Fuck you!"

The vampire used his free hand to wipe as much blood from his face as he could—his own and that of Rorke's dead friends. "I vill give you vone last chance," he told him. "Eizer tell me vhat I vant to know, or I vill subject you to a vorld of pain zhat your tiny 'uman mind could never compre'end," he growled, tightening his grip.

Rorke spat blood in his face. "You're all gonna fucking burn!"

Alucard scoffed amusedly and moved closer to Rorke, glowering at him. "'Ave you ever vondered vhat is like vor your skin to burn and melt in zhe sunlight?" he asked him.

The man's scowl thickened, but there was fear in his eyes.

"Virst, zhere's zhis intense 'eat…like you're sitting inches avay vrom a vaging vire. And zhen your skin starts to boil. Zhe 'eat burns zhe virst layer avay, and as zhat melts and trickles down, zhe vlesh and muscle burn next. I've 'eard some people say zhat vire burns your nerve endings, and eventually, you veel noving, but vith zhe sun, you veel *everyving*," he explained slowly, watching as the desperation on Rorke's face grew. "And zhen zhe adrenaline kicks in. You vant to vun, and you know zhat you can, but at zhat point, you look like vone of zhose children's dolls zhat got vhrown into an oven, covered in your own melted vlesh. And zhen zhe vire consumes vhatever is levt of you, burning you down to a pile of ash. You veel zhat, too."

Rorke choked, looking a little nauseous.

"I vink…virst, I'll leave you out just long enough so your vace becomes unvecognizable. Vampires zon't 'eal vrom severe vounds invlicted by zhe sun, so if you survive, you'll spend eternity veeling like somevone 'as vrapped leather avound your 'ead."

The man gagged. "G-get off me!"

Alucard tightened his grip even more. "Last chance," he warned him. "Who do you vork vor and did you kill Loyde and Sophina Klarke?"

Rorke growled frustratedly, and it looked like he was thinking, but after only a few seconds, he shook his head. "Undead freak!" he yelled.

The vampire crashed his fist into Rorke's face, breaking his nose. As the man groaned painfully, Alucard let him drop to the ground like a sack of potatoes. He held out his hand and summoned Luther, and moments later, a black bat raced through the darkness and transformed into the long-haired, white suit-wearing man.

"What the hell happened here?" Luther questioned worriedly, but when he saw Alucard's face, his eyes widened in shock. "W-what the fuck happened to your face?!"

"'Oly vater," he muttered. "Take zhis piece of shit back to my castle and put 'im in vone of zhe vindowless cells. Vonce all zhe 'emlock is out of 'is system, turn 'im."

Rorke looked absolutely horrified. "No!" he yelled as he tried to get up, but Luther grabbed him and pulled his arms behind his back. "Get off!" he shouted, almost screaming. "Fuck off!"

Alucard punched his face again. "If 'e breaks bevore is time to turn 'im, vind out who 'e vorks vor and who keeps 'elping 'im get avay vith 'is crimes."

Luther frowned, still holding Rorke. "Is he involved in the murders?"

"*Da.* Is likely zhat 'e killed Loyde and Sophina, and maybe zhe ozzers, too."

"Fuck...."

"I'll kill all of—"

With an aggravated snarl, Alucard slammed his fist into Rorke's face one last time, knocking him out. "Vhreaten 'im vith zhe sun. Cut 'is vingers off, I zon't care. Vind out vhat I vant to know."

Luther nodded. "Yeah, understood."

"I'll 'ave to talk to zhe council zhis evening and tell zhem vhat 'appened. Zhe last ving ve need is zhem getting upset because I vas vonce again doing zheir jobs vor zhem."

"Do you want me to come?" he asked.

"No. Vork on 'im," he muttered, nodding at Rorke.

"All right. But...Alucard?"

He sighed deeply. "Vhat?"

"That...looks pretty bad," he said, gesturing to his face. "Are you feeding properly? It's sort of hard to tell when you're hungry because your eyes don't get darker like the rest of us vampires. I mean your *pupils* do get thinner when you're mad...and you look kind of mad right now...so I'll stop...but I'm worried about you."

Alucard let out another sigh. He was tired of Luther asking him if he was okay or if he was hungry or whatever the fuck else he'd been asking recently. "Take 'im back to zhe castle and send a group to dispose of zhese bodies properly. I zon't vant anyvone vinding zhem."

Luther nodded. "Yeah, no problem. Just...make sure you feed when you need it. Don't wait for Zalith's per—"

"Vill you mind your own business?" the vampire snarled. "Do your job."

Although he looked irritated and as if he wanted to argue, Luther threw Rorke over his shoulder and started heading back towards the castle.

Alucard huffed irritably and carefully dragged his hand over his face. He could feel the burns healing, and the rest of his body was recovering, too. Now that he had Rorke, he wanted to head home and sleep, but the thought of returning to an empty bed made him feel empty.

He couldn't go yet, anyway. Bernie's information had come through, and he wanted to keep up his end of the bargain. So, he summoned another vampire, and when the woman landed beside him, he turned to face her. "I need you to 'ead to zhe Shire Inn on St. Marseus Street. Is a ma'ogany and vhite building betveen a bar and a café. To zhe vight, zhere's an alley 'idden be'ind some crooked vence, and at zhe end is a door. Knock. Zhere is a man called Bernie who lives zhere. Tell 'im zhat I sent you, and vor 'is savety, 'e needs to stay at my castle until 'e can leave vor Elescaster. Get Luther to give 'im a voom on my side of zhe castle."

"Yes, My Lord," she said with a humble nod. Then, she transformed into a bat and hurried off towards Dargamoore.

And now Alucard could go home. He exhaled heavily as the sadness quickly returned, outweighing his anger and annoyance. But he tried his best not to think about it. He may have Rorke, but it wasn't over yet. Rorke worked for someone, and if Alucard wanted to stop the murders, he needed to find out who that someone was.

# Chapter Fifteen

## Answers

| Alucard |

When Alucard returned home, the absence of Zalith hung in the air. With a heavy heart, he took his shoes and cloak off, the weight of loneliness pressing down upon him with each deliberate movement. He wasn't hungry, and he didn't want to eat without Zalith, anyway. So he cast a weary glance towards the staircase, and he decided to resign himself to the solitude that awaited him.

Ascending the stairs with leaden steps, the vampire entered the dimly lit confines of his bedroom. First, he took off his bloody clothes and climbed into the shower. The warm water didn't bring any relief, though. He felt empty, and he felt alone.

Once he was done, he dried off and collapsed onto the bed; the scars on his back stung when they met the blanket, reminding Alucard how much he hated his body. He felt revolting, and he was sure that Zalith didn't want to see them anymore, either. Maybe the grotesque marks of his past were starting to revolt Zalith, and Alucard wouldn't blame him if that were the truth.

He got up, slipped a t-shirt on, and then got back into bed.

As he lay there, his gaze drifted listlessly towards the blank wall beside him. Each passing moment seemed to stretch into eternity, a relentless march towards an uncertain future. Perhaps tomorrow would bring clarity, a beacon of hope amidst the suffocating darkness that threatened to engulf him. Or perhaps tomorrow would herald the final reckoning, the inevitable end to their relationship. Only time would tell.

Alucard woke when he felt Zalith getting into bed beside him. He opened his eyes and glanced at the clock as the demon moved his arms around him. It was just past 3 a.m.

Zalith pulled him closer and made himself comfortable. Why? Why cling to him now if he wasn't going to do it when Alucard needed it? All this did was confuse him further.

The demon soon realized that he'd woken him up and leaned over so that he could see Alucard's face. "I'm sorry if I woke you," he mumbled tiredly. Then, he rested the side of his head on Alucard's, holding him tightly.

A short silence fell over them. Alucard had nothing to say, nor did he want to think. He just wanted to go back to sleep. He could feel his sorrow tearing at him; he didn't want to sink back into it—he wanted to forget.

"Did you have dinner?" Zalith asked.

Alucard closed his eyes, trying his best to ignore his sadness. "No."

"Do you want something to eat?"

He went to answer, but the pain of his sorrow built up in the back of his throat, keeping him from using words. He felt as though he had lost the ability to breathe and remained silent, turning his head to hide his face from Zalith as much as he could. He didn't understand; he didn't want to try and understand.

Zalith placed his hand on Alucard's shoulder. "What's wrong?"

So many things were wrong. It was all that Alucard could think about recently, and right now, he was trying his best not to.

"Are you cold?" the demon then asked, rubbing Alucard's sleeve.

The vampire didn't want to answer that, either. He scowled in distress, trying to understand what was happening. Why was Zalith doing this? Why was he asking these questions? Why was he acting as though things were okay, as though he hadn't noticed the change in things recently? How could he not? *He* was the one causing them—*he* was the one causing Alucard to feel so much hurt and confusion. Why did he have to act as though he didn't know what was wrong?

"Alucard?" Zalith insisted, leaning over him again.

With a scowl still on his face, Alucard rolled onto his back and stared up at Zalith, who placed his right hand down beside him.

"Vhat?" the vampire uttered.

Zalith frowned in concern. "What's wrong?"

Glaring up at him, Alucard began to feel a crushing heartbreak. If he was ever going to find out what was going on, maybe now was the time. His sadness wasn't going to relent—he could feel the tears forming in his eyes as he tried to work out what to say or ask. What *should* he say? Should he tell Zalith that it was okay that he didn't want him anymore, or should he ask him if he wanted this to go on?

The confoundment kept him silent. He scowled, turning his head away from Zalith again so that he wouldn't see tears trickling down his face, but before he could turn his head to rest the side of his face on his pillow, Zalith placed his hand on his cheek and turned his head back to look at him.

"What's wrong?" he asked sadly.

Alucard stuttered, frowned, and gave in, letting his tears fall. "Vhy are you doing zhis?" he questioned despondently.

The demon slowly took his hand off Alucard's face and dragged it to his chest. "Doing what?"

"Zhis," he answered, his frown becoming a distressed scowl. "You make me vink you zon't vant me anymore, and zhen you do zhis and act like everyving is okay."

Zalith shook his head slightly. "Of course I want you, Alucard. Is…this because I'm not around as often?"

He took his eyes off the demon and turned his head to scowl over at the wall. "Everyving is divverent," he answered. "I zon't understand vhy you're alvays gone, vhy you zon't talk to me as much anymore, or vhy you zon't touch me. If someving is vrong, just tell me," he insisted, his frown and sadness thickening as he spoke each word. Why hold back now? He'd already let Zalith know that he wasn't content, so why hesitate in telling him why? Why postpone hearing his answer? If tonight was the last night he'd spend here, then so be it.

But Zalith sighed quietly as silence fell between them again.

Alucard felt his heart begin to race a little faster as his angst, worry, and pain all came together as one. He had no idea what Zalith was about to say, but whatever it was, his sigh made it seem as though it couldn't be anything good.

"Alucard…."

The vampire tensed up. He wasn't as ready to hear it as he thought he was.

"As far as I'm concerned, there's nothing wrong between the two of us. I never stopped loving you, and I never will," he said as he moved a strand of Alucard's hair away from his face and tucked it behind his ear. "I'm so, *so* sorry if my absence has hurt and upset you. I didn't realize it would have this much of an effect on you. I genuinely thought that you knew in one way or another what was happening on my end, but…I see now that obviously, I didn't communicate with you well enough. I never meant to push you this far, and I never wanted anything like this to happen," he insisted despondently.

Alucard wasn't sure what to say. As much as he wanted to accept Zalith's apology and go back to hoping that things would get better, he couldn't. He'd done so far too often, and he didn't want to feel the disappointment again.

But Zalith wasn't finished. "There are people in Eltaria who are still in my care; most of them are refugees, but a handful of them are people who work for me and have worked for me for quite some time. I told you before about the deity that the humans manifested, and it's just getting stronger, and those who work directly for it are getting smarter and far more capable. My people and colleagues are being slaughtered like animals, and I've been doing my absolute best to keep everybody alive. But that task is only becoming more and more difficult," he explained sullenly but then paused.

Alucard looked up at him, noticing a look of hesitation and dismay on his face.

"I'm…prone to putting every piece of myself into everything that I do; I throw myself entirely into my work—it sort of…envelopes me," he explained slowly. "Or maybe I envelope myself in it, I don't know. It's almost a compulsion. But even on a good day, I can't rest until I've either solved the issue at hand or at least made decent steps towards solving it, and right now, there are two important things in my life, Alucard, and one of them is you, and the other is Eltaria. You both give me tunnel vision; when I'm with you, it's like every single care and worry I ever had is gone, and even when you're not around, you're still in my head almost every minute of every day. On the other hand, the people I'm supposed to be taking care of are dying. I've never had to balance my work with any relationship before; I'm six hundred years old, but this is still new to me. I never wanted to upset you, Alucard, and I'm so sorry," he insisted, placing both his hands on either side of Alucard's face. "I never wanted this to happen, and if I'd known that you were this upset, I would've explained myself sooner."

Staring at him, Alucard frowned in confliction.

"Why didn't you tell me sooner?" Zalith then asked.

Taking his eyes off him, Alucard looked over at the wall. He'd just heard so much that he didn't know how to respond. It made sense, though. He knew what it was like to focus so much on work that he forgot about the world around him. And he'd suspected that maybe Zalith's work had something to do with his absence.

"Alucard?"

He sighed quietly, closing his eyes as he tried to hide his sorrow. "I vas…I zidn't know vhat you might say, and I vas avraid you vould tell me zhat you zidn't vant me anymore."

"I always want you, Alucard," Zalith insisted, dragging his thumb down the side of his face.

"Zhen vhy…." He hesitated. Zalith just told him why he'd been acting the way he had lately; he didn't want to question him any more and risk aggravating him. He'd got the answers he'd been looking for. His confusion and dismay started lifting as he let the demon's response sink in; what Zalith said meant that things weren't going to be like they were for a while, but Alucard now understood why, and although it upset him, he wasn't as depressed about it.

He sighed, pondering for a few moments. All that really mattered was that Zalith still loved him and that he didn't wish for their relationship to end. He was busy with work and trying to save the people he cared about. Alucard knew how that felt, and he didn't want to stress Zalith out any more than he already was. What he did want to do, however, was help Zalith in any way he could.

So, he set his eyes back on the demon and frowned. "Let me 'elp you with vings in Eltaria. Vould be easier vor us both if I vas zhere vith you vather zhan 'ere doing noving."

"I want you to be with me always, Alucard, but…I'm afraid that you're going to get hurt, and I don't want that to happen."

Alucard sat up with an irritated huff. "I'm not going to get 'urt. You've been vith me long enough to know zhat I can take care of myselv."

The demon hesitated. "Everyone I love has died in Eltaria; my enemies are just getting stronger, and if *anything* were to happen to you, I'd never be able to forgive myself. I never know what to expect with these people. I thought my father could handle them, I thought my mother and my brother could handle them, but they were taken from me by these same people, and I'll not lose you to them, too. I want you to stay here because I know you're safe. I can't bear to lose you."

Staring at him, Alucard found himself without words again. He didn't know what to say. He just wanted to help Zalith—that was all he could focus on right now. "'Ow many people are you trying to save?"

"There are only around sixty of them left."

He then thought to himself for a moment. If he couldn't go to Eltaria to help Zalith— he'd not force the demon to take him—then all he could think of as the next best thing would be to bring Zalith's people to Aegisguard. He was sure that Zalith had probably already thought about the idea—after all, he was living there to escape the war that had ravaged his homeworld—so why couldn't *everyone* take advantage of that? Of course, if Zalith's people were demons, Alucard was sure he would've already moved them here. But the fact that he hadn't done that made it clear to Alucard that they *weren't*, and so Zalith couldn't move them using the Underworld because phasing could only be done by demons, and if a demon tried to bring along someone not of demon blood, they'd burn up and die.

With a quiet sigh, the vampire frowned. "Zhen bring all of zhem 'ere vhere zhey'll be safe vrom zhe war."

Zalith looked reluctant. "I don't want to put your body through that."

"I'll be vine. I just vant to 'elp you," he insisted, staring into the demon's dark, conflicted eyes.

Zalith frowned and sighed, placing his right hand on the side of Alucard's neck. "Thank you. It's very nice of you to offer." He exhaled deeply, resting his forehead against Alucard's. But then he was silent. He hadn't agreed nor disagreed, and as he closed his eyes and huffed tiredly, Alucard frowned in confliction.

"Do you…vant me to do zhat?" he asked him.

He hesitated again, slowly opening his eyes to look at him. "But what if something happens to you?"

"Noving vill 'appen to me," he said confidently. "Zhe only veason I suffered last time vas because of vhatever Zamien 'ad done to my ethos. But ever since 'e took zhose vunes avay, I've velt divverent…like I 'ave more…of everyving," he explained slowly. "And I veel as zhough taking people vhrough a portal von't 'urt me zhe same vay did bevore."

Zalith sighed as he moved his hand from the side of Alucard's neck and to the back of his head. "I believe you," he said, "I'm just worried. I can't…ignore my worry."

"Just let me 'elp you," Alucard pleaded. "If you move zhem 'ere, you von't 'ave to vorry about zhem anymore."

For a few moments, Zalith stared at him…but then exhaled sullenly. "Okay," he answered. "Thank you, baby." Then, before Alucard could say anything, Zalith leaned closer and kissed him.

Alucard expected their kiss to be short and snappy, just like every other kiss they'd shared lately, but Zalith didn't stop to look at him or to speak another word. He kissed Alucard again and again, almost as if he was making sure that it was what Alucard wanted. Of course, the vampire wanted the moment to last longer than a few seconds, so he placed his hand on the side of Zalith's neck and kissed him back.

Their lips met in a fervent embrace, a mingling of desire and desperation that transcended words. As the kiss deepened, Alucard felt Zalith draw nearer, a silent reassurance in the gentle press of their bodies. With a tender urgency, Zalith guided him backwards; Alucard yielded, surrendering himself to the weight of Zalith's presence as he reclined upon the cool embrace of the sheets, their lips never breaking contact. In that moment, time seemed to stand still, the world shrinking to the intimate space they shared, where nothing else mattered but the intoxicating symphony of their entwined souls.

Alucard felt his sadness wither as each moment passed; his worries, his anger, his despair…all of it disappeared as Zalith's explanation buried deeper into his mind. Their kisses became more intense, and it didn't take long for Alucard to feel relieved.

He turned his head away, taking a moment to breathe. The demon kissed the side of his face and down to his neck, and Alucard felt a familiar, pleasing shiver spiral through his body; it felt as though it had been so long since he'd felt the captivating warmth of Zalith's lips against his neck. He moved his hand to the back of the demon's head but then turned his own head to stop the demon from kissing his neck.

Zalith looked down at him, moving a strand of his crimson hair out of his face. "I love you," he said quietly. "So much, Alucard. And I always will."

Alucard smiled happily for the first time in a while. He felt content. All his concerns had been silenced, and although Zalith was still going to be busy with his work in Eltaria, it might not last much longer. Alucard was going to help him bring his people to Aegisguard, and once they were here, Zalith wouldn't have to worry or stress over them anymore. Then, things would return to the way they were, Alucard was certain.

He moved his hand to the side of Zalith's face, taking a moment to stare at him now that he actually had the chance to. "I love you, too," he said softly.

Zalith smiled, caressing the vampire's hair for a few moments. He shuffled back into bed beside him and rested his head on Alucard's chest, wrapping his arms around him.

Alucard didn't really know what else to say. He just…felt okay. It had been so long since he'd felt happy, and right now, he felt better than that. He knew why Zalith had been distant and distracted, and it wasn't because of him or his feelings. He was simply stressed out and busy with work—work that Alucard was going to help him with. And tomorrow would most likely be when he'd be doing that, so he should probably sleep.

He moved his arm around Zalith, holding him tightly as he made himself comfortable. He didn't want to think about tomorrow or anything beyond now. Zalith was beside him, he felt a whole lot less overwrought, and everything was going to be fine.

That was all he needed to focus on.

# Chapter Sixteen

⤙ ⸱ ✝ ⸱ ⤚

# An Alleviating Morning

**| Zalith |**

The morning felt a lot less wearying than usual. Zalith slowly opened his eyes, setting his sights on Alucard, who slept silently beside him. Every morning for the past few months, he'd woken and left the vampire without much of a goodbye, and he hated it. He missed Alucard so much and knowing that the vampire was hurting a whole lot more than he thought made Zalith feel like shit. All he wanted to do was make it up to him and continue showing and telling him just how much he meant to him.

He tightened his embrace around Alucard, keeping his head rested on his chest. At least today he wouldn't have to leave him. But he still felt terrified about Alucard going to Eltaria; he had a lot of confidence in Alucard and his abilities, but so many terrible things had happened in Eltaria…things he'd always believed wouldn't, and he didn't want to lose Alucard. He didn't want him to get hurt even the slightest.

His worry was overbearing, but the sooner his people were safe, the sooner he could live his life with Alucard once more, and the sooner he'd be relieved of his stress. He knew today would be yet another irritating string of events dealing with people and situations he'd rather not, but hopefully, it would be the last day of travelling between worlds.

With a soft exhalation, Zalith reluctantly withdrew his arm from around Alucard, his fingers lingering over the contours of the vampire's form as if seeking solace in the touch. With a heavy heart, he made a feeble attempt to extricate himself from the embrace of the bed, his movements sluggish with the weight of remorse that hung over him like a shroud.

As he sat upright, his gaze drifted down to Alucard's slumbering figure, a pang of guilt gnawing at his insides. How could he have been so blind to the depth of Alucard's distress, so unaware of the turmoil that brewed beneath the surface of their shared moments? The realization pierced him like a dagger, leaving him grappling with the inadequacy of his own words, the hollow echo of unspoken gratitude reverberating within the recesses of his mind.

Yet, amidst the tumult of emotions, one truth remained steadfast: he would never again allow Alucard to languish in solitude, adrift in the void of his own despair. With a silent vow etched upon his heart, Zalith resolved to stand by Alucard's side, no matter what the worlds might throw at them.

The demon stroked his thumb over the side of Alucard's face, moving a strand of his hair behind his ear. Then, he leaned closer and kissed the vampire's cheek before sitting up and moving to the edge of the bed.

He dragged his hand over the back of his neck and pulled the thin gold chain hanging around it; it twisted around to his back while he slept. Once he sorted his chain, he rested his elbows on his knees and sighed. He needed to contact his people in Eltaria and tell them that he'd be arriving later with Alucard. He'd go right now if it weren't for his vampire—he didn't want to wake him up; he'd let him sleep a little longer before getting ready.

What he *would* do, however, was summon an izuret and let his people know. And with the thought of an izuret lingering on his mind, one appeared through a small rift in the air. It floated down towards him, landing on the edge of the bed not too far from where he was sitting.

"Tell Greymore and Orin to get everyone together at a safe location near the Gateway. I'll be arriving today with my partner to transfer everyone from Eltaria to Aegisguard. I'll give you a solid time to share with them once I have it."

The small creature nodded, chirped quietly, and then disappeared as silently and swiftly as it arrived.

Zalith sighed quietly and sunk into his thoughts while he waited for Alucard to wake. A lot of plans were going to need to be made for his people, so he might as well get a head start.

| Alucard |

Alucard frowned when he heard Zalith's quiet, tired voice. He opened his eyes, turning his head to glance at the demon, who was sitting on the edge of his side of their bed.

Zalith looked down at him, and as their eyes met, the demon smiled. "Good morning, baby," he said as he leaned back towards him, and then he kissed the vampire's lips. "Did you sleep okay?" he asked, resting his weight on his arm as he lay beside him.

The vampire nodded, rolling onto his side as he sighed quietly. "Who vere you talking to?"

"I sent an izuret to tell my people we'd be arriving sometime today." He smiled, placing his free hand on the side of Alucard's neck. "I didn't want to give a definite time in case you have things to do first."

Alucard nodded slightly. "I 'ave to 'ead to Dor-Sanguis to vinish someving I vas vorking on last night, so I'll stop by zhe Citadel docks and tell my people to take my galleon to zhe island; zhe ship I 'ave 'ere vill take too long to get zhere vithout Drac. Vhere are zhey going vonce I get zhem to Aegisguard?"

"I'm going to keep them somewhere in Nefastus, on my land. I'm going to have a compound or something built for them, so they all have a place to live. The place I have in mind already has a few barns here and there, so they can stay there while their homes are being built. There is, however, one particular person I would like to have stay here in one of the guest rooms for a couple of weeks… as long as that's okay with you."

Alucard frowned. "Who?"

"Idina, the woman you met along with my other two alphas. Her husband died yesterday, and she's a mess. I want her to have somewhere nicer than a barn to stay."

He felt no need to question or refuse. "Okay."

Zalith then shuffled closer and pulled him into a hug.

Alucard rested his forehead against the demon's chest and sighed quietly; there was nothing he loved more than Zalith's embrace, and he'd hold onto every moment he got to spend in it. But as much as he wanted to sink into Zalith's arms, he had to tell him what he'd been dealing with in Dor-Sanguis; he wanted to get it over with before heading to Eltaria, so now was probably the best time to explain.

"I need to tell you someving," the vampire said slowly.

Zalith frowned, looking a little concerned. "What?"

"Somevone in Dargamoore 'as been murdering vampires, and two of zhe bodies ve vound vere Loyde and Sophina Klarke… Eltarian vampires."

"What?" he asked again, this time with sadness in his voice.

"I vink I vound zheir killer. I'm going to get answers vrom 'im today. Zhe vest of zhe Eltarian vampires are okay, zhough. Zhose who are too avraid to stay in zhe city vight now moved back to my castle."

The demon frowned despondently. "Who do you think it is?" he asked quietly.

"I vound zhis kid who told me zhat zhey're a group of 'umans who call zhemselves zhe Dargamoore Saviours or someving stupid like zhat. Zhere's zhis guy, Rorke, who's involved; I captured 'im last night, and Luther is vorking on getting answers out of 'im.

I 'ave to deliver 'im to zhe city council later and let zhem do zheir own investigation, zhough. I'm not going to visk zhe treaty."

Zalith nodded. "Thank you for helping them."

"Should only take a vew hours, and zhen ve can go to Eltaria."

The demon nodded again while he fiddled with Alucard's hair. He looked a little nervous and asked, "At the risk of sounding selfish, what do we do if you get hurt and can't help the people in Eltaria?"

"I von't get 'urt. I killed Rorke's little gang, so is just 'im."

Zalith sighed quietly and said, "Just be careful though… please." He kissed Alucard's lips.

"I vill."

The demon then tightened his arms around him. "Do you want blood?"

Alucard frowned at him. Blood? He wasn't sure if Zalith meant his own or that of some human; he'd had no choice but to revert to drinking human blood since Zalith started becoming busier and busier, and the vampire was now sure that it was because Zalith didn't want to feel either the high or fatigue he'd get when he let Alucard drink from him. Had he changed his mind? Or was he offering because he felt bad?

The vampire felt conflicted. He leaned out of Zalith's embrace so that he could see his face. "Vhat… do you mean?"

Zalith smiled and laughed slightly as he placed his hand on the side of Alucard's face. "Do you want some of *my* blood?" he rephrased.

Still with a conflicted frown, Alucard took his eyes off Zalith's face and looked down at the blanket between them. "But… you 'aven't given me your blood in months, and I zon't vant to take if you zon't vant to veel zhe side effects."

The demon pulled Alucard back into his embrace as sadness flickered across his face. "I'm so sorry, Alucard," he said quietly, nuzzling the vampire's hair. "Please take some. It's the least I can do right now."

Alucard's confliction started weighing down on him. He was already so sick of human blood; having to go back to drinking it made him feel so tired, revolted, and uncomfortable no matter where he was or what he was doing. Being told that he wouldn't have to drink it today gave him relief, but he cared more about Zalith than he did his own comfort. Zalith had been so busy these past months; he must have been fighting and dealing with people who he obviously didn't want to, and he needed his strength. Alucard didn't want to take any of that away from him because of his irritating need to consume blood.

But he missed Zalith so much, and he craved his blood unlike anything he'd ever craved before. And then there was the fact that he'd need his own strength today, especially since he would be taking around sixty people through the Gateway. He knew how awful that portal made him feel, and he didn't want to let Zalith down.

He sighed quietly and leaned back again, but Zalith sat up, pulling him with him. As he sat in front of Zalith, the vampire took a moment to stare at him, thinking—or at least that's what he made it look like. He hadn't seen Zalith naked in so long, and he just wanted a moment to gaze at the man he loved. It had been so long since they'd spent a moment together that he started to feel the sort of nervousness he'd felt at the very beginning of their relationship, but he wouldn't let it consume him.

When he placed his hand on the side of Zalith's neck, the demon pulled him closer. Zalith leaned back against the headboard and pulled Alucard into his lap, making him straddle it as he kept his hands on either side of Alucard's waist. The demon smiled, gazing into Alucard's eyes; Alucard was sure that Zalith missed him too; something about the look in his dark eyes made it evident, or perhaps it was the connection that their imprints gave them, a connection that he'd been too afraid to allow himself to experience before Zalith gave him answers.

But he wasn't afraid anymore. Despite the confusion and sadness, everything Zalith told him last night seemed to make everything awful wither away while he slept. Right now, Alucard felt happy, and as he gazed into Zalith's eyes, he couldn't keep himself from smiling.

"What?" Zalith asked with a quiet laugh.

"Noving," Alucard mumbled, turning his face away so that Zalith couldn't see him.

The demon smirked as he placed his hand on the back of Alucard's head and made him face him again. Then, he kissed his lips, and as he did, Alucard smiled once more. He dragged his fingers through Zalith's hair, tilting his head aside while the demon started kissing his neck; he closed his eyes, allowing himself to sink into the moment. He missed Zalith's affection so much that he felt as if a single kiss on his neck had him entirely enthralled. He waited, moving his hand from Zalith's head to his shoulder, and soon enough, he set his eyes on the demon's neck.

Alucard could feel his eagerness increasing; he didn't think or hesitate for much longer. He wanted Zalith's blood, and Zalith told him that he could have it, so he wasn't going to refuse his hunger, nor would he refuse the demon's offer.

He moved his face closer to the left side of Zalith's neck; he could feel the demon pulling him closer, and as Zalith kissed his neck one last time, the vampire sank his four fangs into the demon's skin.

The moment Zalith's blood oozed into his mouth, Alucard hummed quietly in relief. He listened to the demon groan in satisfaction, tilting his head back as he gripped a fistful of Alucard's hair in his fingers. The sweet, captivating taste aroused Alucard; the more he swallowed, the harder he got—he couldn't help it. Something about drinking from the man he loved after *so long* made him feel euphoric, it made him feel desperate. His fatigue faded, his body began to relax, and as the delight enthralled him, he let go of any remaining confliction and concern. Nothing else mattered right now.

Zalith dragged his hand down Alucard's back and then squeezed the vampire's ass with both his hands. Alucard tensed up, and when he felt the demon's arousal rubbing against his leg, a shiver of excitement raced through him.

Alucard pulled his fangs from the demon's neck, and Zalith lightly gripped his jaw in his hand, staring into his eyes. He urged Alucard closer, kissing his lips a few times; Alucard felt the demon shudder with anticipation as he dragged his right hand up Zalith's arm to grip his bicep.

The demon gently bit Alucard's bottom lip and slowly moved his face from the vampire's. He gazed for a moment and then moved closer again, kissing the vampire one last time. He took a moment to breathe, resting his forehead against Alucard's as they both opened their eyes to stare at one another.

"You're so beautiful," Zalith said with a sigh, moving a strand of Alucard's hair from over his left eye. "I don't deserve you."

Alucard frowned through his shy smile. "You *do*."

Zalith shook his head. "I don't deserve someone so kind and forgiving, someone as beautiful in every way as you. I just…I feel so awful for neglecting you the way I did, and not only that," he said with a sorrowful frown. "I feel like my years of using people shouldn't have led me to someone like *you*. I love you so much, Alucard, and all I want to do is make you happy."

The vampire didn't really know what to say. Of course, a little sadness lingered, especially now that the high from Zalith's blood was slowly fading. But he *did* forgive him. He understood why he'd been distant and busy, and he wasn't going to hold it over his head. He stroked the side of Zalith's face and said, "You *do* deserve me, Zaliv. And if I zidn't vink so, I vould 'ave levt. I love you, too, and I vorgive you, okay?"

Zalith shrugged slightly, smiling as he pulled the vampire closer to kiss him again. He then dragged his fingers through Alucard's hair; his dismayed stare seemed to fade…and a look of desire lingered in his eyes. "Can I bite you, too?" he whispered.

The vampire didn't hesitate and nodded shyly. Zalith smiled and kept kissing him for a few moments; he kissed his lips, his cheek, and down his neck until he reached the same place where the scars that his fangs had left were.

Alucard exhaled quietly as the demon caressed his chosen place to bite with a kiss, moving his left hand from Alucard's waist, up his body, and over his shoulder to the back of his neck. He gripped the vampire's hair and then pulled, making him tilt his head to the side. Then, Zalith sank his fangs into Alucard's neck.

The vampire flinched lightly, letting out a quiet, pleased sigh as he lightly dug his claws into Zalith's arm, waiting for the brief moment of pain to pass. And as Zalith drank the blood from his neck, the demon groaned in satisfaction.

Alucard tightened his grip on Zalith's hair and his right bicep, sinking deeper and deeper into the euphoria of the demon's blood and venom. He smiled contently as Zalith pulled his fangs from his neck, but then frowned when the demon moved so close that Alucard fell onto his back.

They laughed as Zalith rested his forehead against the vampire's and started kissing him once again. But once the demon started to kiss his way down Alucard's neck, he stopped and leaned into his ear.

"Alucard," he whispered, smirking.

The vampire smiled amusedly as he opened his eyes to stare at the ceiling. "Zaliv," he replied.

Zalith snickered quietly, taking a moment as if he'd forgotten what he wanted to say. But he soon fell silent and leaned in closer. "Can I suck your dick?" he asked, his voice still a whisper.

Enthralled by euphoria, Alucard closed his eyes and nodded, moving his hand to Zalith's shoulder. He pushed Zalith down and away from his neck, and as he did, the demon smiled excitedly and made his way to Alucard's crotch.

Alucard sighed quietly, closing his eyes as he sank deeper and deeper into the delightful high. He felt the demon unbuckle and pull off his belt, and as he did, the vampire frowned in confliction. It had been so long since he'd felt pleasure, and he was *so* eager to feel it again.

The vampire gripped the blanket, murmuring contently as the demon dragged his tongue up his shaft. He lay there, utterly ensnared inside the pleasure of Zalith's bite and his lips around his dick. He scowled, frowned, and tightened his grip on the blankets as he fidgeted with pleasing anticipation. Each stroke of the demon's warm tongue pushed him nearer to his peak; he moaned when Zalith playfully stroked his tip with his teeth, and he whined as the demon eased his hard dick down his throat.

"You feel so fucking good," Zalith moaned, sucking the vampire's tip before swallowing his inches once again.

It wasn't very long until Alucard felt himself reaching his climax; the unbearable feeling of Zalith's throat around his dick urged him nearer and nearer to the edge, and when he couldn't take it anymore, he grimaced in struggle and moaned loudly, desperately, as his shaft throbbed. He looked down and watched Zalith hum contently as his cum oozed into him, and he swallowed it with a pleased groan.

And then Alucard lay there, his body trembling, overwrought with pleasure and satisfaction. Zalith kissed the vampire's thigh and slowly made his way back up to his neck. He kissed him once, twice, and then stared down at him as he gazed back. Alucard's thoughts were silent; all he could focus on was how content he felt and how much he loved Zalith.

A smile graced Alucard's lips as his hand caressed the side of Zalith's neck, the touch of the demon's skin igniting a warmth within him that defied description. In Zalith's presence, time seemed to lose its relevance, each moment stretched out into an eternity of bliss. Never before had he experienced such a profound sense of contentment; with Zalith, every uncertainty melted away, leaving only a serene sense of rightness in its wake.

Despite the trials and tribulations of the past few months, Alucard found himself anchored in the present moment, unburdened by the weight of past sorrows. The answers he sought lay within the depths of Zalith's gaze, a beacon of hope that illuminated the darkness of his soul. In that fleeting moment, happiness blossomed within him, a fragile yet potent reminder of the transformative power of Zalith's affection.

# Chapter Seventeen

─ ⟨ † ⟩ ─

# Preparatory

| **Alucard** |

Alucard's contentedness didn't last forever. As the high faded, the thought of helping Zalith and his people started possessing every corner of his mind. He was going to be helping Zalith bring his people from Eltaria to Aegisguard in a few hours, and he hadn't even made sure he knew *exactly* what it was that he was getting himself into.

He had questions, and they all flooded his mind one after the other. He needed to know *what* Zalith's people were, because if they were all demons, surely they could have phased over to this world themselves. And then there was Zalith's enemy, the being that the humans had manifested. He needed to know more about it in case it decided to make an appearance…and Alucard had a horrible, awful feeling that it might, and he had to make sure that he knew what to look out for.

The vampire frowned hesitantly. The last thing he wanted to do was end his and Zalith's content moment, especially after he'd waited so long to have one…but he had to know the answers to his questions.

With his arm around Zalith, he glanced down at what he could see of the demon and sighed quietly. "Zaliv," he said, making sure that the demon hadn't fallen asleep.

"Alucard," the demon said with a smirk.

"I vant to ask you vings bevore ve go to Eltaria."

"Go ahead," he said, looking up at him.

"Vell, I vant to know more about zhe manivestation you told me about, zhe vone zhat zhe 'umans created. Vhat is zhe ving, vhat can do, and vhat if vinds you 'ere?"

"If it does find its way here, then we're going to have a lot more to worry about than just Damien and Lilith," he answered with distress in his voice. "Whatever it is, it keeps changing and adapting; every time I hear about it or come across it, it's always capable of new things. It seems to become capable of whatever the humans collectively imagine it to be capable of. That's why it's so strong. The more they believe, the stronger it gets," he explained slowly.

Alucard frowned in concern, listening to Zalith's every word.

"It gets in your head; it tries to confuse and torment you, and if it *does* talk to you, you have to do your best not to respond, because if you reply, it buries itself deeper and deeper until there's no way for you to fight it off...like a parasite. Its light is blinding, and it also seems to be its greatest defence; if you get too close, it begins melting the flesh from your body until you no longer exist. We have noticed, however, that its light is also its greatest weakness as well as its strength. If the light isn't touching you, it can't hurt you so much," he explained, the dread in his voice increasing. "And it's not even worth it trying to fight it; if it does show up, we should focus all our efforts on getting away from it," he insisted, looking up at him.

Alucard frowned and slowly set his eyes on the ceiling. From everything Zalith had said, it sounded as though this manifestation of power was, in fact, a Numen. After all, that's all Damien, Lilith, and Letholdus were...masses of power and energy existing off the sole beliefs of their followers. Somewhere, elsewhere, a long time ago, Damien and the others had been created through belief.

He sighed and looked down at Zalith. "I vink might be a Numen, and if zhe 'umans manivested zhis in Eltaria, zhen von't be able to leave zhat vorld."

Zalith frowned. "If Numen can't leave the worlds they're manifested in, how did Damien and the others get here?"

"I zon't know everyving about zhem, but Zamien vould talk a lot sometimes. Numen can break and make vules. Vherever Zamien and zhe ozzers came vrom, zhey must 'ave some'ow broken vree of zhe vorld zhey vere created vithin. But considering 'ow much Zamien boasts about zhat, I'm sure takes *a lot* of power to do zhat. Zhis possible Numen vas also manivested in Eltaria, so...if tried to leave—zhat is, if became powervul enough—I'm sure zhat Zamien and zhe ozzers vouldn't vant zhe ving 'ere; not only zhat but a vorld can only 'arbour so many Numen at vonce. Vould die if tried to come 'ere because zhe number of Numen zhis vorld can 'old 'as been met," he explained, trying his best to convince Zalith that the manifested, Eltarian Numen wouldn't be able to come to Aegisguard...because it wouldn't unless one of the other Numen were to somehow change the rules. But Alucard knew how selfish and arrogant the Numen were, and there was no way that they'd help out some unknown, newly-formed Numen.

Zalith seemed conflicted, though.

"Zhe only vay zhis manivestation vould get out of Eltaria vould be vith zhe 'elp of zhe current Numen; zhey vould 'ave to give up zheir place in zhis vorld, and none of zhem are going to do zhat," he assured him, and as he watched a look of relief appear on the demon's face, he looked back up at the ceiling. "Ve are safe 'ere."

The demon smiled and leaned over Alucard, staring down at him for a few moments. Then, he moved closer and kissed him.

Alucard wasn't yet done with his questions, though. He looked away shyly as Zalith stopped kissing him to smirk down at him. "I 'ave vone more question."

"What is it?" the demon asked with a smile.

"You said zhere are sixty people zhat need to come 'ere; I gazzer not all of zhem are zemons. Who and vhat am I taking vhrough zhat portal?"

"Most of them are werewolves, some shapeshifters, and then some of the vampires who stayed behind," he answered, moving a strand of Alucard's hair away from his face. "But…I *do* need to talk to you about one of the werewolves," he added, looking concerned.

"Vhy?" Alucard asked with a confused frown.

He sighed quietly. "One of them is Danford, one of the men that Varana mentioned to you last year. We were never an actual couple, but we did have sex a few times, but that was years ago before I even met you. If you're not comfortable bringing him here, let me know, and I'll have someone put him out of his misery because he's not going to survive in Eltaria on his own," he explained.

Alucard took his eyes off Zalith and glared at the wall beside him. He didn't know how to feel about it…to bring one of Zalith's old lovers to not only the world he lived in but the *country* he lived in, too…and so very close to the house in which they lived. A part of him felt strange, as though he didn't like the idea of Danford being so close; his name made Alucard scowl upon its mention. But Zalith had insisted before that Danford meant nothing, and he trusted the demon, so he'd not condemn a man to death simply because he felt a little weird about him being in Aegisguard. He'd get over it.

But that didn't mean he wouldn't feel odd about it. He shrugged at Zalith. "Zoesn't matter," he mumbled and sat up, making the demon move aside, and then he started buckling his belt as he moved to the end of the bed. "I should get veady," he said, standing up. "I 'ave a gang of vampire murderers to vind."

"I don't have any kind of feelings for him," Zalith insisted, watching Alucard as he made his way over to the dressing rooms. "He's just good at his job."

Alucard's irritancy quickly thickened. "I bet 'e vas good at *my* job," he snarled, disappearing into the dressing rooms.

"If you don't want to bring him, just say no," Zalith called from outside.

Rolling his eyes, Alucard snatched some clean clothes and walked back into the bedroom. He spared not a glance for Zalith and made his way over to the door. "Vhatever," he muttered, pulling the bedroom door open. "I'll be back soon."

He left the room. The thought of bringing Danford to Aegisguard made him feel more and more annoyed as each moment passed. He already had to hear that he was someone whom Zalith used to sleep with and that he was still around—he'd probably been there talking to Zalith every day these past few months, the past few months which were nothing but confusing and upsetting for Alucard.

The vampire gritted his teeth as he went into his study and closed the door behind him—perhaps a little harder than intended. He slumped down onto the couch and scowled at the clothes in his lap. His aggravation boiled into anger, and his anger soon simmered into frustration. He wasn't going to leave Danford to die just because he was someone Zalith had sex with…or was he? The thought crossed his mind…and he was angry enough to do it, but…it wasn't exactly the man's fault, was it?

Alucard didn't know what to say or think. All he could do was sit there and feel angry. He was irritated with Zalith and annoyed by the fact that this old conquest of Zalith's had been seeing *his* boyfriend more than he had for the past few months.

Whatever. He rolled his eyes, snarled irritably, and got dressed. What more could he do about it? Nothing. He'd agreed to assist Zalith and help his people, and that was what he was going to do.

His door then opened, and Alucard set his annoyed glare on Zalith, who stood in the doorway in a black suit and a grey shirt. He leaned against the doorframe and frowned slightly, but there was clearly a faint smile on his face.

"I'm not happy with the way we ended that conversation," the demon said.

Alucard scoffed as he took his eyes off Zalith and continued buttoning his shirt. "And I'm not 'appy to 'ave just been told zhat you've been 'anging avound vith vone of your old boyvriends," he sneered.

"He was *not* my boyfriend, and I definitely don't hang out with him," Zalith responded with a calm and assuring tone. "I nor he will ever have any desire for one another, and it was only something I did because I was lonely. You don't have to feel threatened by him or his presence—he isn't even going to be around that much."

The vampire rolled his eyes, keeping his sights on the window as he finished buttoning his shirt. "I zon't veel vhreatened by some ugly verevolf."

"I'll fire him if you want, Alucard. You mean a million times more to me than he ever will."

Alucard had nothing to say.

"Would you feel better if we put him somewhere in a town instead? He doesn't have to be as close as everyone else."

"I'd veel better if you zidn't keep all zhe people you put your dick into avound," Alucard snarled, standing up.

Zalith watched him as he snatched his blazer from his desk. "Do you want me to kill him?" he asked, but with that same hinted smile on his face.

Was this funny to him? Clearly it was, and Alucard wasn't *at all* in the mood for it. "No," he muttered, glowering at him as he pulled his blazer on. "I zon't vant you to kill anyvone; if you 'ad to kill all zhe people you fucked, you vould probably 'ave to kill *all* your people, vight?" He headed for the door as he took his eyes off Zalith.

But Zalith evidently didn't want him to leave; as Alucard reached the door, the demon snatched his shoulders and lightly pinned his back against the door. He then sighed calmly and stared at the vampire's irritated face. "What do you want me to do?" he asked calmly. "Tell me how I can make it easier on you."

Beyond aggravated, Alucard gritted his teeth and scowled in hostility. "You can get zhe fuck off me so I can leave and prepare to bring your whore 'ere," he growled, shoving Zalith back.

The demon sighed and relented. "Okay."

Then, Alucard left his study.

He made his way across the hall and downstairs. As he walked down them, he glanced at Zalith, who quickly followed him. He felt so agitated right now that he didn't even want to look at the stupid smile on Zalith's stupid face.

When he reached the front door, he grabbed his fur-collared cape and left the house.

"I'll see you a little later," Zalith called. "I love you."

The vampire snarled irritably and dematerialized into vermillion smoke. It was time to get back to work.

# Chapter Eighteen

# Justice

| Alucard |

When Alucard got to Dor-Sanguis, he landed by his castle docks and followed the wooden walkway around the cliff until he found the entrance to the cave where his galleon was moored. Most of the crew lived in Dargamoore City, but once he sent for them, they'd arrive pretty quickly.

"Anton," the vampire called as he approached the bridge leading up to the deck.

"Aye?" came the captain's voice.

Alucard made his way up to the deck, where the brown-eyed, almost-navy-blue-haired human met him with a smile.

"Good afternoon, sir," Anton said.

"I need you to call zhe crew over and take zhe galleon to Aditus-Insula. In a vew 'ours, I'll be zhere vith a large group of people. Zon't be late."

Anton nodded. "Should I have the ship restocked, sir? Food, water, and medical?"

"*Da*. Be as vast as you can vith everyving."

"Understood," he said with a nod.

Alucard then turned around and headed back down to the docks. As he made his way around the cliff and up to his castle, he tried to focus on what he'd come to do, but he couldn't stop thinking about that werewolf, Danford. He didn't like the idea of Zalith being around one of the people he used to sleep with, and he hated the idea of bringing him to Aegisguard even more. But as uncomfortable as it made him, he wouldn't leave the man behind to die. He'd never be happy about any of it, though.

He sighed quietly as he reached the castle courtyard, and when he headed inside, the vampires standing guard by the doors greeted him with humble bows.

"Is Luther still 'ere?" he asked one of them.

"Yes, My Lord. Down in the dungeons."

Alucard acknowledged his answer with a terse nod before crossing the hall. Once he reached the door, he descended into the dungeons, where the scent of blood lingered as a grim testament to his domain. As he ventured deeper, the echoes of Luther's commands and the pained cries of his latest prisoner ricocheted off the cracked, mossy walls.

With each step, Alucard's presence loomed over his prisoners like a spectre of dread; those who'd been begging at their doors backed off, and the few men who tried communicating with one another fell silent. They were all guilty of something, from attacking his vampires to harassing the people who worked with the Nosferatu, and they all deserved to be exactly where they were.

Once he reached the unlocked door with a vacant-faced guard standing outside, Alucard lost his Danford-induced irritated scowl and stepped into the room.

Luther crashed his fist into Rorke's bloody, swollen face, but when he noticed Alucard walk in, he stood up straight, and his aggravated frown turned into a relieved one. "Oh, I wasn't expecting you until much later," he said with a hint of amusement in his voice.

"'As 'e said anyving usevul?" he questioned, standing a few feet from the door.

Before Luther could answer, Rorke groaned feverishly and drawled, "Fuck…you."

Luther punched his face, wiped his bloody fist on his trousers, and then looked at Alucard again. "He confirmed that there are still a lot of these Dargamoore Saviours in the city when I started ripping his nails off, but that's all."

Alucard glanced at Rorke's bruised, nail-less fingers.

"I was just about to get started on his teeth."

Rorke groaned again. "You can…take all you fucking…want," he growled, glaring at them with his right eye—the other was swollen shut. "I ain't…telling you shit!"

Luther went to punch him again, but Alucard snatched his wrist.

"Is all zhe 'emlock out of 'is system?"

"Not yet. He's on some sort of overtime release solution," Luther answered as Alucard let go of him. He went over to the table where a collection of medical instruments sat and picked up a syringe. "Intermuscular," he said, showing it to him. "They have a doctor working with them."

Rorke started laughing.

Ignoring him, Alucard stared at the syringe for a moment. It was filled with a lilac liquid, and he could smell the hemlock on the needle. "Do you know who zhe doctor is?"

"No, but I'll find out," he said, glowering at Rorke.

Alucard shifted his sights to Rorke. If Luther hadn't broken him by now, then they were going to have to resort to much more effective methods. When he threatened Rorke yesterday, he seemed horrified when he told him what it was like to burn in the sunlight. Perhaps *that* would get him talking.

He slowly walked around Rorke and stood behind him. The man flinched when Alucard harshly slammed his hands down on his shoulders, and when the vampire slowly dug his claws into his skin, Rorke grimaced and grunted painfully.

"I'll give you vone last chance to tell me vhat I vant to know," he said, digging his claws deeper.

Rorke growled frustratedly. "Get your filthy fucking hands—"

The vampire dug his claws as deep as they'd go, making Rorke yelp. Then, he concentrated on his fire ethos, quickly heating the human's blood inside his body. Rorke started sweating, grunting and exhaling painfully. He tried to stifle his cries, but Alucard increased his blood's temperature as each second passed, and in a matter of seconds, the man's subtle complaints turned into agonized groans and wails.

"Get off!" he cried, losing his pathetic tough composure. "Get the fuck off me!"

Alucard kept going for a few more seconds, and just as Rorke started screaming, he let go and returned to where Luther was watching from. "Tell me zhe names of *every* person vorking vor zhis Dargamoore Saviours group," he demanded as he took the clean rag that Luther offered to him. He cleaned his bloody claws and watched as Rorke trembled and breathed frantically.

For a moment, it looked like Rorke was considering giving him what he wanted; the expression on his face journeyed from desperate, to pondering, and ended with anger. "I ain't…telling you…shit!"

"Should I get the Deathcoil?" Luther asked.

Alucard shook his head. "Zhat vould be a mercy." He handed the rag back to Luther and stood behind Rorke again.

"Get the fuck away from me, you undead freak!" the man growled, trying to pull free from the chair; the ropes around his wrists were cutting into his skin, and the flesh around his ankles was tearing away as he struggled and thrashed.

The vampire dug his claws into Rorke's shoulders again. He started heating the man's blood, and when he began trembling and groaning once more, Alucard asked him, "Vhat are zheir names?"

Rorke winced and groaned, shaking his head. He was still trying to escape, and the rope cut deeper into his skin. His cries grew more agonized as Alucard kept increasing the temperature; he thrashed, he whined, and he yelled out. After just a few more seconds, the man cried out, "Fuck, okay! I'll tell you!"

Alucard didn't remove his claws or stop, though. "Who's zhe doctor?"

The man wailed. "Stop!"

"Who is zhe doctor who made zhe 'emlock solution?"

Rorke gritted his teeth and thrashed around violently. "Fucking…Brăescu!" he yelled. "Denisa Brăescu!"

"And who is zhe person covering up your involvement in several divverent crimes?"

He cried out again and growled frustratedly. "Fucking…Hargot!"

Alucard frowned. "'Argot Mann?" he asked.

"The fucking…council bitch! She hates your guts—*all* of you!"

The vampire scowled irritably. *Of course* it was someone on the council. He pulled his claws from Rorke's shoulders. "You're going to answer all of my subordinate's questions. If you zon't, vhen I get back, I'll boil your blood until you melt vrom zhe inside out. Understood?"

Rorke scowled at him, but when the vampire stepped closer, he nodded and exhaled painfully. "All right," he groaned. "All right."

"Are you going to find Hargot?" Luther asked as he handed him the rag again.

Alucard nodded, cleaning his claws. "Get vhat you can out of 'im."

The vampire then left the room and headed upstairs. He wasn't surprised that one of the council members was involved; he knew that they didn't like him much, and at least one of them was bound to try something to dissolve the treaty at some point. But he wasn't going to let that happen. He'd expose Hargot, and he'd find *everyone* else who was involved, including Doctor Denisa Brăescu.

He knew who she was. Denisa was a renowned Dargamoore doctor, and it was going to be a huge blow for the city to lose her, but he didn't care. That woman was involved in the murders of his people, and he wasn't going to let that go unanswered. A new city doctor would inevitably emerge.

Alucard left the castle, dematerialized into vermillion smoke, and headed towards Dargamoore. He arrived in a few moments, and when he landed outside the House of Commons, the surrounding people gasped and exclaimed at his sudden appearance.

The vampire headed into the building, ignoring the doorman, who insisted that he needed an appointment. He shoved past the nervous guards, went upstairs, and pushed open the door to the chamber where all the council members were sitting. Their conversation came to a swift halt when they set their eyes on him, and each of them looked horribly anxious, including Dirk.

"Sorry, sir, but uh…did we have a meeting scheduled for today?" Dirk asked.

"No," Alucard said as he slowly moved towards their table. "But ve ought to."

The council members glanced at one another, looking unnerved.

"What about?" Dirk questioned.

Alucard shifted his sights from each of the council members, and when he looked at Hargot, a flicker of dread danced across her face. "You're avare of zhe vampire murders, no?" he asked them all.

Each of them nodded.

"Yes, we're very sorry," Dirk replied.

"Are you?" Alucard tested.

The man frowned and glanced at his colleagues. "Of…course we are."

"Vell, vould appear zhat vone of you is involved."

Every one of them looked astonished, but Hargot looked *astounded*.

"How dare you accuse us!" Hargot exclaimed. "We are the city council. It is our job to protect all citizens, including—"

"Does your protection include covering up zhe crimes of Vorke?" he interjected.

Hargot lost her scowl and frowned unsurely. "What?" she questioned, looking to her colleagues. "I don't know anybody by that—"

"I 'ave Vorke in my custody. Last night, 'e and several of your *ozzer* colleagues tried to murder me not var vrom Ekacaster Varmstead. Only took less zhan a day to break 'im, and not only did 'e tell me zhat you're covering up 'is crimes, but 'e also told me zhat Doctor Denisa Brăescu is vorking vith zhis group of killers."

"I would never do such a thing!" Hargot exclaimed as her colleagues frowned skeptically at her. She then scowled at Alucard. "How dare you!"

"Zhey call zhemselves zhe Dargamoore Saviours. Zhey are vesponsible vor zhe deaths of Georgina 'ale, Daniel 'emming, Loyde and Sophina Klarke, Noelle Veed, Vrank Jameson, and Vicktoria Vess. I vould've been zheir eighth victim."

"Hargot?" Dirk questioned.

The woman started panicking. She shook her head and glared at Alucard. "I would never!"

"Vould you like me to bring Vorke 'ere? I'm sure 'e'd be very 'appy to tell everyvone at zhis table exactly vhat 'argot 'as 'elped cover up."

Hargot's face turned red as she jumped to her feet. "This is outrageous! Are you seriously going to take the word of this…this thing?!" she shouted, desperately eyeing her fellow council members. "He's not even following the rules! He's taken it upon himself to look into this without *our* assistance!"

Everyone glanced unsurely at each other.

After a few moments of concerned mumbling—and Hargot's loud, angry huffing— Dirk stood up and said, "Hargot, I think we better all calm down and—"

"Calm down?!" she yelled. "This creature is accusing me of—"

Dirk interrupted her, "While Mr Aleksei didn't follow the *suggested* rules regarding crimes between our peoples, he has no reason to lie. We would, of course, like to speak to this Rorke ourselves." He looked at Alucard. "You said you have him in custody?"

He nodded. "At my castle. I'll 'ave vone of my subordinates bring 'im over."

As he sat back down, Dirk said, "That would be appreciated."

Hargot huffed and shook her head. "And you're going to trust the word of a criminal?" she questioned her peers.

"Hargot, please," Clyde then said. "I'm sure that there's been a big misunderstanding. Let us all just wait and talk to this Rorke."

"Or you can tell us zhe truth yourselv bevore 'e gets 'ere," Alucard suggested as he twisted his hand and summoned Luther, telling him to bring Rorke along.

The woman remained standing, glaring at him. "There is no truth to tell."

"Why would Aleksei be lying?" Lars questioned.

"Why? Do you really have to ask?" Hargot scoffed. "He's one of *them*. They *all* want to take our city over, and he's starting with alienating us."

Dirk shook his head. "Aleksei has been working with us for years, and I trust him."

"Of course you do," the woman sneered, sounding threatened. "We all know that you're friends."

"I vouldn't go zhat var," Alucard said irritably.

"Why would he go for you?" Silas, one of the council members who was usually silent, asked with a frown. "Why not Lars or Clyde or any of us?"

"Because he knows that I'll never believe in that treaty. He feels threatened."

Just then, a knock came at the door, and when Alucard looked over there, he watched as Luther dragged Rorke in.

The council all jumped to their feet.

"What did you do to him?" Dirk asked in disbelief.

"I know this man," Sebastian, another of the usually quiet members, said, pointing at him. "He's the man who burgled Lady Eliade's home!"

"He was involved in that robbery outside Winsemoore," Lars said, wide-eyed.

Luther dragged the bloody, bruised man over to where Alucard was standing. "Sorry it took me a sec. He was being difficult."

Alucard watched as the angered, disgusted look faded from Hargot's face. She went red again, and her eyes shifted to the door. She was going to try and make a run for it, wasn't she?

"W-who is this…this…filthy man?!" she exclaimed. "How dare you bring him into our chamber and—"

"Shut up," Alucard snapped. "You know exactly who zhis is." He grabbed Rorke's shoulder and dug his claws into the open wounds he'd earlier left there. "Vhy zon't you tell us who 'argot is, Vorke?"

The man grunted and groaned, breathing heavily. His eyes shifted between each council member, and when Alucard dug his claws a little deeper, he winced and blurted, "She's working with us!"

"Vith who?" Alucard questioned.

"The fucking…Dargamoore Saviours! She helped us cover up the murders."

"I-I did no such thing!" Hargot exclaimed, panicking.

"Is this true?" Clyde asked, astounded.

Alucard dug his claws a little deeper.

"Sh-she told us to go for the couple that went to the Ruby Lounge, all right?!" Rorke cried. "She made sure that there wouldn't be any officers around to see us doing it. Same with the rest of them. She told us to lure that fucking Georgina woman to the tavern on Baron Street because there weren't any officers there, either. We only meant to kill her, but she brought her boyfriend."

Alucard wanted to know what happened to Georgina and Daniel, and why they ended up in an alley beside a tavern that wouldn't serve vampires. Now he knew.

"Vhat about Noelle Veed?" he asked.

Rorke grunted—

"It's all lies!" Hargot insisted and tried to move away from the table.

Clyde grabbed her. "I think it's best if you wait here for the authorities." He looked at Lars. "Contact them. Tell them we have a major situation and some prisoners."

Lars nodded and hurried out of the room.

"Vhat 'appened to Noelle?" Alucard demanded, moving his claws around inside Rorke's wounds.

With a painful grunt, the man trembled and said, "That was…that was Gavrila. She works at the Green Eagle on Deena Road." He groaned and winced. "She lured her into the alley under the pretence that she was going to give her blood."

Alucard snarled angrily. "And Vrank Jameson?"

"He's lying!" Hargot shouted, trying to escape Clyde's grip. "Why are you listening to these people?! They've clearly threatened him or—"

"If I 'ave to tell you to shut up vone more time, I vill come over zhere and break your fucking jaw," Alucard growled impatiently.

Hargot, breathing frantically, gawped at him and then looked to her peers for assistance, but they all looked ashamed of her.

"Vrank," Alucard repeated.

"I-I don't know who—"

"The blonde guy," the vampire snarled at him. "'E vasn't even tventy years old."

Rorke whined painfully and tried to pull free from Luther's grip, but when Luther tutted irritably and yanked on the rope that was binding his ankles and wrists, the man winced again and shook his head. "I-I don't know, man. One of the guys must have just jumped him in the street! Hargot told us to always dump the bodies in alleys or someplace they wouldn't be found until morning!"

"I never said—"

Alucard sharply turned his head and snarled viciously at her.

The woman flinched in Clyde's grip and stared with a stressed, horrified glare.

"Vicktoria Vess. Vhat 'appened to 'er?"

Rorke didn't try to fight this time. Instead, he laughed a little and shook his head. "Fucking Marian. He was seeing that bitch for *weeks* until he finally figured out that she was an undead freak," he growled, glaring at Alucard. "He fucked her and everything before he realized. And when he *did* realize, he gutted that bitch like a pig!" he spat.

Alucard smashed his fist into Rorke's face with a furious snarl.

"Do you have to with the violence?" Dirk complained.

Rorke fell back against the force, and then Luther made him get down on his knees.

That was when Hargot started crying. "It's lies! It's all part of their plot to take our city from us!"

Clyde sighed deeply. "Why, Hargot? You were the last person I thought would stoop to these levels. You're going to hang for this."

"Are you serious right now?!" she exclaimed anxiously. "Are you all so blind that you can't see what's going on here?!"

"All I see is a desperate, prejudiced woman who couldn't stand the idea of sharing this city with another species," Silas said firmly. "We've all had to make adjustments, but we've made them with open minds, just as we have all had to adjust our understanding. And the fact that—"

"Oh, shut your fucking mouth!" the woman shouted. "We all know you're fucking that undead bitch, Elena!"

Silas scowled at her. "How dare you, you rotten—"

"Don't," Sebastian said as he grabbed Silas, keeping him from lunging at her.

Alucard admittedly found it a little amusing to see them fighting among themselves. He watched as Clyde pulled the struggling, screaming woman to the other side of the room while Sebastian tried to calm Silas down.

Another knock then came at the door.

The vampire watched as Lars returned with a whole squad of law officers. They filed into the room and stood against the wall, waiting with expectant looks on their faces.

"Ah, thank you, Lars," Dirk said with a nod. "Officers, please arrest these two. We have significant evidence that they were involved in the recent vampire murders. This man," he said, pointing to Rorke, "has been involved in several robberies, and Hargot here has been covering for him. They are both members of an anti-vampire hate group called...uh...."

"The Dargamoore Saviours," Luther said.

"Right, the Dargamoore Saviours."

"Zhere are ozzer members zhat ve know of," Alucard then said. "Doctor Denisa Brăescu. Gavrila..." he paused and dug his claws into Rorke's shoulder again.

The man winced before he said, "Gavrila Faur."

"She vorks at zhe Green Eagle on Deena Voad," Alucard continued. "And Marian...."

"Marian...Pintea," Rorke breathed defeatedly.

Alucard patted Rorke's shoulder. "My subordinate 'ere," he said, looking at Luther, "vill vork vith your interrogation ovvicers to get zhe names of every ozzer person vorking vor zhis group out of zhis man."

The officers glanced at one another and nodded in response.

"Will they all hang?" Dirk asked as Hargot continued struggling in Clyde's grip.

"Anyone directly involved in the murders will hang," the chief officer answered as he fiddled with his moustache. "Everyone else who is a part of this gang will serve time."

Dirk nodded.

"It wasn't me!" Hargot cried. "He's mistaken!"

Clyde sighed loudly and escorted the woman over to the officers. "You can take her away."

She screamed and cried as two of the officers handcuffed her.

Alucard felt a little reluctant to let Rorke go before knowing the names of everyone else involved, but Luther would be going with him, and he trusted him to keep him updated. "Make sure you veport everyving back to me," he told his subordinate as two more officers walked over and took Rorke away.

"Yeah, you got it," Luther said with a nod.

The vampire then looked at the chief officer. "I vill send over a vew more of my 'igher vanking vampires to assist vith zhe 'unting and capturing of zhe vest of zhe gang."

With a nod, the man said, "That would be appreciated."

Then, as the chief led the way out, the officers took Rorke and Hargot.

"Are you staying in Dor-Sanguis?" Luther asked.

"No. I'm 'eading back to Nevastus to 'elp Zaliv vith someving."

A look of disappointment and confusion struck his face. "Helping him with what? I thought you were having problems."

Alucard didn't want to tell him his business, but he didn't want to be hounded about it. "Ve vesolved everyving. Go."

Luther looked like he wanted to ask more questions, but he clearly knew better than to wait around when he should be doing his job. He nodded and wordlessly left the room, following the officers out.

The vampire then shifted his sights to Dirk and the other council members. "I trust zhat vrom now on, you'll vet any new council members."

Dirk nodded. "Of course. We're sorry that this happened."

"We had no idea," Lars insisted.

Alucard sighed deeply. "Just make sure zhat zhis gets sorted. A lot of my vampires 'ave 'ad to move back to zhe castle out of vear."

"Don't worry," Dirk said with a nod. "We'll make sure that it's safe for them to move back as soon as possible."

With a quiet grunt, Alucard left the chamber.

He made his way through the building and out onto the street. When he thought about heading back home, he wasn't struck with loneliness or despair but aggravation. He was never going to be happy about bringing Danford to Aegisguard; however, he *did* want to help Zalith, and he *was* happy about the fact that things were okay with them and that the demon had just been busy trying to keep his people alive. He just hoped that Danford wouldn't end up causing drama. That was the last thing he wanted to deal with, especially after going through the past months wondering if Zalith's attention was going elsewhere.

With a quiet exhale, he dematerialized into vermillion smoke and began his journey back to Nefastus.

# Chapter Nineteen

# To Eltaria

**| Zalith |**

Zalith wasn't sure when Alucard would get back. While he waited, he sat in his office and looked through all the work that had piled up over the past few months. He'd been so distracted with the situation in Eltaria that he hadn't been able to deal with the Imperito gang in the Citadel. Updates from Margo and Sheriff Reed told him that Don Lorenzo Armani had smuggled more weapons into the Citadel recently, and he now owned three more businesses, which he'd acquired by scaring off the previous owners.

The demon sighed deeply. He was going to have to deal with them once his people were safe. He still had a duty to the city, and he wasn't going to let the entire place fall under Armani's control.

He leaned back in his seat and tapped his claws on his desk. He couldn't stop thinking about Alucard, and he felt a lot more than just guilty for asking him to bring Danford over to Aegisguard. He felt as though it was wrong of him. Before, he'd never really considered what his actions might make the people around him think or feel, but Alucard mattered to him more than anything else, and so did his feelings. Clearly, the revelation had upset the vampire, and Zalith felt awful.

Should he just kill Danford? There wasn't anything special about him other than the fact that he did his job well. He wasn't worth the bother it was causing Alucard. The man wouldn't last very long if he were to be left in Eltaria alone, so killing him was the best thing Zalith could think to do—it was the better choice for everyone.

He needed to assure Alucard that Danford meant absolutely nothing to him and never had. He cared about Danford just as much as every employer cared about their employees, and that was it. But would Alucard understand? He wasn't sure. He knew that this was Alucard's first relationship, so he might have to try and help him make sense of it.

The demon glanced at the clock, and just when he was about to consider focusing on his imprint on Alucard to find out if he was still in Dor-Sanguis, he heard the front door open. He got up and left his office, and when he set his eyes on the vampire, who was hanging his coat by the front door, he smiled and headed over to him.

"Hey," he said when he reached him; he took hold of his hand and kissed his lips. "Did everything go okay?"

Alucard nodded. "I levt Luther to 'elp zhe city law envorcement vind zhe vest of zhe killers. Vone of zhe council members vas involved."

"Dirk?" he said, not surprised.

"No. 'Argot."

"I thought it'd be Dirk."

"'E's too avraid to even vink about starting a movement, let alone actually starting vone," he mumbled. He then sighed and said, "I sent zhe galleon to zhe island. If ve leave now, ve'll probably veach zhe vessel bevore gets to zhe island. Zhat gives us a little time to make plans."

Zalith wanted to ask him if he wanted to talk about the Danford situation some more, but he *did* want to get to Eltaria as soon as possible, so he'd ask him when he next got a chance. "Okay," he said with a nod. "Do you not want to sit down for a moment, though?"

"I'm okay. Zhe sooner ve get zhere, zhe better, no?"

He smiled a little and said, "Okay. Thank you again for doing this."

The vampire smiled, too, and took his coat back off the coatrack. Once he put it on, Zalith helped him with his cape and took his hand again. They left the house, and without any hindrance whatsoever, Alucard dematerialized them both and started racing to their destination.

Zalith was nervous. His heart was racing, and his body was trembling. He was terrified that something might happen to the man he loved, but he trusted Alucard and his abilities. The vampire *was* the only one who could save the rest of his people, and he still wasn't sure what he could do to show just how much he appreciated both his help and his patience. He'd pretty much abandoned him the past few months, and there probably wasn't anything he could do to make up for it. But he'd try his best, and he'd make sure Alucard never had to feel like that again.

| **Alucard** |

It was dark when Alucard reached his galleon. He raced down towards the vessel, and when he landed and rematerialized with Zalith, he immediately felt the weight of how much he'd been travelling lately. His body ached, and he felt a little dizzy for a moment, but it passed when the demon held him in his embrace, shielding him from the cold wind that raced past.

"Aleksei, sir!" came Anton's voice.

Alucard looked up at the forecastle deck, where the captain was standing and steering the ship. A shoal of differently sized and shaped skyfish glided around the lantern hanging above the wheel, and when thunder rumbled through the thick clouds, they dispersed.

"We're not far from the island, sir!" the captain called.

The vampire nodded and then nuzzled Zalith's neck. He could feel the demon's heart racing in his chest, and he was trembling, too. "Are you okay?" he asked quietly.

"Yeah. Are you?"

"I'm okay."

"Do you want to talk about the Danford situation some more? If you don't want him here, I won't make you bring him."

That name was beginning to irritate Alucard as much as Varana's did. He sighed and backed out of Zalith's embrace.

"I'm yours and only yours, Alucard," Zalith said, and then he smiled, moved closer, and guided his hands down the sides of the vampire's body. "And yours is the only ass I will ever want and need," he added, squeezing his ass.

Alucard pouted as he felt his anger wither—he'd not let Zalith know he felt amused, though. Instead, he glared at him, watching as the demon's smile grew.

"Do you want to kiss?" he then asked.

"No," he grumbled.

Zalith laughed quietly and pulled Alucard closer. "You're very cute when you're angry." He moved his hand to the back of the vampire's neck and said, "Come here." He wrapped his arms around him again and held him tightly.

Alucard kept his stubborn pout, but it soon faded as he relaxed in Zalith's embrace. The demon kissed his forehead, and when his irritancy started to decline, he exhaled quietly and moved his arms around Zalith. The demon's embrace had a way of always making him feel better, and it was something he'd never be able to say no to.

He started thinking about what was going to happen once they got to Eltaria. Zalith's mention of Danford had distracted him, and he hadn't asked for specifics about the people he'd be taking through the portal. "I need to know 'ow many people I'm taking vhrough zhis portal and 'ow old zhey are," he said, his voice muffled against Zalith's blazer.

"There are sixty-three people in total, but twelve of them are demons who have already been here, so you won't need to bring them," he answered and tightened his embrace when a cold wind raced by again, making Alucard shiver. "There are twenty-seven werewolves, all within usual mortal ages, and three shapeshifters and eighteen vampires. The eldest vampire is only eighty-six. As for the rest, they're all younger than that. One of the shapeshifters is a child, a druid; the eldest is two or three hundred, and he's a förvandlare. The second isn't far off that, and I think he's a druid, too."

"A child?" Alucard asked with a frown. "Are zhey orphan?"

"His parents were killed. Greymore found him whilst he was hunting; he was hiding under the roots of a tree in the form of a small rabbit."

"Do zhe ozzer shapeshivters look avter 'im?"

"Everybody looks after him, but he sticks closely to Idina."

"War is alvays vorse on children," he muttered sadly.

"He's been very upset," Zalith continued. "But he's slowly adjusting; I imagine he'll feel better once he has a stable home."

"I imagine zhat vith Idina staying in zhe 'ouse, zhis child vill be staying vith 'er?"

"That would be up to her, but...now that I think about it, I think I'd rather the child stay in the house where it's safer and warmer."

Alucard nodded. "Is vine," he agreed.

They then hugged in silence for a few moments.

"Do you remember when I did hand stuff to you in there?" Zalith abruptly asked.

"Vhat?" Alucard frowned, leaning out of his embrace to look at him. When he saw that Zalith was looking over his shoulder, he glanced over there and set his eyes on the door to his quarters. It didn't take him long to understand what Zalith was referring to, and embarrassment warped his face. He pouted and sharply turned his head, scowling as he glared at the sea.

"And then when I did mouth stuff downstairs?" The demon smirked. "Maybe one day, we'll do other stuff, too."

Alucard wasn't sure whether Zalith was trying to embarrass him or if he was trying to tell him that he wanted to have sex. *Did* he want him right now? Alucard frowned, glancing at the demon, who had taken his eyes off him to stare at the sea. Did *he* want *Zalith*? He glared down at the deck as confusion started consuming him, as well as a familiar, unseemly desire. The thought of Zalith wanting sex made Alucard want the same thing.

The vampire shifted his sights from Zalith to the door to his quarters. Maybe...he and Zalith should retreat into that room? Was that what he wanted? Was that what Zalith wanted? Alucard was sure that *he* wanted it—he wanted Zalith, but...he felt far too nervous to tell him or even *hint* that he wanted him. Maybe he should just lead the way into his room; would Zalith understand what he wanted *then*? But what if he didn't?

What if they got in there and Zalith asked why he'd taken him into his quarters? He didn't want to deal with the humiliation.

He'd wait until Zalith initiated something again; maybe once they were done in Eltaria or tonight when they got back home. Why was he even thinking about it? He felt—for the lack of a better word—awkward for having these thoughts right now. It wasn't the time *at all*, was it? They were on their way to save Zalith's people from annihilation. His thoughts should be focused on that.

"Ve can probably vly zhe vest of zhe vay if you vant to get zhere now," he offered.

The demon shook his head. "You should get a little rest first. Please."

He wasn't going to lie, he *did* need to sit down. "Okay."

Zalith smiled at him. "Thank you again." Then, gently pulled Alucard with him as he headed across the deck.

Alucard followed him, and with a relieved sigh, he and Zalith retreated into his quarters.

| **Zalith** |

When they got into the room, Zalith closed the door behind them and sighed heavily, following Alucard over to the couch.

"Everyving vill be vine," the vampire said, obviously trying to assure him. "Ve'll meet your people and zhen 'ead straight vor zhe portal. Vill be over and done vith in less zhan hour."

Zalith frowned worriedly as they sat down and placed his hands on Alucard's waist. He pulled him closer, moved his arms around the vampire, and held him in a tight embrace as he buried his face in Alucard's neck. For a moment, he sat there, trying to keep himself as calm as he could; as it always did, the vampire's intoxicating scent of warm amber, cinnamon, and roses alleviated him, and the hint of cedar among it only enthralled him more. He could lay in Alucard's embrace forever, and right now, it was all he needed.

He didn't want to let go of him, and he still didn't want Alucard to go to Eltaria. So many people had been taken from him—so many of the people he loved. He didn't want to lose Alucard to the manifestation, either.

As he felt the vampire's arms around him, he scowled in distress. Why couldn't it all just be over? He'd grown so tired of the war back home, and so very tired of the worry and uncertainty. If only there was another way to get his people to safety.

But there wasn't.

The portal was the *only* way they'd get to Aegisguard, and Alucard was the only one who could transport them without alerting Letholdus.

Why did it have to be Alucard? All he wanted to do was keep his vampire safe, but now he was taking him to the most dangerous place he knew. He didn't want to, but…Alucard wanted to help him help his people, and he felt so conflicted. He knew how dangerous it was, and if anything happened to Alucard over there, he'd never forgive himself. And if he were to lose him? The thought alone made him feel sick, and if he did lose Alucard…then he knew he'd lose his will to live.

Despite how much he trusted Alucard—despite knowing just how capable his vampire was—his fear didn't wane. Maybe his fear would never leave him. He loved Alucard so much; he didn't want to go back to a life without him, and every time they came across something even the least bit dangerous, he'd always find himself fearing losing him.

He tightened his grip, nuzzling the vampire's neck. Just one more hour, and then it would be over. He wouldn't have to worry about his people or that manifestation of light anymore. All he'd have to worry about was his life in Aegisguard—his life with Alucard.

Alucard then stepped back, and as he did, Zalith looked at him. "Ve can vly now," the vampire said.

Zalith looked over his shoulder at the back window, seeing that it had gotten *much* darker. How long had he been standing there wrapped up in his thoughts? It didn't matter. He always found that he got a little lost in Alucard's arms, and it was something he'd willingly do whenever he got the chance.

But he couldn't falter anymore. He sighed quietly, setting his sights back on Alucard. For a moment, he stared into the vampire's hell-fiery eyes—they always captivated him; however, as much as he might like to, he couldn't stand there and gaze into them for an eternity.

He nodded and said, "Okay." His heart raced a little faster as anxiety accompanied his fear. He didn't want it to be time to go yet.

They headed for the door, and as Alucard pulled it open, Zalith tensed up. When the vampire led the way outside, the demon tried his best to keep himself composed. But his heart was thumping rapidly, and his instincts were begging him to abort. But they couldn't turn back now.

Alucard wrapped his arms around Zalith, and vermillion smoke enthralled them; he felt his feet leave the ground and waited as they made their way through the sky. It was strange feeling Alucard's dematerialization ethos inside his own body; it made him feel more connected to the man he loved. Perhaps he was just slightly obsessing over how much he loved him, but it felt as though their ethos was rather harmonious together, something Zalith hadn't experienced before.

He then discovered that he could move while in the smoke-like form and turned his head so that he could look at Alucard. The vampire, however, no longer looked like the red-haired man Zalith knew him best as. Alucard seemed to have taken some sort of dragon-like form, but much of it was concealed inside the thickening smoke.

Zalith looked the vampire up and down. He could have sworn he could see wings slashing through the mass of smoke…. Four wings, and a tail, too. What exactly was Alucard beneath the red fog? Was he seeing parts of the vampire's true form? The form that had started seeping through when he was comatose?

What was *he*? Zalith looked down at himself, but just as Alucard appeared to be on the outside, Zalith could see himself as nothing but vermillion smoke. He looked up at Alucard again, catching a glimpse of his right, hell-fiery eye. Whatever he was right now, Zalith was certain that he enjoyed it, but he'd find another time to ask questions.

The demon set his sights on the island as it came into view; its usual downpour of rain and black clouds shrouded it in a haze. Alucard slowed, descended, and landed, rematerializing both himself and Zalith as their usual selves. The vampire had made sure to land under the cover of a towering cliff, avoiding the rain as it splashed down onto the dark rock.

But just as Alucard was about to head for the gateway, Zalith grabbed his hand.

"Wait," Zalith insisted.

Alucard stopped and turned to face him, staring at Zalith's unsettled face.

The demon pulled him closer and placed one hand on Alucard's waist and the other on the side of his face. He then frowned sadly, staring into the vampire's eyes. "Please just…be careful," he pleaded, resting his forehead against Alucard's. "I love you so much."

Alucard frowned in concern. "I love you, too," he replied, placing his hand on the side of Zalith's neck.

The demon then kissed his lips, pulling him as close as they could possibly be to one another. Once he took his lips from Alucard's, he stared into the vampire's eyes again. "Please don't leave my side," he begged softly.

"I von't," Alucard said, dragging his hand down from the side of Zalith's neck and to his hand; he gripped it tightly and waited for the demon to tell him he was ready to go.

But Zalith didn't say anything. He took his sights off Alucard and looked over at the gateway. He had to compose himself before they went through…so he shoved aside as many of his emotions as he could…and led the way.

*Anything* could happen the moment they went through, but he was prepared to do whatever he had to in order to ensure that Alucard got back home safely.

His enemies were smart, though.

He just had to try and be just as unpredictable. It was the only way he'd get his people out of there.

# Chapter Twenty

─ ⟨ † ⟩ ─

## A Cabin in the Woods

| Luther |

Hargot didn't take long to crack. Luther stood outside the interview room, listening to the woman cry and beg every time the interrogation officers told her that she'd hang for her participation in the vampire murders *and* for covering up Rorke's crimes. She pleaded that they let her live and serve a life sentence instead, and eventually, the officers agreed and got her to spill the names of *everyone* involved in both the vampire-killing gang and those who worked with Rorke.

Of course, once they got what they needed, the officers read her her rights and told her that she'd hang next week, no trial. If Hargot had been involved in killing humans, then Luther might say that it was a little harsh, but she played a part in murdering *his* people, *innocent* vampires. She deserved all she got.

He went with the police and Alucard's appointed Paladins to hunt down and arrest the remaining Dargamoore Saviours. The first man they went for was Stefan Keeling, a butcher who'd been assigned with hiding the bodies of dead vampires—of course, he hadn't done a very good job. He was arrested and ordered to serve ten years in prison.

Using Hargot's intel, the next place the police and Paladins went to was 54 Staston Lane. An old Lethidian temple was being used as a meeting spot, and inside, they found seventeen members of the group. Most of them were ordinary citizens, but one of them was a seer able to control her fire ethos, and Luther had to step in, using his speed to subjugate the woman before she could engulf anyone in flames. The Paladins got away fine, but three officers were scathed—they'd live.

And finally, as the night dragged on, Luther and the officers followed the Paladins to a small hut in the woods, a hut which Freja and her pack often scouted, so Alucard's vampires knew exactly where to go.

Everyone stopped just behind the tree line, setting their eyes on the cobblestone hut with broken windows and half of its roof missing. No lights were on inside, but the faint scent of hemlock lingered in the air. There were Dargamoore Saviours inside—what a ridiculous name. Hunters. They were just glorified vampire hunters.

"This it?" Vasile, the police chief, asked.

"Yeah," the lead Paladin, Mihai, answered.

They all then looked at Luther.

"Scout," Luther told Teodora, the best shapeshifting vampire among them.

With a nod, the dark-haired woman morphed into a black cat. She left the cover of the tree line and approached the cabin, and then she pounced up onto the crooked windowsill.

Luther watched her peer through the broken glass, treading silently as she moved along the ledge.

"You can turn into cats?" one of the officers asked quietly.

"Shush," Vasile snapped.

The officer shook his head, his eyes wide. "Cats?"

"Only very few of us," Luther muttered. "The majority of us can turn into bats, though."

"Teodora has an exceptional gift," said Petre, Teodora's lover.

"Be quiet," Luther grumbled irritably.

They fell silent.

Luther's mind wandered for a moment, though. Would Alucard pay more attention to him if *he* had an exceptional gift? If he could turn into a cat or an owl, would he be worthy of more than the cold shoulder? Perhaps he should try honing his abilities. If he put his mind to it, he could be just as impressive as Teodora, he was certain.

Not long later, Teodora returned to the trees and left her cat form. "I counted six men and four women inside, commander," she told Luther. "All armed with silver, and they're burning hemlock in the fireplace."

"Your kind are allergic to that, right?" Chief Vasile questioned.

"It's poisonous to us," Luther confirmed.

"We'll be too vulnerable if we get close," Mihai said.

Luther nodded slowly. There were ten police officers with them; could they handle the men and women inside that cabin? He looked at Vasile and asked, "Can your team deal with them? Your numbers are even."

Vasile adorned a confident stare. "We can," he said, glancing down at the colt attached to his belt.

"What if they have hidden powers like that fire girl?" an officer asked warily.

"Were any of them seers?" Luther asked Teodora.

The woman shook her head and said, "Not as far as I could tell, but seers are sometimes hard to detect. Their ethos is so weak."

That was true, and Luther didn't want to take the risk. The last thing he wanted to do was fuck up a mission that Alucard had trusted him with. "Vasile, you and your team need to lead them outside and away from the cabin so that we can help fight without the hemlock affecting us."

Vasile nodded. "Understood. Everyone got it?"

His human team nodded and quietly said, "Yes, chief."

"All right, your call," Luther then said to Vasile.

"We'll head to the other side of the glade," the chief said. "Then, we'll move in and draw them out."

"Got it," Luther muttered.

The police officers then left, following their chief as he led them along the tree line.

Luther focused on the cabin. The hemlock was obscuring his senses, but the harder he tried, the stronger the scent of humans grew from inside. He could hear their faint beating hearts, and it was making him hungry. When was the last time he fed?

Thinking about that made him remember the starved look he'd often see on Alucard's face when he visited to give him updates…and thinking about Alucard…that made him think about Zalith. That creature of a man. His heart hurt, and he couldn't seem to wrap his head around what Alucard told him earlier. How had he and Zalith fixed things? He knew that Zalith must have done something…manipulated him or played with his feelings. That atrocious man didn't deserve Alucard.

He frowned as he stared at the cabin. Now that Zalith had convinced Alucard to forgive him, would Luther and him drift again? He didn't want that. He missed Alucard and the times that they and Attila spent together, and he longed to have them back. That wouldn't happen if Alucard was wasting his time on a man who evidently didn't love him, would it?

Luther had to do something…but what? *What* could he do? Would anything he said convince Alucard that he deserved better? That Zalith didn't deserve him? He'd try—he had to try. He couldn't sit idly by and watch someone he cared about be used and fooled only to later be shoved aside again. He couldn't bear to see Alucard go through it all over again.

But if he wanted to take action…if he wanted to be able to save his friend from the pain and sorrow that Zalith was leading him to, he needed more information. He needed to know who Zalith was and what he was planning. He needed facts to present to Alucard, a man who Luther knew wouldn't listen unless the facts were laid out right in front of him.

Where would he get that information, though?

He pondered…recalling the faces he'd seen around Alucard's estate. The butler didn't seem the talkative type, and it was likely that he was paid to keep silent. And the same could be said for the staff. But what about that woman? Alucard's sister, Varana. Would *she* be able to give him what he was looking for?

Alucard's sister. Not only could she be a great source of information…but maybe comfort, too. If he was close with her, in a way, he'd be closer to Alucard, and *that* was what he wanted.

"Commander," Mihai said, snapping Luther out of his thoughts.

"What?"

"They're heading in," the hazel-haired Paladin told him.

Luther watched as Chief Vasile slowly and quietly led his officers towards the cabin's back door.

"They better not fuck this up," Constantin muttered, scratching his bald head.

The other Paladins chuckled quietly.

"Humans," Petre mumbled.

"You've got to give it to them, though," Teodora said, sounding as if she was trying to be the voice of reason. "They're kinda…cute, don't you think? With their little guns and their tools," she continued as the others laughed.

Luther laughed, too. He could see her point.

"Some of them are a little smarter than others, though," Mihai butted in. "These ones knew to use hemlock, which not very many of us know as a deadly poison to our kind. The herb was meant to have become extinct."

"Someone started growing it again," Luther said with a sigh. "I'm sure that Lord Alucard will find out who, though. He'll stop it."

They all looked hopeful.

"Now, stop with the chatter. The *last* thing we need is one of you dying because you weren't paying attention," Luther grumbled. "I don't want to have to face the Vampire Council and try to explain that you were too busy chatting."

"You know what I've been thinking about?" Constantin asked, ignoring Luther. "Felix." He chuckled with the others. "He fucked up so bad that he didn't even have to stand before the Council; Lord Alucard just outright erased him."

The vampires laughed again.

"That guy was creepy as all hell, though. Obsessed," Teodora said.

"I said stop," Luther snapped. "Insubordination will get you a trial, too."

They fell silent.

Commotion then snatched their attention—a loud bang and shouting voices. Luther watched as the officers burst into the cabin; gunfire, screaming, slicing, and the smell of blood and ash. Moments later, two women scurried out through a window and darted for the trees, but just as they made the tree line, Luther ordered Teodora and Constantin to kill them.

Both Paladins executed the fleeing woman without mercy.

And then Chief Vasile dragged one of his men out of the cabin, his face smothered in blood and desperation. The man he pulled was already dead, but the chief evidently couldn't accept that. He tried resuscitating the man, but his efforts were futile.

"Should we help?" Mihai asked.

Luther shook his head. "The hemlock." But that wasn't the only reason for his answer. They were humans. Why would he risk his life for humans? He nor the Paladins were going to step a single toe past the tree line.

So they kept watching.

The smell of death thickened in the air, and after several more shots, just three people emerged from the cabin: one of Vasile's officers and two hunters. The officer was injured, grasping a bleeding wound on her leg while the hunters stumbled after her, yelling at her to stop trying to get away. She fell when she reached Vasile, who fired his colt at one of the men, ending his life. But when he fired at the second man, his gun clicked.

It was empty.

"Stay where you are!" Vasile shouted. "You're under arrest!"

The hunted laughed and pulled a knife from his belt.

"For fuck's sake," Mihai muttered with a sigh. "If I get burned up in there, I'm going to make sure you all bear the same scars." Then, without Luther's order, he left the tree line and hurried to help the remaining police. In the blink of an eye, he grabbed the hunter, tore his head off, and then helped Vasile and the woman to their feet.

"Th-they had…they had guns," Vasile stuttered, shell-shocked. "Why didn't you tell us they had guns?!"

The Paladins looked at Teodora.

"I-I didn't see them," she said with a shrug, looking a little overwhelmed. "I swear."

Mihai helped both humans back into the trees.

Luther didn't want to deal with the aftermath, nor did he want to have to sit through trials before the Vampire Council. His job was to help the city law enforcement deal with the remaining Dargamoore Saviours, and he'd just completed that task. Now, he wanted to go and see if Varana would go to dinner with him; his mission to help Alucard was far more important than this. "Mihai, you're in charge of clean up. Make sure you send me updates—and leave out anything that'll ignite a trial because none of us want or deserve that. We did the job. And tell the rest of the castle that the killers have been dealt with; everyone will likely be able to return to the city within the next few days."

"Uh…of course, commander, but…where are you going?" Mihai questioned.

"To take care of other business. Get to work."

"Why…didn't you tell us they had guns?!" Vasile cried.

Luther sighed heavily and transformed into a bat. Then, he raced up into the sky and began his journey to Nefastus.

# Chapter Twenty-One

— ‹ † › —

# Greymore and Addison

As Eltaria's skies transitioned from late afternoon to early evening, streaks of orange mingled with patches of darkness, casting an eerie glow over the vast expanse below. The sprawling forest, veiled in shadows, extended for miles, its dense canopy alive with the flickering dance of fireflies and the gentle hum of nocturnal insects. Despite the encroaching night, the lingering heat of summer refused to yield, adding to the sense of foreboding that hung heavy in the air.

Within the heart of the forest, mere moments from the shimmering gateway, stood a solitary, dilapidated house. Its once-sturdy stone walls were now weathered and worn, the thatched roof torn and scorched, and the second floor collapsed into ruin. Around the crumbling structure, a weary gathering of people had assembled, their exhaustion palpable as if mirroring the decay of their surroundings.

The worn souls, dirt-streaked and weary, sought refuge wherever they could find it, whether on rough-hewn logs or the unforgiving forest floor. Comfort was a distant memory, replaced by the grim camaraderie born of shared hardship and despair. Amidst the encroaching darkness, they clung to each other, finding solace in the companionship that transcended their collective plight. No one sat alone; each individual found strength in the solidarity of their small groups, a flickering beacon of resilience amidst the encroaching shadows.

Hushed whispers rode the evening breeze, weaving a tapestry of fear and uncertainty among the assembled crowd. Hope lingered on the horizon, promising aid yet refusing to disclose its arrival time or method. In the oppressive darkness, questions loomed like spectres: when would help arrive? From where would it come? How much longer must they endure the interminable wait in the shadows?

Each passing moment felt like an eternity, stretching endlessly as they grappled with the unknown. Time seemed suspended, trapping them in a perpetual cycle of anticipation and dread. How many more sunsets would they witness through the veil of uncertainty, each one tinged with the bittersweet knowledge that it might be their last?

Yet, amidst the uncertainty, a flicker of resilience remained. Despite the lingering despair, they clung to the fragile hope that tomorrow might bring deliverance from the darkness that threatened to engulf them all.

A black and red tear oozed down the cobblestone chimney, a sinister gateway manifesting through sheer force of will. Parting like the jaws of a slumbering beast, it disgorged two demons into the mortal realm. Leading the way was Zalith, his eyes darting warily from tree to tree, scouring the oppressive darkness for any lurking threats. Yet, to his relief, no imminent danger revealed itself within the ominous shadows.

Behind him, in the tight grip of his hand, was his red-haired mate, Alucard. He stepped out of the rift, and as it closed behind him, he set his hellish eyes on Zalith.

Zalith scowled skeptically; all of his senses were as heightened as he could make them. Within the dark, he detected nought but his demon allies, who were protecting the camp in which he and his partner had arrived—it might not be any use searching for hostiles, though. The demon hunters who had long haunted his life knew how to hide from his detection, and as much as he hated to know it, they could be out there…watching.

Were they?

He looked back at Alucard, tightening his grip on his hand; it had never been so clear to anyone that this vampire was everything to Zalith, and if the demon were to lose him, the consequences of his grief would very well be destructive.

Amidst the camp, the demon's trusted subordinates stood vigilant, flanked by two formidable Alphas who doubled as confidants—Orin and Idina. Orin's once-pristine silvery-blonde locks cascaded untamed around his weary face, the fatigue etched into his silver eyes a testament to the trials they faced. Nearby, Idina's braided brunette hair framed her features, her verdant gaze scanning the encroaching darkness with a mixture of resolve and trepidation.

At the sight of Zalith and his vampire companion approaching, both Orin and Idina rose to their feet, their movements quickened by a palpable sense of urgency. With determined strides, they closed the distance, their presence a steadfast reminder of the unwavering loyalty that bound them together.

Two imposing figures, stationed a short distance from the house, raised their gazes as Orin and Idina abandoned their posts. The first man, his eyes a deep shade of brown reminiscent of rich coffee, fixed his attention on the approaching demons. Spotting Zalith and his fiery-haired companion joining the camp, he swiftly abandoned his position as well. His companion, with tousled shoulder-length black hair, turned sharply to follow suit, the strands dancing in the light breeze.

As the three groups converged, they came to a halt before each other, a silent tension lingering in the air.

Orin immediately set his eyes on Zalith. "Everyone's accounted for, Sir. We made sure to cover all tracks on our way up; hopefully, no human knows we're here. Tyrus and his men are watching the perimeter, but so far, we haven't detected a single sign of anything worrisome."

"Good," Zalith said, taking a moment to eye each of his subordinates.

Then, Orin turned his attention to Alucard. He held out his hand in an offering of greeting. "It's very nice to see you again. Thank you so much for helping us, truly."

Alucard slowly took the man's hand and nodded. "You're velcome."

Zalith nodded at the other two men. "These are the two werewolf Alphas that I work with," he said to Alucard. "They were originally the Primes of very large territories, but as pack numbers dwindled and we all had to come together, they naturally became Alphas again," he explained.

"Vhy did zhey become Alphas?" Alucard asked.

"There aren't any Alphas left to lead; one can't be a Prime without Alphas," the demon answered.

The vampire nodded in understanding.

"This is Warner Addison," Zalith then said, looking at the man with brown eyes and hair.

Warner extended his hand, and Alucard met it with a firm shake, his gaze sweeping over the man's dishevelled form. The air around Warner seemed to crackle with unsettling energy as the vampire took in the scruffy tangle of hair framing his face and the unkempt beard that sprawled across his jawline like tangled vines. Dark circles etched beneath his eyes hinted at a weariness that belied his status as an Alpha, while his gaunt frame seemed ill-suited for the role of a leader. Despite his apparent fatigue, there was a palpable intensity to Warner's presence, a sense of foreboding that lingered in the air like a shadow.

The vampire's sights shifted to the second Alpha, poised on the brink of introduction. Towering over both Alucard and Zalith, he exuded an imposing presence, his broad frame eclipsing theirs with an aura of undeniable strength. His jet-black hair, cascading in unruly waves to his shoulders, was swept back from his face, offering a glimpse of dark brown eyes that seemed to hold untold depths of secrets. Across his rugged countenance, a network of scars marred his stubble-adorned cheeks, a testament to battles fought and wounds endured. Two fresh slashes, stark against his weathered skin, traced a path from jaw to temple, hinting at a history steeped in violence and strife.

"And this is Thomas Greymore," Zalith introduced.

Greymore seized Alucard's hand with a fervour that bordered on eagerness, his grip firm and unyielding as if trying to convey something beyond mere greeting. A glimmer of excitement danced in his eyes, betraying a fervent enthusiasm that seemed almost palpable. "Thank you so much; we'll forever be in your debt, uh…vampire…." He frowned and glanced at Zalith; clearly, he didn't know Alucard's name and wasn't sure what to call him. "Vampire…King…" he drawled, setting his eyes back on Alucard.

Alucard frowned slightly, taking his hand out of Greymore's. "Is actually Lord," he corrected. "But my name is Aleksei."

"Aleksei—so sorry," he laughed with relief in his voice. "Thank you again," he repeated. "When this is all over, we should all get a beer, huh?" he suggested nervously. "Get to know each other a little. Do Vampire Lords even like beer?"

The vampire frowned and said, "Considering zhat I'm zhe only vone, is safe to say zhat no, Vampire Lords do not like beer. I'm more of a vine person."

As Zalith smiled at Alucard, the demon's four subordinates chuckled.

"Well, la-de-da," Greymore sung in amusement.

"It doesn't take a Lord to know that wine is superior, Greymore," Orin said.

Greymore rolled his eyes. "Yeah, yeah, yeah, okay. I'm not getting into the weeds with you about this again."

A solitary snap shattered the quiet of the forest, sending a jolt of apprehension through the gathered group. Alucard felt Zalith's hand tighten around his own, a silent gesture of shared unease as they both cast wary glances over their shoulders. In the flickering shadows, Zalith's subordinates braced themselves, ready to confront whatever unseen threat lurked in the darkness.

But as the source of the disturbance revealed itself, a collective sigh of relief washed over the assembly. The tension dissipated like mist in the morning sun as a small boy burst forth from the murk, his hurried footsteps carrying him towards Idina. With each step, the angst that had gripped them moments before melted away, replaced by a sense of fleeting calm.

Alucard frowned as he watched the boy wrap his arms around Idina's leg and look up at him fearfully. Clearly, the little freckle-faced child was the one Zalith had told him about. Small, scared, and eyes as green as emeralds and hair a similar brown to Idina's. He was also only six years old, and the red in his eyes made it clear that he had been crying—and Alucard felt that was understandable, given the circumstances.

Idina placed her hand on the boy's shoulder and looked down at him as he held onto her leg, hiding as much of his face behind it as he could while staring up at Alucard. "Are you okay?" she asked.

The boy nodded, keeping his eyes on Alucard. He looked afraid of the vampire but didn't take his eyes off him.

Smiling, Idina then glanced at Alucard. "Colt, this is Zalith's partner, Aleksei. He's going to help us find somewhere safe to stay."

Keeping his eyes on Alucard, the boy frowned shyly. "Hi," he murmured.

Alucard was certain that the boy was terrified, and the last thing he wanted to do was make him feel any more afraid. He wasn't as experienced with children as much as the people around him seemed to be, but he *did* remember very well what it had been like for himself when he was just a child in the midst of war. He knew what he needed back then, and that made him think that maybe he knew what this boy needed, too.

The vampire smiled slightly, slowly crouching until he was at eye level with Colt. As his hand slipped from Zalith's, he held it out towards the boy. "*Salut*," he greeted.

Colt slowly relaxed as his eyes wandered down to Alucard's hand and then back to the vampire's face. Slowly, he held out his small hand and placed it in Alucard's.

"Everyvone calls me Aleksei," he said as he shook the kid's hand. "But you can call me Alucard—zhat's my veal name," he said, smirking.

Colt smiled and giggled a little as Alucard let go of his hand.

"Vhat vould be your veal name?"

The boy left the safety of Idina's leg and moved closer. "Colt," he mumbled shyly, twisting the heel of his shoe into the dirt.

"Vell, Colt, you zon't 'ave to vorry about anyving. I'll take you to your new 'ome, and you'll be safe here."

Observing Alucard with a tentative nod, Colt slowly extended his right hand, a hesitant gesture that spoke volumes of his shyness. Despite the apprehension that came with knowing that Colt was going to touch him, Alucard remained rooted in place, torn between his own discomfort and the child's fragile emotions. In the end, he chose to prioritize Colt's well-being over his own unease, offering the boy a reassuring presence in the face of uncertainty.

As Colt's hand made contact with the side of Alucard's pale face, the vampire watched in quiet astonishment as the boy's appearance began to shift. His hair, once a nondescript shade, transformed into the same fiery hue as Alucard's, while his eyes mirrored the depths of the vampire's own gaze. Colt was obviously the shapeshifter child Zalith had mentioned, and it looked like he was already warming up to Alucard.

Offering a tentative smile, the vampire found himself at a loss for words as the others around them chuckled affectionately. However, their laughter seemed to unsettle Colt, and with a flicker of hesitation, he retreated behind Idina's protective stance, his borrowed features fading back to their original state. Though uncertain of his own role in the exchange, Alucard couldn't help but feel a newfound sense of connection with the shy shapeshifter, a silent promise of acceptance and understanding.

"I'm sorry," Idina said, looking at Alucard as he stood back up. "He's shy."

"No, I'm not," Colt mumbled, his voice muffled as he hid his face against her shin.

As everyone laughed again, Alucard looked at Zalith, slipping his hand back into the demon's grasp. Zalith smiled at him but shifted his attention to Orin as the man's face went from amused to vacant.

The silvery-blonde-haired man placed two fingers on his temple and set his eyes on Zalith. "Tyrus tells me that his scouts just got back from the portal, and from what they can tell, the coast is clear."

Zalith nodded. "Tell him to let them know to watch the path. We'll move out immediately."

"Yes, sir," Orin said with a nod.

Greymore held out his hand towards Colt. "Colt, come with Uncle Grey; we'll get everyone ready to go. Come on," he encouraged, taking the boy's hand. Greymore then picked him up and made his way over to the rest of the waiting people with Warner following behind him.

Idina turned to face Zalith. "What about supplies? Can those be transported, too?"

"I can provide whatever everyone needs in terms of shelter, food, healthcare, and clothing for the foreseeable future," Zalith explained. "Living quarters may be cramped for now, but I'll have a compound built on my land as soon as possible. In the meantime, however, I want both you and Colt to stay in our home until we can arrange something safe for the two of you," he said, glancing at Alucard. "Tyrus and Orin have their own homes in Aegisguard, and I'd like for you to have one nearby as well."

The woman held her hand to her face, smiling as tears started forming in her eyes. "Thank you so much," she said, her voice breaking.

"Of course," Zalith said with a nod.

"I vant to calculate ages bevore ve leave," Alucard said to Zalith.

"Okay," the demon agreed.

Zalith led the way over to his people as Alucard, Idina, and Orin followed. He kept a tight grip on Alucard's hand, walking towards everyone who'd gathered around outside the house, preparing to leave.

Idina glanced at Zalith while they approached the group and wiped away the tears from her eyes. "We weren't sure what instructions to give them regarding the portal; the vampires seemed somewhat familiar with the process, but obviously, no one here has made the trip."

The demon nodded in response. They then stopped a few feet away from the crowd.

Alucard took a moment, eyeing everyone he could see. First, he set his sights on each vampire, evaluating their ages one after the other. He located the eldest vampire—eighty-six years old. The rest—sixty-seven, seventy-three, seventy-four, forty-five, thirty-eight, eighty, sixty-one, fifty-six, sixty-seven, twenty-four, seventy-nine, thirty-one, twenty-nine, sixty-seven, fifty-nine, fifty-two, and seventy-eight. All the vampires totalled a thousand and sixty-six years of age. Before, that might have been a concern, but he was confident that the removal of Damien's runes raised his limits.

Zalith then started to speak, "Everybody, this is Aleksei," he called, taking his hand from Alucard's; he put his arm around Alucard's waist, gripped the side of it with his hand, and pulled him closer. "He's the one who will be transporting you all through a portal and to Aegisguard. Once we've all made it to the other side, we'll escort you to a ship, which will take you to my land. *That* is where you'll be living. It won't be perfect at the beginning, but it'll be much safer for you than anywhere here in Eltaria."

Alucard set his sights on the werewolves, all of whom were grouped up rather closely together. There were twenty-seven of those. Their ages brought the total to two thousand seven hundred and nine. Right now, the number was already over three thousand including Zalith—close to ten times his age.

With a hint of concern on his face, he looked over at Zalith.

"Aleksei will lead the way through the portal, and you'll all be following behind him in a single file line. There needs to be skin-to-skin contact for this to work, so please make sure you are holding each other's hands. It is extremely important that you do not let go of each other and break the chain until you have *all* reached the other side. Please keep in mind that this is a one-way trip; once you're in Aegisguard, there is absolutely no returning to Eltaria."

The crowd started looking at one another, murmuring and mumbling in what sounded like uncertainty. Alucard stared at them, locating the three shapeshifters. Little Colt was only six, and the eldest was two hundred and seventy-one. The third was two hundred and three. That made the total age of this group four thousand two hundred and fifty-five.

"If you change your mind about making the trip, then let one of us know by the time we get to the portal. However, keep in mind that if you *do* stay here, you're on your own, and myself and my colleagues will no longer be responsible for your well-being," Zalith continued.

Alucard took his eyes off the group and looked down at the ground. Could he take a group totalling ten times his age? He'd not done it before, but he was sure that this group was close to that of the last of the vampires he'd taken through a few years ago. Back then, it had almost killed him… but now he felt confident in himself and his ethos. He knew he was capable of more, and he'd not fret.

"I'm sure I don't have to tell you that we need to move soundlessly, so unless you see something worth alerting the group about, please refrain from speaking as we make our way to the portal," Zalith concluded.

As the group started to mumble to one another again, Zalith turned to face Alucard.

"All of your zemons are phasing over, vight?" the vampire asked.

Zalith frowned slightly as he placed both his hands on either side of the vampire's waist. "Yes…. Is something wrong?"

"No," he mumbled, looking down at the ground. "Are you okay?" he then asked, staring into Zalith's dark, worried eyes.

But the demon smiled and placed his hand on the side of Alucard's face. "I'm just anxious. But as long as you're okay, I'm okay," he said.

Alucard saw the worry in Zalith's smile, a smile that he was sure Zalith forced to try and convince *himself* more than anyone else that everything was okay.

The vampire refrained from voicing his concerns, unwilling to incite panic in Zalith or unsettle the crowd. Instead, he conveyed his reassurance through a gentle touch on Zalith's shoulder, a silent gesture of solidarity amidst the gathering tension. As he felt Zalith's gaze drift to his lips, Alucard leaned in, anticipating the reciprocal movement from the demon.

Their kiss was brief, a fleeting exchange of comfort amidst the looming uncertainty; as the group's readiness to depart became evident in their collective silence, Alucard reluctantly withdrew, tearing his gaze away from Zalith's and fixing it on the looming darkness ahead. With a heavy heart, he steeled himself for the challenges that lay ahead, silently determined to face them alongside the man he loved.

"Let's go," Zalith said, taking hold of Alucard's hand once again.

And then, without any further hindrance, Zalith and Alucard led the way from the small house into the murky forest.

# Chapter Twenty-Two

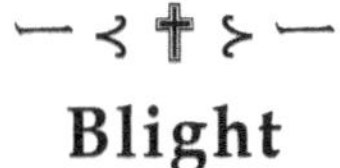

# Blight

| Alucard |

As they trekked through the mist-laden woods, Alucard stole a glance at Zalith by his side. The portal loomed tantalizingly close now, a mere twenty minutes' walk away. Soon, they would reach it, and this chapter of their journey would draw to a close. Zalith's burden of responsibility would be lifted, and Alucard's constant worry for his safety in this perilous realm would finally ease. All that remained was to guide the group safely to Aegisguard.

Suddenly, the crisp sound of approaching footsteps cut through the silence. Alucard felt Zalith's grip on his hand tighten instinctively, and they both turned sharply; the vampire's heart raced with apprehension, but when they recognized the approaching figure as one of Zalith's people, they both exhaled a mixture of relief and irritation.

The man, with sandy-blonde hair and a weathered eye patch concealing one of his dull blue eyes, stumbled to a halt beside Idina, his expression a mix of contrition and apology. Zalith's eyes narrowed briefly before he returned his focus to the path ahead, his annoyance thinly veiled by a mask of stoicism. Alucard couldn't help but feel a pang of angst gnaw at his heart as he watched Zalith's facade harden, a silent reminder of the burdens they both carried.

Alucard set his sights on Colt and then watched the blonde man hand him a stuffed tiger toy. "You forgot Maurice down near that fallen tree."

"Maurice!" Colt cried happily, snatching it from him, and then he hugged it tightly.

Idina smiled at the man. "Thanks, Danford," she said, glancing down at the boy in her arms. "What do you say, Colt?"

"Thank you," Colt said with a shy smile.

"No problem," Danford said with a smile. "Make sure you keep an eye on him, eh? He's a good cat." He flicked the toy tiger's ear.

Colt laughed quietly. "Yeah."

Alucard's gaze thickened with hostility as he observed Danford's interaction with Colt. The sight of his mate's ex filled him with a tumult of emotions he struggled to contain. When Danford's gaze shifted and met his own, the vampire's scowl deepened, making the man visibly shiver in dread.

With a quick glance over his shoulder, Danford searched for the source of Alucard's intense scrutiny, clearly hoping that it was directed at someone else. However, the realization that he was the target of the vampire's piercing gaze only intensified his fear. Shrinking back, he sought refuge behind the towering figures of his companions, a feeble attempt to escape the weight of Alucard's silent judgment as they followed Zalith through the enveloping darkness.

And for the next while, they travelled in silence.

## | Zalith |

As they neared the tree line, the ethereal glow of the gateway shimmered ahead, casting a faint illumination on their path. Zalith glanced at Alucard, his heart heavy with apprehension. With each step, his anxiety swelled, a relentless tide threatening to engulf him. All he wished for was a peaceful passage, a quiet journey home for Alucard and his people.

Yet, as his gaze lingered on Alucard, a sense of unease crept over him, gnawing at his insides with a relentless intensity. Each moment brought a fresh wave of worry, each beat of his heart echoing with a dull ache. Just a few more minutes, he reassured himself, and it would all be over.

However, his focus shifted as the tell-tale sound of Tyrus's materialization echoed nearby. With a steadying breath, Zalith kept his gaze fixed on the darkness ahead, leading the way toward the portal. As Tyrus's hand settled on his shoulder, Zalith spared a brief glance in his direction, acknowledging the silent support of his ally amidst the looming uncertainty.

"Everything looks good, boss," the man muttered.

"Good," Zalith replied. Then, as Tyrus backed off into the darkness, the demon looked at Alucard. "Are you ready?" he asked, placing his left hand on the vampire's arm, still holding his hand with his right.

Alucard nodded. "Are *zhey*?" he mumbled, looking over his shoulder at the people following them.

Zalith nodded, keeping his eyes on Alucard. He could see the concern on his face, but he wasn't sure whether it was for his people or for himself. "If you reach a point where you feel you have to stop, that's okay. We can work something out. I don't want you to push yourself too hard," he said quietly.

"I'll be vine," he assured him.

"Okay," Zalith murmured, releasing his grip from Alucard's arm. With a subtle shift, he manoeuvred his hand to the right side of Alucard's waist, drawing him into a comforting side embrace as they pressed onward. The warmth of their closeness offered a fleeting sense of reassurance amidst the encroaching darkness.

As Zalith reclaimed Alucard's hand, their fingers intertwining in silent solidarity, they shared a resolute glare ahead. In that shared gaze, unspoken understanding passed between them, a silent vow to face whatever lay ahead together, hand in hand.

The oppressive darkness of the night deepened, its weight bearing down on Zalith and his people like a suffocating blanket. Despite the feeble attempts of a half-hidden moon to pierce through the dense clouds, the forest remained shrouded in impenetrable gloom. Murky tendrils of fog snaked through the underbrush, coiling around them like the arms of a malevolent force, ensnaring their progress.

Zalith's gut clenched with a mounting sense of dread as the fog thickened, its oppressive weight drowning him in a suffocating embrace. Panic clawed at the edges of his mind as he struggled to navigate through the swirling mists. What had started as a mere inconvenience now morphed into an ominous presence that seemed to seep into his very bones.

Frantically, he cast his gaze around, his heart hammering in his chest as he fought against the rising tide of fear. The fog, once a dull grey, now shimmered with an eerie pallor, its ghostly glow casting long shadows that danced menacingly at the edge of his vision. For a fleeting moment, he entertained the notion that it might be the moonlight filtering through the fog, but the oppressive weight of it dispelled any semblance of comfort.

Halting in his tracks, Zalith squeezed Alucard's hand in a vice-like grip, his gaze fixated on the swirling murk before them. The group behind them erupted into a frenzied chorus of whispered questions, their fear palpable in the air. But Zalith had no answers to offer, his own unease mirroring theirs in the oppressive silence.

With a sense of foreboding weighing heavily on his shoulders, Zalith intensified his grip on Alucard's hand, his senses straining against the suffocating fog. Though they searched in tandem, their efforts yielded nought but a sense of ominous emptiness. It was as if the fog itself had become a living entity, lurking in the darkness with malevolent intent, and Zalith couldn't shake the feeling that they were being watched, even as the mist obscured all sight.

He searched the darkness with both his eyes and his sensory ethos, but his search yielded nothing. He also felt Alucard searching, but as far as either of them could tell, there was nothing out there.

It was just fog.

But something was wrong. Zalith *knew* something was wrong.

The once vibrant forest fell into an eerie stillness, suffocating under a heavy blanket of oppressive silence. The air grew frigid, its icy claws digging into them. Dread hung heavy in the darkness, a horrifying presence that seemed to leech the very life from the surroundings.

Anxious breaths echoed through the gloom, the only sound amidst the unnerving silence that enveloped them. Zalith's heart pounded in his chest, a frantic rhythm that matched the escalating sense of unease gnawing at his insides. It was as if the very essence of life had been drained from the forest, leaving behind nothing but an overwhelming sense of foreboding.

Whispers.

Voices.

The wind carried a distant murmur.

*Everyone* stood still. The dark became endless. The night became timeless. And the dread became the very air they breathed.

A furious scowl struck Zalith's face when he heard it.

The macabre, distorted voice called, "*I was wondering when we'd find each other again, Eladarin.*"

A confused frown warped Alucard's face when Zalith heard the voice call out again. "*Caedis…how nice it is to finally meet you.*"

Zalith's people started panicking as the dark filled with strange, ghostly apparitions, moving as though they were groundless. Everyone searched the darkness for their allies, and Zalith grabbed Alucard's arm.

Twisted, distorted breathing.

The macabre exhaled, snarling in laughter.

"*Would you like to meet me….*"

"*Caedis?*"

Alucard sharply turned his head, and when Zalith looked in the same direction, he saw the incoming spiralling ball of light that the fog made impossible for anyone else to detect.

And Zalith had no time to evade—

Without hesitation, the vampire pulled free from Zalith's grasp, his movements quick and decisive. Holding out both hands, Alucard intercepted the pulsating light, the sheer force of it pushing him back with a staggering impact. His boots skidded against the ground, leaving faint trails in the earth as he struggled against the onslaught.

All eyes turned to Alucard, their gazes heavy with concern and apprehension. Despite his scowl of determination, Zalith could sense the inner turmoil raging within his vampire. It was not the physical pain that tormented him, but the insidious assault on his very essence. Like a relentless parasite, the light drained Alucard's ethos, sapping his strength with each passing moment.

Yet, even amidst his struggle, Alucard remained resolute. He clearly understood the consequences of releasing his hold on the light, knowing that it would unleash devastation upon the area they stood. With grim determination etched upon his features, he braced himself against the relentless force, unwilling to let it consume them all.

But then a second light flew towards them.

Alucard didn't have a free hand.

Zalith knew that if *he* tried to stop it, the light would tear him apart, but he wouldn't let it take Alucard.

He flung himself in Alucard's way, putting himself between his vampire and the incoming blight—

**Light.**

Bright white consumed the dark.

The earth quaked beneath them, a violent upheaval that shattered the stillness of the night. Before anyone could react, a blinding explosion erupted, hurling them all off their feet with a deafening roar. A shockwave reverberated through the air, slicing through the darkness with its sheer force, leaving them all reeling in its wake. Anything else in its immediate vicinity was rent asunder, torn apart, and shattered by the sheer force of the explosion.

Zalith hit the ground with a painful grunt. He tumbled, growled, and scowled in both anger and trepidation as he slowly came to a halt. The area swiftly became toxic, the air plagued with rhodium, silver, and platinum, everything deadly to himself and his people. He choked, laying on his front with the side of his face resting on the grass. For a moment, his body was still and limp, failing to catch up with his racing thoughts.

Alucard—where was Alucard?

He struggled to his hands and knees as the poisonous air challenged every move he made. With dread in his heart and terror in his eyes, he searched the space around him. Where there was once forest now lay a stretching battlefield of shattered trees, mangled corpses, and blood—blood everywhere. And the light…he'd recognize that white glow anywhere, breaking the darkness and lighting the world as if it were a day brighter than ever.

The demon's body jolted upright, his muscles tensing as a surge of adrenaline coursed through his veins. There, looming before him in the darkness, descended the embodiment of his deepest fears—the nameless Light, a grotesque aberration birthed from human belief. Its ethereal form pierced the night sky, casting an oppressive glow that swallowed everything in its path.

Dread clawed at Zalith's insides, a suffocating weight that threatened to crush him under its relentless grip. As the Light neared the ground, its radiance blinding in its intensity, a primal terror gripped the demon like a vice. His heart thundered in his chest, each beat echoing in the silence of his terror-stricken mind.

The screams of his people reverberated around him, their cries mingling with the cacophony of chaos and despair that engulfed the poisoned air. The metallic tang of fear hung heavy, choking him with its suffocating embrace. As death loomed ever closer, an overwhelming sense of horror consumed him, threatening to drown him in its merciless tide.

But Alucard. The vampire possessed his thoughts, even through his panic. Where was he?

Zalith forced himself upright, his muscles protesting with each movement as he surveyed the battlefield through eyes blurred with pain and exhaustion. Despite the anguish that gnawed at his soul and the raw, unyielding fear that coiled in the pit of his stomach, he refused to succumb to despair.

With a grim resolve, he hurled himself into the fray, his steps unsteady yet determined as he joined the desperate struggle unfolding around him. The werewolves, their primal instincts driving them forward, unleashed their bestial fury upon the demon hunters who had come with the Light to extinguish them. Blades glinted in the moonlight, silver and rhodium gleaming with lethal intent as they clashed against the darkness.

Every swing of a blade and howl of pain served as a grim reminder of the stakes at hand. Zalith fought alongside his people, their numbers dwindling with each passing moment, but their spirits were unbroken. They were warriors in a battle for survival, facing an enemy who sought to annihilate them at any cost. And despite the odds stacked against them, they refused to yield, determined to fight until their last breath. Just as they'd been trained.

But where was Alucard?

The question throbbed in his head.

Zalith snarled in revolt, tearing the head from his first foe. He searched the battlefield, desperately hunting for a sign of his vampire, but Alucard wasn't within sight. "Alucard?!" he yelled, his voice thick with panic, and the dread on his face grew as the battle became louder.

Snarling wolves, yelling voices, the thick scent of blood, and the sound of metal clashing—but no Alucard.

Zalith's heart hammered in his chest as he turned sharply, locking eyes with Tyrus amidst the chaos of battle. Despite the gaping wound that marred his side, the man fought on with a ferocity that bordered on madness—allocer demons were relentless, though, so he wasn't surprised by Tyrus' resolve. But the acrid tang of rhodium poison hung heavy in the air, a grim reminder of the peril they *all* faced. Even Tyrus had his weaknesses.

A surge of urgency pulsed through Zalith's veins, his mind racing with the desperate need to find a way out of this nightmare. His demons, weakened by the toxic atmosphere, were unable to phase away to safety. The only escape lay through the portal, but without Alucard, it remained impassable. Yet, in the midst of the hell unfolding before him, finding Alucard was not just a means of escape or a matter of survival. He just wanted to find him. He *needed* to find him.

Dread tightened its grip around Zalith's heart as he sprinted over the bodies of fallen comrades, his claws cutting through the ranks of their enemies with ruthless efficiency. "Alucard?!" he called out, his voice strained with desperation as he scanned the battlefield for any sign of his vampire.

A fleeting moment of stillness descended as Zalith halted in his tracks, his chest heaving with exertion. Blood trickled down the side of his face from wounds he had unknowingly sustained in the heat of battle. But in that moment, amid the chaos and carnage, all that mattered was finding Alucard. Nothing else could quell the rising tide of fear that threatened to consume him whole.

But his decision to halt invited the Light to focus on him.

"*Where's Caedis?*" it asked, its voice echoing through his head, trying so sorely to snatch his attention.

He'd not listen to it. He'd not respond to it.

He scowled, bursting forward, continuing to aid his people where he could, all whilst searching for Alucard. But his thoughts raced as fast as his heart. Where was Alucard? How did this happen? Why was this happening? Was Alucard okay? Why couldn't he see, hear, or even *feel* his vampire?

He stopped again, frantically searching the light-flooded battleground.

"*Can't you find him?*" the voice called again, louder this time.

Zalith kept ignoring it. He turned his head and set his eyes on Idina; a group of demon hunters was headed her way, and she was already struggling with the group that had surrounded her. But behind him, some of his werewolves were failing against the enemy, too. To his left, more of his people battled with little chance of winning— everywhere he looked, his people were falling, suffering… and as the Light grew brighter and thicker, still… there was no sign of Alucard.

The demon's scowl thickened with panic, dread, and heartache. He didn't want to assume anything, but there was no sign of his vampire—

It called to him again, "*Where is he?*"

He ignored the voice and the pain of his injuries; he just wanted to find Alucard.

Zalith moved forward, searching, panicking, his eyes scouring every inch of the battlefield—

*"Where's Caedis?"*

Alucard wouldn't have left—he couldn't have. He wasn't on the ground, nor was he fighting—he wasn't *anywhere!*

*"You can't ignore me forever, Eladarin,"* the voice whispered.

He could, and he would. His heart raced, his fear intensified, and his aching body began to defy his will. He stopped running, slowing to a panicked walk as he turned, frantically searching the blinding battlefield.

But then he felt the grip of a hand on his right shoulder, and he was spun around before he could react. And when his sights met those of the man who now had *both* his hands on the demon's shoulders, his eyes widened in both shock and horror, and confusion constricted him where he stood.

Blue eyes, dark brown hair, and a face so much like his own. The man before him was unmistakeably Xurian, his brother…but…how?

Xurian, with a dismayed frown, stared into Zalith's eyes. "Z, I think they got Alucard," he said—even his voice was Xurian's.

Zalith stared at his brother. His body was still, his thoughts were tangled, and he could do nothing but stand there and gaze at Xurian's slowly changing face. One moment, his face adorned a worried, concerned expression, but as his words were spoken, his face slowly twisted into a crazed, maniacal grin, and malice filled his eyes.

"Maybe he's dead like me," he said as his grin stretched across his face.

With a surge of anger coursing through him like a bolt of lightning, Zalith's initial confusion morphed into a scowl of pure fury. Gritting his teeth against the onslaught of emotions, he wrenched himself free from Xurian's grip, his muscles coiling with tension. With a primal roar, he lashed out with his fist, aiming for his spectral adversary. "Fuck you!" he yelled, his voice dripping with venom. But to his dismay, his blow passed straight through Xurian as if he were nothing but smoke, dissipating into the air like a wisp of fog. Enraged and frustrated, Zalith's gaze snapped forward, only to find himself ensnared by the blinding brilliance of his enemy's light.

Realization dawned on him like a cold chill down his spine—he'd fallen prey to the illusions spun by the malevolent entity. He'd unknowingly played into its hands, responding to its taunts and provocations. Now, it sought to ensnare him further, drawing him ever closer into its grasp.

With every fibre of his being, Zalith fought against the inexorable pull of the Light, his willpower a barrier against its insidious influence. He refused to become another victim of its twisted machinations, his resolve burning brightly amidst the encroaching darkness.

Zalith grimaced, trying to pull himself from the Light's enticing glare. He struggled, he fought, he tried—but his weakening body began to fail him. No ethos, little to no strength…. Was this it?

Another hand gripped his arm. He sharply turned his head, and as his sights met with the hell-fiery eyes of his vampire, relief flooded through him.

Alucard uttered words, but Zalith couldn't hear them. He lifted his hands, placing them on the sides of Alucard's face—he couldn't express his relief; to see him alive, to see him right in front of him, to see him.... Behind him.... Someone was sprinting through the dark; Zalith had no time, Alucard had no time—there was *no* time!

The vampire's frown of concern twisted suddenly into a look of startled horror as Zalith's delayed response unfolded before him. In an instant, the air was thick with shock and disbelief as Alucard's features contorted with anguish.

Zalith's gaze followed Alucard's downward, only to be met with a scene of unimaginable dismay. A silver blade cut through Alucard's back, its deadly edge piercing out through his chest with merciless precision. A strangled gasp escaped the vampire's lips, and Zalith's heart shattered as he watched in horror, feeling a surge of helplessness grip his soul.

As Alucard's attacker withdrew their weapon, a sickening lurch of dread washed over Zalith. The world blurred around him when he fell with Alucard. Zalith dropped to his knees, holding the vampire in his arms as he desperately clamped his hands against his wound. But the life left his face faster than Zalith could comprehend—he didn't understand, he didn't want to understand. Alucard went limp, his head resting in Zalith's lap, and the fire raging in his eyes was extinguished.

Everything fell still and silent.

Zalith couldn't accept it—he wouldn't, but…he stared down at his vampire, and there wasn't a flicker of life on his face. Was…he—

**Light.**

Zalith stared in horror, in confusion.

Alucard appeared before him again; it was as though everything Zalith had just seen wasn't real.

Standing on his feet once more, Zalith stared in disbelief, his voice stuttering as he struggled to comprehend what was unfolding before him. His gaze locked with Alucard's hell-fiery eyes, confusion swirling in his mind like a tempest.

Tears threatened to spill from his eyes, but he fought to hold them back, his emotions in turmoil. His thoughts raced, a jumble of questions and fears clamouring for attention. What was happening? How could this be real? Every beat of his heart echoed the frantic rhythm of his mind, a cacophony of uncertainty and dread.

Alucard gripped both of Zalith's arms and stared at his confounded face. "Vhat are you doing?" he asked in confusion, trying to pull him away from the Light's gaze.

A faint tick…

Tick…

Tick…

Zalith felt so confused, so horrified. But if this was the same as what he'd just seen, then Alucard was about to suffer.

He scowled and pulled Alucard aside, and as a blade-wielding attacker came at them both, the demon reached out and snatched the silver sword. Silver didn't affect him, so he tore the weapon from the hands of their foe.

Zalith set his eyes on him, and his confusion deepened.

Addison?

Why was Addison attacking Alucard?

He'd always been a questionable man, and Zalith had never placed as much trust in him as he did in Greymore. He asked himself whether this was reality or merely a trick of the mind; nevertheless, it was enough to fuel Zalith's growing suspicion that Addison had betrayed them, perhaps colluding with the hunters to lead them into this ambush.

The thought filled Zalith with disgust. He loathed traitors, and now it seemed his worst fears were being realized. His suspicions about the presence of turncoats among their ranks had been confirmed, and if Addison was indeed working with their enemies, it would explain how the Light had tracked them down.

Anger simmered beneath the surface as Zalith grappled with the unsettling revelation. Without remorse, without any desire to ask for confirmation, he tore Addison's throat out and then desperately grasped Alucard's hand.

It was time to leave.

He surged forward, pulling Alucard alongside him as they sprinted across the chaotic battlefield. Together, they dispatched every foe that dared to block their path, Zalith steadfastly refusing to let Alucard stray from his protective grip.

But then a familiar shriek tore through the air, chilling Zalith's blood. Instinctively, he glanced skyward, Alucard mirroring his movement. Above them, the ominous silhouette of a winged beast eclipsed the Light's blinding spread, casting a shadow of dread over their hearts.

With a horrifying screech, an armoured, battle-ready gryphon landed in the middle of the battlefield, crushing a group of Zalith's people as it scoured the carnage for its target. Clearly, that was Zalith. He had no time to grieve his people or scowl at the creature; the winged beast charged at him and Alucard.

The toxic air obviously kept Alucard from morphing into a form that would better help them fight the beast, or he would have done it by now. Instead, they stood side by side, preparing to fight the monster.

But the sound of incoming ethos snatched both their attention. Zalith sharply turned his head, staring in the same direction Alucard did, and set his eyes on the red-black mass of energy spiralling towards them.

Gryphon on his left, demon-repelling ethos on his right, and Alucard right in front of him. Panic consumed Zalith again as each hostile raced closer. He had no time to make a choice; he threw himself forward and wrapped his arms around Alucard as he tried to dive out of the way of both attackers.

But the gryphon was faster than Zalith.

Alucard yelled out painfully, and Zalith grunted as he hit the ground, agony starting to electrify his own body when the vampire landed atop him.

His arms remained tightly wrapped around Alucard, but his hold proved futile against the force that tore the vampire from his grasp. Zalith's heart clenched in agony as Alucard was wrenched away, leaving him to stumble in a haze of pain.

Ignoring his own injuries, Zalith scrambled to his feet, his gaze instantly drawn to Alucard's prone form lying motionless on the ground. Blood pooled around him, a stark contrast to his pallid skin. With a sickening dread coiling in his gut, Zalith watched as the gryphon withdrew its silver-plated claws from Alucard's body, the glint of their metallic sheen sending a shiver of ice down his spine.

Panic filled Zalith's eyes once more. "Alucard!" he yelled in dismay, rushing over to the vampire as the gryphon fled.

Zalith skidded to his knees, his heart pounding with urgency as he reached Alucard's side. With trembling hands, he gently turned the vampire onto his back, his fingers tightening around Alucard's arms in a desperate attempt to anchor him to life.

Alucard stuttered and grimaced, his grip on Zalith's shirt faltering as blood spilt from his mouth. Zalith's own breath caught in his throat as he watched the life ebb from Alucard's once vibrant features. Panic surged through him, rendering his thoughts a tangled mess of confusion and despair.

He shook his head in disbelief, his voice faltering as he struggled to form coherent words. The weight of helplessness bore down on him, leaving him paralyzed with indecision. In that moment of heart-wrenching uncertainty, Zalith could only cling to Alucard's fading presence, hoping for a miracle that seemed increasingly out of reach.

**Light.**

  Tick…

    Tick…

      Zalith's gasp echoed through the air as he found himself back on his feet, rooted to the spot where he'd stood before Alucard's arrival. Confusion enveloped him like a suffocating fog, mingling with the dread and horror that gripped his heart. Yet, amidst the turmoil, a chilling realization settled over him like a shadow. This time, as he surveyed his surroundings, he couldn't shake the sensation of detachment from the world around him. It was as though a veil had been drawn between him and reality, leaving him feeling adrift in a sea of uncertainty and unease.

Alucard grabbed his shoulders—

"What are you doing?!" the vampire panicked, trying to pull the demon away from the Light.

Tick...

Tick...

Tick...

Zalith set his eyes on Addison. Just like before, the man wielded a silver blade and headed straight for Alucard, who was oblivious to his approach. The demon swiftly grabbed the weapon, tore Addison's throat out, and sprinted into the battle with Alucard.

The shadow of a gryphon crept overhead—it wasn't going to get them this time.

Zalith turned his back on the landing beast and raced towards the portal, but he'd forgotten the attack of boiling black-red light. He stopped in his tracks, both he and Alucard like deer in lantern light. The spiralling ethos hit the ground at their feet inches from where they stood, and they were both thrown off their feet.

The demon landed with a pained, aggravated grunt. He opened his eyes, searching for Alucard, but it wasn't his vampire that his eyes found.

Idina.

Her eyes were glazed over, and her skin was covered in blood. She lay before him, crimson seeping from her eyes, mouth, and ears. And tears seeped down her face as she held onto the Colt, who was lifeless at her side.

Ticking....

It was getting louder and louder.

Zalith's eyes followed the sound, and when he located a gold pocket watch in the grasp of the dead boy, he frowned in horrified confoundment. He didn't even know what was going on anymore.

But the ticking.

It didn't stop. It tick, tick, ticked....

Zalith scowled when he was pulled back to where he'd been standing, and Alucard's grip snatched his arms once more.

"Ve 'ave to go," the vampire insisted, holding a bloody, bleeding wound in his side as he set his eyes on the portal in the distance.

The demon complied, limping as a new wound in his leg tore with each step. Those of his people who remained lingered around the portal, fighting, crying, and screaming as the demon hunters and Light's allies tried taking their lives. They had to go; Zalith had to get away with Alucard—with whoever they could take.

But reaching the portal brought no relief. From its darkened light, a familiar, disgusting face emerged before either Zalith or Alucard had a chance to comprehend.

Detlaff—with a grin so wide and white on his face—stepped out of the portal. Immediately, Zalith grasped Alucard's arms and pulled him back, ready to fight for their lives—for their escape. But Detlaff? Here? Why?

He wasn't alone. Behind him, an army of men and women broke free from the portal. Each wielding silver, and all grinning maniacally. The demon hunters, the Light, the gryphons, and Detlaff and his allies—all Zalith could think to do was run.

The demon turned to face Alucard, preparing to flee, but he had no chance to even look at his vampire.

Zalith's shoulders were grabbed—something pulled him back.

The demon managed to set his horrified eyes on Alucard but only got to witness what Detlaff had prepared for him. With a laugh and a grin, the maniac snatched Alucard by his throat and pinned him down on the grass. Detlaff's allies chanted as Alucard fought and struggled; he tried with what looked to be all the might he could manage to escape, but he couldn't, and Zalith couldn't do anything to help.

Clawed hands burst from the ground, stabbing their talons into Alucard as he lay there helplessly. Hellfire, demonic chanting, hissing, and gnawing—the ground caved in, Alucard yelled in horror, and in just moments, Zalith's vampire was pulled into the earth, and hellfire rained from the chasm that took him away.

Laughing, Detlaff turned to Zalith and grinned. But the watch… a watch which Zalith felt appear in his pocket—tick, tick, tick… and then darkness.

**Light.**


Tick…


Tick…


Tick…


Tick…


Tick…

Tick...

Tick...

Tick...

Tick...

Tick...

Tick...

Tick...

Tick...

Tick...

Tick...

Tick...

Tick...

Tick...

Tick...

Tick...

Tick...

Tick...

Tick...

Tick...

Tick...

Zalith's thoughts were silent.

His confusion enthralled everything.

Where was he?

What was going on?

Where was—

Alucard—standing before him. He gripped Zalith's shoulders, preparing to speak—

"What's happening?" Zalith asked, his voice just as dismayed as his face.

What *was* happening? The world felt so strange. But Alucard…. He was right in front of him. His eyes, his scent, his aura: it was all the same, as it should be, and it brought him hope. But…he didn't know what to think, what to feel, or what to say; it almost didn't make sense. He'd just seen the man he loved die *three* times.

Was it going to happen again? How was it going to happen this time? Or this time…would it *not* happen?

"Ve 'ave to go," Alucard insisted, tightening his grip on Zalith's shoulders.

As before, Addison came at them with a blade—

Tick….

Tick….

Tick….

Zalith stopped and killed him.

They ran.

The demon pulled Alucard with him.

Tick….

Tick….

Tick….

The Shadow of a gryphon.

Left, right, back, forward. Where?

Zalith couldn't stand to see Alucard die again.

He ran back with him—the way they had come.

The gryphon landed, and it slaughtered his people.

The spiralling ethos hit the ground, killing more and more of his people. But Alucard was safe. Alucard's hand was still in his. Maybe…maybe this time, it was different. Idina was still alive. Colt was still alive. Everyone was heading towards the portal.

That was where he had to take Alucard.

He gripped his vampire's hand tighter, setting his determined gaze on the gateway to their escape—to safety…to home. He hurried, his heart racing, and his strength waning, but that didn't matter. He needed to get Alucard home—they needed to leave Eltaria, a place he never wanted to see again. Aegisguard was his home now— *Alucard* was his home. He didn't need anything else.

The demon looked back at his vampire, who adorned a look of confused horror, but continued following him. They reached the portal, and Zalith wasn't going to waste any time. These were his people, he had to take care of them, but Alucard was more important to him than anyone.

"Go," he insisted, forcing Alucard to take the lead.

Alucard didn't hesitate. The vampire headed straight for the portal.

Detlaff didn't come out this time.

Maybe this time it *was* real. Maybe they were going to escape.

As Alucard hurried through, Zalith snatched Idina's hand; in her arms, the woman held Colt, and with her free hand, she grabbed hold of Tyrus. Zalith didn't see who else managed to grab onto the link, but as soon as the rain hit his face, he felt…relief.

He continued forward, pulling Idina and whoever she had managed to bring with her. He kept his eyes on Alucard, frantically searching the rainy island for anything that might come for him. But there was nothing. Just rain. Rain and Alucard. And Idina, Colt, Tyrus, Greymore, Orin, Danford, and one last vampire.

That was it. No one else came through.

But Alucard's grip on his hand weakened. He felt his heart stop for a moment when he took his eyes off the portal to look at his vampire.

Alucard, as blood oozed from his face, dropped to his knees with an agonized grunt. Zalith whined in grief, dropping with him; his first thought, his loudest thought was: was he about to lose him again?

The demon gritted his teeth and grimaced, placing his hands on either side of Alucard's face. He stared into his eyes; the last time this had happened, he needed blood, so he'd give him blood.

He anxiously pulled the collar of his shirt from his neck, the rain pouring down his face. Then, he moved his hand to the back of Alucard's head, pulling him closer—

Screams and cries burst through the quiet.

Zalith's dread constricted him. He looked over his shoulder and watched vines of light creep out from the portal. Before he had a chance, the tendrils burst towards him, forcing him off and away from Alucard.

He wouldn't let it happen again—he *couldn't*.

The demon got up, setting his eyes on Alucard—but it was too late. In the blink of an eye, the vampire was ensnared in light and pulled into the portal.

Gone.

A suffocating, *drowning* emptiness consumed Zalith.

His heart, soul, and body shattered beneath the weight of horror, confusion, and heartbreak. Unable to bear the overwhelming anguish, Zalith sank to his knees, the relentless rain pouring over his upturned face. Around him, the horrified whispers of his surviving people faded into silence, their voices swallowed by the torrential downpour.

Light.

# Chapter Twenty-Three

─ ≺ ✝ ≻ ─

## Escape

**| Alucard |**

Pain engulfed Alucard, searing through every fibre of his being. It was as if his resistance to fire no longer existed, and his very essence had become kindling for an inferno, flames clawing at his skin with unrelenting fervour. Each breath he drew felt like swallowing molten lava, scorching his throat and consuming his essence. In the midst of the torment, silence enveloped him like a shroud, broken only by the relentless throb of agony that pulsed through him.

Amidst the torment, the Light inundated his vision, blinding him to all else. It was everywhere, an all-encompassing blight that offered no reprieve from the searing pain that ravaged his senses.

He stared at the ground beside him as he lay on his side, his face resting in something thick and red. The fur on his collar was stained crimson, and his vision was distorted and swaying as if the world wasn't still.

So much light…so much…confusion. He remembered—slowly, but surely. They had been standing in the dark…fog came, fog ensnared with ethos, and no one had seen it until it was too late. He'd seen it, he'd felt it, and he'd caught the ball of light that had been thrown their way. But another came, and when it hit the ground beneath them, the ethos he'd caught in his grasp combusted simultaneously.

Now…he lay on the ground—the shaking, trembling ground…or perhaps that was just his body. They…*them*…he'd been with people—Zalith. Where was Zalith?

Gritting his teeth against the waves of agony, the vampire fought to command his battered limbs to action. With as much effort as he could muster, he managed to press his hands into the ash-covered ground, using the earth as leverage to haul himself onto his knees. Every movement sent shards of pain ricocheting through his torn and bleeding body, but he refused to yield to the overwhelming anguish.

Glancing down, he confronted the source of his torment, his hands instinctively clasping against the wound that marred his stomach. Crimson stained his fingers, mingling with the ashen residue of battle, as blood oozed through the gaping wound, tracing rivulets down his trembling form to pool beneath him in a macabre tableau of suffering.

Pain everywhere. Light everywhere. His vision soon became clear enough for him to see the battle happening around him. Embers of silver and blue slowly rained from the sky. Fires were burning in every corner of the opening he found himself in. Werewolves snarling, tearing, running; people with blades of silver, and others attacking with whatever they could find.

It looked so familiar. Armoured gryphons, mages in black robes; the enemy were demon hunters, and that Light…. He looked over his shoulder, setting his eyes on a mass of blinding, white gold-rimmed light—it was as though the sun had come to the world in the form of something much smaller, no taller than a man, but forcing such brightness around itself and out into the world.

*That* was Zalith's enemy, and thus, *his* enemy.

Alucard winced, his fingers tightening around the searing wound as he turned away from the blinding Light. His mind raced with concern for Zalith—where was he amidst this chaos? The air hung heavy around him, thick with the oppressive weight of silver and rhodium, weapons sourced to sap the strength of Zalith's people.

His very essence struggled against the suffocating miasma, his senses reeling from the onslaught. Wounds refused to close, pain persisted with unyielding intensity, and the world itself seemed to warp and twist, amplifying his confusion with each passing moment.

But he had to find Zalith.

The fog of disorientation began to lift as a familiar figure hurried over, silvery hair glinting through the battle. It wasn't Zalith, but Orin, the seir demon who was one of Zalith's Alphas, who knelt before him. With hands firmly planted on the vampire's shoulders, Orin's eyes bore into his own, words tumbling from his lips in urgent but indistinct tones. Behind him, a colossal black werewolf stood sentinel on its hind legs, its towering form eclipsing the surroundings, a formidable guardian amidst the turmoil.

"Aleksei!" Orin yelled, shaking him slightly.

Alucard scowled, snapping out of his confusion.

Seeing that he had the vampire's attention, Orin clearly tried his best to banish the panic from his face. "Can you stand?"

Could he? He frowned, slowly pulling himself to his feet with Orin's help. Then, ignoring the pain surging through his body, he took a moment to stare around the battlefield. There was no sign of Zalith.

"The enemy attacked us, and we can't find Zalith," Orin said desperately. "They've poisoned the air with rhodium, silver—everything toxic to us. We can't use our ethos, and our numbers are falling. What do you suggest we do?"

What *would* he suggest? Obviously, they couldn't find Zalith, so they were looking to him for their orders. What was the plan? The plan was to get everyone to Aegisguard, as it always had been. But not yet—not until he found Zalith.

However, they were in the middle of a battlefield. Alucard had promised to get everyone Zalith cared for back to Aegisguard, and that was what he was going to do. But how? The air was full of poison.… All of his ethos was useless…apart from his Numen ethos. Silver had nothing over the ethos he got from his father's blood. But if he was going to use it, he was going to have to be a lot more careful and use much more focus than he did with his normal ethos.

Zalith's people weren't going to be able to do anything in the field of poison, so the first thing he had to do was get rid of the toxic air. Then, the Light.… He looked over his shoulder. He wasn't entirely sure what to expect, but from what Zalith had told him and from what he was seeing, it was safe to assume that the light coming from that manifestation was its power. If he could blind its light, he might slow it down.

As for finding Zalith, he couldn't use the ethos of his imprint or his demon senses. He'd have to search the entire battlefield, all whilst trying to keep Zalith's people safe *and* fighting off the enemy. It was going to take a lot, but he had a lot at his disposal.

He set his eyes back on Orin. "I'll clear zhe air, zhen you'll be able to vight. Vork on getting everyvone to zhe gatevay, and vait vor me and Zaliv zhere," he instructed.

Orin nodded, and then, with his werewolf ally, he raced back off to join the fight.

Alucard didn't have any time to waste. But his injuries; he looked down at his blood-soaked hands, the unseen wound in his side or stomach or wherever it was—it was still bleeding, and his Numen ethos was something he hadn't used enough to know how to control. Would he heal once he summoned it? He wasn't sure, but he might as well make use of all the blood that he was losing.

He closed his eyes, and everything around him slowed as he allowed his once dormant Numen power to consume everything he was. Darkness seeped from his skin, and he effortlessly transformed the blood that had left his body into a black fog ensnared with shimmering red and silver embers; it banished the Light in front of him as it draped to the ground as though it were weighted, just as it had the day he'd turned on Damien.

Then, he opened his eyes, his sclera black, his irises as hellish as always.

First, the air.

He scowled, focusing on what he had to do. This power made his body feel numb enough that he could ignore his pain and leave his wounds open so he could continue turning his pouring blood into fog. The world around him slowed so much that it looked as if it had come to a halt. But his unparalleled eyesight kept him from thinking everything had become still. Time continued ticking, and the world *was* spinning, but he was moving so fast that everything seemed to be lagging.

In the form of darkness, Alucard burst forward, the very air around him sizzling out of existence as he moved through it. He spared a glance at the Light—the enemy. Within the brightness, his speed granted him the ability to see that the manifestation was, in fact, very human-looking—in shape, at least—and inside the brightness, a familiar figure.

Zalith.

He was so very far inside that Light, and the creature inside was reaching its arm out to grab him. Soon, Zalith would be within its grasp.

Alucard wouldn't let that happen.

The vampire focused on cleansing the air, but he was only clearing that which he ran through. He wasn't going to get it done fast enough; he needed to cover more ground. So, he switched his tactic. Why do two things one at a time when he could do both at once?

With everything around him still slowed, he reached the centre of the battlefield and tore at his own wrists. And then darkness seeped from his body in place of his blood; it flooded the battlefield, banishing the light, battling it like both ethos' were monsters in form.

As the dark spread, Alucard's strength waned, but once the air was clear, he'd be able to use his other ethos; his Numen ethos wasn't low in supply, he just slipped a little further into the dark of his mind the more he used it… and he didn't wish to lose himself. Not now that he had something to live for.

Once he'd banished the light which ensnared the field, Alucard relented. With a grimace and pained exhale, he stumbled back. Around him, nothing but darkness lingered. Darkness filled with shimmers of silver and red—his ethos, his blood, his very being, even. It burned the toxic air, leaving it clear of anything that would harm Zalith's allies. Their enemies wouldn't be able to see in his fog, but Alucard had made sure that Zalith's people *could*.

For a moment, Alucard listened as the demon's allies fought back against the enemy, slaying them with the drastic advantage he had given them.

But now… Zalith.

With a scowl in response to his aching body, Alucard cut off all his Numen ethos other than that which he needed to keep the area ensnared in his darkness. Then, he raced forward, focusing on Zalith's location. He was still alive; his aura was strange and distorted, but that had to be because of how close he was to the Light—the Light whose power could no longer be seen, and Alucard suspected that it had become desperate. But that didn't matter. His plan was to get Zalith and leave.

He raced through the fog, keeping his focus on Zalith, but he soon burst out of the dark and into the light once more—the light that his ethos couldn't penetrate. In the centre of the small opening was Zalith, and the glowing outline of something like a man. It held out its hand, reaching for Zalith, but Alucard wasn't going to let it have him.

The vampire hurried over to the demon; he stood in front of him, trying to block out the light, assuming that it somehow had Zalith ensnared, enticing him to walk closer and closer until it snatched hold of him. Alucard gripped the demon's shoulders, staring at his bloodied, vacant face. His once dark eyes were flooded with golden light—it was like they had been infected with the Light's blinding gold—and his confused expression seemed to thicken as his sights flickered from the Light to Alucard.

"Zaliv?" he asked desperately. He'd never seen him like this. What had happened to him? What had this Light done? Why did he look so confounded to see that he was standing in front of him?

So many questions, but no time. Whatever this Light had done to Zalith, Alucard had to get him into the cover of darkness before he'd get to learn.

But the demon stared at him, stuttering as if he was about to say something, but no words left his mouth. He stared in horror, turmoil. It confused Alucard so much that he didn't detect his incoming attacker until it was too late.

Alucard's body tensed with agony as a blade tore through his flesh, skewering him and Zalith in a single, brutal thrust. Yet, despite the searing pain, he refused to yield. With a guttural grunt, he tore himself free away from Zalith, wrenching the blade from his own body with grim determination. Whirling around to face his assailant, Alucard's eyes narrowed with a mix of shock and betrayal as he beheld Addison, the once-trusted ally now a traitor. Without hesitation, the vampire drove the blade back, aiming squarely for Addison's chest. The man tried to fight, but his attempts were pathetic, and when the blade sliced through him, he stared at Alucard as if he couldn't believe that he'd lost

His body dropped to the ground with a thump. Alucard then yanked the blade from his chest and sliced the man's head off, keeping him from transforming into a hellhound. It only then hit him that Zalith's dead lycan allies might start turning any moment, but when he took a quick glance through the chaos using his fog, he saw that their enemies had been beheading them. Hellhounds were nobody's allies.

As quickly as he could, Alucard grabbed hold of Zalith and pulled him into the darkness. The Light screeched out in frustration, but Alucard was too fast for it to even attempt to give chase. He kept running, getting as far from the manifestation as he could before he had to stop and assess both their conditions.

Beside one of the only standing trees for miles, Alucard stopped and pushed Zalith against it so that he'd lean back in case the wound Alucard had just noticed on his leg made it hard for him to stand.

He then placed his right hand on Zalith's shoulder and his left on the side of the demon's neck, staring into his disorientated, dark eyes. The gold had vanished, and that relieved him. "Zaliv?" he asked again, unsure why he hadn't said a word.

Alucard looked the demon up and down; the wound that Addison's blade left on Zalith had already healed in the no-longer-toxic air, and whatever was causing blood to seep from the demon's leg seemed to heal, too, as had the wound on the side of his head, leaving a trail of dried blood from his temple to his jaw.

"Are you okay?" Alucard asked desperately.

The demon stared at him in silence for a moment. A small frown broke his confused expression, and as his eyes stared into Alucard's, Zalith shakily answered, "I don't…know."

He didn't know? Alucard grimaced and looked down at his own wounds; the cut in his stomach was healing—he could feel it. He didn't care about wherever else he was wounded. He was healing, and that was all that mattered. But Zalith…. The demon looked so confused, disoriented, distressed. What happened to him?

"Vhat 'appened?" the vampire asked, but he was sure that he wasn't going to get an answer.

Zalith continued staring at him, almost aimlessly. "I…don't know."

Alucard frowned, thinking, trying to work out what might have happened. Zalith had warned him that the Light used people's minds as a weapon; it would enter a person's thoughts. He'd warned Alucard not to listen to it, to talk to it—maybe…Zalith had done something he shouldn't have. He'd been so close to that Light, and he looked so confused—turmoiled. Had the Light got to him? Was it still in his head? It couldn't be…he'd blocked the Light's brightness out with his darkness. Unless the creature's light wasn't its source of power or influence…. If it was still in Zalith's head, he had to banish it.

He dragged his hand up from Zalith's neck and placed his fingers on his face as though to read his thoughts—but that was when Zalith did more than stare in confusion. The demon scowled and defensively shoved Alucard back, scrambled to his feet, and stood prepared to fight him. If Alucard didn't know better, he'd say that Zalith looked traumatized, unsure, and as though every despairing feeling had consumed him.

The vampire moved back towards Zalith—but slowly and calmly—and placed his hands on his shoulders again. He had to convince Zalith that he was free of the Light and that Alucard was going to take him to safety; he had to help Zalith understand that the Light didn't have hold of him anymore. He had to help him block out the Light if it was still in his head, and then keep it from getting to him again. He had a way, but it would leave himself vulnerable. He didn't care. Zalith mattered more to him than his own life did.

Before, that creature had been able to speak to him because he only had a single line of thought-blocking defence—the Aegis fur on his cape; all Aegis dragons who possessed fur were immune to thought-reading ethos. Now, he was using both the ethos of that fur and his own to block out the Light's influence. Zalith only had his own ethos—he needed more, and Alucard had exactly that.

With a scowl on his face, Alucard reached for the small clip inside his cape and unfastened it. "Zaliv," he said, making sure that he had the demon's attention.

Zalith stared at him in turmoil, waiting.

"I zon't know vhat zhat ving did to you, but zhis vill keep vrom knowing vhere you are," he said, pulling off his cape. He then put it around Zalith's shoulders and clipped it in place. "Zhe vur possesses anti-ethos compounds—stops anyving and anyvone vrom being able to vead and manipulate zhe vhoughts of zhe vone vearing—zhat's vhy ve couldn't detect Boreas in Avalmoor last year. Zhat Light von't know vhere you are, von't be able to get into your mind, and you vill be safe."

Zalith slowly lifted his hand and placed it over his.

"Ve 'ave to go to zhe portal now," he said, trying his best to ignore the distorted whispers that began seeping into his mind the moment he took his cape off. Obviously, with Zalith's aura now invisible, the Light must be becoming a whole lot more desperate to find and grasp him.

The demon nodded weakly in response to Alucard's words.

It was time to go.

Whatever the Light was, Numen or not, it had to be powerful if it could do something like this to Zalith. Alucard looked at him as he led the way through the darkness, heading for the portal. He had no idea what was going on inside Zalith's head—he had no idea what that creature had done to him. All he knew was that he needed to get Zalith back to Aegisguard, where the Light couldn't possibly follow.

But his worry increased as each second passed. Zalith's eyes were still full of anguish, and his expression even more so. He walked, he breathed, but it didn't feel as though he lived. It was like a part of Zalith had almost died. He didn't adorn his usual devious look, nor did he emit his familiar dark and deadly aura. He was…silent. Empty in a way that Alucard hated. It hurt his heart, his soul, and his body to see Zalith so unlike himself—physical and ethosal. What had happened?

"*What…did you do with him, Caedis?*" the Light's distorted voice called.

Alucard ignored its call. He could hear the confusion in the Light's voice, the desperation. How sorely it wanted Zalith, but how severely Alucard would protect him. He led him through the dark, the gateway just minutes ahead of them; all that remained of Zalith's people had gathered around it, cutting down any enemy that came close. They were ready to leave…but were Zalith and Alucard?

The vampire had never been so ready to leave a place—

"*Do you think…if I kill you, Caedis…he'll show himself?*" the Light called.

Alucard scowled, gripping Zalith's hand as they both reached the portal. Everyone stared at them, waiting for instructions.

"Take somevone's 'and," Alucard instructed, glancing at Zalith as he stood in front of the portal. "And all of you take 'old of vone anozzer—ve are leaving."

"*You can leave… but that doesn't mean I won't find you,*" the Light called.

Alucard closed his eyes and stepped through….

His ethos shuddered, and Alucard grimaced, stepping out onto the island as the cold rain hit his blood-covered face. He pulled Zalith with him, and Zalith pulled Orin. Orin pulled Tyrus and Tyrus tugged on Idina. One after the other, Zalith's allies emerged from the portal.

But as each person walked out, Alucard felt his ethos ebb away, drained with every passing moment until he was left with nought but the remnants of his power. Blood trickled from his every orifice, a crimson testament to the strain of his efforts. Despite the mounting agony, he clung to Zalith's hand, refusing to let go as he called upon the depths of his Numen ethos.

With a grunt of exertion and a grimace of pain etched across his face, Alucard strained against the overwhelming weight of his depleted energy. His grip tightened on Zalith's hand, his knees buckling beneath him as he fought to maintain his footing, and when he fell, the demon fell with him. They kept hold of each other's hands, and Zalith kept hold of Orin's while his people continued to come through the portal.

Alucard's grimace thickened, his pain increasing until it became unbearable. He searched for Zalith's embrace, but when he looked at the demon, all he saw was his conflicted face. Nothing had changed despite their escape, and it caused him more pain deep within his heart. But Zalith *did* move closer, and Alucard rested his forehead on the demon's shoulder while he breathed frantically, trying to cope. However, his pain soon forced him to cry out in agony, gripping Zalith's shoulder with his free hand. He gritted his teeth in an attempt to silence himself, but with every breath he took and let go of, he uttered a sound of pain.

Moments passed, his ethos dwindled, and as the last person came through, Alucard felt no relief. His free hand slipped from Zalith's shoulder; his racing heart didn't slow, and the agony reached a point that made him feel numb. Four-thousand years' worth of age was already a stretch, but with Zalith and his demons on top of that… Alucard was surprised to still be conscious. But he sat there in Zalith's embrace, relief caressing him as he felt the demon wrap his arms around him.

"Alucard?" Zalith asked quietly, confusion in his voice.

The vampire looked up at him. Zalith's distressed frown hadn't faded, but he moved his left arm from around the vampire and pulled the collar of the furred cape away from his neck.

An invitation?

Whether it was or not, Alucard didn't refuse. He moved his face closer to Zalith's neck and sunk his fangs into his skin without a moment's hesitation. He felt the demon flinch, but Zalith didn't try to pull him away; he moved his hand to the back of Alucard's head, waiting as the vampire gulped his blood down.

With each desperate mouthful, Alucard felt his strength slowly returning, but he'd not get it all from Zalith—he had to stop. Zalith needed his strength, too.

Alucard frowned and pulled his fangs from the demon and then nuzzled his neck, moving his arms around him. All he wanted now was to rest in Zalith's embrace—it was all he *ever* wanted.

But his rest wouldn't come yet. The petrified cry of a woman caught his *and* Zalith's attention. They both looked over at the gateway, setting their eyes on Idina, who was looking around in sheer panic, and the confused people watched her anxiously.

"Colt!" Idina cried, looking around at the confounded, exhausted faces of her people. "I must…I must have—he let go of me!" she cried. "Where is he?!"

Colt, the little shapeshifter boy Alucard had met not too long before the battle. Idina had been holding him—*he* was probably clinging onto her when they went through the portal. But the kid must have let go, and Alucard suspected he knew exactly where the boy was.

He had to go and get him.

But when he went to stand up, Zalith lightly grabbed both his arms and stopped him. "Don't go," he pleaded.

"I 'ave to save 'im," Alucard insisted as a conflicted frown struck his face.

Zalith stared at him like he was searching his eyes for something, but he soon relented and nodded. "Okay," he said sullenly.

Alucard stood up and made his way over to the gateway. Colt wasn't going to survive in there for long, and he had to be quick.

When he reached the portal, he turned his back on it and exhaled deeply…and then he stepped backwards into the darkness.

# Chapter Twenty-Four

— ⸲ ✝ ⸱ —

# Adellum


**| Alucard |**

As Alucard stepped backwards into the gateway, the familiar world dissolved into obscurity, replaced by the engulfing darkness of the portal. The solid ground vanished beneath his feet, leaving him suspended in the void, weightless and adrift. There was no sensation of gravity, only the eerie emptiness between the realms—a desolate expanse that enveloped him in its icy embrace.

The chill seeped into his bones, a palpable reminder of the solitude that pervaded this boundless void. Amidst the cold, Alucard's thoughts turned to the boy—where had he gone?

Alucard turned around to behold the breath-taking display of hues sprawling before him. Reds, oranges, purples, and blues danced in a vibrant explosion, while countless white specks shimmered like distant stars strewn across a disordered celestial canvas. Despite the mesmerizing spectacle, he couldn't afford to linger.

Amidst the kaleidoscope of colours, a lone figure floated motionless—a mile distant yet achingly close. It was Colt, the defenceless boy, adrift and unconscious. Alucard had to reach him, no matter the obstacles.

He morphed into vermillion smoke and raced towards the boy at lightning speed, reaching him in no time at all. He rematerialized, grabbing Colt in his arms—but that was when it appeared.

Light.

Brighter than anything Alucard had seen.

And all too familiar.

It burst out of the emptiness before him, so bright that he had to hold his arm up to cover his eyes. Colt slipped from his grip, and they were both blown back—but a pair of burning, bright claws gripped Alucard's shin.

"Caedis…" the Light called, its voice a lot more distinct here. Cold and empty, just like the space around it.

But as Alucard stared, he could have sworn he saw a grin on that creature's face, a creature barely visible through its light, but this close, Alucard could see its faceless head, its human-like body, and the single eye in its forehead, wide open and projecting the light that surrounded its form and the world it existed in.

"Did you think you could run?" it asked, but this time, with its mouth—a gaping black hole lined with teeth so sharp. "From me?" it laughed. "I…am Adellum…I am…Light—not even *you* can keep him from me."

Alucard knew better than to respond, but as he tried to pull free, the creature tugged him closer.

"Why do you try to escape?" it questioned, pulling him so close that their faces were just inches apart. "You are…exactly what I need."

With a scowl, Alucard pulled free of the creature's grip—or so he thought. He morphed into vermillion smoke, but the creature snatched hold of his throat, pulling him out of it. The Light grinned, Alucard grimaced in pain and panic—and Colt…the boy drifted further and further into the void space.

Whatever the creature had planned, Alucard wasn't going to be a part of it. He'd get Colt, and then he'd leave—this Light couldn't enter Aegisguard; Letholdus would kill it before it had a chance to even look at Zalith. Maybe…maybe *that* was exactly what needed to happen. To free Zalith of this creature for good…only a Numen could kill a Numen.

Was this creature a Numen? Alucard couldn't think of anything else. As he stared at it, his thoughts began to wither, and his strength began to wane. There was no time to think. He snatched the creature's face, glaring back with as much hatred as he felt the creature emitting through its white light. His ethos shivered, his very being struggled—he'd not give in to whatever this was. He'd fight—for himself and Zalith.

Adellum—what was it? With his own Numen ethos shrouding him from this creature's influence, he stared into the eye in its forehead. Zalith was right about everything he said; it *had* been born of collective human belief, born of the very will the humans had to find and kill Zalith and his people. It *was* a Numen, and that was probably one of the biggest weaknesses it could possess.

However, Alucard couldn't use his ability to absorb a Numen's life force here. If he did, he wouldn't be able to leave this place—he'd have to go back to Eltaria, dispose of Adellum's ethos there, and then leave. If he wanted to get rid of this creature—if he wanted to stop it from entering Aegisguard and haunting Zalith's life any further—*that* was what he would have to do.

But Colt—Alucard glanced to his left, setting his eyes on the boy as he slowly drifted away. Then, he set his scowl back on Adellum.

"You can't resist forever, Caedis," it said, its grin becoming a struggled grimace as it gripped Alucard's wrist and tried to pull his hand from its face.

Alucard had decided what to do. This creature's days of making Zalith's life hell were over, and it was about to suffer what might be its first devastating defeat. Clearly, it hadn't expected Alucard's knowledge, his power, or his presence—Adellum was just as arrogant as all Numen, and that brought a smile to Alucard's face. "Neizer can you," he answered.

Locking his gaze with Adellum, Alucard watched as the entity seemed to quiver with uncertainty. The frantic twitching of its eye betrayed its struggle to comprehend why the vampire remained unaffected by its attempts at manipulation. Alucard knew that Adellum was delving into his mind, probing for weaknesses, listening to his every thought.

The realization evidently dawned upon Adellum—the creature faced not just any adversary, but one purpose-built to thwart beings like itself, to thwart Numen. A flicker of fear danced across its luminous, light-drenched visage as Alucard's resolute determination echoed within his mind, laying bare the truth for Adellum to see.

"Vemember who I am vhen you next vink of 'urting Zaliv," he warned, his voice starting to distort, Adellum's power quickly becoming his own. As the creature let out deafening, confused screams of agony, Alucard continued tearing Adellum's life force away. "And suffer," the vampire added, a smile creeping across his face as the Light let go of him and placed both his human-like hands on his head, wailing.

Alucard watched, waiting, absorbing Adellum's ethos the same way he had absorbed Lilith's. His once-lost wings appeared, as did his horns—all of them. His body changed the more he absorbed; he began to feel the Numen ethos constrict him, but he didn't stop, he wouldn't stop until Adellum was nothing but an empty shell—a shell he would throw back into the world it was born into.

The vampire didn't care to see what Adellum's lightless, powerless form looked like. The moment he had all of Adellum's ethos, he snatched the unconscious body of Zalith's enemy and frantically searched the void space for the doorway to Eltaria—and he surely found it. But he'd leave Colt here—in this place, non-Numen-blooded beings would simply fall into stasis if they became adrift. The boy would be fine; he could live within the void space for years and never age. He'd be perfectly okay for five minutes.

With the Numen ethos beginning to overwhelm him, Alucard snarled, opened his wings, and sped toward the doorway to Eltaria, pulling Adellum's corpse with him. He'd go through, leave Adellum's body on the battlefield, remove its ethos from his own body, and then leave. This was the last time he wanted to be in Eltaria—and the last time he wanted Zalith to have been there, too. Aegisguard was their home, and nothing or no one was going to take it from them, least of all some arrogant Numen.

He reached the doorway and took a moment to stare into the darkness. All he had to do was step through, and he'd be back in Eltaria. The battlefield would no longer be consumed by his darkness, and there was a possibility that the enemy might still be there…but it didn't matter. He had more than enough power to deal with them if they were there—he'd just use the ethos he'd stolen from Adellum.

With a quiet sigh, he turned his back on the portal, and then he propelled himself backwards with his wings, breaking out of the void space and into the world connected to it.

As soon as his feet hit the ground, he dropped Adellum's corpse and searched the battlefield for hostiles, but it was barren. All that remained on the black, ash-covered field were the corpses of those who had died, and small, withering fires. Alucard could sense people nearby, however—most likely the enemy looking for anyone who might not have gotten away. But he hadn't left anyone behind, and no one would be found. The battle was over. It was won, and Zalith and his people would never have to suffer again.

The vampire folded his wings against his back, picked up Adellum's lifeless body and threw it forward, watching it tumble onto the battlefield. It deserved to join its fallen followers, and what a fitting end for something so foolish.

Alucard held out his hand—he felt regret in relinquishing this power; how he loved it so…to possess his wings, to be what he really was. But…it just wasn't *him*. And he'd rather not become his true self through stolen power. Everything he had, he'd earned, and he'd not have it any other way.

The white, shimmering Numen power started to seep from his body, but he didn't let it return to Adellum. Alucard didn't want to be around when the Numen woke up. He lifted his hand to face the sky, and Adellum's power slowly seeped into the air. It'd be a few hours before it would all return to the Numen's body—the vessel that allowed Adellum to exist in this world. And that was plenty of time for Alucard to get back, to help Zalith and his people get to Nefastus, and to bask in their victory.

He snapped out of his thoughts, keeping his focus on his task; it didn't take him long to dispose of Adellum's ethos—such…ugly ethos. He felt a whole lot of relief once it left his body; he felt lighter, free as though a huge burden had left his soul. Was that what it felt like to be a fully-fledged Numen? A constant weight on their shoulders because of their infinite power?

With a roll of his eyes, he lowered his hand, stepped back, and kicked back into the portal, leaving Adellum in the field that had become—in a sense—its grave.

Alucard didn't waste time once he was back within the void space. He set his hell-fiery eyes on Colt, morphed into vermillion smoke, and hurried over to him. Now, all he had to do was get back to Aegisguard, and all of this would be over.

He hoped.

# Chapter Twenty-Five

— ≷ ✝ ≷ —

## Safe...?

| **Zalith** |

Zalith remained on his knees, his gaze fixed on the portal's swirling vortex. With each passing moment, his dread intensified, a relentless tide that threatened to engulf him. His heart hammered in his chest, the weight of uncertainty pressing down on him like a suffocating blanket. Panic clawed at the edges of his consciousness, etching lines of worry onto his brow. What was Alucard enduring within that enigmatic void? Was his vampire okay, or had the Light taken him? The uncertainty gnawed at him, leaving him adrift in a sea of doubt. Was this even reality, or merely a twisted illusion? The question lingered, haunting him with its elusive answer.

He stared into the dark portal while the rain trickled down his face, dripping in through a small crack in the rock above him. What if something was happening? He knew there was a void space between the portal and Eltaria; he knew that was where his vampire must have gone to retrieve Colt—but...Zalith had never seen it. He didn't know what the void space might do to someone—to *Alucard*. His angst gripped him as he clasped the crimson cape around his shoulders. Alucard could lose his focus in there; he could become lost within the void forever. What if something grabbed him? What if...the Light was with him? What if it had left the confines of Eltaria?

The demon scowled, staring, waiting, trying to remain where he was. Sure, he could phase over to Eltaria in case that was where Alucard ended up, but what if he wasn't there? The Light could be waiting on the other side—this could be a trap, a façade. But...he couldn't just sit there and dread what might be happening to the man he loved. He could use his imprint to see what Alucard might be feeling or doing...but that could be a trap, too. If this was another fake life, he was sure that his enemy would love to know that he possessed such a connection to Alucard, and he'd not jeopardise himself or his vampire like that.

But where was he? Why wasn't he back yet? Each second passed, each moment lingered...but...in the silence, Zalith expected to hear that infernal ticking; however, there was nothing. What if…this *was* real? But that could be another trick, a way to make him believe that this was reality—that Alucard wasn't going to die before his eyes once again.

"Are you okay?" Orin then asked, appearing beside him.

For a moment, Zalith took his eyes off the portal to look up at him…but he then set his gaze back on the darkness within the gateway. He wanted to see Alucard come through—to see his vampire come back to him. The confused, panicking people around him didn't matter right now. He just wanted to see Alucard.

He waited…and waited…and waited…and as soon as he saw the tip of a boot emerge from the darkness, he climbed to his feet. Relief started to drown out his dread, and the moment Alucard stepped out of the portal, he was left with nothing but utter relief—it warped his face, his heart, and his body. He hurried through the crowd, keeping his eyes on his vampire, who handed Colt to Idina. Instantly, he threw himself at Alucard and tightly wrapped his arms around him—he'd never let him go again, whether this was real or not. He'd not let Alucard out of his sight.

The vampire moved his arms around Zalith, too, holding him just as tightly as the demon pressed his face into Alucard's neck. His fear, however, quickly increased when he set his eyes on the darkness inside the gateway. Was something going to come out and grab Alucard again? He held onto him a little tighter, waiting for whatever was going to happen.

Something *was* going to happen…wasn't it? Just as it had every time before.

Scowling, he nuzzled the vampire's neck, his familiar, alleviating scent calming him a little.

Alucard stood there in his embrace; Zalith could feel the vampire's tense body relaxing, and as Alucard tightened his grip, he pressed his face into Zalith's neck. The demon tried to settle his own trembling body, but he couldn't. He was so overwhelmed with fear and relief and worry and agitation—it was so much at once.

And Alucard evidently noticed.

The vampire frowned as he leaned back so that he could see Zalith's face. "Are you okay?" he asked, staring into the demon's eyes as he stared back.

Zalith didn't want to answer, nor did he want to think about it. He wasn't okay, but he didn't want to speak of it. He just wanted to rest—to leave this island…and to make sure Alucard wasn't taken from him again. So, he shrugged in response and dragged his hand down Alucard's arm to grip his hand. "Let's go."

With a nod from Alucard, Zalith fell into step behind him, his gaze drawn to the silhouette of the galleon looming on the horizon. In the distance, small rowing boats bobbed steadily toward the island, ready to ferry him and his people away.

Zalith stared at his vampire when they stopped by the edge of the island, waiting for the boats to arrive. He felt so paranoid, confused, and worried…. What was going to happen? When? He looked over his shoulder, eyeing every person who made it out, watching as they grouped up behind him and Alucard. Would another one of them kill him? Would they turn heel like Addison? Or…was something going to happen with the water? He looked down at the black sea below. Would something come out and take Alucard from him? Would the island suddenly crack and throw everyone into the water? His heart ached with turmoil as he looked at Alucard, down at the water, and back at the vampire.

"Zhey vill take us to my ship," the vampire said, glancing back at Zalith's nervous people. Then, the vampire looked at Zalith and frowned in concern. "Vhat?" he asked, moving a little closer to him as the demon tightened his grip on Alucard's hand.

Zalith shook his head slightly but then frowned in worry. "Are you okay?"

The vampire nodded. "I'm vine, Zaliv," he answered quietly. "Ve're both vine."

With a slight nod and weak smile, Zalith set his eyes back on the horizon.

The small boats soon arrived, and everyone started to board. Zalith sat with Alucard, staring, waiting for whatever might come for his vampire next. Would something come out of the water and grab him? Would the boat suddenly sink? Was Alucard going to drown this time? He wasn't sure, and he'd not let his guard down.

He sat at the helm of the boat, searching everything before him, ready for whatever might happen. Something *was* coming, wasn't it? This wasn't real…just as it had been every time before, the world he was sitting in was false—and just as before, something would eventually come and take his vampire from him.

As sharp thorns of worry and dismay ensnared his heart, he glanced at Alucard. The vampire shuffled closer to him and rested his head on his shoulder, holding him as he sat there under the suffocating weight of dread. Each time the boat jolted against the waves, his heart beat a little faster, his body shuddering in trepidation—he almost jumped to his feet every time, ready to attack, ready to protect Alucard. But nothing came.

It wasn't long until the rowing boats were lifted up onto the galleon deck, and everyone climbed out.

"Vollow 'im," Alucard instructed Zalith's people as he waved his hand in the direction of the ship's captain. He then took hold of the demon's hand and started leading him towards the cabin.

Zalith followed, not uttering a word as he continued waiting in dread for whatever was inevitably going to happen. Would they start sailing only for something to attack the ship? Was a creature going to burst up out of the water and grab hold of Alucard? Was something going to attack the ship from above…or below? What was going to happen?

He kept hold of Alucard's hand as they stepped into the cabin. Alucard shut the door behind them and led the way over to the bed, and then he made the demon sit down.

Alucard placed his hand on Zalith's shoulder, gripping his cape. "Let me take zhis," he said, but Zalith quickly lifted his hand and placed it over Alucard's.

For a moment, the demon felt hesitant, but Alucard was only trying to help, so he let go of the vampire's hand, staring up at him as he took his cape from over his shoulders.

The vampire carefully placed it on the nearest table and then stared down at him for a moment. "I should go and make sure everyvone is on board. I'll be vight back—"

But Zalith desperately snatched Alucard's hand before he could back off. "No," he insisted fearfully, but as Alucard stared down at him in confusion, he stood up. "I'm coming with you," he said firmly.

The vampire, however, frowned in hesitation and made him sit back down. "You need to vest. Your vounds 'aven't 'ealed properly yet."

"I'll be fine," Zalith said, shaking his head. "I just…don't want to be without you right now."

As Zalith leaned forward and rested his head against the vampire's stomach, Alucard looked down at him and placed his hand on the back of the demon's head. "I von't leave."

Zalith felt bad; he knew that he was being clingy, but what if something happened to Alucard once he left the room? He didn't want to let him out of his sight. "Thank you," he said, tightening the grip he had on Alucard's coat. He didn't care whether this was reality or not; he didn't want to let his vampire go.

"Is vine," Alucard said softly. "Ve can vest until ve get back."

With the weight of his turmoil pressing down upon him like an unrelenting storm, Zalith offered a faint nod. Alucard assisted him in shedding his garments before tucking him into bed and crawling in beside him. As he reclined, Zalith held onto Alucard's hand tightly, their eyes locked in a silent exchange of understanding. Despite their closeness, the demon's worry refused to dissipate. He remained vigilant, unwilling to lower his guard.

He frowned, moving a little closer to Alucard. His eyes slowly drifted to the vampire's hand, as did his fingers. He dragged them over the faint creases on the palm of Alucard's hand, his angst beginning to slowly settle the longer he lay there in silence. The ship started moving, and for a moment, he felt his heart beat a little faster, but nothing happened. The ship sailed, and he and Alucard rested together.

Maybe…maybe this *was* real…. *Was* it? He had no idea, and as he started to think about it again, his anxiety began to outweigh the relief he felt while lying next to Alucard. He took his sights off the vampire's hand and stared into his hell-fiery eyes. He loved Alucard so much and having to see him die so many times…. It left a pain in his heart— a pain he couldn't explain. He didn't want to see it happen again; he *wouldn't* let it happen again.

The onslaught of confusion, turmoil, and anguish left Zalith reeling. Why was he repeatedly subjected to the torment of witnessing Alucard's demise? Each occurrence carved a deeper wound into his psyche, threatening to unravel his sanity with every passing moment. The relentless cycle of dread weighed heavily upon him, intensifying his fears of what might transpire next. Would this be the moment when Alucard was torn away from him yet again? With a furrowed brow, Zalith's gaze drifted to Alucard's hand, seeking solace and reassurance amidst the uncertainty. But as he pondered the authenticity of their reality, a nagging doubt crept in: was this world merely another illusion, woven by the insidious presence lurking within his mind?

He set his eyes on Alucard again. Was it real? Was... *he* real? Alucard... everything about him was right. His face, his eyes, his smell, and even his aura. No illusion could replicate everything so well, could it? But... this Light that the humans manifested was always changing and getting stronger. What if it was strong enough to make all of this seem so real? Zalith wasn't sure, and he might never be sure. But what he *was* sure about was that he wasn't going to let Alucard out of his sight... no matter what. He'd stay with him, and he'd stop whatever might happen to him next.

| Alucard |

They lay in silence for a few hours. Alucard dozed off a couple of times, but he kept himself from falling asleep entirely.

When the ship jolted, he opened his eyes and stared at Zalith. His worry hadn't faded at all. He'd seen how traumatized Zalith looked back in Eltaria, on the island, and even now. Alucard had never seen him in such a state before. He wasn't like himself at all. The vampire didn't really know what to do for him, but he would try his best to ensure that he helped Zalith through this.

What mattered right now was that they were *both* alive, Adellum wouldn't dare to come after Zalith again—even if he could—and they had also managed to find another traitor among Zalith's people. Addison. He was dead, though, so that was another thing that Zalith wouldn't have to deal with. Zalith's people were safe, too. All that was left to do was to get them back to Nefastus.

Right now, though... despite lying down, Zalith didn't look calm or relaxed. He looked tense, he *felt* tense, and Alucard had no idea what to do for him except be there with him. He knew Adellum had done something to him... something to make him look as though he had seen death—could that be what it was? Could Adellum have corrupted Zalith's mind by making him see someone die? Had... he made Zalith see himself die? Or... maybe Adellum had made Zalith watch *him* die. He knew how a Numen's mind worked, and most of them—especially Damien—thought it was fun to show people their loved ones dying. What if that was the thing causing Zalith to look so daunted?

His worried expression thickened as he placed his hand on the side of Zalith's neck. The demon's wounds still hadn't fully healed, and he wasn't going to get or feel any better if he didn't get some rest. As much as Alucard wanted to help him, he knew they'd both have an easier time helping Zalith get better if he got some sleep.

As he stared into Zalith's eyes, he did his best to look calm. "You'll 'eal vaster if you sleep. Ve can sleep—"

"I can't," Zalith responded sullenly.

The vampire frowned. "Vhy?"

"What if you die again?" Zalith muttered, but it was as though his question wasn't directed at Alucard—not entirely. His eyes flickered from Alucard for half a moment, down to the sheets, and then back to him.

"Vhat?" Alucard asked, but Zalith's answer pretty much confirmed his suspicions. Adellum must have made the demon watch him die…but…only once? No…seeing him die once couldn't unsettle Zalith *this* much…could it? He frowned again, shaking his head a little. "Vhat are you talking about? I'm not dead. I'm vight 'ere—I vill alvays be vight 'ere," he insisted softly.

The demon, however, shook his head and hid his face against the side of the pillow.

"Zaliv?" Alucard insisted, his worry worsening.

Still hiding his face, the demon scowled in distress. "You keep dying. I don't want you to die anymore," he cried painfully.

Staring at him, Alucard frowned in dismay. Evidently, Adellum *had* made Zalith watch him die over and over—so many times that it had Zalith in this terrorized way, and it hurt so much to see him like this. Despite them leaving Eltaria, Zalith hadn't gotten any better. His aura was still strange, his voice, his actions—there was something so very wrong with him, and it felt like a dagger had been plunged through Alucard's chest. He didn't know what to do or what to say; all he could really think to do was try and convince Zalith that this wasn't another of Adellum's fantasies and that he nor Zalith were going to die. They were safe. Adellum was gone. And they could now be together without having to worry about anyone else.

He shuffled closer, resting his forehead against Zalith's as he lay beside him. "I'm vight 'ere," he said quietly, closing his eyes as he moved his hand to the side of Zalith's face. "Zamien couldn't take me vrom you, Liliv couldn't take me vrom you, and zhis Light vill not take me vrom you, eizer. I can only imagine vhat 'e showed you, but 'e is gone, and you and I are veally 'ere now. Ve are safe, and ve vill be 'ome soon. You zon't 'ave to vorry about me, your people, or zhat Light anymore. All of zhat is over."

Zalith stared at him, fiddling with a few strands of the vampire's crimson hair. But he sighed quietly, the look of distress on his face thickening. It was obvious that he didn't want to talk about it. Alucard could only hope that what he said would get through to him.

The vampire exhaled slightly, staring into the demon's dark, tormented eyes. "Sleep vith me now," he pleaded. "Ve both need to vest." He knew Zalith wasn't going to agree, so he'd already moved his index and middle fingers to the centre of the demon's head. "Sleep," he whispered. Zalith's eyes slowly yielded, and the demon fell into what Alucard hoped to be a deep, relaxing sleep.

Alucard then found himself enveloped in the unsettling silence, his gaze fixed on Zalith, his worry unabated. The limited knowledge he possessed about the demon's predicament gnawed at him, casting a shadow of unease over his thoughts. He could only hope for Zalith's well-being, uncertain of the extent of the visions Adellum had subjected him to. Whatever they entailed, they clearly haunted Zalith, rendering sleep a daunting prospect. While Alucard couldn't comprehend the depths of Zalith's torment, he understood fear all too well. Determined to offer support, he resolved to remain by Zalith's side, reassuring him of their safety as often as needed and steadfastly demonstrating his unwavering presence.

He moved his arm around Zalith, holding him tightly as he closed his eyes. The journey home wouldn't be too long, but he'd not pass up on time to rest with Zalith. So, as the ship slowly glided along the water, Alucard allowed himself to fall into a light sleep.

# Chapter Twenty-Six

## Recover

**| Alucard |**

Alucard woke to a quiet knock on the door. He sat up, took a moment to wake a little, and then frowned. "Vhat?" he called irritably.

The door opened, and the captain leaned in. "We've just docked, sir."

"Vight, vank you," he mumbled, waving his hand in dismissal as he laid back down.

Once the captain left, the vampire took a few moments to stare at Zalith. He didn't want to wake him, but they had to get home. The moons were climbing higher and higher into the sky as the night got later, and Alucard was sure that they'd both just go back to bed once they got back to their house.

With a hesitant look on his face, he placed his hand on the side of Zalith's face. "Zaliv?" he asked quietly.

Slowly, a frown appeared on Zalith's face, and as he opened his eyes to stare at Alucard, they seemed to flood with dread and confusion almost instantly. He sat up, looking around as if he had no idea where he was—

Alucard sat beside him, keeping his hand on the side of his neck. "Zaliv," he said calmly. "Is okay. Ve're in Nevastus."

The demon looked at him, breathing frantically, the panic in his eyes slowly fading the longer he gazed at the vampire. But then he frowned in confoundment.

"You vere asleep…vor only a vew hours," the vampire explained.

Zalith nodded stiffly. "Okay."

"Your people can live on my ship vor now," he said, sure that Zalith would need at least a few days' rest before getting to work on assigning his people homes and jobs. "Is big ship—a 'undred people could live on 'ere vor months. Zhey vill be safe, and you can vest until you're veady to velocate zhem."

A slight smile of appreciation flickered across Zalith's dread-smothered face. "Thank you, baby."

Hearing him call him baby filled Alucard with happiness and relief. At least Zalith wasn't so utterly traumatized that he was *nothing* like himself. He was still Zalith—the vampire was sure he just needed time to heal and recuperate.

He smiled, slowly dragging his hand down from Zalith's neck, over his shoulder, and to the blanket. "Ve can 'ead 'ome now."

The demon nodded slightly. "Okay."

Alucard shuffled to the end of the bed, took one of his shirts from the cabinet, and then handed it to Zalith. "Zhis vone is cleaner," he said, glancing down at Zalith's bloody shirt, which lay on the floor. He waited for the demon to get dressed, and once he was ready, Alucard grabbed his cape, pulled it on over his shoulders, and led the way out.

They stepped onto the deck together; the moment Idina saw them emerge from the cabin, she rushed over and stopped in front of them.

She looked at Zalith. "Are you okay?"

Zalith shrugged in response.

Alucard was convinced that Zalith wasn't okay, but he didn't want to panic the demon's people. "'E's vine. 'E just needs vest."

Idina nodded, taking her eyes off the demon to look at Alucard. "What's the plan now that we've docked? Will you be taking us to the place Zalith mentioned?"

"No," Alucard answered. "Ve all need a vew days to vest. You can all live 'ere on my ship vor now. Zhere are more zhan enough vooms—zhere's a bar, too," he said, glancing over at two of the werewolves who were eyeing a tavern not too far from the docks. "Keep all your people on zhis ship until Zaliv or I come to escort you elsevhere. I vill send a subordinate of mine tomorrow to keep an eye on you. As vor now, if you need anyving zhat isn't alveady on board, ask vone of zhe crew. Zhey vill go to zhe city and get," he explained.

With relief on her face, Idina nodded. But her eyes then shifted to the sky. "I'm not entirely sure how the phases of the moon work here, but… if we were back in Eltaria, the next full moon would be in three days," she said with concern in her voice.

"Zhe silver moon is zhe veal vone," Alucard said, "and zhe only vone vith phases. Vorks zhe same as your moon. If Zaliv is not vecovered in vree days, I vill vind somevhere vor your verevolves to safely vait out zhe moon."

"Thank you," Idina said, smiling. "If either of you needs anything, I'm ready to help—we all are."

Alucard nodded. "Just make sure no vone leaves zhe ship. Zhe people 'ere are…not very velcoming of anyvone who is not 'uman or elf."

"Of course," she said with a nod.

"Ve're leaving now."

With another nod, Idina made her way back over to where Tyrus and Orin had been waiting for her.

Alucard clutched Zalith's hand tightly in the cloak of night, their solitary figures navigating the deserted docks. Side by side, they traversed the stone piers, their destination set on the cobblestone road ahead. A carriage awaited them by a lamppost, the coachman's presence acknowledged by the extinguished cigarette and the firm grasp on the horse's reins as soon as he caught sight of them.

The vampire pulled the door open and invited Zalith to get in first. Once the demon got in and sat down, Alucard followed, sitting beside him as he shut the door.

When the carriage started moving, Alucard glanced at Zalith. The demon still looked confused, like he was dealing with denial—like he wasn't sure he was where he was. But that didn't confound Alucard. Adellum really must have messed with his mind so much that Zalith wasn't sure what was real anymore. But Alucard wasn't going to give up on him. He moved closer, guiding his left hand to Zalith's shoulder, and then rested his head on the demon's. "Are you okay?" he asked quietly.

"I'll be fine," Zalith mumbled, moving his arm around Alucard.

He would be fine, wouldn't he? It was Zalith… there had never been a thing that could stop or destroy him. He might be hurt and confused right now, but Alucard knew he'd get through it. But for now, all he could think to do was hold him and help him feel safe. Zalith's embrace always made *him* feel safe, and he could only hope that it did the same for him.

Alucard wanted to talk to him; he just wanted to hear his voice and know that he was okay—but was he? How long would he be like this? The vampire frowned and hugged him a little tighter. He loved Zalith so much and seeing him like this… knowing what he might be going through…. It hurt him that he couldn't do more. What *could* he do? What should he do? There had to be something that would help Zalith through this… right? He glanced up at him, but the look of turmoil still clung to the demon's face. Maybe he'd feel better tomorrow.

Maybe.

Holding him, Alucard closed his eyes and did his best to relax for the rest of the journey home, hoping Zalith might do the same.

The carriage soon eased to a halt, and they reached the familiar comforts of home. Alucard swung open the door, gesturing for Zalith to step out first into the welcoming embrace of the gardens. Hand in hand once more, they made their way towards the front door, ready to leave the night's journey behind them.

But just as they crossed the threshold, Varana's startled gasp shattered the silence, her worried eyes searching Zalith's form. Alucard watched her approach, her hands outstretched in concern. However, as she moved closer to touch Zalith's face, the demon recoiled with a defensive snarl, causing her to halt mid-step.

"W-what happened to you?!" she exclaimed, horrified.

But Zalith didn't seem to want to talk to her. He scowled, refusing to even look at the woman.

The moment she realized that he wasn't going to answer, she set her hostile gaze on Alucard. "What did you do to him?!" she growled.

Alucard wasn't surprised that she'd blame him, but he wasn't in the mood for her right now. He snarled in aggravation and snapped, "I did noving. I'm trying to 'elp 'im."

Varana glowered, slowly taking her eyes off Alucard to look at Zalith again. "Z? What happened?"

But he ignored her.

Alucard was sure that the conversation was over and started leading the way towards the stairs—and Zalith followed, leaving Varana standing in the middle of the hall with a confused, irritated scowl on her face.

"Hello?!" she called, but when she *finally* worked out that no one was going to answer, she shrieked, stropped, and stormed off down the hall.

Alucard sighed softly, knowing that after such an eventful day, rest was the only sensible option. He guided Zalith up the stairs to their bedroom, shutting the door behind them with a gentle click. Then, he assisted Zalith in undressing, followed suit, and then slipped under the covers beside him.

For a short while, they lay there in silence. Alucard wanted to lay on his side to avoid his scars aching against the sheets, but he chose to rest on his back so that Zalith could nuzzle his neck and hold his arm around him. Alucard didn't know what else to do or whether he should say anything to try and comfort Zalith; all he could seem to think about was how worried he felt—how much it hurt to know that Zalith was struggling.

He glanced down at what he could see of him. Maybe it was better to let Zalith rest until tomorrow—maybe a night of sleep would help him feel a little better. Alucard was sure that the demon probably wouldn't let himself sleep, so he was more than likely going to have to help him again.

"Zaliv?" he asked quietly.

The demon uttered a sound of acknowledgement. But then, he sighed and sat up—

Alucard also sat up, placing his hand on Zalith's shoulder. "You need to sleep."

Zalith gazed at him and shook his head as a sullen expression appeared on his face. "I can't."

Alucard frowned in sorrow. He still didn't know what to say or do; all he knew was that Zalith needed to rest. If he had to fool him into doing so, then he would. "Okay," he said quietly, pulling Zalith so that he'd lie down. "Ve can just lay 'ere," he mumbled, moving his arm around Zalith as they both lay on their sides, facing one another. "I'll stay vith you."

"Okay," the demon said quietly, staring into Alucard's eyes once more.

The vampire placed his hand on the side of Zalith's face. "I love you," he mumbled, trying his best to ignore his sudden nervousness.

Something flickered through Zalith's eyes, but Alucard wasn't sure what it was. Hope? Relief? Maybe both.

The demon moved his hand to the side of Alucard's neck and leaned a little closer, placing a single kiss on his lips. "I love you, too."

Regret filled Alucard's heart; he didn't like having to do this, but there was no other way Zalith would get the rest he needed. With a smile, he struggled to hold back the tears that had so suddenly begun forming in his eyes; he moved his index and middle fingers to the centre of Zalith's forehead and whispered, "Sleep," and surely enough, the demon's eyes closed, and Zalith drifted off to sleep.

Guilt warped every inch of Alucard's being. Guilt and pain. But what more could he do now? Nothing. He had to let Zalith sleep and at least try to get some more rest himself. There was no telling what tomorrow might hold for them both, and he wanted to do whatever he could to try and help Zalith through what he was dealing with.

For a few moments, he stared at the demon's tired face and sighed quietly. Maybe tomorrow things would be better for everyone. The day had been long, harsh, and full of pain, anger, and terror. Sleep was one of many things they both sorely needed.

Alucard closed his eyes, keeping his arm around Zalith, holding him tightly. Tomorrow…they'd both continue their road to recovery and maybe Zalith wouldn't feel so…strange.

As sleep began to claim him, Alucard's final conscious thought, as it often was, was of Zalith—his steadfast mate, his unwavering support. With a silent vow, he pledged to do whatever it took to help Zalith find his way back to his true self, no matter the obstacles they faced.

# Chapter Twenty-Seven

— ⸲ ✝ ⸱ —

## Alucard's Subordinate

| **Varana** |

As she stared into her vanity mirror, Varana glowered frustratedly. Zalith had been acting differently lately, but tonight, he'd been a complete asshole. Why the hell did he look like he'd been through hell? Why did he snarl at her like that? She didn't do anything; she just wanted to know what was wrong with him.

She pouted sadly, brushing her hair. He'd pushed her away, and it was getting worse with every day. No matter how many times she tried to talk to him, he acted like she didn't exist, and she was beginning to feel like maybe she didn't. Ever since he started seeing Alucard...*him*...he'd changed. He wasn't the same, and she didn't like it at all. But was there anything she could do to stop what she felt was the imminent end to their friendship?

The thought made her heart hurt. She didn't want to lose Zalith—she *couldn't* lose Zalith. But she was powerless, wasn't she? She knew that he wouldn't listen to her if she suggested that Alucard was coming between them. He'd just tell her to stop being dramatic.

She wasn't being dramatic, was she? She just wanted her friend back.

A knock suddenly came at her door.

With an irritated sigh, she called, "What?!"

The door opened, and Edwin peeked in. "Sorry, milady, but someone is asking for you. A man named Luther."

Varana frowned. It took her a moment to recall the name. She remembered that Luther was one of Alucard's subordinates. What could he possibly want...and at this hour? She was admittedly a little curious. "Send him up," she replied.

Edwin nodded and left her room, closing the door behind him.

She finished brushing her hair and put some of her red lipstick on. Then, when her door knocked again, she called, "Come in," and Alucard's long-haired subordinate stepped into her room.

"Hey," Luther said with a smile. "Sorry it's so late, but I thought I'd see if you were available to have dinner or something."

Varana smiled sweetly at him as she stood up. "Oh, how kind of you to ask. Well, if you don't mind dining in, I'd be delighted."

"Sure," he said with a nod.

The fact that he'd come over himself made Varana's plan to seduce him a little easier; she didn't have to put in the effort of trying to get him to go home with her—they were already there. But she was tired and frustrated, and she wasn't really hungry, either. Maybe she could skip the dinner part. "Or," she said as she slowly strutted towards him, "we could forget dinner and just skip to what you *really* came here for."

Luther laughed nervously. "Uh…what…did I come here for?"

She giggled and stroked her hand over his shoulder. "Don't play hard to get with me," she warned him with a sweet but venomous smile. "I know what everybody wants."

The man smirked and placed his hands on her hips as she pressed her body against his. "I'll admit, I'm a tad surprised. I thought I'd have to wine and dine you first."

Varana giggled again and caressed the side of his face. "Usually, I'd prefer a man to pine, but…" she paused and grasped his crotch—he was already hard; what a pathetic little man. "I think I can make an exception for someone as handsome as you." He wasn't handsome, but stroking his ego would get her what she wanted, wouldn't it?

A creepy grin stretched across Luther's pale face. His hands traversed her curved body, and when he guided his palm up under her nightgown, she hummed quietly and rested her forehead against his shoulder. He slipped his hand into her underwear, and when his fingertip met her clit, Varana's quiet hums grew louder and thicker with anticipation.

"You're so fucking wet already," Luther breathed, slipping two of his fingers inside her.

Varana moaned softly, squeezing the man's dick. "Don't make me wait," she pleaded.

Luther hastily unbuttoned and pulled Varana's nightgown off. He gripped her bare waist, kissing her wetly—and rather disgustingly—as he guided her back towards her bed. As she lay down, she watched him undress; his body wasn't much to look at, though. He was skinny and had barely any muscle on his frame, and his dick wasn't very impressive, either—below average. But she'd put up with it. She wanted to draw him deeper into her web, and she wasn't going to lie, if this man could make her orgasm, she might just feel a little less frustrated tonight.

She smiled at him when he crawled over her, and she exaggerated a pleased moan when he eased his dick inside her. He started thrusting, and his moans were like claws on a chalkboard, scraping against her eardrums, but she did her best to ignore the disgust and sighed pleasurably—that was what he wanted, right? To hear her moan, to hear her react as though he was the best lay she'd ever had. But he wasn't. She couldn't even feel him inside her. How disappointing.

Varana endured it, though, humming and groaning, dragging her hands down his back and her legs up his. When he *finally* climaxed, he sounded like a bleating sheep mixed with a dying animal. At least he was respectful enough to pull out.

"Fucking hell," Luther breathed, staring down at her.

She smiled as best she could but didn't know what to say. She grabbed some tissues from the box on her nightstand and handed them to him. "Be a darling and clean up."

Luther used the tissues to clean his cum off her skin, but Varana felt as if even a shower wouldn't be enough to make her feel completely void of it.

The man then laid down beside her with a long, loud sigh.

She glanced at him and seeing that he looked utterly pleased with himself made her feel more frustrated than she had been before he showed up. "How long have you known Alucard?" she asked. Now that he'd gotten what he wanted, she wasn't going to wait to ask her questions.

"Uh…" he drawled. "A few hundred years. He, Attila and I used to work together a lot of the time." He looked at her. "How long have you known Zalith?"

Varana sighed sadly at the mention of his name. "Nearly all my life."

"So, you're close, then?"

"As close as close can be without all the kissing and sex," she grumbled.

Luther frowned and asked, "I guess you've lived through all his other relationships, then."

"Unfortunately."

He leaned up on his arm to look down at her. "Why do you say that?"

She glanced at him and rolled her eyes. "He gets through people like I get through outfits. A new one for every occasion." But then she held her hand to her mouth; guilt and hesitation started consuming her. She didn't like talking shit about Zalith, nor did she want to expose his private life to someone neither of them knew—to anyone, for that matter. "Has Alucard dated anyone before him?" she questioned, trying to divert the subject.

"No," Luther muttered—he sounded a little upset by that fact. "He was never the dating type until Zalith showed up."

"Not surprising," she grumbled. Who'd want to date a miserable little vampire?

"How long do Zalith's relationships usually last?"

Varana frowned and glared at him. "Why are you so interested in them?"

He shrugged. "Just curious—we all are, his vampires. He's never been romantically involved with anyone before and some of us are a little worried that his priorities are shifting."

She scoffed and stared up at the ceiling. She wondered the same thing about Zalith.

"So?"

Varana sighed irritably. "I don't know. Some last days, some last weeks, others can last months or even a few years on or off. It depends on the person. Your little red-haired leader has been with him longer than anyone else, though—at least the longest period without breaking up, that is."

"You think they're gonna break up?"

"It's inevitable," she said confidently. They *had* to break up soon, right? That was Zalith's pattern, that was how he worked. His little relationship with Alucard wouldn't last much longer, would it?

She exhaled deeply and shook her head. She didn't want to lay there and think about Zalith and Alucard; she wanted to forget about them for a while. Maybe Luther would be able to make her cum if she gave him another chance.

"Fuck me again," she commanded.

Luther looked nervous. "Uh…right this second?"

"Right this second. Or are you unable to—"

"No, I got it," he mumbled, and then he leaned in to kiss her.

She turned her head to the side. "I don't want to kiss."

"Okay…" he drawled unsurely, and then he kissed his way down her body and dragged his tongue over her clit.

Varana sighed loudly and closed her eyes, trying to focus on Luther and forget about everything else for a while. She didn't know what happened to Zalith tonight, and she was convinced that she might never find out. He'd pushed her away; he was giving all of his time to Alucard, and she wondered how long it would be until he forgot her entirely.

ARC TWO
— † —
THE SLOW
DESCENT INTO
DEREALIZATION

# Chapter Twenty-Eight

— ⸲ † ⸱ —

## Disarray

| **Zalith** |

*S*omething roused Zalith from an uneasy slumber, and a chill ran through his body as if the very air held a foreboding secret. His eyes snapped open to an empty space beside him, where Alucard should have been. Panic clawed at his chest, its icy fingers tightening with each passing moment. Where had his vampire disappeared to?

*The room seemed to close in around him, shadows deepening into menacing shapes. Zalith's gaze darted around, seeking any sign of his missing mate. But it was the unnatural mist creeping along the floor that sent shivers down his spine, its ethereal presence whispering of unseen dangers. Without Alucard's reassuring presence, the darkness felt suffocating, suffused with an eerie silence that echoed his growing dread.*

*Zalith hurriedly climbed out of bed and slipped into his trousers, a sense of urgency propelling his movements. With each step, the darkness seemed to press closer, an oppressive weight on his shoulders. He flung open the door, stepping into the dimly lit hallway, where shadows danced like spectres in the gloom. The faint glow at the end of the corridor offered little solace, its feeble illumination casting long, eerie streaks of gloom along the walls. Despite the distant light, panic still clutched at Zalith's heart as he hastened towards Varana's room, his every footfall echoing in the empty silence of the hall.*

*His hand trembled as he pushed open Varana's door, the creak of the hinges reverberating in the tense silence. But what he found inside was a scene straight from his worst nightmares: Varana's room bathed in blood, her lifeless form sprawled amidst the crimson tide. The thick, swirling fog seemed to clutch at her, hastening the decay of her once vibrant form. Horror etched deep lines into Zalith's face as he stood frozen in the doorway, disbelief and anguish warring within him.*

*The horror intensified when he thought about Alucard. What if the same had happened to him?*

*With fear on his face and in his frantic breaths, he hurried back across the hall and down the stairs. The main hall was as murky as the floor above, but a bitter coldness lingered in the silent air, so cold that it made even Zalith shiver.*

*He sharply turned his head, a muffled shuffle coming from Alucard's office. Without hesitation, he raced over, pushed the door open, and hoped he'd got there in time—but he hadn't. He opened the door to see Damien drop the still, dead body of his vampire, blood smothering both Alucard's neck and the Daegelus' hand.*

*"Eladarin." Damien grinned, but his voice…. It was distorted and dreadfully familiar—the voice of Adellum.*

*Zalith had no time to evade; as the Daegelus' eyes filled with bright, blinding white light, he lunged at the demon, snarling cruelly as he reached for him—but then…*

*Darkness.*

Zalith's eyes snapped open, his heart pounding against his ribs as he sucked in a ragged breath. Panic seized him, driving him to sit up abruptly, his fingers clutching the blanket in a tight grip. His gaze darted around the dimly lit room, searching for any sign of danger lurking in the shadows. A flicker of movement caught his attention to his left, and he turned towards it, his muscles tense with dread. Yet, as his eyes met Alucard stirring in sleep, a wave of relief washed over him, dispelling the lingering fear.

However, his anxiety didn't fade.

He leaned closer to Alucard and placed his hand on his arm; he seemed perfectly fine as far as he could tell, and with that, his worry started to wither.

The vivid images lingered in Zalith's mind, haunting him with their gruesome reality. Was it all just a terrible dream? He frowned, withdrawing his hand from Alucard's arm, and settled back down beside him. Despite the doubts gnawing at him, a longing for solace tugged at his heart. With a sigh, he shifted closer to the vampire, rolling onto his left side. Wrapping his arms around him, he pressed his cheek against Alucard's, seeking refuge in the warmth of their embrace. Holding him tightly, Zalith allowed himself to be enveloped by the reassuring presence of Alucard's body against his own.

Zalith lay there for a while, staring at the wall, holding his vampire. He still didn't understand whether this was real or not—this world that he lay in. It could all be a façade…just as every other had been before. And his dream—his nightmare…did it mean something? Why had he just seen both Varana and Alucard dead? Was…he going to lose them? Was he going to start seeing them *both* die?

Varana—he wanted to go and see if she was okay, but…what if he left Alucard and came back to him gone…or worse? He frowned in distress, holding Alucard in his arms. He wasn't going to leave him. Whether this was real or not, nothing would make him leave his vampire alone ever again.

As soft birdsong filled the air, Zalith stirred, blinking his eyes open to the glow of daylight filtering through the curtains. The warm rays illuminated nearly half of the room, casting a tranquil ambience. Remaining nestled on his side, Zalith found himself still wrapped around Alucard, the vampire peacefully lost in slumber beside him.

He didn't want to move. He remained where he was, sighing quietly as he closed his eyes once more, holding Alucard in his embrace. Despite his confusion and turmoil, he felt alleviated enough to remain calm in the vampire's presence. There was nothing or no one that made Zalith feel more comfortable than Alucard, and right now, he just wanted to lay in the quiet with him. He didn't want to think about his dream or his inability to grasp reality.

But it didn't take long for Alucard to wake up, too. The vampire frowned and slowly moved his palm along the sheets and placed it on Zalith's hand.

Zalith smiled slightly in response; he felt better knowing that Alucard was awake, but he didn't say his usual morning greeting. For some reason, his motivation to use his voice had left him. All he could feel was his festering dread and the confusion as to whether this was even real or not. He didn't know what to do or what to say, so he just lay there, holding Alucard.

Alucard, however, seemed to be able to tell that he wasn't feeling so great. "Are you okay?" he asked, glancing up at him as best as he could from the corner of his eye.

*Was* he okay? The longer he lay there, the more he began to think about the dream he had last night. The sight of Varana and Alucard…. Both of them had been taken from him, and he couldn't get the thought of it nor the feeling of horror out of his head. And when he tried *not* to think about it, the thoughts intensified.

He didn't want to talk about it, nor did he want to think about it—he also didn't really want to worry Alucard with it, either. So he sighed quietly and nuzzled the side of the vampire's neck before saying, "I'm fine."

For a few moments, Alucard stayed silent, but he then turned onto his right side so that he was facing Zalith. He frowned, gazing at him. "You zon't look vine," he said, concern in his voice.

Zalith adorned a hesitant expression as he moved his hand to the side of Alucard's face. As his frown thickened, so did his confliction. He fiddled with the vampire's hair, debating whether or not he wanted to tell Alucard how he felt; should he tell him how he had no idea whether this was real or another façade? Or how he'd seen Alucard die so many times, and how he was terrified of seeing it again?

He slowly dragged his fingers down the side of Alucard's face and over his neck, and then he started dragging them over his arm in a circular motion. He didn't want to worry Alucard with his problems, but he also didn't want to *not* tell him. He loved

Alucard so much, and he didn't want to keep things from him—Alucard deserved to know. And *he* always made Alucard tell him things, even when the vampire clearly didn't want to.

But what if this *was* a façade? What if the Light still had hold of him? Telling Alucard how he felt might be telling the Light how he felt…and if this was fake—if this was a trick—he didn't want to expose his feelings, his confusion, or his terror. But…what if it wasn't? What if this was real? Alucard was entitled to know what was going on.

He slowly lowered his hand, placed it on Alucard's bicep, and stared into his sleepy, hell-fiery eyes. "I keep…seeing you die," he mumbled.

Alucard frowned slightly. "In…dreams? Or visions?"

"I don't know whether it's dreams or visions or if it's real," he said with a sigh, taking his eyes off Alucard to look down at the sheets. "I…was…or *am*…trapped in a continuous loop of some kind—it always ends with you dying and then starts over again. The same thing happened each time, but I was able to prevent what killed you the time before from killing you again the next time…and I don't know if any of that was real, or if this is real…or what's going to happen next. But this…" he said, tightening his grip on Alucard's arm, "it *feels* real, but…so did everything else that happened before now. Every time I saw you die, all of it felt so real, and I had and *still* have no idea whether this is the real world or not," he explained, his dread thickening and his frown growing— even his heart started to race a little faster as his turmoil constricted him tighter and tighter with each word he spoke.

As Zalith then set his eyes back on Alucard, the vampire also frowned. He sat up and looked down at Zalith, his frown becoming one of confusion and worry, almost as if he was trying to work out what to say.

"Vell…*zhis* is veal…. If zhis vasn't veal, vings vould veel so divverent," he assured him.

Staring up at him, Zalith slowly shook his head. But he then sat up, climbed over Alucard, and straddled his lap. As Alucard gazed nervously at him, Zalith placed one of his hands on Alucard's shoulder. "I saw Xurian, and when he touched me, it felt just like this," he insisted, lightly squeezing Alucard's shoulder. "It felt as real as anything else."

Alucard frowned again, staring into Zalith's eyes. "Vell…not everyving vill seem veal if zhis vas vake. No Numen can get everyving completely pervect in an illusion. Does anyving veel…vrong?" he asked slowly.

The demon retreated into his thoughts again. Back in Eltaria, the situations he found himself in had been wrong…. However, right now, everything seemed right. Nothing was out of place, and nothing strange was happening…he just couldn't stop worrying that it might not be real. *He* still felt terrified; Alucard could be taken at any moment, and he could wake up right back in Eltaria again. He couldn't stop worrying about that.

He looked at Alucard with a distressed frown. "I do. *I* feel wrong."

"Vhat…veels vrong about you?"

Zalith wasn't entirely sure, and he knew that, with time, he'd figure himself out and get over it. He shrugged, sighed, and moved from Alucard's lap. He sat beside him and rested his head on the vampire's shoulder. "I just need time," he mumbled.

Alucard frowned in confliction as he looked down at him. "I vant to 'elp you vhrough zhis," he said, insistency in his voice. "So tell me vhy you veel vrong."

The demon sighed again and slowly shook his head before glancing at him. "The Light…it just…took something from me. I *never* doubt my mind like this, and I'm never afraid like this, either. It's made me so paranoid. Last night, I dreamt that you and Varana were killed, and there wasn't a thing I could do about it. I know that it was just a dream—and I know that you're safe and alive right here—but I can't help but worry that Varana might actually be dead like she was in my dream," he explained, distressed.

Alucard took hold of Zalith's hand and squeezed it lightly. "Ve can go check on 'er," he suggested, preparing to get out of bed.

But Zalith stopped him from pulling the cover off and shook his head. "I don't want to give in to the paranoia."

"Is better to go and see if she's okay vather zhan sit 'ere and vorry about, no? Is vine to be avraid vor a vhile, especially avter vhat 'appened."

Zalith shrugged lightly. "I'm just glad you're here with me—that's all I need," he said quietly, squeezing Alucard's hand. "It was just a dream, and I want to treat it as such."

Alucard nodded and rested the side of his head on Zalith's head. "I vill alvays be 'ere vor you if you need anyving. I'm not going anyvhere. No vone and noving vill take me vrom you, I promise."

The demon smiled as best he could through his dismay. "I love you, Alucard."

"I love you, too," Alucard mumbled, but there was despondency in his voice.

Noticing the sadness, Zalith frowned and glanced up at him. "What's wrong?"

"Noving," Alucard mumbled. "I'm vine. I just vish I could do more to 'elp you."

Zalith turned his head so that he could nuzzle the vampire's neck. "You do so much for me, Alucard. Just you being here is enough." He placed a single, soft kiss on the vampire's skin. But he didn't want to sit there and let his thoughts continue eating away at him, nor did he want to talk about it anymore. He needed to distract himself, and he knew exactly how to do that. "Do you want to join me for a shower?" he asked, lightly dragging his fingers up Alucard's arm and over his chest.

Alucard responded with a nod. "Ve can do zhat."

With a smile on his face, Zalith climbed out of bed, pulling Alucard with him. Then, they made their way into the bathroom, where Zalith hoped he'd be able to escape his paranoid thoughts for a while.

# Chapter Nine

—⟨✝⟩—

## Perturbation

**| Zalith |**

Zalith took Alucard into the bathroom. Once they got into the shower, Alucard switched the warm water on, and they both stood under it for a few moments before Zalith grabbed one of the many bottles of soap. He poured some onto his hand and smiled as he offered the bottle to Alucard. The vampire, who looked almost as if he wanted to go back to sleep, took it from him and smiled slightly in thanks.

As Zalith washed the dried blood from his skin, he found himself worrying about *why* Alucard looked tired; he'd been through so much yesterday, and he probably needed to feed. The demon suspected that the blood Alucard took from him on the island last night wasn't enough and that he needed more. He didn't want Alucard to feel sluggish or tired because he hadn't fully recovered yet, so he'd make sure the vampire got what he needed.

First, however, he just wanted to kiss the man he loved. So once Alucard finished cleaning the soap from his hair, Zalith moved closer and smiled at him. The vampire frowned shyly as he looked away from him and instead set his gaze on the floor. Zalith dragged his fingers through Alucard's crimson hair and placed his free hand on the vampire's waist. As he moved his hand from Alucard's hair and to his chin, he made the vampire look at him so he could kiss him.

The demon pressed his lips against Alucard's, resting his body against the vampire's as his back hit the wall. He kissed him once, twice, and a third time as his smile grew wider. All his turmoil and dread seemed to slowly wither away the longer he spent with his vampire, and he couldn't find the words needed to express how thankful he was to Alucard. He kissed him again, and the vampire moved his hand to the back of Zalith's head as he kissed him back. A few moments later, though, the demon rested his forehead against Alucard's and let his smile fade.

"Do you want blood?" he asked, not forgetting Alucard's evident fatigue.

For a few moments, Alucard stared at him as if he was pondering. However, a look of hesitation soon appeared on his face. "I zon't vant to take any more vrom you."

Zalith smiled slightly as he placed his hand on the side of Alucard's neck. "I'll be fine. I just want you to feel better."

As the vampire's initial hesitation began to wane, Zalith sensed the need for gentle encouragement. He shifted his hand to the back of Alucard's head, guiding the vampire's face closer to his neck with deliberate slowness. Anticipation sent a shiver through Zalith's body as he felt the subtle pressure of the vampire's fangs against his skin, a moment heavy with both vulnerability and desire.

When Alucard's fangs penetrated Zalith's skin, the demon couldn't suppress a flinch followed by a soft sigh of delight. Tilting his head to the side, he wore a contented smile, the sensation of the vampire's venom coursing through him awakening a symphony of sensations, enthralling his body, senses, and emotions. With a subtle increase in the grip on the handful of Alucard's hair, Zalith relished the familiar pleasure of the vampire's bite, a sensation he realized he had sorely missed during the months without it.

He basked in the euphoria for a few moments longer, letting out a quiet, pleased groan as the enthralling elation aroused him. After a brief pause, the vampire then withdrew his fangs from Zalith's neck; however, the intoxicating effect of the demon's blood appeared to envelop Alucard so profoundly that he leaned against the wall once more, tilting his head back to gaze up at the ceiling.

"Do you feel better?" Zalith asked with a slight smirk on his face.

A content smile slowly appeared on Alucard's face as he closed his eyes.

Zalith's lips trailed a slow path along the vampire's neck, the steam from the shower wrapping around them like a sultry embrace. As Alucard traced teasing patterns down the demon's sleek, wet body with his fingertips, fiery anticipation ignited within Zalith, making his heart beat faster, and as their eyes locked in a heated gaze, the demon couldn't resist capturing Alucard's lips in a fervent kiss.

Drawing closer, Zalith molded his body against Alucard's, every touch sending shivers down his spine and mingling with the warm cascade from above. With Alucard's hands firmly gripping his waist, the intensity of their embrace only escalated, fueled by months of pent-up desire. Zalith's arousal surged to life, the steamy mist and falling water heightening every sensation as their connection deepened amidst the intimate confines of the shower. His dick started hardening, rubbing against Alucard's inner thigh, but just as their desire threatened to consume them, a sharp knock shattered the intense atmosphere, pulling them back to the harsh reality beyond the bathroom door.

"Vhat?!" Alucard snapped frustratedly.

"Luther has arrived, sir," Edwin called from outside as Zalith laughed quietly in amusement.

Alucard rolled his eyes and leaned his head back against the wall.

"Do you want me to tell him to tell Luther to leave?" Zalith asked.

The vampire looked like he was pondering again. But he shook his head and sighed. "I should go and see vhat 'e vants. If 'e's vinished vrapping up zhe situation vith zhe murderers, I 'ave to send 'im to your people."

Zalith moved his hand to the side of Alucard's face and stared into his eyes. "Can I come with you?" he asked. He didn't want to be alone right now.

Alucard nodded. "If you vant to."

The demon smiled and kissed him. "Thank you."

Alucard led the way out of the shower. They wrapped towels around their waists, headed over to the countertops, and started to dry and tidy their hair. Once they brushed their teeth, they walked into their bedroom and went into the dressing rooms, where they both got dressed. Zalith pulled on a grey shirt, whereas Alucard chose a white one with long sleeves, and they both dressed in black trousers.

Zalith took Alucard's hand and followed him out of the room, through the hall, and down the stairs towards the vampire's office. The door was already a few inches ajar, which had to mean that Edwin had sent Luther inside to wait for Alucard.

When Zalith and Alucard headed into the room, Luther—who was sitting in one of the chairs in front of Alucard's desk—looked over his shoulder at them. He frowned bitterly when he set his eyes on Zalith, who trailed behind the vampire. The man wasn't in his usual white suit and had instead arrived in a short-sleeved shirt, and his usually tied hair was loose and looked as though he hadn't put much effort into tidying it. Was he under the impression that things between him and Alucard were casual? Zalith didn't like that.

"Morning," Luther called.

Zalith let go of Alucard's hand and wandered over to one of the two couches. Sabazios instantly got up out of his bed and trotted over to where he sat down and curled up on the floor at his feet.

"Vhy are you dressed like Elvin?" Alucard mumbled, waving his hand towards Luther as he sat behind his desk. "Did someving attack you on your vay 'ere?"

Luther laughed slightly. "No. I met someone and spent the night with her."

Alucard didn't look interested. He leaned back in his seat and exhaled quietly. "'Ow did vings go vith zhe vest of zhe Dargamoore Saviours?"

"Pretty smoothly, actually. Hargot was feeling very talkative when the sheriff offered her a deal. She told us the names of everyone involved, and with the help of the vampires you sent over, it wasn't hard to catch them all. The ones directly involved with the murders are going to hang next week, and everyone else is serving fifteen years in prison."

"And 'argot?"

"Twenty-five years."

Alucard rolled his eyes. "She should 'ang, too."

"She probably would have if the sheriff didn't make that deal in front of witnesses."

With another sigh, Alucard crossed his arms. "'Ow are zhe vampires doing?"

"I haven't been to check on them since last night, but I told Mihai to tell them all the good news. I can go and check on them when I leave and send you—"

"No. I 'ave someving else vor you to do vor zhe next couple of days—maybe a bit longer," he interjected, glancing at Zalith, who started petting Sabazios' head.

"Please tell me it's getting rid of that ugly guest in the dungeon."

"No. Zetlaff vill stay vhere 'e is. I need you to go to zhe Citadel docks; zhere, you vill vind my galleon and Zaliv's people. Zhey vill be living zhere until ve 'ave avanged proper accommodation vor zhem. Zhey're all non-'umans, so I'll need you to make sure none of zhem start unnecessary drama in zhe city. If zhey need someving zhat is not onboard, you vill go and vetch vor zhem," he explained.

Luther's once relaxed expression faded into a confused one. Evidently, he thought the job was beneath him, and that made Zalith smirk. Luther was going to hate it.

"You'll make sure zhey're all okay, and vill also make sure zhey zon't leave zhe ship."

The man scoffed quietly in what seemed to be shock. "Are you punishing me or something? You're giving me babysitting duty?"

Alucard didn't look as though he was in the mood to deal with complaints. "Do you 'ave problem?"

"No," Luther answered, backing down—*everyone* probably knew better than to answer that question with a yes. "How many of them are there?"

"No more zhan…sixty. Verevolves, zemons, vampires, and shapeshivters."

Zalith could see that Alucard looked a little despondent with that number, just as Zalith did. They couldn't save everyone. But Zalith tried his best not to sink into his dismaying thoughts.

"Werewolves?" Luther asked in astonishment. "I thought you were through with those animals."

"Zhese volves are Zaliv's people, so you vill take care of zhem as equally as everyvone else."

"Right," Luther agreed.

"Do you 'ave ozzer updates vor me?" Alucard then asked.

For a moment, Luther eyed Zalith with a condescending stare but then proceeded to tell Alucard of his updates.

Zalith took his eyes off Luther and stared down at Sabazios. He patted the hellhound's head as the dog wagged its tail excitedly. He didn't really care much for what Luther had to say; he just wanted to be in Alucard's presence if he couldn't currently be within his embrace.

He glanced at his vampire and felt slightly amused seeing the look of total disinterest on his face while Luther nattered on about something Zalith didn't care to listen to.

However, when he heard Varana's heels clicking through the hall outside, he immediately stood up and headed for the door, leaving as silently as he could. He set his eyes on Varana; she was walking towards the front door in an emerald-green ballgown-like dress and a hat to match. Obviously, she was going out with her friends again, but Zalith didn't want to let her go yet.

"V," he called.

As Varana stopped in her tracks and turned to face him, Zalith reached and wrapped his arms around her, hugging her tightly.

"What's wrong?" she asked worriedly, hugging him back.

He was overly relieved to see that she was okay, even though he didn't want to give in to the fear that she wasn't. He just had to express how alleviated it made him feel to know that she was fine. "Nothing," he answered, kissing her head. Then, he stepped back to look at her. "I've just had to deal with a lot lately, and I'm glad that you're here."

Staring up at him, Varana's concerned frown didn't fade, but she *did* smile a little. "I'm glad you're here, too."

"Alucard and I transported the remainder of my people here last night," he informed her. But he then smiled weakly. "I'll let you get back to it," he said, and when she nodded, he turned around and headed back towards Alucard's office. He heard the quiet clicking of her heels as she left the house, and he glanced over his shoulder, watching her leave. He really was glad that she was okay—that both she *and* Alucard were okay.

He went back into Alucard's office; he met Alucard's concerned gaze as he stopped to close the door behind him but smiled over at the vampire to assure him that he was okay. Then, he walked to the couch he'd been sitting on and sat down.

The demon resumed petting Sabazios, but he almost instantly began to feel his conflicting thoughts returning. He looked at Alucard, trying to focus on his words to try and find comfort, but he just wanted to be within the vampire's embrace and having to wait for it only made him sink deeper.

He loved Alucard so much, and he loved Varana, too. Where would he be without either of them? He couldn't escape the dread that this might all be another façade—that Alucard would be taken from him again, that Varana would be taken from him again. He didn't want to lose either of them. What would he do with himself if they were to die? How could he live surrounded by all of their possessions? He couldn't—he wouldn't— and the thought of losing them dragged him so far down into despair.

Was this real? Was any of it real? As he became more and more entangled in his distress, his eyes darted around the room, almost as if he was searching for an answer, for an escape of some sort. He felt so confused, so worried, so...panicked. And he hated it. He had no idea what to think, and all he could do was hope that sometime soon, he'd be able to grip reality, even if it was only a little.

Suddenly, Alucard said to Luther, "You can go."

Zalith snapped out of his thoughts and stared over at them.

Luther stuttered and stopped talking. "What?"

"Go," Alucard repeated with an impatient scowl on his face.

"But I haven't finished ta—"

"Vould you like me to make you leave? Go and do vhat I asked."

Luther frowned but stood up and walked out of Alucard's office, leaving him and Zalith alone.

Alucard left his desk and headed over to where Zalith was sitting. The demon looked up at him as he stood in front of him, but he then sat down and stared down at Zalith's hand as the demon placed it over his.

"Are you okay?" the vampire asked, lifting his head to gaze into Zalith's eyes.

"I'm okay," the demon replied, staring back. "Is this all you had to do for today?"

The vampire shrugged slightly. "I sent Luther to go and check on your people, so...I zon't veally 'ave anyving else to do."

Zalith sighed as he leaned closer and rested his head on Alucard's shoulder. "I really need to get the compound sorted out for them...I just...don't feel like it right now."

Moving his arm around Zalith, Alucard relaxed a little. "You zon't 'ave to vorry about zhem vight now. Zhey're safe and 'ave everyving zhey need on my ship. Zhey'll be vine staying zhere vor 'owever long you need," he assured him.

"Thank you for letting them stay there—and for lending them Luther."

"Is vine. I zon't 'ave to do anyving else today, so...maybe ve can do someving togezzer?" he suggested.

Zalith looked up at him and smiled slightly. He didn't really want to do anything other than stay there and hold Alucard, but if the vampire wanted to go out, then he'd go with him. After all, at least he'd still be in his presence.

"Ve could...go to zhe lake again. I 'aven't vidden my new 'orse much yet."

Still looking up at him, the demon nodded. "That sounds good."

They stood up as Alucard took hold of Zalith's hand. Sabazios followed them out of the room, and as they headed for the front door, Zalith did his best to keep calm and focus on Alucard. He didn't want to let his dismay get the better of him, but it was slowly gripping his heart more and more with each passing moment.

# Chapter Thirty

— ⸱ ✝ ⸱ —

## Stories

**| Alucard |**

Alucard guided Zalith out of the house and to the stables. There, amidst the rustic scent of hay and leather, stood the vampire's ebony stallion, patiently awaiting their arrival. Zalith trailed beside him, their fingers intertwined; as they approached the horse, Alucard deftly took hold of the reins, leading the horse out into the open. He then mounted it, inviting Zalith to join him. The demon settled in behind him, his touch reassuring as he enveloped Alucard in a warm embrace, his chin finding a comfortable perch upon Alucard's broad shoulder.

And then, they set off on their journey.

The pair sat in silence while the horse took them through the estate's grounds, along the path outside, and towards the forest that would eventually lead them to the lake.

As calming as it felt to be in Zalith's embrace, Alucard found the silence rather unsettling. He knew that, when *he* sat in silence, his thoughts quickly consumed him; he didn't want Zalith to sink into sadness and the confusion that Alucard now knew had gripped the demon so tightly since they'd left Eltaria, but he didn't know what to say. How did Zalith make it seem so easy to just start a conversation out of nowhere?

He stared ahead, watching each tree pass by. What Zalith had said about nightmares stuck to Alucard. *He* knew too well how horrifying dreams could be, and he knew how they could make someone feel. He wasn't sure how Zalith was dealing with it, but he knew the man he loved well enough to know that the demon was probably trying to hide how he felt. Alucard wanted to assure Zalith that it was okay to be afraid—that he had nothing to be embarrassed about. He wanted to reassure him, hold him, and tell him that everything would be okay. Because it would. Adellum was gone, and Alucard was going to make sure that Light never hurt Zalith again.

But he wouldn't push or insist. He didn't want to upset, annoy, or overwhelm Zalith. He'd wait until the demon was ready to talk about it again. He felt irritated with himself, though. He didn't know what more to do other than be with Zalith and wait. Maybe that was the best thing he could do right now. Zalith said he needed time, so that was what Alucard would give him.

With a quiet sigh, the vampire glanced at what he could see of Zalith's face from the corner of his eye. "Are you okay?" he asked, a question which he found himself asking a whole lot more often than usual.

From what Alucard could see, it looked as though Zalith smiled.

"I'm okay," the demon answered. "It's nice out today."

Alucard stared up at the sky and nodded slightly in agreement.

"Is your new horse well-behaved?" the demon then asked.

"Mm-hmm. I called 'im Noir," he answered, stroking the stallion's mane.

"It's a beautiful name. How is Drac doing in the sanctuary? Does he get along with the female dragon?"

The thought of Drac's loneliness having ended made Alucard smile. "Yes," he said, glancing at Zalith again. "I checked on 'im a vew months ago, and 'e seemed veally 'appy zhere. I miss 'im, but…I veel better knowing 'e's vith 'is own kind. I 'aven't gone to see 'im much…maybe ve can go see 'im soon," he suggested.

"That would be nice," Zalith agreed. "I'm sorry for my absence as well," he then said sullenly. "I let myself become so busy, and I didn't even think about how it might be affecting you. I'm so sorry that I let you down and made you feel abandoned. I'll never do that to you again," he explained with severity, moving one of Alucard's hands off the horse's reins so that he could hold it.

Alucard frowned slightly as he heard Zalith's tone become sadder. "Is okay," he insisted softly. "I know zhat you 'ave vork to do and zhat you vere busy. Your people are important to you, as mine are important to me. I vill 'elp you vith zhem in any vay I can."

"I don't think I'll ever be able to thank you enough for helping me move them," Zalith said, squeezing Alucard's hand. "But thank you," he mumbled, kissing the side of the vampire's face. "So much."

"You zon't 'ave to vank me," Alucard said with a smile. "Vhat do you 'ave planned in vegard to zheir living space?" he then asked.

The demon sighed quietly. "Well, I'm going to have to look around myself, but there's a spot on our land that I'm thinking about moving them to. It's far away enough that we won't have to concern ourselves with their noise and their comings and goings, but it's close enough so that I can be there if I need to be."

As he spoke, Alucard nodded in acknowledgement.

"And I'm going to have to make a deal with a contractor to build them a compound so that they can live comfortably. I assume that some of them are going to leave the compound at some point to start lives elsewhere, but I can see the werewolves and the demons staying for a very long time—perhaps *too* long."

"If zhey do leave, zhey'll 'ave to stay clear of zhe city—zhe people aren't very vond of non-'umans."

Zalith nodded. "I'll make sure they're all aware of the rules."

They then went silent. Alucard didn't want to let it drag on too long, though.

"I killed Addison," he told him.

The demon didn't immediately reply. After a few moments, he said, "Thank you. I suspected since Idina's husband that we had more than one defector."

Alucard frowned. "Idina's 'usband?" He knew that the woman's husband died, but how was that linked to finding defectors?

"He was the traitor that I had to find the other night. He was trading information with our enemies and trying to leverage himself into a role where the humans would see him as an ally rather than one of us," he explained. "I'm going to have to get Orin and Tyrus to question the rest of my people. I'm not taking any more risks."

The vampire nodded. "Let me know if zhere's anyving I can do to 'elp."

Zalith kissed his cheek. "Thank you, baby."

Throughout the rest of the ride, a serene quietude settled between them. Zalith leaned forward, enfolding Alucard in a tight embrace, finding solace in the steady rhythm of the horse's movement through the dense forest. As they approached the clearing where the glistening lake awaited, Alucard's firm command urged the horse into a trot, seamlessly guiding them towards their destination.

When they emerged into the clearing, Alucard directed the horse towards the towering tree that stood sentinel by the tranquil waters of the lake. With a gentle pull on the reins, he brought the stallion to a graceful halt. Together, he and Zalith dismounted, and they settled beneath the comforting shade of the ancient tree.

Alucard leaned against the bark, and Zalith sat in front of Alucard—almost in his lap—leaning his back against the vampire's body. Alucard moved his arms around Zalith, and the demon held both his hands, a faint but noticeable smile on his face. Then, in the afternoon sun, the pair sat in a calming silence, staring out at the lake.

Alucard's thoughts were calm…but they weren't quiet. He couldn't stop thinking about Zalith—he couldn't stop *worrying* about Zalith. He felt as if he only knew a fraction of what the demon must be going through, and he wanted to do whatever he could to help, but he still couldn't think of a thing to do. Zalith seemed okay now…but Alucard still felt like the silence might be causing Zalith to drift into his despondent, worrying thoughts. He didn't want that to happen, so he tried his best to think of a conversation—even if he just talked and Zalith listened…that would help, right?

He frowned, trying to think of something that might help Zalith feel better. What if he were to show Zalith what he did to Adellum? Would it help Zalith feel a lot less worried if he knew that Adellum wasn't coming back? That he was gone and wouldn't be able to get into Aegisguard. That would help, right?

With an unsure frown, he looked down at Zalith. "If vill 'elp you, I can show you vhat I did to zhe Light…in zhe void space," he offered.

Alucard couldn't see Zalith's face, so he wasn't sure what kind of expression currently clung to it.

"No," the demon refused. "Thank you, though."

The vampire frowned in dismay. Why wouldn't Zalith want to see proof that his foe had been defeated? That his foe wouldn't be able to get into this world to continue haunting him? Alucard wasn't sure, but he felt as though it was best not to question him. So, he sunk into the silence, staring at the lake.

As time stretched on in the quiet of their shared respite, Alucard's concern deepened. If Zalith's reticence stemmed from a reluctance to witness Adellum's downfall, then perhaps conversation could serve as a welcome distraction. But what subject could bridge the gap of their silence? Alucard pondered, sifting through the recesses of his memories for anecdotes or tales worth sharing. Though doubts crept in about the interest of his own past exploits, he resolved that the content mattered less than the companionship it could provide. With a determined resolve, he steeled himself to engage Zalith, if only to stave off the weight of undue introspection.

The vampire smiled slightly, glancing down at what he could see of Zalith. "Do you vant to 'ear about zhe time Luther almost got eaten by a giant rat?"

Zalith laughed quietly. "I would love to hear that."

"Vell," Alucard started, staring at the calm water. "Vas…two…maybe vree 'undred years ago—avound zhe time I started zhe war in DeiganLupus. A lot of my vampires 'ad become trapped in zhe city avter zhe 'umans discovered zhey could poison zhe air vith 'emlock, vhich is toxic to vampires. To get zhem out of zhe city, ve 'ad to use zhe underground tunnels—zhat place vas a vell-known 'ome vor verevolves, crocodiles, and so many ozzer vings. Vhat ve *zidn't* know vas zhat zhere vere zhese disgusting giant rats about zhe size of a 'orse down zhere."

The demon laughed quietly—obviously, he knew where the story was leading.

"Zhese rats vere zhe vesult of discarded potions and alchemic ingredients being tossed into zhe rivers and zhe pipes and vhatever. Eventually, zhe rats living down zhere got massive. So, ve vere leading zhe vampires vhrough zhese underground tunnels vhen ve 'ear zhis disgusting sound—Attila vhought vas verevolf, but verevolves zon't sound like screaming 'ogs. Ve continued as ve only 'ad so much time until vould be daylight. About tventy or so minutes later, zhe ground starts shaking, and zhis 'uge, ugly rat drags its body out of vone of zhe tunnels opposite us—everyvone panicked and started vunning avound, and Attila, Luther, and myselv 'ad to deal vith zhe ving.

"I tried vire, but…zhat only pissed zhe ving off. Zhen Luther came up vith zhis smart idea to try and slit throat—'e got close, only to vind out zhat zhis rat's skin vas vhicker zhan leather. Zhis rat sank teeth into Luther; zhe bottom 'alf of 'is body vas stuck in zhat ving's mouth vor about ten minutes vhile Attila and I tried to tear into zhe ving's skin. Obviously, ve vinally killed zhe rat, ozzervise Luther vould 'ave been dead a long time ago."

Zalith scoffed a little through his laughter. "You probably didn't even have to help Luther. He would have most likely turned the rat's stomach."

Alucard smirked, gazing at what he could see of Zalith as the demon started to drag his fingers over his hands.

The vampire then sunk into his thoughts. Maybe he should keep talking; Zalith seemed to have enjoyed his first story…but what else to tell? There were so many stupid things that happened during his days of moving around with Attila and Luther, but he wasn't sure if Zalith wanted to hear about his homophobic subordinate or his estranged one. He'd ask before he'd tell.

The vampire glanced down at Zalith and frowned. "I can tell you about zhe time Attila pissed off an entire country."

"Tell me," the demon said with a smile, looking up at him.

Alucard thought to himself for a few moments, recalling the story. "Vas…a short vhile avter ve killed Janus. Attila and Luther vanted to celebrate, and I vhought, vhy not, so I vent vith zhem to some city in Solitudinem. Vas zhe voyal city and Attila some'ow ended up in a game of…poker, I vink, vith zhe king's son. Zhey played vor hours until Attila beat 'im—and zhis little brat vent running to 'is vather and told 'im Attila 'ad stolen vrom 'im. Zhere vas a vight; zhe king sent some of 'is men, and ve vhought zhem. Ve vere all a little drunk, too, so zhat zidn't 'elp.

"Anyvay, ve beat zhose guys, more guys came, and eventually, vone small ving turned into a man'unt. Zhere vere vather large bounties vor all of us—mostly Attila, zhough. All of zhe king's guards vere looking vor us, bounty 'unters…and even normal citizens. Now, ve all avoid Solitudinem, vor I am sure zhey are still vaiting vor us to show our vaces."

The demon laughed quietly. "I can imagine how horrifying it would be to see an artist's rendition of Attila's face on a wanted poster."

"If you go to Solitudinem, you vill probably vind vone and get to see 'ow bad is."

"Maybe I'll make a point of it one day," Zalith answered, staring at the lake. "I remember…centuries ago when my brother and I were much younger, we used to spend a lot of time in the less-wealthier parts of our city because we had a lot of friends down there. One night, we went to a tavern, and our friend Cliffton—who was a very good artist—happened to stop in on his way home from a job he was working on. My brother and I used to ask him to draw things for us *all* the time, but he always refused to do it.

"Just the day before, Xurian had become infatuated with a beautiful blonde woman he happened to meet at the market, and he spent the day with her and walked her home. When my brother and I were at the tavern, we were all drinking, and Xurian got a little too drunk. He begged Cliffton to draw a picture of this woman for him so that he could give it to her as a gift. Eventually, Xurian started to cry about it, and Cliffton gave in. He drew this amazing drawing of the woman based solely on Xurian's description of her.

"Then, in a drunken stupor, Xurian dragged me out of the bar, and we wandered around the city until we got to her house. My brother knocked on the door and called her name over and over until she woke up; just as Xurian had given up and slipped the drawing through her mailbox, the lights turned on in the house, and the woman came out. However, it turned out that we weren't at the blonde woman's house, but Xurian's most recent ex-girlfriend's house, and she was infuriated with us. She called us a fair few things, slammed the door in our faces, and we left. I think it took us a while to get home after that, but…we made it," he said with a slight laugh. "I might add that Xurian actually married this woman years later—his ex-girlfriend."

Amused, Alucard laughed a little and leaned his head back against the tree. "Zhe amount of time I spent getting drvunk and doing stupid vings in my past is uncountable. Girlvriend drama, too—vor Attila and Luther. Zhey spent a lot of zheir time valtzing avound zhe place trying to woo vomen. Zhey vould usually leave me by myselv vhile zhey vent to do vhatever zhey did; I vould alvays vind zhem zhe next morning passed out in alleys vith all zheir belongings stolen. Zhey never learned zheir lesson," he said with a shrug.

Zalith laughed quietly as he started stroking Alucard's hand again. "If I'd been there, I wouldn't have dreamed of leaving your side. But I would've let Luther and Attila leave, and then I would have flirted with you all night," he said, smirking.

Alucard felt a little flustered, but luckily, Zalith couldn't see his face, so he'd not have to hide it. "If I 'ad met you any time bevore now…I zon't vink vings vould 'ave turned out the same."

The demon laughed again. "They might have. But if not, I would have pined after you until the end of time."

"Back zhen…vings vere…strange. I never knew when I vould be leaving, or vhen I vould be coming back. Zamien vould come to me at any time and any place and pull me avay vor any time betveen a veek and ten years. 'E took me avay vor a good 'undred years vonce, and all zhe people I knew in zhat lifetime vere dead by zhe time I got back. I guess zhat's anozzer veason I started to keep avay vrom people. I never knew 'ow long I vould get to know zhem," he admitted sadly. "But I zon't vant to talk about Zamien," he said with a scowl on his face. He didn't even want to *think* about Damien.

Zalith looked up at him and smiled. "Well, we have each other now, and that's all that matters."

Alucard smiled slightly. "Zhat's true," he agreed.

"And if we want to get drunk and be stupid, then we can do it in the comfort of our own home—we don't have to go anywhere," he said contently.

Still staring down at him, Alucard nodded in response. Then, they both stared out at the lake.

Silence fell over them again, but this time, it felt a lot more relaxing. Alucard enjoyed telling Zalith about his past and hearing about the demon's; of course, he wanted to know more, but they had all the time in the world to tell one another about their lives before they met. Alucard still felt as though his life might not be so interesting, but Zalith seemed to enjoy his talks. Maybe he wasn't as boring as he thought…maybe *he* just found the events of his past uninteresting. But, if such things were entertaining to Zalith, he'd not stop sharing.

# Chapter Thirty-One

## Babysitting

| **Luther** |

Luther's steps echoed through the bustling streets of the Citadel's city centre as his expression twisted into a grimace of resentment. The mere thought of his new assignment soured his mood further. Babysitting duty? And not for Alucard's own, but for Zalith's entourage.... The very idea grated against Luther's pride like coarse sandpaper. He harboured a deep-seated animosity towards that demon, a festering resentment that gnawed at him with every passing moment. To Luther, Zalith was an interloper, an unworthy recipient of Alucard's affections, and, by extension, of Luther's begrudging assistance.

But despite his simmering antipathy, Luther knew better than to openly defy Alucard's wishes. The consequences of crossing the formidable vampire were far too dire to risk—the idea of facing the Vampire Council for insubordination made him feel a little sick; he hadn't even thought about the possibility until last night when the vampires he was working with started talking about it. Besides, beneath his layers of disdain, there lingered a steadfast loyalty to his friend. Luther recognized that Alucard was going through a lot right now, and if providing aid, even to Zalith, could alleviate some of his burden, then he would begrudgingly comply. After all, his allegiance to Alucard outweighed his personal disdain for his arrogant demon boyfriend.

His glare became a scowl the more he thought about Zalith. The things he'd learned from Varana last night lingered in the back of his mind, and he wondered... did *Alucard* know the things Varana had told him about Zalith? Did Alucard know how promiscuous his boyfriend really was? It sickened him to think that Alucard might just be another temporary fix for Zalith, and if he had to warn Alucard about this demon's behaviour, then he would. The last thing he wanted was for his friend to feel used and unwanted, just as he surely must have been all this time.

And then he thought about when Alucard told him that he and Zalith resolved everything. Had that revolting man somehow convinced Alucard that he loved him again? His anger worsened at the mere thought of Alucard falling victim to Zalith's endless lies.

With a deep sigh, he lost his scowl and set his eyes on the docks as he made his way closer. He could see Alucard's galleon docked ahead and could almost smell the repugnant stench of dog. Why in the world would someone like Alucard look after werewolves? Luther scowled again; Alucard did far too much for that demon—a demon who didn't even care that Alucard was suffering because of him.

He rolled his eyes, shook his head, and followed the pier until he reached the steps that led up onto the deck of Alucard's ship.

However, as Luther's hand tightened on the railing, a voice sliced through the din of the bustling promenade, calling out his name. He halted in his tracks, the familiarity of the voice drawing his attention like a magnet. Turning slightly, he cast his gaze over his shoulder, his eyes falling upon the figure of Varana. There she sat, amidst the vibrant scenery of the promenade, a striking contrast in her green dress, her crimson eyes gleaming with recognition as she waved a white handkerchief in his direction. She sat outside a quaint restaurant, flanked by three other women bedecked in equally resplendent attire, their brightly coloured dresses and hats adding to the kaleidoscope of hues that adorned the promenade.

Luther sighed a little and smiled. He might as well go and say hello; he wanted to keep her sweet. Right now, she was his best chance at getting closer to both Alucard and Zalith.

He left the docks and made his way through the crowd of people and cut the line of couples waiting to get into the restaurant. When he approached her table, the giggles of her friends died down.

"Hey," he said with a smile.

"Hello," she said, and as her friends whispered to one another, she glanced at them. "Girls, this is Luther," she introduced.

"Hi." The blonde smiled. "I'm Cadence."

"I'm Selena," the other greeted.

"Hi." The third giggled. "I'm Mary-Beth. Varana's told us *so* much about you," she said as her friends laughed quietly.

Varana then smiled as Luther set his eyes back on her after nodding at each of the women. "Where are you heading? I didn't expect to see you out here."

"I'm on a job for Luca," he said, having not forgotten that Luca was the name that Alucard's little sister had given him.

"Out here...by the docks?" she asked with a frown.

Luther sighed as he slipped his hands into his pockets. "He has me looking after Zalith's people. They're staying on his ship."

"Oh. Do you mind if I go with you? I should probably make an appearance—it's the least I can do."

He didn't see a problem with it. "Sure."

Selena leaned forward as Varana finished her drink. "Why is it the least you can do? What's happening?"

"Why don't you mind your own business for once?" Varana snapped, placing her glass down. Then, she stood up, linked her arm with his, and smiled. "Lead the way."

Luther led the way away from the restaurant, leaving Varana's friends alone.

They walked through the crowds, down to the docks, and approached Alucard's ship. He glanced at Varana as they continued forward and caught her staring at the galleon with a rather sour look on her face.

"Is this it?" she asked, unimpressed.

While Luther led the way up onto the deck, he nodded. "Yeah. I heard it cost him more than what I earn in ten years or something. He used to use it a lot back in the wars."

Varana scoffed when they reached the deck. "Hmph. I used to have *fleets* of these things."

"I'm sure you did," he said, smirking.

She laughed quietly and smiled as they walked along the deck. "I did. Luca needs to start paying you better, and then maybe you'll have a boat like this one day."

Luther shrugged as they stopped walking. "I don't need a ship. Why sail when I can just fly everywhere? And he pays me more than enough."

She kept her smile. "You can fly all the way across the ocean?"

"I do it every day," he said with a smirk. "I live all the way back in Dor-Sanguis."

"That's very impressive," she giggled.

"Please," he said, turning to face her. "You haven't seen *half* of what I can do," he flirted.

Varana giggled again. "Is that so?"

He smirked suggestively in response.

"I can't wait to see what else you've got hidden," she murmured.

Luther grinned but held back his response as he set his eyes on the dark-skinned, bald-headed demon making his way down off the quarterdeck; his orange eyes and cold aura were tell-tale signs that he was an allocer demon. Both Luther and Varana turned to face the man, and once he reached them, he bowed respectively to Varana.

The man then held his hand out towards her; she took it, and with a smile on her face, she followed him up onto the quarterdeck. However, when Luther followed, two other demons who'd been guarding the steps moved in front of him and blocked his way. Varana didn't stop to tell them to stand down—she didn't even look back at him. She seemed far too focused on the small crowd of people that had run over to her the moment she'd been seen as if she was some sort of celebrity.

Glaring at the two demons blocking his path, Luther scoffed in revolt. "Get out of my way," he warned.

"Name?" the left guard asked challengingly.

Obviously, this had to be some sort of security measure Alucard had set in place. With a vacant stare on his face, Luther crossed his arms. "Luther," he answered.

"Luther what?" the right guard asked just as bitterly.

"Why does it matter?" he complained.

"You're not permitted to be on this ship without proper identification," the first guard said, eyeing Luther up and down.

With his patience dwindling, Luther rolled his eyes and glowered at the two guards. "My boss…who *owns* this ship, sent me here," he said.

But they just glared at him, waiting.

Luther rolled his eyes again and uncrossed his arms as he sighed impatiently. "Aleksei."

"Aleksei who?" the second guard asked.

"Do I look like I fucking know?" Luther snapped—he didn't know Alucard's surname and his irritancy was becoming overbearing.

"You don't know your boss' name?" the second guard muttered.

The first guard scoffed and looked over his shoulder. "Tyrus," he called, nodding at the bald man who hadn't long taken Varana away.

Luther set his eyes on the bald man once again, watching as he made his way over with a red apple in his hand. He stopped between the two guards and started to eye him slowly.

"Who are you?" he asked.

"Just like I told your ugly friends here, I'm Luther."

"Hmm." Tyrus frowned, polishing the apple on his shirt. Then, he took a bite, chewed it for a few moments, and then looked Luther up and down once again. After a few moments of silence, he scowled ever so slightly. "Pat him down."

"Are you fucking serious?" Luther growled, but as the two guards stepped towards him, he backed off defensively. "Don't touch me," he snarled in disgust.

"Do you want to be on this boat or not?" Tyrus asked. "Don't waste my time."

Luther hesitated as he glared at the bald man, who chewed loudly on his apple. But he then relented and held his arms out. The last thing he wanted to do was cause a scene that might get back to Alucard. He was trying to do whatever he could to make things easier for his boss—he didn't want to make things worse by refusing to go through his security procedures.

"Did you come here with her?" Tyrus asked, nodding over at Varana as the two demons continued to search Luther for weapons.

"Obviously," Luther grumbled. Then, he set his sights on Varana. "Varana!" he called, but the woman didn't seem to hear him; she continued talking to the people who'd swarmed her.

"Are you two…together?" Tyrus asked, amused.

"Yes…" Luther uttered.

"Hmm…." Tyrus frowned skeptically. "You're pretty spindly…you look like a newborn horse," he said, smirking. "I don't believe you."

Luther scowled irritably at him. "And yet, I'm still more attractive than you," he sneered.

Tyrus laughed amusedly. "Skinny *and* can't afford a mirror. Unless you've got a big dick, I don't know what she sees in you," he mocked as the two guards finally stepped away from him.

One of the guards, however, looked at Tyrus and shrugged. "He doesn't," he said.

Irritated and unable to come up with a comeback, Luther glared at all three of them. He *hated* demons; they always thought they were so funny and smart and better than everyone else. If these people weren't important to Alucard, he would have taught them a lesson by now.

Chuckling, Tyrus shook his head and tossed his half-eaten apple into the ocean. "Let's go," he said, turning around to lead the way over to where Varana was.

"There you are," Varana said as Luther reached her. "What took you so long?"

Rolling his eyes, Luther stopped in front of her and glanced back at the two guards. "I got held up by some idiots," he grumbled.

"Who?" she asked and looked at Tyrus, who stopped beside her. "Him?"

"No," Luther uttered, looking back at the guards again. "Those imbeciles," he said, nodding over at them as they stood with their backs to him.

Varana rolled her eyes and turned to face the people who had come to greet her: a brunette woman with a small boy at her side and a silver-haired man—both demons.

Luther sighed angrily; he'd seen enough demons for today, but it seemed as though he wasn't yet done dealing with them.

Tyrus shot a glance at Luther. "These are the people you need to talk to. Good luck, Speckle," he mocked with a smirk and walked off.

With a smile, the silver-haired man ignored Luther and bowed to Varana. "It's so good to see you, your majesty," he said humbly. "You're looking as beautiful as ever."

"Thank you," Varana replied, taking her eyes off him to smile at the woman.

"I was wondering when we might see you again," the brunette said as she let go of the boy's hand to shake Varana's, and then they kissed each other's cheeks. "I'm so glad to see that you're doing okay."

"I'm glad to see that *you're* doing okay," Varana replied. "When I heard a few years ago that you were still based in Eltaria, I was worried. Thank goodness you got out okay, though." But she then adorned a sympathetic expression. "I heard about your husband, too. I'm so sorry, Idina."

Idina frowned sadly and looked down at the floor. "Thank you; it's been hard, but I'm getting through it. One day at a time," she said, looking back at Varana.

Varana smiled and took hold of her hands. "You're more than welcome to come visit Z and me," she said, waving her arm to point in the direction of the house, but her hand slapped Luther's face—he was smacked out of his vacant stare and gawped in both shock and confusion as Varana held her hand to her face. "Oops," she gasped.

Luther shook his head and looked the other way, staring down at the few vampires gathered on the deck. He wasn't entirely sure what to think. Clearly, Idina and Varana were acquainted—maybe even friends; Idina was also an eligos demon, which was surprising. He didn't think a Lethidian demon would work so closely with someone related to Lucifer. He wasn't sure who the kid was or the silver-haired guy—who looked pretty strange, even for a demon—but they both waited in silence while Varana and Idina spoke. He wasn't exactly sure what to say; he didn't even know if these people were expecting him. After what happened with those two guards, he was beginning to feel as though Alucard had thrown him into another situation without much guidance.

But he couldn't complain. He should know by now that Alucard wasted no time sharing details that didn't matter. He'd been sent there to talk to these people, to look after these people, and that was what he would do. Surely, Alucard had told them that he would be coming; if not, this was going to be a lot more tedious than it needed to be.

"This is Luther," Varana then said, standing beside him.

"Aleksei sent me," he said, setting his eyes on Idina as the child clung to her leg.

"Oh, good," Idina said. "I'm Idina, and this is Orin," she said, looking back at the silent silvery-blonde-haired seir demon, who had been observing since greeting Varana. "I imagine we have to discuss many things, so would you prefer to come and sit down? There's a bar just below the second deck."

"I know," Luther grumbled. "Let's go," he said and started leading the way.

"Oh, do you mind if I come?" Varana asked.

He stopped walking, looked back at her, and shrugged. "Sure," he said and walked down from the quarterdeck; he led the way along the deck and deeper into the ship.

Luther's memory guided him through the labyrinthine halls of Alucard's majestic vessel, a floating fortress akin to a hotel on the seas. Amidst the lively hum of chatter and clinking glasses, he made his way to the heart of camaraderie aboard the ship—the bustling bar. Here, a tapestry of voices intermingled with the scent of spirits, enveloping the room in a comforting haze. The crew and the people entrusted to Luther's watchful eye occupied most tables, each engaged in their own pursuits; be it savouring drinks, engaging in animated conversations, or partaking in the timeless pastime of cards.

Amidst the throng, one lone figure captured Luther's attention—a solitary soul, bent over parchment, the dance of charcoal bringing life to his thoughts.

He led the way over to one of the only vacant tables, pulled out a seat for Varana, and once she sat down, he pulled out his own seat. He watched Idina send the child off to the scribbling man, and then she joined them.

Luther didn't see or feel any need to falter. "Has Aleksei told you anything specific yet?" he asked, looking at Idina.

"He told us to remain on the ship and that if Zalith hasn't recovered in three days, he'd be organizing somewhere for the werewolves to wait out the full moon."

With a quiet sigh, Luther rested his arms on the table. He was probably going to have to see to that, too. He kept his eyes on Idina and frowned slightly. "This is Nefastus," he started. "Here, there are more rules than you might find elsewhere—unspoken rules. If you know, you know; that kind of deal," he explained.

Idina nodded, listening carefully.

"No non-humans whatsoever are allowed to live here—the only exception is elves, and anyone who might look like one can get away with pretending to be one. There *are* werewolves here, as far as I am aware…a small pack to the west. But they stay clear of the Citadel."

She nodded again.

"There are vampires here, I see, and obviously, they're going to need to feed. Aleksei's crewmen are human, and all of them are pretty much willing vampire fodder."

"So, just so I'm completely sure, the vampires are free to feed on these crewmen whenever they need?" Idina asked.

"Just don't kill them," Luther warned her. "Dead people in this city start too much shit. So, make sure no one gets greedy."

"Understood," she said.

"No one leaves the ship for reasons of safety and precaution. Aleksei will meet us here in a few days, I'm sure, and he'll bring updates. Or he'll send some kind of correspondence. Until then, you'll all find everything you need here, and if you need anything else, ask me, and I'll see what I can do."

"Thank you," Idina said.

"You can tell everyone else this," he muttered, standing up. "I need to send word to Aleksei that I got here."

"Of course," Idina said.

Luther didn't have anything else to say. "I'll be right back," he said with a smile, glancing down at Varana, who looked as though she was content sitting where she was.

Varana nodded in response.

He then left the table and headed to his old room. A few moments of peace and quiet were something he sorely needed right now.

# Chapter Thirty-Two

— ⸲ ✝ ⸰ —

## Options

| **Luther** |

Seated at the familiar desk within the confines of his old quarters, Luther found solace in the unchanged surroundings. Every detail, from the neatly arranged books to the cherished photographs adorning the walls, whispered tales of memories past. Even the bed, a haven of chaos he had abandoned years prior, remained a testament to his autonomy, untouched by foreign hands. In this sanctuary of solitude, he found reassurance in the knowledge that his space remained inviolate, a sanctuary where his presence reigned supreme.

He sighed quietly, folding up the paper he'd written a quick message on. He then handed it to the owl that was waiting in his open window, and once it took hold of the paper in its beak, it turned around and took off, heading to where Alucard was.

Luther didn't have much else to do other than sit around thinking about how irritated he felt about babysitting Zalith's people; he didn't work for Zalith, so why was he doing something for *him*? He rolled his eyes and stood up, leaving his room. He locked the door, slipped the key into his pocket, and made his way through the ship.

When he emerged into the bar, he set his sights on Varana, who was still sitting at the same table talking to Idina. A few moments later, though, the Brunette woman stood up, and it looked as though she was about to leave. That gave Luther some relief—at least he wouldn't be stuck talking business *all* day.

He headed over to Varana once Idina left, but Varana stood up and smiled when he stopped in front of her.

"Let's get a drink," she said before he could speak.

Luther nodded and followed her to the bar.

"A mojito," she ordered and looked to Luther.

"Whiskey," he uttered. Then, as the server disappeared, he looked at Varana. "So, why are you so popular here?" he asked, thinking about the greetings and attention she received upon her arrival.

She smiled when she was handed her drink. "Oh, I'm just a queen," she laughed. "They *all* adore me."

"Huh…." He frowned, taking his drink from the server. "So…are any of these people your friends or are they all just subjects?" he asked—he also wanted to ask if that made Alucard royalty; he really didn't know all that much about Alucard, and since his interest in The Vampire Lord had become more intense lately, he found himself wanting to know everything he could about him.

Varana took a quick glance around the room. "Well, I know Tyrus, Orin, and Idina well—and…Danford," she said, looking over at the man who was sitting at a table alone scribbling on paper with a piece of charcoal; Idina was over there talking to him while the little boy held onto her leg again. "That's about it."

Danford was the only person whom Luther hadn't yet had the 'pleasure' of meeting. However, he was a werewolf, so he suspected that he might not be as annoying—just repulsive. His curiosity, though, was somewhat piqued. "Who is he?"

Taking her eyes off Danford as Idina left with the boy, Varana shrugged. "Werewolf…but he's not the strongest. I don't know how he's survived this long to be perfectly honest; maybe it's because Z favoured him."

"Favoured him?" he questioned, his interest spiking. He'd love to know more about a man Zalith seemed to be interested in.

She rolled her eyes. "They slept together on multiple occasions; of course, it never lasted—it never does. But Z might still have a soft spot for him," she mumbled.

Interesting. Why was Zalith keeping a man he used to sleep with around? Was Luther right in suspecting that Zalith's lack of attention for Alucard lately was because that demon was seeing someone else? Or perhaps planning to? Was that someone else Danford? A man Zalith 'favoured'? Luther frowned, taking his eyes off Varana to look over at Danford again. Why would Zalith keep an ex nearby?

"Are you okay?" Varana then asked, snapping him out of his silent thinking.

"Yeah," he uttered and sipped from his drink. "Did Zalith date him?"

"Date?" she repeated, sounding shocked. "No, never. He was just someone Z had sex with because he was bored."

Luther then scoffed, remembering a conversation he and Varana had about Zalith's promiscuous past. "Oh, so he's just another one of those guys you told me about on our date, huh?" he asked with a smirk.

Varana shrugged. "One of many. Actually, I think he was one of the last ones before he started seeing…Luca," she mumbled.

With a frown on his face, Luther moved a little closer to her. "How do you feel about that? About them—Zalith and Alucard."

A sour look clung to her face as she sipped from her drink. "I'm just waiting for it to end, honestly. Initially, they seemed happy, but lately, I haven't seen them together as much. Maybe Z is having second thoughts; he's been so busy, too, and barely has time for me," she said sadly.

"You're *that* sure it will end?"

"I know him, Luther. He gets bored. I really think he had nothing but good intentions here, but it's only a matter of time before he sees someone else that interests him and starts chasing after them. This relationship of theirs has lasted longer than any of his others…but all things have to come to an end."

Anger started to simmer within him. Of course, he already knew of Zalith's past, but knowing that he was the type of man who used people until he considered them 'expired'…. Luther hated that, and he hated knowing that Alucard was just another victim. He did his best to keep a scowl off his face and sipped from his drink, glancing at Danford again. "Do you think he's already seen someone new?"

She shrugged. "Not that I've noticed. I'm sure if he had, though, he'd be reluctant to tell me because that would mean I was right about the Luca situation. I did tell him that it wouldn't last and that this was just another temporary thing. But maybe he *would* tell me…he always surprises me."

"What would happen if they did break up? Would they keep in touch? Or does he toss people aside like garbage?"

Varana laughed a little. "Well, that depends entirely on Luca. Z always goes back and forth between people, and I wouldn't be surprised if they broke up but kept seeing each other here and there for a few years."

Luther's anger increased. "How many people has he done this to?"

With a deep sigh, Varana took a sip of her drink. "Out of respect for my best friend, I will not say. But I *will* say that the number is very shocking, and that's not including the ones I don't know about."

He scowled harder, trying his best not to give into the anger that came with knowing Alucard was just another temporary use for Zalith. "I guess…it's just a waiting game then."

Varana giggled. "Why? Are you interested? Should I put in a good word for you, Luthy?"

"No," he grumbled. "I'm just concerned for my friend."

"Aw, that's so sweet of you," she said, placing her hand on his arm.

Luther's attention, however, reverted to Danford. He took his eyes off Varana and looked over at the man, watching as he continued drawing on his paper. He couldn't help but wonder…was this Danford guy involved? Was he a part of the reason why Zalith had been ignoring Alucard?

He didn't want to be right about Zalith seeing someone else…or did he? He didn't want Alucard to be any more upset than he already was; he was already quite sure that Alucard loved Zalith, and it would hurt the vampire so much to find out that he'd been seeing someone else. But…if things played out that way, at least Luther could be there to show Alucard that he didn't need someone as selfish and rude as Zalith. He could show Alucard that *he* could be more than just his work subordinate.

Luther looked down at the floor, finishing the rest of his drink. Why had he just thought that? Was that what he wanted? It was. What he wanted was to be something more to Alucard than just some errand boy. He could be so much more—he could give Alucard what Zalith couldn't. He wouldn't cheat or lie or make Alucard feel unwanted. He'd do a much better job of taking care of him than some demon who didn't know when to put his dick away. Zalith didn't deserve Alucard, and Luther wouldn't rest until his friend was free of a man who didn't value him for all he was.

Just then, Idina came over and snapped Luther out of his thoughts. He took his eyes off the door and looked at the brunette woman, watching as she spoke to Varana.

"Is it okay if Orin and I steal you away for a few minutes?" she asked quietly. "We need to talk to you privately."

Varana put her drink down. "Oh, sure," she answered. Then, she looked at Luther. "I'll be right back."

"Sure," he mumbled, leaning back against the bar.

As Varana walked off, Luther set his eyes back on Danford and frowned. Maybe now that Varana was busy, he could ask the man himself if Zalith was sneaking around with him. He wasn't going to find out from Varana, nor would he get anywhere with that demon—not that he wanted to talk to him, anyway. Danford looked pretty reasonable and like the type to blab if Luther said the right things.

Luther signalled for a refill before strolling over to where Danford was sitting. Pausing beside the table, he cast a casual glance at the canvas, noting the outline of a portrait taking shape beneath Danford's skilled hand. Yet, to Luther's bemusement, the subject bore no semblance to anyone familiar—an enigma amidst the familiar faces that populated Alucard's vessel. With an amused shake of his head, Luther redirected his focus to the man himself, a figure whose attire belied a certain lack of refinement. Eyeing him with a mix of curiosity and skepticism, he took in the man's appearance and asked, "You're Danford, right?"

Danford looked up at him. "Uh…yeah," he said, a cautious, confused look on his face as he glanced around the room.

"Luther," he greeted, holding out his free hand.

Still with an unsure expression, Danford slowly reached out and shook his hand.

Luther did his best not to show the revolt he felt. A werewolf touching him…gross. But he had to do what he had to do to get close and get the information he wanted. He pulled out the seat beside Danford and sat down, placing his drink on the table.

"What's up?" Danford asked unsurely.

Luther wasn't sure whether he should just get right to it or wear him down a little first. There was the possibility that Danford wouldn't answer his questions unless he felt comfortable, so he was going to have to try and become this man's friend.

He leaned his arms on the table and glanced down at Danford's drawing. "Who are you drawing?" he asked, suspecting that talking about his art might be a good start.

"Um…nobody, really," he answered. "Sometimes, I just draw with no intent."

"Well, it looks really good so far."

He looked down at his drawing. "Oh…thanks," he said with surprise in his voice. "It's just a sketch. I probably won't finish it."

"Why won't you finish it?"

Danford shrugged. "I'm not crazy about it."

"Then why are you drawing it?" Luther asked with a hint of unintended harshness in his voice. He was doing his best to ignore the hate he had for werewolves.

"To pass the time," Danford said with another shrug.

With a frown on his face, Luther looked down at the picture and then back at Danford. A smirk crept across his face; flirting always got him to the places he needed and wanted to be, so…this probably wasn't going to be any different. "Is that all you do to pass the time?"

Danford smiled slightly, almost as if he was humoured and confused. "No," he answered. "But there's not much to do on this ship. I've been thinking about painting again when we're all settled, though."

Luther nodded, keeping a smile on his face. "What else do you do?"

"Read. Sometimes I write, but I work mostly—especially these days."

Just then, one of the bar crew came over and took the empty glass sitting beside Danford.

"Can I get another one, please?" Danford asked, looking up at the server. Then, he looked at Luther. "Do you want anything?"

"Another whiskey," he said, looking up at the guy.

"What about you?" the werewolf asked. "What do you do?"

"Work mostly, too. I was sent here to keep an eye on you and all your people," he said with a smirk, leaning slightly closer as he finished what was left of his drink.

"Oh, you work for Zalith? I haven't seen you around before."

"No," Luther grumbled—but he quickly smiled again. "I work for his partner."

Danford's face lit up a little. "Oh, Aleksei?"

"Yeah," he said, a little disappointed that Danford showed no sign of shock, but his suspicions that this was the man Zalith was giving his time to hadn't waned.

"He's great. He's done a lot for us. But…he's kinda intimidating, eh?"

Luther laughed slightly. "More often than not. But he's actually the kindest man I know. As for Zalith…" he said, his tone turning sour. "I don't like him much at all."

With a hesitant frown, Danford laughed. "Oh…why not?"

Just then, the server returned with their drinks. Luther waited until he was gone to look back at Danford. "Well…." he sighed—he had but a moment to examine Danford's response. The man looked cautious again, almost as if he wasn't sure about how he felt about Zalith.

Luther wasn't sure if expressing his dislike for Zalith was a good idea, especially if he was going to try and use his subordinate to try and get information about him. The best thing to do here was to act as if he was curious and like he was looking to get to know Zalith a little better. That might get him somewhere.

"I guess I don't really know him all that much," Luther lied—well, he didn't, did he? All he knew was that Zalith was a stuck-up demon and one who was taking advantage of someone he cared about. "He whisked Aleksei away from Dor-Sanguis—which is where *his* work is based—and none of his friends really see him anymore. He spends all his time with Zalith, and I guess that makes me a little…upset."

"Oh." Danford frowned. "Have you…tried talking to him about it?"

As Luther prepared to interject, his attention was drawn to the approach of a figure commanding the room with his imposing stature. Towering above the crowd, the man exuded an air of rugged confidence, his features adorned with a shadow of stubble that hinted at a life lived on the edge. With a drink clasped casually in one hand, his dark hair cascading behind his ears, he exuded an aura of authority that brooked no dissent. The scent of the outdoors clung to him, reminiscent of the wild, and his very presence spoke volumes—this man was unquestionably Danford's Alpha. A subtle shift in Danford's demeanour betrayed his subservience as he gazed up at the newcomer, his posture instantly morphing into one of deference and obedience.

"Just came to check in on that drawing you've been working on," the Alpha said, looking at Danford. Then, he sat down across from Danford and set his dark brown eyes on Luther.

"Oh," Danford said—but with more interest in his voice than when he had been talking to Luther. "Here," he said, turning the paper so that he could see.

The werewolf Alpha didn't take his eyes off Luther.

Luther glared back, sure that this guy wasn't happy with him talking to one of his packmates, but Luther didn't care what he thought. He was going to get the information he wanted, and this ugly, disgusting dog wasn't going to stop him.

The guy glanced down at Danford's drawing. "Shit, this is amazing," he said, slowly setting his eyes back on Luther. "How you draw like this, I'll never understand." Then, he raised his drink a little. "Cheers," he said, sipping from his drink. "So, who's your friend?"

Danford looked at Luther. "Oh, uh…Luther."

"It's nice to meet you, Luther. I'm Greymore," he said, keeping his eyes fixed on him. "You're a new face. I've never seen you around here before. Are you two friends?"

"Oh, no," Danford answered. "We just met."

Luther smiled slightly, keeping his eyes on Greymore. "I'm just getting to know the people I was sent to keep an eye on."

Greymore laughed. "Well, there's a lot of people for you to get to know; you've got your work cut out for you."

"I like to take my time," Luther said with a smirk as he glanced at Danford.

Danford frowned in embarrassment and looked away.

In response, Greymore raised his eyebrows slightly and scoffed. Then, he sipped from his drink, placed his glass down, and cleared his throat. "Oh," he said to Danford. "You know who that drawing looks like?"

"Who?" he asked, intrigued.

"Oliver."

"Oh, uh…you really think so?" he asked, looking down at his drawing with an unconvinced frown.

Luther rolled his eyes, sipping from his drink. Clearly, this Greymore guy was about to ask Luther what he was doing here talking to Danford and wanted to get Danford out of the way before doing so.

"Yeah," Greymore confirmed. "It really does. You should go and show it to him—he'll get a kick out of it."

"Uh…" Danford mumbled, glancing at Luther and then at Greymore again.

Greymore nodded.

"O-okay," Danford said, picking up his drawing as he stood up. Then, he wandered off, leaving Luther alone with Greymore.

"So," Greymore said, his frown becoming a skeptical glare, "what exactly are you looking after?"

Luther glared right back at him. Not only had he had to deal with annoying demons, but he was also now going to have to deal with a nosey werewolf. He really hated having to explain himself more than once, but in order to keep his intentions hidden, he'd be…nice. "Aleksei sent me here to keep an eye on all of you until Zalith has a place ready for you to live."

"Oh," he said, frowning in realization. "Aleksei sent you?"

"He did."

Greymore leaned back in his seat with his drink in his hand. "He's a nice guy. From what I heard, he and Zalith make a good team."

Luther kept his smile. "So I've heard, too."

"Of course, I haven't seen them together much, so I can't really speak to it myself personally. Have you known them long?"

"I've known Aleksei pretty much all my life. As for Zalith, I first met him about a year ago. I don't see much of him, nor do I know much, but he seems nice," he said, holding back a gag. He hated calling Zalith anything but what he was: an asshole.

Greymore laughed amusedly. "When you see him, is it from a great distance? Don't get me wrong, I could talk about how great he is for hours, but the typical first impression one gets when looking at him is not that he seems nice."

"Well," Luther said, leaning back in his seat, "I've only ever really seen him while he's with Aleksei, and when he's with Aleksei, he always seems to be having a good time. Perhaps my opinion will change when I see him *not* with Aleksei."

With a smile and a shrug, Greymore sipped from his drink. He then smirked a little, keeping his eyes on Luther. "So, word on the deck is that you and Varana are an item."

Luther also smirked. "Is that so?"

He laughed again. "Is it?"

"I'm pursuing my options."

Surprised, Greymore chuckled. "Really? You have the opportunity to be with someone who looks like her, and you're still gonna peruse your options? That's crazy. Looks aside, but the money? The power? Who else do you have on the side? A literal god?" he exclaimed, shaking his head as he placed his drink down and stared at Luther, waiting for him to answer.

"It's not all about looks, money, and power," Luther uttered.

"True. But still, *that* is the opportunity of a lifetime right there," he said, crossing his arms as he paused for a few moments. "I've never been with a demon before. What's it like? Amazing, I imagine."

Luther shrugged, finishing his drink. "It's not really any different than being with anyone else," he mumbled—he didn't feel anything amazing about sleeping with Varana. Maybe it was because he was simply using her to get information.

"But their capabilities? And their venom—I don't know. In the right setting, I imagine that could be a pretty good time. You should ask Aleksei what he thinks," he suggested with yet another laugh.

Starting to feel his irritancy breaking through his façade, Luther rolled his eyes and looked over at the bar. He didn't want to ask Alucard *anything* about that. He didn't even want to think about the things he and Zalith did—things that Zalith didn't deserve. How Zalith got to touch him; how he got to know the things Alucard would never tell anyone else. How he got to see the side of Alucard that Luther felt he always wanted to know. And how Zalith had been the one to help Alucard out of his solitude.

Luther so sorely wished it had been *him*, and that he had known Alucard was gay before he gave up trying to woo him and started a job that would force him to marry woman after woman. But he hadn't lost hope. Now that he knew, he was going to do whatever he could to prove to Alucard that he deserved better than that arrogant demon…and that *Luther* was better for him.

His thoughts became a little discombobulated for a moment. Of course, he knew that *Alucard* was a demon, but he'd never thought of him as one; that was mainly because so many years ago, Alucard had told him his story and asked him *not* to consider him a demon. Both he and Attila respected that, and thinking about it now came to him as a surprise. Alucard *was* a demon, and Luther felt his hatred for them was now a little hypocritical. Not *all* demons were like Zalith…. Alucard was nothing like that selfish, rude, arrogant creature. But…he didn't consider Alucard a demon, so when he thought about how all demons were the same, Alucard was excluded from that statement.

Luther rolled his eyes again and sighed, shuffling in his seat as he looked at Greymore again. He felt a little awful for doing what he was doing just to get what he needed to know about Alucard and Zalith—what he needed to know so that he could give Alucard the happiness he deserved. Screwing his sister, talking to one of Zalith's exes and possibly the guy he was sleeping with behind Alucard's back. It was the kind of behaviour he didn't often find himself partaking in, but…it was for Alucard, and for Alucard, he'd do anything.

"Well, Luther," Greymore then said and gulped down the rest of his drink. He loudly placed his glass on the table. "I don't suspect all of us will be on this boat for very long, so if you really want to get to know everyone, I suggest you start as soon as you can," he said, standing up. "Nice meeting ya."

Luther sunk deeper into his thoughts, the sound of Greymore's loud call for a round of drinks for everyone drowning out as he stared at his empty glass. He wasn't sure how long of a mission this was going to be—learning what he needed to learn—but the longer he spent knowing Zalith was upsetting Alucard, the worse he began to feel. However, he had to be patient; he'd learn what he needed to know, and he'd get what he wanted.

Just then, Varana stopped beside him. "Let's go," she said.

He looked up at her, ignoring the stupid, drunken cheers coming from the people in the bar aimed at the woman. He felt no need to stay any longer. Now that he knew who Danford was, he'd be able to find him again later. For now, he needed time alone with his thoughts—or maybe time with Varana. Perhaps she'd give him more information.

So, he stood up and left the bar with her, heading back to his room.

# Chapter Thirty-Three

## Fish Tank

**| Zalith |**

As dusk lingered in the air, Zalith and Alucard arrived back home.

Zalith led the way into the house, firmly holding Alucard's hand as they made their way through the entrance hall. He felt a lot more relaxed than he had earlier; he'd had a nice time with Alucard today. But with his enjoyment came guilt, and that upset him. The whole time he spent occupying himself with work, he could have been enjoying moments like today with his vampire, and knowing how much it hurt him only made him feel worse. He wanted to make it up to Alucard, but…he had no idea what to do for him.

He looked over his shoulder at the vampire while he led the way forward, and when Alucard shyly stared back, Zalith smiled at him. He wasn't sure where else to go, so he took the vampire into the lounge next to his office and sat on one of the couches.

Alucard sat beside him, and as he did, Zalith leaned his head on the vampire's shoulder, sighing quietly. The demon missed the warmth of the sun on his face as well as sitting down at the lake with the man he loved; he hadn't been out much with him in the past few months, and now that he had been, he remembered how much he loved it. Being able to share something even as simple as a walk with Alucard made him feel content.

Zalith moved his arm around his vampire, holding him as they both relaxed. Perhaps they could do something tomorrow, too. He'd missed out on so much time with Alucard that he wanted to make up for *all* of what they'd lost. Even if they just went on another walk or had dinner somewhere; time out of the house with Alucard at his side was one of his favourite things.

The vampire rested his head on Zalith's, staring at the wall in front of them, and for a while, they sat in silence.

But with the silence came Zalith's dismaying thoughts. He could hear the clock ticking on the wall; it was getting louder and louder. Maybe he should send someone to fetch a violinist to come and play for them or ask Alucard to tell him another story.

Alucard then smiled at him. "If you vant, ve can go to my study; I 'ave someving more intervesting to stare at zhan zhese valls," he suggested excitedly.

Curiosity tried shoving Zalith's dismay aside. "Is that so?" he asked with a sultry tone. Was he being too bold assuming that Alucard might just be trying to flirt with him?

The vampire looked away shyly and nodded. Then, he took hold of Zalith's hand and stood up. "Let's go."

Zalith got up and followed Alucard out of the room and towards the stairs. He watched Alucard's every move as they headed up, waiting for the vampire to glance back at him so that he could smirk and see his flustered face. But the vampire didn't look at him. He took Zalith to the top of the stairs, across the hall, and then into his study.

When they stepped into the room, Zalith watched Alucard look to his left, so that was where *he* looked, too. Sitting between the bookshelves was a glass tank filled with water and tropical fish. Alucard stood there with a proud smile on his face, waiting for Zalith to take a closer look, so he moved a little nearer and gazed into the tank.

He was admittedly surprised. He hadn't been expecting to see what he was now standing in front of, and it took a moment for him to work out what he wanted to say. The glass, water-filled tank was at least six feet in length and half that in height. The water was home to both aquatic plants and so many fish of different shapes, sizes, and colours—and Zalith had no idea what they were called.

He looked at Alucard. "When did you get this?" he asked, slowly looking back at the tank. "It's nice," he added, staring at a small group of fish as they swam around the other fish that chose to swim alone.

"I got zhe idea avter I took Drac to zhe sanctuary," the vampire answered. "I vigured I could vork out a vay to make a smaller version of zhe 'abitat Drac vas moved into."

Impressed, Zalith leaned forward and peered into the glass. Drac's new habitat possessed a rather large waterfall to oxygenate the water, and this tank appeared to have a smaller one that must surely be powered by some kind of mechanism he wasn't aware of. There was even a current in the water—the plants closer to one side of the tank were moving around as they would in a current.

"How does it work?" Zalith asked as he stood up straight and set his gaze back on Alucard.

The vampire shrugged slightly. "Is boring conversation," he said, but when Zalith smiled to assure him that he wanted to listen, he smiled and looked at the tank. "Zhere's an intake inside zhe tank—takes zhe vater into a vilter zhat cleans. And zhen comes back out zhere," he said, pointing to the miniature waterfall.

Looking back into the tank, Zalith nodded and watched as the fish inside it continued to swim around. He didn't recognize any of the species, so he glanced at Alucard and asked him, "What kinds of fish are they?"

Alucard moved closer and stared into the tank. "Zhose are angelvish," he said, pointing to the large, almost triangular-shaped fish that were sticking close to one another. "Zhese are silver dollars, but zhey look like piranhas," he said with a smile, pointing to the rounded, shimmering silver fish that were just a little bigger than the angelfish. He next pointed to an eel-like fish that was rapidly darting along the gravel-lined bottom of the tank. "Zhose are veather loaches. And zhat's a catvish," he said, pointing to a small black fish which looked like it had whiskers. "Zhere are some tetras in zhere, too, but zhey're small and 'ard to see."

Zalith's smile grew. He was certain that Alucard had named every single one of these fish, and he had to ask, "What are their names?"

"Zhis is Marbella," Alucard said, pointing to the angelfish with a greyish-white body and a few white patches. "'Ana," he said, pointing to the dull orange angelfish, "she veminds me of 'ana zhe chicken. And zhat ozzer vone is Conrad," he said, pointing to the third and final angelfish.

"And this guy?" Zalith asked, pointing to the weather loach as it darted past again.

"Vinny," he said. "Vas Vincent but…I like Vinny better."

Zalith watched one of the silver dollars. "Him?"

"Is a she," Alucard corrected. "She's greedy vith vood, so I call 'er Snappy. Zhis is a male, and I got 'im vrom somevone who 'ad alveady named 'im Pete, so…zhat's 'is name. And zhat vone is T. I did 'ave anozzer vone zhat came vith Pete, but 'e zidn't last long because zhe man I got zhem vrom vasn't veally taking care of zhem."

"Where did you get them?"

"A mage," he answered sadly. "Zhey use small vish like zhese in practices. I zon't like zhat."

Zalith watched the fish swim around for a few more moments. But his guilt started to consume him again. It seemed as though Alucard must have been working on this for quite a while, and the fact that he hadn't had time to notice made him feel worse. And he was quite sure this wasn't the only thing he'd not taken the time to notice these past few months.

As Alucard wandered over to the couch not too far from the tank, Zalith followed and sat with him. Once again, he leaned his head on Alucard's shoulder and took a moment to glance around the room. He hadn't been in there all that much since Alucard moved in and seeing how comfortable the vampire had made it brought a smile to his face. However, his smile faded when his gaze wandered to a shelf of books, all of which possessed Deiganish titles.

He frowned harder as his guilt grew heavier. He was supposed to be helping Alucard to better understand, read, *and* write Deiganish, but he'd failed to do that, too. He wasn't sure if Alucard had been learning on his own, but the fact that there were now Deiganish-written books in his study made Zalith assume that Alucard *had* been learning by himself.

Zalith took his eyes off the books and looked down at the floor, his guilt increasing. He really had neglected Alucard, hadn't he?

With a dismayed scowl on his face, he nuzzled Alucard's neck and moved his arm around him. He *needed* to make things up to him, but…how? He had no idea, and he needed to think about it. Sooner or later, he'd work out what he could do for Alucard—or so he hoped.

For a short while, they both lay in silence, watching the fish as they swam around. But the silence started gnawing at Zalith. He couldn't think of anything to say, so he tried distracting himself by thinking about the things he had to catch up on now that his people were safe. He still needed to deal with the Imperito, and to his relief, there were no concerning reports regarding the Numen. But he still wanted them dead, and he needed to ask Alucard how he felt about the situation.

Before he could ask, though a knock soon came at the door, and as they looked over at it, Edwin stepped in.

"Dinner is ready, sir," he said, setting his eyes on Zalith.

"Okay, thank you," Zalith said, and as Edwin left, he looked at Alucard. "Are you hungry? Do you want to eat now?"

Alucard nodded. "Ve can 'ave dinner."

"Okay," Zalith said with a smile, and then he stood up. "Let's go," he said, taking Alucard's hand. He'd ask him about the Numen later.

Then, without further hindrance, he led the way out of Alucard's study.

**| Alucard |**

Alucard followed Zalith through the house. He felt content and couldn't keep a smile off his face. He'd had a nice time with Zalith today, and he liked to think that he'd at least been able to improve Zalith's mood a little. He still wanted to find new ways to help Zalith through this, but right now, he couldn't think of anything other than being there for him. He *had* offered to show Zalith how he'd stopped Adellum, but Zalith didn't want to see that, and even though he didn't understand why, he wasn't going to force him. Maybe it had something to do with the fact that Zalith would have to let him into his mind…and maybe the demon wasn't ready to do that just yet.

He followed him downstairs, and when the demon glanced back at him and smiled, he thought about the flirtatious look Zalith had given him before they'd headed up to see the fish tank. He felt a little selfish about it now, but when they'd been in his office, he couldn't help but feel like he wanted him to make a move. Of course, he knew that Zalith was going through a lot, but it had been so long since they'd had sex. He sorely missed Zalith's affection, and sometimes, it was all he could think about…especially now that he had his demon back.

But the last thing he was going to do right now was put his needs before Zalith's. He didn't want to make the demon do anything he wasn't ready for. So, he'd keep his desires to himself and let Zalith set the pace. And right now, Zalith wanted to sit and have dinner, so that was what Alucard was going to do, too.

# Chapter Thirty-Four

— ⸲ † ⸱ —

## The Numen Dilemma

**| Alucard |**

Alucard and Zalith sat at the dining table, a palpable silence enveloping them. While Zalith methodically sliced into his steak, Alucard's gaze lingered on his own plate, the desire to eat warring with a weariness that settled deep within him. The day had stretched on endlessly, and all he craved was the solace of his bed, the weight of exhaustion heavy upon his shoulders.

Zalith looked at him with a pondering expression. "I know you don't like talking about it," he started, watching as Alucard shifted his gaze to him, "but have you put any thought into the Damien and Lilith situation?"

The vampire frowned and looked down at his food. He hadn't thought about Damien or Lilith much at all since the Daegelus' last appearance. All he'd really thought about was how awful he felt about the fact that Zalith had gotten hurt by Damien because of him and that Zalith's late, strange behaviour might have been because of that.

But he knew that wasn't the case now. He was sure that at some point, he and Zalith would have to talk about their plans involving the Numen. Zalith had said he was going to kill Damien, and as much as Alucard would love for that creature to die, he knew that it was going to be an almost impossible task. So much would have to be done, and so much would happen that Alucard didn't feel as though it was worth the stress. Hunting and killing a Numen was no simple task, especially one like Damien.

He shrugged, staring down at his plate. "In vhat sense?" he asked, looking for clarification—maybe Zalith was simply referring to the fact that they were hiding from the Numen and that Alucard had to be discreet with his work and subordinates.

"I want them dead," Zalith answered.

Alucard frowned again and looked down at his plate. Did Zalith know what it would take to kill a Numen? "Do you know 'ow to kill zhem?"

"No," he answered, "but I'll find out, and then I'll kill them." The demon put his knife and fork down, rested his arms on the table, and stared at him. "Do *you* know?"

*Did* he?

Alucard stared into his wine. He *did* know… and that was one of the reasons why the Numen took it upon themselves to mess with his memory. He knew what it took to create a Numen, to weaken a Numen, and to even kill one.

But Alucard couldn't do that. All he could do was take their power from them for a limited time. To kill them? It took a whole lot more than simply taking their power from them, and it was something near impossible. Alucard didn't want to let Zalith take on such a dangerous mission—he didn't want to lose him, and that was something that was most likely going to happen if the demon went ahead with his promise to kill Damien.

He looked at Zalith with a conflicted frown on his face. "I zon't know," he said slowly. "If ve *should*," he added. "Is dangerous, and… I zon't vant you to put your life at visk vhich is vhat you vill be doing if you actually vant to try and kill zhem."

Zalith looked down at his plate, sighed slightly, and set his eyes back on the vampire. "I know. And that doesn't make me change my mind. Our lives are at risk regardless."

Alucard sipped from his wine and frowned in hesitation. They were already hiding from the Numen and they would be for the rest of their lives if they didn't do anything about it. It wasn't exactly *totally* impossible to kill them; it was just a lot of hard, long work. But Zalith seemed to know that and still wanted to kill them. He'd told Alucard many times before that he would kill Damien, and the thought of that creature being dead and gone forever brought relief to Alucard—relief he wished to feel for the rest of his life. And hiding right now *did* make him feel safe, but it was inevitable that one day, Lilith and or Damien would find them.

He sighed quietly and said, "I know. But is not simple. Zhere's more to zhis zhan taking zheir power avay and ending zheir lives. Vill take us years to kill just vone of zhem, and ve'll need 'elp."

"I'm willing to put in the time and effort; if it's going to ensure our safety, then no time is too long."

"Vell…." Alucard exhaled, looking down at his food. "Ve vill also need to go to some of zhe ozzer vorlds. A Numen's power comes vrom zheir vollowers, and I know zhat Zamien's believers live in Tengetso. Ve vould 'ave to go zhere and eradicate 'is influence, and zhat vould take a long time. Ovten, a Numen's power comes vrom people's admiration and love vor zhem, but… Zamien's comes vrom 'ate. Zhe people in Tengetso loath 'im because of zhe destruction 'e brought down upon zheir vorld. Tengetso is enthralled by death, depravity, and everyving awvul. All vas birthed by Zamien, and 'e goes back zhere every so ovten to curse zhe land vith more 'orror."

Zalith nodded as he picked his knife and fork up again. "Well, it's going to take a while, but at least ageing isn't an issue for us."

Alucard glanced down at his plate. "I guess," he mumbled.

The demon frowned. "They're never going to stop looking for you, and they won't stop making our lives hell unless we do something about it."

"I know," Alucard said with a sigh as he looked over at the door. He was beginning to feel irritated—not at Zalith, but at the fact that the Numen would never stop looking for him, and they wouldn't stop making his life hell unless he and Zalith did something to stop them. It was going to be a lot of work, and even though Zalith said he was prepared for the amount of time and effort it would take, Alucard felt guilty that this even needed to happen. He sighed again, glancing at Zalith, who was staring at him, clearly waiting for him to answer. "Ve vould need numbers—zhe Numen vill start wars. Ve vill need to go to zhe ozzer vorlds, and zhere isn't anyvone I know as powervul as ve are to stay 'ere and look avter vings vhile ve are gone."

"It will take time," Zalith assured him, "but I believe there are solutions out there."

Alucard nodded. "Vell, depending on vhen ve plan to declare zhis war, I can 'ave people veady; is easy to turn a vampire, but to make sure zhey von't die takes time."

Zalith finished eating his food. "We can arrange and have a meeting soon with our subordinates and work out numbers and everything we need. Even if it takes years, it doesn't matter. We're still going to kill them."

The vampire nodded again, picking up his glass to take another sip of his wine. "Vine," he agreed. "Vhen should ve arrange zhis meeting?" he asked. Although it was going to take much time and even more resources, he believed that he and Zalith could eradicate Damien, and maybe even Lilith, too, freeing themselves of their most dangerous enemies. Maybe once the Numen were no longer after him, he might actually be able to live a full life, a life that he didn't have to spend hiding and running; although doing so with Zalith felt much more comforting, he *would* like to stop hiding one day.

"The sooner, the better, preferably," Zalith answered, refilling Alucard's almost empty wine glass.

"Vank you," Alucard mumbled. Then, he sighed quietly. "Maybe…in a veek?" he suggested.

"That sounds good. Thank you for letting me do this, and for letting me become involved. I know it's going to be dangerous and a lot of work, but I believe we can do it."

Alucard nodded, placing his glass down. "I just 'ope none of zhe ozzer Numen get involved. Zamien and Liliv are not very much liked by zhe ozzers, but…zhey may stick togezzer vonce ve take vone of zhem down. Zhe same as vhen I killed Janus—all zhe dragon gods 'ated vone anozzer, but vhen Janus died, zhey all grouped up vor safety. I zon't know if zhe Numen vill do zhat, but zhere is a possibility. Zhey von't physically group up—zhey are veaker vhen zhey are close to vone anozzer, but zhey may band zheir vorces togezzer."

Zalith thought to himself for a few moments. Then, he said, "I wonder if we can organize something in such a way that they don't find out that it's us."

"Do you 'ave any ideas? Or vill ve need to vink about zhat?"

"We could run things from the shadows and have stand-ins who would appear to be in charge. Or we could find out who the Numens' enemies are, and we could either masquerade as them or work with them," he suggested with a devious tone.

Alucard pondered for a moment. Everything Zalith said sounded smart, and if the Numen didn't know that it was he and Zalith who were after them, then maybe it would be easier to work on doing what needed to be done in order to end their lives for good.

He nodded at Zalith. "Both sound like good ideas. But zhen do ve know or trust anyvone to stand in vor us? And zhen I zon't veally know who Zamien's enemies are…or Liliv's."

"Perhaps one of my Alphas could stand in, but I want to think about all of the options before we make decisions. As for their enemies, we can send people out to look for the information we need—they are bound to have enemies considering how deplorable they both are," he said with a roll of his eyes and sipped from his wine.

Alucard nodded, glancing down at his glass. "Zhen ve vill reconvene vith zhis next veek."

"It's a date," Zalith said with a smirk.

# Chapter Thirty-Five

## Light's End

**| Zalith |**

As Zalith lay in bed, ensconced in Alucard's embrace, his mind wandered through the labyrinth of his thoughts. The relentless question gnawed at him: was this reality true or merely a fleeting illusion? Despite the perplexing uncertainty, today had unfolded serenely alongside Alucard. No turmoil had marred the day; not even a whisper of horror had crossed their path, and it was starting to seem as though nothing was going to happen to take away the grasp he felt he was finally getting.

He frowned, staring at the wall across from where he lay. Maybe Alucard was safe; maybe things were okay, and maybe this wasn't some façade. Perhaps…it *was* the real world, and perhaps it really was over. Unless…it wasn't, and this was a fake world…but he couldn't avoid thinking about the fact that, if this was real, he'd be wasting his life sitting around acting as though it wasn't. He wouldn't waste his life like that, and he wouldn't hurt Alucard by not being himself.

The demon looked down at what he could see of Alucard, listening to the calm, relaxing beat of his heart as he started falling asleep. Alucard offered to show him what happened when he went into the void space—he offered to show him what happened to the Light. Perhaps if he allowed himself to see it, he'd get some closure and be able to move on with his life.

"Alucard?" he asked, unsure whether the vampire had fallen asleep yet or not.

But he hadn't. Alucard murmured a sound in response, letting Zalith know that he was awake.

"Can you show me what you did to the Light?"

"I vhought you zidn't vant to see," he responded.

"I'm ready to see it now."

Alucard went quiet for a moment but then rolled onto his right side so that he was facing the demon. He placed his fingers on his face as though to connect their minds, and then he closed his eyes.

Zalith did the same, preparing for whatever he was about to see, and as darkness engulfed his vision, he allowed Alucard's memory to be seen as if it were his own.

*He witnessed Alucard leaving the island and stepping back into the void space where he went to collect Colt. He witnessed how the Light startled Alucard, yet Alucard didn't cower nor even think about running. He stole the Light's power until it was nought but an empty vessel, and then he dragged its corpse into Eltaria, left it on the battlefield, and returned to the island. And from Alucard's thoughts during that memory, he learned that Adellum would take a very long time to recover from what the vampire did.*

Once the memory was over, Zalith opened his eyes and stared into Alucard's. His adoration for Alucard was paramount, and right now, he began to think about that and how much he really did love him. The fact that Alucard had gone out of his way to stop the Light for him—he didn't know how to explain how it made him feel. He loved and appreciated Alucard so much, and the things he did for him…Zalith could probably never repay him.

Although he wasn't quite convinced it was over—Adellum had come back from many devastating blows before—he allowed himself to relax and bask in the fact that Alucard banished the Light to stay in Eltaria forever.

"Alucard," Zalith murmured, his hand tenderly caressing the side of the vampire's face. Meeting Alucard's gaze, he offered a gentle smile, his heart heavy with the weight of his affection. Words seemed inadequate to convey the depth of his love and longing for him. Silently, he leaned in, pressing his lips against Alucard's in a fervent kiss. As their embrace deepened, the demon shifted, positioning himself above the vampire, his arms cradling Alucard on either side with a tender embrace that spoke volumes where words faltered.

Zalith's kisses grew more passionate, his desire for Alucard consuming him as he tangled his fingers in the vampire's crimson hair, pulling him closer. Every touch and every caress was a testament to the hunger that burned within him—not just for Alucard's body, but for his very essence, his soul, his heart. But as Zalith's lips trailed down to Alucard's neck, a moment of reluctance gripped him. The primal urge to taste and claim Alucard's essence as his own warred with the weight of his guilt. He felt unworthy, undeserving of the euphoria that would flood his senses with the taste of Alucard's blood. So with a conflicted sigh, the demon withdrew from the brink of temptation, returning his lips to Alucard's in a searing kiss. His hand, now trailing down Alucard's body, conveyed his ardor as it explored every curve and contour, seeking solace in the intimacy they shared.

When Alucard's hand trailed to the side of Zalith's neck, the demon felt a shiver of anticipation course through the vampire's body; Alucard evidently sensed his desire and inclined his head, offering his neck once more to Zalith's fervent kisses. With each tender caress, Zalith's fingers traced a path of longing over Alucard's sculpted abdomen. The vampire fidgeted, and Zalith could tell that his excitement was growing as quickly as his own.

Alucard reciprocated the longing, his touch a dance of desire as he explored Zalith's form with eager fingers. From the curve of his waist to the strength of his muscles, Alucard's touch conveyed an unspoken yearning for more. Yet, in the midst of their shared ardor, a moment of uncertainty flickered in Alucard's eyes as he met Zalith's gaze.

Halting his affections, Zalith met Alucard's gaze with understanding, granting him the space to decide their course. And then, with a sudden surge of determination, Alucard seized Zalith's arms, flipping their positions with a swift motion that left Zalith pinned beneath him, a silent invitation for their passion to ignite anew.

Zalith stared up at him in surprise, but he quickly smirked as his excitement and desire for more quickly consumed him. He loved it when Alucard took control.

Alucard released his grip on Zalith's arms, positioning himself with deliberate intent, his arms now serving as pillars of support on either side of the demon. With a steady hand, he caressed the side of Zalith's neck while clutching the pillow in his other, his gaze fixated with primal hunger.

Yet, instead of yielding to his evident urge to bite, Alucard hesitated, savoring the anticipation that hung heavy in the air. As Zalith drew him closer, the vampire's lips met the demon's skin in a series of soft kisses, each touch a symphony of pleasure that reverberated through Zalith's being. From shoulder to pec, Alucard's trail of kisses blazed a path of desire down Zalith's body, igniting a feverish yearning within him.

Zalith's anticipation peaked when Alucard reached his waist; he watched the vampire's jaw widen, and he braced himself for the impending sensation of the vampire's bite. And when Alucard's fangs sank into his side, a rush of pleasure mingled with a tinge of pain coursed through the demon's veins, eliciting a primal groan of ecstasy from his lips. Gripping Alucard's hair with fervent need, Zalith surrendered to the intoxicating embrace of the vampire's venom, relishing in the exquisite agony as Alucard's bite deepened.

"Fuck," Zalith breathed, tightening his grip as the pleasing pain enthralled him. And of course, it aroused him. It pleased him so much that he could feel his hard shaft throbbing, eager to plunge into Alucard's body.

But he had to wait.

Alucard soon pulled his fangs from his side and made his way back up the demon's body, and once his face was near his, Zalith lightly snatched his jaw and smirked up at him.

"I liked that," he told him, his voice hushed and seductive. And after he spoke, he felt Alucard shiver once more in anticipation. He hastily flipped them over, pinning the vampire beneath him.

Zalith's lips tenderly met Alucard's once more, a gentle caress rather than a fiery embrace, yet beneath the surface, a simmering desperation lingered. With a soft sigh, he deepened the kiss, their mouths melding together in a sweet exchange of affection. As his heart raced in his chest, Zalith's fingers trailed down Alucard's body, a soothing touch that spoke of comfort even as a faint sense of urgency tugged at him.

Feeling the warmth of their shared breaths, Zalith couldn't help but be overwhelmed by a sense of tenderness mingled with a quiet desperation to hold onto this moment. With a tender stroke, he guided Alucard onto his back, his movements careful and measured, matching the rhythm of their affection.

Continuing to kiss Alucard's lips, Zalith's hand trailed down the vampire's body again. This time, his touch encompassed more than desire; it held a quiet reassurance, a promise of unwavering affection even as an undercurrent of longing pulsed through him. And as his fingers met Alucard's shaft, the vampire hummed quietly in anticipation, turning his head to the side as Zalith started kissing his neck. Mere moments later, though, Alucard moved his hand to the back of Zalith's head and urged his face closer, evidently waiting for him to bite.

Zalith wasn't going to wait any longer. He knew what Alucard wanted…and he wanted it just as sorely. As he stroked the vampire's hardening dick, he sank his fangs into his neck, making Alucard tighten his grip on his hair and whine in delight. The moment Alucard's blood touched his tongue, Zalith groaned in satisfaction and swallowed it like a starved beast; he missed Alucard's sweet, enthralling taste, and he wanted to make the most of every second he got to taste it.

But he couldn't take too much. He had to control himself…so he pulled his fangs away and leaned into the vampire's ear. "Can I fuck you?" he asked as he let go of Alucard's shaft and slowly dragged his fingertips up his body.

Alucard exhaled deeply and nodded in response.

Zalith couldn't explain how relieved he felt by his answer. He didn't waste a moment. While his heart raced in his chest, he reached over to his nightstand and took the small tincture bottle of lube from inside.

He glanced at Alucard, who shyly turned his head away once he saw that Zalith was looking at him. The demon smiled down at him and moved a strand of his crimson hair from over his eye. He loved him so much; he could simply stare at him for hours, but it wasn't enough right now. He needed to be as close as he could to his vampire, and this was the only way he knew.

The demon poured some of the lube onto his fingers, and while he eagerly kissed Alucard, he gently massaged it into the vampire's ass. Alucard hummed quietly in content as Zalith slowly pushed his fingers in and pulled them back; he pressed his tips against the vampire's tight walls, making him moan hushedly, and once he was done, he gradually pulled them out again before rubbing some of the viscous liquid onto his own dick.

He couldn't wait a moment longer.

Zalith gripped Alucard's left leg and positioned it over his back as he leaned closer. He then grabbed his dick and started carefully easing it into the vampire's ass.

With a struggled frown, Alucard turned his head to the side, inviting Zalith to kiss his neck again. The demon pressed his lips against the vampire's soft skin as he gradually moved his shaft deeper inside him. He listened to Alucard's hushed breaths, and when he pressed his chest against his, he felt the vampire's heart racing in sync with his. His body started aching out of sheer desperation; he hadn't had sex in months; every ounce of energy he'd been surviving on had come from the brief kisses he'd managed to share with Alucard, and that filled him with guilt. But the guilt couldn't outweigh the pleasure, it couldn't outweigh his thoughts about how much he loved Alucard and how much he needed and wanted him.

And how much he wanted to please him.

Alucard guided his hand to the back of Zalith's head, gripping a fistful of his hair; Zalith knew he was trying to keep himself from moaning, which made him smirk and feel the need to please him further, forcing him to whine in delight.

But as he moved his dick deeper, he felt Alucard flinch, tense up, and hesitate, so he pulled back a little and lifted his head to look down at him. "Are you okay?" he breathed.

The vampire glanced at him and nodded. And as he turned his head away again, he said, "'As just been a vhile."

Zalith's guilt was growing, so much that it started breaking through the desperation and desire. All those months he'd been focusing solely on his work, he hadn't spent much time with Alucard at all. But he didn't want to let his negative feelings consume him. Not right now. They both needed this.

"I'll be gentle," he told him and eased his shaft in a little slower.

As the demon nuzzled Alucard's neck, he started thrusting gently, pushing his dick a little deeper each time. Alucard's tight, warm walls ensnared his shaft, making him hum contently against the vampire's neck, and when every inch was inside, he slowly pulled back, listening as Alucard exhaled deeply, stifling a moan.

Zalith smirked and pinned Alucard's arms above his head, breathing against his neck as he thrusted his shaft back into him. The vampire grimaced and moaned, turning his head to the side as his face turned a little red. Zalith started moving faster, and while he did, Alucard moved his other leg over Zalith's back, pulling him closer.

With a pleased, *relieved* expression on his face, Zalith thrusted in and out of Alucard's body, moaning quietly against the vampire's neck as that feeling of utter delight quickly ensnared him. He let go of one of Alucard's hands and gripped the sheets below him in an attempt to keep himself from losing control. But his body urged him to thrust deeper and harder—it begged him to take everything he wanted from Alucard.

But he resisted. He moaned and whined, burying his face against Alucard's neck, moving his body back and forth as he listened to the vampire's pleased cries. He felt Alucard drag his hand up his back, and when the vampire dug his claws into his skin and tensed up, a flurry of overwhelmingly pleasing surges coursed through him. There were no words to explain how utterly delighted Alucard's body made him feel; he wanted every part of him all the time—he wanted to hold on to this feeling for as long as he could.

However, he could feel Alucard approaching his peak. The vampire fidgeted beanth him, urging Zalith to push Alucard's body to its limit. And he complied. He thrusted deeper and harder, giving the vampire the same overbearing pleasure that he gave to Zalith, and just moments later, with a struggled and delighted whine, Alucard climaxed, and his enthralling walls lightly throbbed around the demon's dick in response.

Zalith grunted in desperation—he wanted to feel the sheer contentedness that came with an orgasm, the same delight that Alucard was feeling right now, moaning and digging his claws deeper into his skin. So he thrusted aggressively, pushing his own body to its peak, and when he couldn't hold on any longer, he halted after a final, deep thrust and moaned pleasurably as his shaft convulsed inside Alucard, and his body was consumed by alleviating relief.

He let out a long, gratified moan as his cum filled the vampire's ass, each throb increasing his satisfaction. This was his favourite way to claim Alucard, to remind him that he belonged to him, to remind him that he loved him, and that he'd never stop loving him. And as the last of his climax oozed from his dick, he kissed the vampire's neck and lightly dragged his tongue over the wounds left by his fangs.

After a few deep, calming breaths, Zalith loosened his grip on Alucard's wrist, his heart thumping in his chest and his body trembling. With a deep, shaky sigh, he rested his aching body against Alucard's and listened to his gradually slowing heart.

Alucard pulled his legs from around Zalith's waist and rested them on the bed. He kept his hand on Zalith's back, his eyes closed, and his head to the side. Zalith didn't want to move, though. He breathed against Alucard's neck, keeping his face nuzzled into it. And he grasped Alucard's hand firmly.

"I love you, Alucard," he whispered as he tightened his grip on the vampire's hand. "And thank you for loving me so much."

As Zalith then lifted his head from Alucard's neck, the vampire turned his head so that he could look up at him.

"Vhy do you vank me?" he asked with a confused frown.

Zalith stared down at him, moving his hair away from his eyes. "Because I'm thankful I met you. I don't know where I'd even be right now if you weren't here. My life…would be empty."

Alucard moved his hand from Zalith's back and placed it on the side of his face. "I von't be going anyvhere. You make my time vorth living," he said as nervousness flickered across his flustered face.

But that made Zalith smile. He leaned in and kissed the vampire's lips for a few moments. Then, he pulled his shaft from the vampire's body, used a nearby shirt to clean both himself and Alucard, and then lay beside him. They both made themselves comfortable, facing one another as they lay on their sides.

"I love you, too," Alucard then said.

Still smiling, Zalith kissed the vampire's forehead and pulled him closer. Alucard moved his arms around him, resting his forehead against his chest as Zalith held him in a tight, protective embrace.

Zalith could lay like this forever, and right now, he felt nothing but sheer happiness. Nothing was going to take that from him.

# Chapter Thirty-Six

— ⵣ ✝ ⵣ —

## Magic Trick

| **Alucard** |

As dawn's gentle light seeped through the parted curtains, it found its mark upon Alucard's face, stirring him from slumber. He scowled irritably, though not in response to the sun's intrusion.

"Daddy? Papa?" came the voice of a small child—a girl.

Alucard didn't want to reply. One thing he hated most in the world was being woken from his sleep; he groaned in dismissal, pulling the blankets over his face to block the sun—but then the confusion hit him. Daddy? Papa? A girl? He opened his eyes, pulled the blankets away from his face, and slowly looked over his shoulder.

"Can I show you something?" asked the small, strawberry-blonde demon sitting cross-legged between him and Zalith.

Her eyes looked so much like Zalith's, and her hair was a much lighter shade than Alucard's. But who was she?

"Papa?" she asked, staring at him with a frown on her face.

"Vhat?" he asked—but as if he was asking himself: what the hell was this?

"Can I show you something?" she pleaded. "Daddy won't wake up," she said with a pout, looking at Zalith, who had his back to Alucard, sleeping quietly. "But you woke up." She smiled, setting her dark eyes on him.

Alucard stared at her. Why was she calling him her father? He wasn't a dad, and neither was Zalith… as far as he was aware, anyway. He glanced at Zalith and then back at the girl. He sat up, looking down at her as she excitedly shuffled a deck of black cards in her hands.

"I want to show you a trick. But… a magic trick," she whispered, leaning closer.

With a tired exhale, Alucard dragged his hand over his face and waited, staring at her, trying to work out who she was, where he was…. A dream?

*The girl shuffled the cards, wriggling around excitedly. Then, she held them out towards Alucard and smiled. "Okay, you have to pick one—don't think about it too much—just pick one," she urged.*

*Despite his confusion, he did as she said, almost as if he was compelled to do so. With a quiet sigh, he reached forward and went to grab a card, but stopped for a moment to stare at the rings on his left hand. He should only possess one—the one that hid him from the Numen—but he had four; two on his ring finger, one on his middle, and the last on his index finger.*

*"Okay, now I have to guess what you got," the girl said.*

*Alucard looked down at the card in his hand; it was a tarot card, the high priestess to be specific.*

*"Is it... three of cups?" she asked him.*

*Alucard took his eyes off the card and looked down at her. "No," he answered.*

*"Damn it," she mumbled but brought the cards up to cover her mouth and frowned in surprise. "Oops," she said. "Sorry Papa."*

*The vampire had no idea what to say... or what to think; all he could do was let her take the card back from him and watch as she started to reshuffle the deck. He had no idea what was going on, and the first thing that came to mind in the midst of his confusion was Zalith. He looked at the demon—maybe he'd know what was going on. So, he leaned over and placed his hand on Zalith's shoulder. "Zaliv?"*

*Zalith stirred and mumbled quietly but rolled onto his back and looked up at him. The demon smiled and moved his hand to the side of Alucard's face. "Good morning, baby," he said sleepily.*

*Before Alucard could ask him what was going on, the girl wriggled into Zalith's lap. "Daddy!" she said contently.*

*Zalith sat up, smiling down at her.*

*Alucard gazed at them; his eyes wandered to the thin gold chain around Zalith's neck and then to the rather ghastly scar cutting deep into the centre of his chest. That was new, too.*

*"What is it?" Zalith asked with a smile.*

*"A magic trick!" she insisted, holding out the cards to him. "Pick one."*

*As told, Zalith picked one of the cards.*

*"Okay, now I have to guess."*

*Waiting, Zalith glanced at Alucard and smiled at him.*

*"Is it... three of cups?"*

*"No," Zalith said with a smirk, looking down at her as he flipped the card around to show her what it was. "It's death," he revealed.*

*Alucard couldn't keep his eyes off the both of them—all of this seemed so right, but... so wrong. Why? It wasn't real... was it? It felt real... or... maybe he wanted it to be real? He wasn't sure, but as he looked at both the girl and Zalith, he felt nothing but contentedness.*

*However... it couldn't be real. Zalith had no scars, they had no small girl in their lives... and as Alucard looked down at the rings on his fingers, the symbols etched into them changed.*

*This was a dream. But... what a random dream.... He looked at Zalith and the girl again, trying to work out why his mind would create such a situation. Was this... supposed to be their daughter? Was that what this was? He looked down at his hands again—once more, the symbols on his rings had changed. It wasn't real— but... why did he feel like he wanted it to be?*

*It wasn't. And the moment he accepted that, he felt the world withering away. Before his eyes, everything—Zalith and the girl included—faded into darkness, and he was left with a bitter, drowning emptiness in his heart.*

Alucard opened his eyes. Before him stood the wall of his and Zalith's room, and the sun was shining on his face. Was *this* the real world? He could feel Zalith's arm around him, he could hear the demon quietly breathing, and the pain of Zalith's bite lingered in his shoulder. He *was* really awake this time. But... why had he seen those things?

He pulled free of Zalith's embrace, sitting up; he found himself searching the room... but why? It was only a dream, so... why did he feel as though he would see the girl again?

"Alucard?" Zalith asked, sitting up beside him. "What's wrong?"

The vampire slowly turned his head to look at him. For a moment, he stared at the demon's face; his eyes wandered down to the thin gold chain around his neck, and then he searched his chest for the scar he'd seen in his dream, but it wasn't there. Of course it wasn't there. But still... he lifted his hand and placed it over Zalith's chest. Did it mean something? Was the fact that he couldn't seem to let go important?

Zalith frowned and placed his hand over Alucard's, staring into his eyes. "What's wrong?" he asked again.

Alucard, with a confused frown, shook his head slightly. "I 'ad... a veird dream."

"What happened?" he asked, concern in his voice and on his face.

"I...." Alucard frowned and looked down at his lap, pulling his hand from beneath Zalith's. "Ve vere... 'ere," he started, thinking about what he saw before he'd woken up. "But... vasn't just you and me," he said, setting his eyes back on Zalith. "Zhere vas... a girl—I vink... *maybe*... she vas our daughter—she called us Zaddy... and Papa," he explained slowly.

Zalith laughed quietly. "What?" he asked. Then, as Alucard frowned hesitantly, the demon slipped his hand into Alucard's. "What did she look like?"

Alucard shrugged; he felt pretty stupid about it now. He had no idea why his mind had come up with such a thing, but he didn't feel the need to keep it from Zalith. "She vas…maybe vour," he said, looking down at his lap again. "She 'ad your eyes, and 'er 'air vas kind of…orange."

The demon smiled and started fiddling with Alucard's fringe. "What was she doing?"

"Showing us…cards or someving," he mumbled.

"What was her name?"

"I zon't know."

Zalith frowned slightly and moved his hand to the side of Alucard's face. "Maybe one day we'll meet her for real."

Alucard adorned a confused expression. Was he joking around, or was he being serious? He wasn't sure…and he was even less sure whether or not he wanted to know. So, he sighed and looked down at his lap again. "Did you sleep okay?" he asked, changing the subject.

The demon laughed again. "Deflection? You don't want to have a baby with me?"

Alucard took his eyes off Zalith and scowled down at the bed. He still wasn't sure if Zalith was trying to embarrass him, but…he couldn't help but consider the question for a moment. *Did* he? Did Zalith want a child with him? He sighed quietly, unsure if Zalith was waiting for an answer or not.

But the demon moved his hand to Alucard's shoulder. "No pressure—I'm just joking with you…," he said amusedly. A moment later, though, he mumbled, "Maybe one day."

With a conflicted sigh, Alucard gazed at him. Did Zalith really want a child? With *him*? Or was he just looking to see how he might react? He wasn't sure, yet…maybe one day…they *would* have a family. But with what had happened and with what was due to happen with the Numen, it might not be any time soon. That was okay, though. Although the idea of a family did sound nice, Alucard wasn't yet ready for a commitment like that, nor did he feel like he was good enough to parent a child.

He smiled slightly in what he hoped Zalith would take as agreement and then laid back down.

"Of course, we should probably get married first," Zalith said with a smirk, lying beside him.

Alucard immediately felt flustered despite being unsure whether that was a joke. Maybe this time, though, he'd play along rather than let Zalith watch him become embarrassed. "Of course," he agreed. "Is zhis a proposal?"

Zalith laughed. "Why? Are you interested?"

"Are *you*?" Alucard asked him.

The demon smiled slightly as he stared at Alucard. For a moment, it looked like he was thinking, but then he placed his hand on the side of Alucard's face. "I'm interested, but I'm not going to get engaged to you in bed. I'd prefer to do it someplace much nicer. So, you're going to have to wait," he said and kissed his forehead.

Alucard stared down at the sheets; despite the talk of marriage, his mind drifted towards a growing desire. He might have gotten enough of Zalith's affection last night, but he wanted more. He shoved his shyness away and asked him, "Vhat *vill* you do in bed, zhen?"

Zalith smirked excitedly. "You know what we do in bed," he said, dragging his fingers over the side of Alucard's face, along his arm, and down to his waist. Then, he leaned in and started to kiss him.

The vampire felt content with Zalith's answer and rolled onto his back so that the demon could lean over him. Their kisses grew more aggressive, and it wasn't long before Zalith's hand was wandering down to Alucard's crotch.

Alucard set his eyes on the demon's neck; even though he fed last night, he still felt hungry. He wasn't sure if it was because he needed it or because he wanted it; either way, he was going to sink his fangs into Zalith's neck. It was what he wanted, and he'd had to go so long without all the things he wanted, so he'd not wait.

He placed his hand on the back of Zalith's head and pulled the demon's face closer; he then exhaled deeply in relief when the demon both kissed his neck and caressed his arousal. As the pleasure quickly consumed him, Alucard turned his head to the side and closed his eyes, dragging his fingers through Zalith's hair. But once he reached the top of Zalith's head, he took a fistful of his hair in his hand, turned his own head, and savagely sank his fangs into the demon's neck.

Zalith flinched a little but groaned contently, dragging his thumb over the tip of Alucard's shaft, which made Alucard's body shiver and tense up. The vampire murmured in delight, the taste of Zalith's blood enthralling him in euphoria, and as the demon continued to tend to his dick, he sank deeper into the satisfaction.

But then the demon started moving his hand a little faster, holding Alucard's dick firmly in his grasp. As the anticipation became too much, Alucard pulled his fangs from Zalith's neck and turned his head to the side, letting out a euphoric moan.

The demon leaned into his ear. "Can you still feel my cum inside you?" he whispered seductively, stroking his thumb over the tip of Alucard's dick; he smeared the vampire's pre-cum down his shaft and grinned against his neck as Alucard groaned hushedly in response.

Alucard closed his eyes and breathed, "Yes," his answer filled with desperation. His heart was starting to race, and he fidgeted beneath the demon.

When Zalith started sucking his neck, he gripped the demon's hair tighter; he was approaching his peak already. He didn't want to dig his claws into the demon's skin, though, so he let go of him and instead grasped the pillows on either side of his head. He couldn't banish the struggled but pleasured grimace from his face; he scowled, he squirmed, and as he finally climaxed, he gritted his teeth and whined pleasurably into the pillow beside him.

Waves of pleasure surged through his body, overwhelming him. He waited until the orgasm was over, leaving him in a state of relieved, pleased euphoria, but when he started to relax, he felt Zalith kissing his way down his body. The demon dragged his tongue over the vampire's shaft, eagerly cleaning up his cum with a delighted groan, and once he was done, he kissed his way back up to Alucard's neck, where he placed one final kiss before resting beside him with his head on Alucard's shoulder.

Alucard smiled contently and retreated into his thoughts. He felt content, yet he couldn't keep himself from thinking about something that made him feel…confounded. Yesterday, he'd taken Zalith into his study in hopes that he'd understand that he wanted the demon's attention; usually, when he led him to a place he wanted to be, Zalith would take the opportunity to flirt with him—and more. But last night, Zalith hadn't even flirted much, really. And then just now, Alucard made it *specifically* clear that he wanted Zalith. Maybe…he needed to start seeking his attention in different, more obvious ways. His subtle hints didn't seem to be getting him what he wanted anymore—either that or it was because Zalith was still dealing with his trauma.

Frowning, Alucard stared up at the ceiling. He didn't like to ask for Zalith's attention; he felt that no matter how long they'd been together, he'd always feel too nervous to tell Zalith what he wanted. But he'd managed to initiate sex right now, hadn't he? Well, it wasn't exactly sex…but it was the attention he wanted. So, surely, he could do it again. All he had to do was find a way to twist something either of them said into a suggestive comment, right?

He didn't want to overthink it. Right now, all he wanted to do was enjoy what time he had left to lay in bed with the man he loved. He'd work out what to do when the time came.

And it *would* come. He craved Zalith so much more than he let on, and now that he had Zalith back, he wouldn't ignore his desires as much anymore.

# Chapter Thirty-Seven

— ⸲ ✝ ⸳ —

## The Pocket Watch

**| Zalith |**

When the sun climbed higher and the morning grew later, Zalith exhaled quietly and nuzzled the side of Alucard's face. "What are you going to do today?" he asked the vampire.

Alucard glanced at him. "Hmm…maybe…ve can go and see your people?" he suggested. "Zhey 'ave Luther, but…."

"But…" Zalith continued. "I'd be surprised if they haven't all jumped overboard to get away from him," he said with a roll of his eyes.

Alucard frowned and sighed quietly. "*But*," he said, "'e's not zhe best person to send to a ship vull mostly of verevolves. Also, 'e 'as probably upset a vew people alveady vith 'is need to…charm."

"How does he ever manage to charm people?"

"Zon't ask me," Alucard muttered. "All I know is zhat people eizer end up in bed vith 'im or chasing 'im avay vith pitchvorks."

"I don't know why anyone would want to see him without clothes. I imagine he's nothing but a skeleton under that suit he seems to wear every day."

Alucard glanced at him again. "Vhy do you say zhese vings about 'im?"

"Because I'm not a fan," he said with a smile, staring up at him. He didn't want to upset Alucard, though, or make him feel like he couldn't hang around with Luther. "If you'd like me to stop, though, I'll try my best."

The vampire looked back up at the ceiling. "I zon't care," he mumbled. "Just zon't let me vind you two zhe vay I vound you vith Attila."

Zalith laughed amusedly. "Luther should do well to watch his mouth, then," he said, moving his hand up Alucard's body to grip his shoulder.

Alucard smiled a little in response, and then he sighed and asked, "Do you vant to go and see your people?"

"I'd like to if that's okay," he answered, sure that Alucard was trying to divert the subject away from Luther.

"Vhen do you vant to go?"

"We can have breakfast first, and then we can head out," the demon said.

Alucard nodded and sat up, and as he did, so did Zalith.

They headed into the bathroom, showered, and got ready for the day. Then, they headed downstairs and outside onto the patio, where they sat at the table and waited for Edwin to bring out their breakfast.

Coffee was already on the table, and once they sat down, the demon started to pour himself some. When he poured a cup for Alucard, though, he noticed that the vampire was staring at the guest house which was being built for Varana. It looked a lot like his house—both he and Varana wanted them to match and not clash—and inside, the place looked exactly like what he imagined *his* house would now look like if he allowed Varana to have full design control.

He smiled a little at the memory of her reaction when he'd told her she couldn't design *all* the rooms, and then he glanced at Alucard. "I think it'll be finished in no more than two months. I was very picky about everything with it, so Varana better not complain; all the changes she requested were made, and I'm sure she'll be happy over there."

"Do you vink she'll actually stay zhere?" he grumbled, adding his usual amount of sugar to his coffee.

"Here's hoping," Zalith said with a sigh. "As long as her friends don't mind taking an extra minute or two to travel across the courtyard, she'll be fine."

Alucard sighed and nodded, staring down at his coffee.

"Is she bothering you at all?"

"No," he said with a pout.

"Good," Zalith said and sipped from his coffee.

Edwin walked out of the house with two platters in his hands and placed them on the table. Both displayed an assortment of breakfast foods, and one had a few glasses and a selection of drinks to choose from.

The butler bowed respectfully and went to walk off—

"Did you move zhe black box zhat vas on zhe table a vew days ago?" Alucard asked, glancing up at him.

The butler looked down at him. "I did, sir, yes."

"I vant you to go and get vor me and bring 'ere," he instructed.

"Of course," Edwin said with a nod. Then, the butler left.

Zalith frowned curiously. A black box? He smiled at Alucard. "What did you send him to get?"

Alucard looked at him, but a nervous frown plastered itself to his face. "Is…surprise," he answered.

A surprise? "Oh, *I* see." He didn't want to make Alucard feel more nervous than he obviously was right now, so he'd just wait and see.

Edwin soon came back with a small black box in his hands and handed it to Alucard before leaving as silently as he had arrived.

Zalith sipped from his coffee and waited for Alucard to explain.

The vampire, with a shy little frown, pushed the box across the table and placed it in front of him. "Is vor you. I got zhis zhe day bevore ve vent to Eltaria."

Zalith's gaze fixated on the box, a tumult of emotions swirling within him. Guilt, like tendrils of darkness, coiled around his heart. Alucard's gesture pierced through the veil of his absence, a stark reminder of his own neglect. Despite his withdrawal, Alucard had gone out of his way to get him a gift, igniting a pang of remorse within the demon's chest, and the weight of indebtedness settled heavily upon him. Each thoughtful act of Alucard's served as a silent reproach, amplifying Zalith's awareness of his own failings. The urge to reconcile, to bridge the chasm he had allowed to widen, surged within him with newfound intensity.

"Thank you," he said, trying to hide his guilt. Then, he looked at Alucard. "You didn't have to get me anything."

Alucard glanced down at his coffee and shrugged. "I vanted to do someving vor you; you do so much vor me all zhe time."

The demon's guilt intensified. *All* he felt was guilt. He made Alucard feel so alone and so abandoned, and yet, Alucard hadn't grown bitter and still did something nice for him. He didn't know what to do, say, or think. All he could do was look down at the box and then back over at Alucard. "You do a lot for me too, baby," he said, placing his hand on Alucard's arm as he smiled at him.

Then, as Alucard smiled back, Zalith looked down at the box again. He had no idea what could be inside and considering that it was a gift from Alucard, his excitement was something unique—it was something he hadn't felt before, or if he had, he didn't quite remember when.

With both hands, Zalith carefully lifted the lid off the box to reveal the navy silk within. A shimmer of gold flickered in the sunlight as he picked up the silk and whatever was wrapped inside it, and then he started unwrapping it. It had a little bit of weight to it, so he felt it must be something made of gold—the flicker made that obvious. However, as he pulled away the silk to reveal that it was, in fact, a gold pocket watch, he felt his heart stop for a moment.

As Zalith fixated on the box, his mind became a battleground, the quietened torment of his past writhing its way back into his consciousness with each passing second. In the recesses of his memory, a vision imposed by the Light seared itself into his psyche:

Idina's lifeless form, adorned with a golden pocket watch. The mere sight of the watch before him elicited a visceral reaction, stirring memories too painful to confront yet impossible to ignore. He couldn't tear his gaze away, each tick of the watch echoing like a relentless drumbeat in the caverns of his mind. A chilling realization crept over him, a whisper of dread coiling around his soul: could this be the same watch, a haunting relic from a vicious cycle that he could never escape?

But he knew Alucard was gazing at him, so he smiled as best as he could and looked at the vampire. "Where did you get this?" he asked, trying to hide how distressed he felt.

"In Dor-Sanguis," Alucard answered. "Zhere vere cakes, too, but zhey're likely stale by now."

Zalith's sights remained fixed on the watch, his thoughts swirling in a tempest of uncertainty. Perhaps it was mere coincidence, a trick of fate playing upon his fears. With a furrowed brow, he gingerly flicked open the watch's small cap, revealing its inner sanctum. But as his eyes fell upon the intricate carvings of carnations nestled beneath the ticking hands, a wave of torment engulfed him, twisting his very essence. It was as though the hands of time had reached out to ensnare him in their grasp once more, transporting him back to the haunting memory of Eltaria. Doubt clawed at his consciousness, the insidious notion of illusion taking root in his mind. Could this be another cruel mirage, a phantom conjured to torment him anew? The dread of realization hung heavy in the air, each tick of the watch echoing like a sinister refrain of his past.

His heart started racing, his hands began to tremble, and as he looked at Alucard, he felt dread and angst constricting him so tightly that it became hard to breathe steadily. Moments after he'd seen this watch before, Alucard was taken from him, and he couldn't shake the fear that it was going to happen again.

But…what if…it *was* just a coincidence? The Light couldn't have known Alucard got him this gift; Alucard said he got it *before* they went to Eltaria. And even so, the Light hadn't got into Alucard's head, so how could it have known about this watch?

His blood ran cold. Was this real? Was this life reality? Or was this another thing meant to confuse him and pull him deeper into Adellum's grasp?

The demon's hands trembled, but he did his best to hide it. If this *was* real, he didn't want to upset or alarm Alucard. He dragged his thumb over the glass containing the watch hands, and then told Alucard, "I love it," but his dread was quickly consuming him, and it might be too late to try and hide his feelings.

"Vhat's vrong?" Alucard asked worriedly.

Zalith glanced at him and then back down at the watch. "Nothing," he said with a shake of his head. "It just reminded me of something—I really do love it," he insisted.

"Vhat…does vemind you of?"

The demon sighed, staring down at the watch. He shrugged, frowned in confliction, and glanced at him. "Something I saw in Eltaria when I was trapped by the Light."

Alucard didn't say anything else, and when Zalith glanced at him, he saw a dismayed look on his face. He was certain that the vampire was beating himself up about it—he always had that certain look of dismay and embarrassment on his face. He didn't want Alucard to blame himself.

Zalith placed his free hand on Alucard's arm. "Alucard, please don't be sad—I really do love it," he assured him. Then, he reached into his trouser pocket and pulled out the watch he already had inside. He put it on the table and put the new one in his pocket.

"Zon't…keep vor my sake," Alucard said sullenly. "If makes you veel strange, zhen get vid of."

"No, I'm keeping it," Zalith said and lightly gripped Alucard's jaw. He turned the vampire's face towards his own and kissed his lips once, twice, and a third time.

When Zalith stopped, Alucard smiled a little before he sipped from his coffee and turned his head to stare out at the guest house again.

Zalith knew that Alucard was sinking into his thoughts; he knew that he was still beating himself up, but he didn't really know what more to tell him right now. His paranoid thoughts were making it hard for him to concentrate.

He tried his best to focus on breakfast, but his dread and angst lingered over him. He thought that he was moving on—and he *was*. He wasn't going to let what happened in Eltaria ruin the rest of his life. Whether this was real or not, he was going to live his life with Alucard and enjoy his time with him. The watch may have made and may still be making his heart beat a little faster out of worry, but…he really did love it, and he also adored the fact that Alucard had gone out of his way to get him a gift despite the pain Zalith put him through.

Right now, he just wanted to focus on all the positive things his vampire made him feel and enjoy breakfast.

| **Alucard** |

Alucard wasn't sure how long he and Zalith were sitting on the patio, but by the time they were done with breakfast, the sun was much higher in the sky, and his eyes were aching because of it.

But he couldn't shake the dismay. What Zalith said…when he told him that the pocket watch reminded him of something the Light showed him…it made Alucard feel like an idiot. He was supposed to be trying to help Zalith get over what happened in Eltaria, but he'd obviously made it worse, hadn't he? All because he'd tried to do something so stupid as to get Zalith's attention by doing something he thought was nice for him. But it wasn't nice—it was upsetting Zalith, and Alucard didn't want that. He glanced at the demon and then glared down at his coffee, sinking into his sadness. He really couldn't do anything right, could he?

"Stop worrying, it's okay," Zalith suddenly said with a saddened frown. He always seemed to know when Alucard was worrying.

But Alucard shook his head. "Is not okay," he mumbled. "I'm supposed to be 'elping you veel better, not making vings vorse."

"Alucard, you couldn't have possibly known, so it's not your fault. It's a very thoughtful gift, and I've already made the decision that I'm going to think of you and how much I love you every time I look at it instead of what happened in Eltaria, which is going to be very helpful, so thank you," he insisted.

The vampire shrugged slightly, keeping his eyes on the table. "Okay," he said. He didn't know what else to say. He didn't know what to think, what to feel, or what to do. As he glanced at Zalith—who was finishing his coffee—he didn't fail to notice the conflicted look on the demon's face. He was sure that Zalith was just putting on a brave face *and* act to keep him from getting upset, and that only made him feel worse.

He sat there, waiting without any idea what to do. He'd given that watch to him, Zalith took it, and now they were both left in a cloud of despair. What else could either of them really do? Alucard told him to get rid of it if it made him feel afraid, and Zalith insisted that he wanted to keep it. Alucard wasn't going to argue with him; Zalith could make his own decisions. Alucard just wanted to do something to help him—something to make him feel better. But his attempt at doing so had failed, and he felt as though he should just stop trying; all trying ever did was cause despair, whether it be his, Zalith's, or both.

So, for the rest of their morning, he sat in silence, trying his best not to show just how disappointed he was with himself.

# Chapter Thirty-Eight

— ⸲ ✝ ⸱ —

## Disconcert

**| Zalith |**

Zalith and Alucard sat in the horse-drawn carriage as it pulled them towards the Citadel. The demon leaned his head on Alucard's shoulder with his arm around him, holding him tightly. He was trying his best to hide his anxiety, but the further away from the house they got, the worse he felt.

His feelings were all over the place. He felt terrible for upsetting Alucard; the vampire had done something so nice for him, and he'd made the vampire believe that he didn't like the gift. He loved it, and he loved that Alucard went out of his way to get something for him, even when he was spending his time neglecting the vampire.

But…he couldn't stop thinking about the fact that he'd seen the same pocket watch in Eltaria—in one of the realities that the Light made him live through. And he couldn't help but sit there and ask himself…was this even real? Was this world also a façade? Was he going to lose Alucard *again*? He glanced up at what he could see of Alucard with a look of dread lingering on his face. Was he going to have to see Alucard die again?

He stared ahead, his heart beating a little faster as his worry intensified. He couldn't escape the feeling of eyes on him. Was the Light watching them? Was it watching *him*? Had it always been watching? Was it still playing with him and his mind? He had no idea what was real and what wasn't anymore. Was the Light dead? No…Alucard hadn't killed it…so what was stopping it from getting into Aegisguard? What was stopping it from creeping its way over to where he and Alucard felt they were safe?

The demon scowled, trying to hide his angst. But the watch—how had the Light known about the watch that sat in his pocket? A watch that Alucard had picked up before they'd gone to Eltaria—before any of that had happened. Had…Alucard spoken to the Light before the void space? How had it found out?

That wasn't the only thing worrying him. He overlooked the importance of seeing that pocket watch before, and it made him wonder, what else had he overlooked? What else had he seen that might make its way into this world, real or not? Detlaff…the

Diabolus and Lucifer—were they going to make their way into his and Alucard's lives the way this pocket watch had? Was he going to have to look out for them now, too? Where were they? Alucard hadn't said anything about Detlaff or Lucifer or the Diabolus in so long; Zalith had no idea where they might be and when they'd show up—*if* they'd show up.

But… first of all, how did the Light know to show him everything it had?

"Did you talk to it?" Zalith abruptly asked.

Alucard frowned and looked down at him. "Vhat?"

"The Light," Zalith answered. "Did you talk to it?"

The vampire shifted his gaze to the carriage window. "No. Zhe only time I spoke to vas vhen I stole 'is power."

Zalith nodded. "Okay," he said quietly.

"Vhy?" Alucard asked.

The demon shook his head and sighed. "I'm just… wondering how it knew about the pocket watch."

"I zon't know," he mumbled. The sadness in his voice was very clear.

But Zalith needed answers. "Where is Detlaff?"

His abrupt and random questions made Alucard look confused. "Vhat? Zetlaff?"

"Yes. Is he still locked away?"

With a perplexed frown, Alucard nodded slowly. "Yes…. E's been down zhere vor months."

"Are you sure?" Zalith asked, finding it harder and harder to hide the panic that was slowly eating away at him. "When was the last time you checked on him?"

"Luther checks on 'im ovten, and vhen I vas down in zhe dungeons zhe ozzer day, 'e vas still zhere. Everyving's vine, Zaliv."

"Hmph. I wouldn't be surprised if Luther fucked up," Zalith mumbled.

"'E vouldn't. 'E's an idiot, but 'e takes 'is job seriously."

"Mm."

And that was where the conversation ended. Zalith tried to keep himself from sinking deeper into his paranoia and focus on what he was going to say to everyone when they reached Alucard's ship. He was sure that all his people were going to want to know how he was and what was going on, and he needed to prepare for their barrage of questions.

| **Alucard** |

When they reached the city, Alucard climbed out of the carriage and helped Zalith out. There weren't many people around the docks, but there were enough for Alucard to frown hesitantly as Zalith went to take hold of his hand, but the demon stopped before he took it, seeming to remember where they were—Alucard knew that he still didn't want the people of the Citadel to know that he was gay. The demon frowned despondently as he looked at Alucard, and the vampire stared back in worry; Zalith was clearly struggling, and despite his own feelings of dismay, the vampire wanted to do whatever he could to make it easier for him.

While the carriage left behind them, Alucard did his best to remain as close to Zalith as he could and started leading the way to the docks. He stared down at the ground as they walked, unable to shake the awful feeling he got every time he thought about how his gift had only made things worse for Zalith and how he had no idea what to do for him. Zalith was most likely convinced that he was still trapped in an illusion created by Adellum and probably wouldn't believe any attempt Alucard made at trying to convince him that this wasn't a dream—that this was the real world. And Alucard didn't know what to do anymore.

He frowned sullenly, leading the way towards the docks. His attention, however, shifted to a small billboard not too far away. On it were several pantomime and show posters, but one was advertising an opera—an opera which had been going on all week and would be ending in a few days. He thought back to the time when he and Zalith went to an opera; it was their first real date, in fact, since being together officially. It made him feel content remembering the fun he and Zalith had, despite the Diabolus spy. Maybe…he and Zalith would have just as much fun if they went to another?

Taking his eyes off the billboard, he looked at Zalith, but the despondent stare on the demon's face made him hesitate, and since they were now already in the docks and on their way towards his ship, he felt that it was best to wait. They should probably get business out of the way first.

He invited Zalith to lead the way up onto the ship's deck, and as he did, Alucard followed. The vampire spotted two of Zalith's Alphas on deck—Tyrus and Idina—and watched as they noticed Zalith's arrival and hurried over. Alucard was sure that he wasn't going to be needed and planned to head off whilst Zalith dealt with his people, but the demon snatched his hand the moment they were out of the Citadel's view. He wasn't going to argue, so he walked beside him.

"I'm so glad you came," Idina said with a smile as she and Tyrus stopped in front of Zalith and Alucard. "It's so good to see you," she said, shaking both their hands.

Zalith smiled at her and nodded in response to Tyrus' nod as he, too, shook their hands.

Tyrus—once he started shaking Zalith's hand—however, didn't let go, and that made Alucard scowl in hostility. Why did this guy feel the need to hold Zalith's hand for so long? And why did he feel so irritated about it? This Alpha was Zalith's subordinate, so…why did he feel like he might say something if Tyrus didn't let go in the next few seconds?

"Did you know Varana's sleeping with that skinny guy?" Tyrus then asked, still keeping hold of Zalith's hand.

The demon smiled with a look of malice in his eyes. "What?"

"Tyrus!" Idina exclaimed in disapproval, smacking his arm.

He let go of Zalith's hand. "Am I wrong, though? We heard it."

Idina looked flustered. "Yes, but we don't need to gossip about it."

Zalith—still with his hostile smile—kept his eyes on them both. "To confirm, we're talking about Luther, right?"

"Yeah," Tyrus grumbled. "I don't know what she sees in him when she could be with me, but whatever."

Idina sighed and shook her head, taking her eyes off Tyrus.

Alucard had no time to think about the revelation; Zalith turned to him and asked, "Did you know about this?"

"No," Alucard answered with a frown because he *didn't* know. He had no idea that Luther was seeing Varana. Of course, he'd been aware that Luther was pretty adamant to tell him about his latest conquest, but he'd ignored it—and he was glad he had. He'd have rather found out right now from these people than from Luther himself; that would have been a rather disgusting conversation.

Zalith sighed and looked back at his Alphas. "Thank you. I'll deal with it."

Tyrus smiled, and Idina adorned a look of dread.

"How have things been here?" Zalith then asked.

"Well," Idina started, taking her eyes off Tyrus. "People are getting a little restless. Some of them are wondering if it's okay to leave the ship while they wait for accommodation."

Zalith took his eyes off Idina and looked at Alucard.

Alucard—who hadn't really been paying too much attention—frowned and looked at her, and then at Zalith. "Vhat?" he asked, realizing he'd been too busy scowling at Tyrus. But he then set his eyes on Idina. "Luther told you zhe vules, no?"

"He did," she confirmed. "But some people are getting a little stir-crazy, and if we can allow some coming and going, I think things might go a little smoother. Might I suggest, maybe…small groups of no more than ten could head into the city just for a little while—one group per day?"

The vampire sighed and glanced at Zalith. Alucard wasn't the one trying to establish a reputation or a governing role here. It was Zalith's choice to make, and they were *his* people, after all. "Is up to you," he told the demon.

Zalith glanced at Idina and Tyrus. "It'll be fine. Tell Orin and work out who gets to leave between the three of you."

Idina and Tyrus nodded.

Tyrus then left, but Idina watched him go before she moved a little closer to Zalith and asked him with worry in her voice, "Can I talk to you?"

The demon nodded.

Alucard felt discontent when Zalith let go of his hand and turned a little to his right to face Idina, but the demon *did* move his hand to Alucard's back, keeping it on him. Alucard then set his sights on the horizon, waiting for Zalith to be done with whatever it was Idina wanted. He wasn't going to purposely listen…but he couldn't help but overhear with how close he was to them.

"Are you okay?" Idina whispered.

"I'm fine," he said with an assuring tone. Evidently, he didn't want his people to know about his experience with the Light. "How about you?"

"It's still hard. But I've mostly been worried about you and Colt, though."

Zalith was quiet for a moment; he must be thinking. But then he said to her, "Go and pack your and Colt's things; you can take the carriage home with Alucard and me."

Idina gasped quietly in relief. "Thank you so much, Zalith," she said and lightly hugged him. Then, she looked at Alucard. "And thank you, too, Aleksei," she said as Alucard glanced back at her. The woman then hurried off to do as Zalith had said.

Alucard watched her leave, and when Zalith turned to face him, the demon took hold of his hand again. Zalith led them over to the edge of the deck and stared out at the water. Alucard didn't know what to say, so he stood beside him and stared, too.

"Will we take another boat trip one day?" Zalith asked.

The vampire looked at him and frowned. "Ve can take vone vhenever you vant."

"Maybe after all these people have a place to live, and we can be alone."

Alucard nodded in agreement, looking back out at the water. "Ve can do zhat."

However, the sound of smashing glass then caught both his and Zalith's attention—they sharply turned their heads, staring over at the door that led down to the lower decks. The ruffle of commotion came from below, and considering that everything on this ship was expensive, Alucard felt the urge to hurry to wherever the sounds were coming from. And as he rushed off, Zalith followed.

# Chapter Thirty-Nine

## Rivals

**| Alucard |**

Alucard led the way below deck, Zalith's presence a silent echo beside him. The clamour was coming from the bar, where he could sense the auras of almost all of Zalith's people. He traversed the corridor, anticipation thrumming through his veins like a drumbeat. As he neared the entrance to the bar, a scene of chaos unfolded before him. Greymore, ever the enforcer, intervened between two quarrelling men, preventing further discord. Alucard's entrance was met with neither surprise nor deference; the devastation around him took precedence over pleasantries.

Surveying the aftermath, Alucard's gaze swept over the wreckage. Chairs lay strewn across the floor, alcohol staining the wooden planks, and shards of shattered glass littered the scene. His lips curled in a silent snarl at the wanton destruction; the absence of a chair from its rightful place, now a projectile through the broken window, spoke volumes of the altercation's intensity.

With a steely resolve, Alucard's gaze settled on the two men, their faces etched with the remnants of anger. They would soon learn the extent of their little conflict, the depths of the vampire's irritation laid bare.

He reached them as Zalith stepped off to the side, leaning against one of the walls to spectate. Alucard snatched the back of both men's shirts and pulled them from Greymore's grip before anyone could intervene. A lot of the people in the room gasped in shock when the vampire threw both men to the floor; Greymore looked as though he was about to intervene, but he calmed down when he clearly realized that it was Alucard who'd taken the men from his grip.

One of the spectators pounced forward, ready to defend one of the men, but Zalith snatched the man's arm and glared at him as he stared back. "Touch him, and I'll kill you," he said calmly. As the man shuddered in fear, Zalith let go of him and set his eyes on Alucard.

As soon as Alucard's hands sent the first man crashing to the floor, recognition flashed across his face, freezing him in place. He remained motionless, a silent acknowledgement of the authority the vampire wielded. In contrast, the second man's defiance simmered beneath a scowl directed at Alucard. Ignoring the warning implicit in his rival's submission, he made a futile attempt to rise, only to be met with the weight of Alucard's boot pressing down firmly on his chest, pinning him to the floor.

Their altercation unfolded dangerously close to Danford's table, the proximity unsettling the timid man. As Danford scrambled to distance himself from the escalating chaos, Alucard's firm hand intercepted him, shoving him back into his seat with a forceful push. Danford's eyes widened in horror, a silent witness to the raw power and unpredictability that surrounded him.

Zalith's amused laugh cut through the crowd. He was evidently enjoying the show.

Alucard's glare bore down upon the two men sprawled on the floor, their expressions a mix of bewilderment and defiance. While the first man seemed resigned to his fate, the second met Alucard's gaze with a venomous scowl, his hands clenching around the vampire's shin in a futile attempt to dislodge his foot from his chest.

A surge of irritation coursed through Alucard, a primal urge to mete out punishment clawing at the edges of his composure. The thought of casting them into the ocean flickered briefly in his mind, a tempting punishment for their insolence. Yet, a sense of restraint tethered him; these were Zalith's people, and he wouldn't overstep his bounds.

With a measured exhale, Alucard suppressed his simmering frustration, opting for a more tempered approach. His voice, cold and authoritative, cut through the tension-laden air as he addressed the men, his words dripping with unspoken threat; they would learn, one way or another, the consequences of their actions. "Do you 'ave any idea 'ow much zhat is going to cost me to veplace?"

The man not currently restrained beneath Alucard's boot frowned in sorrow. "S-sorry, sir. We'll pay you back, sir."

"No. Vhat you vill do is show some more vespect to zhe place you've been allowed to stay in," he snarled angrily. "Vhen I said you could all stay 'ere, I zidn't expect to vind you destroying my bar," he said, glancing around the room. "Get zhe fuck up, and get zhe fuck out," he warned them, taking his foot off the man's chest. He stepped back and watched them climb to their feet. Then, they swiftly left the bar without another word.

Alucard rolled his eyes, ignoring all the gawping people as he set his gaze on Zalith.

"Who even is this?" one of the spectators near Zalith asked as he stared at Alucard.

"My husband," Zalith answered, glowering at the man who had asked—but when the demon caught sight of Alucard's confused stare, he smiled.

Alucard looked away and tried to hide his fluster. Why would Zalith say that? They weren't married....

Greymore then sighed loudly. "All right, get back to what you were doing. Show's over," he called irritably, waving his arms to encourage everyone to do so. And on his call, everyone resumed what they were doing before the two men started fighting.

Zalith made his way over to Alucard and didn't look too happy at all. He took hold of Alucard's hand and sighed quietly. "Let's go home."

However, Greymore rushed over to them with a frown and called, "Hey, hey, hey," he urged, catching up with them as they headed for the door. "I'm sorry about the mess," he said, stopping in front of them when they turned to face him. "I'll pay for it—let me get you a drink," he offered.

"I zon't vant anyvone to pay vor anyving," Alucard grumbled.

"No, no, no," Greymore declined. "You *graciously* let us stay here on your ship; those two morons were rude as fuck. Let me pay you back," he insisted calmly.

Alucard didn't want to stay. Zalith said he wanted to go home, and Alucard concurred with his choice.

But the demon huffed quietly and said, "We might as well get a drink while we wait for Idina."

Of course, they had to wait for Idina and Colt to have everything ready; they were coming to stay with them until the compound was built, and there was no telling how long they might take to be done. So, as Greymore led the way, the vampire and Zalith followed him over to the bar.

"What are you guys having?" Greymore asked as he leaned his arm onto the bar, summoning the bartender with his other hand.

"Black spiced rum," Zalith said.

Alucard shrugged as Greymore looked at him. "'E vill know," he said, setting his eyes on the bartender, who stopped in front of Greymore.

Nodding, Greymore looked at the man. "I'll take another pint. The usual for Aleksei, and black spiced rum for my boss," he said. Then, as the bartender wandered off to get what he'd asked for, Greymore turned to face both Zalith and Alucard. "So, how are you two doing? You didn't get scraped up too bad in the fight the other day, did you?"

"We're good," Zalith answered. "How are you and everyone else doing?"

Greymore shrugged. "Good. Some people obviously aren't adjusting as well as others, and some people are getting restless—as we all just saw—but it's nice to not have to be afraid and paranoid all the time. Most of the disagreements have been between my wolves and Addison's…traitorous fucker." He adorned an assuring smile. "I'll deal with it, though. They're all one pack now; they'll learn to get along."

Zalith nodded and explained, "I'm sorry that we weren't more prepared for everyone, but we're working on a solution for you. You may all be stuck here a little bit longer than I would like, but as long as people behave and stop breaking things, it shouldn't be an issue." The demon turned his head and gazed at Alucard for what looked like confirmation.

Alucard felt no need to disagree. "I zon't vant to come 'ere and see more of my vings broken."

Zalith smiled and set his eyes on Greymore.

With a frown on his face, Greymore shook his head a little. "If anyone breaks anything else, I'm going to throw them into the ocean… and maybe a shark will get them, who knows," he said with an amused smile.

The vampire sighed quietly and watched the bartender place their drinks in front of them. Then, he looked down at his wine. "Zhere are no sharks in zhese vaters, only eels."

"Are these eels mean?" Greymore asked.

A perturbed frown appeared on Alucard's face. By mean, he assumed Greymore meant hostile. "No. Unless you get too close to zhem, zhen yes."

Greymore laughed slightly and sipped from his beer. "Are they the type that shock you or do they just bite?"

"Zhey vill paralyse you, vatch you drown, and zhen take you to zheir offspring, vhich vill live inside your corpse vor up to a month."

"Sounds like Varana," Greymore muttered and took another sip from his drink.

Amused, Alucard smirked, and he could see that Zalith was trying *not* to smile.

But then Greymore laughed. "I'm just joking; she's a very nice lady." He took a large gulp of his drink before asking, "So, Aleksei, what else lives in these waters? I guess… dolphins?"

"No," Alucard answered. "Zhey zon't live zhis close to 'umans. All 'umans do is 'unt and kill zhem vor no veason. Zhere are very minimal vings in zhe vater zhat people von't try to eat or do someving vith, so most of zhe in'abitants keep miles and miles avay vrom big cities like zhis."

"Yeah, makes sense," Greymore said with a sigh. His face suddenly lit up, and he grinned at Zalith and Alucard. "Once, I was on a week-long trip on my own ship and happened to catch a glimpse of a sea dragon; it was so beautiful. I don't think I'll ever see anything like it again. I'm glad it wasn't close to civilisation because it would have probably ended up turning into steak."

Alucard finished his drink and set his eyes on Greymore. "Do you… like dragons?" he asked, but the look on Greymore's face had already given him his answer.

"I love them," he said with a smile. "Unfortunately, I never got to see one up close— they all sorta just disappeared in Eltaria because of the war, but… they've always been an interest of mine."

The vampire tried to think of an answer, but his thoughts were quickly consumed by his worry for Zalith. The demon had been awfully quiet all day, and even more so right now. He'd only taken a small sip of his drink, and Alucard wasn't sure whether Zalith was waiting for him and Greymore to stop talking so that they could go home. Maybe... he should try and end the conversation quickly so that he and Zalith could head back to the house.

"You von't see many 'ere in Nevastus," the vampire answered. "You von't see many vandering avound at all, veally. But zhey are 'ere if you know vhere to vind zhem."

"Ah, secretive, I see," Greymore said with a smirk. "Just like Zalith," he added, setting his eyes on the demon, who had just finished his drink.

"A man after my own heart," Zalith said as he leaned over a little, resting his head on the side of Alucard's for a few moments.

Alucard smiled as Zalith stood up straight again. However, his smile faded when he felt the aura of someone irritating pierce his and Zalith's space.

"Alucard," Luther said, appearing beside him.

The vampire took his eyes off Greymore and looked at him. Zalith also glanced at him but rolled his eyes in irritancy as he, too, realized their conversation was now most likely at an end.

"Vhat?" Alucard grumbled. He didn't want to talk to him right now.

"I need to talk to you," Luther said.

"Vhy?"

Luther took his eyes off Alucard to glance at Zalith and Greymore for a few moments. He then frowned and stared back at Alucard. "Alone. It's sensitive."

The vampire glanced at Zalith, who shook his head a little in what looked like an attempt to hold back a comment. Then, Alucard sighed and scowled. He didn't want to leave Zalith's side for many reasons, and he was quite enjoying the conversation with Greymore. "You can tell me 'ere."

Once again, Luther eyed Zalith and Greymore. But he exhaled irritably and crossed his arms as he set his eyes back on Alucard. "It's to do with what happened on your last visit to Dor-Sanguis," he revealed. "The woman."

Of course, Alucard hadn't forgotten about the Numen spy he'd caught the other day—the scout sent by Erich to find out who was looking for information on Charlotte, Alucard's own mother. He hadn't told Zalith about it, and he didn't think that now would be a good time to do so. He didn't want to worry Zalith with his personal problems, not while he was dealing with his confusion and paranoia. But he didn't want to leave Zalith there alone, so if Zalith wished to hear his and Luther's conversation, he'd invite him along.

He looked at Zalith. "Do you vant to come?"

"Sure," the demon answered.

"Oh, I guess we'll talk about dragons another time," Greymore said with a smile.

Alucard glanced back at him as he prepared to follow Luther. "*Da*," he agreed. Then, he and Zalith followed Luther out of the bar. He was eager to hear what Luther had found, and although he wasn't sure how Zalith was going to take it, he was just as eager to let the demon know what happened with Erich's scout.

# Chapter Forty

— ⸜ ✝ ⸝ —

## A Discussion of Witchery

**| Alucard |**

Alucard, Zalith, and Luther headed into the vampire's study. Once they entered, Alucard made his way over to his desk and sat behind it while Zalith leaned against it beside him. Luther slumped down in one of the seats in front of them as he exhaled deeply.

While he made himself comfortable, Alucard glanced down at the glass floor and watched a few fish swim around an old crab cage at the bottom of the dock. But when he set his eyes on Luther, he watched his subordinate glance at Zalith with a sour look on his face. Alucard impatiently tapped his clawed fingers on the desk, snatching Luther's attention.

He looked at Alucard. "You told me to get rid of that spy's body," he started. "Well, I can't."

Alucard scowled impatiently. "Vhat?"

"What spy?" Zalith questioned, looking at Alucard.

The vampire glanced up at him. "I vent to Dor-Sanguis vhen you vere… busy; Luther told me zhat people 'ad been vatching my castle. Ve caught vone of zhem and interrogated 'er. I vill… tell you more later," he said, watching a horribly concerned expression steal Zalith's frown. But now that he said something, he was sure that Zalith would insist he let him get involved. He'd work that out later, though. Right now, he wanted to know why Luther couldn't dispose of the body.

As Zalith nodded slightly in agreement, Alucard set his eyes back on Luther, waiting.

"Usually, we'd feed them to Drac, but Drac's not around," Luther continued with a bitter tone in his voice and a stubborn look on his face.

Alucard was almost certain that Luther's tone and expression weren't because of the spy situation but because of the company Alucard had with him.

"So, we started burning the bodies. This girl, however, would not burn," Luther revealed. "We did the next thing on your 'how to dispose of a body' list and cut her up—

or at least tried to. We cut off a limb, but it turned to dust and reattached itself. Attila then suggested we just bury and forget about her, so we did that. The ground wouldn't hold her. I got a letter this morning from Attila telling me the ground has literally thrown this body up like an out-of-date meal," he explained.

"Vhat?" Alucard asked with a confused frown.

"Yeah," Luther said with a nod, reaching into his pocket. He placed a white envelope on the table and slid it across to Alucard. "All the details are in there, but it pretty much says what I just told you. Attila's going to try dumping her in the bottom of the ocean, but something tells me that won't work, either."

Perturbed, Alucard picked up the letter. He didn't even want to open it. He'd heard enough from Luther. Never had he ever heard of such a thing—a body that wouldn't burn, tear, or stay in the ground. Even a Numen's body burned, tore, and remained buried; granted, it would heal and return to its normal state, but it would still do all those things first. So, what the hell could this woman have been for her *dead* body to survive and fight off means of disposal?

He looked up at Zalith. "'Ave you ever 'eard of such a ving?"

"Witchery, perhaps," the demon suggested. "I have heard of cases where bodies have been hexed before and or after death, making it hard to dispose of them."

Luther scoffed in disagreement. "If it were witchery, we'd know. Witch ethos involves runes, and we noticed none on her body at all—inside or out."

Zalith seemed to smile in an attempt to tolerate Luther. "You cut up every inch of her body? Her organs? Looked underneath her skin? In her skull? Her eyes?"

"Yes, I did," Luther said, scowling.

"But she heals," Zalith said condescendingly. "So, did you take her apart or just fish around inside her body?"

"Why the hell should I answer you?" Luther then snarled.

"Okay, so you obviously just fished around in her body then since you're not saying otherwise," Zalith said.

Before Luther could argue anymore, Alucard sighed and shook his head. "Enough," he grumbled. "Continue," he then said, looking at Luther.

Zalith didn't say anything in response, but Alucard didn't fail to notice the smug smile on his face.

Luther rolled his eyes and set them back on Alucard. "I did some digging because I suspected you might not know what was going on. You should check yourself for a rune," he suggested.

With a confounded, almost offended frown, Alucard scowled at him. "Excuse me?"

"If she's what I think she is, then you're about to have a whole lot of shit to deal with."

Alucard's scowl thickened. He had no idea why Luther was being so vague and bitter—it was unlike him. But he didn't care for Luther's personal issues. Rune? What rune? And what the hell was he talking about? "If you vould like to keep your job, I suggest you tell me vhat zhe fuck you're talking about, and drop zhe attitude," he warned.

As a flicker of startlement ran across Luther's face, he frowned and cleared his throat. "Sorry. Something happened yesterday. I'm just irritated."

"I zon't care."

Luther nodded. "It's called a mark of death—the rune you might have on you. This woman may have been a grim reaper."

Alucard glanced up at Zalith as angst began consuming him. He didn't know how to feel about that.

"I haven't seen anything on him," Zalith said, and as he took his eyes off Luther to look down at Alucard, he smiled.

The vampire's inner turmoil churned like a tempest, drowning out any sense of embarrassment that might have crept in. A grim reaper—a concept that sent shivers down his spine. He'd heard the whispers, the tales spun by humans of their relentless pursuit of souls. But why would one seek him out? The question gnawed at Alucard's mind, a puzzle with pieces too sinister to ignore.

He knew of their allegiance to Erich, the puppet master pulling strings from the darkness. Yet, the notion that such a formidable entity would be dispatched for mere reconnaissance unsettled him. Doubt coiled around his thoughts, casting shadows over his once-solid convictions. Were the spies seen in Dor-Sanguis mere observers, or were they heralds of impending conflict?

With each passing moment, Alucard's belief in Erich's intentions dwindled, replaced by a growing sense of foreboding. Was Erich planning something? Were he and Zalith going to have to make preparations to hide from and fight another Numen?

"I found this," Luther said, reaching into his pocket. He pulled out a torn book page and handed it to Alucard with a quiet sigh. "It looks like that; it doesn't do anything, really," he said, pointing to the piece of paper in Alucard's hand. "It just acts as a beacon for other grim reapers to come and find the killer of their comrade. You killed that girl, and it says right there that grim reaper bodies can't be destroyed until their killer is brought to justice. It all makes sense, right?"

With a perturbed frown, Alucard opened the piece of paper and stared down at the drawing in the page's centre. The rune appeared as an X, but something sword-shaped stabbed down through its centre, and vines spewed from its blade to wrap around the X, constricting it very tightly—so tightly that the vines were cutting into the X as though it were flesh. He hadn't noticed the rune anywhere on his body, and he was sure that Zalith would have pointed it out if he had. But…then again, he hadn't really been looking at his own body, let alone searching for things that shouldn't be there.

He looked up at Zalith and turned the piece of paper so that the demon could see what was on it. "You 'aven't…seen zhis on me?"

"Not that I've noticed, at least," he answered.

So, it looked like Alucard was going to have to search and see if he did have the rune on himself somewhere. He'd not do that with Luther there, though, and he'd heard all he needed to know from him. Taking his eyes off Zalith, he looked at Luther. "You can go," he told him.

Luther, however, frowned in discontent. "You…do realize that this mark means you could have a bunch of—"

"I know vhat zhis means," Alucard snapped irritably. "You told me vhat you 'ad to tell me, now leave."

With an aggravated frown, Luther glanced at Zalith but stood up. "If you need anything else, I'll be here, as ordered."

"Good. Go," Alucard said with a wave of dismissal.

With an irritated huff, Luther left.

Alucard looked up at Zalith again "Are you sure you zidn't see zhis on me?" he asked, placing the piece of paper down on the table.

The demon smirked slightly. "Yes, but I can look again if you like," he suggested.

Alucard felt that it was a good idea, so he nodded. "Zhe last ving I need are grim veapers chasing me," he muttered, standing up.

Zalith followed Alucard into the bathroom.

For the second time this week, however, Alucard felt a familiar hesitation to take his shirt off and reveal his scarred back. It hadn't really bothered him again until he started thinking that Zalith didn't want him anymore, and despite the fact that the confusion was cleared up, he still felt…reluctant. He started to slowly unbutton it, but he stopped when his hesitation became concern.

The demon then moved in front of him and continued unbuttoning his shirt for him.

Alucard wasn't at all content with his old fears returning, so he did his best to ignore it and stared down at the floor while Zalith pulled his shirt off for him. Then, he waited as the demon dragged his hand over his left pec and down his arm as he searched his skin for signs of a death mark, and as each moment passed, Alucard's dread concerning the possibility began to worsen. All he could do was stand there and hope that he didn't have it.

He frowned, though, as Zalith—who was now standing behind him—rested his chin on his shoulder and sighed quietly. "There's nothing as far as I can see," he said, lightly grabbing the vampire's ass in his hand. "I haven't checked here, though," he mumbled.

Alucard pouted, refusing to look and see Zalith's face; he was certain that the demon was smirking, and he didn't want to let Zalith see his flustered expression. He glared ahead and waited. But he began to feel a little strange about it now. The only time he ever really got undressed was for bed, or…when he and Zalith were having sex. That wasn't happening right now, and he felt nervous with Zalith's focus being purely on what he looked like beneath his layers of clothing. Zalith wasn't going to be distracted by his desire to please him but would instead be focusing on searching every inch of his body, and that made him feel a little uncomfortable.

When Zalith gripped his belt, Alucard gently snatched his wrist and frowned. "Ve can look more later."

The demon frowned. "I don't mind looking now. I won't be handsy," he said with a smirk. "But if you'd rather do it at home, that's okay."

Alucard took his shirt from the counter where Zalith had put it and pulled it back on. "Ve can go 'ome now, anyvay," he said, turning to face Zalith. "Unless you 'ave anyving you need to do 'ere."

"Okay," Zalith answered. "We can head home."

With a nod, Alucard led the way out. As nervous as he was about Zalith searching every inch of him, he wanted to know for sure if he had a death mark. So, the sooner they collected Colt and Idina, the sooner they could get home and get it over with. And if he *was* marked…he wasn't sure what he should do about it. But that was something to figure out once he knew whether it was there or not.

# Chapter Forty-One

— ⋜ ✝ ⋝ —

## Opera Tickets

| **Alucard** |

Alucard stood on the deck beside Zalith, waiting for Idina and Colt. As the afternoon sun waned, a chill crept into the air, its icy tendrils cutting through the usual humidity. The vampire shivered, folding his arms tightly around himself in a futile attempt to ward off the biting cold. His gaze drifted to the distant silhouette of the cityscape, obscured by the veil of dusk. Impatience gnawed at him; should he send someone to find out what was taking so long?

He frowned, setting his eyes on the billboard advertising the opera. Seeing it again made him feel a little eager to suggest that he and Zalith go; he wanted to spend time with him and also wanted to try and help distract him from his worries. But when he went to ask, he began to feel nervous. How *should* he ask? What if Zalith said no? What if Zalith just wanted to go home, where he probably felt most safe?

The vampire shivered as the breeze picked up, and when he pouted irritably, Zalith moved as close as he could get to him and wrapped his arms around him. Alucard moved his arms around him, too; but after a few moments, Zalith didn't let go, and it was then that Alucard realized the demon was trying to shield him from the cold with his embrace. So, Alucard moved his arms and rested them against the demon's chest as he huddled closer to him.

While they continued waiting, Alucard buried his face in Zalith's shirt, sinking into the demon's naturally warm body temperature as it quickly helped him escape the cold. Zalith's embrace was something he loved and craved pretty much all the time, even when he was mad or upset. Something about being in Zalith's arms made him feel safe and content, and he never wanted to leave his arms, but the time to do so always came.

"Zaliv," he said quietly, fighting his angst off.

"Yes?"

"Do you…vant…to go and see an opera vith me?" he invited, trying to sound less nervous than he currently felt. But not having to face Zalith made it a little easier.

"Really?" Zalith asked with what sounded like surprise in his voice.

Alucard nodded, turning his head to glance over at the billboard in the distance. "I vould like to go vith you. I zon't know if zhere vould be any seats levt, but ve can go and see, and if not, ve can alvays do someving else," he suggested.

"I'd love to go," the demon said, holding him tightly. "We'll have to tell the coachman to take Idina and Colt home and to come back for us later."

The vampire nodded. "Okay," he said. Then, as Idina and Colt came to mind, he started to think about where they might be staying in his and Zalith's home. "Vhere vill zhey be staying?"

"One of the guest rooms on the second floor, most likely," Zalith answered. "They've got five to choose from."

"Okay," Alucard mumbled, burying his face back into Zalith's shirt.

Then, as the minutes dragged on, they waited for Idina and Colt. Alucard wasn't sure how long they might take, but he was content standing within Zalith's embrace. The thought of heading to another opera with him was exciting, and even if they couldn't get in, he was sure that they'd find something else to do. He just wanted to spend time with Zalith, whether it be at an opera or simply walking through the city. Any time he got to spend with the demon was his favourite time of the day—and night.


Eventually, Idina came up onto the deck with Colt following closely behind. The woman was carrying a small bag in the hand she wasn't using to hold Colt's palm, and as she made her way over, she smiled slightly.

"Sorry I took so long. I had to wrangle up Colt," the woman said, glancing down at the shy boy who had almost immediately set his eyes on Alucard. "I'm ready now, though."

Zalith took Idina's bag, letting go of Alucard's hand as he then led the way down to the docks. Alucard followed behind, slipping his hands into his trouser pockets. Then, they walked through the docks and down the street, heading to the nearby carriage stand.

"You'll be heading back without us," Zalith explained, looking at Idina. "The carriage will take you to our home, and once you get there, Varana will show you to a room."

"Thank you so much again," Idina said.

The demon nodded, leading the way into a large, paved area where a few other carriages and some hitched horses were waiting. He took Idina and Colt over to their carriage and pulled the door open. Idina stepped inside, and once Colt got in and sat down, Zalith handed Idina her bag and shut the door.

"Take them home," Zalith then instructed, looking up at the coachman, who nodded in response. "Come back for us later."

As the carriage prepared to leave, Zalith returned to Alucard's side. Obviously, they couldn't hold hands there, so they stuck close to one another as they left the carriage stand and returned to the Citadel's busy streets.

"So, what's *this* opera about?" Zalith asked with a smile.

Alucard glanced at the demon. "I zon't know," he admitted. "I just…vanted to spend time vith you," he said nervously.

The demon smiled a little brighter. "Thank you. I love spending time with you."

"I love spending time vith you, too," Alucard said quietly.

But Zalith heard him; when Alucard glanced at the demon's face, he saw both happiness and surprise. The vampire could feel his own heart almost pounding as his angst gripped him tightly, but he didn't want to let his nervousness stop him from telling Zalith the things that he needed and deserved to hear.

When they reached the opera house, Alucard spotted the long line of people slowly filing inside, and he was immediately filled with disappointment. There weren't going to be any tickets left, were there?

He and the demon joined the line anyway, and it didn't take long for Alucard to see that everybody ahead of and behind them already had their tickets in their hands. Of course, just like in Dor-Sanguis, it looked like he would have needed to book tickets ahead of time. But there was still the possibility that they could buy any spare tickets once they reached the doorman, so he'd wait.

They moved closer to the entrance, and when they reached the doorman, he held his hand out, expecting them to place their tickets on it.

Zalith frowned a little, staring at the man. "Are there any seats left to purchase?"

"Unfortunately not," the doorman replied, just as Alucard had suspected he would.

"Tell me who bought the most expensive seat here," Zalith then requested.

Alucard frowned strangely. What was he up to?

The doorman looked a little confused. "I…can't exactly share that information with you, sir. Sorry."

The vampire looked at Zalith, but just as he was about to suggest they either book for another time or leave, he noticed the same expression on Zalith's face that the demon would always have when he was searching somebody's mind. So, Alucard waited, sure that Zalith was most likely finding out who had the tickets he wanted so that he could go and buy them. After all, Zalith knew all the wealthier people in Nefastus, didn't he? There was no doubt in Alucard's mind that Zalith was acquainted with whoever bought the most expensive tickets possible.

Zalith soon smiled and led the way out of the line, and he seemed to be searching the crowd for someone.

Alucard followed him over to an expensively dressed man and his blonde-haired, blue-eyed female companion—in fact, the woman looked just like the one he'd seen a little less than a year ago when he was on the grounds of his home looking after that chicken, Hana. He frowned sadly at the thought of the short-lived friendship he'd had with the bird and stood silently at Zalith's side when they stopped in front of the man and woman. While she looked to be in her twenties, the man looked at least fifty. He didn't like to assume, but it looked like someone was using the other, or maybe they were both using each other.

"Good afternoon, Mathew," Zalith greeted, holding out his hand to the man. As Mathew took and shook his hand with a smile, the demon looked at the man's wife. "Cadence," he said.

Cadence smiled but giggled a little as she held her hand over her mouth, glancing at Alucard.

"What might you be doing here at this time of the day?" Mathew asked, looking around the busy square.

"It seemed like a nice day for a walk," Zalith answered.

"I see," the man said with a nod. "I trust you and Varana are well?"

"Quite," Zalith answered.

"Oh, Luca." Cadence smiled, setting her eyes on Alucard. "It's nice to see you again."

Looking at her, Alucard nodded. "Likevise."

Mathew set his eyes on Alucard. "Oh, you must be the foreign chap Cadence told me about. Where's your accent from?"

The vampire hated that word. Foreign. He wasn't going to answer.

"Mathew," Zalith then said with a more serious tone in his voice. "This might be a little unprecedented, but would you mind if I bought the tickets for this show from you?"

Mathew frowned but smiled in what looked like confusion as he glanced at Cadence and then back at Zalith. "Oh, well…I don't know. My wife was really looking forward to this."

But Cadence laughed slightly and waved her hand. "Oh, don't worry about it, sweetie," she said with what sounded like relief. "We could just go to the pantomime instead."

Mathew frowned in confliction, sighed deeply, and reached into his pocket. "Sure, it's no problem."

"How much were they?" Zalith asked, reaching into his own pocket.

"Two coronam each," Mathew said.

The demon pulled more than two coronam out of his pocket; Alucard was sure that was to avoid suspicion of the fact that he didn't actually carry his money around and instead stored it in a vault that he could reach into using ethos. "Here," he said with a smile, taking four of the white coronam notes from his hand, and then he slipped the other two back into his pocket.

"Enjoy the show," Mathew said, handing Zalith the tickets after taking his money. Then, he took hold of his wife's hand. "I've heard many good things about it."

"Thank you," Zalith said, handing one of the tickets to Alucard. "Have a good night."

"And you," Mathew said with a nod, stepping out of the line so that Zalith and Alucard could take their places. And then, the couple left, leaving Alucard and Zalith in peace.

As the line moved forward, Alucard looked at Zalith. He'd not deny that he enjoyed and appreciated the demon's methods; however, he couldn't help but wonder what Zalith might have done if Mathew had refused. "Vhat if 'e 'ad said no?" he asked him.

"It would have been fine. I have my ways," he said, tapping the side of his head with his finger.

Of course, he would have probably used some sort of mind manipulation to get Mathew to agree, whether he wanted to or not. And Alucard had no reason to disagree. So, with a slight smile, he stared ahead again, waiting to enter the opera house.

However, as they approached the doorman once more, he stared at them with a skeptical, disapproving look—and even more so when they both offered their tickets to him.

"Where did you get these tickets?" the doorman asked. "It wasn't just five minutes ago you were asking me—"

"Vhy does zhis matter?" Alucard interjected. "Ve 'ave our tickets, and I'm sure zhe next part of your job tells you to let us enter—or did you vorget zhat part?" he asked as Zalith smiled in amusement beside him.

The doorman scoffed and snatched the tickets from their hands. "Enjoy the show," he mumbled, handing them a small piece of card telling them where to find their seats.

Then, as they headed inside, Zalith leaned into Alucard's ear and told him, "You're so hot when you're mean."

Alucard smirked in response and led the way through the entrance hall and up a flight of carpeted stairs. Whatever the show was about, he was sure that he was going to enjoy it, but not as much as he'd just enjoyed the look of defeat on the doorman's face.

# Chapter Forty-Two

— ⸲ ✝ ⸱ —

## Another Opera Date

**| Alucard |**

Alucard and Zalith made their way up towards their seats.

As they climbed a third set of stairs, Zalith glanced at him and smirked. "Does it feel strange to not be attending our second opera as a married couple as we did the first time?"

Alucard scowled in embarrassment, remembering how he'd not fully understood the booking form when he took Zalith to an opera back in Dor-Sanguis. However, he didn't let the humiliation consume him. He felt the need to respond with the same attitude—something he found himself doing a lot lately. "No," he answered. "I'm your 'usband, am I not? You called me so earlier."

The demon smiled and laughed slightly as they reached the next floor. "I did, you're right."

"Vhy?" Alucard then asked, leading the way along the seat-lined balcony and towards another staircase.

Zalith moved his arm around Alucard's shoulders to hug him while they made their way up the next staircase. "Because it sounds better than boyfriend," he answered. "And in a situation such as the one we were in, the word demanded respect."

Alucard stared in front of him; the demon's smile was making him feel nervous, just like it always did. He was right that such a word demanded respect; he was sure that Zalith's people weren't too content with some vampire throwing them around, but they all seemed to calm down a little more after Zalith called him his husband.

Glancing at the demon, Alucard smiled back, walking up the final staircase. The mention of marriage and children this morning had stuck with him more than he thought it might, and the thought of one day marrying Zalith made him feel content. He wasn't sure when it might happen, but now he knew that it probably would, and as anxious as it made him feel to think about the future—to think about a family and a wedding—he didn't let it take away his happiness. He was sure neither thing would happen too soon and that when it *did* happen, it would be the right time for both of them.

After a short walk through a quiet hallway, Alucard and Zalith located their seats. Perched atop a grand balcony, nestled amidst the swirling currents of conversation and anticipation below, lay their sanctuary. At the apex of the lavish opera house, their view commanded a panorama of the entire auditorium below, a sea of elegantly adorned patrons awaiting the performance. There, ensconced in luxury, rested a plush velvet divan, inviting in its sumptuousness. Flanking the entrance to their private enclave, heavy drapes whispered of exclusivity, veiling the world beyond in an aura of mystery and refinement. This was not merely a seat; it was a throne of privilege, an enclave of indulgence reserved for those who dwelled in the rarified air of society's elite, perfect for him and Zalith—and worth the money paid.

Once Zalith closed the curtains behind them, they made their way over to the couch. Alucard sat down, making himself comfortable as Zalith sat beside him; there was no indication as to when the show would be starting, but Alucard felt it wouldn't be too long.

It was then that a server peeked through the curtains, clearing his throat loudly to alert them of his arrival. "Good evening, sirs. Would you like any refreshments?" he asked pleasantly.

"A bottle of red wine," Zalith requested, glancing back at him. "The best you have. Do you want anything?" he then asked, looking at Alucard as the server searched for what he'd asked for from his trolley.

Alucard wasn't entirely sure what he wanted. As soon as the opportunity for food was presented, he felt like something sweet, but what? His mind was blank; all he could seem to think about was the conversation they had this morning and how eager he was for the show to start so that he and Zalith could relax. "Vell…someving…sveet, maybe," he said with a shrug.

Zalith looked back over his shoulder at the server, who placed a bottle of wine and two glasses on a small round table beside the demon's end of the couch. "Do you have anything with chocolate?"

The man nodded and looked at his trolley in the hall. "There are gateau slices—"

"Perfect," Zalith said. "We'll have one of those, please."

Nodding, the server placed a slice of chocolate gateau on a small plate and handed it to Zalith. The demon then paid and tipped the man before sending him on his way.

Alucard waited to be handed his snack, but as Zalith turned back to face him, he didn't hand the plate and its fork to him. Instead, the demon cut a small piece of the cake with the fork.

The demon smirked suggestively. "If you want some, you have to kiss me for it."

Staring at him, Alucard pouted. *Of course* Zalith was going to use this as an opportunity to make him feel flustered, and his nervousness increased as each moment of the demon smiling at him passed by. He wanted that cake; it looked so delicious, and seeing it only made him crave it a whole lot more. His eyes shifted from Zalith's smile to the cake and then back to the demon's face. He wasn't going to deny that he'd like to try and get over his anxiety and kiss him; there were so many things he felt he wanted to do for Zalith, but his fear stopped him every time. Maybe this time, he'd not let it stop him. After all, he *really* wanted that cake.

Alucard's brows furrowed in a silent battle with his own apprehension, his gaze momentarily diverted to the safety of the floor below. Summoning a shard of resolve, he raised his eyes to meet Zalith's, a tumult of emotions swirling within him. But he did his best to shove aside the doubt that threatened to ensnare him. His hand, guided by a mixture of longing and uncertainty, found its place at the back of Zalith's head, fingers entwining in the silken strands of his hair. Slowly, hesitantly, he bridged the gap between them, drawing their faces closer in an unspoken invitation. As their lips met, a surge of conflicting sensations washed over him, mingling with the electric pulse of their connection. He felt the startled flutter of Zalith's response—he obviously hadn't been expecting Alucard to be so brave. But despite the façade of confidence that he projected, Alucard's heart thundered within him.

However, he ignored it. He kept kissing the demon as he kissed back, and in his free hand, he gripped the plate on which his slice of cake sat. Now that Zalith was distracted, he could take what he wanted. Without any hindrance, he abruptly snatched the plate from Zalith's loose grip and hastily moved back to his side of the couch. He didn't manage to get the fork, but he didn't care. He just wanted the cake.

Alucard then glanced at the demon, watching as he smiled and rolled his eyes before eating the cake that was on the fork, which he then handed to Alucard. As Zalith started to pour them both a glass of wine, the vampire tried the cake. It wasn't as delicious as it looked—in fact, it was a little dry—but he'd still eat it.

The demon took a sip of his wine and placed his glass back down. "Come back here. I miss you," he said quietly, holding his arm out.

Alucard didn't hesitate. He wanted to be in Zalith's embrace, and he'd not deny his invitation. The vampire placed the cake on the table and shuffled closer to the demon. He rested his head on his chest and moved his arm around him while Zalith held him tightly. Now, he felt utterly content. All that needed to happen now was for the show to start.

And it didn't take very long for that to happen.

When the stage curtains opened, revealing the performers, Zalith tightened his embrace around Alucard. The show began, and as the silent hall was filled with opera music and vocals, Alucard glanced up at Zalith's face and saw him smile. A feeling of content ensnared him in response; all he wanted to do was make Zalith happy and seeing that he was enjoying himself made him feel like he was doing *something* right.

However, after about ten minutes, Alucard felt Zalith tense up. He looked at him again, and when he saw a scowl of distress on the demon's face, Alucard frowned in worry. Zalith was overthinking again, wasn't he? He was giving in to his paranoia, and Alucard could hear his heart beating faster in his chest. The demon shuffled around a little, so Alucard sat up straight, and Zalith leaned on him and nuzzled his neck; he wrapped his arms around the vampire, clinging on to his left shoulder, and then softly kissed his neck a single time.

"Are you okay?" Alucard asked as he rubbed the demon's thigh.

"Yeah," Zalith replied quietly.

"Are you sure?"

Zalith nodded. "Mm-hmm."

The vampire made himself comfortable and looked down at the stage. But then he felt Zalith sniffing him after kissing his neck again.

"You smell good," the demon mumbled, dragging his hand down from the vampire's shoulder and to his chest.

His fingers moved over the crucifix around Alucard's neck, and as Alucard tensed up nervously, Zalith began to fiddle with the platinum chain. But he stopped after a few moments and slowly guided his hand down Alucard's body and to his leg, and that was where he kept it.

But it wasn't too long after that he started gently rubbing Alucard's leg. The vampire's nervousness was slowly increasing, and when Zalith moved his hand around to his inner thigh, Alucard tensed up a little more.

"Vhat are you doing?" he asked quietly.

"Do you want me to stop?"

The vampire pondered for a few moments. Although he wasn't entirely sure where Zalith was going with it, he was curious to find out. "No," he answered.

Zalith smirked and continued rubbing the vampire's inner thigh.

Alucard stared out at the performers. He felt slightly conflicted, though; he enjoyed Zalith's attention more than anything, but it wasn't like they were at home right now. He'd feel a whole lot more comfortable there, but... despite his worry that people may see, he found he didn't want Zalith to stop.

The vampire frowned as his body began to succumb to Zalith's affection. He dragged his hand to Alucard's crotch, and as the demon stroked his fingers over the bulge in his trousers, the vampire exhaled quietly in struggle. Excitement and angst consumed him, and his thoughts started battling one another. He didn't want to say no to Zalith's attention, but he was afraid that someone might see or hear. Neither of them would want that. But when the demon breathed onto his neck through what Alucard knew was a smile on his face, his worry started to wither.

He relaxed as best he could, moving his right hand to the back of Zalith's head to grip his hair. Anticipation shivered through his body as Zalith lightly kissed his neck; Alucard leaned his head back, staring up at the ceiling, finally taking his eyes off the show. He didn't care for it anymore.

As Zalith moved his face from the vampire's neck to look down at his waist, Alucard turned his head to hide his expression, sure that Zalith would enjoy seeing just how flustered he made him feel. All it ever really took was one touch of Zalith's hand and he'd lose the control he had over himself. Alucard had come to find that Zalith always knew how to make him lose himself a little, but he enjoyed that. He enjoyed just how serene Zalith made him feel.

Zalith unbuckled the vampire's belt and moved his hand inside his trousers. Alucard did his best not to utter a sound in response to the delight that wandered through his tensing body at the touch of Zalith's hand. He frowned pleasurably as the demon started to caress his hardening shaft, and when Zalith returned to nuzzling and kissing his neck, Alucard tightly gripped the cushion beside him in an attempt to keep himself quiet. The opera was still loud, and his and Zalith's seats were out of the view of everyone else, but Alucard didn't want to make a single noise that might cause someone to suspect what might be going on above them.

Sitting there, he scowled, finding it harder to stay still while the demon continued to pleasure him with his hand. But after a few moments, Zalith kissed Alucard's neck one last time and moved his head down towards the vampire's waist. Alucard felt his angst return as the demon unbuttoned his trousers and pulled his shaft out. Zalith didn't waste any time at all and dragged his tongue over it, and then he took it into his mouth.

Still gripping a fistful of Zalith's hair, Alucard fidgeted and exhaled shakily, leaning his head back as he closed his eyes. The pleasure was quickly consuming him, gripping him fiercely as his heart beat faster and his legs trembled.

Zalith gripped Alucard's left thigh with his free hand as he sucked a little faster, exhaling content hums as he did. Alucard tightened his grip on the demon's hair; his heart was now racing, his breaths were becoming harder to control, and the longer the demon pleased him, the more he struggled to keep himself silent.

Alucard dug his claws into the cushion, a whisper of a struggled whine upon his long, deep breaths. He frowned pleasurably, his once angst-filled body now giving in to the delight of Zalith's attention. The vampire sighed in enjoyment, tightening his grip even more; pleasure electrified through his body as the demon swiftly led him to his peak, and when he climaxed, he gritted his teeth and attempted to keep himself from letting a euphoric, pleased moan escape his hushed breaths. And then, his pleasure-enthralled body was left to tremble as Zalith returned the vampire's shaft to his trousers.

Zalith kissed the vampire's body over his shirt, making his way back up to his neck; he nuzzled it, exhaling deeply against Alucard's skin as he wrapped his arms around him once more. "What did I miss?" he asked quietly.

Alucard, trying to control the shivering ache of his alleviated body, rested what he could of his head on top of Zalith's, moving his arm around him again. "Not much."

"Okay, good."

The vampire's excitement didn't wane as quickly as he thought—in fact, as he had a few times before, he wanted to do something for Zalith. If they weren't in an opera house, he might even ask Zalith if he wanted him to do anything for him, but the fact that they were in public kept him from acting on his curiosity.

He sat there, staring down at the performance, letting his body slowly calm down as he enjoyed the bewildering scent of Zalith's natural aroma. He wasn't sure how much longer the show would go on, but he knew he would enjoy the rest of it sitting there with Zalith. He felt utterly content right now, and he hoped Zalith felt the same.

# Chapter Forty-Three

─ ⸱ ✝ ⸱ ─

## Apologies

**| Zalith |**

When Zalith and Alucard left the opera house, it was dark and cold; the demon felt Alucard shiver beside him and rubbed his back. He wanted to hold his hand and pull him into his embrace, but there were a lot of people leaving the building behind them, and the square was also packed with crowds outside each tavern and restaurant. The smell of food clashed with the scent of alcohol, and lively music echoed from several buildings, bright lights flashing at their entrances. The Citadel felt more alive than it ever had during the day.

"Come on," he said, leading the way forward. "Let's get to the carriage."

Alucard nodded and followed on his right as they crossed the busy square.

But a flurry of loud, angry voices snatched the demon's attention. He looked in the direction of the commotion, setting his sights on a group of what at first glance looked like drunks, but half of the men were wearing grey-striped, black suits and black fedoras.

Imperito.

Zalith kept walking but watched as the gang fought with the tavern patrons while the security tried to break it up. He felt guilty seeing that Imperito still walking the streets and causing shit; he was supposed to have dealt with them already. But he hadn't forgot, and he *would* live up to his promise to the city council. Just like he'd disposed of the Meshuga, he'd chase the Imperito out, too—or kill them all if need be.

He wasn't going to intervene now, though. The security was managing, and before Zalith could take any action, he needed to discuss a plan with the council. He should probably send them a letter once he got home asking for a meeting. The sooner the Imperito were dealt with, the better.

"Should ve 'elp?" Alucard then asked.

Zalith shook his head. "I don't want to get involved on my own. I need to talk to the city council and come up with a plan. Come on, let's get home," he said as they left the square and headed for the carriage stand.

Once they reached the place, Zalith set his sights on their black carriage. He walked Alucard over there and opened the door for him, and once the vampire climbed inside, Zalith followed. All he wanted to do was get home and relax.

As the carriage started moving, the demon rested his head on Alucard's shoulder and moved his arm around him. The vampire shivered for a few moments, but once Zalith's embrace warmed him, he relaxed, too.

And while they journeyed home, they sat quietly in one another's embrace.

The night grew darker, and the moons were high in the dark purple-orange sky when Zalith and Alucard got home. Opening the carriage door, the demon invited Alucard to climb out first, and then he followed the vampire into the house.

Zalith pulled his blazer off while Alucard shut the door behind them, and then he smiled at him when he came over to the coat rack and took his cape off. The demon felt a little better being home where he felt safe, but his conflicting thoughts still lingered. There was no way for him to tell whether this was a façade or not, but he didn't want to think about it. He had so many more important things to do. Not only did he have to get things started with a home for his people, but he and Alucard also had to start looking into killing Damien and Lilith. And there was the Imperito, too.

He was worried about the possibility that Alucard might have a death mark, though. Alucard's safety was one of his greatest concerns…and he found himself wondering if this was the way he was going to lose Alucard next. Was a grim reaper going to come and kill him?

But he didn't want to give in to his paranoia—not now. Not after he'd had a good time at the opera, despite his moment of dismay before distracting himself by pleasing his vampire. He wanted to think about how ready he was for their future together, a future that he so sorely wanted and would do whatever it took to get.

What if he'd never get it, though? What if he was actually dead? What if Alucard was actually dead and they were all still back in Eltaria right now trapped by Adellum's blinding light?

As he and Alucard slowly walked through the hall, he scowled in distress. What would happen if he saw Alucard die again, and then woke up from this fake reality? Would he become desensitized? Would he stop caring about having to witness the man he loved dying over and over and over again? His scowl thickened when he started to picture Alucard's cold, dead eyes and the sight of his bloody face. He never wanted to see that again.

He exhaled deeply and tried to keep himself from sinking too deep into his dismay. There had to be something else he could focus on—something that would distract him enough—and his mind chose the fact that he had to contact the contractor he'd used since moving to Aegisguard. He needed to discuss the compound he wanted to have built for his people.

As he took hold of Alucard's hand, he spotted Edwin making his way across the hall with a linen basket. "Edwin," he called.

The butler turned to look at them and made his way over. "Yes, sir?"

"I need you to contact Leonard; tell him to meet me here tomorrow."

"Yes, sir," Edwin said with a nod. Then, he swiftly left the hall and disappeared into one of the other rooms.

"Leonard?" Alucard asked.

"The contractor I've been working with since I got to Aegisguard. I need to talk to him about the compound I want to have built for my people."

Alucard nodded, walking beside him.

"Thank you for taking me out," Zalith then said. "I had a nice time, and it was fun."

Glancing at him, the vampire smiled shyly. "Ve can go out more if you vant. I'm…never veally busy," he suggested with a shrug.

Zalith smiled. "I'd love that."

With his shy expression growing, Alucard looked away.

Zalith stopped walking and pulled the vampire closer. He wrapped his arms around him and hugged him tightly, taking the chance to get a little lost in Alucard's delightful scent. He loved his unique, enticing natural aroma; it captivated Zalith the very first time he entered Alucard's home. Cedarwood, warm amber, roses, and cinnamon. It was unlike anything he'd smelled before.

He kissed the vampire's lips and smiled at him. "You're so cute," he murmured, moving his hand to the side of Alucard's neck.

The vampire's face reddened as he looked down at the floor and pouted.

"You're even cuter when you make that face," the demon said, smirking.

Alucard looked around in fluster as he clearly tried to figure out what to say.

Zalith took hold of the vampire's hand. "Let's go and check on Idina and Colt," he suggested, starting to lead the way to the stairs.

But as their conversation drew to a close, Zalith found himself engulfed once more by the relentless cacophony of his thoughts. The urgency to kickstart the construction of the compound gnawed at him, a relentless drumbeat echoing the pressing need for his people to find solace and sanctuary. Guilt coiled around his conscience like a suffocating embrace; the burden of their displacement weighed heavily upon him. The image of his people cramped within the confines of Alucard's ship tugged at his heartstrings, a stark reminder of his own shortcomings. They deserved more than makeshift accommodations; they deserved a haven to call their own. The responsibility for their plight weighed heavily upon his shoulders, a heavy mantle of regret that threatened to crush him beneath its weight.

Turning his gaze towards the vampire at his side, a surge of apprehension gripped Zalith. His once-content thoughts now poisoned by worry, he scrutinized Alucard's form for any hint of danger. His fingers itched with the urge to scour every inch of the vampire's body, searching for the telltale mark of impending doom. Uncertainty gnawed at his resolve, fueling an anxious desperation to ensure their safety. They couldn't afford to overlook any potential threat; not when the stakes were so perilously high.

However, his eyes then shifted from Alucard to Varana. From where he stopped walking, he could see her sitting in the lounge on the pile of cushions with a book in her right hand and a bowl to her left filled with red grapes, which she was contently eating while enjoying her novel.

He remembered how he'd found out that she and Luther were sleeping together. How could he forget? He needed to talk to her about that, and he didn't exactly want to wait. He glanced at Alucard. "One moment," he said, still holding his hand as he made his way towards the lounge. Then, as he stepped inside, he let go of the vampire's hand and walked over to where Varana was sitting.

"Varana," he said.

The woman, however, didn't acknowledge his presence or his voice.

"Varana," he repeated irritably.

"What?!" she snapped, lowering her book to scowl at him.

Zalith frowned with just as much aggravation. "We need to talk," he said sternly.

"About what?" she asked but then rolled her eyes. "Just spit it out! I'm trying to read!" she insisted, glancing down at her book as she ate the grape she'd been holding between her thumb and finger.

He wasn't going to dance around the reason he'd come to her. "Are you sleeping with Luther?"

Varana's annoyed scowl slowly transformed into a snide little smile as she picked her book back up and pretended to read it. "I don't know what you're talking about," she mumbled.

Zalith knew she was lying, and it only made him feel even more vexed about what she'd been up to. "Did you fall down the stairs and hit your head multiple times on the way down?" he questioned.

She scowled but didn't utter a word to him.

With his impatience growing, Zalith then snatched her book—

"Hey! Give that back!" she shouted, preparing to stand up.

But Zalith held it over his shoulder, letting her know she wasn't getting it back. "I'll give it back when you explain to me what the hell is going on in your head."

With an exasperated snarl, Varana threw a grape at Zalith. "It's *none* of your business!" she insisted, watching as the grape bounded off his shoulder and hit the floor.

Ignoring it, he scowled in revolt. "*Why* Luther?"

She glared again, but her irritated eyes shifted to something behind Zalith. The demon looked over his shoulder, setting his eyes on Alucard, who was leaning against the doorframe with a vacant expression on his face.

Realizing that Varana was looking at the vampire, Zalith frowned and looked back at her. "Is it because of *him*?"

"I thought sleeping with somebody that he works with would be funny, and obviously, I was right because here you are acting like a court jester."

With his *anger* now boiling, Zalith rolled his eyes *hard*. "Well, I hope it was worth it, V—"

Varana snatched her book back and slumped down into the cushions. "Why does it matter to you so much?"

"Because I don't like him, Varana. I care about you, and I don't want you associating with people like Luther."

She scoffed a little as she flipped through the pages of her book. "So, *you* can involve yourself in *my* affairs any time you want, but when *I* do it, it's deserving of capital punishment?"

He scowled again, slowly becoming more and more aggravated as each moment passed. "What you did to Alucard was an entirely different situation and you know it."

"I don't know," she said with a sing-song tone. "I think someone's jealous."

"Varana—"

She abruptly slammed her book shut and glowered up at him. "You've been gone for *months*, Zalith. You can't just show up and spend a grand total of three minutes with me and with Alucard and then suddenly start acting like you give a shit! My reasons for getting together with Luther were petty, but frankly, he and I are adults, and we can do whatever we like."

Zalith's thoughts fumbled, and he went silent for a moment. He knew he'd neglected them both so much recently and being told so made all the guilt come back. He looked over his shoulder at Alucard; the vampire *was* looking at him, but it seemed as though he wasn't the only one who felt upset by Varana's words.

He took his eyes off the vampire before he let Alucard's frown of confliction get to him and set his eyes back on Varana. "I'm sorry—"

"And everyone keeps asking me why you're acting so strange, but honestly, I think that you've been gone for so long that you've managed to change without us noticing," she said with a bitter frown.

His guilt thickened; it weighed so heavy on his mind and in his heart that he began to feel as though he might drown. But he didn't want to let that happen. Both Varana and Alucard deserved his apology, and he needed to work out how to make it up to them.

"Varana," he said, losing his irritated scowl. "I didn't mean to upset you."

She rolled her eyes and looked back down at her book. "Whatever."

Zalith wasn't going to argue with her anymore, and there really wasn't much point in saying sorry over and over again to the both of them until he knew how to *show* that he was sorry. So, he turned around—

"At least Luther knows how to take care of me," Varana mumbled quietly.

But Zalith heard, and his anger returned. For *centuries,* he'd been taking care of her; he'd been devoted to looking after that woman, and to hear her disregard that so easily made him madder than he'd been in a while. He wasn't going to express his anger, though. Instead, he started walking away as a scowl appeared on his face. "I fucked Alucard on those pillows, by the way, so you might want to move," he called.

Varana gasped and shrieked in revolt.

Zalith heard a *thump* as she surely hit the floor after launching herself off the pillows, which made him smirk in amusement. He took hold of Alucard's hand and left the room, closing the door behind them.

## | Alucard |

Alucard followed Zalith across the hall and towards the stairs. He wasn't going to lie to himself; he *was* still upset about the fact that Zalith had neglected him, but they'd moved on from that. All he wanted to do now was focus on helping Zalith get better.

Zalith suddenly stopped in front of the stairs and turned to face Alucard. "Alucard," he said as he frowned sorrowfully. "I know that I neglected you for far too long, and…I need you to tell me what I can do to make it up to you," he pleaded softly.

The vampire frowned, staring at Zalith's face. He looked almost *desperate*, and Alucard wasn't sure why. He didn't know if it was because of his recent turmoil or because he really did feel so awful about prioritizing his work. But Alucard chose to ignore the lingering pain caused by his absence for Zalith's sake. After all, why should his need for the demon's attention outweigh the need Zalith's people had for him?

He shook his head, looking to his side. "You zon't 'ave to do anyving. You vere doing vings vor your people, and zhey are more important. You zon't 'ave to do anyving to show me you're sorry. You told me you are, and zhat's enough."

Zalith's expression grew sullen. "Nothing is more important to me than you are, Alucard," he said, placing his hand on the side of his face.

The vampire didn't want Zalith to feel sad or burdened with needing to find a way to show him that he was sorry. Alucard would get over his sadness; he needed a little more time, just as Zalith needed time to get over his paranoia.

So, he shook his head again, staring into the demon's dark, guilt-filled eyes. "I'm vine," he insisted. "You should vocus on your people."

Zalith's sad stare only seemed to worsen. Distress smothered his face, but he kept his eyes on Alucard. "You know I'd do anything for you, right?"

Alucard wasn't sure why Zalith was saying such a thing. "I know," he answered, nodding. "I vould do anyving vor you, too."

"I love you," the demon said and kissed his lips.

As Zalith gazed at him, Alucard stared back. "I love you," he said as he moved his arms around him and hugged him tightly, resting his head on Zalith's shoulder. However, when he started thinking about a way to change the subject and maybe make Zalith feel better, he thought about Hana. "You know vhat you can do?" he asked, leaning out of Zalith's embrace to see his face. "You can get me a new chicken—vone zhat isn't going to end up on my dinner plate."

The demon laughed amusedly. "I'll get you a whole flock of chickens."

Alucard shook his head. "I only vant vone—vone zhat looks just like 'ana did," he said sternly.

"Is it okay to keep just one chicken?"

Frowning, Alucard thought to himself for a moment. Was it okay to keep a chicken on its own? Or did it need friends? "I zon't know," he admitted.

"Well, I'm not a chicken farmer," Zalith said, smirking, "but I'll ask around and see what actual chicken farmers have to say."

"Okay," Alucard said with a small, amused laugh.

"Would you like to pick them out, or should I surprise you?" Zalith asked, leading the way upstairs.

Alucard shrugged. "Zoesn't matter. Just zon't get any males. I'd vather not be voken up at zhe crack of dawn," he mumbled.

"Agreed," Zalith said. "Perhaps we could train a rooster to wake you up at noon," he then suggested when they reached the top of the stairs.

Looking at him again, Alucard pouted. He knew that he slept *a lot*, and now he wasn't sure whether Zalith disliked that. He frowned, glancing down at the floor as he followed Zalith across the hall to the next set of stairs. "Do you…'ave problem vith 'ow long I sleep?" he asked nervously.

"I've never met someone who can sleep quite as long as you, Alucard, but I'm joking. I really don't mind how long you sleep, and I want you to get all the sleep you need," he said, smiling at him as they made their way up to the second floor.

When they reached the top of the stairs, Alucard sighed quietly. "I zon't know vhy I sleep so much," he admitted. For as long as he could remember, he'd always sleep *so* much—more than the average person seemed to—and he never really knew why.

Zalith stopped walking once they reached the room that Idina was in and smiled at him. "As long as you're sleeping next to me, I'm not too worried about it, baby," he said.

Then, after Zalith knocked and Idina told them to enter, they headed into the room.

# Chapter Forty-Four

—⸲ ✝ ⸱—

## Revelations

**| Zalith |**

Zalith pushed the door open, and when they stepped inside, both he and Alucard set their eyes on a small wolf-like puppy whining and crying on the bed. Idina was sitting beside it with a flustered look on her face while staring at them.

Why had Colt chosen to take the form of a dog? Zalith frowned strangely but then noticed that Sabazios followed them upstairs and was standing beside him, staring at Colt with his head tilted, almost as if he wasn't sure what he was looking at.

"Vhy does 'e cry?" Alucard asked, nodding at Colt.

"Oh," Idina said, taking her eyes off them to look at Colt. "He lost his stuffed tiger—Maurice—and he's been having a hard time coping with it. He was very special to him. The last time I saw it was when we went through the portal," she explained.

The vampire took his eyes off the crying puppy and glanced at Zalith.

Zalith's attention drifted away, though. Idina's mention of the portal set off his paranoia again. It made him think about the moment he'd seen Adellum's glowing vines seep through the darkness…. It reminded him of all the times he'd seen Alucard die, and *that* forced him to think about the death mark again. He wanted to search the rest of Alucard's body for it as soon as possible.

But he wasn't going to just storm out of the room and confuse Colt and Idina. His eyes shifted from the boy to Idina's pretty much empty bag. He knew that she—like the rest of his people—had close to no belongings whatsoever, and that made him feel even more guilty than he already did. So, he offered her, "Would you and Colt like to head into the Citadel and get some new clothes? Perhaps something to replace Maurice?" he suggested, setting his eyes back on her.

Tears of gratitude started to form in Idina's eyes again. "Thank you so much," she exclaimed happily. "I'll pay you back every single dime—"

"Don't worry about it," he said, smiling. "You should probably head out soon, though—before the stores close. Varana might want to go; you'll find her in the lounge.

Just avoid the theatre square. I saw some troublesome faces down there." The last thing he wanted was for the Imperito to bother them.

Idina nodded. "Thank you," she repeated. Then, she looked down at Colt. "Do you want to go out to the shops?"

Looking up at her, his whining finally silencing, Colt nodded slowly.

Then, Zalith smiled and took hold of Alucard's hand. "If you need anything, just ask one of the butlers. Alucard and I have something to see to."

She nodded as she ushered Colt to change back and get ready. "Thank you so much, Zalith—and thank you, too, Alucard."

It looked like Idina was settling in well, and hopefully, some new clothes and toys would help Colt calm down a little, too. There wasn't much more Zalith could do right now, but if there was anything either of them needed, he'd make sure to get it for them.

Now, he wanted to go and search Alucard.

"We'll see you a little later," the demon said to Idina. Then, he left the room, taking Alucard with him.

"Vhat is…dime?" Alucard asked curiously, glancing at him as they started to make their way downstairs.

Zalith smiled at him. "A certain coin in Eltaria."

"Oh…okay."

"Alucard," Zalith then said, looking over at him.

"Vhat?"

"Can we check for that mark now?" he asked as they reached the bottom of the stairs.

The vampire frowned hesitantly.

Zalith hadn't failed to notice Alucard's nervousness earlier, too. For some reason, the vampire seemed worried about him seeing the bottom half of his body; it felt like he was also beginning to feel insecure about his scars. A few nights ago, Zalith went to bed and saw Alucard wearing a shirt beneath the blankets, something he only did when he was concerned about someone seeing his scars. The demon wasn't sure why Alucard's insecurities might be returning, but he assumed that it was because of his negligence; his absence probably made Alucard think that he didn't find him attractive anymore, and that brought an aching sadness to the demon's heart.

"Okay," the vampire then said quietly, snapping Zalith out of his thoughts.

"Where would you like to go?" he asked as he stopped in the middle of the hall.

Alucard shrugged. "Ve can just…go to zhe bedvoom," he mumbled, glancing over at their bedroom door.

"Okay," Zalith said and started leading the way over there as Sabazios trotted off downstairs.

He hoped that his search proved that the death mark didn't exist, but if it did…then he was going to do whatever he had to to get rid of it.

## | Alucard |

When they got into their bedroom, Alucard wandered over to the bed and watched Zalith close the door behind them. The vampire didn't sit down, though. Instead, he stood there with a nervous frown on his face, waiting for Zalith to join him.

The demon made his way over to him, but when he reached him, Alucard glanced over at the windows. Their house might be in the middle of a forest, but he didn't want to risk something or someone seeing him naked.

Zalith evidently noticed; with a wave of his hand, the demon pulled all the black curtains shut with his telekinesis. Then, he stood in front of Alucard. "Should I double-check under your shirt?"

Alucard shrugged, staring down at the floor. "If you vant."

"I *do* want to," Zalith confirmed as he started unbuttoning the vampire's shirt.

The vampire stood there and waited. His nervous frown didn't fade, and once Zalith pulled his shirt off and dropped it on the bed, Alucard watched as the demon gently dragged his hands over his pecs and abs. It looked like Zalith was searching but also enjoying the opportunity to see and feel him, and Alucard didn't mind the affection.

Zalith didn't find anything on his front, arms, or neck, though. So, he moved behind him to search his back. As the demon's hand came to rest upon his shoulder, though, a chill raced down Alucard's spine, setting his nerves alight with a primal sense of unease. Despite knowing that Zalith would never hurt him, his body reacted instinctively, recoiling from the touch as if stung by unseen forces. A light shrug betrayed the discomfort gnawing at him from within; it was a familiar dance with his own trauma, a relentless shadow that loomed over his every interaction. Rationality waged war against instinct, each skirmish leaving Alucard teetering on the edge of vulnerability. He knew, deep down, that he could trust Zalith, yet the spectre of past wounds cast a long shadow over his present. The scars of his previous life, invisible yet ever-present, whispered tales of betrayal and pain, leaving Alucard caught in a tangled web of trust and trepidation.

"I'm sorry," the demon said quietly, taking his hand off him. "I won't touch."

Alucard shook his head. He trusted Zalith's touch and didn't want to make him doubt that. And now that he was thinking about it, he never really told Zalith where all those scars came from, did he? Perhaps now was a better time than any. "'E vould..." he started, struggling to find the words. "Zamien vould ovten vhrash me vor every minute I vas late back vrom 'is tasks. Sometimes, 'e vould just do because 'e vas angry at somevone or someving else. And zhe scars stay zhere because 'e did vith someving zhat must 'ave 'ad silver; I zidn't 'eal so good back zhen; my body vas a lot veaker…because 'e vouldn't let me 'ave 'uman blood. I 'ad to survive on zhe blood of vhatever I could vind in zhe castle," he explained quietly, and when he felt his heart growing heavier with dismay, he exhaled deeply and tried to keep calm. He didn't want to remember that part of his past…but Zalith deserved to know.

Zalith carefully wrapped his arms around the vampire and hugged him tightly.

Alucard shrugged and continued, "You see zhem every day, and you must vonder vhy zhey are zhere." He paused and exhaled again, looking up at the ceiling in an attempt to keep himself from crying. "I…used to vonder vhy vas alvays my back, but…I guess now vas because 'e zidn't vant zhe people avound 'im to know what 'e did to me. 'E used to be so proud, showing me off to all 'is associates like I vas some kind of trophy, and zhey vould all treat 'im like a king. I zon't know vhy I used to vink I vanted to be like 'im—vhy I vhought I deserved vhat I got vrom 'im."

Holding him, Zalith nuzzled his neck and shook his head. "Damien and Lilith are both repulsive cowards," he said, and although he was clearly trying to hide it, there was anger in his voice. "They used you, lied to you, and treated you in a way *no* person deserves to be treated. Whatever happened back then, you don't have to worry about it now. They're *never* going to find you, and you're not alone anymore, either. I'm here, and I'm not going anywhere; there's nothing that would make me change my mind, Alucard. I love you more than I've ever loved anyone, and for you, there's nothing I wouldn't do. We're going to kill Damien, Lilith, Lucifer, and whoever else we have to in order to keep you safe and keep anything like that from happening again."

Alucard gripped Zalith's arms and held them firmly. His assurance helped him relax a little, but dismay still lingered inside him. "No matter 'ow many times you tell me, I still can't seem to understand vhy you do so much vor me," he mumbled sullenly. "No vone ever did anyving vor me. Zhere vas a time vhen I expected somevone to 'elp me, and zhen zhey let Zamien do zhis. I guess zhat lingers in zhe back of my mind every time anyvone says zhey vill do someving vor me. And every time you tell me I matter more to you zhan anyving…I just can't seem to accept zhat, and I alvays vant you *not* to prioritize me because no vone ever 'as, and I zon't expect to come virst vor anyvone." The tears forming in his eyes wanted to fall, but he didn't want to let them. He closed his eyes and scowled, trying to stay composed, and then he continued, "I say zhose vings, and I guess you probably vonder vhy I zon't seem to vant you to prioritize me. You are…zhe virst person to treat me like I mean someving and is taking longer zhan I vhought vor me to get used to," he explained, struggling again to find the right words.

"Alucard," he said quietly, still nuzzling his neck. "You don't have to explain yourself to me. I understand, and never have I ever wondered why. I love you just the way you are, and I understand more than you might think I do—"

"I vant to tell you, Zaliv," Alucard interjected. "If ve're going to be togezzer vor as long as I vant, zhen…you deserve to know. Zhere could be someving I do vone day zhat upsets you, and I von't know; I zon't vant *you* to vink I did someving because I zon't love you or vant you or vhatever. I ovten ignore my desires vor you and your attention because I zon't know 'ow to tell you vhat I vant.

"You compliment me and say all zhese nice vings to me, and I vant to tell you vings like zhat, too, but I zon't know vhen or 'ow. I alvays 'ave to put so much vhought into vhat I say bevore I say because vor vour 'undred years I *alvays* 'ad to vatch vhat I said and 'ow I said. And now, is like a 'abit; every time I try to ignore zhat, I veel strange and panic, and zhen I just sit zhere and do or say noving," he explained, starting to feel distressed.

Alucard felt Zalith tense up. He could feel the demon's heart beating a little harder than normal, and then something wet trickled down his chest. Was Zalith crying?

The vampire took a deep breath and tightened his grip on the demon's arms; he wasn't done yet. "You've been so patient vith me, and I zon't know 'ow to vank you. You make me veel safer zhan I've ever velt, and you make me veel loved. I 'ave…never velt loved bevore, nor 'ave I velt so 'appy vith somevone. You know and 'ave seen my scars, and you're still 'ere, and I zon't 'ave zhe vords to tell you 'ow vankful I am. I zon't know 'ow to vank you for everyving you do vor me. I just vish I could do more vor you—I vish I could get over zhis shit and tell you vings like you tell me—and do vings vor you. Because I vant to, I just—"

Zalith squeezed him affectionately. "You don't have to be careful with what you say," he started. "You don't have to watch what you say or do and feel uncomfortable; there's nothing to be afraid of, and I'm not going to get angry or belittle you or anything like that. But I don't want you to do anything you're not ready for because you're worried about how I feel about it. I want you to take your time, I want you to be comfortable, and I want you to just be you.

"You don't have to thank me either," he said, nuzzling his neck again. "I'm not going anywhere, and I've always been able to be so very patient with you; that will never change. And if you not knowing *how* to do these things plays a part, you know I can talk you through it."

The vampire opened his eyes as his tears stopped trying so hard to fall and gazed ahead. His thoughts were racing just as fast as his heart was. He felt more nervous than he had in a long time, but he needed to say the things he was saying. He needed to tell Zalith why he said and did the things he did; he was sure that Zalith wondered why he still hadn't done anything for him or said anything to him, and he didn't want the demon to think it was because he wasn't attracted to him or because he didn't want him. He wanted Zalith in so many ways and more than he had ever wanted anything. But he had no idea how to approach it or how to tell Zalith when and how he wanted him.

And above all, he had no idea how to do the things Zalith did for him.

He wasn't going to let his anxiety get the better of him now. He told Zalith so much already, and he wasn't going to cower when they came close to solving one of the problems Alucard knew he had.

With a slow nod, he said, "I vink zhat…I vant you to tell me 'ow to do vings."

"I can teach you whenever you'd like," Zalith agreed quietly, leaning into his ear.

Alucard felt slightly more confident now that Zalith understood and offered to help *him* understand. A part of him wanted to take advantage of this situation, but they hadn't yet searched him entirely for a death mark. They should probably focus on that.

With a frown on his face, Alucard glanced back at what he could see of Zalith. "Vank you," he mumbled. "But…ve should probably look vor zhis mark," he suggested.

"Agreed," the demon said and resumed searching Alucard's back.

The vampire waited, his nervousness fading enough for him to stand there without worrying about what Zalith might be thinking. Zalith slowly dragged his fingers over his back and his shoulders; the demon seemed to be very thorough, checking the back of his neck, beneath his hair, behind his ears—everywhere.

"I don't see anything here," Zalith then said. "I need to check your legs."

Alucard felt his once-settled angst begin to return, but he wouldn't let it stop them. He moved his hands down to his belt and unbuckled it; without a word, but with a frown, Alucard pulled off his trousers and threw them to the bed with his shirt. While the cold started to gnaw at his skin, he stood there in his underwear, waiting for Zalith to check the rest of him.

The demon crouched, slowly dragging his hand down Alucard's right leg, presumably searching for any sign of a rune. He even made the vampire lift his feet so he could check them.

But when he stood back up, Zalith moved to Alucard's front. "I didn't find anything," he said. "I should probably check beneath these," he said, pinching the side of the vampire's underwear. "Although I didn't see anything last night…this morning…or at the opera," he said with a smirk.

With an embarrassed pout, Alucard looked away.

Zalith, however, lightly gripped his jaw in his hand and made him look at him. "Let me check your mouth."

"Vhat?" Alucard questioned, but he quickly lost his frown and sighed. Of course, Zalith was just being thorough, and for all Alucard knew, the mark could have very well branded itself somewhere he wouldn't see it, such as within his mouth. So, he nodded and slowly opened his mouth.

He waited once more, staring up at the ceiling. He frowned when he felt Zalith drag his thumb over the pointed tip of one of his bottom fangs, but as the demon made him tilt his head back, his frown became one of concern. He felt the demon's grip on his jaw weaken, and as confusion filled him, Alucard lowered his head and stared at Zalith's conflicted face.

"It's on the roof of your mouth," the demon said, dread in his voice *and* on his face.

Staring at him, Alucard frowned again, and his thoughts began to overwhelm him. The mark of death was something that pretty much invited any and all grim reapers to come and avenge their fallen comrade. But…it didn't make him feel as afraid as it might anyone else. After all, he'd been running and hiding all his life; what difference was this? Just as the Numen couldn't, no grim reaper would find him, would they? The ring he wore kept him hidden from everyone and everything. He was safe, death mark or not.

"What do we do?" Zalith panicked.

Alucard snatched his hand before he could say another word. "Noving. Zhey von't vind me. I 'ave zhis," he said, looking down at the ring on his left middle finger. "Zhis is probably vhy zhey zidn't vind me moments avter I killed zhat voman. Maybe…zhe vay zhis 'ides me vrom zhe Numen also keeps me 'idden vrom vhatever tracing ethos zhey use. Zhey are Erich's soldiers, avter all, so zhey must use Numen ethos to locate zhe people zhat get zhis mark." He squeezed Zalith's hand. "Zhey von't vind me," he said firmly.

Zalith, who didn't look very assured, nodded slightly. "Okay," he mumbled.

As Alucard stared into the demon's turmoil-filled eyes, he frowned in worry. "Zaliv," he said with an insistent voice; he didn't want him to sink into his thoughts again, nor did he want him to panic. "Vill be *vine*."

"I know," Zalith said, staring back at him—but he still didn't look convinced.

"Ve 'ave been safe vor zhis long vrom zhe Numen. Zhey von't vind us now, and neizer vill zhese grim veapers. If zhey vere going to vind me, zhey vould 'ave alveady. 'As been days and no vone 'as come."

The demon *still* didn't look convinced. He frowned, shaking his head slightly. "I don't…want to act like things are fine and regret it," he said sullenly. "I'm not going to go out and do anything rash, but I'm not going to let my guard down, either. I don't want to lose you, and I certainly won't lose you because I chose to ignore something and thought we were safe."

Alucard kept his frown and tightened his grip on Zalith's hand. He was right. They shouldn't let their guard down just because something hadn't happened yet. After all, Alucard didn't really know too much about grim reapers or Erich, and for all he knew, he could be wrong about their location methods. Both he and Zalith needed to stay alert, and he'd not let *his* guard down.

He nodded, gazing into Zalith's conflicted eyes. "Ve vill be cautious," he agreed.

The demon then glanced down at the vampire's clothes. "Let's get you dressed," he said, reaching over to pick them up. "I don't want you to get cold."

"Okay," Alucard mumbled, and then let Zalith help him dress.

# Chapter Forty-Five

— ⹂ ✟ ⹁ —

## Talk of Stubborn Bosses

**| Luther |**

In the snug confines of one of the small loungers on Alucard's galleon, Luther reclined with a drink cradled in his grasp, lost in the labyrinth of his ruminations. Today had proven itself a tempest, the fruits of his labour overshadowed by the sour exchange with his boss. Despite unearthing invaluable information, his efforts were met with only disdain, compounded by an irritating altercation with that demon, Zalith.

Why did Zalith have to be there? This wasn't his ship, nor was it his business; what Alucard had him looking for had nothing to do with that demon, so why was he sticking his nose in? He already annoyed Luther *so* much, but today was probably the worst he'd ever felt.

He rolled his eyes and sipped from his whiskey. Clearly, Alucard spoke to and forgave Zalith for neglecting him; why else would he have let Zalith come with him? Why else would he look so comfortable with him? Zalith had obviously somehow convinced Alucard to forgive him, and Luther didn't like that at all. No one should be forgiven for forgetting and mistreating Alucard the way that demon had, and Luther still suspected that Zalith was being unfaithful and just didn't want to lose Alucard because he was the son of a god.

Zalith was the most insufferable person he'd ever met. He was rude and selfish, and from what Luther had seen *and* heard, it seemed like Zalith would always choose himself over anyone else. Today, if Alucard hadn't been present, then Luther would have given that demon a piece of his mind. The fact that Zalith thought he could sit there and berate him and his work…. Luther couldn't let go of his anger.

That demon had no idea how hard he worked to find out the information he gave Alucard, and he also had no idea how hard he worked for Alucard in general. Luther felt his loyalty and devotion to Alucard was so very much more than Zalith's, and he didn't understand why Alucard couldn't see that.

Just then, someone stopped in the lounge doorway, and when Luther noticed them in the corner of his eye, he looked over at the door to see Danford, the blonde-haired, blue-eyed werewolf he'd spoken to yesterday.

"Oh, hi," Danford said with a smile, standing there looking as though he was lost; he had his sketchbook clenched in his arms against his chest.

Luther didn't feel like talking or continuing his mission to get close to this guy right now, but if he sent him away, he felt it might shatter whatever sort of friendship they already had. Building on it would get him one step closer to finding out the things he needed to know about Zalith, and he felt more determined than ever to get what he needed. So, he lost his frown and smiled at the werewolf. "Hey," he called.

"Sorry we didn't get to finish talking the other day," Danford said.

Sipping from his drink, Luther leaned his arms on the table and frowned. "Nah, it's fine," he said. But a smirk then appeared on his face. "We can always continue now if you want."

Danford seemed surprised. "Oh, sure," he agreed. Then, he made his way into the lounge, placed his sketchbook and a few pieces of charcoal onto the table, and sat opposite Luther. "How has your day been going?"

With a roll of his eyes, Luther leaned back in his seat and sighed irritably. "Same old, same old."

"You don't look too happy. What happened if you don't mind telling me?"

"Sometimes, I feel like people don't appreciate the things I do for them," he muttered, thinking about his small conversation with Alucard and that demon.

Danford frowned slightly. "Is it…anyone in Greymore's pack? We're all really happy to be here, but I know sometimes tempers can run high."

Luther shook his head. "No." He exhaled deeply. "It's just my stubborn as all fuck boss," he grumbled, trying *not* to feel anger towards Alucard, but how could he not? Alucard not only ignored his interest but never seemed to show him that he appreciated the things he did for him. But…such a thing had never really bothered him until Zalith came along. Before, Luther was content helping Alucard, but now that his boss was giving himself and all his attention to someone who *didn't* appreciate him, he couldn't ignore just how angry that made him feel.

"Oh, Aleksei, eh?"

"Yup."

Danford looked like he was considering how to reply. "Ah, that sucks. I know what it's like to have a stubborn boss, too," he said with a slight laugh. "Hopefully, things get better for you."

Luther sighed again and looked down at his drink. He didn't really want to think or talk about what happened earlier. A subject change was something he wanted for multiple reasons, and he'd not falter in presenting one. To his right sat the bottle of whiskey he'd been pouring for himself—a bottle he'd taken from Alucard's own private stash. The Vampire Lord never seemed to drink dark liquor, and Luther wished not to see it go to waste, especially when one single bottle cost around the same as what he earned each fortnight.

He glanced at the bottle and then looked at Danford, who sat there with an awkward stare on his face. "You want a drink?" he offered, snatching another glass from the cabinet behind him.

"Sure," he said, smiling.

"So," Luther said as he started pouring Danford a glass. "I heard that you and Zalith were a thing not too long ago," he started, focusing on his wish to find out whether or not this was the man Zalith was being unfaithful with.

Danford laughed nervously. "Um…sure. I guess so."

"You guess so?" he asked, sliding Danford's glass across the table to him. "What happened with that?"

With a nervous look on his face, Danford took his eyes off Luther, opened his sketchbook, and started slowly drawing. "Well, we were never really a *thing*," he said with a shrug. "It was more just uh…well just sex, I guess," he muttered.

A disgusted look struck Luther's face. "I've heard that's all it ever is with him," he said and sipped from his drink. His frown only grew thicker with revolt as he thought about his next question. "Do you think that's what it is with Alucard—Aleksei, I mean?"

Once more, Danford shrugged and frowned but kept his eyes on his drawing. "It's possible," he answered. "But I've never seen him be quite so affectionate with someone. But he's old as shit, right? So who am I to say, eh?"

Luther's hate for Zalith grew deeper. Of course, he already suspected that that demon wasn't with Alucard because he genuinely loved him, especially after what Varana shared with him the other day, and now, he was more convinced that Zalith was just using Alucard as a distraction, just as he did with every other man who came before him. He wasn't sure when that demon was going to be done with his boss, but he knew for a fact that it wasn't going to be long now and that it was probably going to destroy Alucard.

He then wondered…just how long had Zalith been doing this to people? Pretending to love them, using them for attention and sex. Alucard wasn't going to be the last, and the more he thought about it, the more he just wanted to go and convince Alucard that it was time for him to leave before Zalith decided he was done with him.

Taking his eyes off his drink, he looked back at Danford. "How old is he?"

Danford scoffed a little. "God," he muttered, thinking to himself for a few moments as he stopped drawing. "Probably over five hundred. I'm not too sure, though. Greymore might know, or one of his guys," he suggested and took a sip of his drink as he glanced at Luther.

Luther rolled his eyes. "You'd think if he's been around that long, he would have learnt how to treat people properly—with respect, even," he muttered, refilling his glass.

"Eh," Danford mumbled, resuming his drawing. "He grew up rich; old-money kids are different than the rest of us," he said with a shrug. "Based on what I've heard, though, he's gotten kinder with age."

"Was he kind to *you*?" Luther asked bitterly.

"Well...." He frowned. "I wouldn't say he's ever been mean to me or treated me poorly, but he can be cold for sure. Even when we were sleeping together, he wasn't very affectionate—but he has his favourites."

"Favourites?"

"Oh, yeah, like uh..." he paused and looked around, probably looking to see if anyone would hear. But when he realized they were alone, he adorned an embarrassed expression. "Well, Greymore...Orin, Idina, Tyrus...there were others, but they're all dead," he explained. "He was also kind of nice to his cousin, I guess...but I think he had him killed so that probably doesn't count," he mumbled.

Luther scoffed and sipped from his glass. "Has he slept with all of them, too?"

Danford smiled slightly in amusement, "Well, Greymore is straight, so no, but I really don't think Zalith's into him at all. I think if he and Orin were going to get together, it would have happened already, but maybe it did. I'm not too sure. Idina is a woman, so no there, too, and Tyrus is straight as well. As for his cousin, they were related, so I don't see that having happened, either."

Luther downed his drink. He was already tired of this subject. He wasn't really learning anything he didn't already know, and he wasn't getting any closer to finding out whether or not Zalith was cheating on Alucard. Clearly, Danford was a dead-end, which made him feel defeated. He was good at finding out what he needed to know, yet this time, the person he'd chosen to ask didn't prove to be useful but instead proved to be...interesting.

He looked at Danford. Despite the fact that he was just using this werewolf to fish for information, he'd not deny that he was actually quite nice to talk to—and *easy* to talk to, too. With most people, Luther found he was simply talking to get what he needed, but he felt that even without an agenda on his mind, he would enjoy talking to Danford. The fact that he was a werewolf still made him feel slightly reluctant to explore whether this man might actually become a real friend of his, but it was time to stop fishing around and ask Danford straight up. He was tired of waiting.

"Aleksei's convinced that Zalith's cheating on him," he started as Danford stopped drawing. "He's a close friend—*very* close—so I want to find out whether it's true or not. To be honest, I suspected Zalith might be seeing you again, but I'm not convinced. I know you don't want to speak against your boss, so I'll stop hounding you for information," he said with a sigh. "And...I actually kinda like you, so, now that you know why I've been asking everything I've asked, it's your choice if you want to keep talking to me or not."

Danford frowned in surprise and looked down at his drawing. For a few moments, he didn't utter a word, clearly thinking to himself. "Well, I mean…it's really nice of you to look out for your friend like that, but…Zalith's not cheating on him with me." He shuffled around and adorned a nervous expression. "I don't mind if we keep talking, though," he said, resuming his drawing.

Luther felt relieved; he'd rather not Danford hate him because he seemed like the kind of man who he felt might be nice to have around while he spent however long on this ship waiting to go back home to Dor-Sanguis.

He stared at him, watching as he scribbled into his sketchbook with a piece of charcoal. The first time he'd seen Danford, he'd been drawing, and there he was, drawing once again, and Luther wouldn't deny that he felt intrigued. "What are you drawing?"

"I can't show you yet," Danford said, smiling as he glanced at him.

With a quiet sigh, Luther refilled his glass and stared over at the window. It seemed as though he and Danford might be becoming friends, and if that were so, maybe he'd be able to use this werewolf to get more information where he needed it. He was convinced that Danford wasn't the one Zalith was seeing behind Alucard's back, and there was a chance that Danford could actually help him find out who it really was. If they were friends, perhaps Danford would be more willing to share things about his boss.

Luther looked at him and skeptically asked, "I don't suppose I could rely on you to tell me if you hear anything about Aleksei's suspicions regarding Zalith, could I?"

A pondering expression appeared on Danford's face. Luther wasn't sure what he might be thinking or what he might say, but either way, he'd got what he wanted from this guy.

Danford slowly took his eyes off his drawing, glanced at Luther, and shrugged. "Sure, as long as you leave me out of it," he agreed.

Smirking, Luther sipped from his drink again. How pleased it made him feel to know that one of Zalith's trusted subordinates—and an ex, too—would help him on his mission to free Alucard from that demon. "Don't worry, I won't say anything about you."

"Thanks," Danford said with a smile as he stopped drawing. Then, he lifted his sketchbook and showed Luther what he'd been drawing. "This is for you."

Luther stared at the drawing. It was a portrait of *him*, and it looked better than any piece of art he'd ever seen. How had Danford managed to draw something so good so quickly? A look of surprise surely appeared on his face. "Wow, that's…really good, actually."

With a triumphant smile, Danford placed his sketchbook down, carefully tore out the page he'd drawn on, and slid it across the table to Luther.

As Luther took it, he also smiled. "Thanks."

"That's okay," Danford said, clapping his hands together to try and get the charcoal off them, but his attempts failed, and after a few moments, he slowly lowered his charcoal-smudged hands in defeat. He then started trying to remove it by rubbing his hands together beneath the table.

"That's not going to come off, you know," Luther said, resting his arms on the table as he finished his drink.

Danford sighed. "Yeah," he drawled. "I was going to wipe my hands on my shirt, but…I don't want to look like a slob," he said with a quiet laugh.

Luther laughed a little and leaned back in his seat. "I have something in my room that'll get it off," he offered.

Looking down at his hands, Danford frowned shyly. "What is it?"

"Uh…" he mumbled, trying to recall what it was named, but he had no idea. "I don't know what it's called to be honest, but it'll work," he assured him, standing up. "We use it to get blood stains out all the time. Something from an herbalist."

"Oh, okay," Danford replied, flustered. He got up, grabbed his sketchbook, and started to follow him.

And without hindrance, Luther led the way back to his room.

# Chapter Forty-Six

## Habits

**| Luther |**

Luther led Danford through the halls and to his bedroom. He unlocked the door and headed inside; he turned left into his bathroom, where he snatched a small bottle sitting by the sink.

He turned around and held it out towards Danford. "Here," he said, handing it to him. "It gets pretty much everything out, so I can't imagine it not helping with that," he muttered, waving his hand towards Danford's charcoal-smothered hands. Then, he left Danford to clean his hands and made his way over to his desk. He placed the drawing that Danford gave him on top of a stack of papers.

"I see you got the good room," Danford called.

Luther looked back over his shoulder, shrugged, and turned to face the werewolf. "Eh, it's not the best. Where are *you* staying?"

"Oh, some…room on the third floor down," he said, leaning against the wall beside the bathroom door. "You're lucky you get your own room; I have to share with someone else."

"Who are you sharing with?"

"Gregory," Danford answered with a displeased tone in his voice.

Luther had no idea who that was; he didn't particularly care, but he was enjoying talking to him. "I have no idea who that is. He nice?"

"He's a nice guy, but he snores like a bear," he mumbled.

Luther laughed a little.

Danford sighed heavily. "I'd rather have my own room, of course, but we've all been close quarters for so long, I guess I'm kinda used to it. And his shoes *stink*," he abruptly added with a revolted look on his face. "He has to leave them in the hall; they're *that* bad," he complained.

"Ew," Luther uttered, pulling open a small box on his desk. "Well," he then said, pulling out a small metal tin, "now that we're friends, Danny, maybe I can find a way to get you away from Gregory and his nasty shoes," he said with a smirk, opening the tin, in which sat his tobacco, cigarette papers, and matches. He set his eyes on Danford, waiting for him to reply.

With a smile on his face, Danford shrugged slightly. "And put me where?"

"I have this friend—Attila, he used to have a room here—but he doesn't need it anymore. He works on the other side of the world."

"Oh, really? That'd be awesome."

"I know what it's like to have to share a space with someone you'd really rather not."

"Who?"

Luther sighed. "Well," he started, thinking back to the time he, Attila, and Alucard shared a very small space with many other people. "There was a time Attila, Aleksei, and I were hiding from some bad people. We had to cramp into a single bedsit to wait for our window to escape the city without bloodshed, and there were like…fifteen other people with us. Aleksei wouldn't let *anyone* into the bedroom with him, so we had to share the lounge-diner area. There was a really, *really* annoying elf named Dargron; he never shut the fuck up—always singing, dancing, humming—he talked in his sleep and sleepwalked naked every night. On the second night, he tripped over Attila's leg, and one of the other guys got his dick in his face," he laughed, remembering that Attila had actually tripped the elf on purpose.

Amused, Danford laughed. "Was he any good at singing?"

"No," Luther scoffed. "His voice made me want to stick knives in my ears."

Danford laughed again but then smiled curiously. "Can *you* sing?"

"Never tried to," he admitted. "But I've heard my boss a few times—a long time ago, though."

"You don't even sing quietly to yourself?"

"Nah. I mean…I'll whistle here and there, but that's about it." He looked down at his hands as he rolled two cigarettes. Once he was finished, he looked at Danford, who seemed to be looking around his room. "Do you want one?" he offered, holding up one of the cigarettes.

As Danford looked at him, his face lit up. "I'd love one, thank you," he said, making his way over to him. "We've had to pretty much beg for them off the crew since we got here."

"Well," Luther said as he handed one to Danford, who stood beside him, "this stuff's a lot better than you've probably ever had," he said, reaching for the small box of matches. He lit both of their cigarettes and then inhaled a single time from his before sighing quietly.

After smoking a little of his cigarette, Danford frowned unsurely. "Are we allowed to be smoking inside?"

"Yeah, there's a window open," Luther said, looking over his shoulder at the open window behind his desk.

With a nod, Danford leaned against the desk and continued to smoke in silence, as did Luther.

Luther wasn't exactly sure what else to say, but he was enjoying the silence for a moment.

"Can I ask you something?" Danford then asked.

"Mm-hmm," Luther murmured, tapping the ash from his cigarette into a small glass bowl.

With a curious yet concerned look on his face, Danford glanced over at him with a smile. "Are you straight?"

Luther laughed quietly, smirked, and looked down at his cigarette. "If I were, do you think I would have invited you into my room?"

Blushing, Danford looked down at his cigarette and chuckled. "I thought you just wanted to wash my hands."

However, Luther's smile dimmed. He realized he'd strayed from his mission to assist Alucard, entangled in his own selfish pursuits. Or was he? He was acutely aware of his penchant for debauchery; what else was there to fill the void? He simply couldn't resist. True, he leveraged Danford for information, but now he found himself drawing the man into his latest circle of conquests—a circle presently limited to Varana and that other guy he'd picked up in that bar after his date with her.

He smirked, not at all ashamed that he'd managed to form another little group of interesting and useful people; it was a questionable habit, one he felt he might only give up once Alucard understood how he felt. But he didn't want to think about that. Alucard wasn't there, Danford *was*, and Luther wasn't going to pass up the chance to reel yet another attractive individual into his little web.

Keeping his eyes on Danford, he shrugged and smiled suggestively. "I don't offer to wash just anyone's hands, you know."

Danford smiled and took a drag from his cigarette, then placed it in the ashtray and turned to face Luther. Luther, setting his own cigarette down, smirked as the werewolf leaned closer. With a swift, confident motion, Luther moved his hand to the back of Danford's head, pulling him in for a kiss. Danford responded eagerly, and soon their hands were all over each other. Luther gripped a fistful of Danford's hair with his hand, while Danford's fingers found Luther's shirt collar. As their kisses deepened, Danford began to unbutton Luther's.

However, Luther wasn't interested in anything drawn-out or especially intimate, he just wanted to let Danford know that he was going to be more than his friend. As his shirt came undone, Luther pulled Danford's face from his own and then pushed him down onto his knees.

As his knees hit the floor, Danford laughed slightly. "That was quick."

With an impatient roll of his eyes, Luther unbuckled his belt. "Shush," he mumbled.

"Okay," Danford said, surprised.

Then, as Luther leaned his hands back on the desk and set his eyes on the ceiling, Danford reached into his trousers. But that was when the door opened.

Luther scowled angrily but surprise struck his face when he saw Varana standing in the doorway with a revolted frown.

"Ew!" she snarled, watching as Danford scrambled to his feet. "Get off him, Danford!"

"I-I'm so sorry," he stuttered in what was very clearly fear.

"Get the hell out," she warned.

Nodding, Danford scurried across the room and darted out the door—

"And tell someone to send up something for me to drink. I'm parched," she ordered.

"O-okay," Danford responded, and then, his footsteps disappeared down the hall.

Varana closed the door and set her scowl on Luther.

He rolled his eyes and turned around, picking up both his and Danford's finished cigarettes. He flicked them out the window and glanced over his shoulder, watching Varana as she slumped down and laid back on his bed, staring up at the ceiling with a loud sigh.

Luther buckled his belt while he made his way over to her. "What's up with you?" he asked, sitting beside her.

She looked up at him from where she lay. "I know we're not exclusive, but Danford? Really? He's like if a dust bunny grew legs and started talking."

He laughed slightly and shook his head. "I was just passing the time; what the hell else do I got to do around here?" he mumbled.

Varana shrugged, looking back up at the ceiling. "Z talked to me about us today, by the way," she said with a smile. "He wasn't very thrilled."

"I'm sure he wasn't," Luther said with a smirk. "What did he say?"

"He was mostly wondering why, but then I told him that it's not his business, especially considering the fact that he's been gone for so long now," she explained. Then, she looked at him and smiled. "He really doesn't like you."

"Good," he mumbled, laying back. "I have no reason to be liked by him, nor do I want to be liked by him," he said, glancing at her.

She looked back up at the ceiling. "Oh, and then he told me he fucked Luca on the pillow pile I was sitting on, and it ruined the fun for me," she grumbled.

Luther scowled. His hate for Zalith was growing day by day. Not only did he lord around like he owned everyone and everything, but it now seemed like he used Alucard in more ways than Luther was aware of. "Does he lord around about fucking Alucard often?" he uttered in disgust.

Varana shrugged. "Not really, but knowing Z, I'm sure they fuck like rabbits."

With an irritated snarl, Luther abruptly got up and made his way over to his drink cabinet. He poured himself some whiskey and glared down into his glass for a moment. He didn't want to think about the things that Zalith got to share with Alucard—the things *he* wanted to share with Alucard. Hearing that that demon spoke so crudely about it only made him feel worse. He hated Zalith, and he wasn't going to stop trying to show Alucard that he deserved better than some guy who talked about having sex with him like it was a casual conversation.

As his door opened, he looked back over his shoulder, watching as one of the crew handed Varana what looked like a glass of lemonade. She didn't thank the man, and once he left, Luther made his way back over and sat beside her as she sat up.

Varana frowned at him. "Do you think Luca's any good at sex?"

Luther took a sip from his drink as a conflicted frown appeared on his face. He wasn't going to tell her that he thought about it—of course he had—but he'd rather not think about it or discuss it. "I don't know," he grumbled. "I don't really sit here and think about how my boss fucks," he muttered and took another sip from his drink. "I never actually knew he was gay," he then said with a shrug. "Guy's so damn secretive. But…I don't see him as a bottom."

She laughed, drank from her glass, and looked at him. "I do," she said, amused.

"Why? Is he?"

"That's what I heard, but I wasn't surprised when Z told me."

"Does he tell you how big his fucking dick is, too?" Luther scowled with disgust and anger. "Why does he tell you everything like it's public information?"

She smiled amusedly. "I'm sure he'd tell me if I asked, but it's also nothing I haven't seen before, so," she said.

Luther choked on his drink. "What?" he frowned, glaring at her.

"What?"

He shook his head, confused. "What did you mean by that?" he asked, unsure whether she was saying she'd seen Zalith naked or Alucard.

"That I've seen Z naked many times," she answered simply.

"Oh…I thought you were talking about Alucard."

She then laughed slightly. "I saw his dick, too, but only for a second."

Luther looked down at his drink. "Does Alucard know Zalith tells you all of this?"

Varana shrugged. "I don't know, probably. I don't really talk to him. He kind of looks like a sad little strawberry," she mumbled and sipped from her drink again.

A scowl then appeared on Luther's face. "He's depressed," he defended, almost snapping at her. He didn't like when *anyone* spoke disrespectfully about Alucard, and he'd always jump to defend him, not only because he was his boss but because he was his friend. "He didn't exactly have the best upbringing."

"Okay, and?" she asked, staring at him. "My dad literally has six other personalities, but I'm fine, aren't I?"

Knowing that Alucard and Varana shared the same father, he frowned and glared at her. "Why didn't your father hunt *you* down like an animal?"

"Because he loves me very much," she said with a content smile.

Luther started thinking about how he didn't know all that much about Alucard's upbringing. He'd seen glimpses of scars on his body; he'd learned from being around him so much that he wasn't exactly the most empathic person and had assumed it was all because of his childhood. Both he and Attila knew that Alucard's father had been looking for him his entire life, and Luther felt it was safe to assume that Lucifer was the reason why Alucard was the way he was… and he wanted to know why.

He looked down at his drink, took a sip, and then looked back at her. "Why did your father treat him as poorly as he did and never lay a hand on you?"

"Because I'm his favourite, obviously. My father doesn't even consider Luca his son and just wants the power back that he took from him."

"Okay, so why didn't he just take it back when he was a baby rather than let him grow up through all that shit?" he asked angrily.

Varana then scowled. "Why are you so nosy?" she questioned. "Are you writing a book or something?"

"No," he grumbled. "I just think he'd like some answers; he doesn't seem to know why he went through all of that… at least that's how he made it seem, anyway."

"Well, he's more than welcome to come and ask me."

Luther scoffed. "Clearly, you two don't like each other, so why would he come and ask you?"

She laughed quietly. "Aw, did he send you to me to get answers?" she asked, smiling. "Is he scared of me? He's scared of me, isn't he?" she giggled.

"No one sent me, Varana. I'm just curious. I'm Alucard's best friend, but he never really tells me anything."

"I'm not talking about Lucifer," she said firmly.

He rolled his eyes and scowled at the window.

"What?" she then asked with a smile.

Luther glanced at her. "Did you even know what was going on?"

"With Luca?"

"Yes."

"No," she mumbled. "None of us had any idea where he was—in fact, my siblings and I were actually supposed to be tracking him down so Daddy could eat him," she said, glancing down at her nails.

That didn't surprise Luther. He knew how cruel and barbaric demons were and learning that Varana and her siblings had been sent to basically sentence Alucard to death didn't shock him. "I guess you're demons, so killing your own family is second nature," he mumbled.

"Excuse me?" she asked in what sounded like astonishment.

"What?" he laughed. "It's literally in every single history book you might find anywhere in Aegisguard. Demons killing demons for fun, demons killing demons to start wars, demons killing demons because some demon killed another demon and *that* started a war. Where've you been for the last…five hundred years?"

She glowered at him. "Angels kill other angels…humans kill other humans, and *vampires* kill other vampires. It would seem that there is not *one* dominant sentient species that doesn't display such behaviour," she insisted. "What's the point you're trying to make, Luther?"

"In every single war-linked event, shit has always started because of demons killing demons, or because some demon wants another demon dead so some demon can kill his brother or mother or sister or something. Demons here love the conflict, the war, and most of all, killing their family, it would seem," he said, finishing his drink.

"You're right," she then said with a sarcastic tone in her voice. "I love killing my family; maybe I'll kill Alucard. Are you going to wage war just to avenge your beloved boss, Luthy? Once you're done sucking his dick, of course."

He rolled his eyes. "I'd do a better job than Zalith," he mumbled. "Good luck killing him, though. I'm sure Zalith would stop you…unless he's tired of Alucard, then he'd probably welcome you, wouldn't he?"

"If I wanted him dead, he'd be dead, Luther," she said sternly. "You can hate Zalith all you like, but the fact of the matter is that if he wasn't such a good person with a good heart, I would have made the call, and your precious leader would be gone—*and* you'd be crying all over his gravestone right now, and not here swapping fluids with Danford," she said with a roll of her eyes.

"You underestimate Alucard," he said, disregarding everything else she said. "He managed to hide for four hundred years—do you really think calling your father would end his freedom?"

She then glowered at him. "Should I do it? Then we can find out."

He scoffed and looked down at his empty glass before looking back at her. "I'd rather not fight another war, thanks."

"What war?" she asked, amused. "Once he's gone, he's gone. The only thing keeping that man safe from Lucifer is Z and my discretion," she proclaimed.

"He isn't going to just go so easily." Luther frowned. "He's going to run, and then his people are going to fight Lucifer's people just like they did years ago. It would just be a repeat of the last few times Lucifer thought he'd found him."

Varana laughed again and sipped from her drink.

"Why is that funny?"

She looked at him and smiled. "You're very devoted to a man who doesn't seem to spend a lot of time with you. It's cute."

"Takes one to know one, doesn't it?"

The woman then fell silent. Clearly, what he said hit a nerve, and it stopped her arguing. He glanced at her as she stared into her drink with a despondent look on her face.

Varana soon rolled her eyes and glared at him. "Are you going to fuck me or not?" she then asked.

Luther scoffed and placed his glass on the closest table. He wasn't going to say no—he'd not finished with Danford, or even really started with him for that matter. So, he started to crawl over to her—

She placed her hand on his face, covering most of it as she scowled. "Wait, take me to dinner first," she requested.

"Fine," he mumbled, his voice muffled through her hand.

"But," she said, taking her hand off his face and wiping it on his blanket, "have a shower first so you can wash the Danford stink off your body."

He huffed irritably, stood up, and slipped his hands into his pockets. "Fine," he said, making his way over to the bathroom.

"Thank you," she called.

"Yep," he mumbled. Then, he disappeared inside, leaving Varana on her own.

# Chapter Forty-Seven

— ⸱ ✝ ⸱ —

## Reading

| **Alucard** |

As the night neared its end, Alucard and Zalith sat in bed and read their books by the light of the lamps on their nightstands.

Alucard looked through the history book that had sat on his shelf for many long years, a book he hadn't been able to read since it was written in Deiganish. Now that he was so much better at both reading it and writing it—after teaching himself over the past few months—he took it upon himself to read more Deiganish-written books, which would help him understand it more.

He stopped reading, however, as the thought of Zalith's absence plagued his mind. Before Varana said something earlier, he hadn't really thought about it after he helped Zalith and his people out of Eltaria; he felt like he'd forgiven Zalith, but every time he thought about how alone and confused he felt, it brought a dismaying feeling to his heart. He didn't want to think about it, though—why would he? He and Zalith were fine now, everything was the way it should be—apart from Zalith's post-battle anxiety, but that was something Alucard was confident he could help the demon through.

Silencing his thoughts, he continued to read.

"What are you reading?" Zalith soon asked, lowering his book to look at the vampire.

Alucard glanced at him. "Is uh…Deiganish…book of lore," he explained.

A despondent frown appeared on Zalith's face, but it didn't stay there for long. He looked down at the book in Alucard's hands and then back at his face. "Have you read it before?"

"No," Alucard admitted. "Zhere vere no copies in Dor-Sanguian."

Zalith frowned. "Why is it only exclusive to Deiganish people when it's world lore?"

"Most of zhe 'istorians are vrom DeiganLupus, and since war 'as been 'appening so much in zhe past vour 'undred years, zhere just 'asn't been time to translate," he mumbled tiredly.

"Hmm," Zalith murmured, looking back down at his own book.

"Vhat are *you* veading?"

"A history book," he said, smiling as he glanced at him.

"Vhich era?"

"Primulus…Diabolus," he said, flipping to the beginning of his book to look. "Currently, it's covering the year five-fifty," he added as he flipped back to the page he'd been reading.

Alucard nodded. Of course, he knew all about the Primulus Diabolus era; it was the very era in which he fought his first war and the one in which the Diabolus came to be the world-spread cult it was today. He didn't want to talk about it, nor did he want to think about it, so he returned to reading the Letholdus-preaching babble in front of him.

Moments later, though, Zalith looked at him again, holding his book out so that Alucard would look at it. "Is this you?" he asked with an amused smile as he pointed to a specific paragraph.

The vampire stared at the page, reading the long description speaking of a tall, ice-pale man with hair as red as blood and eyes that looked as though they had fire raging in them. That *was* him, and he wasn't surprised to learn that he'd made it into a history book. He'd been all over the world, fought many, many battles—waged multiple, too—and there were bound to be people who would have survived and gone on to write about him.

He shrugged, sitting up straight. "Yes."

With a smirk on his face, Zalith leaned back and continued reading. "They made you sound nearly as handsome as you are. And they made you sound a lot eviler."

Staring at his pages, Alucard pouted. He didn't want to know what some history book said about him.

Smiling, Zalith turned his attention back to reading.


A short while passed, and when Alucard looked at Zalith, the demon seemed to be *extremely* into what he was reading. A concerned frown warped the vampire's face, unsure of what that book might be saying about him. It was probably all over-exaggerated; no one knew Alucard close to well enough to be able to write a good story about him, and he hoped that Zalith wasn't taking what he was reading too seriously.

"Alucard," Zalith then said with a confused tone in his voice, yet there was an entertained look on his face. "Who is Seraphina?"

"Vhat?" Alucard frowned—he had no idea who Seraphina was; he didn't even know *anyone* by such a name.

Zalith cleared his throat quietly and read from the book, "Seraphina, just a wisp of a woman. Her blonde hair was dirtied with mud and blood, all from her long, hard day of work. Before today, she'd never really enjoyed being a nurse on the front lines—that was until her eyes met with that man…no, that creature. She'd caught him staring at her heaving bosoms, and the look of hunger that lingered in his eyes forced her to forget the rule that kept her from associating with her patients."

Alucard stared at him, listening as he read from the book. None of what he was saying sparked any kind of memory—a nurse? And bosoms? Why would he *ever* stare at such a thing?

The demon then skipped a page before clearing his throat again. "How startled she felt to see him in her tent—her private space. Why had he come? Her hands trembled, her body cried for the touch of such a strong, dangerous man. Seraphina let out a wince of shock and longing as the creature's cold hands gripped her soft, warm skin. He didn't seem to be the patient type. With his free hand, he gripped her left bosom—"

"Stop," Alucard insisted, trying to snatch the book from him.

Laughing, Zalith moved away, holding the book out of Alucard's reach. "Seraphina revelled in excitement, pulling Aleksei's shirt apart. The buttons dropped to the floor, and she hastily placed her hands on his beautifully muscular body—"

With an embarrassed, irritated scowl, Alucard snarled and threw himself at Zalith, trying to reach for the book, but Zalith fought back, holding him off as he laughed and continued to read.

"'Aleksei', she cried," Zalith read, putting on a unique voice for the woman. "'Touch me', she begged, gripping a handful of his hair in her hand—'"

"Stop," Alucard snarled, snatching the corner of the book.

But Zalith snatched it back, turning onto his side and holding the book as far away from himself as he could, keeping Alucard back with his left hand—*still* laughing. "*A*leksei grinned eagerly—"

Alucard snatched the book from him and slammed it shut in his hands. Then, he tried to make off with it, but before he even managed to get back over to his side of the bed, Zalith grabbed hold of him with his arms, pulled him back, and tried to take the book from him, laughing as Alucard grunted in struggle.

"I wasn't done with that," Zalith insisted, pulling the book free from both of Alucard's hands. He kept the vampire pinned down on his front, laying on Alucard's back as he opened the book, trying to find the page he was on as Alucard snarled and gave in, stopping his struggle. "Seraphina whined in delight. Aleksei plunged his manhood into her body, holding her wrists tightly as—"

Revolted, Alucard abruptly moved to his side, throwing Zalith off his back and making him stop with his close-to-hysterical laughter. As Zalith stumbled back, Alucard swung around and tried to snatch the book from him again, but the demon held tightly onto it.

Alucard was tired of hearing him quote that stupid book, so he wasn't going to give up this time. He scowled as they struggled; both of them tried to pull the book from the other's hands as Zalith laughed and Alucard snarled. However, the more they struggled, the further they moved to the edge of the bed, and before either of them could stop, they fell off and hit the floor.

The vampire took his chance to pin Zalith's back against the floor. He took the book from him in one hand, holding him down with the other. Then, as Zalith smirked up at him, the vampire chucked the book across the room and scowled down at the demon.

"Is this the view you had of Seraphina?" Zalith asked, still smiling.

Alucard scowled, unamused. "No."

"What a shame. I have such a good view down here."

"Zhen you can stay down zhere," Alucard sneered, keeping his hand on Zalith's chest.

Zalith smirked again. "I'd like to."

Not at all in the mood for Zalith's flirting, Alucard rolled his eyes and went to stand up; that book had put him off *everything* for what he felt might be a while.

But before he could get up, Zalith grabbed his waist with both his hands. "Wait," he said with a sad frown.

Alucard stared down at him, waiting.

"I have a question," the demon said, still with a sullen look on his face.

Alucard could see his smile, and he knew that this sadness of Zalith's was just a façade. It wasn't the first time Zalith would have pretended to be sad or upset to get his attention… and more.

The vampire waited but then frowned skeptically. "Vhat… is your question?"

"Is this Seraphina real? Do you know her?" he asked, still with his fake sadness. "Do I have to worry about women, too?"

Alucard deadpanned. "No," he grumbled. "I zon't know who she is because I zon't care to try and vemember."

"Oh, so it was a one-night stand sort of thing?" Zalith asked, amused.

With both his anger and embarrassment increasing, Alucard glowered at him. "Zhat zidn't 'appen!" he insisted.

"So, you didn't plunge your manhood into her body?"

"No," Alucard growled.

The demon laughed slightly. "Aw." He smiled, reaching up to touch the vampire's hair. "You really don't know who she is? Who wrote the book?"

Alucard pouted, still holding him down. "I zon't know."

"If only the author knew how often you had your tongue down my throat—among other things. I wonder if they'd revise it."

With a humiliated frown, Alucard took his glare off Zalith and tried to get up again, but the demon pulled him back into his lap. The vampire struggled, trying to move away; right now, he just wanted to be back in bed, but Zalith wasn't letting him go.

"At least you have fans," he continued, ignoring Alucard's disapproving grunts. "I can only imagine the horrid things someone would write about me."

"Veally?" Alucard glared down at him again. "You zon't vink zhat vas 'orrid? I veel veird now knowing zhere are 'owever many copies of a novel out zhere zhat say I slept vith some voman," he complained.

Zalith laughed again. "At least she seemed to enjoy it."

Irritated, Alucard seethed quietly in disapproval.

The demon kept laughing.

Growing weary of the demon's laughter, Alucard clamped his hand over Zalith's mouth, hoping to silence him. Instead, Zalith began to lick his palm, clearly an attempt to force him to release his grip. Alucard, however, was resolute. He could both see and feel the demon's smirk beneath his fingers, but he wasn't about to let go.

Zalith then gripped the vampire's ass with both hands, slowly dragging them up over his waist, his sides, and then across his pecs.

Alucard refused to let go, his glare intensifying as he battled the urge to retreat beneath a blanket. The cold was starting to bite at his skin, and his nervousness compounded it. Utterly naked, he felt increasingly exposed; the longer he sat there, the more vulnerable he became, especially with Zalith's hands trailing over each of his abs and his piercing gaze fixed on him.

He scowled and pouted, averting his eyes from Zalith as the demon's hands reached his pelvic area. Zalith's fingers traced the defined lines of his body, and with each moment of contact, Alucard found his initial discomfort melting away. Sitting there, he began to enjoy Zalith's attention. Despite Alucard's hand still covering his mouth, the demon continued his exploration unabated, which led Alucard to suspect that Zalith probably liked it.

Alucard sighed quietly and removed his hand from Zalith's mouth, but the demon's hands didn't stop roaming. Zalith seemed entirely content with what he was doing, and Alucard couldn't deny that he liked it, too. So he remained silent, letting Zalith continue as he pleased.

But after a short while passed, Alucard began to feel his fatigue getting the better of him. His eyes felt heavy, his face was cold, and all he wanted to do was get back into bed. So he sighed quietly, moving to get up again. "Ve should—"

"No," Zalith said sadly, gripping his waist once more to keep him where he was. "Wait," he pleaded with that same look of sadness.

"Ve need to get back into bed," Alucard mumbled.

The demon frowned sadly. "But I like touching your body." Then, his saddened frown faded into a smirk. "Especially here," he said, dragging his fingers around the vampire's crotch.

Alucard pouted and looked away, trying to hide his flustered scowl. But he felt the need to fight his nervousness. Earlier, he told Zalith that he wanted to be braver when it came to sex and intimacy, and right now was a good opportunity. So, with a nervous frown, he looked down at him again. "I…like zhis too," he muttered, staring down at the hand he had on Zalith's chest.

Zalith smiled up at him. "Yeah?"

The vampire nodded.

Zalith smirked, moving his hand to the side of Alucard's face. "I also like touching you here." He sat up and started kissing the vampire.

Alucard kissed him back, their tongues entwining in a heated dance. The vampire stood, leading them towards their bed without breaking the kiss. Just as Alucard was about to turn and slip under the covers, though, the demon smirked through their kisses and playfully pushed him down onto the bed. The vampire shifted to the centre, his anticipation growing; Zalith crawled over him, trailing slow, tantalizing kisses up his body before finally straddling his lap.

The demon leaned into Alucard's face, resting his arms on either side of the vampire as he started kissing his lips. Alucard moved his right hand to the back of the demon's head and gripped Zalith's thigh with his left. At first, he felt like he wanted to put his hand on the demon's ass, but despite his attempts to not be so nervous, he lost this time.

Zalith, however, seemed to know how he was feeling and gripped Alucard's wrist. He moved the vampire's hand so that he'd grip his ass, smirking as he did. Before Alucard could frown nervously and look away, the demon placed his hand on the side of his face and continued to kiss him. Alucard kept his hands where they were, excitement starting to simmer through him as Zalith moved his kisses from his lips to his neck.

But Zalith only kissed his neck a few times before leaning into Alucard's ear. "I want you to touch me," he whispered, pulling the vampire's hand around to his crotch.

Alucard felt his nervousness peak; he lightly gripped the demon's arousal as Zalith wanted, fighting the urge to let go and cower because he was worried that he might do it wrong.

The demon kept his hand over Alucard's and smiled, still leaning into the vampire's ear. "Do this," he said quietly, making Alucard slowly pull his hand back and forth whilst keeping hold of the demon's shaft.

While Alucard did as Zalith said, the demon continued pressing his lips against his neck and let go of the vampire's hand, leaving him to touch him by himself. Alucard's fear of doing something wrong lingered, but he tried to ignore it. He wasn't sure if what he was doing was right, but Zalith hadn't told him otherwise, nor had he stopped to correct him, so he felt as if it were safe to assume that what he was doing *was* right. As he moved his hand, the demon's dick hardened in his grip, and a quiet exhale of what sounded like contentment escaped through the demon's kisses.

But when Zalith stopped kissing his neck, Alucard was struck by anxiety—

"We don't want to do it dry the whole time, so give me your hand," Zalith instructed seductively.

Alucard let go of the demon's shaft and moved his hand towards Zalith's. The demon took hold of his wrist and dragged his tongue over the palm of the vampire's hand. He then smirked as he let go, kissing the side of Alucard's face a few times before starting to kiss his lips again. Alucard returned his wet hand to Zalith's dick and gripped hold of it. Then, he started caressing it again, just as Zalith showed him.

Zalith exhaled in delight, moving his face to kiss Alucard's neck again. "Go faster," he whispered as he pinned the vampire's free hand above his head, breathing against his neck when Alucard started moving his hand a little faster.

He was sure that Zalith was enjoying it, and his nervous thoughts were pretty much silenced by the demon's quiet breaths of contentedness. He felt Zalith ever so slightly flinch with what could only be pleasure as he nuzzled Alucard's neck, exhaling deeply onto his skin.

"You're doing good, baby," the demon mumbled, playfully biting Alucard's neck.

Zalith's assurance made him feel confident. He kept stroking his hand up and down the demon's dick, relaxing his body as Zalith kissed his neck again and tightened his grip on Alucard's wrist. Zalith started drifting back and forth as if he were fucking him; Alucard wasn't sure whether it was because he wasn't doing it right or because it was something Zalith simply wanted to do.

"Faster," Zalith whispered.

Alucard did as he asked, moving his hand even faster. He felt Zalith's body tense up; the demon started breathing a little faster, gripping a fistful of Alucard's hair in his free hand. He thrusted into Alucard's hand, groaning as the pleasured look on his face intensified, and just moments later, with a loud, pleased whine, the demon climaxed. His hot cum erupted from his tip, dripping onto Alucard's skin, and as the vampire watched, a satisfying sense of victory ensnared him. He felt pleased with himself that he'd actually managed to make Zalith orgasm by himself.

With a pleasured exhale, Zalith sighed quietly. "Shit," he breathed, nuzzling Alucard's neck. He laughed a little, and as the vampire let go of his dick, he said with a smirk, "You did it." He kissed Alucard's cheek.

Alucard felt his nervousness abruptly return, so he looked away and pouted.

"Thank you," Zalith said, kissing the side of his face again. Then, he stared down at him. "How do you feel?"

Glancing up at him, Alucard struggled to keep a nervous smile off his face. "Good," he said, keeping himself from responding with his usual answer of 'fine'—he didn't want Zalith to think he wasn't content. "'Ow do *you* veel?"

"Good," the demon answered as he took a few tissues from his nightstand and cleaned them both up. Once he was done, he rested his forehead against Alucard's and stared into his eyes, smirking. "I want to do something for you because you did such a good job."

With his shyness returning, Alucard took his eyes off Zalith and stared over at the wall.

"What do you want?" he asked, dragging his fingers over the vampire's abs.

"I vant..." he instantly said, but then paused for a moment, his sudden eager desire for Zalith's affection confusing him. But with his pause came angst. He frowned, still staring at the wall; he couldn't fall silent now. "I vant...you to fuck me," he mumbled shyly.

The demon smirked deviously, moving his hand to the back of Alucard's head to grip his hair once more. "Okay," he said, caressing his hair, "I just need a moment first," he said. Then, he started to kiss him again.

Alucard gripped a fistful of the demon's hair in his hand, placing his other on Zalith's right bicep. As they kissed, the vampire's eager desire for the demon's affection grew more demanding, and as each moment of waiting passed, Alucard felt himself edging nearer to desperation. Despite the attention he got from Zalith the past few days, he still felt deprived; those long months of nothing seemed to have a much larger effect on him than he'd initially thought.

He sighed longingly, turning his head to the side as Zalith started kissing his neck.

However, the demon then stopped to lean into Alucard's ear. "I'm glad Seraphina isn't still in your life because she'd hate what I'm about to do to you, vampire," he mumbled, dragging the tips of his fingers down from the right side of Alucard's neck and to his waist. "Turn around," he instructed.

Alucard frowned nervously and turned around, moving onto his hands and knees as Zalith gripped either side of his waist. The vampire's hands sunk into the blankets as he stared down at them, waiting as patiently as he could as the demon reached over to his nightstand.

A familiar angst gripped Alucard tightly when he felt the demon's lube-smothered dick easing into his ass. He grasped the blanket, exhaling quietly; the deeper Zalith went, the more eager Alucard felt, and once every inch of the demon's shaft was inside him, the vampire groaned hushedly, waiting to become enthralled by pleasure.

The demon began thrusting back and forth, gripping Alucard's waist tightly. As he sighed pleasurably, satisfaction started to consume each and every one of Alucard's senses, and any longing he felt began to fade as Zalith sped up, moving faster than he usually did. His once softer movements became harder thrusts, and although it was new, Alucard didn't feel confused or anxious. He moaned in delight as he closed his eyes, tightening his grasp on the blanket.

The demon then leaned forward, still moving back and forth as he groaned quietly. Alucard responded with a whine of anticipation as the demon lightly bit his back between his shoulder and his neck. Although his bite was only a playful one, Alucard wanted Zalith to sink his fangs into his skin. But it didn't take long at all for pleasure to begin surging through his body, making his legs and arms tremble. He was already starting to become lost in the euphoria, and as Zalith's breathing became as erratic as his, Alucard's desire for closeness made its way through the pleasure.

Zalith somehow seemed to know what he wanted—he always did. The demon stopped for a moment, hastily turning Alucard onto his back. He then leaned over the vampire and moved Alucard's right leg over his back as he started kissing his lips. Alucard grimaced in struggled delight as the demon eagerly moved his dick back into his ass, gripping his thigh tightly as he continued to undulate his body against Alucard's.

Alucard soon turned his head to the side, his heart racing, his breathing even more frantic than before. He grimaced and tried to cope, gripping Zalith's arm in his hand once more, struggling not to dig his claws into the demon's skin.

Zalith then gripped the vampire's shaft in his hand and abruptly sunk his fangs into Alucard's neck. He tended to Alucard's arousal, still moving back and forth as his venom oozed into the vampire's body.

A grimace smothered Alucard's struggled face, and he had no control over the whine of pleasure that escaped his lips. The confusion of it all constricted him; the drowning pleasure of Zalith's venom, the delightful rapture of the demon's dick inside him, and the pleasing, satisfying grip of Zalith's hand on his arousal.

Alucard closed his eyes and moaned pleasurably, "Zaliv." A part of him wanted to ask Zalith to stop for a moment so that he could catch his breath, but he couldn't find his voice. Despite the confoundment, he didn't want Zalith to stop. Not really. He grimaced again, breathing quickly, fidgeting as the demon bit down a little harder.

But Zalith then let go of the vampire's shaft and gripped hold of his throat. Alucard frowned, but not in disapproval. He liked it when Zalith became aggressive and assertive.

Alucard murmured in delight, gripping Zalith's wrist and pulling his hand closer to let him know that he wanted him to hold his throat a little tighter. And he did. The demon tightened his grip, pulling his fangs from Alucard's neck to moan quietly through his own struggled breaths.

The euphoria quickly drowned Alucard in bliss; he scowled, the intensifying pleasure pulling him closer to climax. And once he peaked, he unintentionally dug his claws into Zalith's arm, grimacing in struggle as he tried to quieten his pleasured moan.

Zalith flinched but hummed contently as he continued thrusting his shaft into and out of the vampire's ass. He moved a little faster, still gripping the vampire's throat, pressing his face against his neck.

And not too long later, the demon moaned feverishly and climaxed, plunging his dick as deeply inside him as he could. Alucard felt the demon's thick shaft throb, filling him with his warm cum, which sent a shiver of sheer delight through his trembling body.

For a few moments, Zalith stayed where he was, breathing deeply against Alucard's neck as he let go of it. He relaxed his body against Alucard's and started caressing the vampire's hair, but he didn't stay there long. He soon moved from over Alucard and cleaned himself and the vampire with some more tissues, and then they made themselves comfortable in bed. Alucard, with his eyes beginning to get heavy, rested on his left side; Zalith lay beside him, resting the side of his face on Alucard's, wrapping his arms around his body to hold him tightly.

Alucard felt content about the fact that he'd conquered his fear of doing something wrong because he'd never done it before; he managed to do something for Zalith. He was sure the demon was also satisfied. Zalith had most likely been waiting a while for him to do things like that for him, and he'd finally done it. Of course, there was more to come, though; he wanted to learn how to do everything that Zalith did for him. Zalith always did so much for him, and he knew it was about time he started to do things for him, too.

Suddenly, Zalith's quiet, amused laugh snapped him out of his content thoughts.

Alucard frowned, looking at what he could see of Zalith in the corner of his eye. "Vhat's vunny?"

Zalith tightened his embrace around him. "Nothing. I was just thinking about how far we've come together and how mean you used to be to me."

The vampire's confused frown thickened. "Vhat?" he asked in astonishment. "I vasn't mean to you."

Zalith laughed again. "You used to push me away and yell at me all the time."

Alucard pouted, glaring at the wall. "I never yelled at you," he grumbled. "And I used to push you avay because zhat stupid smile of yours used to make me veel so irritated."

Once again, Zalith laughed and nuzzled the side of the vampire's face. "How does it make you feel now?"

Still pouting, Alucard scowled. He took a moment to think about his answer. Zalith's smile made him feel so many different things; it still made him feel irritated from time to time, but that only seemed to be the case when Zalith was *trying* to annoy him. He sighed, shrugging slightly. "Only good vings."

"Good," Zalith said contently.

Alucard then frowned curiously. "Vas zhere…anyving I ever did zhat irritated you?"

"No, nothing," Zalith answered quietly. "At first, when we met in that tavern in Dor-Sanguis—and on the tower in Eltaria with Damien—I did think that you were a little rude, but I liked it, and I can't think of a point where I ever felt irritated by you. I liked everything about you, and I still do," he said and kissed the side of his face.

As content as that made Alucard feel, he was sure that there had to have been at least *one* thing he'd done that annoyed Zalith back when they were associates. Was Zalith keeping quiet in an attempt to keep him from getting upset? He wasn't going to get upset; he just wanted to know what Zalith had really thought of him back then.

"Are you just saying zhat?"

"No, I'm not just saying that, baby," he assured him. "I always thought you were so cute, especially when you were angry."

The vampire's pout returned. "I'm not supposed to be cute vhen I'm angry."

"I know, but I can't help it; I think you're cute all the time."

Alucard sighed, giving in. He was too tired to argue about whether he was cute or not. He felt fine with Zalith thinking it; if it were anyone else, he'd scold them. But he let Zalith get away with a lot, and Zalith was also the only person he'd back down to— that, and he was also so very tired. "Vine," he mumbled, closing his eyes. "I vink you're cute vhen you're mad, too," he said, his fatigue helping him fight his nervousness. "And vhen you zon't comb your 'air back."

The demon made Alucard roll onto his back so that he could look down at him. Then, Zalith kissed his lips before smiling at his tired face. "Thank you."

Staring up at him, Alucard slowly raised his hand and flicked the demon's uncombed fringe. "Vhy *do* you comb back?"

"Because it looks neater that way," he answered, fiddling with the vampire's hair. "When it's like this, I look more approachable, and I want people to see me as their boss, not their brother. It's also a habit; I've been doing it for however many hundred years," he explained.

Alucard smiled slightly, staring into the demon's dark eyes. "I like 'ow you look eizer vay."

Zalith smirked again. "Thank you," he said, but then he laughed. "What if I was a woman?"

Confused by his abrupt question, yet too tired to work out why he'd asked it, Alucard frowned. "Vhy are you asking me zhat?"

"I'm just wondering."

The vampire sighed and took his eyes off Zalith. "I'm…gay," he mumbled shyly. "So, zon't turn into a voman any time soon," he warned sleepily.

He laughed again. "I won't," he said, dragging the tips of his fingers over the side of Alucard's face. Then, he placed his hand on his neck. "I love you," he said quietly.

Alucard turned his head to look up at him and smiled despite his tiredness quickly dragging him into a daze. "I love you," he mumbled, placing his hand over Zalith's.

Then, with a smile on his face, Zalith lay beside him as Alucard moved back onto his left side. The demon wrapped his arms around him, holding him tightly as he allowed the weight of his exhaustion to swiftly drag him off to sleep.

# Chapter Forty-Eight

— ⊰ ✝ ⊱ —

## A Morning of Sullen Realizations

| Zalith |

Zalith sighed quietly as he glanced at the light shining in through the bedroom curtains. The moment he woke, a familiar flurry of thoughts struck him; where was he? Was this real? Where was Alucard?

The demon frowned, taking a moment to realize that he was in his and Alucard's bedroom… in *their* bed, and in his arms, he was holding the vampire tightly, resting the side of his face on Alucard's right bicep. Seeing and feeling his vampire calmed his turmoil; the feeling of overwhelming contentedness he'd feel when waking up to see Alucard beside him warmed him in the cold morning, but as he stared at what he could see of Alucard's face, sadness and guilt started to grip his heart once more.

He still hadn't gotten over the fact he'd basically neglected Alucard—*abandoned* him. Last night, he learned that Alucard had to teach himself to both read and write Deiganish because he'd failed to live up to his promise to help him. That was just one of many things that started to inflate his sorrow. Yesterday, he saw that Alucard had become so nervous once again, and that could only be because he'd not touched his vampire in such a long time; a few months might not seem long, but for Alucard, it clearly was, and Zalith hated that he'd failed to notice just how horribly his absence had affected him.

With a despondent expression, Zalith stared across the room at the window. He was certain that Alucard was still upset with him—that his acceptance of the apologies was only surface-deep. Zalith understood how Alucard thought and suspected that his vampire was merely pretending everything was fine to ease his own guilt. But the pretence didn't bring any comfort. Zalith knew Alucard wasn't entirely okay, and it gnawed at him. He lay there, trying to decipher what Alucard might truly be feeling, and pondering the notion that his vampire should have abandoned him instead of waiting. Alucard had endured months of pain and sorrow for his sake, and Zalith felt undeserving of such loyalty. He couldn't shake the feeling that he didn't deserve the sacrifices Alucard made for him.

Tightening his embrace around Alucard, he looked down at what he could see of his peaceful face again. He was so cute when he slept, and Zalith couldn't keep himself from smiling. However, as the urge to kiss him presented itself, Zalith frowned once more. He made sure to kiss Alucard each and every morning when he had to leave without getting to say goodbye or explain to him that he would be gone for most of the day *and* night. But it wasn't enough, and he should have known that. Alucard deserved to know what was going on, but he'd been left to assume that Zalith didn't want him anymore, and nothing could hurt the demon greater.

Why would he not want Alucard? He loved him more than he'd ever loved anyone, and he'd never wanted to be with someone as much as he wanted Alucard—he'd never wanted to spend his life with someone just as much as he wanted to spend it with his vampire. In fact, he'd never actually wanted to share his life or so much of his space with *anyone* at all. But with Alucard, he wanted to share everything he had to offer.

Usually, thinking about how much he loved Alucard would help him get over whatever was stressing him out, but right now, it only seemed to make him feel worse. Despite Alucard's sadness and nervous disposition, he'd shown Zalith some of the worst parts of himself—at least the parts of himself that *he* considered to be his worst. But Zalith didn't care; he wasn't bothered by the fact that Alucard was smothered in scars, de-winged, and cast out. He understood the vampire's reasons and trauma, and yet, Alucard did his best to conquer his fears to make Zalith feel happy.

What Zalith had done—not prioritising his relationships over his work was an awful habit—but Alucard still stuck around despite becoming so very sad and alone, and Zalith had no idea how to show Alucard how much he loved him or how much he appreciated him, and he had no idea how to make it up to him, either.

He sighed again, taking a few more moments to enjoy holding Alucard before getting up to start his day. He had to meet with the contractor today to get things started on the compound for his people, and that was going to be something of a strain, especially when he just wanted to spend time with Alucard now that his people were safe and away from Eltaria. He also needed to meet with Margo and deal with the Imperito.

However, his thoughts quickly shifted back to Alucard and the mark of death they'd found on the roof of his mouth. Zalith wasn't entirely sure what to suspect, and that deep, drowning fear that this might be the way Alucard was taken from him this time lingered in the back of his mind. They may be veiled from the world, but what if the ethos that they were using to conceal themselves failed to keep Alucard hidden from the grim reapers who were going to be looking for him to avenge their fallen comrade?

He sat up, staring down at Alucard, overwrought with worry. What could he do, though? He'd done everything he really could to keep Alucard undetectable and safe. As much as it unsettled him, all he could do was stay alert and prepared for anything that might happen.

With a quiet sigh, he left a long, meaningful kiss on the side of Alucard's face, and then he carefully got out of bed and headed into the bathroom to get ready for the day.

| **Alucard** |

Alucard opened his eyes just enough to glare at the wall opposite him. He felt Zalith leave their bed and heard him head into the bathroom. The sound of running water followed, bringing with it a familiar pang of confusion and worry. He dreaded the thought of waking up alone every morning, fearing that history might be repeating itself. But he refused to dwell on it and closed his eyes, willing himself back to sleep. His exhaustion clung to him, a heavy shroud, and he wasn't even sure how much rest he'd managed to get last night.

After a short while of lying there without success in falling back asleep, pain began to surge through Alucard's head. A headache was the last thing he needed right now—the persistent ache in his shoulder was already more than enough. Shoulder? He scowled, slowly pulling his hand from beneath the pillow to grip his shoulder. He dragged his fingers over his skin, tracing the scars left by Zalith's fangs; he found two fresh wounds from last night. Normally, the wounds from Zalith's bite took a few days to heal but never caused lingering pain like this. It was likely because Alucard hadn't fed off Zalith in return. Blood typically helped not only to heal his wounds faster but also to numb the pain, and his lack of reciprocation was clearly why he felt so fatigued and irritable now.

He moved his hand back under his pillow as he listened to the running water from the bathroom. With his current loss of blood came an almost eager need for something sweet. His thoughts were suddenly plagued by all the things he'd love to eat right now, and the distant smell of breakfast being prepared in the kitchen started to make him feel nauseous. He scowled, hiding his face beneath the blanket in an attempt to ignore his senses. But as the bathroom door opened, he pouted irritably.

Slowly, he pulled the blanket away from his face and set his eyes on Zalith. The demon walked out of the bathroom utterly naked, presumably heading for the dressing rooms. But he noticed Alucard staring, so he smiled and altered his course, making his way over to the bed. Alucard took his eyes off the demon and stared over at the wall again, pouting as Zalith sat beside him.

"Good morning," Zalith said, placing his hand on Alucard's right shoulder.

Alucard couldn't find the strength nor motivation to form a proper reply and simply uttered a sound of irritated recognition.

The demon laughed quietly. "Are you grumpy?"

Snarling quietly, Alucard pulled the blanket over his face.

Zalith then pulled the blanket away from his face and leaned in. He kissed his cheek with a purposely loud smooch.

Alucard grumbled quietly and tried to push him away. "Stop," he complained. He wasn't in the mood for Zalith's playfulness.

"What if I don't want to?" Zalith asked with a smirk, nuzzling the side of his face.

With an aggravated sigh, Alucard tried to pull the blanket over his face again, but Zalith snatched it, stopped him, and kissed his cheek once more.

A quiet knock suddenly came at the door. Zalith's smile faded into a perturbed frown as he stood up and headed to the door, but when he was halfway there, he clearly remembered that he was naked, so he snatched a pair of trousers from a nearby dresser. He put them on as he continued to the door, and when he reached it, he opened it and set his eyes on Edwin.

"Sir, Leonard has sent word that he will arrive in around an hour," the butler said.

"Thank you," Zalith said, and as the butler then wandered off, the demon closed the door and made his way back over to the bed. As he sat down, he placed his hand back on Alucard's shoulder and smiled. "Would you like to come and have breakfast with me, or do you want to get some more sleep?"

Alucard didn't really know what he wanted, but what he *did* know was that whatever he could smell cooking was *not* what he desired. As for sleep, he was sure that he wouldn't get any more with the headache he had—a headache that wouldn't wane unless he ate something to help him with his blood loss. He didn't exactly feel like drinking Zalith's blood, though, and his usual go-to—which was often cake—didn't sound very appealing either. So, as his confusion and irritancy grew, he shrugged in response.

Zalith smiled down at him but then got up again, walked over to the door, and pulled it open. "Edwin," he called, and as the sound of the butler's footsteps echoed from outside, Alucard glared at the door. "Bring breakfast up here for us, please," the demon instructed.

"Yes, Sir," came Edwin's voice.

The demon then shut the door and returned to Alucard. "Are you okay?" he asked quietly, stroking the side of the vampire's face.

Alucard nodded, trying to ignore both his headache and his craving for something sweet.

"The contractor will be here in around an hour," Zalith said, moving into the bed. He made himself comfortable beside Alucard and wrapped his arms around him. "I have to take him to the place I want the compound to be built so that he can get a lay of the land. You can come with me if you like," he offered.

"Maybe," Alucard mumbled, and then he quietly sighed and closed his eyes.

"Do you have to do anything today?"

Alucard was busy trying to work out what he wanted—what he *needed*. Cake? No. Candy? No. Chocolate? No again.

"Alucard?"

The vampire frowned and sighed quietly. "I 'ave Luther coming. I vas also vorking on someving," he said, remembering that he'd been researching dream ethos to find a way to stop his nightmares. "I vill probably vork on zhat more. I also 'ave to vink about zhe Numen and everyving I vill need to share vhen ve 'ave zhat meeting next veek."

"What are you working on?" the demon asked curiously.

"Just someving to stop my nightmares."

Before Zalith could respond, another knock came at their door. "Yes?" he called with a hint of irritancy in his voice.

The door opened and Edwin walked in with one of the kitchen staff, carrying their breakfast into the room.

Alucard didn't bother to sit up; he glanced up at the plate and mug placed on his nightstand, but he already knew that he didn't want any of it.

The butler and staff member left the room in silence, closing the door behind them.

Zalith looked down at Alucard as he sat up beside him. He sipped from his coffee and asked, "Are you going to eat something?"

"No," Alucard mumbled with a pout.

The demon sighed and glanced at Alucard's plate. "You should at least have a bite of toast—or some coffee."

"I zon't vant," Alucard mumbled stubbornly.

"What if I feed it to you?" Zalith asked, smirking.

"No," Alucard muttered again, pulling the blanket over his head.

Zalith took another sip of his coffee. Then, he placed his mug on his nightstand and leaned over to look down at Alucard again. "Baby," he said quietly.

"Vhat?" Alucard muttered from beneath the blanket.

"Baby," he called again.

Alucard pulled the blanket from over his head and glared at him. "Vhat?" he snarled impatiently.

Laughing, Zalith leaned a little closer so that his face was just inches from his. "Would you like some of my blood?"

The vampire took his eyes off him and turned back to face the wall. "No."

"Why not?" Zalith asked, concerned.

"Because I zon't veel like," he said quietly.

Confused, Zalith frowned. "Do you not like it anymore?" he asked with a forced laugh.

"No," Alucard said with a sigh. He didn't want Zalith to think he didn't like it anymore or something. "I just zon't vant."

With a saddened frown, Zalith sat up straight and leaned back against the bed's headboard. He picked up his coffee and stared into it for a few moments. Then, he sighed and sipped from his mug. "Okay. If you change your mind, you can have it whenever."

Alucard nodded in response.

But not even a second later, Zalith put his coffee mug onto his nightstand and then crawled under the blanket. He wrapped his arms around the vampire and held him tightly, burying his face into his neck. "Are you grumpy because of me?" he asked quietly.

Alucard frowned as he pondered. He felt a little less irritated in Zalith's embrace, and as he recognized the sadness in the demon's voice, guilt started to outweigh his annoyance. "No," he answered. He *wasn't* mad or upset because of Zalith, he just felt exhausted and confused. He had such an intense, confounding craving for something so specific, and he was still trying to work out what it was.

"Okay," the demon said quietly, sadness still in his voice.

He didn't want Zalith to be sad, and he didn't want him to think that he was irritated because of him, either. His first thought was to change the subject, and all he really had was what was currently on his mind. "Do ve 'ave…anyving…vith strawberry?" he asked, narrowing down his strange craving to that fruit.

Zalith smiled against Alucard's neck. "Like what?"

"Cake…" he said but then frowned. "No, vait…ice cream," he said, sure that that was what he wanted.

Zalith hugged him a little tighter. "There's probably some downstairs in the kitchen. If not, we can send someone out to go and get some for you."

Hearing that there could be some downstairs urged Alucard to get out of bed. "I vant to go and see," he said, gripping the blanket, preparing to pull it from over himself—

The demon grabbed the blanket and stopped him from getting up. He then stared down at him. "Right now?" he asked.

Alucard frowned. "Yes."

"It's seven in the morning."

"So?" Alucard pouted. "I vant."

Zalith laughed quietly. "Okay."

Alucard didn't waste any time getting out of bed. He took the clothes that had been laid out for him last night, pulled them on, and made his way over to the door as Zalith—who had also finished getting dressed—followed him.

They made their way through the hall and down the stairs. When they reached the bottom of the stairs, however, Zalith stopped walking and lightly grabbed Alucard's hand.

"I'll be in my office if you need anything…and if you change your mind about coming with Leonard and me to look at the land. I'll let you know when I'm leaving either way," Zalith said, smiling.

Looking at him, Alucard nodded. "Okay," he said. Then, as Zalith left to head for his office, Alucard made his way down the hall, heading for the kitchen, where he hoped to find what he was looking for.

# Chapter Forty-Nine

## Commit

**| Varana |**

Varana woke up when she felt Luther moving closer to her. He moved his arm around her and started grinding his strangely cold body against hers, and in response, she rolled her eyes.

"Are you awake?" he asked her.

Varana uttered a sound of annoyance, swatting his arm so that he'd let go of her.

Luther frowned, leaning on his arm as he stared down at her. "What's wrong, sugar walls?"

"I'm sleeping," she grumbled, but she lightly pushed her ass back against his crotch to aggravate him.

Luther moved his arm back around her and gripped her right breast in his hand. He then moved closer, smiling down at the side of her face. "If you're sleeping, why are you pushing your ass against my dick?"

She didn't answer, but she exhaled quietly and placed her hand on his head, and a slight smile appeared on her face as he nuzzled the back of her neck. He pinched her nipple, kissed the back of her neck and over her arm, and then rested the side of his face on hers as he gripped her hip.

But he seemed like he was in a rush. He swiftly kissed his way down her body and disappeared beneath the blanket. Then, he parted her legs with his hands and dragged his tongue over her clit and into her pussy, and as he pleased her with his mouth, she hummed contently.

He didn't eat her out for very long, though. After a few moments, he kissed his way back up her body; he smiled down at her, gripping his dick in his hand, but before he could slide it into her, she grabbed his shoulder.

"Wait," she said. She didn't want to face him right now. He made the ugliest expressions while he was fucking her. So, she turned over onto her stomach. Then, she sighed, letting him know he was free to continue.

Varana let out a quiet moan of pleasure as Luther slowly moved his dick into her. She rested her arms in front of her, closing her eyes as he began eagerly thrusting. She'd not deny that it felt quite pleasing, and as off-putting as she first found Luther, it turned out that he actually knew what he was doing when it came to pleasing a woman.

However, she didn't care, nor was she enjoying it enough to focus on him and what was happening. Instead, she retreated into her thoughts. She wasn't sure what time it was, but it was early, and she found herself wondering what she might do with her day. She didn't have any plans, although she heard a group of people were waiting to head into the Citadel to look around, so she thought she might accompany them.

She wasn't going to stay there with Luther; she'd already spent the entirety of last night with him, and she didn't want him to think she'd become attached to him. Having casual sex didn't mean much to her, and she was convinced that it didn't mean anything to him, either. Just mutual…enjoyment.

When she remembered that they were having sex, she moaned delightfully, gripping a handful of Luther's hair in her hand as he moved his face to her neck, breathing rather heavily onto her skin. She rolled her eyes, somewhat matching his erratic breathing. She didn't want him to think that she wasn't interested; the last thing she wanted was an argument.

Luther: did she even like him? He wasn't *that* bad to look at; she'd been with much more attractive men, but she didn't need to complain. However, he was selfish in bed. He often made everything about himself, but she couldn't really judge him because she was just as selfish—again, at least Luther knew what he was doing, despite his haste and need to please himself. But…did she *like* him? She wasn't sure, and she needed to decide.

With a quiet, pleasured sigh, she rolled onto her back so that they were facing one another. Luther smirked and eased his dick back into her, making her moan quietly. Varana dragged her hands over his arms; she felt nothing special at all when she touched him, nor did she feel anything when he touched her. She felt nothing different when they had sex, when they spent time together, or when they did pretty much anything.

He *was* nice to her, though, and gave her attention. But she then thought, how long would they be together until either of them made their true intentions known? She was almost sure that it wouldn't bother Luther if she told him that she was just sleeping with him to aggravate Zalith and Alucard. Alucard…. She rolled her eyes again, tilting her head back a little as Luther playfully bit her neck.

While Luther continued thrusting into her, Varana glanced down at the hideous rat tattoo he had on his stomach, a rat with not only Luther's hairstyle but a rat wearing a white suit, something she saw this vampire wearing *a lot*. Perhaps this image was an indication of his character; maybe he purposefully wanted to show the world who he was on the inside. Why did he have such an ugly tattoo?

She sighed pleasurably, resting her head back on her pillow to stare up at the ceiling. Luther was no marble statue; he *did* possess enough muscle to avoid being classed as skinny, but now that was ruined by the tattoo. With a revolted stare, she glared over at the wall. She'd rather have not seen the rat. He'd look so much better with something else…like a dragon…no, *she* would look good with a dragon tattoo. If she didn't have such nice skin and wasn't so beautiful, she'd get a dragon tattoo.

Varana then sighed happily, thinking about how stunning she really was, but she did her best to make it sound like a sigh of pleasure so that Luther wouldn't discover that she really wasn't into the sex at all.

After a few moments, Luther moved his face from her neck and leaned in to kiss her lips, but she hesitated and looked away. Luther wasn't her boyfriend, and she really didn't want him kissing her right now—or at all. Instead, with her hand on the back of his head, she pulled him back down to her neck.

Luther didn't comply, however, and stopped moving his body to look down at her. "What's wrong?" he asked, but clearly with no concern for her. "Why can't I kiss you?"

She frowned up at him. "Did you brush your teeth?"

He laughed slightly. "Babe, I just woke up, and so did you. Have you brushed *your* teeth?"

"No, so I'm sure you don't want me kissing *you*, do you?" she sneered.

Luther shrugged as he moved his face back into hers, moving a strand of her hair away from her face. "I don't care."

"Well, *I* do," she denied.

He lost his smirk and frowned. "Whatever. It's not like I *need* to brush them, is it? I don't eat."

"Luther, shut up," she said, scowling.

"Pshh, whatever," he uttered, moving his face to her neck.

As Luther turned his attention back to fucking her, Varana scowled up at the ceiling. He was lucky that she even let him enter her body, and *that* should be good enough for him. Why did he think he was in control? He hadn't earned it; *Varana* was the one in control, and she wasn't going to let him think for a moment longer that it was the other way around.

She placed her hand on his chest, making him stop moving once more. "Lie down," she instructed.

Luther did as she told him and lay on his back as she straddled his lap. Varana felt so unimpressed by this man right now, but she wasn't going to cut this off. She gripped his dick and moved it back into her pussy as he gripped either side of her waist.

But he soon frowned in response to her unenthusiastic gyrating. "You don't really seem into it, babe," he mumbled. "It's putting me off."

Irritated, she deadpanned and stared down at him, falling still. She knew she wasn't really expressing her enjoyment as much as she usually might, but if she wasn't enjoying herself at all, she'd not be doing it. She blinked in annoyance but then took his hands off her waist and made him grip her breasts. Then, she started moving with a little more enthusiasm.

Varana retreated into her thoughts, ignoring Luther's irritating moans of pleasure. Where was this relationship even going? Well, it wasn't even a relationship, was it? All she and Luther really did was have sex and talk, and what they spoke about was mostly just Zalith and Alucard. She rolled her eyes again, tilting her head back as she made Luther tighten his grip on her breasts. Why was Luther so interested in Alucard and Zalith? Was it because they were the only thing she and he had in common? She felt as if she couldn't blame him for going on and on about them because she had more stories about Zalith than she did anything or anyone else, so of course, *that* was going to get her talking.

It wasn't like she had anyone else to talk to, anyway. Her friends—Mary-Beth, Selena, and Cadence—were dull and boring. Zalith was always too busy screwing around with his boyfriend…Alucard…*him*. She wasn't going to talk to Alucard, either, and she couldn't just head into town and find someone else because everyone in the Citadel knew her as Zalith's wife, and she wasn't going to ruin all his plans by fooling around with some other guy or by making it known that he was actually gay. So, who did that leave for her? The staff—they really weren't that attractive—and Luther.

With another pleased sigh, she glanced at Luther. She felt annoyed remembering how Zalith spoke to her about Luther the other day. If Zalith didn't like it, then so be it. She didn't care. If Zalith was allowed to have a secret boyfriend, then she was allowed to have one, too.

She then scowled. Did she just call Luther her boyfriend?

Luther suddenly gripped her shoulder and pulled her down so that her face was just inches from his. At first, she felt a little startled, but as her face came closer to his, she frowned in annoyance.

"I want you to bite me," he panted.

Varana sighed again, moving her face to his neck. But she hesitated. She only ever bit her actual boyfriends and men she liked. Did she like Luther? She didn't *not* like him…. She rolled her eyes again and sank her two fangs into his skin, and when Luther moaned loudly in satisfaction, she adorned a look of fatigue.

She waited a few moments…and then pulled her fangs from his neck, not bothering to sit up straight as she stared at the bed's headboard. What if Luther *was* her boyfriend? Would such a thing please her? She hadn't had an actual boyfriend in such a long time, and she felt it might actually be a nice change of pace. But would Luther even say yes? She wasn't sure. Yesterday, she'd interrupted him and Danford; she wasn't jealous, and she didn't even want to think about what they might have done if she hadn't walked in when she did.

How dare Luther spend his time with someone else? Especially someone like Danford. Was *she* not enough for him? She *should* be. She had everything any guy could ever want in a woman. She was rich, royalty, and hot as all hell. What the fuck was Luther doing? If Danford was someone like Zalith who had everything going for him, then she'd understand and might even be fine with sharing Luther with him, but what did Danford have? Some paper and a stick of old, crusty charcoal? One eye? Did…this mean that Luther saw her on the same level as Danford? That wasn't right at all—she was a mystifying, intoxicating minx and should be the only one Luther wanted!

She scowled as anger started consuming her. He was going to have to choose because she wasn't going to continue to have a dick inside her that had been God knows where, and to think that it had been touched by a peasant like Danford? She shuddered at the thought, and she was going to make Luther choose *her*.

Luther uttered in aspiration. "I'm getting close," he breathed, moving his hands from her breasts and to her thighs. "Where do you want it?"

She frowned, sitting up to look down at him as she placed her hands on either side of his head. "Where do *you* want it?" she muttered, leaning forward, her face not too far from his.

"I don't wanna get you pregnant," Luther said with a confused scowl.

Varana sighed in annoyance. "I'm a matriarch—I just *won't* get pregnant." She frowned at him and added, "You're a vampire; you can't get anyone pregnant."

Looking up at her, Luther shrugged and took his eyes off her face to stare down at her breasts as they bounced against his chest.

She glared at him, staring at his stupid face. He was just seconds away from climax, and that was when she slid back. Luther gritted his teeth and uttered a sound of confusion as she gripped hold of his dick, restricting him from reaching the end of his peak.

"I want you to commit to me," she said with a scowl.

Panting, Luther took his eyes off her body and stared up at her irritated face. The look of high induced by her venom seemed to fade as he frowned in hesitation. "What?" he asked, still breathing erratically.

"I want you to commit to me," she repeated. "No more Danford, no more whoever else. Just us," she demanded.

He then scoffed, dragging his hand over his face. "Why should I commit to you if you're not gonna commit to me?"

"Where are you getting that impression from?" she asked, offended. "Why would I ask you if I'm not going to commit?"

Luther laughed through his struggled frown. "I heard things about you."

"Like what?!"

He shook his head and gripped her waist again. "Can I finish?"

"That depends on whether or not you're going to commit to me, Luther," she said, irritated.

"Why?" he asked with another scoff. "Do you really like me *that* much?"

Varana forced a smile onto her face. "Yes," she said, dragging her fingers over his throbbing shaft. "Are you going to do it or not?"

Luther, who looked very desperate to finish, sighed, looked to his left and his right, and then frowned in defeat. "Fine," he uttered.

She smiled victoriously. "Thank you." Then, she moved his dick back into her pussy.

Luther didn't waste any time. He pushed and pulled on her waist as she leaned forward again. She thought she might as well kiss him and put in a little more effort now that he was actually her boyfriend. But she felt a little disappointed that not even thirty seconds later, Luther climaxed and moaned feverishly, tightening the grip he had on her with his hands.

Varana sighed quietly in disappointment. She didn't even feel his dick throbbing when he came, and she was nowhere near reaching her peak, so she wasn't going to bother. She moved from over him; she wasn't expecting him to roll over and cuddle her, so she got back under the blanket and stared over at the wall. At least now she didn't have to think about Luther and Danford doing unspeakable things behind her back. She'd rather not share Luther, and now that he had agreed to commit to her, she felt she could like him just a little more.

# Chapter Fifty

—  ≺ ✝ ≻ —

## Building Plans

| **Alucard** |

Alucard sat behind his study desk with an entire tub of strawberry ice cream in his lap. He'd already eaten his way through half of it, but he still wanted more—or perhaps he was just eating because he didn't know what else to do while waiting for Luther to arrive.

He laid out the notes he made in preparation for making something to stop his nightmares alongside the crystals he bought. His violin also lay atop some sheet music he'd been writing. The last time he worked on music was months ago…before the sadness caused by Zalith's absence became too much.

The vampire frowned. His thoughts were a little more discombobulated than usual. Now that he could actually think about more than just ice cream, he started to ponder over what happened yesterday—more specifically, what was said and what he felt. Despite trying to assure himself *and* Zalith that he had no issues with the abandonment, he couldn't help but think about what Varana said and how it made him feel. For the past near-week, he'd been ignoring his sadness for Zalith's sake; Zalith was dealing with the trauma of the battle that took place in Eltaria before he'd gotten his people to Aegisguard, and Alucard didn't want to overwhelm him with concern and worry by telling him that he wasn't content.

With a quiet sigh, he stared down into his ice cream, slowly eating it from the steel spoon he'd taken from the kitchen. But as his thoughts became sadder, he placed the ice cream down and picked up his violin. It often helped him settle his thoughts, and that was what he needed right now. So, he rested his face on the violin and started playing. He spent so long working on his latest piece, and he didn't want to neglect it, for it was one of his favourite hobbies.

He slowly dragged the bow over its strings, trying to lose himself in his music. But his thoughts didn't silence. The first thing that came to mind was…perhaps the lingering sadness had something to do with the fact that he didn't want Zalith's blood this morning.

He had to go without it for months, and he didn't want to get attached to having it all the time again, only for him to have to resort back to human blood when Zalith got busy again.

*Was* Zalith going to get busy again? It happened before, and Alucard was convinced that it might happen again, especially after hearing Zalith confess that his tendency to focus on work to ignore his problems and deny himself pleasure was a habit he'd had for years.

Alucard scowled, trying to concentrate on his tune. He didn't want to think about it; he didn't want to think about the anger he felt when he thought about himself being more important than Zalith's work and his people, because he shouldn't be, should he? Why would one person matter over hundreds? Alucard didn't expect to be so important, but…maybe he was? Zalith insisted many times that he was the most important person in his life, and despite his constant denial to accept that statement, he was starting to feel like…perhaps he should actually listen. After all, Zalith was the most important person in *his* life, and he'd prioritise him over anything and everyone. But then again, Zalith hadn't exactly done that for the past few months, had he? So, why *should* Alucard believe that he was as important as Zalith constantly said he was?

Guilt warped his thoughts. He stopped playing and lowered his bow and violin. With a frown on his face, he stared at the unfinished sheet music on his desk. He didn't want to feel angry at Zalith, nor did he want to blame him. Zalith had obviously been so stressed, and to fight against a Numen? To try and keep what remained of his people safe from something like Adellum? He just wished Zalith asked him for help sooner—he just wished…that he'd stopped sulking about Zalith's absence and spoken to him about it sooner, then maybe more of Zalith's people would still be alive.

He picked up his quill and scribbled down the next few notes of his song, and then, he resumed playing. But he scowled in discontent. He didn't know how to feel. He felt so sad and confused when he thought about the months he'd spent wondering whether Zalith still wanted him or not, but his guilt became heavier in his heart when he thought about telling Zalith just how upset it all made him. He thought he'd be so happy for things to go back to the way they were, but he wasn't. He felt…strange. It didn't feel right for things to have just so suddenly returned to how they were. Zalith left him in pain for months, and that was finally catching up with him. His confliction was finally becoming the problem that he wished it wouldn't.

Alucard stopped playing again and sat up straight when he heard the front door open. He glanced out of the window to his left, listening as a pair of footsteps made their way through the hall downstairs. At first, he thought it might be Edwin escorting Luther to his office, but the knock didn't come at his door.

He listened while Edwin presented Zalith with Leonard, and as they greeted each other, Alucard turned his attention back to his violin. He rested his face on it again and started playing from the beginning.

Maybe he was overthinking everything. He hadn't seen much of Zalith in months, and the past few days were brimmed with the demon's attention. Perhaps he just needed more of that? Maybe a few more nights of affection and embrace would silence these conflicting, upsetting thoughts. Perhaps he only needed to get used to Zalith being around all the time again, and maybe he needed to accept that Zalith did what he needed to do and that he never considered leaving Alucard…he was just busy.

He stopped playing again; he focused so that he could hear Zalith speaking to Leonard, the contractor. His feeling of guilt returned as he put his violin down so that he could start eating his ice cream again. This morning, he felt so irritated, and he felt like Zalith probably thought it was his fault. *Was* it his fault? No…Alucard wasn't angry with him; he'd just woken up feeling aggravated because of his blood loss. He'd not taken blood back from Zalith last night, and whenever he lost so much, he'd feel tired and unmotivated.

Sighing, he stared into his ice cream. Zalith offered him blood, and he'd said no. Why did he say no? Why did he often feel the need to act so stubborn? Maybe it was because he didn't want to allow himself to make Zalith the solution to all his problems, or perhaps it was just who he was. But why? He knew Zalith didn't mind him feeding off him, *and* the demon very clearly enjoyed it, but Alucard almost felt as if he was a parasite, especially since both he and Zalith knew he could survive off the blood of humans.

There were also other solutions to his fatigue, such as the ice cream in his lap. Sugar was a great help in restoring his energy after losing blood, but drinking Zalith's blood wasn't only easier, but he always found pleasure in doing so…and he didn't want to become addicted to it.

Listening to Zalith's voice, however—and thinking about him in general—always had a way of making Alucard change his mind. Along with thinking about him came a quickly increasing need for Zalith's attention, a need that was greater than usual considering he'd turned it down this morning, and a need so much more intense since he'd been deprived of Zalith's attention for so long. He didn't want to think about that anymore, though.

Now that he was a lot less irritated, he wanted to sit with Zalith; he wanted to be in his embrace…and maybe more, too. Perhaps that would help him silence his thoughts. But once again, the idea of having to go without Zalith's attention for months possessed his thoughts, and a desire to simply take it started to enthral him. He told himself he'd get over his nervousness when it came to getting what he wanted from Zalith and now would be no exception. He wanted to see him, touch him, feel him, and taste him, and he'd not waste his time sitting there thinking about whether or not he should do it.

The vampire put his almost-empty tub of ice cream on his desk, stood up, and then made his way down into his office. He headed for the door, left, and turned to his right, reaching the door to Zalith's office. He pushed it open, and when he stood in the doorway, he set his eyes on *his* demon and Leonard, the contractor, who was sitting in front of Zalith's desk. Zalith, of course, was sitting behind it, and immediately set his dark eyes on Alucard.

As Alucard entered, Leonard stumbled over his words and glanced back at him. The man was short, pudgy, and tanned, and his face adorned a thick black moustache. His black hair was neat and combed, and he dressed smartly in a beige suit. He took a small look at Alucard with his dull green eyes and then turned back to face Zalith.

Zalith smiled at the vampire and held out his arm, inviting him to sit with him.

Alucard closed the door behind him, walked over there, and made himself comfortable on the arm of Zalith's chair as the demon moved his arm around him.

"Where was I?" Leonard asked himself, keeping his eyes on Zalith; his accent was one Alucard immediately recognized; this man was from Lupa. "Ah, a road into this compound. Would you like it to be bricked or not?"

The demon shook his head slightly. "No. I don't want the area to look too developed so I can claim ignorance if something were to happen out there."

Leonard nodded in understanding. "How far out on your property do you want these homes to be built?"

Zalith looked down at a map on his desk and placed his finger over a spot that looked to be about two miles away from their house. "Around here," he said. "The land is flat, there's a lake nearby, and it's not too far nor too close to the Citadel. Close enough so that I can be there if I need to be, but far enough so that they won't bother me. And so that it won't look too suspicious…preferably to the northwest, too."

As Leonard stared down at the map, Alucard looked at Zalith. He felt somewhat content with the demon's arm around him and sitting beside him, but it wasn't what he'd come here for. He wanted what he refused to take this morning, but he wasn't going to cut Zalith's meeting short. He'd just have to wait and ignore his increasing eagerness.

Leonard pulled a small notebook from his pocket and started writing.

"I don't want it *too* close to the lake, though," the demon said.

The contractor nodded again. Then, once he'd taken down his notes, he looked at Zalith. "Do you mind if we head out there and take a look? I'd like to survey the land a bit."

Zalith nodded. "Edwin will take you out there on the horses. I'll meet you shortly."

Tucking his notebook into his pocket, Leonard stood up. "All right, I'll meet you soon," he said. Then, the man turned around, left Zalith's office, and pulled the door shut behind him.

The demon looked up at Alucard and smiled. "Hey. Did you find your ice cream?"

"Mm-hmm," Alucard answered, staring down at him.

"I'm glad. I heard you playing; I love it when you play," he said with a smirk. But then he frowned curiously. "Do you feel better now?"

Gazing at him, Alucard's impatience became something he couldn't ignore. Before, he might have ignored his urges, but not anymore. He wanted Zalith, and he wasn't going to let his nervousness get in the way of that—he wasn't going to let anything get in the way of it. He was going to get what he wanted, and he was also going to let Zalith know that he was doing it because *he* wanted to and not because the demon had enticed or convinced him.

He frowned but stood up, gripping Zalith's shirt as he did. He pulled the demon out of his seat and then pinned him back against the wall.

The demon smiled and laughed quietly as Alucard held him against it. "You shouldn't push me around, vampire. I might start to get used to it," he said quietly.

With an impatient snarl, Alucard moved his face to Zalith's neck, hiding his embarrassed expression before it became visible. He then exhaled quietly, moving his hands to grip either side of Zalith's waist. For a moment, he wanted to enjoy being close to him, and to his relief, Zalith didn't try to move things along. He stood there, leaning against the wall, waiting.

Alucard rested the side of his face on Zalith's, closing his eyes, enjoying to demon's intoxicating, natural scent of bergamot and sandalwood. This close to him, he could also detect the so very faint scent of white sage, a scent which became stronger when the demon bled, and that was what Alucard wanted from him. He *needed* his blood. But his desire to taste it calmed as he held Zalith where he was. It wasn't often he got to touch him, and now that he seemed to be finding it easier to get over his shyness, he wanted to do more than sink his fangs into Zalith's neck.

He stared down, slowly moving his hands under Zalith's shirt as he rested his forehead on the demon's shoulder. He wanted to take the shirt off him so that he could stare and touch, but he didn't want to appear too eager. So, for a few moments, he dragged his hands over Zalith's abs, guiding his fingers over the demon's defined body. Then, as he heard a content sigh come from Zalith, he guided his hands from beneath his shirt and gripped its top button.

As Alucard started unbuttoning the demon's shirt, Zalith moved his hands to Alucard's waist. He pulled the vampire closer and then started to slowly move his hands down to Alucard's belt. Zalith's hands traversed around Alucard's waist, and he eventually moved his fingers beneath the vampire's belt. But Alucard was more focused on removing the demon's shirt, and once he untied its last button, he pulled it off Zalith's body.

Alucard then moved his face back to Zalith's neck, nuzzling it as he dragged his hands down the demon's body once more. The feel of Zalith's soft, warm skin always gave him comfort, as did feeling his body against his own. He sighed quietly, placing a kiss on the demon's neck in the area where he planned to sink his fangs.

But Alucard's desire for touching and closeness started to intensify as Zalith gently gripped his crotch over his trousers. He frowned, moving his left hand up Zalith's body; he gripped Zalith's throat, slowly tightening his grip as he made the demon tilt his head aside. He glanced at the demon's face, seeing that he was staring at him with a smile on his face, and that seemed to hinder Alucard's bravery for a moment.

He frowned as a pout appeared on his face. "Zon't look at me," he mumbled.

Zalith smirked. "Okay. Should I close my eyes?"

"No," Alucard snarled, moving his hand from Zalith's throat to grip his jaw. He then made the demon turn his head to the side so that he couldn't stare at him.

"I like it when you boss me around, vampire," Zalith said quietly.

Alucard, who didn't really have anything else to say, huffed quietly in response. He felt eager, and he just wanted what he'd come for. So, he dragged his hand back to Zalith's throat, keeping his other hand on the demon's waist.

Zalith moved his hand from Alucard's crotch and started unbuttoning his shirt. As he did so, Alucard guided his hand up from Zalith's waist and gripped his bicep. He moved his face closer to the demon's neck, but just as he thought he was about to savagely sink his fangs into it, he hesitated. He didn't want it to be over so quickly with just one bite; he wanted to enjoy Zalith. After all, this was *his* demon, and he could do with him what he wanted.

With his eagerness settling, he used his thumb to move the demon's thin, golden chain away from where he wished to bite; he then widened his jaw and sank his fangs into Zalith's neck, but he didn't keep them there for as long as usual. Instead, just moments after his top two fangs pierced Zalith's skin, he slowly pulled them out again, allowing the demon's blood to quickly trickle down his body.

For a few moments, he gazed, holding Zalith where he was despite hearing the demon's confused murmur. Zalith stopped unbuttoning the vampire's shirt and waited, surely confounded by Alucard's decision to let his sage-scented blood seep from the two wounds in his neck. It trickled over his left pec and trailed its way through the lines of each of his abs.

Alucard didn't want to keep Zalith waiting too long, but he couldn't ignore the delight he found in watching. However, his desire to taste outweighed that. Without further hindrance, Alucard leaned forward and pressed his tongue against the demon's stomach. He slowly dragged it up Zalith's body, licking his blood away; he dragged it to his abs, over his left pec, and to his neck where he'd left the two small wounds.

As Zalith sighed contently, Alucard sank his fangs back into his neck. He didn't bite the place he first had; this time, he sank all four fangs into Zalith's neck just above the first two wounds, and as the demon flinched, he uttered a long sigh of pleasure. The demon's sigh made Alucard feel content, too, and as the demon resumed unbuttoning his shirt, Alucard bit down a little harder and groaned in satisfaction as Zalith's tantalizing blood sated his hunger. The demon pulled Alucard's shirt off, dragged his hands over his body, and soon moved them to grip the vampire's ass, pulling him even closer. Alucard could then feel the demon's arousal against his crotch, and that excited him further.

He pulled his fangs from Zalith's neck, but he didn't get much time to decide what he wanted to do next. Zalith became a little more assertive, pulling away from the wall as he turned his head to stare at Alucard despite the fact that the vampire was holding his throat. The demon smirked, leaning his face into Alucard's, and then, he started kissing him. Zalith guided Alucard back until his ass hit his desk; the demon made him shuffle back to sit on it and continued kissing him, his excitement clear in his sudden aggression.

Alucard didn't feel hesitant; he'd gotten what he wanted, and now, he was obviously going to get more. He gripped Zalith's arm tightly, kissing back, his eagerness starting to become uncontainable once again. The demon moved his hand into Alucard's trousers, gripping hold of his arousal as he smirked through their kisses.

With a frown, Alucard lightly pushed Zalith back; as the demon fell back into his seat, Alucard straddled his lap. Zalith grinned, and then they continued kissing. Alucard could feel the demon already trying to unbuckle his belt, and once he did, he pulled it from around his waist and dropped it on the floor. Alucard knew he'd have to get up so that his trousers could come off, and his growing excitement didn't keep him from doing so. He stood up, leaning forward so that he and Zalith could keep kissing as the demon removed Alucard's trousers. As Alucard then moved back into Zalith's lap, the demon unbuckled his own belt and unbuttoned his trousers.

The vampire waited while Zalith reached over to one of his desk drawers. He rested his head on the side of Zalith's, taking a moment to breathe, but his aspiration returned as he felt the demon move his cold, lube-smothered fingers into his ass. Alucard exhaled quietly, tightening the grip he had on Zalith's arm as he waited as patiently as he could. And Zalith didn't seem to want to take too long, either. After a few moments, the demon gripped Alucard's waist with one of his hands and slowly pulled him down over his hard dick.

Alucard groaned pleasurably as Zalith breathed onto his neck, burying his shaft deep inside him. He tightened the grip he had on Zalith's arm, digging his claws into his skin; usually, he'd try not to, but he craved Zalith's affection so intensely that he had no room to try and control himself. He silenced all his thoughts, focusing solely on Zalith and the pleasure he made him feel.

For a short while, the demon guided Alucard's body up and down over his dick as they both breathed deeply onto one another's neck. Alucard hummed in delight but frowned in confusion when Zalith suddenly gripped his waist with both hands. Before he could question him, the demon lifted him up and pinned his back down on his desk. Zalith leaned over him, resting his arms on either side of him as he started to kiss him again, thrusting his shaft into and out of his ass. Alucard guided his left leg over Zalith's back as he turned his head to the side so the demon could kiss his neck. Then, he lay there, quickly becoming enthralled by the pleasure of Zalith's movements and the soft kisses to his neck.

But then a sudden knock came at the door, and before either of them said a word in response, it swung open.

They both sharply turned their heads. Zalith adorned a furious glare, and Alucard stared in horror as he set his eyes on Luther, who stood in the doorway.

"Can I fucking help you?!" Zalith yelled, glowering at Luther as he did his best to conceal Alucard from him. "A closed door is *not* an invitation to enter—have some fucking respect!"

Alucard had no words to describe how mortified he felt. He was so intensely embarrassed that he couldn't bear another moment where he was. So he instantly disappeared, leaving Zalith's office and reappearing up in their bedroom. His look of horror didn't fade when he realized that he was in their bedroom dressing rooms and leaned back against the wall as he stared ahead in utter humiliation. Not only had he just been caught naked, but he'd been seen in such an intimate moment…and he felt like he couldn't face Luther after that.

He shook his head and looked down at the floor, trying to calm down. But that was when he heard Zalith yelling. And although he was sure that the demon was going to kill Luther…Alucard found himself considering keeping out of it.

But was he going to let Zalith kill his subordinate?

# Chapter Fifty-One

— ⸰ ✝ ⸰ —

# Confrontation

**| Zalith |**

Zalith seethed with anger. The moment Alucard disappeared, his scowl thickened, and before Luther could say anything, the demon lifted his hand and used his telekinesis to slam the door shut in his face.

The demon snarled as he stood up and buttoned his trousers. He took a moment to locate Alucard, whom he'd never seen so horrified before. The audacity Luther had to just walk into his office like that; even if he and Alucard weren't sharing a private moment, there was no reason for Luther to be bursting in. Clearly, he'd become a little *too* comfortable here, and Zalith felt no hesitation in his choice to show Luther how furious he was.

He made his way over to his door, pulled it open, and set his eyes on Luther, who was now heading for Alucard's office. Zalith grabbed the man, and before he could make a sound in response, the demon shoved him back and scowled at him. "*This* is *my* fucking house, and if I catch you waltzing into my office like that again, you'll live to regret it," he warned him.

Luther—after he stumbled back and took a moment to regain his balance—straightened his suit and glared at Zalith in disgust. "Can you not fucking touch me?" he snarled back. "And last time I checked, *you* are not my goddamn boss!" he yelled, gesturing his hand towards him.

With a hostile smile, Zalith pushed Luther against the closest wall. "Oh, I'm sorry. It's annoying when I cross your personal boundaries, isn't it?" he growled as Luther grunted in disgust. "If you don't want to be told what to do, try not acting like a socially inept child."

Luther stepped forward and shoved Zalith away. "You best get the hell out of my face before I make you regret touching me," he shouted, eyeing the half-naked demon with revolt. "I'm sick of you. Alucard might not see how heinous you are, but *I* do, and I'm tired of seeing you lord around the place!"

Zalith stood where he'd stumbled back to and scowled. "If you don't want to see me, then don't come to my house, genius," he sneered. "You should also take a long, hard look at yourself before you start calling people heinous—"

"I'll call you whatever the fuck I want," Luther interjected, moving closer, raising his hand to point at him. "I have every right to be here, walk around, and open whatever doors I want—"

The demon laughed, cutting him off. "It's going to be hard to walk if you don't have any legs," he threatened.

"And it's going to be hard to keep using Alucard if he finds out about your dirty little secrets, isn't it?" he threatened in return.

"What the fuck are you talking about?" Zalith scoffed.

Luther also scoffed. "You know *exactly* what I'm talking about."

"Evidently, I don't, so either enlighten me or get the fuck out of my house."

The ugly man's expression grew sour. "You don't deserve him."

"Who's he better off with? You?" Zalith snapped angrily but with an amused frown.

"As a matter of fact, yes. At least I'd take care of him the way he deserves and not abandon him for months on end, leaving him to feel like he means shit," he growled, glaring at Zalith.

Zalith's scowl thickened. "Stay the fuck away from him."

"Why?" Luther questioned, sounding smug. "If I were to do that, he'd be utterly alone, wouldn't he? Because you sure as fuck won't be around—"

Zalith abruptly smashed his fist into Luther's face. His nose broke, his back hit the wall, and with a confused grunt, Luther moved his hands to his face. Then, he lunged at Zalith, and the demon lunged too—

But that was when Varana appeared out of nowhere and moved between them, holding out her arms and pressing her hands against both their chests, stopping them from reaching one another. Luther stopped moving, but Zalith tried to move her aside. He wasn't going to let that disgusting piece of shit get away with saying what he'd said.

Varana sharply turned her head to glare up at Zalith, pushing him back a little. "What the hell is wrong with you? I said stop!" she insisted angrily.

Zalith wasn't interested. He shoved her aside, ignoring her screech as he zeroed in on Luther. Luther stumbled back, trying to ready himself for a fight, but Zalith was much faster. The demon effortlessly blocked Luther's punch with his right arm, and as Luther staggered again, Zalith seized his shoulders. With a swift, calculated motion, he drove his knee into Luther's side, pulling him down into the impact for maximum force.

Varana screamed as the crack of Luther's ribs echoed through the hall; Luther almost yelped in agony as he dropped to the floor, hunching up in a fetal position like the pathetic little child he was.

"What the hell is wrong with you?!" Varana yelled, glaring at Zalith as she hurried to Luther's side; she placed her hands on his arm as he trembled where he lay, exhaling painful breaths as blood oozed through his teeth.

Zalith just stood there, glowering down at Luther as he struggled to breathe. He deserved everything he got.

Luther clearly wasn't going to give up, though. He pushed Varana away and pulled himself to his feet, setting his eyes back on Zalith.

"Luther, stop," she insisted quietly as she stood up and tried to grab him before he could lunge at Zalith again.

But Luther broke free... and Zalith prepared to beat the shit out of him.

| **Alucard** |

Alucard could hear the commotion downstairs. He frowned and listened to the grunts and snarls; the smell of blood quickly filled the air, and that was all he needed to know that Zalith and Luther were fighting.

He knew he should go down there and break it up before Zalith killed Luther, but he was so embarrassed that he couldn't move. He just wanted to stand there and wait for Luther to leave, but that wasn't going to happen. Even Varana's intervention wasn't enough.

With a deep, shaky sigh, he shoved as much of his embarrassment aside as he could and grabbed a pair of trousers. He hurriedly pulled them on as well as a shirt and some socks and then left the closet.

The vampire rushed out of his bedroom, headed downstairs, and moved between Zalith and Luther, stopping either of them from landing another blow. He snatched Luther's throat before he could reach Zalith, and then shot a disapproving glare at the demon.

Luther stopped struggling and stared at Alucard like a lost child as blood sept from both his mouth and his broken nose.

And Zalith huffed in frustration but calmed down.

"Vhat zhe fuck is going on?" Alucard asked, glancing back at Zalith.

"Your friend doesn't know how to act," the demon replied angrily.

However, before Alucard could speak another word, Varana suddenly gasped in horror. All three of them looked over at her, watching as her mortified face was quickly adorned with a heartbroken stare. Tears formed in her eyes, and as she scowled painfully, she set her glare on Zalith.

A shriek of anger broke the moment of silence, and without a word, Varana threw herself at Zalith.

Alucard—once again—had no idea why it was happening and had no time to let go of Luther and stop her from harshly slapping Zalith's face. By the time Alucard did let go of Luther—who fell to the floor—he snatched Varana's arm and pulled her away from the demon.

"What the fuck is wrong with you?" Zalith asked, astounded, holding his hand over his reddening cheek.

Varana stumbled back as Alucard pushed her a small distance away; she didn't seem to care that he'd shoved her and instantly lunged towards Zalith again, but Alucard wasn't going to let the insane woman touch him. She tried to get around him as he stood in front of Zalith, but the vampire snatched her throat before she could get close enough to lay another hand on the demon. He had no idea why she so suddenly attacked Zalith, but he didn't care; he'd stop her, whatever her reason was.

Flailing in his grip, Varana tried to escape; she tried to push him away, but he wasn't going to move. Then, she started thrashing, attempting to fight to get to Zalith, who—as far as Alucard was aware—was just standing behind him. But Varana couldn't move an inch. He felt her try harder with each passing moment, and he had no intention of letting her go until she either calmed down or did something to deserve more than subjugation.

But then the woman abruptly burst into tears, wailing as she dropped to the floor after Alucard let go of her.

"Varana, what's wrong?" Zalith asked irritably as Alucard stood beside him.

She wailed louder.

With an aggravated scowl, Zalith deadpanned. "Varana."

"How *could you* imprint on him?!" she cried, her voice shrill and cracking.

Zalith's vacant stare became a conflicted one as Alucard glanced at him. He suspected—no, he actually *hoped* that Zalith had told Varana they'd imprinted on each other, but clearly, he hadn't, and she was now only just finding out more than eight months after it happened. Why hadn't he told her? Something like that was a thing that Alucard would have expected Zalith to tell a woman who was obsessed with him. Obviously, he'd not told her, and that made Alucard feel conflicted. Why wouldn't he have told her something as serious as this? Zalith seemed to tell her just about anything, so why was this an exception?

The demon crouched and placed his hand on her shoulder as she cried loudly in grief. "Get up so we can go and talk about this somewhere else," he said, glancing at Luther for half a second as he watched in confusion.

But Varana slapped his hand away and glared up at him. "Don't touch me!" she yelled.

Alucard had seen enough. His irritancy was quickly returning the more he thought about how Zalith neglected to tell her something this important. Zalith told Varana *everything*, but not this, and that made Alucard feel not only annoyed but upset, too, and he didn't really want to see either of them right now.

Without uttering a word, he left Zalith's side, snatched Luther's wrist, and pulled him to his feet, ignoring his painful grunts. Alucard then dragged him into his office, slamming the door shut behind him.

## | Zalith |

Zalith's confliction began to strangle him. He was certain that Alucard was upset, and Varana was wailing on the floor in front of him. He had no idea what to do: go to Alucard and ask him what was wrong, talk to Varana about imprinting on Alucard, or make sure Luther knew to stay away from Alucard. He felt so confused.

He looked down at Varana as a saddened frown appeared on his face. "Varana, can you please get up," he pleaded softly.

She ignored him and kept crying. After a few moments, though, she abruptly stood up. Zalith reached out to place a hand on her arm, but she shoved him back, tears streaming down her face. Her eyes flashed with anger and hurt as she stormed towards the front door. She yanked it open with such force that the hinges creaked in protest, and without a backward glance, she stepped out and slammed the door behind her, the sound reverberating through the house and making the fixtures rattle violently. The intensity of her exit left an echo of her fury hanging in the air.

Zalith stood there. That was *two* doors he'd had slammed at him in the space of five minutes, leaving him feeling defeated and alone; he wasn't sure if Alucard was mad at him or Luther or Varana, and he didn't want to head into the vampire's office and try to talk it out with him only to make things worse. Varana was furious with him, and he didn't want to chase after her and make that worse, either. What more could he do other than wait around for everyone to cool off?

The demon then remembered that Leonard was out on his land with Edwin. He had to head out there, but he really didn't want to right now. So, with a defeated look on his face, he turned around and dragged himself into his office, where he'd probably be spending the next while waiting.

# Chapter Fifty-Two

─ ⸲ † ⸱ ─

## Divulgence

| **Alucard** |

Alucard silently ate what remained of his ice cream while Luther used the towel he'd given him to clean his face. The vampire wasn't entirely sure why a fight broke out between Zalith and Luther, and he could only assume that it was because Luther entered Zalith's office without permission and caught them at a bad time. Alucard didn't want to think about how embarrassed that made him feel.

He sighed and ate the last spoonful of ice cream before swivelling in his seat to face Luther. The man was still holding the towel to his bloody nose with a look of anger and embarrassment. Alucard didn't feel any sympathy for him; he shouldn't have walked in like this was his house. But then again, maybe a simple mishap wasn't worth the punishment Zalith gave him, and Alucard couldn't help but wonder, had something else happened while he was upstairs?

"Your boyfriend's a fucking psychopath," Luther snarled, setting his eyes on Alucard.

"No," Alucard mumbled. "'E is zemon."

"That's no excuse to pretty much almost kill me, Alucard."

Alucard shrugged, turning his head to stare out of the window. "Zaliv vouldn't do zhat to you vor no veason," he defended, but he wasn't very enthusiastic. After finding out that Zalith hadn't told Varana—a woman who was obsessed with Zalith and very clearly wanted him for herself—that he'd imprinted on him, he couldn't help but feel a little upset and annoyed. Zalith always acted so protectively and possessively when it came to people trying to take him away from him, but when it came to Varana, Alucard hadn't seen nor heard of Zalith putting in much effort to let her know that he and Alucard belonged to one another.

Luther scoffed. "Maybe he did it because he was threatened."

Alucard frowned at him. "Vhy vould 'e be vreatened?"

"You tell me," he said, lowering the towel from his bloody face. "He knows I'm onto him, and when I told him—"

The vampire scoffed confusedly. "Zon't try to give your beating a divverent veason."

"What?"

"You valked into a voom vithout permission; you zon't do zhat anyvhere else, so vhat makes you vink you can do zhat 'ere?"

"In case you hadn't noticed, I'm dating Varana, and I'm pretty sure *that* gives me permission to be in this house and open doors so that I can get to places."

"Vhy vould you need to get into Zaliv's office? Obviously, you came knowing I vas zhere, so you should 'ave vaited vor somevone to answer zhe door. Zhat's vhy your vace got broken, Luther, not because Zaliv veels vreatened."

Once again, Luther scoffed and wiped away more blood from his face. "Maybe if I'd known he'd be fucking you in the middle of the day, and in his damn office, I'd have waited to come in," he said as Alucard felt his embarrassment return. "How the fuck was I supposed to know what you were doing? Last time I checked, an office is a place you work."

Alucard scowled angrily. He was tired of Luther's attitude; he might have accepted such behaviour a long time ago when they were closer, but their relationship nowadays wasn't one quite so casual. "Enough," he muttered, resting his arms on his desk.

"I'm not done yet. I'm tired of having to deal with—"

"Zhen leave," Alucard interjected. "If you can't stand to vork avound zemons, I suggest you go look vor vork elsevhere."

Luther scoffed *again*. "Leave you with some waste-of-space demon who has zero respect for you? Not gonna happen," he said sternly.

Alucard's intense need to defend Zalith faltered along with his words. He had no idea where Luther was going with this or what he might be about to say. All he knew was that after the confrontation in the hall just now, he seemed to feel a little less motivated to argue and defend Zalith.

Luther continued, "I don't know what this imprint thing is, but it sounds pretty important. Varana was devastated, and you look depressed—more than usual. Yet another thing he forgot to tell you about, I guess."

"Vhat are you talking about?" Alucard snarled.

"Everything. He didn't tell you that he more or less fucked half a country before meeting you; he didn't tell you one of his exes was coming to live just down the street, and he didn't tell you that Varana was your sister until it came down to telling you that or losing you, did he? I don't like snooping into other people's business, but I'm not going to sit around and watch that asshole use and lie to you," he said sternly. "And what next, huh? He already kicked the shit out of me because I told him I knew what he was up to; what if he kills me next time just to keep it quiet?"

Alucard kept his scowl, glaring at him. He wasn't sure what Luther was going on about, and he really didn't want to think about any of the things he'd just mentioned. But Luther didn't look like he was about to stop.

"I bet he still hasn't told you why he was so distant for *months*, has he?"

"Not zhat zhis is your business, but 'e 'as told me, and—"

"Let me guess: he was in this Eltaria place helping his people? If that were true, why did he take as long as he did to finally bring them here? Why not do it the moment he knew they weren't safe there? Doesn't it all seem a little weird?"

"No," Alucard muttered. "Bringing zhem 'ere vas a last vesort—"

"Probably because he was afraid you might find out he's been sleeping with one of the people you brought back for him."

"Vhat?" Alucard questioned, frowning. Familiar angst gripped him the moment he heard those words leave Luther's mouth. All his past anxiety returned in a tiny moment, all his worry and confusion—but he didn't want to think about it; he didn't want to let the thought that Zalith might have been seeing someone else warp his thoughts. He'd already accepted that Zalith had been busy trying to save his people from Adellum. He hadn't been spending his time and giving his attention to someone else. Zalith wasn't like that…was he?

Luther took a deep breath and sighed as he shook his head. "Ever since you told me about Zalith being so weird and distant, I made it my personal mission to try and help you, to try and find out what was going on—"

"I zidn't ask you—"

"It doesn't matter whether you asked me or not, Alucard. You're my friend, and when you're in pain, all I want to do is help you," he explained calmly. "So, when Zalith's people arrived, I started asking around. I stumbled across a uh…Danford—"

A sour expression instantly appeared on Alucard's face. That name made him feel sick.

Luther frowned skeptically. "I guess you already know about him. I had a conversation with the guy; he told me that when he first started dating Zalith, he was so kind and attentive, but eventually, he became a cold, rude piece of shit that didn't deserve him. It looks like the same is about to happen here. He got what he needed from you, right? You helped his people out of Eltaria—one of those people being the guy he's investing his time and attention into behind your back. What could he possibly need you for now?"

Alucard scowled again and looked down at his desk. He knew that Luther was trying to accuse Zalith of being unfaithful, but Alucard just wouldn't believe it. He'd known Zalith for three years now and he never felt like he'd do something as awful as sleep with someone behind his back. The demon was still attentive and affectionate; even though he was dealing with his trauma, Zalith always seemed to make sure that he was okay.

There was no way Zalith could do all of that and have time and space to cheat on him at the same time. Surely, he would have cracked by now.

"I zon't know vhat you're trying to prove, and I'm sure you're only trying to do because you can't accept zhat Zaliv just 'anded your ass to you, but Zaliv isn't doing anyving zhe slightest bit suspicious, and 'e isn't using me," he said sternly.

Luther scoffed. "I see he's wormed his way back in—"

"Vhy are you so concerned vith zhis?!" Alucard then snapped, standing up.

"I…something's going on, and—"

"Noving is going on!" Alucard insisted, watching as Luther started to cower. "Get zhe fuck out of my vace bevore I break vhat's levt of yours," he growled, slumping back down into his seat.

Staring at him, Luther frowned and slowly shook his head. "I'm sorry. I just…want you to be happy, and even now, you don't seem happy."

"Vhy does my 'appiness concern you?" Alucard muttered, unsure why Luther persisted.

"Because you're my friend. I've known you for centuries, and how long has *he* known you? A few years? Do you *really* know him, Alucard? From what I've seen and heard, he's one of these people who only tell you what they want to tell you; they'll tell you enough so that you think you know them, but in reality, you don't. You didn't know he's got like…eight other demon marks on him, did you?"

Eight demon marks? He knew what a demon mark was; it was an ethos trace that demons could leave on someone when they suspected that they might be mates but imprinting hadn't yet occurred. *Eight* demons had thought that Zalith was their mate?

Luther continued, "And that he might not actually be totally gay. Varana's told me that she's seen him naked countless times, so who's to say he hasn't slept with her, too? Maybe that's why she's so obsessed with him and hates to see him fucking around with other men—especially her brother," he said with a sour tone. "The point is, none of us can be sure if what he's saying is the truth or not. I've also been convinced that once he's tired of you, there's going to be nothing stopping Lucifer from finding you."

Alucard…just didn't want to think about it. He didn't want to think about Zalith's absence; he didn't want to think about Varana or demon marks or all of the people Zalith had been with and abandoned before. He didn't want to sit and worry that he might one day end up being left on his own, too. All he wanted was to be happy, the kind of happy he felt when he and Zalith first started dating. He wanted the serenity, the joy that came with knowing that today was another day he'd get to spend with Zalith.

But now he woke up with a quiet, clawing fear that today might be the last day he got to see him; not because Zalith would leave, but because he himself couldn't deal with the confliction anymore. Zalith had been gone for so long, and Alucard had no idea where he was going or who he was seeing, and as much as he tried to convince himself that it was okay—that it didn't matter because Zalith was there now—he couldn't ignore the lingering sadness. He felt so alone, so lost, and so confused…and Zalith hadn't been there for him.

He shook his head, sighing as he picked up his ice cream to see if there was any left, but the tub was empty. So, he placed it back on his desk and frowned at his arms. "You're telling me vings I alveady know," he said, not much motivation left to defend himself or Zalith. "I know Zaliv enough to know 'e isn't doing and 'asn't done vhat you suspect. I get zhat you zon't like 'im, but you zon't 'ave to try to convince people zhat 'e zoesn't deserve zhe people in 'is life," he mumbled tiredly. "Stop concerning yourselv vith my life and move on vith your own. You are 'ere to do an actual job, not to play investigator. Zhis vill be zhe *last* time I varn you to keep your nose out of my life, or you vill be zhe next corpse Attila is deconstructing."

Luther frowned in what looked like astonishment. "Alucard, I—"

Just then, the door to Alucard's office opened. Both the vampire and Luther looked at it and stared at Zalith. The demon stood there, now fully clothed, leaning against the doorframe with a scowl on his face as he crossed his arms, waiting.

With an irritated sigh, Luther turned his head and looked back at Alucard. "You can't just tell someone to stop caring and expect it to happen," he said. Then, he stood up, gripping his left side as he grunted painfully; the injuries he received obviously hadn't fully healed yet. "I'll see you tomorrow."

Alucard rolled his eyes and watched as Luther made his way over to the door. Zalith just glared at the man and didn't move out of the way to let him through.

"Can you move?" Luther grumbled irritably, stopping in front of him.

"There's plenty of room for you to squeeze by," Zalith replied.

Luther scowled impatiently before abruptly shoving Zalith aside. The demon reacted swiftly, shoving Luther back with equal force. The injured man fell to the floor with an angered snarl but quickly scrambled to his feet, ready to fight back. As Luther swung a punch, Zalith stepped forward and caught his fist, crushing it in his grip. Luther growled and shrieked in pain, but he threw his other hand forward. Zalith intercepted it just as easily, breaking that hand as well.

Alucard was quite sure that Luther was going to end up dead, so before he could attack Zalith again, the vampire swiftly moved behind him and snatched the back of his suit, pulling him away from Zalith, who was standing ready to defend himself.

Luther struggled and grunted but calmed down as Alucard snarled in irritancy.

"I zon't know vhy you 'ave to keep acting like children," Alucard growled as he pulled Luther back.

Luther grunted painfully, holding both his broken hands in front of himself as an agonized grimace lingered on his face.

But then, not at all interested in talking to him for a moment longer, Alucard threw Luther out into the hall. "Get zhe fuck out of 'ere bevore I kill you myselv."

With a horrified look on his face, Luther dragged himself away, leaving Alucard and Zalith alone. He'd sustained enough injuries for one day.

As Luther dragged himself away, Alucard slowly turned his head and set his eyes on Zalith.

"I'm sorry," Zalith said sadly.

Alucard sighed as he turned around and headed back over to his desk. The demon followed, and as Alucard sat down, Zalith sat in one of the seats in front of him. Alucard didn't exactly know what to say or think right now; so much had happened and been said that all he really wanted to do was sit there and do nothing.

But Zalith had obviously come to talk. "Can we talk about the things Luther said?" he asked, staring at him.

"Vhy?" Alucard mumbled. Clearly, Zalith had been listening, but Alucard had no questions.

"Because I heard him talking about a lot of things that aren't true and I'd like to clear things up," the demon explained.

He might as well let Zalith talk if it would make *him* feel better. Alucard felt nothing right now. He just wanted to be by himself, but if Zalith needed to explain, then he'd let him. "Okay."

Zalith sighed quietly. "I'm *not* cheating on you, Alucard. I would never cheat on you, and if you feel insecure about that, then I understand because I know I've been different these past few months, and if you want to look through my mind, you can. I have nothing to hide from you. I'd never seek anything like that with anyone because I love you; you're everything I need."

Alucard waited, taking his eyes off Zalith to stare down at his lap.

"And I'm not using you. You mean far too much to me for me to ever be able to use you for my own personal gain," he continued. "Even if you were some poor, unimportant deadbeat living in the slums or on the street, I'd still feel exactly the same way I do about you now. I don't want anything from you but your love and attention. As for Lucifer, Damien, Lilith, and whoever else might want you, them finding and taking you from me is a very real fear of mine, and even if somehow things did become bad and we did have to end this…I'd never betray the trust you have in me and turn you in like that," he insisted.

"I know," Alucard mumbled.

Zalith frowned sadly. "Good. As for Varana…she and I have *never* slept together. I was gay long before I met her, and I'm not going to change that for her—ever, no matter what she might like to think."

Alucard then frowned, glancing at him. "Is strange…'ow close you are vith 'er. She vas devastated vhen she saw you imprinted on me, almost as if she vasn't expecting zhat to ever 'appen, as if she expected vone day you *vould* change."

"We were both rather co-dependent for a very long time, and I think that somewhere along the way she decided that she and I would end up together despite all the evidence that said otherwise. I've turned her down on so many occasions, but she doesn't seem to understand that she and I will never happen. This is why I was hesitant to tell her about the imprint in the first place because I knew that she'd have a meltdown. But she handled it a lot better than I expected."

Alucard nodded, still staring down at his lap. It seemed as though Zalith hadn't immediately told her to avoid conflict; he was just going to have to accept that. After all, he didn't know Varana all that well, so who was he to say that it would have been better if Zalith told her sooner?

"As for the other people who marked me, they did so despite me displaying questionable behaviour because they idealized me and chose to ignore reality and what was actually going on. I completely broke things off with those people after I found out what happened, and all their marks are gone now because they're all dead. I never marked any of them—obviously, since my imprint is on *you*. I genuinely did not love any of them, and you're the only person who will ever have it—and the only person I *want* to have it."

Staring at his lap, Alucard tried to work out what to say. The sadness he felt in response to Zalith's absence was worsening by the day despite Zalith being right here with him, and the things Luther said made him feel sadder. He knew Zalith hadn't been seeing anyone else—at least he thought so, anyway. He *did* trust Zalith, and he loved him. He knew Zalith loved him, too; why would he be so possessive and protective if he didn't? Why would he go out of his way to explain himself if he was just going to toss him away onto a pile of unwanted men?

Alucard wasn't convinced that Zalith would be unfaithful; what he *was* convinced about was that Zalith might again one day forget to tell him something, that he would continue to keep things from Varana to save an argument. They could be getting married tomorrow and Zalith probably still wouldn't have told Varana, lest she had a meltdown. If Alucard had a friend as close to him as Varana was to Zalith, she would have been the first person he told about imprints the moment it happened, but Zalith hadn't told her, so either Varana wasn't as important to Zalith as she seemed—which was doubtful—or having imprinted on the vampire didn't really mean that much to Zalith as Alucard had thought.

The vampire sighed, glancing at Zalith, who was waiting for him to say something. He couldn't help but wonder what other things Zalith hadn't yet told him or Varana, and the more he thought about it, the sadder it made him feel. He also felt somewhat pressured by Zalith being right in front of him, waiting for him to say something. What *could* he say?

"Alucard, you need to say something," Zalith then said with a worried frown.

"Vhat do you vant me to say?" Alucard replied. "Zhat zhis is okay?"

"No," Zalith said sullenly. "I want you to tell me your thoughts. I want you to tell me how you feel about this situation so we can work through it," he insisted. "I'm sorry you have to keep hearing about my past and all the things I've done. If I could undo all of it, then I would so that we don't have to keep going through this all the time. I'm not that person anymore, Alucard, and if I have to prove it to you somehow, then I will because I love you—I love you so much, and I don't want this to keep coming between us."

"I zon't veally care about your past, Zaliv," Alucard said, frowning. "You could 'ave fucked my dad vor all I care. Vhat I *do* care about is zhe 'ere and now. You levt me sitting avound 'ere vor months to vear and vonder vhere you vere and vhat you vere doing. You made me vink you zidn't vant or need me anymore. I never velt so alone. And even now zhat you're 'ere, I still can't seem to vorget vhat 'appened. Vor all I knew, you *could* 'ave been seeing somevone else. I trusted you veren't, but I eventually started to veel stupid about zhat, too," he explained, unable to keep it to himself for Zalith's sake anymore. The sadness was only going to build, and he felt it was time he not only let Zalith know just how sad he was, but himself, too.

Staring at him, Zalith's frown became sadder. "I'm so sorry I did that to you, Alucard," he started; there was distress in his voice *and* on his face. "I don't know why I'm like this. I've just always been this way, but I don't want to do it to you again, and I'm going to make an effort to change because you're the most important thing in my life. Even when I was working all the time, you were still the only thing I could think about. I think that I isolated myself from you in order to punish myself for not sorting out my work problems as quickly as I wanted to, but it obviously not only punished me, but you as well, and I'm so, *so* sorry," he insisted sadly. "And I always kissed you every morning before I left, too."

Alucard looked down at his lap again. He knew Zalith was sorry, but that didn't take the sorrow away. What happened had happened, and Zalith couldn't undo it. Alucard had been and felt so alone for so long that he'd become used to it. Even *now*, even though Zalith was back and things were just how they had been, Alucard felt that maybe he shouldn't let things return to how they were. Perhaps he shouldn't allow himself to become as attached to Zalith as he had been. For all he knew, Zalith could become distant and busy again, and Alucard didn't want to feel the pain of that all over again. He had once learnt to enjoy his solitude, and maybe it was time to learn to do that again. As much as he loved Zalith, and as much as he loved to be in his presence and receive his attention, maybe it would be better if he learnt to live without it for a few hours.

He didn't want to think about it all with Zalith staring at him, though. Zalith's despondent stare would make him change his mind, and that was something he felt he strongly didn't want to do. He loved Zalith—more than anything—and his attention and affection meant so much to him, but an overabundance of it these past few days hadn't banished his sadness, and he felt it wouldn't ever erase the pain he'd felt.

Perhaps this was some kind of sign that he needed to learn to live without Zalith being around all the time. After all, Zalith was bound to get busy with his work again someday, and Alucard couldn't let that distract him from his own work *or* his happiness. So, he'd have to learn to enjoy his solitude a little more—he had hobbies, he had work—all things he could do here and there so that when Zalith became busy, he'd have things to do to keep him from feeling devastated about Zalith's lack of attention. It hurt to think about it, to keep himself from spending every minute of every day with the man he loved, but it would be better for the both of them if he didn't rely on Zalith's attention as much as he did.

"Do you want me to leave?" Zalith then asked.

Obviously, his silence made Zalith think that he wanted to be alone, and he *did* want to be alone. "Yes," he answered.

Zalith nodded sadly. "Okay," he said.

Then, without another word, the demon got up and walked out of Alucard's office, leaving him on his own to think.

# Chapter Fifty-Three

## A Shattered Ego

| **Luther** |

L uther struggled to wrap his broken hands in bandages, the task nearly impossible with both of them fractured. He'd managed to painfully snap his bones back into place, but the gruesome wounds where the bones had pierced through his skin were still raw and unhealed. He couldn't bear to look at the revolting injuries inflicted by a man he so deeply despised. Determined to cover them up, he persevered despite the difficulty and pain, driven by a need to hide the evidence of his suffering. The last thing he needed was for the people on the ship to see and think that he was weak and pathetic.

He'd also managed to clean his face; his broken nose was somewhat healed, but just like his hands, his face was covered in bruises. And all because of that fucking demon.

He snarled irritably, the very thought of Zalith making him furious—

An abrupt knock came at his door.

Luther sharply turned his head, scowled out through his bathroom door, and gritted his teeth in anger. "What?!"

"It's Danford. Can I come in?" the nervous werewolf whom Luther recently seduced called from outside his door.

Rolling his eyes, Luther looked down at his half-wrapped hands and sighed. He could use some help… and maybe a distraction. Usually, he'd find himself debating it for a few moments, but for some reason, he felt no need to question whether he really wanted company or not when it came to Danford.

So, he sighed and nodded. "Yep," he called.

As the door opened, Luther glanced to his left and watched the blonde-haired man make his way into his room.

"I heard you were hurt… and I just wanted to make sure that you're okay," Danford said, looking around to try and locate Luther. But the moment he set his eyes on him, a horrified frown appeared on his face. He quickly made his way over and ogled his wounds. "W-what happened?" he asked, holding out his hands as if he was going to take hold of one of Luther's, but he hesitated.

"Your psycho boss," Luther grumbled, looking back down at his hands as he tried to wrap them up.

Danford stared in confliction. "Did…you piss him off?" he asked unsurely.

"No," he scoffed. "All I did was tell him that I was concerned about Alucard, and this is what I get," he lied. Of course, he wasn't going to tell anyone how he'd not got a single hit off on Zalith; he didn't even want to think about it.

"He did all of this to you just because you tried to help them?" he asked in disbelief.

Luther's irritancy grew with Danford's clear refusal to believe him. "He's not the fucking saint all of you here think he is, Danford," he snapped, glancing at him. "He's a dirty little liar and a sneaky, rude degenerate. He did this to me because I saw through his lies, and he didn't want me to tell Alucard."

"Uh…Alucard is…Aleksei, right?" he asked unsurely.

"Yes…" Luther said, frowning.

"You're lucky he didn't kill you," he then said worriedly as he moved a little closer to Luther.

"He's lucky *I* didn't kill *him*," Luther grumbled, allowing Danford to take hold of his hand to help him wrap the bandages around it.

Danford frowned, glancing up at him. "Is there anything I can do to help you feel better?"

"No," he grumbled, pulling his hand back as Danford finished tying the bandage around it.

"Are you sure?" he asked in concern.

Irritated, Luther sighed and started to try and finish wrapping his other hand. "I'll be fine," he mumbled.

"Well," Danford said quietly, "if you need anything, just let me know; it's not gonna be easy to do things with no hands."

Luther finished wrapping up his other hand. "Yeah," he mumbled. Then, he moved past Danford and made his way over to his bed.

He sat down, sighing deeply as he tried to ignore the lingering pain of his wounds. Every time he felt the discomfort, all he could think about was that repulsive demon and how much he hated him. But what use was sitting around here thinking angrily to himself? He felt as if he should be back up at Alucard's house trying to convince him that Zalith didn't deserve him. However, he'd not like any more injuries, so he felt he'd wait to heal first.

Danford nervously sat beside him, eyeing him up and down. A small silence fell over them for a few moments until the man cleared his throat quietly. "Now probably isn't a great time, but… can I ask you something?" he asked, looking over at the door and then back at Luther.

"Go for it," he muttered, resting his back against the headboard as he tried to make himself comfortable.

"Is uh…" he paused as an anxious expression appeared on his face. But when his eyes met Luther's again, he frowned unsurely. "Is… Varana going to kill me?" he asked with a nervous laugh.

Luther frowned and scoffed in amusement. "Why would she want to kill you?" he asked as if he didn't already know how irritated Varana had been about finding them together.

"Because she saw us yesterday…. She's kinda crazy, and from what I know, she doesn't really like to share."

With an entertained grunt, Luther shook his head. "She isn't gonna kill you. You'll be fine," he assured him.

Danford sighed in relief. "I've been looking over my shoulder ever since," he said. Then, he looked at Luther. "So… what are you two, then?"

He shrugged. "I fucked her a couple times… that's about it," he said—although she'd made him commit to her, he didn't take it seriously. He didn't want to date just one woman, least of all one as bitter as Varana.

"Oh, good. I've been worried that I might have hurt your relationship or something."

"If anything," Luther said with a smirk, "I've been worried that *she* might have caused unnecessary tension between you and I."

Danford frowned shyly and looked down at his lap. "Oh… well… now that things are cleared up, things are good on my end. What about you?"

Luther shrugged. "Nothing worth mentioning has changed."

"Cool," Danford said, smiling.

After another short moment of silence, Danford looked at Luther again. Luther was sure that he was about to resume talking; as much as he wanted to be alone to rest and heal, he didn't feel a need to send him away.

"I… really don't mind helping you out until your hands get better," Danford said. "Do you… heal fast?"

"I'll be fine," he said with a sigh. "I just need a few days to rest."

"Oh, okay," he said, staring down at his lap again—but he quickly set his eyes back on him and frowned in worry. "Are you hurt anywhere else… or just your hands?"

"Nowhere else notable," he mumbled, sure there was no need to mention at least two of his ribs had been broken.

"Okay, so… you can like… still kiss and stuff… that's cool," he mumbled.

With an amused smile, Luther said, "I guess I can…. Why? Are you interested?"

Danford chuckled. "Yeah."

Luther smiled but then turned to look away from Danford. Usually, he'd find himself jumping at a chance to seduce and have fun with him—with *anyone*. But his recent fight with Zalith and Alucard's lack of care for his injuries left him feeling irritated…and despondent. He just wanted Alucard to care—to see that *he* cared. But it was beginning to seem as though Zalith had dug his claws so deep that Alucard had become blind to the facts. Those facts were that Zalith was a manipulative, toxic asshole, and Luther was much better suited for Alucard. He'd take care of him better than anyone ever could, especially Zalith. But how was he going to get Alucard to see that? How was he going to get past the lies that Zalith forced into Alucard's head?

He sighed again, glancing at Danford, but before he even had a chance to comprehend it, Danford placed his hand on the side of his neck, leaned in, and kissed him once. They stared at each other for a moment, and as Danford's shy frown started to fade, Luther gripped the man's wrist in his spare hand and made him let go.

"I need to be alone," he muttered.

"Oh." Danford frowned sadly. "Okay…I'll go. Sorry," he mumbled, standing up. "Just…let me know if you need anything."

The disappointment in Danford's voice surprisingly made Luther feel guilty. Danford hadn't done anything wrong; he was just trying to help. But Luther wanted to be by himself right now.

"Maybe we can get a drink later," he said, glancing up at him.

Danford nodded. "Okay, cool," he said as he reached the door. "Let me know," he said, and then he left and closed the door behind him.

Once he was gone, Luther sighed deeply and slowly laid back, staring up at the ceiling. His body hurt, as did his heart. Every time he thought about Alucard and Zalith, angst gripped him tightly. He didn't want Alucard to be with that demon, someone who didn't appreciate him. *He* wanted Alucard; he wanted to take care of him and show him that he didn't need Zalith, that he needed someone who'd known him nearly all his life and knew of his flaws and his past, not some demon who *thought* he knew and understood Alucard; someone who just wanted him until he was no longer interesting.

As he slowly turned onto his side, he scowled. Not too long ago, Alucard seemed so miserable and alone; he'd been so sad that he actually told Luther what was wrong, and that was something Alucard hardly ever did. He'd been abandoned and left to worry, but now, suddenly, Alucard seemed to have forgiven him, and Luther didn't like that at all. Zalith didn't deserve Alucard's forgiveness, nor did he deserve *him*. If Luther couldn't get Alucard to see that—if he couldn't get Alucard to leave Zalith—then he'd have to find another way to get him away from that demon. After all, it wasn't really Alucard's fault, was it? It wasn't his fault that a repulsive, manipulative demon had seduced him and made him believe that he was happy. It was all Zalith, and Luther would do whatever it took to get his friend away from that demon.

# Chapter Fifty-Four

— ⋜ ✟ ⋝ —

## Cats From The Mill

**| Alucard |**

Alucard sighed quietly as he made his way through the forest that surrounded his home. He felt that being at home would only make him fall deeper into his conflicting thoughts, and he didn't want to start overthinking. He thought that getting out of the house for a short while might help him clear his mind.

The vampire stared ahead, walking with his hands in his pockets and a vacant expression on his face. He had no idea where he was going but walking aimlessly seemed to be keeping his thoughts somewhat distracted. The fact that he was going to try and spend a little more time by himself in case Zalith ever got busy again made him feel despondent, though; he loved Zalith's company more than anything, but just like the demon's venom, it was a drug, and he needed to free himself of such an addiction so he'd be able to cope better whenever Zalith wasn't around.

As he continued walking, however, a faint sound caught his attention. It sounded a lot like a small feline's meow. Alucard's curiosity instantly drowned out any other emotion he felt, and as he set his eyes on an abandoned mill up ahead, his intrigue grew.

Alucard made his way out into a small glade, keeping his eyes on the eroded mill a few meters in front of him. It had clearly been abandoned for years; the wood was rotten, the turbines had collapsed, and the number of weeds in the area made it seem like this place had never seen a gardener.

Ignoring the state of the place, Alucard followed a second meow, which was accompanied by many quieter squeaks. He wasn't sure what he might find, but he highly suspected there was a cat or two around there somewhere, and of course, he *had* to find them. He'd already set his eyes on the mill's entrance, and as he stepped inside the shattered building, he searched the rubble and hay for the felines.

He heard a rustle to his left, to his right, and then ahead; the distinct sound of purring then broke the silence, and as Alucard followed it, he discovered a small hay-made nest. Curled up inside the nest was a mother cat with matted and bloody fur. She was panting frantically, laying on her side as all five of her kittens suckled from their mother, kneading their small paws into her belly.

The chocolate-brown feline weakly lifted her head to look up at Alucard as he crouched in front of her. She tried to hiss as a warning but struggled and rested her head back down on the hay. Her similarly coloured kittens looked to be no more than a week old; not one of them had their eyes open yet, and out here, they were all so vulnerable, especially since their mother was injured.

Alucard didn't even have to sit there and think about it. He was taking her and her kittens home. He'd clean and heal her up, look after them, and make sure they were safe and healthy. He wasn't going to leave such a small, innocent creature out here; there were foxes and wild dogs, and he wasn't going to let them become a meal.

But he then hesitated for a moment. Zalith probably wasn't going to let him have them in the house; he'd been so strict about Sabazios, and he was sure that he'd be even stricter with the cats. Alucard didn't care. If he couldn't have them in the house, he'd keep them somewhere on the property. It wasn't like the house wasn't his, too. If Zalith didn't like it, then that was his problem, wasn't it?

Alucard moved closer, preparing to pick the cat up, but as his hands came closer to her, she sharply turned her head, hissed, and swatted her paw at him in defence. He frowned, moving his hands away. He didn't want to scare her or stress her out; he had to gain her trust, and luckily, speaking to and understanding animals was something that came with being a demon.

He slowly reached out, moving his hand to place it over the mother cat's head. "Is okay," he said quietly. "I vant to 'elp you."

The cat looked up at him and slowly calmed down as he placed his hand over her head and petted her. Alucard didn't want to leave her or her babies outside for too long, so he didn't waste time picking her up and cradling her in his arms; he picked up each of the five kittens, placing them onto her belly. Then, he stood up and made his way out of the mill, making sure not to walk too fast in case he startled the creatures.

He began his journey home, trying to work out whether he wanted to hide the animals from Zalith or talk to him about it. He'd decide once he was home.

| **Zalith** |

Back at the house, Zalith sat on the stairs in the hall, staring at the front door while he waited for Alucard to return. He heard the vampire leave roughly an hour ago, and that left him with nothing but fear, guilt, and concern. He was sure that Alucard was upset with him—so upset that he had had to leave for a while. Zalith wasn't sure when he might be coming back, but he used his imprint to find out where he was every so often; he wasn't too far away, but the fact that he wasn't in the house made the demon feel sadder.

He rested his chin in his hands. The fear that he ruined his and Alucard's relationship drowned him as each moment without his vampire passed. He left Alucard to wonder and overthink for months, and he hadn't done anything at all to let him know that he was busy with work; he knew that he should have said something, but he didn't, and now, he understood how badly it affected his vampire. Clearly, Alucard was trying to hide how hurt he was, and today, it seemed as though he'd reached a breaking point. It made Zalith feel so disheartened to hear just how much he'd hurt his vampire, and he still didn't know what to do to make it up to him.

Was Alucard going to break up with him? Was Alucard so sad and disappointed that he'd lost hope and faith in him? Had Alucard left to try and work out how he was going to end their relationship?

Zalith didn't want to think about it; he didn't want to lose Alucard. The very thought of having to live without him brought such agony to his heart that he felt like it was breaking. How could he have been such a selfish idiot? He'd become so used to only considering himself before he'd started seeing Alucard that he'd forgotten he couldn't do that anymore. Alucard was so important to him, and he should have known to let him know what was going on rather than leaving him to assume.

He'd ruined it, hadn't he? Of course he had. He'd been purposely ruining his relationships for centuries. Why *wouldn't* it happen subconsciously? He was an idiot for thinking he could do this right. But he wanted it so bad; he loved Alucard so much, but that wasn't enough, was it? He hadn't been there for him, he'd left him to think that he was worthless and unwanted, and despite all of that, Alucard still helped him bring his people to Aegisguard.

He didn't deserve Alucard. Alucard deserved better.


Alucard soon approached the house—Zalith felt his presence become stronger—and the closer the vampire got to the front door, the faster Zalith's anxious heart raced.

He slowly stood up when he heard the door unlock. What was going to happen when Alucard saw him? Was he going to tell him that he was leaving? That he couldn't do this anymore? Zalith grimaced in fear, trying his best not to let the angst get to him. Whatever Alucard had to say, he'd take it calmly.

But as the vampire entered the house and closed the door behind him, an unfightable urge to run to him hit Zalith *hard*. He made his way over and threw his arms around

Alucard before he could utter a sound; the demon embraced him tightly, so tightly as though to never let him go, even if that was what Alucard wanted.

Eventually, though, he let go and stepped back so that he could stare at his vampire. "Where did you go?" he asked worriedly.

Staring at him, Alucard shrugged slightly. "Vor…a valk," he answered, but there was an almost unsure tone to his voice. "By…zhe lake."

Zalith frowned. Why was he being suspicious? "What happened?" he asked, but with dread still in his heart. He had no idea what Alucard was about to say next, and he felt as if he should prepare for the worst.

"Noving," Alucard mumbled, looking away.

His anxiety increased. "It doesn't seem like nothing."

"Is noving," Alucard insisted as he started walking off. "Vhat's vor dinner—"

Zalith gently snatched his arm and stopped him. "Tell me," he insisted softly; Alucard's attempt at changing the subject made the anxiety unbearable.

Alucard frowned and pulled his arm free. "Is noving," he repeated sternly. "I just vent vor a valk."

He didn't like how evasive the vampire was being, but he didn't want to start an argument. He didn't have the strength right now. So, he sighed and said, "Okay."

The vampire then scowled. "Vhy are you mad?"

"Because you're not telling me something, and given our last conversation, I'm assuming it's something that I'm not going to like," he explained calmly.

"'As noving to do vith our last conversation."

"Then what is it?"

For a few moments, Alucard stared at him, glanced away, and then looked back at him. Obviously, he was debating with himself. But eventually, he sighed and shrugged. "I vill show you," he mumbled.

Zalith frowned. "Thank you," he said, but his dread didn't fade. What was Alucard going to show him? What did he need to show him that had him acting so strange and suspicious?

He followed Alucard outside and towards the barn. He felt a little less anxious about what the vampire might have been doing, but he couldn't keep himself from wondering…what was Alucard hiding out here? What was so secret that he had to evade his questions? He wasn't sure, but he was obviously about to find out once they reached the barn. *That* was where Alucard was leading him.

The demon silently followed Alucard to the back of the barn. He frowned when the vampire stopped by one of the paddocks and pulled the gate open, and then, he stepped aside to reveal what he'd been hiding.

Laying on a bed of hay were six chocolate-brown cats, one mother and her five kittens. Zalith was so suddenly overwrought with confusion. Was that what Alucard was hiding from him? Why?

Zalith then smiled discreetly. He thought it was cute that Alucard found the cats; he knew how much he loved animals, but then…dread outweighed his adoration. Alucard was going to want to bring them into the house, wasn't he? But…why did the vampire feel like he had to hide them from him?

With a frown on his face, he looked at Alucard. "Why were you hiding this from me?"

Staring down at the cats, Alucard shrugged. "I vas sure you vouldn't let me 'ave zhem."

Zalith felt a little uncomfortable. The animals in front of him were dirty, and their fur was matted. Clearly, they were feral, outside cats that Alucard probably rescued from somewhere. "Well…you can have whatever you'd like, baby, but…these are feral barn cats—"

"Zhey're not veral," Alucard said with a pout. He then crouched and petted the mother cat's head. "Zhey're vriendly."

Still uncomfortable, Zalith shook his head. "Alucard…what if they have fleas or mites? We don't want that anywhere near our—"

"Zhey zon't 'ave vleas," Alucard interjected, glancing up at him. "Or mites."

"Then why do they look like that?"

"Like vhat?"

"Scruffy, Alucard."

The vampire glanced up at him again and scowled. "Because zhey vere living in some old shack, and I vasn't going to leave zhem zhere," he argued.

"What shack?" Zalith asked, confused.

"In an old, abandoned mill."

"Near the lake?"

"Not zhat var vrom zhere," Alucard confirmed, looking down at the cats again.

For a moment, Zalith frowned reluctantly. He knew there was an old mill on his property, but he wasn't aware of any cats having made it their home. "If they were all the way out there, they're probably dirty at the very least," he said. He really didn't want those animals in the house, and he'd do his best to try and convince Alucard away from the idea of keeping them.

Alucard pouted, still petting the mother. "Vell…I could clean zhem, you know…if I could bring zhem inside."

"Inside…the house?" Zalith asked in dread.

"Yes, inside zhe 'ouse," he confirmed.

"Our house? The house *we* live in?"

"Yes, Zaliv. In our 'ouse vhere ve live. Zhat's vhere I vant to take and clean zhem."

Zalith's conflicted, dread-filled frown didn't fade. Dirty animals inside the house where he worked, lived, ate, and slept? Six feral cats running around…leaving fur everywhere, clawing up the furniture. He shuddered at the thought. "What about the dog?" Maybe that would keep Alucard from wanting to bring them inside. "I'm sure it's not a good idea to have cats around him. What if something happens?"

"Vell…Sabazios isn't allowed in our voom, so…ve can keep zhem in—"

Zalith laughed nervously. "Baby…no," he said, unable to explain how astonished he felt. He didn't want these animals in their house, let alone their *bedroom*.

"But vhy?" Alucard asked, looking up at him again.

"Because we can't have sixteen stray, dirty cats that we know nothing about in our bedroom, Alucard. With our things, with our furniture—"

"Zhere are only six of zhem," Alucard exclaimed. "I'll take care of zhem and keep zhem clean and teach zhem to be'ave."

He sighed quietly. "Alucard, you're very caring and kind, and I love that about you, but I can't have them in our bedroom. I'm sorry."

The vampire huffed stubbornly and sat down, crossing his arms and his legs. "Vine, zhen I vill sleep out 'ere vith zhem," he said firmly.

"You're not sleeping in a barn, either," Zalith denied.

"Zhen let me bring zhem inside. Zhey're not safe out 'ere," he insisted sadly.

With his confliction increasing, Zalith sighed, shook his head, dragged his hand over his face, and looked back down at Alucard. Obviously, the vampire was attached to the family of cats already. Zalith didn't want to try and separate them, not only because Alucard clearly wanted them, but because he felt like he should be a whole lot more lenient with Alucard and what he wanted right now. He'd forced months of sadness onto his vampire that the least he could do was let him keep some cats…. Some dirty, feral cats that had been God knows where….

He sighed again. "You can keep them in one of the *spare* rooms for now, but not in *our* bedroom. And I don't want them roaming around the house, especially not until a vet has checked them over at the very least," he insisted. "God only knows what diseases they could be carrying—"

"I vant zhem in *our* voom," Alucard said sternly; his tone made it clear that he wasn't going to argue about it anymore.

Zalith almost choked on his words. "No, Alucard. I'm sorry, but I just can't," he denied, shaking his head and staring down at the vampire.

"Vine," Alucard said, taking his eyes off him again. "Zhen I'm staying 'ere."

"*Why* do you need them in our room, Alucard? The spare rooms are just as nice, and you can visit them whenever you'd like."

"Because I vant to look avter zhem. I vant to keep an eye on zhem and make sure zhey're safe all zhe time. I zon't vant to 'ave to travel up and down to zhe second vloor."

"So, you're going to just sit in our bedroom all day?"

"So vhat if I am?" the vampire sneered, glancing up at him. But then he set his eyes on the cats. "No, I von't be staying in zhere all day, but zhey vill," he said, nodding at the felines. "Zhey vill be safe in zhere."

Zalith wasn't going to give in yet. "They'll be just as safe in one of the spare bedrooms. Or, better yet, in your office *or* your study where they can go up and down the stairs as they please."

"And I guess I'll be just as comvortable sleeping in vone of zhe spare rooms, zhen."

The demon scoffed in astonishment. Was Alucard *seriously* going to threaten him with sleeping in whatever room he made him put the cats in? He didn't want to lose the comfort of sleeping next to his vampire every night, and Alucard's stubbornness was making it quite clear that Zalith was going to have to give in or face a whole lot of cold, lonely nights.

He sighed deeply, dragging his hand over his face again. "Does this really mean that much to you?"

"Yes, because zhey're vulnerable and need to be taken care of."

With the thought of sleeping alone weighing heavy on his mind, Zalith exhaled deeply and deadpanned, losing his energy to fight. "Fine," he mumbled. "Let's go before I change my mind." Then, he turned around and swiftly left the barn. He was going to regret this, wasn't he?

| **Alucard** |

A victorious smile clung to Alucard's face. He patted the mother cat, listening to Zalith's fading footsteps; not only would he be able to keep the cats, but he'd also get to have them in their bedroom.

However, he wasn't done yet. Zalith often made a point of making him feel uncomfortable in a humorous way, and Alucard felt it was high time to return the favour. It was clear that Zalith had a particular aversion to cats; out of all the animals Alucard had introduced to him, felines seemed to provoke the strongest reaction. Alucard found this amusing and decided to exploit it. He couldn't help but smirk at the thought of turning the tables on the demon, savouring the anticipation of Zalith's inevitable discomfort.

He looked over his shoulder, setting his eyes on the demon, who was waiting by the barn door. "Vas 'ard to get zhem all 'ere alone," he called. "I need you to carry eizer zhe mom or 'er babies," he said as Zalith turned to face him.

A deeply uncomfortable look struck Zalith's face as he took a moment to think to himself. He frowned, looking down at the floor, glancing all around the barn until, once again, he dragged his hand over his face and sighed. "Fine. I'll take the kittens," he said, walking back over to him.

"Vait, *I* vant to carry zhe kittens," Alucard refused.

Zalith frowned hesitantly. "Won't the mother just follow behind if we carry her children?"

"No, you 'ave to carry 'er inside; she's vulnerable, too," he insisted.

"What creature is going to possibly risk its life by approaching us to get to that...thing?!" he exclaimed, looking down at the mother cat, his eyes a little wide as if he couldn't believe what he was seeing or hearing.

"Vill you just pick zhe cat up?!" Alucard snapped in return, trying not to smile. He found it so amusing seeing just how much Zalith hated the whole situation. They were just cats; what was the big deal?

"I don't...I don't want to touch it," Zalith refused sadly, crossing his arms.

Alucard didn't want to keep arguing. As amusing as it was, the family of felines was still vulnerable, and it was going to get dark soon. So, with an irritated pout, he scooped the family up in his arms the same way he had to transport them from the mill, and then he left the barn.

Zalith followed him out and hurried to catch up with him. "Let me help."

"No," Alucard said with a scowl, glaring ahead as he walked towards the house. "Are you not scared you might catch zhe DeiganLupus bubonic plague or someving?" he sneered.

"Yes..." Zalith said with a frown. "But I won't let you struggle. Let me—"

"No," the vampire snarled, turning his body away so that Zalith couldn't reach the cats. He then started walking faster. Zalith had made it clear that he didn't want them and that he didn't want to help, so Alucard wasn't going to let him act like he'd changed his mind.

The demon caught up with him once more, walking at his side as they approached the front door. "Please promise me you won't let them on our bed," he pleaded.

"I von't let zhem on zhe bed," Alucard muttered.

"Thank you," Zalith said before kissing the vampire's cheek with a loud, annoying smooch.

Alucard pouted. "I'll need to vind zhem a bed, and someving zhey can eat out of— and vings to 'ide in," he explained.

"You could use some of the pillows from the pile in the lounge," Zalith suggested. "They can rip those up as much as they like."

"Zhey von't tear zhem up," the vampire said, glancing at him. "Zhey're cats, not vabid dogs."

"Cats have claws, Alucard. They need to file them down somewhere."

He couldn't argue with that.

"Rather the pillows than the furniture," the demon added.

Alucard stopped by the door. "Vhatever," he grumbled, waiting for Zalith to open it. As the demon led the way in, Alucard looked down at the cats. "Ve'll need to tell zhe kitchen staff to make vood vor zhem. Zhe kittens vill need vood soon; maybe a vew veeks."

"What do they eat?" the demon asked, closing the door behind Alucard.

"Zhey'll eat vish."

Zalith nodded, walking beside him as he headed for the stairs. But then a look of dread appeared on his face. "Are they…going to be eating and doing their business in our room, too?"

Alucard frowned at him. "No…I'll teach zhem to go outside."

"How are they supposed to open doors to go out—"

"Ve can leave a vindow open," Alucard mumbled irritably, leading the way upstairs.

They travelled upstairs in silence, but once they reached their bedroom, the demon started to laugh quietly to himself.

Alucard scowled and turned his head to look at him as he walked over to the window. "Vhat?" he grumbled.

Zalith smirked at him. "Are you going to kick them out when we have sex like you did with the dog?" he asked amusedly.

Embarrassed, Alucard scowled and stopped in front of the window. "Who said ve're even going to 'ave sex anymore?" he mumbled, sure that saying such a thing would shut Zalith up and stop him from laughing. But as he looked over at the demon, he saw nothing but a gravely concerned look on his face.

"What?" Zalith asked in what sounded like disbelief—maybe even panic. "Are you joking?" he asked nervously.

"Am I?" Alucard asked challengingly, seeing that he had indeed startled the demon.

"Stop," Zalith said with a frown. He then waited for Alucard to answer, but the vampire crouched and placed the mother cat and her kittens on the floor. "I can't tell if you're joking or not."

With a quiet sigh, Alucard stood up straight and looked at him. "Vhy does zhat concern you so much?" he asked curiously.

Zalith still had a discontent, worried look on his face. "Because I want it, and I need it—and I so happen to like having sex with you."

Alucard frowned, ignoring his quickly increasing embarrassment. "Need?"

"Yes," the demon replied with a desperate tone.

"Vhy?" he asked, looking down at the cats.

The demon kept his eyes on him. "Because I'm an incubus," he revealed. "I can't just not have sex. I can go without it, but it's not a recommendable experience."

Staring down at the cats, Alucard's frown became a perturbed one. What Zalith just said unearthed something that had long been buried in his mind; he was still recovering from the alterations forced upon his memories, and whenever some information or a memory that was once hidden resurfaced, it felt just like this, like someone had reached inside his head and grasped hold of his thoughts.

He'd heard rumours and stories floating around Damien's castle when he was much younger. Incubi were a genetic mutation; they were basically male succubi, and like succubi, they descended from Lilith's bloodline. They were a very rare species of demon because Lilith had never intended for them to exist, and it might even be so that Zalith was the only one.

How had he not pieced it together? Zalith always had a very high sex drive, but Alucard simply thought it was because he was a demon. It didn't matter, though. Incubus or not, Zalith was still Zalith. It just made more sense now.

He glanced at him. "You never told me zhat bevore."

Zalith frowned. "Oh…I thought it was obvious," he said, smiling. "Sorry."

Alucard shrugged. "I zon't know any incubi or succubi, so I vouldn't know 'ow to notice."

"Oh," Zalith responded. But then he frowned in concern. "We can still have sex, right?"

With a flustered, almost irritated frown, Alucard looked back down at the cats.

"Baby?" Zalith asked in worry.

The vampire tried his best to hide his face. "Yes," he mumbled.

Zalith then sighed in relief and laughed quietly. "Thank you."

Alucard nodded as he crouched in front of the cats. He found, however, that his curiosity hadn't faded. He didn't know anything about incubi, and now that he was very close with one, he felt that he should perhaps expand his knowledge. After all, what if Zalith ended up needing something from him and he had no idea what to do? The best way to know more would be to ask, but not yet; he needed a short while to gather his thoughts and work out what it was he wanted to know.

With a quiet sigh, the vampire stood up and looked at him.

"We should have a vet come here as soon as possible," the demon said before Alucard could say anything. "I'll send someone to fetch one."

"Okay," he mumbled. "Ve can go vor dinner now," he then said, turning around to lead the way out of the room. He was sure that Zalith wasn't at all comfortable with the cats, but he didn't want to listen to him complain anymore. He wanted the cats to stay, and they were going to…no matter what.

# Chapter Fifty-Five

─ ⟨ ✝ ⟩ ─

## Incubi

| **Alucard** |

As the day grew later, Alucard and Zalith sat at the table with their dinner. As usual, the vampire focused more on the night's wine than on the roast beef and vegetables. He didn't feel particularly hungry, but he ate anyway; to his surprise, the meal tasted much better than he had anticipated.

While he sat there, however, he couldn't dismiss the constant worry that the kittens and their mother needed him. He found himself trying to resist the urge to head upstairs and see to them every few moments; he didn't want to scare them or stress the mother out, nor did he wish to irritate Zalith, who very clearly disapproved.

Why? Why didn't Zalith seem very fond of the cats? At first, Alucard thought that maybe it was because they were strays and had been living outside, but the further into their earlier conversation they got, the more he started to believe that Zalith didn't like cats altogether.

He took his eyes off his plate and looked at the demon. "Vhy zon't you like cats?"

Zalith finished what he was eating and set his eyes on him. The demon took a sip of his wine while he clearly pondered, and then he rested his arms on the table and sighed quietly. "My mother used to both breed and collect rare cats; they were her pride and joy. However, she had far too many, and it was a little much to deal with. She and my father came to an agreement that she'd keep her cats in a certain wing of the house because we always had guests over, and it was always a huge ordeal with the cats being in the way.

"When I got into trouble—and that happened *a lot*—I'd often end up talking to my mother in a particular lounge in the wing of the house she kept the cats in. She would be yelling at me, and the cats would be walking around me, touching me, kneading into me. The fur would get all over me, too, and I hated it. That—along with the yelling—pretty much ruined cats for me and made them a rather negative experience. I internalized it, and I hadn't really thought about it until today. It's not…that I don't like them, I would just prefer them not to be near me," he explained slowly.

Alucard frowned as he looked down at his food. Clearly, his assumptions were wrong, and he felt incredibly guilty; first, because he'd told himself that he was keeping the cats no matter what Zalith's opinion was, and again because Zalith's reason for being so against the idea of having the cats there was a rather upsetting reason. He didn't want to be the reason Zalith was uncomfortable or reminded of unpleasant things.

He didn't know much about Zalith's mother, though…or his family. He knew that the demon loved his brother dearly and that his mother wasn't exactly happy with his life choices, but that was it. His lack of understanding made him curious, but that wasn't the point of his current pondering. The cats: he had to decide what he was going to do with them. He didn't want to get rid of them; there was no way he'd put them back outside. But…he wasn't going to keep them if it was going to make Zalith uncomfortable. So, what could he do?

Sipping from his wine, he tried to think of a solution, and the only thing that came to mind was giving the cat family to the veterinarian whom Zalith sent for. An animal expert would be able to take care of them, and once they were older, Alucard could find homes for them. That seemed like the best thing for everyone. He'd know they were safe, and Zalith wouldn't have to deal with them and the discomfort that would come with them being in their house.

"Are you okay?" Zalith then asked, placing his glass down before picking up his knife and fork again.

Alucard glanced at him and nodded, but a curious frown made its way onto his face. "Did…you and your mother not veally get on?"

Zalith laughed slightly as he glanced down at his food. "She didn't particularly get along with anybody, but somehow at the same time, she was everybody's dearest friend. It was strange; I don't quite know how she did it. She was always after me about something because nothing was ever really good enough for her, but we were family, and we all loved each other at the end of the day. Once my brother decided to get married to a lower-class woman, though, she was a lot nicer to me—probably to punish Xurian for breaking her heart. She was a very dramatic woman, my mother."

The vampire scoffed. "She sounds like somevone else ve know," he mumbled.

With an amused laugh, Zalith smiled and sipped from his wine. "She was very much like Varana, but somehow both better and worse at the same time. My mother and Varana were very close, too."

Alucard didn't want to talk about Varana. Her name still brought such distaste to his mouth. Zalith mentioned his father, and the vampire wanted to know more about him, too. "Vhat about your vather? Vas 'e better zhan your mother?"

Zalith placed his glass down and thought to himself for a few moments. "Yes," he answered. "But…he was very strict and wouldn't settle with anything below his standards. It all paid off in the end, though, because my family were all very successful in our ways because of how my father ran things. I learned a lot from him, actually; he was always very stoic and quiet, which was nice because my mother was very loud and talked all the time," he said with a slight smile. "I do miss them," he said with a sigh. "I think that they all would have liked you, though. They would have probably asked about you all the time, inviting you over for the holidays and on the boat trips they used to take."

"Vould zhey?" Alucard asked with a doubtful frown. "I vhought zhey disliked zhe vact zhat you're gay."

The demon shook his head. "My father never really cared; he just didn't like me sleeping around. My mother only cared because she wanted me to marry Varana or one of her rich friends' daughters and have a child to carry on our family's legacy. But having a child can be done regardless; I wouldn't have to marry the woman. My mother was just stubborn and traditional. But *you* are very impressive and much better than the people she had in mind for me, and it would have shut her up," he said, smirking.

Alucard smiled slightly, taking his eyes off Zalith to look down at his food. "Sometimes," he started with a sullen tone in his voice, "I vink about vhat might 'ave been like if I got to grow up vith my mother. Even zhough I never knew 'er, I veel like I miss 'er—is stupid, but...I've never 'ad a vamily, and veels strange to 'ear about ozzer people's vamilies because I 'ave no experience of such a thing," he admitted.

"Do you have any memories of her at all?" Zalith asked quietly.

He shrugged and mumbled, "No. None ozzer zhan vhat ve saw avter my memories vere vecovered."

Zalith moved his hand over Alucard's and frowned sadly. "I'm sorry. We'll be making a lot of good memories going forward, and you'll have so many nice things to look back on," he said with a smile.

The vampire smiled again, glancing at him. "I alveady 'ave so many good memories because of you."

Zalith's smile grew. "What's your favourite?"

Alucard pondered for a few moments. There were so many fond memories he had with Zalith, but his favourite? He couldn't decide on just one. "I vink...vhen ve danced at my party," he answered. "Zhat vas zhe virst time in vhat velt like vorever zhat I velt okay," he admitted. "I veally enjoyed our trip to Avalmoor, and both times ve vent to zhe opera, too. And...vhen you asked me to move 'ere vith you."

Zalith tightened his grip a little on Alucard's hand. "That dance is one of my favourite memories, too, and when we first kissed at your house. I loved the boat trip as well, and when you called my house home before it was our house—that made me feel so happy. I also enjoyed it when you beat up Attila."

He snarled at the thought of that man. "'E deserved zhat."

"He did," Zalith concurred, sitting up straight as he went back to eating his food. "How is he doing these days?"

Alucard shrugged. "I zon't care to ask 'im," he said and returned to his dinner, too.

While they ate, Alucard's thoughts returned to Zalith's family and what he learned not too long ago. He'd been told that Zalith was actually an incubus, an incredibly rare species of demon, and since they'd been touching the subject of Zalith's family, Alucard felt that now was a good time to sate his curiosity.

He glanced at Zalith. "Vere… all your vamily incubi and succubi?"

"My mother was a succubus, but my father and brother weren't incubi. I'm special," he said, smirking.

With an amused smile, Alucard looked down at his plate. "Vill you… tell me about incubi?" he asked, glancing at him again. "I zon't… veally know anyving."

"Of course. What do you want to know?"

Alucard shrugged. "Vell… as much as you vant to tell me."

Zalith nodded and sipped from his wine. He then leaned back in his seat and sighed quietly. "Well, being an incubus… it's much like vampirism, except instead of feeding on blood, I feed on life force. Unlike a vampire, though, I won't starve without it, I'll just feel incredibly exhausted and drained. The energy I feed on… I take it when I'm having sex with someone. I can't control that this energy is being taken from them, but I *can* control how much is being taken so that people don't die. I've also found that having sex helps me regulate my emotions—*and* it helps me to heal much faster, too," he said with a smirk. He then leaned a little closer. "I might also go so far as to say that swallowing your cum is a lot like you drinking my blood—like any vampire drinking blood. There's a lot of life force in it," he said with a sultry tone and that little seductive stare in his eyes.

Flustered, Alucard looked away from him.

Instead of continuing his flirting, though, Zalith sat up straight and said, "It's probably also a large part of why I slept around so much… because my body needed it—especially the emotion regulation because I was always so stressed. But, aside from all of that, even if I wasn't an incubus, I'd genuinely like sex—especially with you, because I love you," he said, smiling. "I feel it's something of a relief that I need it to survive because it's one of my favourite things to do."

Alucard fought the embarrassment and asked, "And zhen… vhat about blood? Does blood do anyving vor you?"

"I'm still a demon, so there's life force in blood; it helps me to heal the way it helps you, but it's not as effective as what I get from having sex or sucking your dick," he said with a smirk.

Sure that his face was turning red, Alucard sipped from his wine and nodded in response; at least now he had a better understanding.

They fell silent again as they ate a little more, but when Alucard glanced at Zalith after a few minutes, he saw a pondering stare on his face. What was he thinking so deeply about?

Zalith glanced at Alucard and caught him looking at him.

The vampire looked away and tried to hide his flustered frown.

But the demon suddenly asked him, "What are you going to do about Luther?"

Alucard frowned. "Vhat do you mean?" he questioned and sipped from his wine.

Zalith laughed slightly as he rested his arms on the table. "It would seem that your friend has feelings for you."

The vampire rolled his eyes and cut at his food with an irritated scowl. "Is just a vampire ving; zhey all vink zhey love me like zhat because I made zhem. Zhey all vant to be noticed, zhey all vant my attention. Clearly, Luther is caught up in zhe idea zhat 'e vants to be vith me like you are because of zhis."

"Well, he told me that I don't deserve you—which I agree with—but he also said that you'd be better off with him *instead* of me and that he'd take care of you the way you deserve to be taken care of. That's why I hit him," he said and then finished his wine.

Alucard frowned in disgust. He wouldn't so much as touch Luther even if he was the last man in Aegisguard. Who the hell did he think he was saying all of that to Zalith?

"I can kill him for you if you'd like," Zalith offered with a smile. "Based on today's performance, I'm sure it'll only take me a minute or two."

The vampire shook his head. "No. I need 'im," he mumbled. If that weren't the case, he'd let Zalith do what he wanted. He knew that the demon wanted to kill him, but right now, he was too involved in making sure that Zalith's people were safe and happy.

"Well," the demon mumbled, "I need him to figure out our boundaries; he didn't seem to quite understand what I meant when I told him he can't just go around opening doors in a house he doesn't own. I want him walking on eggshells," he said with an irritated scowl.

"Luther 'as alvays been a dumbass," Alucard muttered. "You give 'im permission to do someving vonce, and zhen 'e vinks 'e can do all zhe time. But I vill make sure 'e knows not to valk avound like zhis is 'is 'ouse. 'E knows 'is place, and sometimes, I just 'ave to kick zhat back into 'im a vew times."

"Thank you. From what I heard, Luther seems rather dedicated to tearing us apart," he then said with an irritated tone returning to his voice. "He's a tenacious little stick bug, so I'm sure he's going to need a few reminders. And for his sake, it's best I don't have to remind him myself. He's lucky he didn't die after saying the things he said."

Alucard nodded and hummed in agreement as he finished his wine.

"I'm sorry I caused a scene twice today," Zalith then said. "I was just angry."

The vampire sighed as he placed his glass down. "No vone—least of all Luther—is going to tear us apart," he said quietly. "And is vine. Luther deserved vhat 'e got."

Zalith smiled and went to answer—

"I zon't vant to talk about 'im anymore," Alucard interjected. The mere thought of Luther was putting him off what was left of his food.

"Neither do I," Zalith concurred.

They went back to their dinner. The veterinarian would be arriving soon, and Alucard wanted to finish eating before that happened.

# Chapter Fifty-Six

— ⸲ ✝ ⸲ —

## Erwin

**| Zalith |**

When a quiet knock came at the dining room door, Zalith finished what he was eating and then said, "Come in."

Edwin stepped into the room. "Sirs, the veterinarian you requested has arrived. He…uh…*they* are waiting in the hall."

"They?" Zalith questioned, confused.

The butler nodded. He looked a little confused himself.

With a quiet sigh, the demon said, "Thank you. We'll be right out."

As the Butler left, Alucard leaned back in his seat. "Ve can go and deal vith zhat now."

More than happy to get the animal business over and done with, Zalith smiled, nodded, and stood up. He led the way out of the dining room and through to the main hall, but the person sitting on the bench by the door wasn't what the demon was expecting. Of course, this person was an elf, so they were bound to look a little…strange…but *this* elf certainly had him intrigued. Zalith wasn't sure whether that was a good thing or not, though.

The elf had blue hair with a streak of red through the centre, and it was tied into a loose ponytail that rested and hung over the elf's shoulder. Their eyes were almost the same blue as their hair but sparkling pink eyeshadow had been applied around them. The elf came dressed in what looked like a beige bathrobe but with white trousers beneath.

Zalith wasn't sure if that was what an average veterinarian elf would wear, but he felt no need to question it. As long as they knew what they were doing, it didn't matter.

However, when the elf lifted their head to look at him and Alucard as they approached, a startled look of delight quickly appeared on their face—

"Oh, my—Alucard?" the elf called, jumping to their feet, their voice more masculine than Zalith had been expecting. "Is that…you?"

Zalith looked at Alucard, watching as an uncomfortable, dread-ridden expression clung to his face. Did they know each other?

"How…how long has it been?" the elf asked, leaving their briefcase by the bench as they hurried over to hug the vampire.

Surprisingly, Alucard didn't refuse the elf's affection.

"How have you been?" the elf asked, stepping back to gawp at Alucard for a few moments, not at all thrown off by the fact Alucard hadn't reciprocated their hug.

Zalith watched closely, trying to figure out who the elf might be. Obviously, they were the veterinarian, and clearly, they and Alucard knew each other.

Alucard looked close to horrified. "Ervin," he said as calmly as he could, holding out his hand.

Erwin smiled brightly, taking hold of Alucard's hand—but not to shake. The elf pulled the vampire's hand to their face, kissed it, and then let go. "I would have never expected to see you here. When I was called to the Cypress Estate, I was expecting to find yet another average couple with a very average, very expensive sick dog."

"Vight," Alucard said awkwardly.

Erwin smiled and looked at Zalith. "Who's this?" they asked with a smile. "So handsome."

"Thank you," Zalith said, smiling.

"Zhis is uh…Zaliv," Alucard introduced, moving closer to the demon. "'E's…my boyvriend."

A look of surprise appeared on Erwin's face. "Oh, how wonderful," they said, holding out their hand. As Zalith shook it, Erwin set their blue eyes back on Alucard. "My husband and I split up a few years ago. It was very sad, but alas, everything sweet must come to an end," they said with a laugh. Then, they moved a little closer and nudged Alucard's shoulder with their hand. "I always suspected you were gay, Ali. Why didn't you tell me?"

Alucard didn't say anything; he looked a little overwhelmed. It seemed that he hadn't been expecting to meet Erwin again, and judging from what the elf said, it appeared that they and Alucard might have known each other for a long time.

Zalith needed more information, but he had enough to know that Alucard was struggling. So, he moved his arm around the vampire's waist and pulled him closer. "So, you're the veterinarian?" he asked Erwin.

Erwin took their eyes off Alucard and looked up at Zalith. "I am…among other things," they said, sounding as if they were trying to be suggestive.

The demon then smiled irritably; he was losing his patience with this elf already. "What other things?"

"Well, now that you asked…." Erwin smiled and crossed their arms. "I'm a doctor of non-ethos medicines; Alucard brought me here to Nefastus so many decades ago, and

I have ever since been in charge of a rather large operation that distributes non-ethos antidotes and medicinal items to the city and beyond. It brings in *so* much money—not that you need it, hey, Ali." Erwin smirked, nudging Alucard's shoulder again.

Zalith quickly pieced it together. This elf must be *the* Erwin whom Alucard mentioned a few months ago; the same Erwin he once thought about looking for to help with the plans he came up with for Eltaria. He didn't want to think about that right now, though. He kept his eyes on the elf, keeping his arm around Alucard. He didn't *not* like Erwin, but he wasn't going to willingly spend time in their presence.

"Vight," Alucard mumbled with a sigh. "Anyvay, zhere are cats."

"Oh, yes—that's what I'm here for," Erwin said, picking up their briefcase. "Perhaps…now that I know you're back, you might want to have a more personal meeting during the week?"

"Maybe," the vampire mumbled as he turned around to lead the way towards the stairs. He took hold of Zalith's hand, pulling him along with him with what looked like an irritated look on his face.

As they made their way up the stairs, Zalith smiled amusedly. It was funny that Alucard didn't seem to like his own friend; he also admittedly enjoyed the way his vampire had taken his hand, for he was usually the one to take Alucard's. He was curious to know why Alucard didn't seem so fond of Erwin, and he'd certainly make sure to ask him later.

He followed the vampire into their bedroom, and Erwin followed after. Alucard led the way over to where the mother cat and her kittens had been placed and stepped aside so that Erwin could move closer.

"Oh, how sweet," the elf said with a babyish tone, kneeling in front of the cats as they placed their briefcase down beside them. "How old are they?" they asked, looking up at Alucard.

"Maybe a vew days. Zheir eyes aren't open, so zhey can't be too old."

Erwin nodded and looked back down at the kittens. The mother cat started purring as the elf stroked her chocolate-brown fur. "And what is it you need me to do?"

"Ve need you to check zhem vor vleas or mites or anyving 'armvul."

The elf stood up and nodded, staring down at the cats. "Well, I'll check one of the kittens; if one has fleas, I'm sure they all will," they said, picking up their briefcase.

As they went to place their briefcase on the side table, though, Zalith let go of Alucard's hand, seeing that he'd left a bottle of lube where Erwin was about to put their briefcase. "Let me move that for you," the demon said, taking the bottle and placing it in one of the drawers. He then returned to Alucard's side, smirking at the vampire as he hid his embarrassed face.

Erwin looked a little flustered but opened their briefcase and said, "I have the necessary treatment with me if they do have fleas. I can either do it for you or leave it here for you to do."

"Check zhem," Alucard urged.

Nodding, Erwin crouched back down and picked up one of the kittens.

As Erwin got to work, Alucard turned to face Zalith. "I'll go and talk to Luther tomorrow."

Zalith smiled, placing his hands on Alucard's arms. "What are you going to do?" He knew that Alucard wouldn't kill him as he'd like, but he was curious to know how the vampire planned to punish his subordinate.

Alucard shrugged. "I zon't exactly know yet."

"Well," Zalith said, dragging his palms down Alucard's arms to grip his hands, "if you'd like to take me up on my offer—"

The vampire frowned. "I zon't vink 'e needs to die," he said with a disapproving tone.

With a quiet sigh, Zalith shrugged and looked down at Erwin. "Yet," he said.

Alucard rolled his eyes and looked down at Erwin, who turned to look up at them after placing the kitten they'd been looking at back down with its mother.

The elf stood up and crossed their arms. "Well, there's no sign of fleas or any parasites for that matter. Of course, I'd have to do a more in-depth examination—"

"Ve can't 'ave zhem 'ere," Alucard interjected.

Zalith frowned in confusion. Why had Alucard so suddenly decided not to keep the cats? He'd put up such a fight to keep them; he went so far as to say he'd sleep out in the barn to be with them. Why the sudden change? Was he doing this…for him? Because of what he told him about his dislike for cats?

He gripped Alucard's wrist. "Are you sure?"

Alucard shrugged, glancing at him. He then looked back at Erwin. "I'll pay you vhatever vee to look avter zhem until zhey're old enough to go to 'omes."

"Oh, of course." Erwin nodded, glancing down at the cat family. "They'll be very well taken care of."

Zalith tugged slightly on Alucard's wrist so that the vampire would look at him again. "Baby, it's okay. They can stay."

"You can send a veekly bill 'ere or vhatever," Alucard mumbled before looking at Zalith. "Is vine," he said, glancing at the demon. "Zhey'll be better vith somevone who knows vhat zhey're doing."

Zalith could see the sadness in his eyes. He didn't want Alucard to feel like he had to get rid of them for his sake, and part of him wanted to tell him that they could come back when they were older…but he didn't exactly want the cats to come back, so confliction quickly gripped hold of him.

He sighed and set his eyes back on the elf. "Why don't you take them for now, and we'll work out what we want to do with them once they're older."

Erwin nodded. "Of course." Then, from their briefcase, they pulled what looked like a sheet of pressed straw; they waved their hand over it as they pulled it from their case, and in an instant, it morphed into a pet carrier. The elf then kneeled and started to carefully move the cat family one by one into the basket.

Watching as Alucard's stare became sadder, Zalith moved his arm around his shoulders, pulled him closer, and kissed the side of his face.

Once all the cats were in the basket, Erwin closed its door and stood up. "Well, unless there's anything else, I think it would be best I got these babies home," they said, smiling.

"Zhis vay," Alucard said, walking out of Zalith's embrace to lead the way out of their room and into the hall.

Zalith frowned, watching as Alucard led the way out of the room. Was he mad at him? He couldn't escape the thought that he might be, but maybe he was just upset—*obviously,* he was upset. He sighed and hurried to catch up, trying his best not to let his guilt increase. He'd upset Alucard already.

## | Alucard |

Alucard led the way downstairs while trying to ignore the sadness he felt about having to say goodbye to the cat family he'd not even had for a day. He wanted to take care of them, but he didn't want Zalith to feel uncomfortable. The cats really would be better off with a vet, and he was going to miss them, but at least he would know they were safe.

He glanced at Erwin. The elf hadn't changed much over the years, but *he* had, and he wasn't the sociable man he once was. Now, he just wanted to be alone with Zalith; he didn't want to go out for lunch or whatever with someone from years and years ago.

When he reached the front door, he pulled it open. Erwin stepped outside and then turned to face Alucard. Before they spoke, though, Zalith appeared at Alucard's side, and a look of startle stole the elf's smile.

"I...I must say it was quite wonderful to see you again, Ali—and to meet Zalith—so unexpected," the elf said with an excited whisper. "Anyway, I hope we can catch up sometime next week. Either way, you'll hear from me," they said, lifting the cat basket. "Toodle-loo," they called as they turned around and strutted off down the path towards the gates.

With a quiet sigh, Alucard closed the door and turned around. He just wanted to go and lay down. But Zalith lightly gripped his arms and turned him to face him.

"Are you okay?" the demon asked quietly as he placed his right hand on the side of Alucard's face.

Alucard shrugged; he wasn't sure what to say. He didn't want to say he wasn't okay because he just had to get rid of something he really wanted so that Zalith would be comfortable. He felt bad for feeling irritated, but he *did* want to prioritise Zalith's comfort.

The demon frowned and wrapped his arms around him, hugging him tightly. "Would some of that ice cream help you to feel better?" he asked quietly.

He pouted, burying his face in Zalith's shoulder. "I ate all of zhat," he admitted.

Zalith clearly tried not to laugh. "Oh, no. Do you want to go and see what else we have in the kitchen?"

"No," Alucard muttered. He didn't feel like eating anything right now; he just wanted to sit somewhere and do nothing.

"Okay," Zalith said, stepping back to look at him. "If you want to do anything, just let me know. I think I'm going to have a bath; would you like to join me?"

A bath sounded relaxing, and relaxing was what he wanted to do. "Okay," he said.

He followed Zalith upstairs and into their bathroom, and while Zalith ran the bath, the vampire stood by the door and leaned against the wall. He didn't want to retreat into his thoughts—they would only irritate him—so, he stood there, staring at the running water, waiting until it was time to undress and climb in.

As the water filled the bath, Zalith turned around and made his way over to where Alucard was waiting. He smiled and lightly gripped the vampire's jaw with his hand to make him look at him, and then he kissed his lips. "Are you sure you're okay?"

"I'm okay," Alucard confirmed.

Zalith sighed and placed his hand on the side of his face after moving his fringe from over his eyes. "All right."

They then undressed and climbed into the hot bath. Alucard sat with his back against Zalith's chest—as usual—and stared sullenly as his silent thoughts dragged him into sadness. But he began to relax when Zalith started gently massaging his shoulders with his soap-covered hands. Alucard sighed, shifting his stare to the bubbles as the demon started dragging his hands down from his shoulders and over his chest.

"So," the demon then said, "tell me about your little elf friend."

"Vhat?"

"Erwin."

Alucard frowned uncomfortably. "Vhat about zhem?"

"Tell me about them," he said. "How did you meet?"

While Zalith continued massaging his shoulders, Alucard frowned and said, "Vas a long time ago—back vhen I vas blowing vings up and vhatnot. Ervin vas just somevone who decided to vollow us avound vor a vhile. I guess zhey velt like zhey became our vriend; zhey veally seemed to like me zhe most even zhough I 'ad no intervest. But ve all met zhem vhen ve vent to a tavern. Zhey are…crossdresser. Luther vound zhem vunny, invited zhem vor a drink, and zhen ve all just did a vew vings 'ere and zhere togezzer. Zhen I levt zhis place and never came back until now. I set up a business vor Ervin since zhey vere particularly skilled vith medicines and vhatever, but zhat vas all done vhrough vriting. I 'aven't seen zhem until now."

"Well, it's nice that you could reconnect with your old friend, even though you don't seem too fond of them," Zalith said with a quiet laugh, still massaging the vampire's shoulders.

Alucard sighed and glared ahead. "Zhey are…just a lot. I met zhem vhen I zidn't exactly care about 'ow much somevone talked, but vonce zhey get going, zhey zon't shut zhe fuck up, and I veally zon't vant to be dealing vith zhat. I von't be catching up vith zhem at all," he grumbled.

The demon laughed amusedly. "Well, that's a shame. They seemed to be looking forward to getting coffee with you, Ali."

An irritated scowl warped his face as he glared back over his shoulder at what he could see of Zalith. "Zon't start calling me zhat," he snarled.

"You don't like it?" Zalith laughed. "I think it's cute."

"I 'ate," Alucard growled, glaring ahead again.

"Then what should I call you?" the demon asked, moving his arms around him as he rested his chin on his shoulder.

"All zhe vings you alveady call me," he mumbled.

Zalith laughed again. "What's your favourite?"

Alucard then frowned nervously. He wasn't sure why he felt so shy about repeating the endearing things Zalith called him, but he just couldn't seem to speak.

The demon appeared to detect his shyness and kissed the side of his face. "You're so cute."

Pouting, Alucard shrugged, trying to ignore his nervousness. "I like…vhen you call me baby," he mumbled. "And vampire."

Laughing once more, the demon nuzzled his neck and held him tightly. Then, he sat up straight. "Lean forward just a bit," he told Alucard.

The vampire did so, and as Zalith started both washing and massaging his back for him, he continued staring at the bubbles.

"Can I ask you something?" Zalith asked.

"Vhat?"

"Did Luther show any signs of being attracted to you before he knew we were together?" he questioned, dragging his hands down his back.

Alucard thought to himself for a few moments. He wouldn't have noticed it before he met Zalith since he wasn't at all open or interested in dating. The vampire admittedly had no idea when someone was flirting with him before because he'd never been aware of what it actually was. Zalith had opened his eyes to many things, and flirting was no exception. He thought he may as well think back; Zalith deserved to know, didn't he?

He sighed and shrugged. "I zon't know," he admitted. "'E vas alvays trying to do vings vith me; 'e alvays tried to get me to go out vith 'im and Attila, or just 'im. But back zhen, I vhought zhat vas just 'im trying to be a vriend. 'E never tried to kiss me or touch me or anyving like zhat, so I zon't veally know vhy 'e so suddenly decided to act like zhis."

"Hmm," the demon mumbled. He then sighed and rested his forehead on the back of Alucard's shoulder. After a few moments, he exhaled deeply and said, "He probably felt some sort of ownership over you because you were all so close, and now that he's realized you don't belong to him, he's become jealous."

"'E can be jealous all 'e likes," Alucard mumbled irritably. "Ve veren't even zhat close. Zhe vree of us spent a lot of time togezzer, but ve zidn't exactly spend zhat time getting to know each ozzer."

"Well, whatever you've been up to recently has obviously made him feel like he knows you a fair bit. He seems to think he's doing you a favour by trying to get rid of me," he said, resting the side of his head on the back of Alucard's.

He rolled his eyes. "Ve 'aven't been up to anyving. 'E just assumes 'e knows best. 'E's alvays been like zhat."

"He's an idiot," Zalith mumbled. He gently kissed the vampire's back a single time before leaning into his ear. "He can try to get rid of me all he wants; it's not going to work."

The demon then tightened his arms around him, and as Alucard frowned, Zalith lightly clamped his jaw over the space between his shoulder and his neck. Alucard thought he might be going to sink his fangs into him, but he didn't. Zalith growled possessively, holding him firmly in his grip.

"You're mine," the demon stated, and it sounded like a warning to whoever might try to challenge his claim.

Alucard kept his conflicted frown. Of course, he enjoyed it when Zalith became possessive, but he wasn't sure whether what he said was a threat aimed at him or just a statement. Either way, it made him feel intimidated in a way he'd not deny he liked. He *was* Zalith's, and as anticipation spiralled through him, he tensed up a little.

"And I'm yours," the demon added with a quiet laugh as he kissed the vampire's neck.

Alucard nodded slowly. He didn't know if Zalith was expecting a response or not, and if he was, he wasn't sure what to say. He leaned back, resting his back against Zalith's chest once again. "I am," he replied quietly.

Zalith then laughed and held him tightly.

And for the next long while, they both relaxed together in silence.

# Chapter Fifty-Seven

─ ⋜ † ⋝ ─

# Whispers

**| Alucard |**

A chilling whisper wrapped around Alucard, constricting him with a paralyzing fear that sent shivers down his spine. He lay there, trembling uncontrollably, his heart pounding in his chest as the darkness seemed to close in around him.

"*Caedis,*" called the woman he hoped never to see nor hear again, a voice that brought anger and resentment unto him.

He opened his eyes to stare at the wall across from him. Murmurs and whispers faded into silence the longer he lay awake. Zalith was sleeping beside him with his arms wrapped around him and his head rested on the side of his. The demon's embrace always helped him feel calm, but this wasn't the first time he'd heard voices call to him. It was, however, the first time in a *very* long time he'd heard *her* voice. That witch of a woman, Lilith. Why could he hear her calling his name?

Alucard didn't want to listen. He just wanted to sleep so that he could wake up tomorrow and spend time with the man he loved. The vampire turned onto his right side so that he was facing Zalith, and as the demon murmured tiredly, Alucard shuffled closer and rested his head against Zalith's chest, wrapping his left arm around him. Then, he closed his eyes and tried to drift off to sleep once again.

*But he soon jolted awake. The bitter air clawed at his bare skin, making him shiver violently as he dragged his hand from behind Zalith—but Zalith wasn't there. Nothing was there. Alucard wasn't in his bed or his home. He lay in an endless, silent darkness.*

*He sat up, looking around in confusion—in dread. Where was Zalith? Where was he? He frowned strangely, slowly searching the still, ominous black.*

*"Caedis," came Lilith's whisper.*

*"Caedis," came another; it was familiar... harrowingly familiar.*

*Alucard scowled, stepping cautiously forward as the ground beneath him flickered strangely. The floor was...peculiar. It appeared like the surface of a lake, and with each step, it rippled as if disturbed by his presence. Yet, there was no water on his foot, and his skin remained dry despite standing there. It felt surreal. If he had to guess, he'd think the ground was made of glass with a delicate, almost ethereal layer of water beneath it. The sight was both mesmerizing and unnerving, making him question the reality of his surroundings.*

*The ground didn't matter, though. What mattered was finding out where he was and where Zalith was. He was almost certain that he was dreaming, so all he had to do was wake up. But a sudden scatter of footsteps snatched his attention. He sharply turned his head, searching the darkness for whatever made the sound. But there was nothing but endless, empty gloom.*

*There it was again—behind him. The faint scatter of footfall echoed in the silence. Alucard turned around, managing to catch a fleeting glimpse of something grey disappearing into the darkness not too far from where he stood. His curiosity was piqued, but so was his unease. The vampire moved closer with the intent to uncover what it was— perhaps it could help him understand where he was—but the more steps he took, the less it felt like he was moving at all. The landscape remained unnervingly static, an unchanging labyrinth that gnawed at his sanity.*

*A rapid scatter of footsteps, a horrifying screech—he spun around, his heart starting to pound in his chest. Something was stalking him, a phantom presence lurking just out of sight. The oppressive darkness and his unfamiliar surroundings only amplified his dread. He just wanted to leave. The longer he spent there, the more his anxiety grew, a creeping terror that threatened to overwhelm him. He could feel panic rising within him, each passing moment pushing him closer to the edge. He just wanted to leave.*

*"Caedis," she called again.*

*With an angered scowl, he swiftly turned around to face the direction the voice had come from.*

*And that was when he saw her.*

*White, waist-length hair, and lips as red as blood.*

*Lilith.*

*She stood in the darkness, barely visible through a quickly forming mist. A twisted smile stretched across her face as she lifted her right hand to slowly point at him.*

*Why? Why was she here? Where even was here?*

*If Lilith was here, though, he had to prepare to fight; her intentions could only be as horrific as her appearance, and Alucard didn't want to risk this not being a dream. However, as Lilith's expression turned sour, something grabbed the back of his shirt.*

*Alucard was abruptly pulled from the darkness and into a room all too familiar. The stone walls, the pungent smell of blood, and the deafening screams of suffering. He knew where he was, and as his back hit the wall, his dread quickly forced a horrified stare onto his face.*

*"Aleksei," Damien said with a grin, leaning into Alucard's face. "Did you really think you could hide from me?" he asked, tilting his head to the side as his smile faded into a frown.*

*Alucard gawped at him. His heart was racing, and his breaths became stifled. His body went numb, his will to fight left him, and all he could do was stand there and stare into the eyes of the creature that he knew had come to tear away everything that made him happy.*

*Damien grinned again, gripping Alucard's throat in his hand. "So long...too long I've been looking for you," he snarled, tightening his grip with every word. "I'm coming for you. I'll take everything from you and your disgusting little demon," he spat.*

*Paralyzed with fear, Alucard shuddered and let out a strained grunt, caught between struggle and terror. His mind remained a chaotic blur, his heart pounding relentlessly in his chest. Desperation clawed at him, and all he could focus on was his overwhelming desire to get back to Zalith. The sheer intensity of his longing was only matched by the suffocating dread that threatened to consume him.*

*"And you'll never even so much as think about betraying me again," he hissed. "I will break you, Aleksei. I will make you understand that you're nothing!"*

*Alucard choked—*

*"Nothing!" Damien yelled—*

Alucard opened his eyes. He gasped for air, immediately sitting up. His heart was still racing, he struggled to breathe, and as he gripped his throat, he frantically looked around the room.

Zalith quickly woke and sat up, placing his hand on the vampire's shoulder as he, too, searched the room for danger. "Alucard?" he asked worriedly. "What happened?"

Still panting and panicking, Alucard looked back over his shoulder at Zalith and stared at his tired but concerned face. He was back in their room, in their house...no Damien, no Lilith, no scurrying creatures...just...Zalith.

He shook his head, exhaling deeply and dragging his hands over his face as he waited for his racing heart to calm. He hadn't had a nightmare like that in a while—at least not one he remembered after waking up.

Zalith moved his arms around him and hugged him tightly. "Are you okay?"

Resting his forehead in his hand, Alucard exhaled and nodded. "Vas just...a nightmare," he mumbled.

The demon sighed quietly and started pulling him back down into bed. "Come lay down with me," he said sleepily. "I'll keep you safe."

As Alucard lay beside him, the demon rested his head on his chest and slowly stroked his fingers through his hair, but he stopped a little over halfway through. Alucard frowned and looked down at him, and he saw that Zalith had already fallen back asleep. He gazed up at the roof of the bed canopy. But the thought of Zalith falling asleep and leaving him on his own made him feel upset. He wasn't sure why, he just didn't want to lay in the dark in silence right now.

"Zaliv?" he asked, looking down at him.

"Mm," the demon hummed in response.

He frowned as his words left him. But he didn't want to think too much about what he was going to say; otherwise, he wouldn't say it. "I zon't…vant to be alone."

"You're not alone," Zalith murmured. "You're with me."

"I know, but…I zon't…vant to go back to sleep."

The demon was quiet for a moment but then moved his hand up onto Alucard's shoulder. "What do you want to do?" he asked sleepily.

Alucard was already sure that he didn't want to go back to sleep; he just wanted to be with Zalith, talk to him, hear his voice, and relax in his embrace. "I vant to stay avake."

Once again, Zalith took a moment to respond. He exhaled quietly, lazily moving his arm around Alucard again. "We can…we can stay awake," he replied tiredly.

Frowning, Alucard dragged his hand up his side to grip Zalith's wrist. After a few moments, the demon seemed to fall silent again. "Zaliv?" he asked, lightly nudging his arm.

"I'm…a…I'm awake," he muttered, shuffling around a little, exhaling deeply once more.

"Can ve go sit somevhere?" he asked. If they left their bedroom, not only did he feel like he'd be more comfortable, but Zalith wouldn't fall back asleep as quickly.

But the demon didn't answer again.

Alucard frowned stubbornly and nudged Zalith's arm again. "Zaliv."

Zalith murmured in response and ever so slightly moved his head.

"Can ve go sit somevhere?"

"Yeah," he whispered.

After a few moments of waiting, however, Zalith didn't get up.

"Zaliv?" Alucard asked again.

The demon murmured and mumbled, "Y-Yeah…I'm getting up."

Alucard waited.

Zalith didn't get up.

A saddened frown made its way onto Alucard's face. "Zaliv?" he asked again with a distressed tone.

But the demon didn't respond, and Alucard didn't want to lay there for another moment. So, he sat up, but the demon grabbed him and pulled him back down.

"Wait," Zalith mumbled, resting his head on Alucard's chest again. "I'm getting up…I just…need a sec."

Alucard waited, but Zalith clearly wasn't going to get up, and Alucard started to feel as though maybe he should just let him sleep. It was late…or early…he wasn't sure which, and he didn't want Zalith to lose out on his sleep because of him. So, he lay there, staring aimlessly.

He let Zalith drift back off to sleep, hoping that he, too, might be able to fall back asleep… but as each empty, silent moment passed, he felt himself slowly sink deeper into dismay. He hadn't seen Damien or heard his harsh voice in so long that seeing him had shaken him a lot more than he thought it might. He couldn't get his face out of his head—his eyes, his warning…. Alucard didn't want to think about it, but… what if Damien knew where they were? What if he was going to find them? They'd been safe for so long that he let himself relax—he allowed himself to forget that Damien had *always* found him whenever he'd run away. Why would now be any different?

Because of Zalith. Everything was different this time because of Zalith. The demon somehow managed to find a way to hide himself *and* Alucard from *all* the Numen, and Alucard didn't have to be afraid and run back to Damien out of fear of being found and used by the other Numen. Zalith would keep him safe, Zalith had always kept him safe, and Alucard would keep *him* safe, too.

The vampire glanced down at the sleeping demon as a smile made its way through his despondent stare. He loved Zalith so much; to think that someone would go so far as to want to kill the Numen for him…. As dangerous as it was, and as much as Alucard didn't want to let Zalith be so reckless, he still adored and appreciated the fact that he would go so far for him.

But he was worried. He knew how dangerous the Numen were. He knew that he and Zalith alone really didn't stand a chance at *killing* them—weakening them, maybe, but killing them? They didn't have the numbers or the tools.

He scowled as the thought of the Numen banished his sadness and replaced it with anger. He wanted them to die just as much as Zalith did. Damien and Lilith…. The world would be a much better place if they were to cease existing. Lilith would be easier to take down than Damien; her number of followers and believers was so much lower than Damien's, and *she* should be their first target.

Why was he even thinking about this right now? Maybe because they had a meeting coming up in a few days, a meeting where they'd gather the allies they needed and get people working on what needed to be worked on.

With a quiet sigh, he looked down at Zalith again. He couldn't sleep. He didn't want to lay there in silence… so he thought he might as well get up and work. The people coming to the meeting in a couple of days would need information, so he thought he'd work on that.

Quietly and carefully, he moved Zalith's head from his chest, made sure that he was comfortable, and then climbed out of bed. He pulled the cover over Zalith; he knew the demon wouldn't get cold, but he still wanted to make sure that he was comfortable. Then, he pulled on a pair of trousers and headed towards the bedroom door. He pulled it open, left the room, and made his way across the hall and towards his study. He wasn't sure what he'd begin with, but not everyone knew what to expect from the Numen, so perhaps getting all of that information down was a good place to start.

# Chapter Fifty-Eight

— ⸲ † ⸲ —

## An Empty Bed

| **Zalith** |

**Z**alith woke as the early morning came around. As always, his first thought was Alucard. With a content, quiet exhale, he smiled and reached his arm over the sheets to locate his vampire, but his hand found nothing. He opened his eyes and sat up to see that Alucard wasn't in their bed at all. His eyes darted around the room as panic abruptly consumed him, but Alucard was nowhere to be seen.

The first question that came to mind was: what happened? Was he dead? Was this it? But he couldn't let his panic overwhelm him, so he immediately concentrated and used his imprint to locate Alucard, and to Zalith's relief, the vampire's life force wasn't far away at all.

He sighed and laid back down, but his relief was soon outweighed by his growing sadness. This was the first time Alucard had gotten out of bed *before* and *without* him, and Zalith was sure that the distress and solitude he was feeling right now was how Alucard must have felt every morning he'd left him alone.

Zalith couldn't help but wonder…was Alucard punishing him? Was this Alucard's way of letting him know just how hurt and upset he was? Zalith deserved it—of course he did. He'd left Alucard on his own to wonder and panic for months, and he was quite sure that there was nothing he could do to make it up to him.

With a sullen frown, he turned onto his side and stared at the place where Alucard would sleep. He knew Alucard was upset with him—maybe even angry at him—and after everything that happened, a crushing angst began to constrict all of his thoughts. Were he and Alucard okay? Had he damaged their relationship with his stupidity? With his failure to prioritise Alucard over his work? Was…was Alucard going to break up with him? Was that why he wasn't there? Was he preparing to end their relationship?

Zalith sat up and rested his elbows on his knees, placing his forehead in his hands. The thought made him feel sick; it made him feel the most crushing heartbreak he'd ever experienced. He didn't want to lose Alucard; he didn't want to see him leave. It hurt him enough to know that Alucard had suffered because of him, but for his actions to be the reason why Alucard left…he'd never, ever be able to forgive himself. But…if Alucard felt that he couldn't be happy here anymore, then he'd not force him to stay. He wanted Alucard to be happy more than anything else, but…he felt his possessive instincts jolt a little inside him. Alucard was *his*, and he'd do whatever it would take to make him happy.

He didn't want to sink into his thoughts or let his instincts take control. The demon shook his head, sighed, and shuffled to the end of the bed. As worried as he was that Alucard was angry with him, he wanted to see his vampire. So, he got up, got dressed, and left the bedroom. He knew that Alucard was in his study, and as he made his way across the hall towards his door, he felt his angst grow just a little bit more. When he opened that door, what was Alucard going to say to him? What expression was going to be on his face? In his eyes?

| **Alucard** |

Alucard flinched in surprise when his office door opened. He took his eyes off his work and looked over at Zalith, who—like him—was wearing only a pair of trousers.

"Good morning," the demon said with a smile. "What are you doing?"

The vampire smiled slightly and looked back down at his desk. "Vorking."

Zalith made his way over, and once he reached him, he kissed the side of his face.

"I couldn't sleep," the vampire mumbled, stacking a few of the loose pieces of paper together. But he didn't want to think about his nightmare; he wanted to keep himself busy so he could ignore the distress that it caused him.

"Oh," Zalith said with a frown. "You should have woken me up."

"I tried to," Alucard said, glancing up at him, "but you kept valling back asleep."

Zalith's frown thickened. "I don't remember. I'm sorry," he said, sitting on Alucard's desk, staring down at him. "How long ago was it?"

Alucard shrugged as he moved more of his scattered papers into neater piles. "I zon't know. Maybe a vew hours."

Nodding, Zalith glanced down at the papers. "What are you working on?"

"Vings ve'll need vor zhe meeting in a vew days," he answered, finishing tidying the papers up. He felt a little embarrassed that his desk was in a complete state.

"Have you had anything to eat yet?" Zalith then asked.

The vampire shook his head. "No," he mumbled.

Zalith smiled and lightly dragged his fingers over the side of Alucard's face, and then he tucked a strand of the vampire's hair behind his ear as Alucard looked up at him. "I'm going to go and have breakfast in a moment if you want to join me. Or, if you prefer, you can have some of my blood," he offered.

Alucard took his eyes off Zalith for a moment and looked down at his work. The demon's offer was an enticing one; in fact, he'd already decided that he wanted his blood, he just didn't want to seem *too* eager. He waited a moment and then looked back up at him. He nodded slowly in response.

Zalith smiled and held out his arm. "Come here," he invited.

Of course, Alucard wanted to go to him, but he felt a little more desperate than yesterday. He stood up, and as Zalith moved his arm around him, he frowned irritably. He enjoyed Zalith's embrace, but he felt a need to do this the way that *he* wanted to this time, just as he had yesterday. So, before Zalith could react, he lightly snatched the demon's throat, made him stand up, and pinned him back against the wall behind his desk.

The demon frowned slightly in surprise, but a smirk of enjoyment stretched across his face as Alucard moved his hand to Zalith's jaw and made him look to his right. Then, he moved his face closer to Zalith's neck; he felt so tempted to sink his fangs into him right away, but he took a moment to enjoy being so close to him, holding him against the wall, obviously overwhelming him with anticipation as he waited for his bite. Alucard could hear the demon's heart beating a little faster, but the longer he held him there, Zalith's angst-ridden aura began to feel… different.

Alucard frowned and moved his face away from Zalith's neck. He let go of the demon's jaw so that he could turn his head and look at him. As he did, Alucard noticed what looked like confliction in Zalith's eyes. Did Zalith not like it when he was forceful? His need to be like this had come so abruptly and it was a need he felt no reason to deny. In fact, he found he enjoyed the few times he got to be the one pinning the other back, but if Zalith didn't like it, he'd stop.

But the demon quickly smiled and moved his hand to the back of the vampire's head; he guided his face back to his neck and then pulled his entire body closer as he waited for him to sink his fangs into him.

Despite his worry, Alucard didn't want to wait. He wanted Zalith's blood, and he was going to take it either way. Without further thought, he sank his fangs into Zalith's skin, tightening the grip he had on the demon as his blood poured into his mouth, drowning him in satisfaction. But he didn't want to take too much—or did he? He now knew that Zalith was an incubus, and he was sure that Zalith would need his energy back the same way Alucard did, and the thought of Zalith's affection right now was a whole lot more enticing than usual.

He tightened his grip, pressing as much of his body against Zalith's as he could as he listened to the demon's quiet, satisfied sigh. Zalith gripped the vampire's waist with his free hand, his other pinned against the wall. But Alucard stopped a few moments later, his thoughts so suddenly becoming conflicted. He wanted Zalith—he craved his attention more than anything—but he didn't want to give in to it. The overabundance of Zalith's affection and attention hadn't helped him get over the sadness he felt in response to Zalith's absence, and he didn't want to let himself think that maybe a little more would help erase the dismay.

Alucard stepped back as he slowly let go of Zalith, and as he sank back down into his seat, Zalith frowned and sat on his desk again.

"Are you okay?" Zalith asked, placing his hand on Alucard's shoulder.

He looked up at the demon's concerned face and nodded. "I'm vine," he mumbled, using the back of his hand to wipe whatever blood might be on his lips. "I just vemembered I 'ave to go and deal vith Luther today," he said, trying to change the subject.

Zalith frowned. "And that made you *this* sad?" he questioned.

"No," Alucard mumbled, swivelling in his seat so that he could rest his arms on his desk. "I'm not sad."

The demon didn't seem convinced. "Did I do something to upset you?" he asked, worry on his face.

"No," Alucard said, glancing up at him. "You zidn't do anyving...." He wanted to add a snarky comment out of anger, but Zalith didn't deserve his irritated attitude. He didn't want to upset him *or* start an argument. He sighed and looked down at his desk as he leaned back in his seat. "I'm just tired."

Zalith obviously didn't believe him, but the demon didn't continue asking. Instead, he nodded. "Okay," he said before leaning forward to kiss his forehead. "Get some rest," he then insisted.

But Alucard shook his head and sighed again. "Zhe sooner I deal vith Luther, zhe better. I'll probably 'ead to zhe ship in a vew minutes."

The demon sighed quietly and nodded. "Okay. I need to get a few things sorted out here, but I'll be home whenever you get back."

Alucard looked up at him. "Vhat do you 'ave to do?"

"I've been putting off sending a message to Margo; I need to deal with the Imperito."

"Oh, vight. Let me know if you need 'elp vith zhat."

Zalith smiled and said, "Thank you." Then, he asked, "Are you sure you're okay?"

Alucard stood up. "I'm vine," he said with a nod. "I just vant to get zhis out of zhe vay."

"Okay," Zalith said quietly. "Well, I'm around if you need me."

The vampire nodded, but he knew that Zalith was worried and he didn't want to leave him to think that he was angry with him. So, as Zalith stood up, he shyly slipped his hand into the demon's and then leaned in to kiss him. When he pressed his lips against Zalith's, he noticed the sadness in his eyes, and his guilt began to outweigh his anger. He didn't want the demon to be sad; he loved him so much, but he just…needed time to get over everything. That didn't stop him from kissing him again, though. As his lips touched Zalith's once more, he moved his hand to the side of the demon's neck, and Zalith kissed back, holding Alucard tightly.

Alucard felt a little less aggravated as he allowed what was meant to be one kiss to become a few slow ones. He didn't enjoy feeling mad or upset at Zalith, and he really *did* just want to ignore it so that he and Zalith could be happy, but he couldn't…no, he *could* right now. He *could* forget his sadness for a while so that he could enjoy a moment with the man he loved.

After a few seconds, though, they stopped kissing, and Zalith rested his forehead against Alucard's with a quiet, sullen sigh. He stared into Alucard's eyes, and as the vampire stared back, the sadness in Zalith's only seemed to have grown, and Alucard didn't want to leave him to suffer.

The vampire frowned. "Vhat's vrong?" he asked.

"Nothing," the demon said with a smile as he fiddled with the vampire's crimson hair. "I'll see you later."

Alucard frowned but nodded. He knew Zalith was upset; he could see it in his eyes and his smile, and he could hear it in his voice, too. But if he didn't want to tell him what was wrong, then Alucard wouldn't force him. His own sadness kept him from feeling as insistent as he knew he'd need to be, but he was sure that Zalith would talk to him later, and Alucard felt as though he'd be able to take it better then, too. Right now, he just wanted to get everything business-related out of the way.

"Okay," he said. Then, as Zalith let go of him, he headed to his study's door.

Zalith followed him into their bedroom, but once he grabbed a shirt for himself, he smiled at Alucard, kissed his cheek, and left, pulling the door shut behind him.

Alucard exhaled quietly and headed into the wardrobe. He wasn't looking forward to seeing Luther again, but it had to be done, and he felt as though this was going to be another long day.

# Chapter Fifty-Nine

— ⋟ ✝ ⋞ —

## The Road To Forgiveness

| **Zalith** |

Zalith made his way downstairs. He couldn't keep himself from thinking about how he'd wronged Alucard and how all of this was his own fault. He still had no idea how he was going to make it up to him or if anything he tried would even be enough. He'd never forgive *himself*, though.

He sighed quietly. What if this was just another loop? What if his next way of watching Alucard suffer was to watch him slowly fall out of love with him? What if they were going to grow further and further apart because of what he did until the point they no longer spoke to each other at all, and Zalith couldn't do anything but sit there and watch it happen? And eventually, Alucard would leave and head home to his castle, and because Zalith wasn't there to protect him, someone would find him and kill him. He didn't want to think about it...but the possibility that this really was just another loop soon to end with Alucard's death was very real.

However, even if this *was* another loop, he was still going to try to fix things between him and Alucard, and himself and Varana, too, who was also upset by his absence. He felt he'd given her enough time to cool down; although she was never really too calm in general, he still had to figure out how to right his wrong.

When he reached the bottom of the stairs, he sighed quietly. "Edwin," he called, summoning the butler.

Immediately, the brown-haired man came running from the hallway to his right and bowed humbly. "Yes, sir?"

"Do you know if Varana is on the property?"

"I did hear yelling coming from the guest house, sir, *and* I have spotted a few of your workers periodically heading back and forth between the guest house and Lady Varana's room with various clothing items," the butler explained.

The house that Zalith said he'd have built on the property for Varana had been ready for a few days, and initially, she was reluctant to move in, just as Zalith had known she would be, but now, obviously, she changed her mind and wanted distance because she was mad. Understandably, though. Zalith knew what he did.

"Sounds like her," he mumbled. "Thank you. Could you also send a message to Margo, please? Tell her that I'd like to meet with her and the sheriff as soon as they're available. Mention that it's about the Imperito."

"Of course, sir."

As the butler wandered off, Zalith made his way through the house, out into the gardens, and followed the trail to the guest house. He liked how it turned out; it looked a lot like his and Alucard's house, but smaller. There was space for a statue in the front garden to go with the small fountain, but the statue wasn't yet in place, so the area looked rather bland. He felt the place looked charming and was worth the money, though. Even if Varana didn't end up staying there very long, he thought he'd get good use out of it one way or another.

The demon headed into the house, where he heard Varana's voice and two sets of footsteps echoing in the foyer.

"If you're going to follow me around so closely, then learn how to breathe quieter!" Varana complained.

"Y-yes, miss," came the nervous voice of another woman.

Varana then came into view, heading towards the staircase that Zalith was standing beside. She had a petite blonde woman at her side, and neither of them noticed the demon yet. So, Zalith watched them curiously, waiting.

"I'm not a pig. You don't need to hover around me as though you're some sort of fly," Varana grumbled.

"Yes, miss. Sorry, miss," the girl uttered.

"Why do you say that so much?" Varana muttered, but then, when she noticed Zalith standing by the stairs, she stopped walking, scowled at him, and adorned a look of repulse. "*You*," she snarled.

Zalith smiled pleasantly. "Good morning."

The woman standing at Varana's side curtsied respectively, and in response, Zalith nodded.

"This is Margaret," Varan introduced. "She's one of my maids. She's on your payroll, of course."

Not surprised to hear that he was paying for Varana's new servant, Zalith chuckled. He found it rather amusing. "Nice to meet you," he said to the girl.

Margaret blushed. "It's very nice to meet you, too, sir."

Varana rolled her eyes and waved her hand in front of the girl's face, dismissing her. "Go...fold a blanket or something. Leave the adults alone."

"B-but...I'm nineteen, miss—"

"Go!" Varana snapped, glaring at Margaret.

Without another word, the maid scurried off, leaving Zalith and Varana alone.

Varana crossed her arms and glowered at Zalith. "Is it just you that's come, or is your sad little soulmate outside hiding in the bushes?"

Zalith rolled his eyes. "Just me, V."

She didn't look very impressed. "What do you want?"

"I came to see how you're settling in."

"Well, I'm fine, Zalith. Thank you for gracing my doorframe with your shadow. Goodbye," she dismissed, gripping the staircase's bannister, preparing to head up.

"Varana, wait," Zalith insisted, stepping closer to her.

She stopped but didn't turn to face him. "What?" she snapped irritably.

"Can we talk?"

She angrily turned to face him and looked him up and down for a few moments with an almost revolted sneer on her bitter face.

"What?" Zalith asked, confused. Why was she looking at him like that?

"Am I a ghost, Z?" she asked. "Can you see right through me?"

"What are you talking about?"

"Well, you haven't felt the need to speak to me in so long that I was starting to think that I've turned invisible."

The demon sighed quietly. "I'm sorry, Varana."

"Well, you better start laying on the affections because I don't believe it," she said, turning her head away from him.

Zalith sighed once more, trailing after Varana as she led him away from the stairs, down the hall, and into one of her lounges. The room bore a striking resemblance to the guest lounge in his own home, with the same pile of cushions nestled in the far corner. However, the couches here were a soft light blue adorned with a delicate white floral print, and vibrant house plants lined the walls, giving the space a lively atmosphere. The air was infused with a pleasant blend of citrus and cinnamon, and the room was noticeably brighter than the interiors of Zalith's home.

Varana sat on the end of the couch and gestured to the pillow pile, letting Zalith know that that was where he would be sitting. Zalith *hated* the idea, and as he sat down, he felt pretty silly about it, but he wanted to weed his way onto her good side. So, he sat there without a word of complaint.

The woman then snapped her fingers, and in came another of her maids.

"Yes, miss?" the girl asked nervously.

"Bring me a nice glass of cherry cordial," Varana requested. Then, she looked over at Zalith. "Do you want anything?"

"Wine, thank you," he answered.

"And he'll have a water. No ice, no lemon," Varana decided, setting her crimson eyes back on her maid.

"Right away!" the girl said, and then she hurried off.

Zalith exhaled quietly, trying to keep an amused smile off his face. "Varana, we—"

"Shh!" she snapped, glancing at him with a scowl on her face.

The demon rolled his eyes, something he did far too often in Varana's presence.

For the next short while, they sat in silence. But soon enough, Varana's maid returned with the drinks she'd asked for. First, she placed Varana's glass on a coaster on the coffee table in front of her and then went to hand Zalith his lukewarm water—

"Oh, I'll take that, sweetheart," Varana interjected. "I know he doesn't look it, but he's so old that if he lifts something heavier than a comb, he might have a stroke," she insulted.

The girl, who looked very confused and even more nervous, handed Varana the water and hurried out of the room.

Varana then turned her head and looked at Zalith. She slowly placed his drink on the edge of the table, which he couldn't reach from where he was sitting. "Your water's ready," she said with a smile.

Zalith sighed irritably. "I see that. Thank you."

She took a sip of her drink. "Are you comfortable?"

"Very," the demon lied.

The woman smiled as if she was keeping a dirty little secret and took her time admiring the crystal glass she was drinking from. Then, she placed it back down on the table and sighed a long, happy sigh. "Well, you'll hate to hear this, but I fucked Luther on there—"

"Varana…" Zalith cringed, disgusted.

She laughed. "I'm kidding," she said, waving her hand. "We did do things on this couch, though," she said, patting the couch.

Zalith grunted in revolt.

As Varana's laughter died down, she took another sip of her drink and turned to face him. "You may speak."

He didn't know where to start, but he knew he needed to apologize. So, he sighed remorsefully. "I'm sorry."

"For what?" she questioned.

A sullen frown appeared on the demon's face. "I shouldn't have spent so much time away these past months, and I should have told you sooner about imprinting on Alucard."

Varana grimaced at the mention of imprint, crossed her arms, and turned her nose up at him. "Is that all you have to say?"

The demon frowned. He knew he owed her an explanation. "I get tunnel vision when it comes to my work, and I know you know that, but—"

"It's no excuse for acting like I don't exist!" she exclaimed.

Zalith nodded. That was exactly what he was going to say if she had let him finish. "Exactly," he said. "I honestly didn't think it would affect you that much, V. I've always been like this, and you accepted it. You've even praised me for it in the past. Why is it such a problem for you *now*?"

Varana clenched her jaw and looked away from him. He could see the tears forming in her eyes, and his guilt started to increase.

"You've changed," she said.

He frowned in confusion. "What?"

"Ever since you laid eyes on *him*, it's like…it's like he's the only person that you have time for—the only person that you care about."

"I care about you, V," he said sullenly.

Tears started trickling down her face. "No, you don't! Not the way you used to! We used to do everything together, Z—we were *inseparable*. Even when you had your little boyfriends, I was always your first priority, and now everything's about your precious little Alucard. When's the last time we went out or read together or even just had a conversation that had nothing to do with him?" she questioned, scowling at him. "You even kicked me out of my own home just because you decided out of the blue that you wanted to shack up with him. And what about this shit?" she questioned, pointing down to the gold anklet she was wearing. "Now I'm in danger, too, just because you decided to defend him and fuck with Damien, who I told you not to get involved with in the first place!"

Zalith hung his head in shame. She was right.

Still crying, she sniffled and flailed her arms around in frustration. "And who do *I* have? I can't talk to my sister about anything that's going on because of *him*, and I can't see anyone in town because I'm supposed to be your fucking wife—"

"Varana, you don't have to—"

"And then when I finally find someone to be with, you suddenly decide that I am indeed worth your time and tell me that I need to stop seeing him! What is it, Zalith? Am I *yours* or not?!"

Zalith felt a little overwhelmed. He felt every kind of guilt and sorrow. He had never specifically claimed any sort of ownership over her, but he knew that he did control most of what was going on in her life, whether he intended to or not. She was, in a way, his, and he hated that this had happened.

He looked at her with a disappointed frown. "Varana, you can do whatever you want. You don't have to listen to me."

Varana scoffed in disbelief and looked away.

"You *can*," he insisted.

"Sure, as long as I don't fuck up a single one of your immeasurable amount of connections, answer immediately to your every call, ignore what my family wants for me, and follow you blindly."

Now aggravated, Zalith scowled. "If you didn't want me to have so much control over your life, you shouldn't have given it to me, Varana. You never said anything before now, and frankly, you look pretty comfortable. If you want to leave, then leave."

Varana turned her back to him, sipping from her drink again.

"All I've done since the day we met is provide for you," Zalith continued.

"With an iron fist—"

"I'm not a perfect person, Varana," he snapped angrily.

"But you *were*!" she insisted, wiping her tears away. "And then you decided to start fucking my brother, and now you don't give a shit about me," she sniffled.

His anger was intensifying. "Look at where you're sitting! I built this entire house for you. I've put my life on the line for you time and time again, Varana—you would have died in Eltaria if I hadn't been there to protect you. Of course I care about you! Do you think I'd even be here if I didn't?" he questioned.

"I think you're just here to save face, honestly. You can't know what Lucifer and the rest of my family are doing if you don't have me, so you probably felt as though you should put some time in," she accused.

Zalith, now utterly enraged, felt it was best that he left before he said something he was going to regret. "You're fucking ridiculous," he said, standing up.

"Wait!" Varana exclaimed as he went to leave the room.

Uninterested, Zalith left the room, but Varana hurried after him, and once she reached him, she threw her arms around him and hugged him tightly.

"Let go," Zalith grumbled, trying to contain his temper.

Varana shook her head. "I didn't mean to be so cruel! I'm sorry," she cried, tears streaming down her face.

Zalith rolled his eyes. *Of course* she was crying *again*.

"I know that you care about me, Z," she wept. "I've just been a mess ever since I found out that you imprinted on him...."

The demon shook his head. "I'm not apologizing for that, V," he said sternly.

"I know," she said, sniffling. "I guess...I *hoped* that if you ever did, after all this time, you'd do it on *me*!"

Varana was still in love with him. Zalith knew that, and he felt very guilty about it. He didn't know what to do with her. He loved her so much—she was his best friend—but he would never be able to be with her romantically. He didn't know whether he should draw the line with her or not because he didn't think that he was stringing her along, and he treated her the way he did because he *did* love her, even though it was just platonic.

He moved his hands up to her wrists and gripped them both as she refused to let go of him, crying into his shoulder. He pulled her arms from around himself and turned to hug her. "I'm sorry," he said.

Nodding, she sniffled, *still* crying. For a few moments, they hugged in silence, and eventually, Varana wiped away her tears and rested her head on his shoulder. "Do you think…that…if I was a man, we would—"

"Don't do this to yourself, V," he refused.

She wiped her face again with her hand. "Why didn't you tell me that you imprinted on him?"

"I didn't want to hurt you."

Varana pouted but nodded. She understood.

As Varana then let go of him, she took his hand and led the way back into the lounge. They both sat on the couch this time and faced one another.

"I'm going to set aside some time to spend with you more often, okay?" Zalith said.

"Okay," Varana muttered sullenly.

"And I'm sorry that I said I didn't want you to see Luther. You can do whatever you'd like, Varana—seriously. I had a bad feeling about him from the get-go, and it turns out that I was right, but if you're happy with him, then that's fine. Just keep an eye on him."

Varana laughed a little. "You know, I caught Luther with Danford's hands down his pants," she revealed.

Zalith rolled his eyes. "Of course." He couldn't tell whether Luther was obsessed with him or Alucard; maybe it was both, considering the way things seemed to be unfolding.

Giggling, Varana picked up her glass. "I made him commit to dating me, though, so we'll see how it all turns out."

Revolted, Zalith sighed. "Do you really want to end up with…that?"

She shook her head and frowned sadly. "No, but I'd take anyone for the time being," she admitted.

Zalith frowned despondently. He knew that Varana had her moments and could be a little too much to deal with sometimes, but she *did* deserve to be loved by someone, especially now since he had Alucard…but…did he *really* have Alucard?

He sighed and looked down at his lap. "I think I've ruined things with Alucard."

Varana rolled her eyes. "You ruin things with everybody—"

"Well, this one's different," he insisted with an irritated snarl.

Varana scowled at him.

He sighed. "I don't know what to do. I guess I could talk to him, but it's not going to undo anything that's happened."

"Just give him time," she said.

The demon shrugged. "I guess…. I just wish there was something I could do for him to make up for it."

Varana grimaced jealously. "What are you going to do for *me*?" she questioned.

Zalith smiled and leaned back on the couch. "I was thinking that I might commission a nice statue of you for the garden in front of your house."

A *thrilled* look appeared on her once pouty face. She placed her glass down and threw her arms around him. "Just for that, I forgive you."

The demon smiled. "Thank you," he said. He knew that a statue wasn't going to fix anything, and he was going to make sure he put in work with their relationship. He was glad, though, that they seemed to be on a path towards forgiveness.

Could the same be said about his and Alucard's relationship, though?

# Chapter Sixty

— ᐊ † ᐅ —

## The Line

| **Alucard** |

Alucard sat in his ship's study, vacantly staring out into the depths of the dock's waters. He missed seeing Drac through the glass, but his dragon was safer and happier where he was.

With a quiet sigh, he fiddled with the crucifix around his neck. As always, Zalith was occupying his thoughts. All he could think about was how sad the demon seemed and how upset *he* felt every time he thought about everything that happened. Every time he thought about how he'd tried to convince himself that he was fine with Zalith's absence, it only made him feel irritated because he'd thought he was over it, but he wasn't, was he? He told Zalith how he felt, and although that was a weight off his shoulders, it saddened him knowing that Zalith was despondent and obviously worrying about how Alucard might be feeling.

But he didn't want to lie to himself or Zalith. He didn't feel like he'd fully forgiven the demon for his absence, and he wasn't sure how long it might take for him to get over it. He thought that continuously getting both Zalith's affection and his attention would help him forget his dismay, but it hadn't, and now the more he thought about it, the worse he began to feel. So maybe he just shouldn't think about it; he shouldn't think about anything.

He swivelled around in his seat and faced his study door, waiting for Luther to walk through. The guy was supposed to be coming to meet him, but for the first time in a long time, he was late. Alucard wasn't surprised, though; after all, Luther had received several injuries, and *that* was probably why he was taking so long.

Alucard could hear him at the other end of the hall outside his door; he just seemed to be taking a relatively long time to get there—and he wasn't alone, either. The repugnant smell of dog lingered in the air, and it was stronger than the stench that had quickly clung to his ship the day Zalith's people boarded it.

Rolling his eyes, he stopped fiddling with his crucifix and rested his arms on his desk. A few more moments passed, and eventually, a knock came at his door, which was surprising since Luther seemed to have taken it upon himself to enter rooms without knocking and waiting first.

"Come," Alucard mumbled, leaning back in his seat.

The door opened, and as Luther walked in, Alucard immediately set his eyes on the man beside him. Blonde hair, blue eyes, and shorter than Luther. What the hell was Luther doing with Danford? Luther was leaning on him, and he seemed to be helping him walk. Luther's injuries weren't *that* bad, were they?

"Sorry I'm a bit late," Luther called as he slowly made his way over with Danford at his side.

"Vhat's 'e doing 'ere?" Alucard asked with a scowl, nodding in Danford's direction.

As Danford's nervous frown thickened, Luther glanced at him and reached Alucard's desk. "Helping me walk…. You didn't forget that your boyfriend kicked the shit out of me, did you?" he asked, astounded.

"Get out," Alucard snarled at Danford.

Danford flinched anxiously. "Uh…sorry," he said but looked at Luther, who sat down in front of the desk. "Are you gonna be okay?"

"Yeah, I'll be fine. Go," Luther ushered, waving his hand in dismissal.

Then, Danford swiftly left the room and pulled the door shut behind him.

Once Danford was gone, Alucard set his vacant gaze on Luther. "Do I even vant to know vhat you're doing vith 'im?"

"I mean, *do* you?" Luther asked, sitting in a discomforted slouch. His face was bruised, his hands were both wrapped in bandages, and he seemed pissed off.

Alucard rolled his eyes and sighed quietly. "'Ow are your vounds?" He should at least ask, right?

Luther scoffed and looked down at his hands. "I can't do shit on my own, you know," he complained. "I have to get that Danny guy to escort me around like some cripple—"

"Vell…you *are* crippled, aren't you?" Alucard said, smirking.

Luther slouched back in his seat and crossed his arms. "All thanks to your questionable choice of companions. I've always been the one to suffer because of that."

Alucard shrugged. "Eh…Attila got beat up vonce or twice back zhen because you both chose to disvespect zhe people I cared about."

A look of defeat clung to Luther's stubborn face. "It wasn't disrespect," he argued quietly. "We were just looking out for you."

"Is valking into a room uninvited and starting unnecessary vights looking out vor me, Luther?"

"I told you why I did that. I don't—"

"I zon't vant to 'ear zhat again," Alucard dismissed.

Sighing, Luther shrugged. "Right, well, I guess it's just business as usual, then," he muttered with an irritated tone. "I guess this is just business too, huh?" he said, lifting his hands. "I guess now I should remember that I might die while trying to protect my best friend's dignity."

Alucard tried to sigh away the guilt that started to build inside him, but it seemed to thicken as each moment passed. Although he decided that Luther deserved what Zalith gave him in response to the things he'd said, he couldn't help but feel a little sorry for him. Ever since seeing Erwin last night, he suddenly thought that the people from his past probably weren't aware of his decision to end all his friendships, and Luther was one such person.

Back then, now that he thought about it, he, Luther, and Attila were actually close, weren't they? They might not have known much about Alucard, but they still went everywhere together, did everything together, and led all their old comrades together. And ever since his return from Damien's castle—the visit that had made him decide to end his friendships—Luther had been in Avalmoor, and Alucard hadn't had the time to tell him.

"Your silence makes me think that doesn't bother you."

Sighing, Alucard shook his head. "Vhy am I your best vriend, Luther? You zon't know *anyving* about me."

Luther scoffed. "Why do I need to know however much about you to call you my best friend?"

He shrugged.

"To be honest, I think you're both mine and Attila's best friend—well…maybe not Attila since you…yeah.…"

Alucard rolled his eyes. "'E crossed a line zhat you have started dancing avound."

"What line? Alucard," he said, leaning forward, "I'm literally just trying to look out for you, same as always. The same thing I've been doing for the two—nearly *three*—hundred years I've known you. Look," he then said, leaning back in his seat again, "I know you love Zalith, okay? I know. But…there's just something about him, and I've always been right about these things, haven't I?"

"No," Alucard said with a frown.

"Come on," Luther scoffed. "DeiganLupus: the monk in the monastery; both you and Attila trusted his little vulnerable act, and I was the one who called him out. He flipped and attacked, the same way Zalith freaked the fuck out and attacked me when I told him I knew he was using you—"

"Zaliv isn't a monk vrom a monastery vith silver in zhe valls keeping me vrom being able to tell vhen somevone is lying—"

"That's not the point!" Luther insisted, but he then grunted painfully and gripped his chest. "I'm trying to tell you that you can't see what he's really up to because you care about him. He's the first person you've ever dated too, right? I know what that feels like—you don't wanna let go. But sometimes, you gotta…just a little to see what's really going on."

"Vhat could 'e possibly vant vrom me?" He scowled irritably. "I zon't 'ave anyving to give 'im—anyving zhat vould be vorth zhe two years ve've been seeing each ozzer."

"Just you," Luther said with a revolted look on his face. "I've spoken to Varana. I know you two don't get along, but she's been with Zalith for centuries, and I'm pretty sure she knows him well enough to judge him. He uses people, Alucard, over and over and always has. He's a demon. I swear Varana even said he was an inkybus or whatever. You know what that is, right—"

"I know vhat an incubus is, Luther."

"Yeah, incubus. They literally need to sleep around and do whatever the hell he does. He's done this for forever, and do you really think after however many hundred years of sleeping around and using people, he'd just stop? People like that don't stop; they might like to think that they could, but they don't. It's like a game to them, and I'm starting to believe that seeing how far he can get with you is all just a part of *his* game."

Alucard scowled as all his conflicting thoughts started swirling around in his head, arising from the graves he'd buried them in. He didn't want to think about Zalith's past, he didn't want to think about any of the things Varana had said, and he didn't want to listen to Luther. He trusted Zalith, and there was no way he'd let Luther try to convince him that choosing to trust Zalith was a horrible mistake.

But Luther then sighed. "I'm not gonna keep going on about it. I know you're tired of hearing it. But honestly, genuinely, I really do care about you, Alucard. I don't want to sit here and watch you get played by some fucking demon. You deserve to find someone who's going to love you, and someone who's going to treat you as their first priority *all* the time, no matter what," he said, moving forward to rest his arms on the desk.

"Zaliv does all of zhat," he mumbled. "I zon't know vhy I'm telling you—maybe is because I 'ope zhis vill shut you up—but Zaliv 'as just been busy vith vork. Is a long story, but to get zhese people 'ere, 'e 'ad to spend a lot of time in Eltaria," he explained. He didn't like explaining his private life *or* Zalith's to Luther, but if Luther really did care and was worrying about him and his relationship, perhaps it was best he knew all the things he was missing.

Luther, however, frowned in what looked like disbelief. "Yeah, Varana filled me in—as did Danny. But why didn't he just ask for your help right away rather than spend months upon months running around in circles trying to avoid the inevitable?"

"Because 'e cares about me, Luther. 'E knows vhat taking people vhrough zhat portal does to me, and so do you. 'E zidn't vant me to suffer just to 'elp 'im and 'is people. Can you just stop now?" He frowned and looked away as the distress of his confliction started increasing. "I zon't need any of zhis."

"I…I'm sorry," Luther said, leaning forward and to the side a little so he could see Alucard's face. "I'm just…worried about you—"

"Vell, stop," Alucard said, glaring at him from the corner of his eye. "I zon't need you intervering with my private life. I vouldn't do zhe same to you, even if you are fucking Varana and whoever zhe fuck else," he snarled angrily.

Sighing, Luther held up his bandaged hands and leaned back in his seat. "You're right," he admitted. "I'll stop."

Alucard rolled his eyes and slowly swivelled back around in his seat to face him.

But Luther looked down at his lap and frowned. "Alucard?" he asked quietly.

"Vhat?" he snarled.

"I didn't mean to upset you."

"I'm not upset," he grumbled.

Luther shuffled forward and moved his arms onto Alucard's desk again. "Look, I've always been there for you, you know? And nothing's changed because you have…*him* now. I'm still here. He's not gonna scare me off, even though he's tried to, and we're not gonna get into that again," he said as he frowned cautiously. "I'm just saying…I'm not ever going anywhere…" he mumbled, slowly moving his hand closer to Alucard's. "And…I'm here for you, okay?" he said, placing his hand over Alucard's.

The instant Luther's hand settled over his, a wave of discomfort surged through Alucard. Despite the bandages encasing the man's hands, the sensation was no less unsettling, an invasive prickle that set his nerves on edge. It mirrored the disquiet he felt whenever anyone but Zalith breached his personal space, and his first instinct was to lash out, to make it clear that such contact was unwelcome and intolerable…but the sight of Luther's injuries tempered his reaction. He didn't want to inflict more pain on someone already suffering, and he recognized the gesture for what it was—an attempt at support.

Instead of attacking, he pulled his hand from under Luther's—but abruptly, making sure that Luther knew he was uncomfortable. "Zon't touch me," he warned, glaring at him.

But Luther didn't back away the way he usually would. "Alucard," he insisted, snatching his wrist—

With a disgusted scowl, Alucard tried to yank his wrist free—he didn't take Luther's injuries into consideration and pulled so fiercely that Luther's fractured fingers broke *again*, and the man yelped painfully as he pulled his hands back towards his chest. He sat back down, holding his trembling hands, slowly setting an irritated glare on Alucard.

"Next time, I'll tear zhem off," Alucard growled.

"Why are you like this?" Luther exclaimed. "I literally just want to help you—"

"I zon't vant your 'elp—"

"Okay, but you're gonna get it anyway," Luther argued. "I ain't talking about this no more, man. I'll just keep getting my bones broken," he muttered.

"You get your bones broken because you piss zhe vrong people off."

"Whatever," he uttered. "Well, if we're here to discuss work, let's just get it over with. Oh, and because of your animal of a boyfriend, I won't be able to work until I've healed," he said, holding out his hands again. "Unless you'd like to risk the people I interrogate getting away because I can't stop them."

Alucard rolled his eyes and stared down at his own hands for a moment. He still felt bad, and he felt worse now that he'd just hurt Luther more. Although he deserved what he got for walking around his and Zalith's house like it was his own, Alucard was beginning to feel that maybe Luther didn't deserve *as much* as he'd got. He was just trying to look out for him, wasn't he? Like he and Attila always had, and maybe part of this was his fault for not telling Zalith that Luther was like this.

He sighed, glancing at Luther's hands. It *was* true that he'd not be able to work until he was healed, and Alucard couldn't deal with the loss that would cause him and his operations. The only solution would be to heal Luther, but did he deserve it?

Alucard felt conflicted. He was certain that Zalith wouldn't be at all happy to learn that he'd not only healed Luther but had also done so with his own blood. *That* would be the most effective method, and he needed Luther to get back to work immediately. After all, he had no idea how his people were doing back home because Luther hadn't been able to travel to Dor-Sanguis. Alucard needed to know if Attila had gotten anywhere with that dead reaper's body, and he needed to know if his people or subordinates needed anything—especially after the vampire murders—and he didn't want to risk leaving another day of no communication between there and here. The stench of war was lingering on the horizon, and if Lilith or Damien made a move, they'd most likely target the place where they knew Alucard kept a lot of his vampires.

Now *that* weighed heavy on his mind. How had he not thought about that before? He'd been so focused on his and Zalith's relationship that he'd become blind to a very real, very dangerous threat. He'd left his own people without warning them that someday, either Damien or Lilith could show up with the intention to destroy their home. Alucard had already lost enough people, and he wasn't going to lose any more. Now that Zalith's people were out of harm's way, he felt like it was time he started looking for a solution for his own people's safety.

At the moment, however, he had to deal with Luther.

"You'll go back to vork today," Alucard said.

Luther scoffed in astonishment. "Honestly, Alucard, do you—"

"I vill 'eal you," he said, and the moment those words left his mouth, Luther's face seemed to glimmer with surprise.

Staring at him, Luther slowly frowned. "You're…gonna heal me?"

"Zhat's vhat I said."

"All right," he muttered. "I guess I'll get back to work sooner than I thought, then."

"Zhat's zhe point."

"Fine," he said, shrugging.

Alucard's eyes darted around the room in search of a glass, his gaze landing on the drink cabinet not too far away. He frowned, realizing Luther's broken hands wouldn't allow him to hold a glass, and feeding it to him like an infant was out of the question. With a resigned sigh and a roll of his eyes, he stood up, deliberately ignoring Luther's expectant gaze. He circled his desk and leaned against it beside the injured man. Shedding his blazer, he draped it over the desk, then unbuttoned the cuffs of his shirt's right sleeve. As he methodically rolled up his sleeve, he extended his wrist to Luther, the gesture a silent offering.

However, Luther didn't frown up at him and ask him if he was sure about this like Alucard had been expecting. Instead, he gripped Alucard's forearm as best he could with his broken hand and pulled it closer to his face. But Alucard quickly changed his mind—he didn't want Luther touching or drinking him. He tried to pull his arm away, but Luther harshly yanked it towards his face and sank his fangs into Alucard's skin before the vampire had a chance to tell him to stop, and Luther was a creature of his own creation, so Alucard felt all the pain of his bite.

With a startled, *furious* snarl, he pulled his arm free and backed away from him. "Vhat zhe fuck vas zhat?!" he shouted angrily. The unwanted contact was quickly drowning him in agitation and discomfort, and the pain reminded him of the agony that his past was infected with.

"What do you mean? I was just doing what—"

"I vas pulling avay!"

Luther scoffed. "No, you weren't. You said—"

"Get zhe fuck out," Alucard growled, trying to fight the distress "Now!"

The man looked hesitant…like he was going to argue. But he evidently decided not to. He got up and walked over to the door. Instead of leaving, though, he turned to face Alucard. "I don't understand. You said—"

"Out!" he yelled, enraged.

Without another word, Luther left the room and pulled the door shut behind him.

Alucard rubbed the two bloody wounds on his wrist as the distress brought tears of frustration to his eyes. The pain matched that which would linger on his forearms even weeks after Damien took those silver shackles off him, and the fact that he didn't consent made it worse. All the humiliation and discomfort came flooding back in, a tidal wave of horrifying memories where he'd had things taken from him, forced on him…things he wanted to keep buried in the back of his mind forever.

He didn't want to think about it. Any of it.

But Luther's unwanted bite awoke the memories, and there was nothing Alucard could do to fight them off.

# Chapter Sixty-One

— ᚲ ✝ ᚲ —

## Greymore

| **Alucard** |

Alucard trembled, staring down at the ocean through the glass floor. His heart was racing, and his throat was so tight that his breaths were stifled. The pain-ridden memories flooded his mind, forcing unto him the agony and the despair that made up the four hundred years of his past. He tried to ignore it; he tried reading the letters on his desk, he tried thinking about Zalith and how much he loved him…but the thought of the demon only made him wonder whether the man he loved would feel disgusted by the things he hadn't seen…the things Alucard kept hidden. How would Zalith feel if he knew what Lilith did to him? How would Zalith feel if he found out the horrible, degrading things that the Numen did?

The vampire scowled despondently, closing his eyes to try and fight the tears. He didn't want to spend any more time than he needed to on his ship…in the silence. He wanted to be back home with Zalith despite worrying that he might find out everything that happened to him as a child. He just wanted to be in the embrace of the man he loved, the man who made him feel safe. And not only that, but the demon's signs of sadness this morning stuck with him; he wanted to speak to him about it. He didn't want Zalith to be upset or worried, so it was probably best he got home so that they could talk about what was making them both feel so despondent.

And hopefully…the dismaying memories would stop consuming his mind.

He glanced at the glass window, wiping the tears from his face and adorning a vacant stare, and then he got up and left his office. The vampire made his way through the halls and up onto the deck. When he headed for the stairs to the docks, however, he heard the irritated snarl of a familiar werewolf and turned his head to look at the quarterdeck. Sitting to the right of the stairs was Greymore, who seemed to have made himself a comfortable set-up. He sat in what looked like one of the seats from the bar, and to his right, he'd obviously dragged one of the supply crates over and was using it as a table. On the crate was a bottle of brandy, a half-filled glass, and an ashtray with a cigar resting in it. Greymore had a fishing pole in both hands and slowly lost his irritated frown as he started whistling quietly. Was he really trying to fish in *these* waters?

Just as he was about to continue down to the docks, Greymore caught sight of him. "Hey!" he called, making Alucard flinch in startlement.

Alucard looked over at Greymore again, staring at him as he waved with a smile. Obviously, he wanted the vampire to head over there, but Alucard wanted to go home and see Zalith. He took his eyes off Greymore and looked at the docks, setting his sights on the carriage that brought him there. He wanted to get home…but he didn't want to be rude to Zalith's people, either, especially not to someone as important as Greymore. Did he really want to socialize right now, though? He was still trembling, and his heart was still racing.

"Come join me, man," Greymore called enthusiastically.

Sighing, Alucard decided that he'd head over and see what he wanted. He turned around and made his way over to Greymore's little perch.

"Hey, how're you doing?" the werewolf asked with a smile as he leaned back in his seat.

Alucard reached him and leaned against the fence that Greymore was fishing over. He shrugged, crossing his arms as he watched the man make himself comfortable in his seat once again. "I'm vine," he answered but then frowned. "Vhy are you vishing out 'ere? Zhe vaters are barren."

Greymore laughed and shook his head, stowing his fishing rod at his side, making sure the line stayed in the water. "You know what, I've been out here for an hour or so, and I think you're right," he agreed. But he shrugged and picked up his glass. "But you never know," he said and finished his drink. He then poured himself another. "Want one?"

Another sigh broke free of Alucard's stifled breaths. He needed a drink after what just happened…and after this morning, too—his conflicted feelings, dealing with Luther—it all made him feel so tired already. So he took the bottle from Greymore and drank from it.

The werewolf laughed again, watching as Alucard took two gulps of the brandy before handing it back to him. "Hard day?" he asked.

Alucard shrugged. "I zidn't get much sleep, and zhen I 'ad to deal vith an annoyance," he grumbled.

Greymore smirked slightly. "You probably don't get much sleep with Zalith around, huh?" he said with a wink.

He rolled his eyes but couldn't ignore the fact that this man made him think of Tobias, someone he still missed more than he might have first thought. Greymore possessed similar humour *and* a casual attitude toward just about everything, and that was why Alucard found it a lot easier to talk to Tobias than with most others. But

Greymore's comment hadn't failed to irritate him; although the man was somewhat nice to be around, he didn't appreciate him involving his private life.

"I'm glad he finally has somebody, though—on the long-term," Greymore continued. "He deserves it. I'm sure you both do," he said, placing down his drink to pick up his cigar, which he then started smoking.

With a nod, Alucard turned his head and looked out at the ocean. He didn't want to sink into his thoughts about Zalith, but he did agree that he and Zalith deserved each other; he'd not rather be with anyone else, despite his current sadness. Instead of thinking about *that*, he focused on his most recent thoughts—those involving his people and the fact that they were in danger. His vampires weren't the only people he had to take care of, though. Although he didn't very much like werewolves, he was still responsible for what remained of Tobias's pack—well, it was Freja's pack now, wasn't it? Freja, the Alpha of the East Pack, had one of her sisters marry one of Tobias' Betas, thus joining their packs. Such a joining only added to Alucard's responsibility; it only added more people for him to consider.

Of course, the best way to keep all of his people safe would be to move them to Nefastus so that he could be there if anything happened, but Zalith had already moved *his* people here, and Alucard didn't want to make it look as though he was doing it just because Zalith had. He didn't have to move them to the Citadel, did he? There were a lot of surrounding towns and villages. But if he was going to be bringing vampires *and* werewolves to Nefastus, he needed to make sure that it was safe and that it wouldn't affect Zalith's plans.

However, he then thought, wouldn't it be better for everyone if *his* werewolves and Zalith's werewolves got along? A larger pack would mean more people and more resources. Of course, though, there were particular methods to joining packs, and they wouldn't just start working together because he and Zalith ordered it. He thought it was a good idea, but he'd not invest in it too much—not yet. First, he needed some information before he could work out exactly what it was that he was going to do with his people.

"So, what's your plan for today, Aleksei?" Greymore asked, placing his cigar down to pick up his drink again. "Cracking skulls?" he laughed. "You're more than welcome to grab a pole and fish with me. I have no plans and *far* too much time."

Alucard looked down at him. "Are you married?" he asked, ignoring his question.

Greymore looked out at the water and shrugged. "Eh, I had a fiancée a few years back, but then the war happened, and I decided to work with Zalith. Her family wasn't too thrilled to hear that; they wanted to hide away and try to assimilate with the humans, but I was far too proud, and my pack needed me. So, ultimately, she packed up her things and left," he explained sadly. "She left a note behind, though; it said that she loved me and if we're meant to be together, then fate will reunite us. But it's been years since I've seen her, and everyone else I used to know is dead, so." He shrugged, smoking his cigar. "Perhaps fate had other plans. Doesn't matter now, though, does it? I don't live in Eltaria anymore," he said with a slight laugh. "Oh well."

Alucard frowned sympathetically. It was probably best *not* to propose his idea to Greymore yet. He didn't want to upset him, nor did he want to be rude. Greymore was actually a particularly nice individual, and Alucard felt a need to be patient with him, just as he had with Tobias. "Do you miss 'er?" he asked, looking down at him.

"Sometimes," he said with a nod, still staring at the water, "but I had to accept that the odds are that she's gone. I mean, this small group of us here was all that was left alive... at least to our knowledge. What I don't miss, however, are her parents." He smiled, looking up at him. "You're lucky you don't have to meet *your* in-laws, Aleksei," he said with a laugh—but a laugh that carried sadness.

Alucard scoffed quietly. "Zaliv is lucky 'e zoesn't 'ave to meet 'is."

"Are you and Zalith the real deal?" he then asked with a more serious but curious tone in his voice. "Do you think you're gonna get married one day?"

The vampire then frowned. *Did* he think that he and Zalith were going to get married? Once again, he didn't want to sink into his thoughts because he knew he'd just become sad and quiet, and he didn't want that right now. He'd spent enough time recently dwelling in his despondency, and he didn't want today to be yet another day of sullen consideration.

He shrugged. "Maybe," he muttered. "Ve spoke about zhat, but I zon't know if Zaliv vas joking or not."

Greymore picked up his drink. "Buddy, I have known Zalith for two decades, and I can say with great certainty that he hadn't liked a *single* person I've seen him with as much as he seems to like you," he said matter-of-factly. "It's all in the body language when you're next to each other," he said and sipped from his drink. "And he talks about you often, too."

Alucard then felt curious. "Vhat... does 'e say?"

"A lot of worrying about you... wanting to get back to you. I've heard lots of 'sigh, I love him' when he's talking to Idina and those other two specifically," he explained, placing his drink back down. "The lack of your involvement in this whole Eltaria situation considering what you seem to be capable of speaks volumes, because when Zalith has tools in his box, he'll use them, but he obviously wanted to protect you at all costs—*that* irritated a few people, but *I* understood." He then smoked for a second. "Yep, he loves you, Aleksei; more than I've ever seen him love anything, including himself."

Staring down at the floor again, doubt started consuming him. "Zaliv does more vor me zhan I could ever do vor 'im," he mumbled. "I veel like I need to do more vor 'im to deserve a life vith 'im," he admitted, not only to Greymore, but to himself, too... because

Zalith really did do so much for him, and he still felt like he didn't do anywhere *near* enough for the demon.

"What do you do for him?" Greymore asked in what looked like curiosity and with a clear, non-confrontational tone.

Alucard shrugged, trying to keep his sadness from breaking free of the restriction he'd put on it. "I zon't know. I alvays…. 'E's alvays my virst priority. I've done and said so many vings I vhought I never vould vor and because of 'im, and I alvays do vhatever I can vhenever I can. I alvays vant to 'elp 'im."

"And you still feel like you don't deserve him?" he asked.

"Maybe," he mumbled. "'E just does so much more vor me."

Greymore glanced up at him before looking back out at the sea. "You know what, Aleksei? I think that if you weren't already perfect in his eyes, he wouldn't settle for you. I don't think he wants a single thing from you because if he did, you would know with absolute certainty. I mean, that's *usually* why he makes relationships with people, whether intimate or otherwise. If he's not whittling you down to a nub or using you for power or your connections or what have you, then he doesn't want anything from you in return for his kindness. You're one of the rare few, my friend," he said, picking up his glass. "Cheers," he then said, lifting his glass before sipping from it.

Alucard stared at the floor, still trying to fight off his sullen thoughts.

Greymore continued, "I think that man has been demonized—no pun intended—and has been put through so much as of these last few years that just loving him and accepting him, warts and all, is something that he'd very much appreciate. A lot of people wanna rag on him because he lost the war, but no one wants to talk about the immense lengths that he's put himself through just to keep entire populations safe from extinction."

"'E does so much vor everyvone," Alucard mumbled sadly.

"Too much," Greymore concurred. "You should take him on a nice vacation," he suggested. "Somewhere tropical." He then looked up at Alucard and smirked. "Take me with you, please," he laughed.

Greymore's suggestion actually sounded good; perhaps a small break would help them both. Zalith told him that he wanted to head out on another journey on his ship, and what better journey to take than one to a vacation destination?

"Maybe," the vampire said, but he'd decided that that was what he was going to do. He'd look into places when he got home and work out exactly where he and Zalith could go. Some time away from everything and everyone sounded delightful; some time where it would be just him and Zalith, something he felt he needed so sorely after everything that happened recently.

"So, what's beyond this city?" Greymore then asked, changing the subject again.

Alucard shrugged. "Most of Nevastus is grassland, varmland, and vorests. Zhere are ozzer cities, but none of zhem are as big and developed as zhe Citadel. Zhis place vas actually lawless and vather disgusting, but ever since Zaliv arrived, zhe place 'as calmed down a lot."

Greymore laughed amusedly. "I'm sure his arrival must have been upsetting for the city folk. But I mean… this place is pretty nice, and I wouldn't have known if you didn't say anything," he said with a sigh. "Are there really no fish here?" he then abruptly asked before Alucard could respond to his former comment.

"No," Alucard confirmed, "and zhere 'asn't been vor about vorty years."

"Forty?" Greymore frowned. "What happened to them?"

"Like I said zhe ozzer day: zhe people over-vished, scared zhem off. Zhere's a lake, zhough, near zhe place Zaliv is 'aving your compound built. You can vish zhere."

"Oh, yeah. I shouldn't be drinking so early in the morning," he exclaimed. "You gotta take me by there one day soon. I'd love to check the place out, maybe catch a fish or two. I make a mean grilled white fish with white wine, mm-mm. I could eat fish *all* day…I'm like a bear," he continued, "I should be a werebear instead of a werewolf, honestly."

"If you vere a verebear, you vould 'ave no conscious vecollection of who you are as a man and a beast—you vould be two diverent people," Alucard said, frowning.

Greymore looked up at him. "Maybe that's what I need…. It would keep things interesting."

"Every berserker I 'ave known 'as been insane…at war vith zhemselves all zhe time," he warned.

"Eh, I can relate," Greymore muttered. "I've been at war with myself all morning; I keep convincing myself that I'll catch something here despite the obvious evidence. Thank god I have alcohol, or I'd be bored."

Alucard sighed. "I'm sure you'll all 'ave a lot to do vonce your new place is veady. I guess I can show you vhere is being built at some point," he said, not forgetting that Greymore had mentioned he'd like to see it.

"That'd be great," he said with a smile. "I like to pretend I know things about stuff before I take the whole pack somewhere," he admitted. "But if it works out, I won't have to pretend this time."

Amused, once again thinking about how this man reminded him of Tobias, Alucard asked, "Vhen do you vant to go?"

"Pshh, my schedule is wide open. I ain't got shit to do out here."

The vampire nodded. "I'll let you know vhen I'm vree."

"Sounds good." Greymore smiled. "I'm looking forward to it—thanks, also."

Alucard nodded, and with that, he felt it was time to head home. "I vill go now," he said.

"All right," Greymore said. "It was nice talking to you again. I'll see you again soon, yeah?"

He nodded once more as he started heading for the docks. "I vill probably send somevone to you to tell you vhen I can take you zhere," he called.

"No probs," Greymore called back.

And then, Alucard made his way down to the docks, focusing on his idea to take Zalith on a vacation. He managed to ignore the festering dismay, and he hoped that by the time he got home, the despair would have dissipated. But the wound on his wrist was still fresh, and the pain was throbbing. He wouldn't be able to escape the memories until the bite had healed. All he could do was try his best to distract himself.

# Chapter Sixty-Two

## Wounds

| **Alucard** |

The vampire stared out of the carriage window, waiting as the horse pulled it towards his home. His racing, despondent thoughts slowed, probably because he was tired and wanted to sleep; he wanted to see Zalith, though, and hoped that he'd get to before he headed upstairs to rest.

Once the carriage pulled into the estate courtyard and stopped, Alucard sighed and unlocked the door. He climbed out and stepped onto the white gravel, and then he turned to make his way over to the front door. But before he reached it, Zalith walked out.

The demon made his way over, so Alucard stopped and waited. When the demon reached him, he took hold of both Alucard's hands and leaned in to kiss him. "Hi," the demon said with a smile, staring at him. "How did things go?"

Alucard stifled a grimace; the wound on his wrist was aggravated by Zalith's grasp, but he did his best to ignore it and smiled, looking down at the ground. "Vent vine," he mumbled. "Vhat 'ave you been doing?" he asked, looking at him again.

The demon laughed slightly. "Not much, but I have a surprise for you."

A surprise? Alucard frowned nervously, unsure of what it could be. "Vhat…suprise?"

Zalith let go of his right hand but kept hold of his left as he turned around and started to lead the way to the right of the house, away from the barn. "Come on," he said with a smile, glancing back at the vampire.

Alucard curiously followed, looking around for whatever the surprise might be. Once they got to the east gardens, the vampire set his eyes on one of the unused animal pens, noticing that there was movement inside. Obviously, there was something in the pen, and whatever it was, Alucard was sure that it was what Zalith was taking him to.

As they got closer, Alucard noticed the chickens inside—four very well-groomed chickens—and the pen would be easily visible from both Alucard's office windows *and* his study, and he suspected that Zalith purposely made sure of that.

They stopped in front of the pen, and as Alucard glanced at Zalith, the demon smiled brightly.

"Surprise," he said, squeezing the vampire's hand.

Alucard couldn't keep a smile from making its way onto his face as he looked back down at the chickens. They walked around in their new home, pecking at the seeds in the grass, stopping to stare up at him and Zalith a few times. One of the four, however, was sitting in the doorway of the coop, keeping its brown eyes on him. The chicken looked a lot like Hana, and Alucard decided that he'd name her that.

He didn't want to wait to greet them. Alucard let go of Zalith's hand to open the pen gate and made his way inside as the demon followed behind him. The darkest of the chickens fled as they walked in, clucking in panic—Alucard didn't blame her. But he had his eyes set on the hen that was still sitting in the coop's doorway.

When he reached her, he scooped her up in his arms and stared down at her as she stared up at him. She didn't make a single sound, and for some reason, didn't seem to be afraid of him.

"Do you like them?" Zalith asked, standing beside him.

The vampire nodded and smiled, glancing at him. "Vank you."

"You're welcome. I'm glad you like them," Zalith said, nuzzling the side of his face before kissing his cheek.

But Alucard then looked down at the calm chicken in his arms and frowned. "Vhere did you get zhem?"

"I know a guy who knows a guy," he said, smirking.

"You…know a guy who knows a chicken varmer?"

"I do," he said with a smile.

Alucard smiled and looked at the chicken in his arms. "I'll 'ave to come up vith names vor zhe ozzer vree; zhis is 'ana," he said. He then smiled again and looked at Zalith. "I vant you to name vone."

Zalith frowned in what looked like surprise and laughed quietly. "Can I think on it?"

The vampire nodded.

His fatigue then struck him. The excitement of the chickens started waning, and as it did, Alucard felt himself sinking back into exhaustion. Of course, he loved the chickens, and he loved Zalith for getting them for him, and he thought he'd be able to enjoy them more later after he'd caught up on his sleep. So, he crouched and placed Hana on the ground.

"Alucard, what is that?" Zalith suddenly asked with concern in his voice.

Frowning, Alucard stood up straight and looked at him. "Vhat is vhat?"

"On your wrist," Zalith said, glancing down at his right hand.

Alucard glanced at his hand. He knew what Zalith must have seen when he'd put the chicken down, and dismay started to overwhelm him. "I vas…going to 'eal Luther, but—"

"You let Luther bite you?" he asked, astounded, his frown becoming an angered scowl.

Seeing and hearing Zalith's anger only made Alucard feel more overwhelmed. The despair of his memories constricted him, keeping him from being able to form a proper explanation…he didn't even know how to explain it without telling Zalith that something from his past had him traumatized. He tried to form an answer, his heart racing in his chest, his body shivering. Was Zalith about to yell at him? "I needed…I needed 'im to vork, and 'e can't vork vith 'is 'ands broken," he explained slowly. "But I—"

"So you let him *bite* you? You let him put his *mouth* on your skin and drink your blood?" Zalith exclaimed angrily.

Alucard shook his head. "I-I…I zidn't…I velt like I 'ad to," he said with a frown, struggling to find the words. Zalith was staring at him so furiously, angrier than he'd ever looked at Alucard. This time, for the first time, the demon was angry with *him*, and it made him feel stupid, small, and pathetic. Why couldn't he just tell him what happened? Why did he feel so confused? Anxious? Conflicted? Why couldn't he just tell Zalith that Luther bit him without his consent, that he changed his mind and tried to pull away?

Zalith scowled and raised his voice, "Are you—" But he didn't finish whatever he was going to say. Instead, he closed his eyes, exhaled sharply, placed his fingers against his forehead, and stood there in silence for a few *very long*, very intense moments.

Alucard's angst became overbearing. He could almost *feel* the anger seething off the demon, and standing just inches from him—watching him try to contain himself—made Alucard feel panicked. He knew what he did was stupid, but he tried to pull away. And when he attempted once more to tell him that Luther forced it, all that came from his mouth was another pathetic attempt at explaining the full story. "I-I…need 'im back in Dor-Sanguis. Someving came up and 'e vouldn't 'ave been able to travel until 'e 'ealed. But I zidn't—"

Zalith then opened his eyes, silencing the vampire. He didn't look at Alucard, though. He started walking towards the pen's exit, glaring at the house. "I have to leave for a minute," he said tiredly.

"Vhat?" Alucard questioned, moving to follow him as he stared at him almost desperately, waiting for him to look at him. "Vhy?"

He still didn't look at him. Zalith pulled the pen gate open and continued walking. "I just…need to go and be mad," he said, irritated.

Alucard stopped as the gate closed in front of him and watched Zalith storm off. "Vait," he insisted. He tried to find the words again. "I zidn't vant—"

Zalith stopped walking but sighed deeply, *still* not setting his eyes on him. "Alucard, please just let me go. We can talk about it later," he pleaded, but still with irritancy in his voice.

Alucard didn't want to let him go. Zalith was clearly angry with him, and he'd prefer to talk it out now rather than sit around panicking for however long because that was exactly what he was going to do. He'd let his thoughts drag him into despair; he'd worry, panic, and start to believe that Zalith was going to leave because he'd done something idiotic, because he'd once again… let someone take from him, because he'd let someone else use him. He had enough of his confusing, overbearing emotions, and he didn't want to become a victim to them once again.

"Vhy can't ve talk about zhis now?" he asked in dread, stopping behind the gate and staring at Zalith.

"Because I need to be alone for a while. Please, just let me leave," he said with the same aggravated tone.

Alucard then hesitated. He didn't want to make it worse; he didn't want to anger Zalith more, nor did he want this to become an argument. So what should he do? Let Zalith go and sit around worrying to the point it made him feel sick, or keep asking Zalith to resolve this with him now? Although the former was going to make him feel worse, he felt it was better than arguing. After all, *that* would probably only cause them both more pain.

So, he backed down. He scowled, both anger and sadness starting to constrict his thoughts *and* his heart, but he had to let him go. "Vine," he uttered.

"Thank you," Zalith said, a little less anger in his voice. And then he left, walking off towards the patio door connected to his office.

Alucard's distress was palpable as he turned, his scowl deepening at the sight of the unnervingly calm chicken gazing up at him. He stood frozen, ears pricked for the sound of Zalith's office door shutting, the finality of it sending a shiver down his spine. Alone now, his dismay swelled; he had never seen Zalith so furious, he'd never been the target of such ire. His mind raced, grappling with the uncharted territory of Zalith's anger directed at him. Should he leave Zalith to cool down, attempt another poor, pathetic explanation, or brace himself for the worst? Inevitably, his thoughts spiralled toward the worst-case scenarios, each more dire than the last.

How could he have been so foolish? He knew that Zalith despised Luther and that any sympathy or assistance toward him would be met with fury, especially after the recent events. Zalith had every right to be enraged, just as he had every right to punish Luther. Alucard should have anticipated Zalith's reaction, but how could he? Nothing like this had ever occurred before. Still, that felt like a poor excuse. The reality was clear: Zalith hated Luther, and Alucard had let Luther engage in something as intimate as drinking his blood…even if he changed his mind. Worse, he allowed the man to bite him.

Perhaps he should have just put his blood in a glass. It wouldn't have prevented Zalith's anger, but it might have lessened it. And maybe Alucard's traumatizing past wouldn't have resurfaced, haunting him, weakening him, turning him into a meek, weak imbecile. The very words Damien used.

What was going to happen now? He'd done something Zalith hated, and that made him feel like he was going to suffer for it. He'd always been made to pay for the things he did that angered the people around him…but he had to remember that it was Zalith, and he trusted the demon with his life. He knew that Zalith wouldn't hurt him the way he had once become so used to, but…this was the first time he was mad at him; he had no idea what to expect, and that only made his growing panic worsen. What *was* Zalith going to do?

He didn't want to think about it. He didn't want to think about any of it. Maybe he should just do what he'd been meaning to do once he got home and sleep. He'd sleep, and when he woke, he'd face whatever Zalith was going to do.

Alucard left the chicken pen. He didn't take the outside stairs up to his study because he'd have to walk past the windows of Zalith's office, and judging by the way Zalith had refused to look at him, he was sure that the demon didn't want to see him. So, he'd make sure Zalith didn't have to look at him. He was convinced that seeing him would only make Zalith angrier, and Alucard didn't want that.

He didn't want to be seen by anyone right now. He felt stupid and embarrassed. He'd come home with so many things to say to Zalith, not at all concerned about what might happen if Zalith saw the wound on his arm. Now, he didn't want to think about any of the things he'd been eager to talk about. He just wanted to forget. After all, who was to say that Zalith would still want him enough anymore to do those things with him? He'd let Luther—a man Zalith hated—do something Alucard had promised he'd only let Zalith do, and that made him feel disgusted with himself. If Zalith didn't want him anymore, he'd understand.

With a sullen frown, he dragged himself around to the front of the house and entered through the front door. He silently made his way upstairs, and when he reached the hall, he hesitated. He wanted to go to bed, but he didn't want to go to his and Zalith's bed. How could he lay in the place where he and Zalith slept and not sink into his despondent thoughts?

Instead, he headed into his study and slumped down on the couch in front of his new fish tank. He stared into the water, watching the fish swim around aimlessly as he thought just as pointlessly. His distress and confusion just sent him round and round in circles: what was Zalith going to do? Was Zalith going to leave? Was Zalith so disgusted that he'd not want him anymore? 'Probably' was always the answer, and there wasn't anything he could do about it, was there? He'd already done the stupid thing that caused this, and he couldn't undo it, could he? All he could do was sit there and dread the moment Zalith came to tell him how he felt.

The sound of Zalith's door opening and closing brought a heavy, suffocating worry to Alucard's heart; the angst felt like heartbreak, and it worsened when he felt Zalith's aura slowly fading further and further away. The demon left, and Alucard had no idea where he was going.

Could he be going to kill Luther? The thought didn't motivate him to get up. If that was going to satisfy Zalith, then Alucard would let him do it. Why should his people matter more than Zalith? Zalith told him many a time that he was more important than *his* people and that he'd always prioritize him and his feelings over them, so why should it be any different for Zalith with his people? He should have chosen to listen to his concern about Zalith's reaction rather than focusing on the fact that his people needed Luther.

The vampire lay on his side as he rested his head on one of the black cushions. He really had made a stupid decision, hadn't he? He thought that maybe his choices weren't ever actually stupid and that Damien had belittled him just because he hated him, but that didn't seem to be the case. He *was* an idiot; he felt so stupid for disregarding how Zalith might react when he found out that he'd thought about helping Luther heal the wounds that the demon gave him for the revolting things he'd said.

He wasn't sure if Zalith was going to forgive him, but one thing was for sure: Luther had become an unnecessary problem. Zalith suggested Luther had feelings for the vampire, and as much as Alucard didn't want to think about it, he had to—and it made sense. Zalith told him the things Luther said. Luther was always talking to him about how he cared and whatnot. Before now, it had been something Alucard could ignore, but he wouldn't anymore—not after he snatched his wrist like that and stole a bite. Zalith mattered more to him than an old, estranged friend, and Luther had to be removed from their lives.

Alucard sat up, unable to find comfort lying there. He felt exhausted, disappointed, overwrought with worry and despair and disgust and utter, sheer humiliation. Zalith was angry at *him*; the demon just left, Alucard had no idea when he'd be back, and he didn't know what Zalith might be thinking right now.

He scowled again, his irritating, despairing thoughts continuing to travel in circles, and Alucard was yet to find any sort of comfort. He couldn't just stop worrying—he couldn't dismiss his thoughts. He loved Zalith so much that just knowing that he was angry with him made him upset enough to have to fight back his tears. But he didn't want to cry about it, and that made him feel frustrated. Zalith knew how conflicting and overbearing his thoughts became, but he'd left him to panic and assume, and that, too, made him feel irritated—irritated, frustrated, upset, worried, distressed—too many emotions at once. All he could do was sit there and try to work out how to shut everything off.

The only thing he could think to do was sleep. Wherever Zalith was, maybe he'd be back when he woke. So, he walked out into the hall, snatched a blanket from one of the cupboards, and disappeared back into his study.

He lay on his couch, staring at the fish tank as he tried to silence his thoughts enough so that he could rest. His conflicting emotions didn't cease, but they *did* calm a little, and as he tried his best to focus on the hope that Zalith would forgive him, he let himself slowly drift off to sleep.

# Chapter Sixty-Three

— ⪦ ✝ ⪧ —

## Worries and Regrets

**| Zalith |**

Zalith sat by the lake under the familiar tree where he first confessed his love to Alucard and heard those cherished words returned. The memories flooded back, starkly contrasting with the turmoil of recent events. Back then, their relationship had been so much simpler, unburdened by the current struggles. Though he still felt love for Alucard, the happiness of those earlier days seemed distant. The strain between them began when he allowed Alucard to believe that his love had faded, a misunderstanding that now threatened to unravel everything they had built together.

He didn't know how to fix it. He wanted to…more than anything because Alucard meant more to him than anything ever could, and he loved him more than he had ever loved anyone, but not even that stopped him from hurting his vampire.

With a distressed scowl, he picked up one of the pebbles and chucked it towards the lake. He watched as it skipped over the water and sighed quietly. Despite his prior thoughts, he couldn't escape his anger. How could Alucard do this? Luther wanted to tear them apart; he wanted to take Alucard from him, and he'd even told the vampire what Luther was up to…yet, Alucard still let Luther drink his blood.

The thought of Luther touching Alucard…the thought of his *mouth* on Alucard's skin—just the thought of any part of that disgusting little man on Alucard's skin made him furious. And that made him wonder, had Luther bit Alucard anywhere else? Had he only seen a fraction of what happened? He cringed at the thought. His anger became something overbearing as he thought about what Luther obviously wanted to do with Alucard—what he might have done. But that was only making him angrier, and he had to stop because none of it was serving him.

He launched another pebble across the lake, trying to calm down even just a little. Did Alucard do this to hurt him? Was it some sort of payback for the pain he'd forced Alucard to endure while he was gone? No…not only did he not see Alucard as the type to make petty little moves of revenge, but the vampire had also looked and seemed genuinely confused as to why he was mad at him for it—it had even seemed to distress Alucard in a way he'd not seen before…or, more admittedly, in a way he'd only seen when Alucard was facing Damien.

That made him feel awful. He didn't want Alucard to be afraid or wary of him; that was the last thing he wanted. But he had to walk away to protect Alucard; if he allowed himself to talk about why he was mad in that moment, it wouldn't have been good for either of them.

Sighing, he leaned back against the tree and picked up another pebble, but he didn't throw it. He stared down at it, fiddling with it as he lingered on his thoughts. He was sure that Luther was going to love to hear about this; he was almost certain that Luther probably encouraged Alucard to let him bite him. Luther probably knew just as well as Zalith did that Alucard had a kind heart. Sometimes, he was *too* kind, and he highly suspected that Luther had used that to get this to happen.

He wanted to *kill* Luther over and over and over again. He wanted to choke the life out of him as many times as it took to give him satisfaction. Then he'd start hurting him; he'd make Luther *beg* for a permanent death, but he'd not give it to him. He'd tear him apart; he'd remove the limbs from his body again and again, and every time he woke back up, he'd repeat the process. He'd make Luther wish he'd never set his eyes on Alucard, least of all laid a hand on him. Luther didn't deserve kindness, especially not Alucard's, and Zalith wanted to make him understand that he should have *never* thought he could actually take Alucard from him.

But Zalith's murderous thoughts evolved into confusion. Why the hell was Luther even involved in their lives as much as he was? Why was he talking to *Danford*? Was he trying to get information? Was he trying to find out whatever he could about Zalith? What the *fuck* did he want? What did Luther think he was going to find? What was he *hoping* to find? Was Danford actually giving Luther what he wanted? Was he speaking about things he knew he shouldn't?

Zalith scowled and threw the pebble into the water. He didn't want to think about Danford. He wanted to think about Alucard, the man he loved with all his heart. He felt awful for being so cruel to him—for walking away from him despite understanding the desperation in Alucard's voice. He had no idea how that might have made him feel and how he might be feeling right now.

He was sure that Alucard now *hated* him. Why wouldn't he? He'd left him to suffer and wonder for months without a word, he'd let Alucard believe that he didn't want him, and it had become so hard for Alucard that he'd returned to being almost as shy and insecure as he had been at the start of their relationship.

They were drifting apart, and it was all Zalith's fault. If he hadn't left Alucard for as long as he did, then Luther wouldn't have gotten to him. That creepy little man had obviously been trying to convince Alucard to leave him. If he hadn't left Alucard for so long, this might not have happened; he might not have let Luther worm his way in, and he wouldn't have let Luther bite him because Zalith wouldn't have almost killed him yesterday.

He scowled at the grass. Now, every time *he* bit Alucard for the next however long, he knew he was going to feel hurt and conflicted about it—angry, even—because he'd be doing it knowing that Luther had bitten him, that Luther had been allowed to touch *his* vampire. He was sure *that* would push them even further apart because he knew Alucard would notice the change in his biting and his reaction to it.

The demon couldn't help but ponder: was he just karmically doomed to never, *ever* be happy because he'd screwed over so many people? Because he'd used and destroyed and killed so many people in his little quest for a connection—a quest he hadn't even realized he was on until he found Alucard. And then there were the people he screwed over just because he could. Was this slow decline in the best relationship he'd ever had with anyone be part of the world making him pay for all the atrocities he'd committed?

Was he going to lose Alucard? Was there even anything he could do to stop that from happening? He knew he didn't deserve him—he would never deserve him. But that didn't stop him from wanting to do whatever he could to keep him. Without Alucard, what did he even have? What would his life even be? He didn't want to think about it, he didn't want to think about losing Alucard… or to think about someone else having the man he loved, the man he wanted to spend his life with… because he knew how things would turn out. He'd start sleeping around again, desperate for something distracting to fulfil the needs he had because of what he was. None of it would mean anything to him, and all he would ever be able to think about was Alucard.

And as for his vampire…. He knew that Alucard would either isolate himself, or he'd be just as desperate as he was for a connection, and the disgusting, revolting people who lived in this world would take advantage of his kind, precious heart. Zalith didn't want that; he didn't want any of that for either of them. And that was why he felt so desperate, why he felt his heart aching and his throat tightening.

He needed to fix it. He needed to fix everything. He needed to tell—no, he needed to *show* Alucard how much he loved him. He needed to show Alucard just how much he meant to him. He wasn't going to lose him; he wasn't going to let Luther or the world or the Numen win. Alucard was his and he always would be. No one would take *his* vampire away. Not Luther, not Damien, not Lilith, not Lucifer… nor would he let his past mistakes ruin it, either. Alucard was everything to him. Despite his anger and distress, nothing ever made him rethink how sorely he wanted to spend his life with Alucard.

The demon sighed deeply, realizing that all his anger faded to sadness and regret. All he could see was the distressed look on Alucard's face. All he could remember was the desperate tone in his vampire's voice. What was Alucard doing right now? Was he okay? No, of course he wasn't. He was most likely sitting around, a prisoner of his own thoughts. Zalith hated himself for leaving Alucard to suffer once more, and he didn't want to waste any time getting back to him and making this all right.

Zalith hastily stood up. He didn't want to scorch the tree that held such wonderful memories for him and Alucard, so he'd not phase through it. Instead, he swiftly disappeared, using the space between what might be the real world and those around it to get home as swiftly as he could.

| **Luther** |

On Alucard's Galleon, Luther lay in his bed with a content look on his face—a smug smile. Getting kicked the shit out of by Zalith had honestly been worth it; he'd love to see Zalith's face when he found out that Alucard had more or less chosen to side with him on the matter. If Alucard supported Zalith's decision to hurt him, he wouldn't have healed him earlier, would he?

Zalith would be so mad—so jealous, even—knowing that Alucard had not only healed his wounds but allowed him to do so by drinking his blood. Alucard *never* let anyone drink his blood, but he'd let Luther do it, and that made him feel…special. After all, he was sure that the only other person he allowed to drink his blood was Zalith, and now, Zalith didn't even have that over him. He had *nothing* over him. He was clearly slowly losing Alucard, and his desperation was clear in his actions. Beating him up was obviously a show, wasn't it? A feebleminded attempt to show Alucard that he was better than Luther, but he wasn't, and Alucard obviously saw that.

Luther smirked, closing his eyes as he let out a quiet murmur of enjoyment. He'd pretty much forgotten that Danford was sucking his dick. He moved his perfectly healed hand over Danford's head, gripping a fistful of his blonde hair as he slowly dragged his mouth over Luther's shaft. He felt so content right now. He had Danford under his thumb, Varana pined for him to commit to her, and now, he was getting somewhere with Alucard, too. And Zalith was sure to soon see that Alucard didn't need him. He felt so accomplished. Everything had paid off in the end, and he didn't even feel bad about looking forward to seeing Alucard tomorrow so that he might see the result of Zalith finding out what had happened.

He moaned deeply. The pleasure of his victory *and* that which he was receiving from Danford made him feel smugger. He couldn't stop basking in all of it. He was pissing Zalith off more and more every day, and he loved it. He loved that he had both Varana and Danford pining after him, two people that meant a lot to Zalith—well, one of them probably hadn't really meant that much, but it was obviously going to anger Zalith knowing Luther was sleeping with one of his exes as well as his best friend. And soon, that demon was going to lose Alucard to him, too.

He grinned, tightening his grip on Danford's hair. He thought coming to Nefastus was going to be a boring, pointless assignment, but it turned out to be something he thoroughly enjoyed.

The same couldn't be said for his time with Danford, though. It was pleasing, yes, but it wasn't enough. It might never be enough. Ever since he'd started yearning for Alucard's attention, that which he received from others didn't exactly do much for him anymore. His desire for Alucard seemed to make it hard for him to feel satisfied with anyone else. But he had come to terms with the fact that he might not get what he wanted from Alucard for quite some time, so he'd have to settle for what he currently *could* get. Although the person in bed with him might not be who he wanted it to be, there was nothing and no one to stop him from *imagining* that Danford was Alucard—and he didn't even feel bad about it.

He abruptly sat up, his eagerness consuming him. Danford stopped sucking and stared at him in concern, but as Luther grabbed him and made him move onto his hands and knees, he uttered a sound of confusion. Luther didn't want to waste a moment. With Alucard on his mind, he eagerly smothered his shaft in lube, gripped either side of Danford's waist, and plunged his dick into his ass. Danford almost gasped in response, but he soon muttered sounds of enjoyment—sounds Luther didn't want to hear.

As he pulled Danford back and forth, he set his sights on the ceiling, focusing on what he *really* wanted. He closed his eyes, the pleasure quickly constricting him as he let himself believe that it was Alucard in his grip. He mumbled and moaned, his contentment swiftly intensifying. And his thoughts: he focused on Alucard. He focused on just how sweet his blood tasted, how satisfied and how overwrought with pleasure he felt the moment his lips touched Alucard's skin. One day, he'd get to do so much more; he'd get to do all the things he wanted. Alucard would be his, and he wouldn't have to fantasize anymore.

Luther grimaced, tightening his grip on Danford's waist, uttering a loud, pleased moan as he wondered what Alucard might sound like when *he* felt pleasure—sounds he'd get to hear someday, he hoped.

He placed his hand on Danford's back, thrusting faster, breathing deeper. Alucard was all he could think about; how he so sorely wished this was Alucard. How he wanted to touch and kiss and please him to the point he couldn't handle it. He wanted to hear him moan, he wanted to feel his tight ass around his dick, and he wanted to make him cum, he wanted to cum inside him and hear him groan in sheer delight.

*Luther* couldn't handle it anymore. He tensed up, the pleasure becoming intoxicating as he tightened his grip even more. And he couldn't help himself—he couldn't stop himself from letting out a quiet, pleased "*Alucard,*" as he climaxed.

Luther then exhaled deeply; his heart was racing, and his body was trembling. He looked down at Danford, but guilt quickly gripped him. He listened to Danford's deep breaths for a moment, sure that the look on his face was one of confusion or sadness. But Luther didn't want to think about him. He pulled his dick from him and slumped down onto his back, staring up at the ceiling. Now, he just wanted to relax.

Danford looked at him but didn't say anything.

Luther had nothing to say. What was he expecting? An apology? He wasn't going to give him one. He wasn't going to apologize for his desires. He wasn't ashamed of what he really wanted—of what he *deserved.*

But Danford got up and pulled his trousers on. "I'm gonna go shower."

"All right," he mumbled, resting his hands behind his head.

Danford hovered for a moment.

Luther glanced at him. "What?"

"Nothing," he mumbled. Then, he turned around, headed into the bathroom, and locked the door behind him.

With a quiet sigh, Luther rolled his eyes and stared at the ceiling. Now that he had a little alone time, he could let himself wonder what things might be like once he had Alucard.

## | Danford |

Danford stood under the pouring warm water. He tried to keep his sadness from gripping him by focusing on all the things he'd felt before Luther said Aleksei's name.

He was glad that they finally had sex; he'd been eager for it since he accepted the fact that he was attracted to Luther. He *liked* him. He'd been so lonely for so long that Luther's attention made him feel better—it made him feel valid again. Although his packmates didn't hate him, they didn't particularly like him, either, and no one spoke to him much. His recent time with Luther was actually the most time he'd spent with someone in a long time.

But…Luther clearly had feelings for his boss. Not only had he just said Aleksei's name instead of his, but he always asked so many questions about Zalith and how *he* felt about Aleksei. That only made him sadder because he wanted Luther to have feelings for *him*, not for Aleksei. But maybe he did. They were together in a way, so why wouldn't he have feelings for him? Luther was attracted to him, wasn't he? He'd said so—he'd made it clear that he was. After all, *he* was the first person Luther had spoken to out of everyone on this ship, and he was also the only person—other than Varana and Greymore—that he'd spent time with.

He'd like to do more with Luther, perhaps a date or something that didn't involve this boat—something that wouldn't involve talking about Aleksei or Zalith or anything other than themselves. He wanted to know more about Luther; he wanted to talk about himself, and he wanted to ask questions. He really, *really* liked Luther, and he wanted to know if he felt the same.

Maybe dinner or something would be nice—it would be, wouldn't it?

He hastily finished showering, switched the water off, and climbed out. Once he grabbed a towel and wrapped it around his waist, he stepped out into the bedroom and looked at Luther, who was still in bed.

Danford opened his mouth to speak—

Suddenly, the door knocked, and Luther immediately sat up.

"Yeah?" Luther called.

The door opened, and one of the crewmen leaned in to hand him a piece of parchment.

"What is it?" Danford asked curiously, making his way over to him.

Luther read the message, scratching the back of his head as he did. "Eh, I gotta go see Varana," he mumbled, pulling the blanket from over himself as he shuffled to the edge of the bed.

Despondency swallowed Danford. They hadn't even had the chance to lay there and cuddle and Luther was getting ready to leave, and that made Danford think that maybe this vampire didn't really like him that much at all.

"Oh, okay," he said quietly. "Is everything okay?" he asked, hoping that maybe she just needed him for business. After all, Luther *had* said that he and Varana weren't a thing.

"Yeah, I just gotta clear some shit up with her," Luther muttered, pulling on his boots after buckling his belt. He then walked over to him and smiled. "Wait here for me," he said with a smirk, and then, he quickly kissed Danford's lips and tucked his shirt into his trousers.

Danford smiled, his sadness and worry disappearing. "Sure," he said contently.

"Do you want me to bring anything back for you?" Luther asked.

His thoughts stumbled a little; he couldn't really think of an answer. He felt so happy that Luther had offered, so relieved that Luther wasn't just leaving right away. He *did* care, didn't he? Why else would he be asking?

Danford kept his content smile and shook his head. "Oh, uh…" he said, thinking for a few moments, but nothing came to mind. "I'm okay, actually. Thanks."

"All right." Luther sighed, pulling on his coat. "I'll see you in a little while."

"Bye," Danford said.

And then Luther left.

Danford looked down at the floor with a smile still on his face. All he could think about was how much he really did like Luther and how it seemed as though Luther liked him, too. He finally felt that his long while of loneliness was coming to an end, and that was all thanks to Luther. Yeah, he was a little weird here and there, but it wasn't so much that he couldn't ignore it. After all, Luther clearly liked him, so it didn't bother him.

He laid back down in bed, taking a few moments to relax. He'd probably go and draw or paint soon to pass the time while he waited for Luther to get back, and when he got back, he'd suggest they go and do something together away from this ship. Maybe then he'd get to know more about the man he was growing fonder of each day.

# Chapter Sixty-Four

## Explanations

| **Alucard** |

Alucard lay on the couch with his back turned to the door. He woke as he heard the front door open, and his head started aching. His heart hurt, too, and he began to feel anxious when he heard footsteps coming up the stairs. He knew it was Zalith, and he was sure that the demon was going to go into their room— he *hoped* that was where he was going. He didn't want to get yelled at right now.

But Zalith *didn't* go into their bedroom. He opened Alucard's study door, and the vampire tensed up in response. Zalith closed the door behind him, and once he made his way over and sat beside him, Alucard tried his best to pretend to still be asleep.

Zalith gently placed his hand on Alucard's right arm. "Alucard?" he asked quietly.

Alucard didn't answer.

"Can we talk about what happened?" the demon asked.

He didn't want to respond, but maybe it was better to get it out of the way now rather than later. Whatever Zalith had to say…he'd listen. He deserved whatever was coming. He'd been an idiot, and if Zalith didn't want anything to do with him, he'd understand.

In response to Zalith's question, Alucard frowned sullenly and nodded.

Zalith moved his hand from Alucard's shoulder and started to fiddle with his crimson hair. "First of all, I'm sorry that I left like I did. I just get very angry sometimes, and I didn't want the anger to cloud my judgement, which it often does," he explained.

Alucard didn't know what to say. He just stared tiredly at the cushions.

Zalith sighed quietly and caressed the vampire's hair. "My issue with the bite isn't that you healed your employee, because I understand that you need him to work; it's the fact that you—knowing what I told you about what he's trying to do—allowed him to have that intimate moment with you. It might not have felt intimate to you, but I'm sure it felt that way for him because your arm was right up against his face and he could feel your skin on his skin and taste your blood as it came out of your body, and *that* is what makes me angry.

"I told you a long time ago that I didn't want you to feed on other people, and that also applies to other people feeding on you," he said sadly. "I can't stand the thought of it," he added with a grimace, looking down at Alucard's face again. "And I'm sorry if I worried you, Alucard. I just…had to be alone with my thoughts for a while."

Alucard stared aimlessly, his fatigue not waning. His headache got worse, his wrist was sore, and his thoughts were as slow as his recovery. He understood everything Zalith said, though; he'd made valid points. Zalith *had* told him so long ago how he felt about him feeding on other people, and it made sense that it would apply to people feeding on him. He *knew* that; he just made a stupid decision and hadn't thought it through as much as he should have. Zalith had every reason to be mad about it, and Alucard didn't blame him for needing to leave—he wouldn't want to see him either if he was Zalith.

He was far too tired to delve into his thoughts and feelings—those that had been so loud earlier seemed to settle, and he took that as himself accepting it. Of course, he'd been expecting so much worse when Zalith finally came to him, but the demon seemed to have calmed down immensely, and he sounded as though he just wanted to make this better. Alucard wanted that, too; this was the first time Zalith had ever been mad at him, and he hoped that it would be the last. What an awful, upsetting experience.

"I'm sorry, Zaliv," he mumbled, unsure of how else to tell him just how much he regretted it; he wanted to try and explain that he changed his mind, but what good would that do? He didn't want to think about his trauma or his past, he just wanted to fix what happened. Zalith hadn't said he'd forgiven him, and he was sure he might not for a while. It was a stupid, horrible thing, and he should have known Zalith would be upset. He didn't expect him to forgive him any time soon, and however this affected their relationship, he knew he deserved it.

"Don't worry about it, baby," Zalith said. He moved under the blanket with him, kissed the side of his face, and held him tightly.

Zalith rested the side of his face on Alucard's and moved his hand over his chest. Then, for a few moments, they lay in silence.

Alucard still wasn't sure what to think. He felt…strange. Zalith being mad at him was something new—something he hated. It made him feel so worried and upset and confused. He *still* felt confused. Zalith hadn't forgiven him, but he was lying beside him, holding him, and touching him as if everything was okay.

He could only hope it *was* okay. He knew what he did was something that might stick with Zalith for a long time, and he also knew that he needed to do something about Luther, who had become overly involved in his and Zalith's lives…and too confident that he could get away with anything. He couldn't kill him; he couldn't fire him—he needed him. He just needed to reduce the amount of time that Luther got to spend with him.

"Alucard, are we okay?" Zalith then asked, snapping him out of his thoughts.

Frowning, Alucard stared ahead. "Vhat do you mean?" he asked as Zalith moved his fingers through the gaps between his shirt buttons and started slowly dragging them over his chest.

"I know that I've made things not so great between us, but I feel like we're slowly drifting apart, and maybe I'm imagining it, but I really don't want that to happen," he confessed quietly with a despondent tone in his voice.

Alucard wanted to immediately answer and tell Zalith that they were fine, but they weren't, were they? Ever since Zalith's absence, Alucard felt sadder and sadder as each day passed and became convinced that the demon didn't want him anymore. Although that might not be the case, he still felt the confliction that it caused him—the doubt.

It recently helped him decide that he needed to learn to spend more time alone because…what would happen if Zalith disappeared again? If Zalith so suddenly started repeating what he'd done over the past few months, Alucard knew that he'd feel the same, and he didn't want that, so he'd decided he needed to prepare for it and learn to count on himself.

He then frowned. Zalith just brought up the fact that he didn't want him feeding on other people, yet…he'd left him for *months* without his blood…but that didn't seem to be a problem. Zalith hadn't even asked him or talked about what he'd done when he needed blood back when he was too busy in Eltaria forgetting that he existed. He didn't ask him what he'd done throughout that period *at all*.

But he then closed his eyes, trying to dismiss his anger. That wasn't what this was about, and he didn't want to bring it up because he was sure that would only make this whole Luther situation worse.

So, he focused on what Zalith asked him. Were they okay? *Were* they drifting apart? It made him not only distressed to think about it but angry, too. Drifting? Drifted was more like it. They'd been drifting ever since Zalith started working more, ever since he'd not told Alucard he was going to be busier and left him to worry that his attention might be going elsewhere. Alucard tried to ignore his confliction since Zalith's return, but it was still there, and no amount of affection helped. It affected him so badly that he'd started losing faith in the only person he trusted never to hurt him; he'd started feeling as though he *needed* to teach himself to live without Zalith.

Alucard didn't want to hold that over him, though. Zalith might have failed to tell him what was going on, but he was actually out in Eltaria trying to save the lives of what remained of his people, *and* he'd not told Alucard because he wanted to keep him safe. He understood that; he would have just appreciated being told that he wasn't seeing someone else and that he was working. It was all so confusing and conflicting. He wanted to be mad, but he felt bad for being mad, and that upset him because holding in how he felt made him feel worse.

He then realized that he was taking a while to answer Zalith's question—a question he was going to answer with complete honesty. "I zon't know," he said because he *didn't* know if they were okay. He didn't want to lose Zalith, but what if that was where this was leading?

Zalith didn't say anything for a few moments. Alucard felt him ever so slightly tighten his embrace around him, and after a short silence, the demon nuzzled the side of his face. "What should we do?" he asked sadly.

"I zon't know," he answered again.

The demon frowned against his face. "I don't know either," he admitted sadly. "But I do know that I love you, and I want to do whatever I can to make this work."

Staring ahead, Alucard started to feel something awful gripping his heart. He didn't want to lose Zalith; he didn't want Zalith to think that they were going to break up. Maybe he should be *telling* this to Zalith rather than thinking it to himself. "Ve'll be okay," he said quietly. "I still vant to spend my life vith you; even zhough vhat's 'appened 'as 'appened, I 'aven't changed my mind about zhat or you or anyving. I'm just trying to get over zhe vact zhat you levt me vor as long as you did to vorry and panic zhat you zidn't vant me anymore. Vecently, zhis is just making me veel 'esitant to velax and allow myselv to believe zhat zhis von't 'appen again. I vink I just need time to see zhat von't," he explained.

Zalith hugged him even tighter, nuzzling his neck. "Baby, I'm so sorry," he insisted sullenly. "I'm going to prove to you that it won't happen again—I promise it won't."

Alucard wanted to believe it. He wanted to trust him so that he could move on and regain the sense of calm and serenity that their relationship gave him at the very start. But he *did* need Zalith to prove it to him, so he'd let him. "Okay," he said.

The demon then leaned up on his arm and gently pulled Alucard so that he'd rest on his back. Alucard stared up at him, and he stared down at Alucard. But Zalith then moved closer and kissed the vampire's lips.

And that seemed to be the end of that conversation.

Alucard gazed up at Zalith again as the demon stared back. He felt relieved now that he'd told Zalith how he felt, but he felt guilty and concerned about Zalith having not said he'd forgiven him for healing Luther. He didn't want to think about any of that, though. He wanted to focus on the fact that both he and Zalith had said what they needed to say and that they could move on. There was nothing but the truth in what he said to Zalith— he *did* want to spend his life with him—he just needed a little time to get over what happened, just as he was sure Zalith needed time to get over the Luther issue.

Right now, though, Alucard wanted to focus on Zalith—on *them*. When was the last time they'd left Nefastus together? Months ago…his birthday. Leaving for Eltaria didn't exactly count because that was for business, and he wanted to leave to do something for them…something relaxing or fun. It wasn't too late, and he was sure Zalith might like the idea of a night out. Alucard felt that getting out of the house for a while would do them some good, and to spend some time alone together would, too.

As Zalith placed his hand on the side of Alucard's face, the vampire frowned shyly. "Do you…vant to go and do someving?"

Zalith smiled and laughed slightly. "Like what?"

Alucard shrugged, taking his eyes off Zalith as he thought for a few moments. Anywhere would be nice. They could go for a walk or for dinner; they could even spend the night somewhere. He just wanted to be alone with Zalith and not have to worry about anyone or anything else.

He needed to make sure that the place he came up with wasn't too far away. They couldn't phase, Drac wasn't around to pull the ship, and Alucard was sure that Zalith wouldn't like to use public transport, so the only option left was for him to fly them to wherever it was they wanted to go—and where he wanted to go was somewhere…romantic. The place that came to mind was Lupa; he'd heard many times how couples spent their anniversaries there, so a *date* must be nice to have there, too. Although it was far away, it didn't make him hesitate; he'd just have to use a little more ethos to get there faster.

Alucard looked back up at Zalith. "Ve could…go to Lupa. I 'eard zhere are so many nice places zhere to 'ave dinner."

"I'd love that," the demon said, smiling.

Alucard then smiled, too.

"How will we get there, though?"

"I vill vly us."

"Okay," Zalith agreed and then smirked. "So, where are you taking me, vampire?"

"Vell," Alucard said, frowning, "zhere is big city in Lupa. Ve could go zhere and pick vone of zhe vestaurants?"

Zalith smiled and dragged his thumb down the side of Alucard's face. "All right. Are we going to be spending the night in Lupa?"

Alucard thought to himself for a few moments. "Maybe. Vould probably be better to do zhat. Vill veally tire me out to vly us zhere and back in zhe same night."

"Okay," the demon said, and then he leaned in and kissed Alucard.

Alucard wasn't in any rush to leave, so he kissed Zalith back, moving his hand to the back of his head. And for a short while, they kissed, and Alucard felt what remained of his conflicting thoughts disappear. Zalith's affection always had a way of calming him down, but it also made him experience a different kind of angst.

He felt Zalith slowly moving his hand down his body, still kissing him as he did, and when the demon reached his crotch, Alucard felt his abrupt excitement begin to grow. He tightened his grip on Zalith's hair, tensing up as the demon lightly gripped his shaft over his trousers. They continued kissing one another while Zalith caressed the vampire's arousal, and Alucard's enjoyment soon became eagerness. As it always did, all it took was a little of Zalith's affection to have him yearning for more.

Zalith's kisses soon moved from his lips to his neck, and as Alucard stared up at the ceiling, he awaited what would come next. But the demon was taking his time. He continued caressing the vampire's shaft, kissing his neck, and smiling as Alucard fidgeted impatiently, quiet utters of both content and desperation escaping his breath.

But to Alucard's relief, Zalith eventually moved his hand up to his waist and moved his fingers under his belt. Alucard waited, gripping Zalith's hair, sighing in anticipation as the demon kissed his neck one last time, moving his hand under his belt and into his trousers.

However, that was when Zalith stopped. He stopped kissing him; he stopped pushing his hand towards his crotch, and he lifted his face from Alucard's neck to look down at him.

Confused, impatient, and concerned, Alucard stared up at him, waiting for an explanation. But Zalith just stared at him with a seductive, amused smirk. Alucard wanted to ask why he was smiling—and why he stopped—but he was sure that he wouldn't get an answer.

Zalith then dragged his thumb down the side of the vampire's face again. "Let's get ready to go," he said, pulling his hand from Alucard's trousers.

Alucard frowned in disbelief. Did he think this was funny? To excite him like this— to make him eager and impatient and then stop? Alucard pouted, taking his eyes off Zalith to glare at the fish tank.

The demon then kissed his cheek once, twice, and a third time before getting up. "Let's go," he said again, still smirking.

As Zalith stood up, Alucard sat up and pulled one of the cushions into his lap to hide his arousal. "*You* go," he grumbled.

Zalith started laughing. "Okay," he said, making his way over to the door. And then, he left, leaving Alucard alone.

Still glaring at the fish tank, Alucard pouted again. He didn't know what to think. All he could focus on was how irritated he felt and how funny Zalith obviously found it. He was certain that Zalith would hate it if he did the same to him, and as the thought came to mind, Alucard decided that he wanted to irritate Zalith. If *he* got to amuse himself, then Alucard would amuse himself, too.

He stood up, left his study, and made his way into their bathroom, where Zalith had just turned on the shower. The demon smirked at Alucard as he made his way in and shut the door behind him, and then they both undressed and stepped into the shower together.

Once they finished showering, they headed out of the bathroom, through their bedroom, and into the dressing rooms.

Alucard walked over to his collection of suits, his gaze settling on a sleek black tuxedo. He decided this would be the one. After all, they were heading to Lupa, where one's attire determined the quality of their seating and dining experience. It had been ages since his last visit to Lupa, but he recalled it as a vibrant, bustling country. He was certain that he and Zalith were in for an interesting night, and he wanted to look his best for the occasion.

The thought excited him. Lupa—more specifically, the city of Alvarez—was well known for its picturesque architecture, its lively, sleepless people, and the seemingly never-ending nights of thrill and celebration. *That* was where he wanted to take Zalith.

He pulled on a white shirt, black trousers, and his black suit. Around his neck, he tied the black bowtie that went with his tuxedo and then started to tidy his hair. Once he was done, he turned around, but Zalith appeared in front of him with a smirk on his face and started straightening the vampire's bowtie.

"You look adorable," the demon said.

Noticing that Zalith was wearing the same thing, Alucard frowned and flicked the demon's bowtie. "So do you," he mumbled.

Zalith laughed amusedly, moved his hand to the side of Alucard's face, and then kissed him. "Thank you." He smirked as he started to fiddle with the vampire's hair. He did so for a few moments but then sighed and moved his hand to Alucard's shoulder. "Are you ready to go?" he asked.

"Are *you*?" Alucard questioned, a testing tone in his voice.

"Are *you*?"

Alucard pouted. "Yes, I'm veady."

The vampire headed towards the dressing room door, but he hadn't forgotten about his wish to amuse himself. So, when Zalith followed him, he walked a little faster, and before Zalith could follow him out of the room, Alucard swiftly turned around and pulled the door shut, sealing Zalith inside. He smirked and laughed quietly, having seen a glimpse of Zalith's confused face.

He heard Zalith laugh from behind the door, though. "What are you doing?"

"Leaving vithout you," Alucard sneered.

"You can't leave if you're here holding the door shut."

Looking down at the hand he was using to hold the door, Alucard rolled his eyes but kept his amused smile. "I could just lock you in," he said, glancing around the room for the key.

"You *could*," Zalith agreed, "but it's not going to keep me from getting out."

"I vould like to see you try and get out," Alucard challenged.

"Okay," Zalith laughed.

The demon turned the doorknob and pulled, but Alucard pulled back, keeping the door from opening. Zalith applied more force. Alucard scowled and applied even more, slamming the door shut once again. However, Zalith didn't try tugging back. Alucard frowned as he felt someone or something move behind him, but before he could even manage to glance over his shoulder, Zalith threw himself at the vampire, wrapping his arms around him as Alucard stumbled forward, startled by Zalith's sudden appearance.

Obviously, Zalith had opened the door just enough to see a space to relocate to, and as he squeezed his arms around Alucard, the vampire pouted stubbornly, regaining his balance. Zalith started kissing the side of his face—frantically and annoyingly—and soon, the demon began playfully biting his neck as he laughed quietly.

But once he was done kissing and biting, Zalith rested his chin on Alucard's shoulder, still holding him tightly.

"Let go," Alucard said with a stubborn pout, trying to pull his arms free. His attempt to amuse himself didn't exactly go to plan.

Zalith smirked. "No."

Irritated, Alucard tried to get free from Zalith's grip; he snatched the demon's wrists and attempted to move his arms from around him, but Zalith laughed and held him tighter. The demon kissed the side of his face again, and again, and again, and Alucard's irritated scowl thickened. As the demon continued laughing, Alucard did his best not to laugh with him. He pouted, struggling, trying to pull free; with each attempt to pull and squirm away, Zalith took a few steps back to keep his balance, something Alucard was determined to have him lose.

After a few more moments of struggling, the back of Zalith's shin hit the bed, and they both fell onto it. Laughing, Zalith *finally* let go of Alucard, who immediately got up, turned around, and glared down at him.

"Sorry," the demon said, smiling up at him. He then moved his hand behind his head, relaxing where he lay. "Are you ready to go?" he asked with a smirk. "You're taking an awfully long time."

Tidying his hair, Alucard pouted irritably. His attempt to make Zalith feel as frustrated as he made him feel obviously failed, as did his attempt to fluster him before. It wasn't really much of an attempt, though, was it? He'd just said 'so are you' in response to Zalith's compliment. If he wanted to fluster Zalith, he was going to have to try harder.

When Zalith stood up and helped him tidy his crimson hair, Alucard sighed quietly. "Ve can go now," he said.

Straightening Alucard's bowtie once more, Zalith smiled. "Okay," he said, slipping his hand into the vampire's. And then, Zalith led the way out of their bedroom.

Once they got outside, Alucard dematerialized them both into vermillion smoke and began their journey to Lupa, where he was sure that they'd have an eventful night.

LIGHT
Numen Chronicles | Volume Three

ARC THREE
+
LUPA

# Chapter Sixty-Five

## Alvarez

| **Alucard** |

Alucard and Zalith arrived in Lupa's capital, Alvarez. The vampire made sure to land in a deserted alley and rematerialized them both from vermillion smoke when they hit the ground. They straightened their blazers, and as Zalith smirked and took hold of Alucard's arm with his, they walked out of the alley and into the busy streets.

The sidewalks were lit by lanterns and the light coming from inside the buildings lined along the road. Every place was either a store or restaurant and despite the fact that it was late, everywhere was still open as it would be during daylight. All the people were dressed expensively or casually, laughing and chattering as they made their way down the bustling streets.

Alucard hadn't been to Lupa in so long, but nothing had changed. Unlike everywhere else, no one was afraid of what might come out after sunset—even the people of Nefastus retreated after a certain time—but here in Lupa, it seemed as though they had nothing to be scared of.

As they continued through the crowds of enthusiastic people, Alucard smiled at Zalith. "Is still as I vemember."

Zalith smiled back at him. "I like it." He then stared ahead, eyeing the city's bright scenery. "Did you use to come here often?"

Alucard shrugged. "A long time ago. I spent some time 'ere vith—" but before he mentioned Luther's name, he frowned, "—Attila and some of zhe ozzer people ve used to valk avound vith."

The demon glanced at him, still smiling. "What did you use to do here?"

"Vas mostly looking vor opportunities. Everyvone who is anyvone comes to Alvarez, so is zhe best place to 'ead to do business. I met a vew of my old subordinates 'ere. Ve vould attend zhe same ball every year vor a vew years in a row; vas vor some vich guy's birvday. Attila knew 'im, so ve vould come 'ere, go to zhe party, and vhile my subordinates got drunk and did vhatever, I sought out people who vould be usevul to me."

"A ball?" Zalith asked as they turned onto another street. "Did you dance?"

"No," he said with a pout, glaring ahead while they continued making their way through the seemingly endless crowds of people. "I vas alvays alone, and I von't dance alone," he mumbled.

"Oh. What about with your friends?"

"No…" he answered. "I only dance vith people I like," he sneered.

"Who have you danced with?" Zalith asked with an amused but curious tone.

Losing his frown, Alucard sighed and slowed down. They kept walking, but Zalith's question stirred the dormant sadness inside him. The only person other than Zalith that he danced with was Vanessa. Every time he remembered her, he remembered the guilt. She and her sons died because of him, and he hadn't had a chance to thank her for taking him in all that time ago.

They stopped walking, and while the muttering crowds walked around them, Alucard looked at Zalith and shrugged. "Vanessa taught me," he told him. "I vas 'eading to a ball vone night and she zidn't vant to let me go vithout knowing 'ow to dance in case I met somevone. She vas… alvays urging me to vind somevone to love back zhen."

Zalith smirked as they started walking again. "Ah, yes, your wife. That was very nice of her," he said. But before Alucard could respond, the demon asked, "Did you ever sleep with her?"

Alucard stopped and glared at him. He wasn't sure if Zalith was asking out of jealousy or in jest. Either way, his question irritated him. "No," he answered sternly. "I told you I've never been vith anyvone bevore you," he mumbled, moving forward again.

The demon laughed and put his arm around Alucard. He pulled him closer, hugging him while they walked. "I'm just joking with you." He kissed the side of Alucard's face. "You looked so mad," he laughed.

Alucard sighed quietly. "She just deserved better," he grumbled, "and every time I vemember 'er, I vemember 'ow everyving zhat 'appened vas my vault."

"I'm sorry if I upset y—"

"You zidn't," Alucard assured him.

"Okay, good."

Then, Alucard stared ahead again and continued leading the way through Alvarez.


After a short while of silence, they turned onto the street that Alucard had been searching for.

"*Via della Pace*?" Zalith asked, reading from the sign as they passed it.

"Means Street of Peace," Alucard translated and set his eyes on the tallest, brightest building—which was made mostly of glass. He wasn't surprised to see that The Glass

House was still around; it was one of the main reasons that people went to Alvarez; it was the best restaurant for miles, maybe even one of the best in all of Aegisguard. He'd *always* wanted to go, and he couldn't think of a better person to eat there with than Zalith. He looked over at the demon as he nodded in the direction of the glass building. "Ve could eat zhere," he suggested. "*La Casa di Vetro.*"

Zalith stared ahead at the building. "Which means?" he asked curiously.

"Zhe Glass 'ouse."

"Have you been before?" he asked, looking at him.

"No. I've alvays vanted to go, zhough."

"Let's try it out, then," Zalith said, smiling.

Content, Alucard led the way towards the huge glass building.

They made their way inside and headed to the attendant waiting behind the desk not too far from the doors. The restaurant's interior exuded opulence, with high, ornately decorated ceilings adorned with intricate frescoes and sparkling chandeliers casting a warm, golden light. Rich, dark wood panelling lined the walls, interspersed with large, gilded mirrors that reflected the elegance of the surroundings. Velvet draperies in deep burgundy framed tall windows, through which the bustling street outside was visible.

As the attendant set her striking green eyes on both of them, she stood up gracefully. Her attire matched the establishment's luxurious ambience—a deep emerald gown with delicate lace accents. She made her way out from behind the mahogany desk, the soft rustle of her dress adding to the atmosphere of refined sophistication. The polished marble floors beneath her feet echoed softly as she approached, her welcoming smile a perfect complement to the grandeur of the luxury restaurant.

"Good evening," she said in Lupanese. "Are you looking for a table or a room?"

A room? Alucard glanced around and judging by the stack of leather suitcases currently being towed towards the stairs by a bellhop, it seemed as though the restaurant was also a hotel. That was rather coincidental, as they had decided they'd spend the night in Alvarez, too.

He looked at Zalith, whom he knew couldn't understand Lupanese. "Should ve get a voom 'ere, too? Or do you vant to look avound vor somevhere else to stay?"

"We can stay here, but make sure to get us the best room they have to offer," Zalith said with a smirk.

Nodding, Alucard set his eyes back on the woman. "Ve vant a room *and* a table," he said in Lupanese.

"Of course," she said. She then led them over to the desk. "Do you know what sort of room you're looking for?" she asked, taking out a small leather book from behind the desk.

"Zhe pent'ouse," Alucard said.

She took her eyes off whatever she was reading and glanced at them both. Her expression made it clear that she was pondering… likely debating whether to ask if they could afford it or if they wanted separate beds or rooms—maybe all those things. But after a few seconds, she nodded and looked back down at her book. "That's going to be fifty coronam a night," she said hesitantly.

"Vine," Alucard muttered as he reached into his pocket and into his vault.

"I can pay," Zalith then said, lightly gripping Alucard's wrist before he could pull the money from his pocket.

But Zalith paid the last time they stayed somewhere, and Alucard felt as if it was his turn to pay for their night out. "Is vine," he said, pulling the money from his pocket. "I vant to."

The demon smiled and relented. "Okay."

Alucard pulled the coronam papers from his pocket and handed them to the woman. As she counted… and *double-counted* the payment, she sighed and looked back at them. "One moment," she said and then disappeared into a small room behind the counter.

Once she was gone, Alucard leaned his back against the desk and sighed quietly, glancing at the few people who were lined up and waiting to be called over. Zalith moved in front of him and smiled, placing his hand on his waist. The vampire waited for him to speak, but instead, Zalith leaned in and kissed his lips. He then kissed his cheek and moved his hand down to lightly grab his ass before the woman returned.

Trying to dismiss his embarrassed frown—and ignore the few quiet rude mumbles from the people waiting—Alucard turned to face the woman as she placed a key onto the desk.

"Okay, you just take the stairs to the right there," she said, pointing over at a flight of stairs. "They'll take you all the way up."

Alucard took the key and placed it in his pocket.

"Now, is there any specific table you gentlemen would like?" she asked.

He looked at Zalith. "Is zhere a specific table you vant?"

"Something with a view," he answered.

"Someving vith a view," Alucard repeated in Lupanese.

The woman nodded and stared down at another book. She took a few moments to read and then set her eyes back on Alucard. "If you'd like to follow me, I can show you to a table," she invited, smiling as she placed her book back down on the desk.

Alucard moved his arm back into Zalith's and then followed her as she led the way into the restaurant. He was eager to try the food, and once they were done, he hoped that they'd find something exciting to do before retreating to their room and heading to bed. But the night was still early, and he was sure that there was plenty of time for him and Zalith to enjoy the city.

# Chapter Sixty-Six

## Pizza

| Alucard |

Alucard glanced around the busy restaurant as the woman led him and Zalith to their table. He was both content and excited to be spending time outside of the house with Zalith, and he hoped that Zalith felt the same, too. It had been a while since they'd left Nefastus together, and it felt relieving to have done so.

He couldn't ignore that Zalith looked a little paranoid, though. He could see the worry on the demon's face, and it looked as though he was glancing around and expecting to spot something dangerous. Alucard didn't want him to be panicking all night, so he'd do whatever he could to help him feel more comfortable.

The demon moved his arm from Alucard's and instead gripped his hand, smiling at him as they followed the woman over to a table beside a window. They sat across the table from one another, and once the woman handed them their menus, they made themselves comfortable.

"What would you like to drink?" the woman then asked in Lupanese.

Alucard looked at Zalith. "Vhat do you vant to drink?" he translated.

"Red wine," Zalith said, smiling.

The woman replied and wandered off.

"She vill send somevone over vith zhem," Alucard told Zalith, setting his sights on him.

"Okay," Zalith said, picking up his menu... but of course, he wouldn't be able to understand what was written on it. He placed it down and smiled at Alucard. "Will you read the menu to me?" he asked, smirking.

Alucard took his eyes off his own menu and glanced at him. He then looked back down at it and nodded. "Zhere are only vree vings vor each course."

"Well," Zalith said as he rested his arms on the table, "I'll have whatever they recommend," he said, glancing at the waiter, who was heading over with their drinks. "Although I'd like something with chicken," he added.

Alucard nodded, and as the waiter placed their drinks down, he told him in Lupanese what they were going to have.

Once the waiter wandered off, the demon poured himself and Alucard a glass of the wine that the man had brought over.

The vampire sipped from his drink and glanced at Zalith, who was smiling at him, and then looked down at his glass as he placed it on the table. He wasn't sure how long they might be waiting for their food, but sitting in silence wasn't exactly what either of them wanted, was it?

But what to talk about? All he really had to discuss were business matters, and he wasn't sure this was the time or place. This was, after all, a date, and he didn't want to start talking about operations or business plans or partnerships over their dinner—unless Zalith was content doing so, but how was he to know? He wanted to tell Zalith about the recent concern for his own people and his plans that involved Greymore, but again, was now really the time?

"So," Zalith said with a smile, sipping from his wine, "have you had any more dreams about our little girl lately?"

Alucard frowned in embarrassment. He thought Zalith had forgotten he'd had such a strange dream, but he obviously hadn't. "No," he said with a pout. "Just zhe vone I told you about."

Zalith frowned sadly. "That's a shame. I'm jealous; I want to meet her."

He shrugged. "Vas just a veird dream."

The demon smiled. "You never know. Sometimes, people's dreams come true," he said with a shrug.

Alucard frowned. There were times when he'd experienced such dreams; he'd dreamt something that later happened. "Vell…'as 'appened to me. Only…veally vonce or twice."

With an interested smile, Zalith leaned his arms on the table. "What happened, if you don't mind me asking?"

"Noving good," he mumbled. "Zhe virst time, I dreamt all zhe children I knew vhen I vas being vaised by Zamien vould die…and zhey did. Zhen, I dreamt zhat Vanessa vould die. She did. "

Zalith lost his smirk and frowned sadly. "Those are…sad dreams."

Alucard shrugged once more, sipping from his wine again. "I 'aven't 'ad vone zhat's come true in a 'undred years or vhatever, so I zon't vink I vill get zhem anymore. Ever since I levt Zamien's castle and stopped going back zhere, I 'aven't veally 'ad dreams about people dying, so…maybe vas a fear ving," he assumed.

"I hope you have only pleasant dreams from now on," Zalith said, smiling.

Nodding, Alucard sipped from his drink. But he didn't want to talk about dreams or people dying anymore. They were supposed to be enjoying themselves, not talking about things that upset them or ruined their mood. So, as he placed his glass down, he rested his arms on the table and set his eyes on Zalith. "Vhat's zhe biggest city you 'ave been to?" he asked, changing the subject.

The demon then frowned something sullen. "I want to answer," he said quietly, "but my answer is a sad one."

Alucard adorned a concerned expression. "You zon't 'ave to answer if you zon't vant to."

Zalith laughed slightly—a laugh that was clearly supposed to mask his sadness. "The city where I grew up," he answered. "Maybe I'll take you there one day. How about you?"

A trip to a city in Eltaria? That excited him. He smiled slightly, keeping his eyes on Zalith. "Zhe Citadel is actually zhe biggest city in Aegisguard, but Alvarez is a close second. I vink I 'ave probably visited every major city 'ere ozzer zhan in Samjang…or Samayo-Akuma."

"Perhaps we can still visit Samjang and Samayo-Akuma together someday soon," he suggested.

Alucard nodded. "I vould like to do zhat."

Just then, the waiter who gave them their drinks made his way over with two plates. He placed one in front of Alucard and the other in front of Zalith. He muttered something in Lupanese and then wandered off again; he had the same dirty look on his face that the people in the reception room had.

"Ooh, risotto." Zalith smirked as he looked at Alucard.

Alucard glanced at him. "Is vhat zhe vaiter vecommended."

"That's good. I like risotto."

Having not tried it himself, Alucard looked down at his risotto, frowned unsurely at the appearance of it, but tried it anyway. He decided that if he was going to be living with someone who ate as regularly as a human, then he should try as many different foods as he could. After all, they weren't going to have the same four things he tried all the time, were they?

He tasted the risotto, and to his surprise, it was actually pretty good.

"Do you like it?" Zalith asked.

Alucard nodded as he sipped from his wine. "I've never 'ad zhis bevore. Do you like yours?"

"I do," Zalith said, smiling. "It's good."

Smiling, Alucard looked back down at his food and continued eating.

While he ate, however, he wanted to find something to talk about. Every time they went silent, he began worrying that Zalith might be thinking about how he was mad at him earlier—about what happened with Luther. Zalith still hadn't said he'd forgiven him, and even though Alucard knew it was going to take some time to get over, he couldn't help but feel anxious about it. But he didn't want to think about it.

He drank his wine, keeping his eyes off Zalith as he tried to think of something else to talk about—something else to *think* about. But his thoughts immediately jumped to what he'd been thinking about earlier. His people: they weren't safe in Dor-Sanguis, and they'd be in even more danger once the fight with the Numen started. He didn't want to leave them there; he'd abandoned them enough lately, and he owed it to them to give them somewhere safer to live until the Numen business was over.

Earlier, he came up with a plan to unite Greymore's pack with Freja's so that he could move his werewolf subordinates to Nefastus. As for the vampires, he'd have to think that through more; after all, not all of them could walk in the sunlight.

The werewolf business, however, required a talk with Zalith, and he wasn't sure that now was the best time to talk about it… but it wasn't like they were talking about anything else, were they?

He looked at Zalith, who had almost finished his risotto. With a quiet sigh, he said, "Zaliv," and as the demon smiled at him, he rested his arms on the table. "Ve zon't 'ave to talk about business if you zon't vant to, but… zhere's someving I need to talk to you about."

Zalith didn't lose his smile. He sipped from his wine and then placed his glass back down. "I don't mind. What is it?"

When Zalith stopped eating to look at him, Alucard thought about how to begin; from the start would be best. "Bringing your people 'ere made me vink about my own, and ever since zhe grim veapers turned up vatching my castle, 'as become clear to me zhat zhey are not safe in Dor-Sanguis, and zhey'll be in more danger vhen ve start zhis Numen 'unt," he explained worriedly. "Zamien knows vhere my castle is, and so does Liliv; I'm surprised zhey 'aven't attacked zhere yet. Anyvay, I vant to bring zhem 'ere— all of zhem."

The demon nodded. "Do you want to keep them on our property like I plan to do with my people?"

"Vell…" Alucard said, looking down at his glass as he picked it up, "I vas 'oping zhat Vreja and Greymore's packs vould unite, zhen zhey can live and vork togezzer. As vor my vampires, I need to vink about zhat more."

"Do you think that Freja and Greymore will have to get married, or would they just be able to join forces and work it out between them?"

"Ovten, is zhe Alphas zhat marry since zhey are zhe leaders of zheir packs, but… I zon't know. Vreja got vone of 'er sisters to marry zhe Beta zhat took over Tobias' pack, and zhat seems to be vorking out, but I zon't know 'ow Greymore's pack vill veact if is not zheir Alpha marrying Vreja."

"They've gotten used to working unconventionally, but if Freja were to marry Greymore, it would probably go smoother," Zalith said slowly. "How old is Freja?"

Alucard wasn't sure. "I vink…late…tventies…maybe early virties," he said, shrugging.

Zalith nodded. "What's she like?"

He didn't know that, either. "I zon't know," he admitted. "She knows 'ow to do 'er job, and zhat's all I veally cared to know back zhen."

"Is Freja going to agree to it?"

"She vill do vhatever I tell 'er to do; zhis is also vor zhe savety of 'er pack, so, yes."

"Well, I'll talk to Greymore, but he's going to have a million questions, and he's going to want to know about her personality."

"Zhey can just…meet…or someving."

"I'll still have to talk to him, but meeting is probably in their best interest." Zalith leaned forward a little and smiled. "Look at you, my little matchmaker," he laughed.

Alucard pouted and looked down at his food. "If zhey agree to zhis, your people and my people vill become our people," he muttered, sure that he should warn Zalith before anything went ahead.

Zalith kept his smile. "Aw."

Unsure of what his reaction meant, Alucard frowned. "Is…zhat okay?"

"It's more than okay," he said, smirking. "It'll be fun."

"Vun?" Alucard questioned.

"I enjoy working with you."

Alucard took his eyes off Zalith, trying to hide his shy smile. "I like vorking vith you, too."

"I like doing a lot of things with you," Zalith said with a flirtatious tone in his voice, accompanying the suggestive look on his face.

As he always did whenever Zalith flirted with him, Alucard became flustered and glanced around the room. Nobody seemed to hear, so he frowned at Zalith and pouted. But he hesitated; maybe he should respond with a similar attitude rather than shy away as usual. After all, he'd told himself that he was going to be less nervous when it came to these sorts of things. So, he asked curiously, "Like vhat?"

Zalith smirked in surprise but kept his flirtatious stare. "I like when we spend time together, and when we eat breakfast together in the morning. I like sleeping next to you in bed at night…and I also like when we touch each other. I like when you let me do mouth stuff to you…and when we have sex," he said, keeping his voice hushed.

Alucard's face reddened as he looked away, but as he did, he noticed the waiter making his way over with a large plate. He and Zalith waited in silence as the man took their empty plates and then placed the new one on the table. On it sat the pizza that the same waiter recommended. He'd never had it before, and it looked…strange. Once the waiter was gone, though, Alucard pouted and refilled both his and Zalith's glasses.

"What do *you* like doing with me?" Zalith asked.

He didn't know what to say. He liked doing everything with Zalith and he enjoyed all the things he'd said. But he didn't want to answer with a simple 'everything you said'; he felt as if he should at least give Zalith something.

The vampire frowned nervously and shrugged. "Everyving you said," he started, "but…I also like vhen ve just sit avound and do noving togezzer. I like vaking up vith you next to me, and I like…vhen you touch my vace," he admitted because he *did*. His face was something he never liked *anyone* touching, not even Zalith at the start. But now, he loved when Zalith put his hand on the side of his face and rested his forehead on his. There were so many things he used to hate that he now loved because it was Zalith doing it, and thinking about it made him smile.

Zalith also smiled as he leaned his arms on the table again. He then reached out, lightly gripped Alucard's chin to pull him closer, and then kissed his lips.

When Zalith then relaxed back in his seat, he looked down at the pizza and smiled. Obviously noticing Alucard's conflicted frown, he frowned, too. "What's wrong?" he asked.

Alucard glanced at him and shrugged. "I…zidn't know vhat pizza vas," he admitted.

The demon laughed quietly. He picked up a slice of the pizza and held it out to him. "Try it."

Staring at it, Alucard frowned hesitantly. But he tried the risotto, and he liked that, so maybe he'd like this, too. He leaned forward, taking a bite of the pizza; it wasn't bad, but he didn't like it as much as the risotto. "Is okay," he mumbled.

"Would you like to get something else instead?"

"Vould you?" Alucard asked.

"Well, I want you to enjoy your dinner."

Alucard shook his head and took the slice he tried from Zalith. "Zhis is vine."

Zalith shook his head. "Tell them to take it back; we can order whatever else was on the menu."

With a stubborn pout, Alucard took another bite of the pizza and frowned. "I'm not calling anyvone over 'ere."

The demon smirked slightly. "Then you better eat every last bite."

"I vill," he sneered.

"If you don't, you won't be getting dessert."

Alucard frowned, finishing the slice of pizza. "I'll do vhat I vant," he grumbled.

Zalith laughed and started eating, too.

After a while, Alucard's attention shifted to a few distinct voices in the crowded restaurant. He ignored them before, but the disgusted comments from a table not too far from their own became more persistent. Part of him was glad that Zalith couldn't understand what they were saying because he might have caused a scene by now, but he didn't like sitting there hearing the things he was hearing and knowing Zalith had no idea.

While Zalith continued eating, Alucard picked up another slice of pizza and glanced at the table where a group of aristocrats were sitting. They laughed, they muttered, and as they looked over at him and the demon, their hushed insults became harsher.

"What's wrong?" Zalith then asked, glancing in the direction Alucard was looking.

Alucard sighed despondently. Could they not have a *single* date that didn't consist of executing their enemies and having to leave to prevent bloodshed because the people around them didn't like the fact they were both men?

He shrugged, placing his food down now that he no longer felt like eating it. "Noving," he mumbled.

Zalith frowned in concern, moving his hand over his. "It can't be nothing. What's wrong?"

"Can ve just…go?" He didn't want to make a huge deal out of it. He'd rather leave and spend the rest of the night elsewhere.

The demon's concerned frown thickened. "Of course. Are you okay, though?"

"I'm vine," he said, standing up. "I just vant to leave."

Zalith nodded and then followed him as he led the way out.

He didn't want to give in to his anger or sadness. He just wanted to leave and spend their night somewhere they wouldn't be looked down upon.

"What happened?" Zalith asked once they stepped outside.

Alucard looked at him as they stopped by one of the building's large windows. He sighed, shrugged, and shook his head. "Zhere vere people in zhere," he muttered. "Zhey zidn't like seeing us, and I vould vather leave zhan start anyving."

Staring at him, Zalith frowned sadly and then pulled him into a tight hug. "Would you rather we go back to our room for a little while? We could head out again later."

"Yes," he agreed. He'd rather have some time to relax and calm down before looking for somewhere else to spend their evening.

"All right," Zalith said, still holding him.

And after a few moments, the demon took hold of his hand and led the way back inside, heading for their room.

# Chapter Sixty-Seven

—⟨ ✟ ⟩—

## Overthinking

**| Alucard |**

In their opulent hotel room, Alucard and Zalith rested on the plush, canopied bed positioned just below the large, arched window. The room exuded Lupanese luxury, with high ceilings adorned with intricate frescoes and a crystal chandelier that cast a soft, ambient glow. The walls were lined with rich damask wallpaper in deep burgundy, accented by dark mahogany wainscoting and ornate gilded mouldings.

The furnishings were equally sumptuous, with a beautifully carved armoire and a marble-topped vanity. Heavy velvet drapes, tied back with gold tassels framed the window, offering a view of the bustling city below. The commotion of the bright city streets was a stark contrast to the serene, almost reverent silence that enveloped the demon and the vampire.

They lay in a tranquil stillness, the weight of the day's events pressing down on them. The luxurious linens and embroidered pillows provided a comforting rest, while the scent of fresh flowers from a porcelain vase on the bedside table mingled with the faint aroma of burning wood from the marble fireplace. Alucard's eyes wandered over the room's ornate details, from the intricate patterns on the fur rug to the delicate lace of the curtains swaying gently in the evening breeze. Despite the elegance surrounding them, a heavy silence lingered as they found solace in each other's presence amidst the grandeur.

However, a sour scowl clung to Alucard's face as he tried to relax with his head on Zalith's chest, but all he could think about was how yet another of their dates had been cut short. Maybe he should have just ignored those people; if he had, he and Zalith would have been able to finish their dinner.

It all bothered him so much, though. Why were people so arrogant? Why should it matter that they were a couple or that they were both men? And why did people have to say such awful things? He didn't want to lay there thinking about it, but how could he not?

He opened his eyes to glare over at the window. Hearing those people only made him understand even more why Zalith decided to hide the fact that he was gay back home in Nefastus, and Alucard was starting to think that maybe it was best they did that *everywhere*. After all, next time, it might be more than some harsh words from afar.

Alucard didn't want himself or Zalith to have to deal with it. They shouldn't *have* to, but then they shouldn't have to act a certain way in public just to please the masses. He didn't want to not hold Zalith's hand; he didn't want Zalith to not kiss him wherever and whenever. He didn't care what people thought…he just didn't want unnecessary drama or conflict. He just wanted to enjoy *one* night with Zalith that wasn't spoiled by either their enemies or people who looked down on them.

"Do you want to talk about how you're feeling?" Zalith suddenly asked quietly, caressing the vampire's crimson hair.

Alucard sighed and buried the side of his face in Zalith's shirt. "I just veel mad," he mumbled irritably.

"Well, we love each other, and that's all that matters. If people don't like it, oh well, they're going to have to get used to it," he stated, tightening his embrace around him.

"Vhy are people so…I zon't know. Vhat is so vrong about zhis? Vhy do people 'ate you if you're anyving but straight?"

The demon shrugged. "Ignorance can breed fear and hatred. Attila once said it was an offence to God. I haven't read much into this world's religions and their views, but from what I have heard, if you're gay, and if you associate with anyone who is gay, you're headed straight for hell, and before that, your life will be long with misery and misfortune," he said amusedly. "Something to do with order and balance, too. Humans seem to believe that they were put in this world to simply please the gods and breed more people to one day please the gods. Perhaps if they knew we weren't humans, they might leave us alone," he said, clearly with a smirk.

"I never veally paid attention to any of zhat," Alucard muttered. "I knew people vrowned upon men who slept vith men and vomen who slept vith vomen, and zhey are especially 'arsh to people who zon't identify vith zhe gender zhey vere born, but I veel like zhe vings I 'eard aren't as bad as vhat else might be said and done to people like us."

"What did they say?"

He frowned hesitantly. "I zon't vant to vink about zhat."

"I want to know," Zalith said sadly.

Although he didn't want to talk about the things he heard, he wouldn't refuse to tell Zalith what people had been saying about them. He sighed, shrugging as he tightened his arm around him. "Zhey said a lot of vings; zhat ve should stay at 'ome so people zon't 'ave to see us and lose zheir appetite. Zhey said ve shouldn't be allowed into zhese kinds of places, and zhat our appearance 'ere vill vuin zhe place's veputation. Vone guy vas pretending to vrow up, and zhe ozzers kept talking about 'ow zhey should complain zhat zhey vere allowing such disgusting vings into zheir vestaurant."

Zalith sighed angrily. "If I could have understood them, I would have done something."

"I know, I just vanted us to 'ave vone night vhere ve zidn't 'ave to deal vith zhis kind of ving, but zhere is alvays somevone somevhere."

The demon kissed his head. "I almost wish we could live in Eltaria; barely anyone cares back there, and we'd actually be able to have dinner in peace."

"I vould like to go back zhere vone day and see more."

Zalith smiled and kissed him again. "One day. I doubt things will look the same by the time I feel like it's safe enough for us to go back, but I'll show you around regardless."

"I look vorward to zhat," Alucard said, smiling.

"Perhaps by the time we go, our daughter will be with us," he said with a quiet laugh.

Alucard then frowned, falling silent as his smile slowly faded. He hadn't thought about the dream he had; he hadn't thought about the little girl or what happened. It was just a dream, so why would it matter?

It *did* matter, though, didn't it? Why else would he and Zalith be thinking about it—*talking* about it? Zalith was obviously interested, and Alucard wouldn't deny that he'd thought about the dream a lot more than he had any other. He always dismissed his other dreams minutes after he woke up, but not this one…and now he was thinking about it *again*.

The little girl—*their* little girl: why had he dreamed of such a thing? Why had he seen a make-believe future where he and Zalith had a child? Was it his subconscious mind telling him what he really wanted now that he felt comfortable with Zalith? Now that he decided he wanted to spend his life with him? *Was* it what he wanted? Did he want a family with Zalith? He did; he wanted to spend his life with him, he wanted to *have* a life with him, and he felt that life would include a family of their own. After all, he'd never had a real family, and Zalith was as close as. But it still felt strange to have such a dream when they'd only known each other for just under three years. But then again, he'd known humans who had families with people they knew for less than that…some even had families together after less than three *months*.

He was overthinking again, wasn't he?

"What's wrong?" Zalith suddenly asked.

Alucard sighed and shrugged slightly. "Noving," he said with an assuring tone. "I'm just vinking."

"About what?"

"Just…about zhe dream I 'ad…vhere ve 'ad a daughter."

Zalith then started caressing his hair again. "I want to see her," he said quietly.

Alucard slowly sat up, leaned on his arm, and looked down at Zalith, who stared up at him. "Vhy?" he asked with a confused frown.

The demon placed his hand on the side of Alucard's face and frowned, but Alucard wasn't sure whether it was a frown of sadness or confliction.

Zalith answered with a smirk, "Because I want to see what she looks like; she's my baby, too."

Staring at Zalith, Alucard thought to himself for a few moments…but he had no reason *not* to show Zalith what he'd seen. So, he nodded. "Okay," he agreed.

But as Zalith took hold of his wrist and placed Alucard's hand on the side of his face, the vampire hesitated. The thought suddenly came to mind: while he was showing Zalith the dream, maybe he could also do something about the fact that the demon couldn't understand Lupanese; he hadn't understood what the people in the restaurant were saying, and Alucard felt it might be nicer for them both if he didn't have to translate for Zalith all night.

"Vait," he then said. "Do you vant me to…'elp you understand Lupanese?"

Zalith smirked. "That could be fun."

Alucard prepared to show Zalith his dream *and* share with him his knowledge on both understanding and speaking Lupanese.

But Zalith suddenly said, "Wait," and placed his hand over Alucard's.

Alucard frowned. "Vhat?" he questioned, but he noticed the hesitant expression on Zalith's face…and the worried look in his eyes.

With his hesitant expression thickening, Zalith moved his hand to the side of Alucard's neck. Then, he sighed, staring into Alucard's confused eyes. "Nothing," he said quietly. "I was just…worried for a moment, but I'm okay now."

Was Zalith hesitant to let him in his mind? It seemed that way, and Alucard didn't want Zalith to feel like that. He didn't want him to feel conflicted or worried or afraid— he wanted him to feel *comfortable*. Zalith always did all he could to help Alucard feel that way, so he would do the same.

He exhaled quietly and gripped Zalith's right arm. He then rolled over onto his back, pulling Zalith so that he would lean over him. As Zalith then stared down at him, he took the demon's hand and placed it on the side of his face. "You can vind zhe dream in *my* mind," he told him. "I von't go into yours. I vill…bury everyving else and leave vhat you need vor you to look at."

"It's okay," Zalith said. "You can—"

"I vould prever zhis," Alucard interjected. He didn't want to argue about it; he wanted to do what was most comfortable for Zalith, and this was it. Surely, Zalith would feel better knowing the vampire hadn't gone into his mind.

Zalith nodded slowly. "Okay."

The demon didn't waste much more time. He closed his eyes, and when Alucard felt him enter his mind, he closed his eyes, too, and let Zalith find what he was looking for. He wasn't sure how the demon might react, but he wanted to know what Zalith thought about the possibility of a family. So, while his heart became ensnared in anxiety with each passing moment, he waited for Zalith to witness what he dreamt.

# Chapter Sixty-Eight

─ ⟨ ✝ ⟩ ─

## A Walk Through Alvarez

**| Zalith |**

Zalith fought through his hesitation as best he could. What if this was all part of some elaborate plan for something or someone to dig deeper into his mind? If this life he was currently living really was a façade, then opening up his mind would give his enemies exactly what they wanted. He'd have to watch Alucard die again… and he'd wake up to a battlefield full of his dead people.

He'd already lost though, hadn't he? If this was a façade, he'd been falling in deeper and deeper since the start. He'd been kissing Alucard, touching him, and having sex with him; he'd practically given in and let himself believe that this was real. What was the point in resisting now?

He loved Alucard so much and he wanted to see what their daughter looked like in the vampire's mind. Real or not, he wasn't going to ruin this moment. So, he delved into Alucard's mind… and then he saw it.

The dream.

He saw through Alucard's eyes as the vampire woke up to the face of their strawberry-blonde daughter. Zalith watched her laugh and offer Alucard cards. She looked so excited, so beautiful, and so much like Alucard.

Zalith then felt Alucard's confusion and the longing Alucard had for this dream to be real. But as he watched himself wake up and turn to face Alucard, he stared at the scar on his chest. Alucard stared at it for a while—*he* stared at it for a while. He had no idea what it was doing there or *how* it got there. Why would he possess such an awful scar in Alucard's dream?

But it didn't last much longer. After a few more moments, he pulled himself from Alucard's mind… and it was over.

## | **Alucard** |

Alucard stared up at Zalith, waiting for him to say something. The demon looked a little overwhelmed, though, and that made Alucard's anxious heart beat faster. Did Zalith not like what he saw? Did he not want a family?

But just then, the demon smiled, and his conflicted stare disappeared. "She's exactly what our daughter would look like," he said with a smirk. "She looks so much like you."

The vampire's angst faded as he pouted and looked away. "I vink she looked more like you."

Zalith smiled and started fiddling with the vampire's hair. "I want a baby."

Alucard's eyes widened a little, and as he gawped at Zalith, a concoction of angst, confusion, and confliction swirled around inside him. Was he being serious? Or was he joking? Alucard couldn't tell. Zalith's words seemed to bring his thoughts to a sudden halt. He couldn't think, he couldn't speak; all he could do was stare at him and try to work out whether or not he was joking.

But then he had to ask himself: did *he* want a baby? Did he want to actually have a child with Zalith? Of course he did. But…right now? He wanted to ask what he meant, but he couldn't seem to find the words. How would they even do it? How would they have a child? A family? Was now even the best time?

Zalith laughed amusedly. "You don't want to have a baby with me?"

Snapping out of his silence, Alucard frowned and shook his head.

Zalith laughed again. "That's very hurtful, Alucard—"

"N-no, I do," he insisted. "I…vant to 'ave a vamily vith you, I just…I zon't know," he said with a frown, unsure of why he felt strangely hesitant.

Fiddling with Alucard's crimson hair, Zalith smiled. "It's a lot to think about right now, but don't worry, you don't have to decide right this second," he assured him.

Alucard felt relieved—

"I'll give you a minute or two to think it over," he said, smirking.

Panic gripped hold of him. A minute or two? He uttered in confusion—

The demon laughed, leaned closer, and kissed his lips. "I'm joking," he said with a smile, and as Alucard pouted, Zalith kissed him again.

Alucard quickly became irritated. Why did Zalith think it was so funny to make him panic like that? He didn't want to be angry, though. He kissed the demon back, moving his hand to the side of Zalith's neck as he tried to dismiss aggravation. He didn't want to sink into his hesitation about starting a family, either. Right now, he just wanted to focus on his and Zalith's night away from home.

But as Zalith's hand started wandering down Alucard's body, he remembered what the demon did before they left home. Zalith flustered him enough today and he wasn't going to let him do it again.

They kept kissing, Zalith started caressing the vampire's arousal over his trousers, and as Alucard's irritancy began to fade, he moved his hand from Zalith's neck and to his shoulder. With a quiet, impatient huff, he turned his head aside, stopping their kissing, and then pushed Zalith down and away from his face.

Zalith laughed quietly as he made his way down Alucard's body and started to unbuckle his belt. Alucard waited as patiently as he could but being denied earlier before they left home made him feel more eager. He waited, though, and as the demon slowly moved his mouth over the tip of his shaft, Alucard exhaled quietly in anticipation.

The vampire gripped a handful of Zalith's hair in his hand, fidgeting lightly in struggle, trying not to utter a sound as the demon sucked his dick. But as he always did, he wasn't able to keep himself from humming contently.

He lay there, gripping Zalith's hair, all of his thoughts falling silent as he allowed the pleasure to consume him. He moaned, he groaned, and he whined as the demon skillfully pleased him, and when he eventually climaxed, he grimaced in delight and cried out in relief, listening to Zalith's content hums as he eagerly swallowed his cum.

Alucard slowly let go of Zalith's hair as he put his dick away for him and buckled his belt. The demon then made his way back up his body and kissed his neck a few times before lying down beside him.

"Was that what you wanted?" Zalith asked with an amused laugh as Alucard turned onto his side, moved his arm around the demon, and rested his head on his chest.

Pouting, Alucard tried to keep his embarrassment from overwhelming him and made himself comfortable as Zalith moved his arm around him. "Maybe," he mumbled.

The demon laughed quietly. "It's always a pleasure to service you."

Undeniably amused, Alucard laughed quietly, tightening his embrace around Zalith as the demon kissed his head. Then, he sighed quietly and frowned. "I love you," he mumbled shyly.

"Thank you," Zalith murmured. "I love you too." The demon then kissed his head again.

With a hushed exhale, Alucard closed his eyes and relaxed, and for a short while, they lay in silence.

Alucard started sinking back into his thoughts, though. Zalith's attention only helped him to ignore it, but now that they were lying there, all he could think about was the conversation they had before and why he felt so conflicted—afraid, even. Why did he feel so anxious when he thought about becoming a father? He loved the idea of having a family with Zalith, but when he thought about being a dad, he panicked.

He frowned and stared aimlessly ahead. Maybe it was because he didn't know how to be a father; he hadn't grown up with one, had he? He'd not had any kind of parental figure in his life, so how was he supposed to know how to be one himself? He didn't want to head into the commitment of raising a child if he had no idea how to do it. If he didn't know what he was doing, surely that would affect their child, and he didn't want to fail them or Zalith.

Perhaps he was so afraid because he felt like he'd be an awful father. He already felt like he had barely anything to offer as a partner, so what did he have to offer as a parent? He didn't want any child that they had to grow up feeling abandoned or unloved by him because he had no idea how to show them that he loved them. So, maybe it was a bad idea; perhaps he shouldn't be hoping for a family. If he had no idea what to do and was lying there sure that he'd be an awful father, why would he be so stupid as to think about actually having a child one day? He shouldn't.

He didn't want to think about it anymore. Tonight was supposed to be about him and Zalith having a good time. He dismissed his thoughts, sighed quietly, and sat up. He gazed at Zalith as he looked up at him. "Do you still vant to go back out?" he asked.

The demon smiled. "Yeah," he said contently.

"Ve can go now."

Zalith smirked. "All right."

Alucard and Zalith got out of bed and pulled their blazers on. Zalith took hold of Alucard's hand, and as they left their room, he smiled at the vampire. Alucard shyly smiled back and walked at the demon's side as they headed downstairs. It was late, and Alucard wasn't sure what they might do with the rest of their night, but he was excited to find out.

## | Zalith |

Zalith led the way outside. He hoped that he and Alucard would find something nice to do with the rest of their night; he wanted Alucard to have fun, and *he* wanted to have fun, too; the last thing he wanted was for Alucard to continue letting what he heard in the restaurant upset him.

If Zalith had known there and then what the people were saying, he would have made sure that they'd never say anything like that to anyone again, but he *hadn't* understood, and in all honesty, Alucard made the right choice by waiting to tell him. Zalith knew how angry he got, especially when ignorant people like that thought they could say whatever they wanted, and the fact that it upset Alucard would have only made his reaction worse.

He exhaled deeply but quietly and looked at Alucard as they made their way along the road which led deeper into the city. Alucard seemed content, and that made Zalith feel happier, too. He smiled and lightly squeezed the vampire's hand as they continued down the road.

However, as they made their way forward, Zalith immediately noticed the group of aristocrats on the other side of the street, standing by what must be their carriage. They were the same insufferable individuals who had driven Alucard from the restaurant; six unattractive, tedious humans, none of whom Zalith deemed worthy of his time. He kept his eyes fixed ahead, doing his best to ignore the derisive laughter that erupted from them as they spotted him and his vampire.

This time, though, Zalith could understand their taunts; Alucard had enabled him to comprehend Lupanese. The newfound understanding only fueled his ire as he clearly heard a derogatory word directed at them; the insult sent a wave of dangerous anger coursing through him, his demonic nature simmering just beneath the surface. The temptation to respond, to unleash his fury was overwhelming, but for Alucard's sake, he restrained himself, channelling his rage into a steely resolve. He vowed silently that those words would not go unpunished, even if the retribution had to wait for another time.

But he'd ignore them—he'd ignore *it*. Alucard was already upset because of them, and he didn't want to make it worse by causing a scene. But he couldn't just do nothing. He and Alucard were simply walking down the street minding their own business, and these people couldn't let them be, could they? They just *had* to say something, and this time, Zalith wasn't going to let it go.

Zalith let go of Alucard's hand as he turned around and made his way over to the snickering people. He dismissed whatever they had to say, and once he reached them, he slammed his fist into the face of the man who first insulted him and Alucard. The guy stumbled back and tripped over his own feet, falling to the ground as his friends all gasped in shock and shuffled back. Wary, confused looks appeared on their faces as they watched Zalith spit in disgust at the fallen man.

One of the men yelled in revolt as he threw his fist towards Zalith, but Alucard— who had swiftly appeared at the demon's side—grabbed the man's wrist and glared at him with so much malice that the guy shuddered and whimpered in fear.

"I vouldn't," Alucard warned with a snarl.

As the humans helped their fallen friend to his feet, Alucard let go of the other guy, and then Alucard and Zalith watched them all scurry off as quickly as they could.

Amused, Zalith smirked, but when he looked at Alucard, he frowned in confliction. "I'm sorry. I couldn't let it go."

Alucard sighed and took hold of his hand again. "Is vine," he muttered. "Let's go."

They continued walking down the narrow cobblestone streets, emerging into the busier, louder heart of the city. Gas lamps cast a warm, golden glow over the lively scene, illuminating the ornate facades of centuries-old buildings. The streets were bustling with life, even at this late hour. Street vendors called out in melodic Lupanese, hawking their wares beneath colourful awnings. Carriages rattled by, their wheels clattering against the stones, while well-dressed couples strolled arm in arm, enjoying the vibrant nightlife.

Zalith and Alucard walked hand-in-hand, weaving through the throngs of people. The air was filled with a symphony of sounds: laughter from open-air cafes, the distant strains of a street musician's violin, and the rhythmic clopping of horses' hooves. The aroma of freshly baked bread mingled with the scent of blooming jasmine from the nearby gardens, creating an intoxicating blend that was uniquely Lupanese.

Every now and then, Zalith glanced at Alucard, his heart heavy with the unspoken question. The recent encounter with the aristocrats weighed on him, and he was anxious to know if Alucard harboured any resentment. Yet, he hesitated to ask, not wanting to spoil the fragile peace between them. He knew he couldn't leave it too long; the uncertainty gnawed at him.

As they passed a grand, ivy-covered opera house, its entrance bustling with elegantly dressed patrons, Zalith took a deep breath. The soft light from the chandeliers within spilled out onto the street, casting a shimmering reflection on the pavement. He gently squeezed Alucard's hand, turning to him with a look of earnest concern.

"Alucard," he began, his voice low and steady, "are you upset with me for what happened back there? I need to know." The night buzzed around them, but in that moment, Zalith's focus was solely on Alucard, hoping for reassurance amidst the city's ceaseless energy.

The vampire sighed. "No, zhey deserved zhat."

Zalith smirked slightly. "They were lucky I only hit him. I wanted to do much worse."

"I vouldn't 'ave stopped you, but zhen I vould 'ave 'ad to pay zhe bond to get you out of vhatever cell zhey vould 'ave taken you to. I 'aven't seen zhe prisons in zhis city, but zhe vones I've seen in ozzer countries vere not to my liking, so I imagine *you* vouldn't like zhem much, eizer."

Laughing, Zalith glanced at him. "What prisons *are* to your liking? I don't think anyone likes prisons."

"Vell, zhere vas zhis vone prison in DeiganLupus vhere zhey served zhese veally good pastries. I vink zhey vere too lazy to 'ire somevone to make vood vor zhe inmates, so zhey'd just go to zhe bakery next door."

"If I ever want to get arrested, I'll commit a crime in DeiganLupus," he said amusedly.

Alucard shrugged. "You zon't vant to go zhere now. DeiganLupus is more or less on zhe brink of civil war. Attila is trying to 'elp zhe new king calm vings down. I vould give a year or two."

"I'll keep that in mind."

The vampire then sighed again but with a smile on his face.

Zalith smiled, too, and squeezed the vampire's hand. "What should we do with the rest of our night?"

Alucard shrugged, staring ahead as they slowly made their way down the long, bustling street. "I zon't know. Is late, and I zon't veally vant to go to a bar. Maybe ve can just... valk or someving."

"I don't really want to go to a bar, either," the demon concurred, taking his eyes off Alucard to stare ahead. That was when his eyes fixed on the mansion-like venue at its end. The crowd thinned, revealing the grand building bathed in the warm glow of numerous lanterns. Several very expensive-looking horse-drawn carriages were stowed along the circular driveway, and a crystal fountain stood majestically at the centre. Around it, a crowd of elegantly dressed men and women chattered loudly; the women in elaborate ball gowns, the men in finely tailored suits, most with cigars or glasses of champagne in their hands.

Excitement quickly enthralled Zalith; he could spot a party miles away, and what lay ahead was exactly that. The lively strains of music emanated from the well-lit venue, blending with the sounds of laughter and clinking glasses. Small groups of people laughed and stumbled around with drinks in their hands, enjoying the revelry. The trees lining the circular road were adorned with small glass lights, casting a festive twinkle over the scene.

It was a familiar, enticing sight. Memories of sneaking into or charming their way into parties like these with his brother flooded Zalith's mind. The thrill of those days surged within him, and he yearned to share such an experience with Alucard. He glanced at his vampire, his eyes sparkling with anticipation. The prospect of mingling among their own class, dancing to the lively music, and losing themselves in the exuberant atmosphere was irresistible. Zalith felt a surge of eagerness, ready to relive those thrilling nights with Alucard by his side, amidst the splendour of the Lupanese luxury and festivity.

He stopped walking, and as Alucard also stopped and looked at him with a confused expression, he smiled enthusiastically. "I know you don't want to go to a bar, but how does a party sound?"

Still frowning, Alucard glanced at the venue at the end of the road and slowly looked back at him. "Is... private party. Ve'll probably get about... hmm... two minutes inside bevore zhey see us and kick us out."

Zalith smirked. "*I* say we'll get *three* minutes," he teased, and as Alucard smirked in amusement, he put his hands on the sides of the vampire's arms. "We're all dressed up *exactly* the way they are," he said, glancing at a small group of laughing men. "They won't even realize we don't belong here. It could be fun."

The vampire looked at the venue again and sighed quietly. "Okay, but if ve get caught, *you* can vace zhe consequences and *I* vill stand zhere and vatch."

Amused, Zalith laughed quietly. "You'd let them throw me out?"

"If you get caught, yes. Is every man vor 'imselv vhen vone is crashing a party," he said with a smirk as he started leading the way towards the party.

"After all we've been through, Alucard. I see how it is," Zalith laughed.

"Is okay. I'll bring some cake back vor you," Alucard said, glancing at him.

"And if *you* get caught, do you expect me to follow *you* out?"

"No. I von't get kicked out. I'll just pretend I vork zhere; zhere are many pros of 'aving zhis accent, you know." He smirked at Zalith. "People like zhis 'ire servers who zon't understand zhem so zhey can talk about vhatever zhey vant and von't get back to anyvone. If zhey approach me, I'll mutter a little Dor-Sanguian, and I'll be vine. Zhe same can't be said vor you; zhey zon't 'ire Deiganish people…someving about zhem being rude."

With a fake look of astonishment, Zalith replied, "Are you saying I'm rude?"

"No. I'm saying zon't try to pretend *you* vork zhere if zhey catch you. Vill be vorse zhan just leaving because you're not meant to be zhere."

Laughing, Zalith took Alucard's arm in his own and stared ahead as they came closer to the venue. "I'll keep that in mind."

But as they walked, Alucard pulled his arm from Zalith's.

Zalith frowned sullenly, but he didn't need to ask Alucard why he didn't want to hold his arm. The people inside the venue could very well treat them the same as the people in the restaurant, and he wanted to have a good night. So, he smiled and looked at Alucard again as he moved his arm around him, lightly squeezed his shoulder with his hand, and pulled him a little closer for a moment. "I know you said you didn't want to go to a bar, but will you drink with me at this party?"

"As long as zhey aren't serving cheap vine," Alucard mumbled.

Zalith laughed amusedly. "If they are, we're leaving."

Smiling slightly, Alucard looked at him again. "You zon't…veally seem like zhe type to sneak into parties," he said quietly as they entered the courtyard where the carriages were parked.

"I don't?"

"No."

Zalith exhaled quietly. "Xurian and I used to do this all the time when we were younger. We had a lot of fun; made a few friends, made a few enemies. It was nice," he explained, remembering the good times he and his brother had.

"Zhen…I 'ope zhis vill be just as vun vor you," Alucard said.

"Even if it's bad, I'll still have fun," he said with a smirk.

Sighing, Alucard nodded. "Okay, vell…just 'ope you zon't get caught," he paused to smirk. "I still stand by vhat I said."

Zalith grinned in response. "As do I."

# Chapter Sixty-Nine

— ⟨ ✝ ⟩ —

## Admirer

**| Alucard |**

Alucard walked beside Zalith into the luxury venue. As they stepped through the grand entrance hall, the air was filled with the sounds of laughter and music. They made their way into a large ballroom teeming with elegantly dressed people; white silk draped gracefully from the high ceilings, creating an ethereal canopy. Confetti and balloons littered the polished marble floor, adding a festive layer underfoot, while an array of colourful lights flickered and danced around the room, casting a vibrant glow on everything.

The vampire's hell-fiery eyes quickly scanned the scene, taking in the extravagant details. It didn't take long for him to spot the hosts of the party. The woman's enormous white dress was a clear indicator that this was no ordinary celebration—it was a wedding party. The joyful atmosphere was palpable, with guests swirling around in elaborate gowns and sharp suits, champagne flutes in hand, and smiles on their faces.

He felt a mix of emotions watching the scene unfold. The lavish decorations, the lively music, and the exuberant crowd reminded him of the nights filled with similar revelry, though this time there was an added layer of romantic celebration. The only wedding parties he'd been to were those Luther had every time he married another princess, and it was a relief that Luther wasn't at *this* one. It was just him and Zalith. He looked at the demon, and as Zalith smiled back at him, Alucard frowned and looked away, his eyes darting around the room, glancing at each and every person.

There weren't just men and women there, either. Alucard frowned while he watched a group of children chase each other; a woman in the far corner was cradling an infant, and someone had even brought their dog—a rather large white, fluffy poodle. He then located two women standing over by the table that Zalith seemed to be heading to, kissing one another without much concern. Maybe he was wrong to assume that the people here might be as ignorant as those in the restaurant, so he slipped his hand into Zalith's.

"Vhere are ve going?" the vampire asked.

Smiling at him, Zalith shrugged. "It's a wedding. Don't all guests leave gifts for the happy couple?"

"Yes…but…ve're not veal guests."

"They don't know that," Zalith said, reaching into his blazer pocket once they reached the table. He took a small piece of ribbon-like confetti and used it to tie a thick stack of coronam notes into a scroll. He then placed the money down on the table between two boxes and turned to face Alucard, putting his hands on both his arms. "I'll go get us a drink," he said, nodding over at a butler wandering around with a tray of champagne and wine glasses. "Don't go anywhere," he said with a smirk before walking off.

Alucard sighed quietly and walked over to the wall beside the table. He leaned back against it, watching the demon as he made his way over to the butler and took two glasses of champagne as well as some cake from another server he passed on his way back over to where the vampire was waiting.

"Here you go." Zalith smiled, handing him one of the glasses.

"Vank you," he said, taking it from him. "Vhat is zhat?" he asked, looking down at the dessert in Zalith's other hand.

"This is a fruit tart." He took a sip of his drink. "Try it."

Alucard frowned and took a sip of his champagne, and to his disgust, his earlier suspicions that they'd be serving cheap beverages weren't wrong. He grimaced and scowled at Zalith, who was now laughing quietly. "I told you zhis vould 'appen," he mumbled.

Smirking, Zalith placed his drink down and then scooped some of the dessert onto the spoon that came with it. "Maybe this will taste better," he said, offering it to him.

"Unlikely," Alucard grumbled, but he tried it anyway. He ate the fruit tart off the spoon, and surprisingly, it actually didn't taste too bad.

"Do you like it?" the demon asked.

Alucard nodded, and as Zalith ate some of it, the vampire sipped from his cheap champagne again. "I veel like zhese people aren't as vich as zhey vould like zheir guests to vink."

As he offered another spoonful of the tart to Alucard, Zalith nodded. "I concur," he said, "but everyone else seems to be happy with the champagne *and* the wine, so maybe they're all pretending to be rich for the night."

Eating the dessert, Alucard shrugged. "Maybe zhat money you gave zhem vill cover zhe debt zhis party 'as clearly pulled zhem into. I vink she is trying to cut some of zhe costs," he said, nodding over at the bride, who had snuck off from her husband to argue with one of the workers.

"Perhaps I should leave them some more," Zalith said, laughing.

"Vhy? You zon't know zhem; you probably just paid vor zhe whole vedding anyvay," he mumbled as they both sipped from their drinks.

"I'm joking," Zalith said, smirking.

Alucard then rolled his eyes and stopped drinking the revolting champagne. "Maybe ve *should* get to know zhem. I'll go and make a vriend, and not only vill ve not 'ave to sneak about, but maybe ve can also start dvinking someving zhat zoesn't taste like piss," he suggested, handing Zalith his glass. "Vait 'ere."

"Okay," Zalith said, smiling.

Then, Alucard turned around—

"Wait," Zalith insisted, abruptly grabbing his arm. He turned Alucard to face him, kissed him once, and smiled again. "Okay, you can go now."

Pouting, Alucard turned around and set his eyes back on the bride. She was still arguing with the worker bringing in more drinks. Alucard didn't know this woman—he didn't know any of these people—but if he and Zalith were going to have a good time, he was going to have to intervene and make the night a little better for *everyone*.

When he reached the woman, she sighed in distress and shook her head. "I told you, we don't need anymore—take it back!" she insisted.

"Take it back where?" the guy argued. "It's all paid for, and we can't just—"

"Is zhere a problem?" Alucard interjected as the woman dragged her hand over her face in frustration.

She looked at him and gestured her hands at the worker. "This moron won't listen to a single word I just said!"

Alucard looked at the guy.

"I told you, ma'am, you can't return this stuff. It's already paid for," he said.

"How can it be paid for if we didn't even give the guy the money yet!?"

"I just work here, lady, I don't know—"

The woman exclaimed in frustration and moved her hands over her face again, letting the guy wander off to hand out more drinks. But when she set her eyes on Alucard, she frowned and shook her head. "Who are you?"

"A vriend of a vriend's vriend," he lied, holding out his hand. "Aleksei."

She frowned and slowly shook his hand. "I don't...recall—"

"Is a long story—I arrived late; my boyvriend just levt a givt on zhe table vor you."

"Oh," she said, glancing over at Zalith as Alucard looked back at him, watching as he placed their unfinished champagne onto one of the passing butler's trays. "Thank you," she said, smiling.

Alucard frowned curiously. "Vhat do you...vink of zhe champagne?"

She rolled her eyes and crossed her arms. "Gerald had us get some cheap shit because we splashed all our savings renting this stupid venue—oh!" she gasped, holding her hand over her mouth.

Amused, Alucard glanced at the woman's new husband. "I own a distillery and distribution company 'ere; is your party, so you can revuse, but if you like, I can 'ave somevone bring over someving...better—and at no cost," he offered, smiling at her.

She frowned in surprise. "I...did Gerald pay you to come over here and pretend you're giving it to us for free, but really, he's already paid for it, hasn't he?!" she exclaimed in panic.

Alucard frowned. "No...you are zhe virst person I spoke to since I got 'ere."

The woman shook her head. "Why would you do that?"

He shrugged. "Is my givt. I 'ave noving on me to leave, so...is zhe best I can do."

Staring at him, she smiled and sniffled quietly. "Really? Thank you so much...you're so sweet."

"And...Gerald...is trying to buy zhat man's vatch, by zhe vay," he warned, nodding over at the woman's husband again as he laughed with the other men he was standing with.

Scowling, the woman rolled up her sleeves—well...she had none, but she didn't seem to realize that. "One day, I'm gonna kill that man," she huffed. She then stormed off, leaving Alucard alone.

Once she was gone, Alucard sighed and concentrated for a moment. He had a vampire, Domenico, running his distillery company, so it took no time at all to send telepathic instructions to let the guy know to bring things over. Then, he made his way back over to Zalith, who greeted him with a smile.

"Did you make a new friend?" the demon asked.

"More or less," Alucard said with a shrug, standing beside him.

"What happened?"

"I just told 'er I vould 'ave somevone bring better vine."

Zalith laughed amusedly. "That's not a very nice thing to say to the bride, vampire."

Alucard pouted. "Zhere vas more to zhe conversation zhan zhat. She told me she 'ated zhe dvinks too, I ovvered to supply better, and she agreed," he explained.

"That's very kind of you," Zalith said before pulling him closer to kiss his lips. "Hopefully it's good."

"Vill be," Alucard assured him.

"Didn't she think it was strange...some man she doesn't know talking to her as if this is his wedding?"

"My vedding vould be so much better," the vampire mumbled, taking what was left of the fruit tart from Zalith.

Zalith laughed *again*. "Yeah? What would you do?"

"I zon't know," he said with a shrug, eating the dessert. "I vouldn't be trying to impress anyvone vith money I zon't 'ave. Vould be about me and...whoever I marry," he muttered shyly. He didn't want to assume that he and Zalith would get married, but he did like the thought of it. "A vedding is supposed to be about 'aving a good time vith zhe person you vant to spend your life vith, and zhe people you care about, vight?" he questioned.

The demon nodded in agreement. "But…having money helps," he said and then adorned a suggestive smile. "When *I* get married, I'm torn between wanting everyone to be impressed and having every other wedding they go to pale in comparison, and having a quiet, reserved little wedding."

"I vouldn't be bovered eizer vay," Alucard said without thought, placing the empty dessert plate on the table beside him. Were they talking about *their* wedding? The thought made Alucard feel…strange. Of course, he'd decided that he wanted to spend his life with Zalith, but would they get married? Did Zalith even want that? He'd joked about it before, and Alucard wasn't sure whether this was a joke, too.

"Regardless," Zalith said, smirking, "the wine and the food will be the best it can be; we won't settle for anything less."

Alucard then realized that they most likely *were* talking about their wedding—if they ever had one. If they got married…of course they'd have a wedding, but…once again, he had to ask himself, *would* they get married? Did Zalith even want him as much as he wanted Zalith? Enough to get married? He'd already been talking about their daughter earlier—a baby, even—and a family was what came after marriage, right?

He frowned and stared ahead, watching as the bride and her husband started dancing along with some of the other couples. "I vouldn't even veally 'ave anyvone to invite," he muttered.

"Maybe we'll just elope and get married on a romantic little beach somewhere all by ourselves," Zalith suggested amusedly.

Alucard glanced at him, still unsure if this was an ongoing joke. "You vouldn't vant your vriends zhere?"

"All I need is you." Zalith smiled, moving his arm around Alucard's waist to pull him closer.

Smiling, Alucard looked away from the demon. "You're all I need, too."

But Zalith then dragged out a sigh, pulling him even closer.

"Vhat?" Alucard frowned, staring at him.

The demon smirked at him. "I want to make out with you, but then I'm going to want to fuck you," he said quietly, "and I'll probably end up finding us a little broom closet to have sex in, but I don't want to have sex in a broom closet," he continued, even though Alucard had already looked away, his face surely reddening. "I want to do it in our nice room that we paid for with the pretty view. So, I can't make out with you right now, sorry."

Staring down at the floor while Zalith laughed quietly, Alucard pouted. Everything the demon just said already made him feel overly embarrassed, and the fact that they were in a room full of people made it worse. To his relief, it seemed like no one heard, but that didn't make him feel any less flustered.

Alongside his embarrassment, however, he felt…enticed, and that was all he needed to decide that he wanted to head back. "Ve can…go back," he mumbled quietly.

Zalith nuzzled the side of his face. "Not yet, baby. I'm having fun."

Disappointed, Alucard pouted again and looked away, but as he did, he noticed that the wine he ordered had arrived and was already being handed out in glasses; he spotted Domenico by the door with several of the distillery workers, unloading a few crates. Before Alucard could say anything, though, an excited squeal caught his attention. He sharply turned his head, setting his eyes on the bride as she scurried over to him with her husband as well as two of his friends and who Alucard assumed to be *their* partners.

Once she reached them, the bride clapped her hands and pointed to Alucard. "Everyone, *this* is Aleksei," she said with a smile. Then, she looked at Zalith. "Oh, you must be his boyfriend; he told me *all* about you."

"No…I zidn't," Alucard muttered in Deiganish so that only Zalith could understand.

Zalith smiled and moved his arm around Alucard's waist, pulling him closer. "Aw, that's sweet. This is a fantastic wedding and a beautiful venue," he then complimented.

The bride giggled and took a huge gulp of the new wine. "This stuff is amazing. Thanks so much again."

Alucard smiled as warmly as he could. "No problem," he said, watching as she wiped the wine from her chin that spilt when she spoke.

"I've not seen you before," her husband then said, a rather unwelcoming frown on his plump face. "Who'd you come with?"

"Oh, shut up, Gerald," his wife dismissed. "Aleksei owns a distillery here…I think you should be nice," she whispered, patting his shoulder. "They both look like businessmen."

A smile instantly appeared on the man's face as he held his hand out to Alucard. "Excuse my manners." Alucard shook his hand, and then he held it out to Zalith. "Champagne's got me a little doo-lally tonight," he laughed as Zalith shook his hand. "The name's Gerald. So, Aleksei and…who's this?" he asked, glancing at his wife.

"Zalith," the demon told them.

"Interesting names," one of the other men said with a smile on his face—a face as dull as any other standard guy's. His combed hair was a light brown, as were his eyes— eyes he couldn't keep off Zalith. "If I were to assume neither of you is actually Lupanese, would I be right?" he asked curiously.

The demon nodded.

"So, a distillery," Gerald said. "Big business, small business?"

Alucard wasn't interested in talking about it. He had already worked out that this man loved to spend money and was probably looking to make more or make some kind of investment—Alucard didn't need it or want it. "Vamily-owned," he answered.

But the other of Gerald's male friends laughed. "Family-owned?" he asked, looking down at the bottle he had in his hand. "I've seen this little symbol here and there, and not just on wine bottles," he said, showing everyone Alucard's Nosferatu signature.

Gerald smirked and prodded Alucard's shoulder. "Come on, what do you say we go and talk business?"

Alucard frowned irritably, but he didn't want to make a scene. "No," he answered as politely as he could. "I'm not looking vor anyving at zhe moment."

"Ah, shame," Gerald mumbled.

His wife then slapped his shoulder. "He's *always* looking for something to invest in as if we haven't invested in enough."

"Where are you from?" the brown-haired man asked Zalith, the same man who had predicted that they weren't Lupanese.

"Another world," Zalith said, smiling.

Everyone laughed amusedly.

"Are you being serious?" Gerald questioned.

"Of course he's not," his wife muttered. "*Are* you?"

"Like space?" one of the other women asked.

"Space?" the man holding the wine bottle scoffed. "No one's from space, Margret, damn," he mumbled, sipping from the bottle.

She tutted and rolled her eyes.

As everyone started bickering about space and people living out there, Alucard took his eyes off the bride and glanced at the man who seemed to be unable to keep his gaze off Zalith. The vampire scowled and glanced at the demon, who was watching Gerald and his wife while they argued.

"Do you like zhe vine?" Alucard asked, glaring at the very standard-looking man, who was *still* staring at Zalith.

He took his beady little brown eyes off Zalith and glanced at Alucard. "Yes, it's quite wonderful," he answered, and then he looked at Zalith again. "Would you like a glass?" he offered, holding out a spare glass of wine he seemed to have been carrying around with him.

"I'd love some—we both would," Zalith said, glancing at Alucard. "But perhaps two fresh glasses would be best so that they're not warm from your body heat," he suggested. "Thank you."

Nodding, the man turned around and hurried off.

As he left, Zalith turned to face Alucard and rolled his eyes.

"I vink somevone 'as taken a liking to you," Alucard muttered.

"I don't blame him. I'm a catch," he said, smirking.

Alucard didn't want to threaten the guy, but he felt as though he might just want to hurt him if he didn't stop staring at Zalith like he was a piece of art.

"…So, therefore, it's totally impossible for people to live out there!" the man with the wine bottle argued as everyone shook their heads.

Alucard sighed quietly. "Is actually called zhe void space," he corrected.

Everyone took their eyes off each other and looked at him.

"Connects all zhe ozzer vorlds," the vampire continued.

"I knew it!" one of the women snapped, pointing at the guy with the wine bottle.

"So, you really *are* from elsewhere, then?" Gerald asked. "How'd you end up here?"

"How does anyone end up anywhere, Gerald?" Zalith replied.

"You tell me," he laughed.

"Maybe I don't want to," the demon responded.

"Here you go," the guy who Zalith sent to get drinks interjected, holding a glass out to him.

Zalith took the glass and handed it to Alucard, and then he took the second glass for himself. "Thank you," he said, turning to face the vampire. "Drink it like a shot," he said with a smirk before Alucard could take a sip.

The vampire frowned. "Vhy?"

"Because it'll be funny," he said, smiling.

Staring at him, Alucard frowned, but he didn't see a reason not to. As the bride and her friends started bickering again, Alucard did as Zalith suggested and downed his glass of wine.

The demon smirked and did the same before placing his hand on the side of Alucard's neck. "Give me a kiss," he said quietly, and he didn't give Alucard much time to do so because he had already leaned in and kissed his lips. He didn't stop with a single kiss, though; they kissed for a few moments before Zalith smirked and looked back at the bride and her friends…who were *still* arguing. A few moments after that, he gazed at Alucard again. "Would you like to dance?"

Alucard smiled. "Yes."

The demon's face lit up with contentedness. He took Alucard's glass and handed both to the guy who went to get their drinks. "Can you hold these for us, please—thanks," he said, taking hold of Alucard's hand. "We'll be right back," he called as he led Alucard towards the dancefloor, where several couples were slow dancing.

But while Zalith escorted him forward, Alucard glanced back at the man who couldn't take his eyes off the demon. He was certain that the guy was going to try and flirt with Zalith, and when he did, Alucard would give him a piece of his mind. But for now, he was going to enjoy a dance with the man he loved.

When they reached the dancefloor, Zalith gently placed his left hand on Alucard's waist and his right on the vampire's shoulder. Alucard mirrored the gesture, his hand resting on Zalith's waist and the other on his shoulder. Their eyes locked, a silent understanding passing between them as the music enveloped them. They began to move in unison, swaying gracefully to the rhythm, lost in their own world amidst the swirling lights and soft melodies. The surrounding couples faded into the background, leaving only the connection between them, their slow dance a delicate expression of their bond.

"Are you having a nice time?" Zalith asked quietly.

Alucard nodded. "Are you?"

"Yeah," he said with a content smile. "I'm glad we came."

"Me too. Veels like 'as been vorever since ve did someving like zhis. I like to be avay vrom 'ome vith you."

"It really does. We should go away more often; I like being away from home with you, too." He paused and smirked at him. "So, where should we go next, vampire?"

Alucard thought to himself for a few moments. "I vant… to maybe go on a vacation," he said, remembering his conversation with Greymore. "Maybe a veek or so avay."

"I love the sound of that." Zalith smiled, resting the side of his head on Alucard's. "Do you have any ideas as to where we could go?"

"I vant to go to Samjang."

"Then Samjang it is," he agreed. "I'm looking forward to it."

Just then, somebody tapped on Alucard's shoulder. "Can I cut in?" the guy who had been staring at Zalith asked as Alucard glanced back at him.

With an irritated, hostile scowl, Alucard glared at the man. "No, you cannot," he snarled, setting his eyes back on Zalith, who looked rather disgusted in response to the man's request.

But the guy laughed slightly. "Please?" he persisted.

Alucard glanced back at him and glowered, and as the man smiled, the vampire gritted his teeth and growled quietly in hostility.

A look of startle appeared on the man's face, and that was all it took to send him scurrying away like a scared child.

The demon smiled when Alucard looked at him again. "I like it when you do that," he said, pulling him a little closer as they resumed dancing. "You're very scary."

Exhaling quietly, Alucard smiled and rested his head on Zalith's shoulder.

And so they danced, losing track of time as the music and their movements melded into a seamless flow. An hour passed, perhaps more, perhaps less—Alucard wasn't sure. He stood in Zalith's embrace, holding him tightly as the night carried on, their surroundings blurring into the background.

At one point, they paused their dancing to mingle with the other guests. They laughed and chatted, sharing stories and sipping the exquisite wine Alucard had gifted to the bride and her party. The conversations flowed as smoothly as the wine, and soon enough, they found themselves back on the dancefloor, moving together once more.

As the evening progressed, guests began to trickle out of the venue, the once lively crowd thinning. Yet, for Alucard and Zalith, the night was far from over. The atmosphere still buzzed with the remnants of celebration, promising more moments to cherish as they continued to enjoy each other's company.

"Let's get a drink," Zalith said with an excited smile, slowing their dance to a halt once more. "And then we'll probably leave in a bit; there's still a lot of people here, so maybe we'll wait until a few more have left before calling it a night," he suggested.

Alucard smiled and nodded, although he wasn't sure if another drink was what either of them needed. Zalith was clearly a little tipsy, and Alucard felt intoxicated himself. But he didn't want their fun to end.

"Okay," the vampire said and then followed Zalith over to a nearby table.

When they reached the table, Zalith went to turn around and face him, but he stumbled a little and almost tripped over his own feet; Alucard grabbed his arms and made him sit down as Zalith laughed quietly to himself.

"Vait zhere," Alucard said. "I'll go vind us vone more drink."

Zalith nodded in response, and as Alucard slowly pulled away, the demon kept hold of his arm, letting it slip from his grip the further Alucard got from him.

Once Alucard was too far for Zalith to reach, he smiled back at the demon and then turned to face the direction he was heading. Just *one* more drink… and they'd head back and call it a night.

# Chapter Seventy

— ⸱ ✝ ⸱ —

## Talk of Forever

**| Zalith |**

Zalith waited where Alucard left him. He leaned his left arm on the table, resting the side of his face in his hand as he gazed at his vampire, watching as he wandered off to one of the last remaining butlers to grab their drinks. His thoughts were clouded and confusing… but in a way that made him feel content. All he could do was stare at and think about Alucard's ass, and that brought a smile to his face— a smile that faded, however, when he caught sight of the same guy who'd been staring at him all night. He was making his way over to him. Of course, the demon's smile faded; taking his eyes off Alucard to look at this guy was like staring at a beautiful masterpiece and then turning to look at someone's mediocre pencil scribble.

"Hey," the guy said with a smile once he reached him and leaned on the table beside him. "I never introduced myself," he said as Zalith glanced up at him but then looked back over at Alucard. "I'm Hamilton."

The demon glanced up at him again for barely a moment before looking at Alucard. "Oh, I thought your name was Gerald."

"No," Hamilton laughed, "that's the groom. I'm Hamilton."

Uninterested, still staring at Alucard, who had been caught by the bride once more, Zalith nodded.

"So," Hamilton said as he slowly sat in the seat beside Zalith. "Are you having fun?"

"I was," he mumbled irritably.

Hamilton frowned curiously. "Do you… want to have fun with me… at my place?" he suggested quietly.

Zalith glanced at him again and laughed amusedly. "Really? You?" he said harshly, but Hamilton didn't seem to pick up on his tone.

"Yeah," Hamilton said, smiling.

"What single thing have I done tonight to give you the indication that I would want to go home with you?" he asked, his eyes still fixated on Alucard.

"Well, I don't know. I thought I'd be able to show you a good time, and we could get to know each other."

Zalith laughed. How stupid was this man? He was obviously here with Alucard; why would he leave his vampire for some random, uninteresting guy? And to his relief, Alucard was now making his way back over with their drinks, having finally escaped the nattering bride's gossip.

He couldn't shake the feeling that what was about to happen was going to be very enjoyable.

| **Alucard** |

As Alucard made his way back to Zalith, his gaze locked onto the man now sitting beside him—the same man who earlier couldn't keep his eyes off Zalith. Anger instantly shattered his sense of calm; he was fed up with this intruder, and a surge of possessiveness flared within him. There was no room for hesitation; he was determined to make it clear that this man had no chance with Zalith. Zalith was his, and no random guest at a wedding was going to come between them.

Zalith smiled up at the vampire when he reached them. "Darling, this is Ham," he introduced, taking his drink from Alucard.

Ham frowned. "People usually call me Hamilton."

At the same time, Zalith tugged on Alucard's sleeve and looked up at him. "He wants me to go home with him," he laughed.

Hamilton laughed unsurely—

Alucard didn't need to hear more. He took his eyes off Zalith, scowled down at Hamilton, and watched as he tried to laugh his way out of it. Alucard felt as though his intoxication might be clouding his judgement, but he didn't care. Some random guy was trying to seduce *his* demon, and he felt a very intense urge to act possessively. But he also wanted to punish this guy for his disrespect; he knew Zalith had a partner, so why was he trying to get him to go home with him?

"It was a joke," Hamilton insisted, leaning back in his seat—

Alucard tipped his glass of red wine into the man's lap. Hamilton jumped out of his seat in startle, gritted his teeth in anger, and threw himself at Alucard. But Alucard snatched hold of his collar and pulled him closer.

"Your vace vill be zhe subject of many jokes unless you get zhe fuck out of mine," the vampire warned with an aggressive snarl, and then, he shoved Hamilton back.

Clearly horrified, Hamilton hastily wiped down his lap and hurried off, leaving Alucard and Zalith alone.

The vampire then looked down at Zalith, who took one last sip of his drink before standing up.

Zalith kissed him and said, "Let's go."

Alucard had no objections. Once Zalith took his hand, he followed him to the hall and out of the building.

The demon led the way through the streets and back to *La Casa di Vetro*, where he ushered Alucard upstairs to their room. Zalith hastily unlocked the door, and once they were inside, the demon pushed Alucard back against the door and immediately started kissing him.

Alucard kissed back, his fingers gripping Zalith's shirt as a sudden, enthralling excitement coursed through him. The demon's hastiness and eagerness only fueled his own desire, the palpable desperation igniting a deep hunger inside him.

Zalith wasted no time, his hands quickly moving to unbutton Alucard's shirt. With a swift motion, he tore it off, his hands roaming possessively over the vampire's body. He paused just long enough to catch his breath, their lips parting briefly before he resumed their passionate kiss.

As their intensity grew, Alucard deftly pulled Zalith's shirt off, their bodies pressing together in a heated embrace. In the dimly lit room, shadows danced around them as they stumbled backwards toward the bed. They fell onto it, their lips never breaking from their aggressive, fervent kisses. The demon's hands wandered down to the vampire's belt, and while still kissing Alucard, Zalith pulled it off and dropped it to the floor, manoeuvring the vampire onto his back.

Zalith crawled over Alucard, their eyes locked with a mixture of desire and urgency. He kissed Alucard's lips deeply, his hands exploring every contour of his body. Alucard turned his head to the side for a brief moment, catching his breath before turning back to face Zalith, their mouths meeting once more in a passionate clash. As they continued kissing, Zalith's hand found its way to the vampire's quickly hardening shaft, caressing it through the fabric of his trousers.

The demon's eagerness was unlike before, and Alucard enjoyed it. His hasty moves, and his eager breaths of anticipation; Alucard exhaled deeply in excitement, tilting his head aside as he gripped a handful of Zalith's hair, pulling him closer to his neck. But Zalith didn't immediately sink his fangs into him as Alucard had been expecting. First, he softly pressed his lips against his skin, tasted him with his tongue, and then gently bit down.

Alucard moaned in delight as his body tensed in response to Zalith's venom, which swiftly enthralled his senses, thoughts, and being. In moments, he felt nothing but euphoria, and as he exhaled deeply in relief, the demon started kissing his way down his body.

Zalith frantically kissed his way down to Alucard's waist and pulled off both their trousers. Alucard hummed excitedly as the demon then moved his mouth over his dick, slowly guiding his left hand back up his body. But Zalith couldn't seem to be able to decide what he wanted to do. As his hand reached Alucard's neck, he lightly gripped the vampire's jaw, turned his head to the side and kissed his way back up his body, and when he reached his neck, he dragged his tongue over the two bleeding wounds he left there.

The demon straddled Alucard's lap and smothered the vampire's shaft in lube; Alucard closed his eyes, exhaling deeply in anticipation while he waited. Zalith eagerly moved the vampire's dick into his ass and placed his hand on Alucard's chest as they both exhaled deeply. Alucard was quickly devoured by his euphoria, sinking deeper as he felt the demon's tight walls ensnaring his shaft. He gripped either side of Zalith's waist, breathing faster as the demon gyrated his hips, guiding Alucard's shaft into and out of his body. Then, Zalith leaned forward and rested his arms next to Alucard's, moving a little more aggressively as he started kissing the vampire's lips.

Alucard tightened his grip on Zalith's waist and moaned in delight; his heart was starting to race as both the euphoria and pleasure consumed him.

Zalith then leaned into his ear and whispered, "I want you to fuck me."

Alucard exhaled deeply in a moment of confliction, but he wouldn't let his nervousness break through the sheer contentedness. Holding Zalith's waist, he rolled and pinned the demon down on his back, and then he leaned over him the same way Zalith always did. The demon stared up at him with excitement in his eyes, and a laugh escaped his almost frantic breaths as he moved his leg over Alucard's back.

With his dick still inside the demon's ass, Alucard moved forward, easing his shaft deeper as he gripped Zalith's jaw in his left hand. When the demon exhaled in delight, Alucard edged his face to Zalith's neck and exhaled deeply. Slowly, he moved his body back; despite his overwhelming euphoria, he still felt his concern. He hadn't ever done this before, but his current high helped him get over his fear of doing it wrong. He just did as Zalith did.

He gripped Zalith's wrist and pinned his arm above his head. Zalith, with *his* free hand, grasped the vampire's hair, pushing his face closer to his neck, and Alucard didn't ignore either of their desires. As he started thrusting faster, he sank his fangs into Zalith's neck. The demon moaned in satisfaction, and so did Alucard as Zalith's blood poured into his mouth. He tightened his grip on Zalith's wrist, moving faster as the pleasure surging through his trembling body intensified.

But the more he moved and the more of Zalith's blood he drank, the more overwhelmed he began to feel. He pulled his fangs from the demon's neck, his heart racing, breathing as frantically as Zalith as they both tightened their grasp on one another.

Alucard grimaced in struggle, allowing a pleasured moan to escape his breath as he approached his peak.

"Cum in me," Zalith pleaded, running his fingers through Alucard's hair.

The vampire kept thrusting, moving deeper and faster as the pleasure completely enthralled him. He got nearer and nearer to the edge, and Zalith's pleased moans pushed him further. Alucard groaned and whined, and when he finally climaxed, he cried out in sheer delight, digging his claws into the sheets as the intoxicating rapture pulsed through him, overwhelming him.

"Fuck," the demon murmured, stroking his fingers down Alucard's back as the vampire's dick throbbed inside him.

Alucard exhaled deeply, slowly relaxing his body as it shivered with satisfaction. But Zalith didn't give him time to calm down. The demon hastily positioned Alucard onto his hands and knees, carefully moved his lube-covered fingers into his ass, and then eased his hard, thick dick into him as he gripped either side of his waist.

The vampire moaned pleasurably, grabbing the blanket beneath him; his heart was still racing, and his breaths were still struggled. But as Zalith started thrusting, he hummed sounds of pleasure and enjoyment, unable to control himself—but he didn't want to. He yearned for Zalith's affection so much that he'd not struggle to try and keep himself silent, and Zalith wasn't exactly keeping himself quiet, either. Alucard enjoyed hearing the demon's pleased, satisfied moans, and he was sure that Zalith enjoyed hearing his, too.

But after a few moments of enthralling pleasure passed by, Alucard frowned. The intense, pleasing euphoria seemed to reach a peak, but it wasn't because he was going to climax again. It was strange.... His body was trembling, his anxious breaths were starting to feel stifled, and his arms felt weak. He became tired; that was the best way to explain it. Despite the amount of energy he'd got from Zalith's blood, he felt as though he could fall asleep any moment, and he could only think that it might be because Zalith wasn't controlling himself.

The demon then repositioned Alucard onto his back. He leaned over him and made the vampire move his legs around his waist as he eased his dick back inside him, and as he moved closer to Alucard, he slowed his thrusts and started kissing him.

Alucard murmured quietly through each kiss, as did Zalith, who soon lightly gripped Alucard's throat in his hand and started moving his shaft into and out of his ass a little faster. The vampire grabbed Zalith's hair, snatching hold of his wrist with his other hand as he grimaced in struggle. He could feel every inch of Zalith's hard shaft, every vein, and the satisfying groove of its tip every time it was almost dragged out of his body. His fatigue waned as the pleasure outweighed it, and when Zalith started kissing his neck, Alucard felt himself creep ever closer to another climax.

He fidgeted in Zalith's grip, tightening his grasp on the demon, who moaned quietly as he nuzzled Alucard's neck, still thrusting. It didn't take much longer for Alucard to reach his peak again, and as he climaxed once more, he moaned feverishly, exhaling deeply, trying to catch his breath as sheer pleasure surged through his body in long, intense waves. Alucard whined quietly with every pulse, and he longed for the feeling of Zalith's climax filling his body.

Zalith started breathing frantically, moving faster as he tightened his grip. With one final, aggressive thrust, Zalith plunged his throbbing shaft as deeping into Alucard's ass as he could, and as the demon climaxed, he moaned in delight into the vampire's ear.

Alucard groaned and exhaled, arching his back a little as he felt the heat of Zalith's cum fill his ass. The warmth shot through his body like venom, ensnaring him in a feeling of utter satisfaction. It lingered for a moment but eventually started fading, and Alucard did his best to try and relax. His heart was still racing, and as Zalith pulled his shaft from his ass, the vampire hummed quietly and stroked the demon's arm.

Zalith grabbed a towel and cleaned them both before lying down beside him. He pulled the covers over them, shuffled closer, and rested his head on Alucard's chest. "I love you," he said quietly. "And thank you for taking me out. I had a really nice time."

Alucard frowned, taking a moment to find his words. "I love *you*," he mumbled. "I 'ad a nice time, too."

Zalith hugged him tightly and then kissed the vampire's chest before sighing contently.

Alucard, however—despite his exhaustion—felt curiosity swiftly warping his once silent thoughts. As he glanced down at what he could see of Zalith, he asked, "'Ave you ever…killed somevone vhen 'aving sex?" he muttered. Of course, he now knew Zalith was an incubus, and he wanted to know more.

The demon laughed quietly. "Why?"

He shrugged. "I'm…curious," he mumbled, his fatigue and euphoria still making it hard for him to find his words.

Holding him, Zalith nodded. "I have…but only ever on purpose," he assured him.

Alucard stared up at the ceiling and frowned. "Okay," he replied. "So, you von't accidentally kill me, no?" he said amusedly.

"No," Zalith replied. "I could never kill you; I'd sooner let you kill me."

The vampire sighed quietly and closed his eyes. "I zon't vant you to die," he mumbled, not even sure of what he was saying anymore. "You'll live vith me vorever."

Zalith looked up at him and shuffled closer so that he could rest his head on Alucard's shoulder. "I'll live with you forever," he agreed.

"Good," Alucard said, pouting.

"So long as *you* live with me forever," Zalith added, nuzzling his neck.

Alucard smiled and rested the side of his face on Zalith's head. "Zhat's all I vant."

"That's all I want, too," the demon whispered sleepily.

Then, as Zalith drifted off to sleep, Alucard allowed himself to sleep, too. He'd had an amazing night, and he could only look forward to what would come next.

# Chapter Seventy-One

— ⸲ ✝ ⸱ —

## By Midnight Tonight

| Alucard |

The afternoon sun shined in on Alucard's face, making him grunt irritably. He stopped fiddling with the gold wires he'd been wrapping around pieces of shungite and leaned back in his seat towards the window. Once he pulled the curtains shut, he got back to work; his dream eater was almost complete, and he hoped that when it was ready, it would stop him from having nightmares.

Although it had only been two days since they left Lupa, he missed it. He missed the break away from work and the city where something was always happening, the city where the Imperito were still at large. Zalith was meeting with Margo and the sheriff soon, and Alucard knew that another attempt at trying to persuade the demon to let him help would be futile. But he wasn't mad. He understood why Zalith wanted to take care of it alone. As far as the city knew, Zalith was a straight, married man. Alucard didn't want to potentially destroy that façade and make the people question Zalith's potion.

He was worried, though. The Imperito were dangerous. Alucard hadn't met Don Lorenzo Armani, but he knew his father's father, Don Paolo Armani; he killed not only hundreds of humans in his time but a long list of demons, lycans, vampires, seers, and even a few mages. He trusted Zalith's abilities *and* his people, but he was certain that some of them would die. The Imperito were equipped for anything. But Zalith knew that, didn't he? He'd had his people watching and investigating them for quite some time now.

A knock came at his study door.

Alucard watched it open, and Zalith stepped in.

"Hey," the demon said as he walked towards his desk. "How's it going?"

The vampire looked down at his half-finished dream eater. "Vine. Vrapping zhe crystals is a little more annoying zhan I vhought, but I'm getting zhere."

"Good," Zalith said as he sat on the desk beside him. "Margo and Sheriff Reed are going to be here soon. I just thought I'd let you know in case you need anything."

Alucard leaned back in his seat. "You know vhat I'm going to say."

The demon laughed a little and fiddled with Alucard's fringe. "I really appreciate the offers but knowing that you're safe here is more than I could ask for."

He nodded and said, "I know I zon't 'ave to tell you, but be carevul. Zhese people aren't like zhe Meshuga; zhey 'ave veapons zhat can 'urt zemons."

Zalith smiled and kissed his lips. "Don't worry, baby. I have a plan, and if it doesn't work out, then I have a back-up plan. My people have been watching them for a while; we know what's waiting for us."

Alucard sighed deeply. "Vell, you know vhere I am if you do vant my 'elp."

"I know. Thank you," he said and kissed him again. "If everything goes to plan, the Imperito will be gone by tomorrow."

"And if not?"

He shrugged and smirked. "Gone by the day after."

The vampire exhaled and nodded. He trusted Zalith, so he wasn't going to hound him with questions. "Vill zhe city make you mayor avter zhis, hmm?"

Zalith laughed quietly in amusement. "I don't imagine…Mayor Benedict Watson would be too pleased about that," he said with a mocking tone. "It solidifies my place on the council, though, and I can start making more changes around here."

Alucard smiled at him. "Maybe you can vun vor mayor vhen is time."

"Maybe," he said, stroking the side of the vampire's face. "And then perhaps we won't have to hide all the time."

"Vill probably take a lot of time to get people to accept us. Gay, *and* zemons? You might start a war."

"If I do, you can be sure that I'll win it," he said with a smirk.

Before Alucard could respond, another knock came at his study door.

Alucard sighed. "Vhat?"

Edwin peered in. "Oh, there you are, sir. Your guests have arrived and are waiting in your office," he said to Zalith.

Zalith nodded. "Thank you, Edwin."

The butler then left.

"Well," Zalith said with a deep sigh. "Duty calls."

Alucard leaned back in his seat. "'Ave vun."

Zalith scoffed amusedly. "I'll try my best." He kissed Alucard's lips, and then he left his study, pulling the door shut behind him.

The vampire shifted his sights back to the dream eater. He wasn't sure how long Zalith would be busy, nor did he know the ins and outs of his plans to deal with the Imperito, but he was certain that he'd be back much later tonight, so he might as well get back to work and finish crafting his nightmare preventative.

## | Zalith |

When he stepped into his office, Zalith greeted Margo and Reed with a smile. "Sorry, I had to see to something upstairs."

"Good to see you again," Reed said as Zalith shook his hand.

"I was beginning to think you'd forgotten about us," Margo laughed as she then shook the demon's hand.

Zalith laughed a little, too, and sat behind his desk. "Things have been a little hectic lately; I had to deal with some family business. However, my people have remained surveying the Imperito and their whereabouts, and I've come up with a plan to remove them from the Citadel."

"We've been eager to hear it," Margo said, making herself comfortable in one of the two armchairs in front of Zalith's desk. "I'm sure you've seen the latest reports. They burned down a family-owned restaurant last week because they refused to sell."

"Two dead," Reed said as he handed Zalith last week's newspaper. "Poor family. Kids are orphaned."

As he read the story, Zalith sighed deeply. "I'm so sorry that it's taken this long."

"We've been reluctant to take action without your guidance," Reed continued. "You did such a good job with the Meshuga, we didn't want to risk making it harder to deal with Armani by attempting to make arrests and build a case. There's no evidence, of course—nothing physical. All the witnesses are too shit scared to come forward."

Zalith put the newspaper down and leaned back in his seat. "Armani is a dangerous man, and his people are equipped to deal with anything. For the sake of the safety of your units and the people of this city, my men will be taking the lead this time. Before forcefully evicting Armani, I plan to offer him a choice to leave peacefully; this would cause less damages and loss of life. However, it is highly likely that Armani will refuse, and we'll have to resort to violence."

Margo nodded slowly. "So…what do you want us to do?"

"I need you to make sure that the streets around Armani's hideout are clear."

"You know where his hideout is?" Reed asked, wide-eyed.

"Thirty-seven, Saint George's Lane," Zalith answered.

Reed and Margo glanced at one another.

"That's…the Saint George Tavern. It's been closed for years," the sheriff said.

"But I guess that's what Armani wants us to believe," Margo muttered.

"Precisely," the demon said with a nod.

"Is it just Saint George's Lane that you need us to clear and blockade?" Margo then asked.

"I think it would be wise to clear the surrounding blocks, too. I'll leave some of my men with your units to ensure capture of any fleeing Imperito," Zalith said. "How long do you think you'll need to clear the streets and have your units in place?"

Margo glanced at Reed and pondered. "Well, if we start as soon as we get back to the city, it could be done by tonight. Maybe nine or ten."

"Perfect," Zalith said and rested his arms on his desk. "I'll prepare my men."

Reed frowned. "Wait, so…we're doing this *right now*?"

Zalith nodded. "That's the plan."

"Don't we need time to let our officers know what to deal with?"

"Your officers need not do anything but keep the streets clear and the blockades up. My men will do everything else," Zalith assured him. He didn't want to waste time with long, drawn-out meetings spent explaining things that his own people already knew. He didn't need the help of Margo and Reed's officers this time.

"What about arrests?" the sheriff asked. "Will we be making any?"

"If any Imperito attempt to flee, my men will capture them. You're free to arrest them." Zalith replied.

Margo and Reed glanced at one another again as if they were wondering if either of them had anything else to say or ask. But neither of them said anything.

"Your officers can handle the clean-up, if you'd prefer," Zalith then said. "There will likely be a lot of bodies."

With a deep sigh, Margo nodded. "I'll inform the morgue to be ready."

Reed leaned forward. "So this is it, right? The Imperito's last day in the Citadel."

"That's the goal," Zalith said with a nod. "My people are very thorough, as you well know. After we deal with Armani and as many Imperito as we find, your officers will be free to arrest and pursue any remaining members—if there are any at all."

"Understood," the sheriff said.

"What about Armani's businesses?" Margo asked.

Zalith thought about that for a moment. "Well, he's stolen plenty from people of the Citadel. I think it would only be right that they're returned to their rightful owners. Those he bought can be handed over to the city; the council can decide what becomes of them."

Margo nodded in agreement. "He's stolen more than businesses, though. Countless lives. He's orphaned too many children. He deserves more than a swift execution."

The demon wanted it over with as soon as possible, but he didn't want to make the council feel like he was taking complete control. "I can try to deliver him to you alive if you'd prefer, but hasn't he stood trial before?"

"Three times," Reed said irritably. "He got off each time, no time, no fine."

"But it's what the people would want," Margo argued.

"The people want him gone, Margo," the sheriff said, looking at her. "And the most effective way to make that happen would be to kill him. I don't want to sit in another courthouse and through another lengthy trial just for him to slip away again."

Zalith tapped his fingers on the desk. "I agree with Reed," he said. "People like Armani are hard to be brought to justice. It's a horrible truth, but the only way you'll be rid of him is to kill him. If you're worried about the people's reactions, though, we can find a way to make this look like an arrest operation gone wrong, or perhaps another hypothetical gang will be responsible. I'm sure that Armani has enemies out there."

The pair adorned conflicted frowns.

"I don't want to scare the people," Margo said, shaking her head. "Talks of another gang strong enough to take out Armani will surely terrify the Citadel."

"Operation gone wrong sounds like the best way to go," Reed said.

Zalith nodded. "All right. I'm going to go and prepare my people. I'll see you both again at…let's say ten."

Margo and Reed nodded, and when Zalith stood up, they did, too.

"Once again, we're truly so grateful for your assistance, Zalith," Reed said as he shook the demon's hand. "I don't know where we'd be without you."

Zalith laughed a little. "I'm just glad to be of use to the city."

Margo then shook his hand and smiled at him. "I'm looking forward to seeing you in action again."

The demon smiled, too. "I won't let you down."

He watched them both leave his office, and then he slumped back down in his seat. He hoped that he could be done with the Imperito tonight; in two days, he was meeting with his subordinates to discuss his intentions to declare war on the Numen, and he didn't want Armani and his silly little human gang causing him any unnecessary distractions.

With a quiet sigh, he got up and left his office. He headed upstairs and to Alucard's study, where his vampire was still working on his little crystal contraption. "Hey," he said as he walked towards his desk.

"I vhought you 'ad to deal vith zhe Imperito stuff?" Alucard asked as he stopped fiddling with the gold wire and leaned back in his seat.

"I do, but I thought I'd come and make out with you before I go," he said with a smirk, sitting on his desk again.

As a flustered expression stole his curious frown, Alucard looked away from him.

Zalith laughed a little and gently grasped his chin. He turned the vampire's head, making him face him, and then he kissed his lips. A drowning, consuming desperation quickly enthralled him when he slipped his tongue into Alucard's mouth, and he couldn't help but say, "I'd fuck you so hard right now if I had the time."

Alucard tried to hide his flustered face again. "Vhy zon't you 'ave time?"

"I have to go and prepare my people for this Imperito take down."

The vampire looked disappointed. "Vell…ve alvays 'ave tonight, no?"

Zalith smiled excitedly. "We do." He kissed his lips and stared seductively into his eyes. "Make sure your ass is ready for me when I get home," he said with a sultry tone. Sex would definitely help him feel a lot more relaxed, and maybe a little less anxious about leaving Alucard alone, but he really didn't have the time. He had to get his people ready for a war in the streets.

A shy little smile appeared on the vampire's face. "Okay."

The demon kissed his lips again and caressed his cheek. "I love you," he said as he gazed into Alucard's hell-fiery eyes. "The operation is happening at ten, but I don't see it taking very long for me and my demons to kill Armani and his gang, so I should be home before midnight."

Alucard nodded. "Okay. I love you, too."

Zalith kissed him one last time and then headed for the door. He knew that if he didn't leave now, he'd start overthinking about what might happen if he left Alucard at home alone, but he knew that his vampire was safe there. Their house was the safest place for him.

He made his way downstairs and left the house. Once he climbed into the carriage, he relaxed as best he could and stared out the window as the world passed by. All he had to do now was head to Alucard's galleon, find his demons, and tell them the plan. And by midnight tonight, the Imperito would no longer exist.

# Chapter Seventy-Two

─ ≼ ✝ ≽ ─

## Operation Gone Wrong

| **Zalith** |

Zalith stared at the ticking clock. Each tick, tick, tick echoed around Alucard's galleon office, making the demon's heart race a little faster. He started tapping his claws on the desk in rhythm with each sound, angst beginning to swirl around inside him. And that question…it clawed beneath his skin, desperate to reach the surface.

Was this world real? Was this *life* real? Would he soon wake up back on the battlefield ensnared by Adellum's light? Was Alucard…okay? He took his eyes off the clock and glanced around the room. Should he send an izuret to check on his vampire? He didn't want to give in to the paranoia, but…his anxiety was starting to get the better of him. He wanted to go home, he wanted to find Alucard and just hold him. But he couldn't. Not yet. He had a job to do.

A knock came at the door.

"Yeah?" he called, sitting up straight.

Tyrus stepped into the room, and Wes, one of Tyrus' Betas, was waiting out in the hallway with some of the demons who Zalith had sent for.

"We're ready, sir," Tyrus told him.

With a nod, Zalith got up and headed for the door.

Tyrus walked beside him as everyone followed Zalith through the halls. "Everyone's waiting on the deck. We've revised the building plans you sent us, and we received word that Margo and Sheriff Reed have positioned their men and created the blockades," he explained.

"Good," Zalith said, heading up to the deck. "Let's move."

When Zalith reached the deck, the rest of his demons joined him. They left the galleon and silently made their way through the Citadel until they reached Saint George's Lane. The Saint George Tavern stood at the end of the street between an abandoned clothing store and a bakery that had been closed ever since Zalith moved to Nefastus—

maybe even before—and inside the tavern, he could sense the life force and hear the heartbeats of at least a hundred humans.

His demons took their positions. Those he'd ordered to stand with the officers at the blockades left to do so, and then half of Tyrus' pack circled around to the back of the building, while a small group headed underground via a manhole and took their positions at the ladder which would take them up into a storeroom inside the tavern.

And once everyone sent Zalith their confirmation that they were ready, he joined Tyrus and the demons who stood against the walls of the surrounding buildings, waiting to burst inside.

Zalith concentrated, listening to the hushed chatter inside. *He* was going to go for Armani; he'd make sure that the man was dead. He shifted his focus between each man, trying to locate their leader. As he recalled the building plans, he knew that there was a storage room with an entrance to the underground tunnels. It was likely that Armani would be nearby in case he needed a quick escape. But he wouldn't be escaping this time. His demons were down there lying in wait.

He glanced at Tyrus, who nodded, letting him know that he was ready.

Then, Zalith set his eyes on the tavern door.

It was time to put an end to the Imperito.

Zalith nodded.

His demons crashed through the tavern door with a ferocious roar, and Zalith was right behind them. As he stormed inside, chaos erupted; the Imperito agents immediately opened fire, their weapons blazing and tearing through the air with deafening gunfire. Shouts of panic and orders filled the room, mingling with the sudden bursts of flame that lit up the darkened tavern.

Darting for cover, Zalith pressed himself against a sturdy wooden beam, narrowly avoiding a hail of bullets. The acrid smell of gunpowder and the heat of nearby explosions surrounded him. His heart pounded in his chest, matching the rapid tempo of the battle unfolding around him.

Without wasting a moment, Zalith surged from his cover, sprinting through the carnage towards the door behind the bar. His path was suddenly blocked by an Imperito goon, rifle raised and firing at one of his demons who had taken refuge behind an overturned table. Snarling with irritation, Zalith lunged forward, his movements swift and brutal. He grabbed the rifle, wrenching it from the man's grip, and with a powerful swing, smashed it into the goon's face. The man crumpled to the ground, lifeless.

Dropping the weapon, Zalith vaulted over the bar, landing smoothly on the other side. His eyes scanned the room through the open door for any threats as the sounds of battle raged on, and then he hurried inside, avoiding the rain of bullets flying around the tavern.

Two large goons emerged from the door to Zalith's right, both carrying automatic rifles. Inside the room before the door swung shut, the demon caught sight of four other men escorting someone towards the back of the building.

That had to be Armani.

Zalith burst into action before the two men could raise and fire their rifles. He sent the first up in ashen flames with a jerk of his wrist, and he grabbed the second's gun and yanked it from his hands. The man stumbled and panicked as his ally screamed beside him, dropping to the floor and rolling around as the fire burned him down to nothing. Zalith snatched the man's throat and tore it out with his claws, and then he pulled the door open and veered left, trailing behind the fleeing men.

The battle raged behind him, the gunfire growing louder, and yells sounding more panicked. But he trusted his men to know what they were doing.

He reached a steel vault door. On the other side were five heartbeats and the sound of metal scraping against metal. They were trying to get into the manhole.

Zalith grasped the vault handle and twisted it, and when he yanked the door open, the five men inside sharply turned their heads to look at him.

The demon set his sights on Armani. Tall, broad, and ugly as fuck; the man looked like he'd been trampled by a herd of horses, dragged through a swamp, and then run over by several carriages. He looked like a man who'd tried to have his face altered but the surgeon had ultimately botched the job.

As the four men dropped their tools and reached for their rifles, Armani raised his shotgun. Zalith dodged to the side, avoiding Armani's first shot, and then he grabbed one of the four guards, tore his heart out, and threw his body at the others. Armani fired again, but his shot hit the ceiling when the dead guard collided with him, knocking him and the three remaining guards to the floor.

Zalith sent the other three up in white flames and grabbed Armani's collar. He pulled the man to his feet and snarled in his face when he struggled and tried to escape. But one of the fire-ensnared men stumbled back and collided with a crate, and when it dropped to the floor and cracked open, a tsunami of gunpowder poured out—

A blinding, deafening white explosion lit up the room, throwing Zalith off his feet. His body hit a wall, and when he landed on the floor with a thump, he stared at the sizzling, crackling white light that engulfed the room.

His heart raced, and his limbs trembled.

Fear constricted him so tightly that his breaths became stifled.

This was it, wasn't it? Adellum. He'd come for him. His life was about to reset. He was going to wake up on that battlefield. He was going to see Alucard die over and over and over and—

A hand grasped Zalith's throat. Someone pulled him to his feet. And then sharp, suffocating pain began surging through his body, originating from his stomach.

The white light soon faded, and when his eyes met the disgusting visage of Armani, Zalith grasped back onto reality.

"Fucking die!" Armani yelled furiously as he stabbed and stabbed and stabbed at Zalith's body.

Zalith snapped out of it, and with a revolted, frustrated growl, he snatched Armani's wrist, broke it and made him drop his pathetic little knife, and then harshly shoved the man back with so much force that he tripped and landed beside the piles of ash which were once his guards.

The wounds in Zalith's stomach quickly healed—a steel knife was anything but lethal.

To him, anyway.

He grabbed the knife as he prowled towards Armani. The man desperately reached for one of the dropped rifles, but Zalith kicked them away and then dropped to his knees. With a flurry of furious yells, he mercilessly stabbed Armani's chest over and over and over again. The man's blood splattered onto his face, staining his clothes, and getting into his hair and his mouth. He snarled in revolt as Armani grunted, choked, and spat blood. And when the man fell silent, Zalith plunged the knife deep into his body, huffing angrily, *seething* as his heart raced in his chest, ensnared by a conflicting concoction of fury, desperation, and angst.

The blinding white light was gone, but a part of him couldn't let go of the fear that his life was still going to restart. He couldn't escape the thought that maybe he was going to find Alucard's body among the battle happening behind him…or the thought that maybe the Light had made him think that the man dead beneath him was Armani.

Zalith stared at the dead man, dread tightening its grip as he waited…waited for the body to transform. But it didn't. The body didn't become Alucard. The blood was human, the fading aura was human…and Alucard…Zalith could feel him through their imprints. He was fine. He was at home, and his aura felt relaxed.

With a long sigh, Zalith let go of the knife and stumbled to his feet. His heart was still racing, and his hands were trembling. But as he breathed deeply, he tried his best to calm down, and as the fear and confusion withered, the sounds of the battle behind him snatched his attention.

Armani was dead, and his demons needed his help.

Zalith shoved Armani's body aside and pulled the manhole cover off. "Get up here," he said to the demons waiting in the tunnels. Then, he hurried out of the room and towards the bar.

When he returned to the battle, he immediately forced his hand through an Imperito goon's back and tore out his heart. He grabbed the man's weapon and cracked it over the head of another, and then he helped one of his fallen, injured demons to his feet and handed him off to another, ordering him to get him to safety.

With an aggravated snarl, Zalith stormed through the gunfire and sliced the throat of another goon with his claws. He grabbed a machete from the floor and launched it across the room, and when it embedded itself in the chest of the goon who was keeping Tyrus pinned down, Tyrus shot him an appreciative nod.

It wasn't over yet, though. Some of the goons tried escaping, but Zalith's demons chased after them. Zalith remained in the tavern, helping his demons take out the last of the goons; most of them tried surrendering when they realized that their leader was gone, but Zalith wasn't going to show any mercy. He ordered their deaths, and once the last man hit the floor, he left the tavern and took a deep, long breath.

He looked down at his trembling, bloody hands, and when he clenched his fists, he closed his eyes and attempted to relax.

"Zalith," came Margo's voice.

The demon opened his eyes and turned to face her.

"Is everything okay?" she asked him.

He pulled his best smile. "Yeah. We've just finished up in there. Armani's dead."

The woman exhaled and crossed her arms. "There's something I never thought I'd hear. But I'm glad it's over. We've made a few arrests, and we're going to interrogate them. There's got to be more Imperito in the Citadel, but we'll find them."

Zalith nodded. "I can lend you my people again to assist."

"Thank you," she said with a smile. "For everything. I meant it when I said that I wouldn't know where we'd be without you."

"I'm glad to help."

"We'll talk to the press tomorrow; we've already got our cover story figured out. There's bound to be a little uproar and skepticism, but that's to be expected. When someone as powerful as Armani dies, people are going to be afraid. But we'll do our best to convince them that the city is safe."

Zalith nodded again and glanced down at his bloody hands. "I better get home and get cleaned up. My people will remain here to help with the clean-up and capture of any more Imperito who might have slipped away. If you need to contact me, speak to Tyrus," he said, nodding in Tyrus' direction.

Margo smiled and said, "Thank you. Tell Varana I said hello, too."

"Goodnight," the demon said, and then he turned around and started walking back towards the docks.

He wanted to adorn his wings and get home as fast as possible, but he didn't want to risk being seen in his demon form by Margo or any of her officers. So he walked and walked…and when he reached the carriage, he climbed inside and did his best to calm down. He didn't want to let his anxiety get the better of him, but he couldn't help but focus on Alucard through their imprints. Feeling connected to the man he loved helped him relax, and as the carriage took him home, he held tightly onto the thought of crawling into bed with his vampire. *That* was all he wanted right now.

# Chapter Seventy-Three

# Dry Blood

| Alucard |

When Alucard heard the front door open, he left his study and headed downstairs. He met Zalith halfway down, and the moment the demon saw him, he wrapped his arms around him and held him tightly.

Alucard frowned worriedly. He saw all the blood on his hands and face, and the tears in his shirt and blazer, too. "Vhat 'appened?" he asked quietly.

Zalith exhaled deeply and nuzzled his neck. "Nothing," he replied. "I just missed you."

The vampire tightened his embrace around him. "I missed you, too." He waited a moment, and then he asked, "Did you deal vith Armani?"

He nodded. "He's dead. My people are dealing with the rest of it. I wanted to get home to you."

Alucard smiled and ran his fingers through Zalith's hair. "I vink you need to shower," he said with a quiet laugh.

The demon laughed a little, too. "I think so, too."

They slowly made their way upstairs and into the bathroom, where Alucard helped Zalith take his bloody clothes off. When he saw the dried blood on the demon's stomach, though, his worried frown returned.

"Did you get 'urt?" he asked, dragging his fingers over the dried blood, but there weren't any wounds below.

Zalith sighed and rested his forehead against Alucard's. "Armani had a stupid little knife, but I'm fine. It was steel."

Alucard sighed and stroked his hand down the side of Zalith's body. "Are you sure?"

He nodded and started unbuttoning the vampire's shirt. "I'll be even more fine once you're naked."

Trying to hide his embarrassed pout, Alucard looked down and watched the demon's hands undress him.

Zalith then took hold of Alucard's hand and led the way into the shower. He switched the water on, and as it fell over them, he placed his hands on the vampire's waist and pulled him closer. "How was your evening?" he asked him.

Alucard shrugged. "Okay. I've almost vinished zhe dream eater."

"That's good." He tucked a few strands of Alucard's wet hair behind his ears, and then he kissed his lips. "Do you still want me to fuck you?" he asked with a smirk.

The vampire tried to hide his flustered face again as excitement abruptly shot through him. He might have thought that after what was clearly a frustrating, painful batter, Zalith would prefer to just shower and head to bed, but he was wrong… and he was glad that he was wrong. Not only was he craving Zalith's affection, but he knew that having sex would help the demon feel better. He wanted to give himself to him—he wanted to give Zalith whatever he needed.

He nodded shyly.

Zalith gently gripped Alucard's chin and made him look at him. He kissed his lips, and as their tongues quickly entwined, Zalith's warm hands traversed down Alucard's body.

With a content hum, Alucard placed his hands against the demon's abs, and when Zalith carefully pushed and pinned him against the wall, he smiled through their kisses and gripped a fistful of Zalith's hair. The demon then grasped Alucard's wrist and guided his hand down to his crotch. Although he was nervous, the vampire gripped the demon's arousal and began caressing it.

As Zalith hummed contently through their kisses, he moved his hands around to Alucard's ass and gripped it, making the vampire groan quietly in delight. The excitement coursing through him intensified, and as the demon's dick hardened in his grip, he kissed back a little more desperately.

Zalith kissed the vampire one last time and then turned him around. As Alucard rested his arms against the wall, the demon massaged cold, viscous lube into his ass. He hummed pleasurably, closing his eyes, sinking into the warmth of the water and the pleasing feeling of Zalith's fingers slowly moving in and out of him.

The demon then pressed the tip of his dick against Alucard's hole. Alucard tensed up, both anticipation and excitement enthralling him. Just the thought of Zalith inside him made him feel aroused; it made him feel desperate, longing as if he'd waited decades for it. And when he finally felt the demon's hard, thick shaft easing inside him, he clenched his fists and moaned pleasurably, relaxing his body as each inch plunged deeper.

Zalith moaned quietly into Alucard's ear, grasping his waist again as he began gently thrusting. The vampire responded with his own pleasured groans, and when Zalith started speeding up, his delighted sighs grew louder.

"Fuck, your ass feels so good," Zalith groaned.

Alucard wanted to reply, but his nervousness gripped him tightly. He did his best, though, to fight through it. "So does your dick," he breathed and then moaned again.

His reply made the demon groan loudly in response, and his thrusts became aggressive, almost as if Alucard's words had intensified Zalith's delight. He fucked him harder and faster, thrusting his dick so deep inside him that all Alucard could do was whine, standing there entirely enthralled by Zalith's dominance. He submitted, relaxing his body so that the demon could plunge deeper, spreading his legs a little more as they trembled.

Zalith groaned again and pleasurably sighed, "Good boy."

A shiver of delight spiralled through Alucard, bringing him nearer to his peak. He responded with a pleasured cry, edging near and near until his body couldn't take it anymore; Zalith's compliment excited him, it made him feel sheer content; he was pleasing the demon, and that was all he wanted. With a feverish moan, he climaxed, the pleasure pulsing through his body as Zalith kept thrusting.

The demon's delighted whines intensified, and he started thrusting so aggressively that with his final plunge, Alucard's body was forced forward, pressed up against the wall as he felt the demon's dick throbbing inside him, filling him with warmth. They groaned together, and it felt like fire coursed through Alucard when the demon dragged his hands down the sides of his body.

"I really fucking needed that," Zalith said as he rested his head against the back of Alucard's. "Thank you."

Alucard smiled through his deep, calming breaths. "I needed zhat, too."

Zalith slowly pulled his dick from his ass and then turned the vampire to face him. He rested his forehead against his, smirking at him, and then he kissed his lips. "I really love you."

The vampire's smile grew. "I veally love you, too."

He caressed the side of Alucard's face. "I mean it. I don't know where I'd be without you, Alucard. You're everything to me, and I know that I fucked up and hurt you, but I promise you…I won't ever do anything like that ever again."

Alucard wiped some blood off Zalith's cheek with his thumb and gazed into his eyes; they were full of guilt and dismay, and that hurt the vampire's heart. "Is okay, Zaliv," he assured him. "You're everyving to me, too. I'm not going anyvhere."

Zalith kissed him again and then sighed quietly. "You know I'd do anything to keep you safe, right?"

He nodded. "I'd do anyving to keep you safe, too."

A small smile flickered across the demon's tired face. "We're going to be talking about fighting the Numen in two days."

"I know," he said quietly. "Ve 'ave all zhe invormation ve need, zon't vorry," he tried to assure him.

He sighed again but nodded. "I just…don't want to lose you."

"You're not going to lose me, Zaliv. Ve 'ave plans, no? And places to vetreat to if ve need. Ve'll be okay."

Although he didn't look entirely convinced, the demon closed his eyes and half-nodded. "I know. There's just…always this thought in the back of my mind that something's going to happen, that something or someone is going to take you away from me," he mumbled sadly.

The ache in Alucard's heart worsened. He placed his hand on the side of Zalith's neck and shook his head. "Noving is going to take me avay vrom you, I promise. I vant to spend my life vith you. Noving vill vuin zhat."

When he opened his eyes to look at him, the demon smiled weakly again. "I want to spend my life with you, too."

Alucard kissed his lips and said, "Try not to vorry too much." Though he knew his words were probably useless; Zalith was still recovering from his traumatic standoff with Adellum. But Alucard could be patient. He'd help him get better, and he'd make sure that Zalith knew he was never leaving. He wanted to spend forever with him, and he'd do whatever it took to ensure it.

# Chapter Seventy-Four

─ ⟨ ✝ ⟩ ─

## Preparatory Declaration

**| Alucard |**

Alucard was in the sunroom surrounded by tropical and carnivorous plants. A conflicted scowl clung to his face while the sun shined in on him, and his ice-blue eyes shimmered brightly as he fed a large flytrap a tiny mouse. The plant had grown too big to sit around waiting for flies, and the vampire took it upon himself to take care of it since Sabazios had been spending his time with Colt, the kid who Zalith let stay on the second floor with Idina whilst their new homes were being built.

As the plant clamped its jaws shut around the dead rodent, Alucard smiled slightly and slipped his hands into his pockets. Some quiet time alone was what he needed before his and Zalith's subordinates started arriving; although it had only been four days since they left Lupa, the vampire missed it terribly. He had a wonderful night, but it was time to get back to business.

Today was the day they were meant to be sharing and devising their plan to take out Damien and Lilith and whichever other Numen wanted to get in their way, which meant Alucard was going to have to talk…a lot. He'd have to tell everyone everything they needed to know to do the jobs he and Zalith had lined up for them, and the vampire had spent the entire week recalling and taking note of everything he knew.

One of the doors then opened, and when Alucard looked over his shoulder, he set his eyes on Zalith, who smiled at him.

"Hey," the demon said, making his way over. "What are you doing?" he asked, resting his chin on Alucard's shoulder as he wrapped his arms around him and hugged him from behind.

Alucard shrugged as he looked back down at the plant. "Veeding Marcy."

Zalith laughed quietly. "Why did you name my plant?"

The vampire pouted. "Vhy 'aven't *you* named your chicken?"

"I did," the demon said.

"Vhat did you name 'er, zhen?" Alucard tested.

Zalith went quiet for a moment but then said, "Marcy."

Alucard tried to hide his smile.

"Do you feed *all* the hungry plants or just Marcy?"

He felt a little embarrassed to admit it, but he shrugged and looked down at the flytrap as it chewed on the mouse. "All of zhem," he mumbled.

Laughing, the demon hugged him tighter. "That's very sweet of you. Have you named any others?"

"Vell..." Alucard said, looking at one of the other carnivorous plants. "Zhat vone is Trent, and zhat is... Sally," he said, looking at another flytrap.

Zalith smiled and turned Alucard around to face him; he lightly gripped his hips and pulled him closer. Then, he placed his right hand on the side of Alucard's face, leaned closer, and kissed his lips. "I always forget how nice this room is," he said, glancing around. "We should do things in here more often," he said, smirking. And then, before Alucard could respond, he continued kissing him.

While they kissed, Alucard frowned hesitantly. The demon dragged his hand down over his waist and to his crotch, caressing it for a few moments. However, once Zalith gripped his belt, the door to the sunroom flung open, startling them both. They sharply turned their heads to look at the door and watched as Colt burst into the room, laughing and panting while Sabazios chased him. But when he reached where Zalith and Alucard were standing, he slowed down and glanced up at them.

In his arms, the boy was clasping a stuffed dolphin toy against his chest, and as Sabazios wandered over, Colt hid behind the dog and frowned shyly. "Thank you, sir, for new Maurice," he said, holding out his dolphin.

Looking down at the dolphin, Alucard nodded. "You're velcome."

Then, Colt turned around and scurried off with Sabazios.

Sighing, Zalith smiled and pulled Alucard closer again. They started kissing—

"O-oh, sorry," Idina then called in shock.

They looked at the door once again, glaring over at her.

"Did Colt come through here? I can't seem to find him," she said with a look of uncertainty on her face, one that was clearly a response to Alucard and Zalith's irritated glares.

"Yes," Zalith grumbled. "He went that way," he said, waving in the direction the boy and Sabazios ran. Then, as Idina left, the demon sighed and rested his forehead against Alucard's. "I think we're going to have to reschedule," he said sadly.

With his own sigh of disappointment, Alucard looked down at the floor. "Is okay. People vill be 'ere soon anyvay."

Zalith smirked. "Unless I do things to you under the table."

Alucard scowled in embarrassment, remembering the time Zalith dragged his foot over his leg the last time he had a large meeting with all his subordinates. "Zon't do zhat again," he muttered. "Vas embarrassing."

The demon tucked a loose strand of Alucard's hair behind his ear. "Sorry."

Staring at him, Alucard sighed quietly, but when a knock came at the sunroom's door, he rolled his eyes and looked in its direction, as did Zalith.

"Sirs, one of your guests has arrived. A Mister Attila," Edwin called from the doorway.

"Oh, good," Zalith grumbled. "Edwin," he called before the butler could leave, "do you remember what we talked about?"

The butler nodded. "Of course, sir. I understand." Then, he left.

Alucard frowned strangely at him. "Vhat did you talk about?"

"Nothing," the demon said, smiling, "just some accommodations for Attila—don't worry about it."

"Okay…" Alucard drawled skeptically. "Ve should go and meet 'im," he mumbled. Attila needed to be invited in by either himself or Zalith, so they had no choice in the matter.

They made their way out of the sunroom, through the hall, and to the front door, where Attila was waiting. He'd come in a formal, traditional Deiganish tailcoat with a frilly-collared shirt beneath it, and his long hair was tied behind his head.

Attila smiled as he set his eyes on Alucard and leaned on the porch's frame. "Been a long time," he said, watching as Alucard and Zalith stopped in the entrance hall. "I was beginning to think you'd forgotten about me."

Alucard rolled his eyes; he wasn't in the mood for Attila's casual attitude. Attila had lost the right to talk to him as if they were friends the day he'd insulted Zalith.

Zalith moved his hand around Alucard's waist and pulled the vampire closer. "Did you have trouble finding the place?" he asked Attila, smiling as Alucard frowned at him.

Attila took his eyes off Alucard, lost his smile, and deadpanned. "No," he answered. "I just followed Alucard's call. It's not hard—"

"Oh, good," Zalith interjected. "Yeah, it's pretty straightforward, but I know some people are a little less intelligent than others," he said with a condescending smile.

Glaring at Zalith, Attila scoffed quietly and shifted his gaze to Alucard—

"Of course, you're smart, though," Zalith continued before Attila could speak. "I mean, you're all dressed up and ready to go," he said, smirking. "Look at us, though— so casual," he said as he started fiddling with the buttons on Alucard's shirt. He then placed his hand on Alucard's chest, gazing at him for a moment.

Alucard stared back, unsure why Zalith was being so…weird, for the lack of a better word. But he was convinced that he was trying to make Attila uncomfortable; the look on Attila's face made it clear that Zalith's plan was working.

The demon sighed and set his sights back on Attila. "You look great, though—like a big baby that's on its way to get anointed—I love it. It works for you," he taunted.

Attila scowled impatiently. "I just came from DeiganLupus, thank you. Every aristocrat dresses up in this shit," he grumbled. "Of course, any smart guy would know that, but obviously, you're not important enough to have seen royalty, are you?"

Alucard scowled and went to scold him—

Zalith, however, laughed and pulled Alucard even closer. "You say that as though I'm not fucking Lucifer's son," he boasted.

"You're unbelievable," Attila said in disgust as he scowled in revolt.

Alucard then sighed irritably. "Can ve just…get on vith zhis?" he snapped before either of them could say another word.

The demon looked at him and smiled. "It's your house too, baby," he said with a content smile, obviously implying that he, too, could invite Attila in.

He sighed, taking his eyes off Zalith to look at Attila. "You can come in," he mumbled.

"Wipe your feet," Zalith said the moment Attila prepared to step over the threshold.

Scowling, Attila did as he was told and started wiping his feet on the doormat. As he did, though, Varana suddenly appeared from around the porch in a tight black dress and made her way into the house.

As soon as she entered, she smiled and twirled around. "How do I look?" she asked Zalith.

"Fantastic, as always," the demon replied as Alucard rolled his eyes.

She smiled but then gasped in shock when she caught sight of Attila. "O-oh…hello?"

"Hello," he replied with a smile, ignoring Zalith's quiet laughter.

"Who…are you?" she asked him.

"My subordinate," Alucard uttered. He suddenly felt so irritated, something that always seemed to happen the moment Varana showed up.

Varana glanced at him with an aggravated expression but then smiled at Attila. "It's nice to meet you. I'm Varana," she greeted, holding out her hand.

Attila took hold of her hand. "Attila," he said and kissed the back of her hand.

She smiled as best she could, and when she backed off and stood beside Zalith, she leaned over to the demon. "Ew," she muttered.

With a quiet sigh, Alucard glanced at the three of them. "Let's go," he mumbled.

However, just then, Edwin came rushing over with a huddle of towels under his arms. He immediately laid one down at Attila's feet and then stood up to look at him. "Right this way sir, if you please," he invited, laying another towel down in front of the other, and he kept laying them down along the floor, creating a path towards the room where Alucard and Zalith planned to have the meeting.

Alucard sighed and shook his head—

"Are you actually serious?" Attila scoffed. "What the fuck?"

"Sorry, we don't want dirty feet walking on the hardwood," Zalith said with a shrug before turning his back on Attila to lead the way.

Attila gawped at Alucard as if he was expecting him to protest.

But Alucard had nothing to say. He followed Zalith, as did Varana.

With an irritated, revolted snarl, Attila followed behind them, walking over the towels that Edwin continued laying out for him.

When they entered the room, Edwin hurried to one of the chairs and placed a towel over its back and its seat before holding his arm out towards it, looking at Attila.

Once again, Attila stared at Alucard as if he were waiting for him to tell Ewin and Zalith to stop, but Alucard had no intention of doing so. Attila deserved to be treated however Zalith wanted to treat him. So, ignoring Attila's stare, Alucard made his way to the head of the table and sat down in one of the two seats that had been placed there.

Everything the vampire prepared prior to the meeting was waiting in three separate neat stacks of paper, each organized by the subjects that would be discussed. As he made himself comfortable, he watched Attila slump into his towel-covered seat with a sour look on his face. Zalith then made his way over and sat next to Alucard, and Varana pulled out the seat closest to the demon. Now all they had to do was wait for everyone else to arrive.

But Alucard felt he needed something to distract him from his irritancy; otherwise, this meeting wasn't going to go as smoothly as he'd like. So, when the butler was about to leave, he frowned at him and called, "Ezvin."

Edwin stopped in his tracks and looked back at him. "Yes, sir?"

"Vill you bring me some of zhat gateau, please," he muttered.

"Of course."

"I'll have some of my punch," Varana called.

"Water with lemon, please," Zalith added, but as Edwin nodded, the demon shook his head. "Perhaps bring out a cheese plate for the table… with some crudités."

The butler nodded. "Of course. Anything for your guest or those that will be arriving?"

"No, thank you," Attila grumbled.

"Everyone else will let you know if they need anything once they arrive," Zalith told Edwin.

Nodding, the butler left the room.

"Where's Luther?" Attila asked.

Alucard glanced at him as he leaned back in his seat. "Occupied," he answered.

"Isn't he on the way?" Varana asked, looking at Alucard.

The vampire said, "No."

"Why not?" she questioned.

"Because I'm sick of 'im," Alucard snarled.

Varana adorned the same irritated glare that lingered on everyone else's face. "Why?"

Alucard scowled. He didn't want to tell her the truth about why he didn't want Luther around anymore because he was sure she'd love that. Attila didn't need to know either, so he had to think of something to say. He rolled his eyes and glared at the door. "'E crossed a line," he muttered.

"What line?" she asked with a little less hostility and more curiosity as she glanced at Zalith.

"Can you mind your own damn business, please?" Zalith snapped.

A hint of excitement flickered across Varana's face. "Oh no…what did he do?" she asked with a slight laugh.

Alucard glowered impatiently. "Maybe you should go and ask 'im unless 'e's too busy fucking Zanvord or zhat ozzer voman on my ship," he snapped.

Varana's smile disappeared. "He's fucking *who*?!" she exclaimed as Zalith rolled his eyes.

To Alucard's knowledge, Luther wasn't actually screwing around with another woman, he'd just said it to piss Varana off, and since Zalith wasn't stopping either of them, he'd not stop just yet. "I zon't know," he said with a shrug, losing his irritated tone. "I've seen 'im vith a lot of people since 'e got 'ere, and ovten, if 'e spends more zhan an hour vith zhem, 'e is most likely going to take zhem to bed vith 'im."

She scoffed. "And you're just going to let one of your guys sleep with the people he's supposed to be watching over?"

"Zhe people zhere can make zheir own decisions, as can Luther," he muttered.

"Not when it comes to using poor, innocent refugees," she mumbled quietly.

"Varana, shut up," Zalith complained as Edwin returned and started handing out the things he'd been sent to get.

Varana set her glare on Zalith as she was handed her punch. "What the hell's wrong with you? Are you grouchy because Luther's sleeping with Danford? Because join the club," she exclaimed.

With an annoyed scowl, he glared back at her, ignoring Edwin as he placed his water in front of him. "I don't give a shit about Danford, Varana; either shut up or leave," he warned her.

"Well, obviously, you must since you're so heated and upset right now!"

"I'm upset because you're already causing issues and we haven't even been here ten minutes yet."

"I'm not causing issues! Your boyfriend was the one who started talking shit about Luther. Was I just supposed to sit here and pretend that I'm deaf?!"

"I would prefer it if you did," he snapped.

She scoffed but then looked at Alucard. "I don't know what you see in Z, Alucard—he's such an asshole," she complained.

"Don't talk to him," Zalith warned.

Ignoring Varana, Alucard took his cake from Edwin and sighed quietly, watching the butler as he then placed the cheese plate in the centre of the table and left as silently as he had come.

Varana continued arguing, "I'll talk to him all I want! Isn't that what we're all sitting here for? To talk? If *he* doesn't want to talk, *he* can leave!"

Zalith exhaled deeply as he closed his eyes and placed his middle and index fingers against his forehead. They both fell silent for a moment, and when Zalith huffed quietly, he opened his eyes and glared ahead, ignoring Varana's glare.

Alucard hoped that their arguing was over, but he knew it wasn't, so he didn't even bother speaking.

"What, you're just going to ignore me now?" Varana scoffed.

"Varana," he grumbled, "shut up."

"If you don't want me here, just say so, Z!"

"Oh my god," Zalith muttered in frustration.

That was when the door swung open and Greymore strutted in with Tyrus and Orin behind him. "Hello, everybody," he announced with a smile on his face.

"Hi," Varana immediately called as if she hadn't been arguing. She set her eyes on Tyrus and smiled brightly. "Oh, Tyrus, sweetheart. Come and sit," she said, patting the seat beside her, and as Zalith rolled his eyes, Tyrus made his way over and sat beside her.

At the same time, Orin sat between Tyrus and Attila, and Greymore made his way over, shook both Zalith and Alucard's hands, and slumped down in the seat closest to Alucard.

"How's everyone doing?" Gryemore asked, looking around the table, and as he set his eyes on Attila, he frowned curiously. "Who's the new guy?"

"Zhat is Attila," Alucard answered. "'E is vone of my subordinates."

"Nice to meet you," Greymore said, smiling.

"Likewise," Attila muttered.

"Is Luther coming?" Greymore then asked, looking at Alucard.

"No, there's been some trouble in paradise," Varana said with a fake, saddened frown *and* tone before Alucard could answer.

"Oh…what happened?" Greymore asked.

"Let's just drop it, please—everyone," Zalith ordered, leaving Varana to laugh quietly to herself.

Alucard glanced at Greymore. "Did you see anyvone else on your vay 'ere?"

"Nope," he answered, leaning over the table to grab a piece of cheese. "But I wasn't keeping an eye out," he said, eating the cheese. Then, he set his eyes on Tyrus. "What about you, Ty? Did you see anyone?"

"I've seen a lot of people," the dark-skinned demon answered.

Greymore nudged Alucard and smirked. "That's his way of asking you to be more specific."

Sighing, Alucard set his eyes on Tyrus. "Verevolf, blonde, vemale…vith a vampire who I 'ave no desire to vemember zhe appearance of," he muttered lazily.

"No, sorry," Tyrus said.

Alucard grunted. "I vouldn't be surprised if zhey got lost," he muttered before slicing a corner off his cake with his fork, and then he ate it.

"Should I send someone to watch the roads for them?" Zalith asked quietly.

"No," Alucard muttered. "Zhey'll get 'ere."

Greymore—who was now on his third piece of cheese—asked Alucard, "How were they getting here? Maybe they got held up?"

"Zhe same vay Attila got 'ere," the vampire replied.

"I didn't see nor detect any other nearby vampires travelling when I was on my way," Attila said.

"Can you even see past the frills on your shirt?" Zalith muttered into his glass as he sipped from his water.

Amused, Alucard smirked.

"I can, thank you," Attila snarled, "and from where I'm sitting, all I can see right now is a despicable child of man."

Greymore snickered and ate yet another piece of cheese.

"Vould you like to end up somevhere vorse zhan Luther?" Alucard then asked with a threatening but curious tone. "I'm sure you've 'eard zhat 'e's currently on babysitting duty, no?"

Attila took his eyes off Zalith and gawped at Alucard. "Sorry."

Laughing, Greymore glanced at Attila and then looked at Alucard. "What's worse than babysitting a bunch of werewolves?" he questioned. "This cheese is fantastic, by the way," he then said, taking another piece of it from the plate that *no one* else had taken any from yet.

"Babysitting the Fledgelings," Attila answered with a grunt.

"Tch, that's true," Greymore agreed. "Has anyone else tried the cheese yet?" he asked, looking around the table as he took *another* piece.

"I think I speak for all of us when I say that we're afraid if we get too close, you'll eat our fingers," Zalith mumbled.

Greymore guwafed. "I'm sorry, it's just so damn good."

"It's good," Orin agreed after trying some.

"Why are we all fussing over cheese?" Attila grumbled.

"Because, unlike some, zhe people 'ere appreciate vine vings," Alucard muttered. "Might be a little 'ard vor you to grasp zhe concept."

Embarrassed, Attila scoffed, crossed his arms, and glared at the wall while Orin and Varana laughed. Greymore nodded with a smile, Zalith smirked, and Tyrus kept a close, skeptical eye on Attila.

The door opened once more, and Idina rushed in. "I'm so sorry I'm late," she huffed, closing the door behind her. She then hurried over to where Varana was sitting and kissed her cheek. Then, she stepped closer to Zalith and did the same. "I was having trouble with Colt; he won't stop playing with the dog," she explained, moving to where Alucard was. She didn't, however, kiss *his* cheek. Instead, she held out her hand and shook his before making her way around to sit beside Greymore.

Alucard was glad that she chose not to push his boundaries.

"How's the little guy doing?" Greymore asked Idina.

Idina sighed while making herself comfortable. "He's been doing good; he's adjusting well. He's just a little bored, so he's acting out."

"Ah, it's unfortunate he's the only kid in the bunch. Shame he doesn't have someone to play with," Greymore said.

Before she could reply, the door opened again. To Alucard's relief, Freja stepped into the room. She sighed deeply, trying to tidy her windswept blonde hair as she set her eyes on Alucard. "Crowell's outside," she muttered. "Somehow, believe it or not, he got lost," she grumbled.

Alucard sighed and got up. "I'll be back," he muttered, glancing at Zalith.

"Okay," Zalith said as he placed his hand on Alucard's back. "And...tell Edwin to bring more cheese," he mumbled, nodding at Greymore, who had just taken three more pieces and an additional piece to offer to Freja as she sat beside Idina.

Sighing, Alucard nodded and left the room. He'd seen enough already to know that it was going to be a *long* meeting. But he'd do his best to get through it...and hopefully, everyone would leave in one piece.

He headed through the hall and to the front door. Outside waiting on the porch was a subordinate he hadn't seen in a few years. Crowell: tall, deadpan stare all the time, and eyes almost as red as Varana's. He was a Paladin, the best of Alucard's vampires, and Crowell was the most experienced of them all. While Attila was his main informant, Crowell would be acting as a more practical one. In cases of gathering allies and information, Attila was best doing so with words, and Crowell specialized with his fists...and whatever other means he decided to use.

As soon as he caught sight of Alucard, Crowell stood up straight, held his right fist against his chest, and bowed humbly. His shoulder-length black hair flowed in the sudden breeze as he said, "My Lord."

"Velax," Alucard muttered, and as Crowell did so, the vampire frowned. "I 'ear you got lost. Explain."

"My apologies. I came straight from my last assignment, and my lack of rest had me a little confused. It won't happen again, My Lord," he said firmly.

"Vight," Alucard mumbled, turning around. "Come in. Zhis vay."

Crowell followed him through the house and back into the conference room, where everyone was waiting in silence.

"Sit," Alucard said, nodding at the empty seat beside Freja.

While Crowell did as he was told, Alucard sat next to Zalith.

"And who do we have here?" Zalith asked.

Crowell set his eyes on him. "Crowell, sir," he answered.

"It's nice to meet you."

"I vorgot to tell Ezvin," Alucard said, looking at Zalith as he realized he'd forgotten to tell Edwin to bring more cheese, and seeing that Greymore had eaten more of it in the short time he was gone made him feel a little stupid.

"That's okay, baby. There's still a lot of food left," Zalith assured him.

Alucard leaned back in his seat, glancing around the table. Everyone was present, and he was sure that Zalith wouldn't wait much longer to start the meeting.

Zalith began, "You're all here because I want to kill Damien and Lilith, and I need your help."

A look of concerned and confused anger struck Varana's face. "Why?"

"Because it's time for them to go," the demon replied.

"Are you serious?" she questioned.

Alucard rolled his eyes and ate more of his cake, trying to ignore his growing irritancy. He didn't know why that woman had to be there, and he was sure that she was only going to keep bellowing at Zalith.

"Yes," Zalith answered.

"Do you have any idea how dangerous this is?!" she exclaimed. Then, she took her eyes off Zalith and looked at Alucard. "You're just going to let him risk his life like this?!"

Uninterested in arguing with her, he replied, "Ve know vhat ve're doing."

"*Do* you? Have you killed many gods before? Because last time I checked, they're all pretty alive!"

"I 'ave, actually," Alucard sneered, glaring at her, "and if you actually kept quiet vor more zhan two minutes and let us continue instead of screeching like an annoying little banshee, zhat vould 'ave been mentioned."

Greymore snickered as he ate his cheese, but when Varana glared at him, he deadpanned and cleared his throat quietly.

Varana set her scowl on Alucard. "Excuse me for being concerned for my best friend of hundreds of years and for everybody else sitting at this table!"

"If anybody zoesn't vant to be 'ere, zhey can go," Alucard snarled. "I'm not vorcing anyvone to visk zheir lives 'elping us."

"What about *him*?" She scowled, looking at Zalith.

Obviously, Varana was under the impression that Alucard was forcing Zalith to help him kill the Numen and deal with his problems, but this whole thing was Zalith's idea.

"I've made my choice, Varana," Zalith stated.

She frowned irritably. "You're both idiots," she said…and then she *finally* shut up.

After a few moments of silence and confused staring, Greymore ate yet another piece of cheese and laughed. "So, who are Damien and Lilith?"

Alucard looked at him. "Zhey are both vhat ve call Numen," he said, glancing around the table at everyone as they listened. "Numen are zhe immortal creators of zhis vorld and zhe ozzers. Liliv is a zemon goddess, and Zamien is a Daegelus—an angel-zemon 'ybrid of sorts," he explained.

"Oh, shit," Greymore blurted. Idina lightly slapped the side of his arm, and as he flinched, he looked over at Alucard. "How do we kill them if they're immortal?"

Sighing, Alucard crossed his arms, preparing to explain all he knew. "Ve start by veakening zhem. Numen get zheir power vrom zheir vollowers—vrom zhe people who believe in zhem, pray to zhem, even zhose who 'ate zhem. Any kind of acknowledgement of zheir existence gives zhem power. So, zhe virst step in killing zhem vould be taking avay zheir power—taking avay zheir vollowers. Zhe less invluence zhey 'ave, zhe veaker zhey vill be, and zhe veaker zhey are, zhe easier zhey vill be to kill vor good."

The vampire then glanced around the table again. Prior to this meeting, after their trip to Lupa, he and Zalith discussed which of the demon's people would be doing what, and Zalith's focused, approving look told him that it was already time to let his people know.

He looked at Tyrus. "You and Orin vill be searching vor Liliv and Zamien's vollowers; zhey are…cults," he explained slowly. "Liliv is vorshipped primarily by zemons. As vor Zamien, 'is invluence is much greater. A whole vorld fears 'im, but Zaliv and I vill deal vith zhat. You vill vind 'is vollowers; 'e 'as spent a long time gazzering particular allies, vone of vhich is called Lucious. If you vind 'im, I'm sure you vill vind zhe vest of Zamien's vollowers. Crowell vas looking vor Lucious—" he said, looking at Crowell.

Crowell nodded and glanced at Tyrus and Orin. "He has created a pocket world in which he hides from Ephriel—another Numen. Damien recently convinced him to join his cause—"

"Vhich is a separate matter," Alucard interjected.

"Yes, and…we discovered where the doorway to get into this world exists," Crowell told them.

Alucard took a small piece of paper from the stacks beside him and pushed it across the table to Tyrus. "Zhese are zhe coordinates."

Tyrus and Orin nodded.

"Zhere is a very 'igh chance zhat a war vill begin zhe moment Liliv or Zamien vind out vhat ve are doing. Zhat is vhere you come in," he said, looking at Freja, Crowell, and Greymore. "Ve vill need people to vight on our side. Zhe Numens' number of vollowers is unknown, but ve are most likely going to need to 'ave our own vorces vor vhen war does break out."

Greymore laughed nervously. "Of course, I'm always happy to help, but…there's not really a lot of us left."

"You vill be vorking vith Vreja," Alucard told him. "Your and 'er packs vill be joining togezzer."

"Oh," he said, seemingly startled. He then looked at Freja and leaned over Idina to hold out his hand. "Nice to meet you. I'm Greymore."

"I hope we get along," Freja said, shaking his hand.

"We can discuss the finer details later," Zalith said as Greymore sat back down.

"And zhen you," Alucard said, nodding at Attila. "You are going to vind out vhat you can about Zamien and Liliv's vhereabouts. Ve 'aven't 'eard vrom or seen zhem in many months, and ve need to know vhether or not zhey are planning someving similar to us. Ve are…enemies and 'ave been vor a vhile, and ve'd like to know if zhey 'ave made any moves since zheir last vreat."

"Of course," Attila said.

Alucard then glanced at the papers beside him. "As vor you two," he said, looking at Orin and Tyrus, "zhis is vhat Zamien and Liliv look like. Vould be 'elpvul to know, no?" he said, sliding two pieces of paper across the table, both of which possessed his hand-drawn likenesses of Damien and Lilith. "If you see eizer of zhem, I advise you to do your best to get avay unseen. Zhere is noving you vill be able to do."

Both Orin and Tyrus examined the drawings in silence.

"You," Alucard said, pointing at Crowell. "I need you to vind zhese," he muttered, handing a few pieces of paper with drawings of a knife and rune-covered cube on them to Greymore, who then handed them to Idina. Idina passed them to Freja, and she gave them to Crowell. "Zhis is vhat vas used long ago to banish Luciver vrom zhis vorld."

"Are you going after *him*, too?!" Varana exclaimed.

Irritated, Alucard rolled his eyes and scowled at her. "So long as 'e stays zhe fuck vhere 'e is, I von't 'ave to," he snarled. Then, he looked back over at Crowell. "Vind zhose. Zhey vere taken a long time ago by Levoldus, and eizer 'e 'as zhem, or vone of 'is children vill. Vind out vhich vone, and zhen I vill kill zhem and take vrom zhem, and if Levoldus 'as zhem, zhen you vill look vor vhat is on zhe next page," he said, and as Crowell flipped to the next piece of paper, Alucard sighed. "Zhat is deridiuz; is a metal known to 'arm zhose vith Numen blood. Von't kill *zhem*, but vill be effective if ve need to get avay. Vhen Crowell vinds zhat, I vill 'ave 'im send some to you," he said, looking at Tyrus and Orin.

Then, Alucard sighed once more and gathered the next lot of thoughts he'd need. "As vor an attack," he started, "in zhe event zhat zhis 'appens bevore ve 'ave vhat ve need to actually vight zhe Numen, all ve can do is vetreat. Ve can't visk zhe Numen knowing our location, so if our enemies vind us, ve leave and make so zhey von't vind us again—and ve do so vith as vew casualties as possible because as Greymore said, ve veally zon't 'ave zhat many people levt.

"I *do* 'ave an entire vace of people veady to vight, but unvortunately, zhey can't alvays be out in zhe daylight. Zhere vill also be several locations to meet set up in zhe event of discovery; zhese places are as vollows," he said, handing everyone a small piece of paper with the coordinates of five different places listed on it. "Zhere is voom in each place vor every vone of us and both your people," he said, looking over at Greymore and Freja.

"What if we're attacked by the Numen themselves?" Attila then asked.

"At zhe moment, is impossible vor zhe Numen to know vhere ve are or who is vorking vith us. If zhey do manage to vind us, a Numen can only vemain in zhis vorld vor about ten to vivteen minutes bevore becoming veaker as each moment passes. I myselv can 'old off Zamien or Liliv vor zhat time, giving everyvone else time to get avay or to deal vith zhe people Zamien or Liliv bring vith zhem.

"Vonce zhat time is up, zhey vill leave, and ve can decide vhether ve vun or take out zhe people zhey levt be'ind. I am…in a vay, Numen, so I can counter zhem if zhis vas to 'appen—but only vor so long," he said, glancing at Zalith to see his concerned face. "Unless ve 'ave zhe deridiuz by zhen…zhen I von't 'ave to be zhe only vone 'olding zhem off."

Crowell asked, "My Lord, should I send the other Paladins in search of the deridiuz whilst I search for these objects?"

"Yes," Alucard confirmed.

After seeing Zalith's concern, he felt it was best that they had a weapon to use against the Numen sooner rather than later. *He* was the best weapon that they had, but Zalith clearly wasn't comfortable with him risking himself like that, and there *were* alternatives, so he'd make sure they had them.

Alucard glanced around at everyone again. "You vill begin zhese tasks immediately; ve vill veconvene every vortnight or sooner if you 'ave invormation zhat needs to be shared in person. Ozzervise, you can send us messages. Do your best not to be seen 'anging avound," he mumbled, looking in Attila's direction. "Zhe last ving ve need is anyvone drawing attention to zhemselves." Then, he leaned back in his seat. "Questions?"

Idina looked at Zalith and frowned in concern. "Are you sure you want to do this? We're all finally settling down here—not just us, but you, too."

"I'm sure," Zalith confirmed.

"Okay," she replied with worry still in her voice.

"Our packs," Freja said. "How do you plan to unite us?"

Alucard set his eyes on her. "Zhat is vor you and Greymore to decide. Traditionally, zhe Alphas marry, but zhat's up to you. As long as all your volves vill vork togezzer, I zon't care 'ow you unite, but needs to 'appen. Ve need as many allies as ve can get."

She nodded and looked at Greymore. "I suppose we should talk about this once we're done here?"

A nervous look appeared on Greymore's face. He cleared his throat and glanced at her. "Of course, uh…do you…want some of this?" he then asked, reaching out to grab the entire cheese plate.

"No," she said, taking her eyes off him to look over at the wall.

"Zhen I believe ve are done 'ere," Alucard said.

Everyone nodded and stood up, and without a word, they all left the room, leaving Alucard, Zalith, and Varana alone.

That had gone a whole lot faster than Alucard thought and that relieved him. Now, he just wanted to head back to the sunroom, finish feeding the plants, and then go to his study to finish building the contraption that would help keep his nightmares at bay. First, though, he had to apologize to Zalith.

As the demon stood up, Alucard set his eyes on him and got up as well. "I should 'ave told you bevore about vhat I said about 'olding Zamien or Liliv off if zhey do vind us. I'm sorry."

Zalith frowned in worry and turned to face him, placing his hands on the vampire's arms. "I just don't want you to get—"

"Is that all you care about?!" Varana exclaimed, cutting Zalith off. "Yourselves?!"

Alucard glared at her as Zalith looked back over his shoulder at her and frowned.

"What?" the demon asked.

She kept a hostile scowl. "You *both* have people who obviously trust you and will work tirelessly for you and you're just going to throw them right back into the middle of another war?! Are you two delusional?!"

"Ve gave zhem zhe opportunity to say no and leave," Alucard snarled. "But zhey zidn't leave; if somebody zoesn't vant to be involved, all zhey 'ave to do is say," he said sternly.

"Yeah, you gave them the option to leave, but where would they be without you?" she asked, looking at both him and Zalith as the demon turned to face her, letting go of

Alucard. "Especially Z's guys. Do you really think that any of them are going to want to leave and face living in this new world alone?! No! You're both stupid!"

Losing what little patience he had left, Alucard sighed deeply and dragged his hand over his face. "I zon't know about you, but I zon't see any ozzer alternatives," he said as calmly as he could.

"Oh, I have one!" she argued. "How about not starting a war with the Numen?!"

He scowled and gritted his teeth. "Zhe only veason you zon't vant me to start zhis war is because you know Luciver is going to get involved, and you zon't vant me to kill your pavhetic vather."

Varana gasped in astoundment and abruptly slapped the side of Alucard's face—and *that* was when he lost his calm. Before she could pull her hand back—and before Zalith could stop either of them—Alucard lunged forward, snatched the woman's throat, and pinned her against the wall. The moment her back hit the wall, Varana screeched and snatched a fistful of Alucard's hair in her hand, pulling harshly on it as the vampire growled in frustration and tightened his grip on her throat.

But Zalith quickly grasped both their arms and pulled them apart; as Varana and Alucard were separated, they hissed at one another, scowling in hostility.

Alucard wanted to tear her apart; she'd pissed him off enough, and he'd put up with her shit for too long. He couldn't stand her; just seeing her made him angry enough to attack, but he didn't because she was Zalith's friend. This time, though, she'd struck him, and her relationship with Zalith wouldn't keep him from lashing back at her.

The demon then scowled at Varana. "Leave," he warned, letting go of her arm.

"No!" she denied, glaring at him. "Why do *I* always have to leave!?"

"Because you're a bitch," Alucard snapped.

With a shriek of anger, Varana tried to throw herself at him again, but Zalith grabbed hold of her. She flailed around and tried to fight *him*, too, but he shoved her towards the door and scowled.

"Get out," he warned her again. "We'll talk later."

Varana growled at him and abruptly tore the table's cloth off, pulling everything to the floor with it. She then stormed out of the room and slammed the door shut behind her.

Still scowling, Alucard rolled his eyes and huffed irritably. He *hated* that woman, and even though she didn't live in the house anymore, the guesthouse wasn't far away enough. He wanted to do more; he wanted to show her *exactly* how he felt about her, but he wouldn't. He was sure that Zalith would get mad at him, and he didn't want that.

The demon sighed and turned to face Alucard. "Are you okay?"

"I'm vine," he grumbled.

Zalith then frowned in what looked like sadness and wrapped his arms around him, hugging him tightly. "I'm sorry she hit you," he said quietly.

"I zon't care about 'er," he muttered. "Vhat's vrong?"

He sighed again. "Everything is going to change," he mumbled, still holding him. "But I'll be okay. I just want you to be safe and happy."

Was Zalith having second thoughts? "Ve zon't 'ave to do zhis," Alucard said, trying to assure him as he placed his hands on Zalith's waist. "You can still change your mind."

"No, I want them to die."

Alucard leaned back so that he could see Zalith's face. "You zon't…'ave to do zhis vor me. Is too much. Zhis von't be easy, and vill probably take years to kill just vone of zhem—years zhat I zon't expect you to vaste. I vant zhem dead too, Zaliv, but…I still zon't vant you to visk your life vor me."

"It could take centuries, I don't even care. I'm going to do this because I love you, and I want you to be free of them," he said, placing his hand on the side of Alucard's face as he stared into his eyes. "And I want to do it for our futures, too. What would we do if we had the baby from your dream and Damien got hold of her because we didn't put the work in to get rid of him?" he asked sadly.

Alucard frowned in just as much concern and looked down at the floor. Zalith was right. How could they possibly have any kind of future let alone a family with Damien and Lilith seeking to destroy them? It wouldn't be possible unless they did something about the Numen, and Alucard wasn't going to give up his chance of a life and family with Zalith because of the people who'd taken that from him before.

He set his eyes back on Zalith. "I know, I…." He frowned and sighed as he looked down again. "I know," he repeated. "I just zon't vant anyving to 'appen to you."

"I'll be fine," Zalith said, moving his hand to Alucard's chin. He then lightly grabbed it and lifted his head so that he'd look at him. "I've got myself out of some pretty bad scrapes before," he said with a smile. "I just don't want anything to happen to *you*."

Gazing at him, Alucard smiled a little. "Ve'll be vine," he assured him.

Then, as Zalith smirked, Alucard felt his curiosity begin to outweigh his anger. Once again, Zalith mentioned having a family, and lately, whenever the subject came up, Alucard felt more and more excited.

He kept his smile, looking down at the floor. "So…ve vill…actually 'ave a vamily vone day?" he asked quietly.

"I'd like to. Are you interested?"

Slowly setting his gaze on the demon's intrigued face, Alucard nodded. "Yes," he answered—he didn't even have to think about it this time. He *did* want a family with Zalith, no matter how long he had to wait and no matter what they had to do to have one.

The demon then grinned. "How many children do you want?"

*That* was when Alucard frowned. It took a while for him to decide that he wanted a family, but to decide how many children they might have? He needed to think about it.

But what he *didn't* need to think about was the fact he actually wanted a son. He wasn't sure why he'd seen their child as a girl; if they did have a baby, he'd want a son.

"I zon't know," he answered with a shrug. "But…if ve 'ad a child, I vink I vould vant a son."

Zalith laughed as he rested his forehead against Alucard's. "Okay, but we have to have the girl first."

Staring into his dark eyes, Alucard sighed quietly. "If zhat's vhat you vant," he agreed.

"It is," he said, smirking. "But I'll find a way to make it up to you."

"'Ow vill you do zhat?"

"What do you want?"

Alucard didn't have to think about that, either. "A cat."

"Really?" Zalith asked with a laugh.

"Yes."

"Out of *all* the things in the world I could give you?"

"Yes."

The demon sighed deeply. "Okay," he agreed, "but you know the rules."

"I do," Alucard confirmed with an excited smile.

Then, Zalith leaned in and kissed him. "Well, I better go and talk to Varana."

Nodding, Alucard let go of Zalith's waist and watched him head for the door.

"Don't go anywhere," the demon said with a smirk as he looked back at him.

"I von't," he said, sitting in his seat.

Then, Zalith left the room.

Alucard sighed quietly as slouched in his seat and stared at the ceiling. He wasn't sure what to expect next; everything was starting to get a whole lot more serious. He and Zalith had started preparing to kill Damien and Lilith. Not only that, but they'd also talked about a family—marriage, even. Alucard couldn't explain how excited and content that made him feel, and he knew that it was what he wanted.

More than anything, he wanted to spend his life with Zalith, and having a family with him was something he wished for just as sorely. It was beginning to look like both of those things would happen; *all* of the things he wanted might actually happen. A family, a life free of the Numen…. After waiting so long, he finally found everything he needed in one single person. And no matter what it took, he'd not let anyone or anything take that from him.

# THE NUMEN CHRONICLES
## SERIES ONE

--------------------------------------------------------------

### Nosferatu
The Numen Chronicles | Volume 1

### Demon's Fate
The Numen Chronicles | Volume 2

### Light
The Numen Chronicles | Volume 3

### Demon's Bane
The Numen Chronicles | Volume 4

### Ascendant
The Numen Chronicles | Volume 5

### Icarus
The Numen Chronicles | Volume 6

### Demon's Curse
The Numen Chronicles | Volume 7

### Renascence
The Numen Chronicles | Volume 8

### Demon's Reclamation
The Numen Chronicles | Volume 9

[And more...]

# THE NUMENVERSE
## OTHER SERIES/STORIES

---

### Aldergrove Chronicles

Set in the year 1176 after Aegisguard's second world war. After being told he has only six months left to live, Clementine decides to track down his sister's murderers, leading him to Aldergrove Academy, a place where a hundred students must fight to the death to earn their right to travel to the New World. But he soon learns that the students aren't the only ones prowling the corridors at night in search of blood.

### Where The Wild Wolves Have Gone

Set in the year 1330. Following Luan, a young transman werewolf who belongs to a pack owned by Lyca Corp., a military-focused organization. The pack have served them for generations, but after a mission goes sideways, Luan begins to learn the horrifying truth about the people they serve.

### Greykin Chronicles

Set in the year 1332, following Jackson, a journalist who heads to the snowy mountains of Ascela in search of his missing best friend, Wilson. But he discovers that not only is there a whole different world hidden out there, but death isn't necessarily the end for some creatures.

### The Numen Chronicles Series Two

Set in the year 1335. While hunting for his missing friend, Elijah stumbles upon a fiery journalist, who so happens to be looking for the same people as him: the doctors who experimented on him when he was a child. But when the two are forced to go on the run together, Elijah's healing wounds are opened, and he realises that Lyca Corp. took more than his childhood.

To stay up to date with future releases, follow the author through their website!

www.numenverse.com/